The Secret of Annexe 3
'A plot of classical cunning and intricacy.'
Times Literary Supplement

The Riddle of the Third Mile
'Runs the gamut of brain-racking unputdownability.'
Observer

The Dead of Jericho
'The writing is highly intelligent, the atmosphere
melancholy, the effect haunting.'
Daily Telegraph

Service of all the Dead
'A brilliantly plotted detective story.'
Evening Standard

The Silent World of Nicholas Quinn
'Morse's superman status is reinforced by an
ending which no ordinary mortal could have
possibly unravelled.'
Financial Times

Last Seen Wearing
'Brilliant characterisation in original whodunnit.'
Sunday Telegraph

Last Bus to Woodstock
'Let those who lament the decline of the English
detective story reach for Colin Dexter.'
Guardian

THE WENCH IS DEAD

Colin Dexter graduated from Cambridge University in 1953 and has lived in Oxford since 1966.

His first novel, *Last Bus to Woodstock*, was published in 1975 and there are now twelve novels in the Inspector Morse series, most recently *The Daughters of Cain* and *Death is Now My Neighbour*.

In 1989 *The Wench is Dead* was awarded a Gold Dagger by the Crime Writers' Association for best crime novel of the year, as was *The Way Through the Woods* in 1992, and Colin Dexter has also been awarded Silver Daggers for *Service of all the Dead* and *The Dead of Jericho*. *Death is Now My Neighbour* went straight to the top of the bestseller lists on first publication in 1996.

Colin Dexter was awarded the CWA Cartier Diamond Dagger for outstanding services to crime literature.

The Inspector Morse novels have been adapted for the small screen, with huge success, in Carlton/Central Television's series starring John Thaw and Kevin Whately. *The Wench is Dead* is the last of the novels to be adapted, and was broadcast in November 1998.

THE INSPECTOR MORSE NOVELS

COLIN DEXTER

THE WENCH
IS DEAD

PAN BOOKS

First published 1989 by Macmillan

This edition published 1990 by Pan Books
an imprint of Pan Macmillan Ltd
Pan Macmillan, 20 New Wharf Road, London N1 9RR
Basingstoke and Oxford
Associated companies throughout the world
www.panmacmillan.com

ISBN 0 330 37030 8

9 8 7 6 5 4 3 2

A CIP catalogue record for this book is available from
the British Library.

Typeset by SetSystems Ltd, Saffron Walden, Essex
Printed and bound in Great Britain by
Mackays of Chatham PLC, Chatham, Kent

For
Harry Judge,
lover of canals, who introduced me to
The Murder of Christine Collins,
a fascinating account of an
early Victorian murder,
by
John Godwin.
To both I am deeply indebted.
(Copies of John Godwin's publication are obtainable
through the Divisional Librarian, Stafford
Borough Library.)

Thou hast committed –
Fornication; but that was in another country,
And besides, the wench is dead
(Christopher Marlowe, *The Jew of Malta*)

ACKNOWLEDGEMENTS

The author and publishers wish to thank the following who have kindly given permission for use of copyright materials:

Map of Oxford Canal reproduced by permission of Oxfordshire Museum Services;

Century Hutchinson Limited for extracts from *Adventures in Wonderland* by David Grayson;

Faber and Faber Ltd for extracts from 'Little Gidding' from *Four Quartets* by T. S. Eliot;

David Higham Associates Limited on behalf of Dorothy L. Sayers for extracts from *The Murder of Julia Wallace*, published by Gollancz;

Methuen London Limited for extracts from *A Man's a Man* by Bertolt Brecht;

Oxfordshire Health Authority for extracts from *Handbook for Patients and Visitors*;

Oxford Illustrated Press for extracts from *The Erosion of Oxford* by James Stevens Curl;

E. O. Parrott for extracts;

Routledge, Chapman and Hall for extracts from *Understanding Media* by Marshall McLuhan;

The Society of Authors on behalf of the Bernard

Shaw Estate for extracts from *Back to Methuselah*, published by Longman.

Every effort has been made to trace all the copyright holders but if any have been inadvertently overlooked, the author and publishers will be pleased to make the necessary arrangement at the first opportunity.

THE OXFORD CANAL

CHAPTER ONE

Thought depends absolutely on the stomach; but, in spite of that, those who have the best stomachs are not the best thinkers

(Voltaire, in a letter to d'Alembert)

INTERMITTENTLY, ON THE Tuesday, he felt sick. Frequently, on the Wednesday, he *was* sick. On the Thursday, he felt sick frequently, but was actually sick only intermittently. With difficulty, early on the Friday morning – drained, listless, and infinitely weary – he found the energy to drag himself from his bed to the telephone, and seek to apologize to his superiors at Kidlington Police HQ for what was going to be an odds-on non-appearance at the office that late November day.

When he awoke on the Saturday morning, he was happily aware that he was feeling considerably better; and, indeed, as he sat in the kitchen of his bachelor flat in North Oxford, dressed in pyjamas as gaudily striped as a Lido deckchair, he was debating whether his stomach could cope with a wafer of Weetabix – when the phone rang.

'Morse here,' he said.

'Good morning, sir.' (A pleasing voice!) 'If you can hold the line a minute, the Superintendent would like a word with you.'

Morse held the line. Little option, was there? No option, really; and he scanned the headlines of *The Times* which had just been pushed through the letter-box in the small entrance hall – late, as usual on Saturdays.

'I'm putting you through to the Superintendent,' said the same pleasing voice – 'just a moment, please!'

Morse said nothing; but he almost prayed (quite something for a low-church atheist) that Strange would get a move on and come to the phone and say whatever it was he'd got to say ... The prickles of sweat were forming on his forehead, and his left hand plucked at his pyjama-top pocket for his handkerchief.

'Ah! Morse? Yes? Ah! Sorry to hear you're a bit off-colour, old boy. Lots of it about, you know. The wife's brother had it – when was it now? – fortnight or so back? No! I tell a lie – must have been three weeks, at least. Still, that's neither here nor there, is it?'

In enlarged globules, the prickles of sweat had re-formed on Morse's forehead, and he wiped his brow once more as he mumbled a few dutifully appreciative noises into the telephone.

'Didn't get you out of bed, I hope?'

'No – no, sir.'

'Good. Good! Thought I'd just have a quick word, that's all. Er ... Look here, Morse!' (Clearly Strange's thoughts had moved to a conclusion.) 'No need for you to come in today – no need at all! Unless you feel suddenly very much better, that is. We can just about cope here, I should think. The cemeteries are full of indispensable men – eh? Huh!'

'Thank you, sir. Very kind of you to ring – I much appreciate it – but I am officially off duty this weekend in any case—'

'Really? Ah! That's good! That's er ... *very* good, isn't it? Give you a chance to stay in bed.'

'Perhaps so, sir,' said Morse wearily.

'You say you're *up*, though?'

'Yes, sir!'

'Well you go back to bed, Morse! This'll give you a chance for a jolly good rest – this weekend, I mean – won't it? Just the thing – bit o' rest – when you're feeling a bit off-colour – eh? It's exactly what the quack told the wife's brother – when was it now . . .?'

Afterwards, Morse thought he remembered concluding this telephone conversation in a seemly manner – with appropriate concern expressed for Strange's convalescent brother-in-law; thought he remembered passing a hand once more over a forehead that now felt very wet and very, very cold – and then taking two or three hugely deep breaths – and then starting to rush for the bathroom . . .

It was Mrs Green, the charlady who came in on Tuesday and Saturday mornings, who rang treble-nine immediately and demanded an ambulance. She had found her

3

employer sitting with his back to the wall in the entrance-hall: conscious, seemingly sober, and passably presentable, except for the deep-maroon stains down the front of his deckchair pyjamas – stains that in both colour and texture served vividly to remind her of the dregs in the bottom of a coffee percolator. And she knew exactly what *they* meant, because that thoughtlessly cruel doctor had made it quite plain – five years ago now, it had been – that if only she'd called him immediately, Mr Green might still . . .

'Yes, that's right,' she heard herself say – surprisingly, imperiously, in command: 'just on the southern side of the Banbury Road roundabout. Yes. I'll be looking out for you.'

At 10.15 a.m. that same morning, an only semi-reluctant Morse condescended to be helped into the back of the ambulance, where, bedroom-slippered and with an itchy, grey blanket draped around a clean pair of pyjamas, he sat defensively opposite a middle-aged, uniformed woman who appeared to have taken his refusal to lie down on the stretcher-bed as a personal affront, and who now sullenly and silently pushed a white enamel kidney-bowl into his lap as he vomited copiously and noisily once more, while the ambulance climbed Headley Way, turned left into the grounds of the John Radcliffe Hospital complex, and finally stopped outside the Accident, Casualty, and Emergency Department.

As he lay supine (on a hospital trolley now) it

occurred to Morse that he might already have died some half a dozen times without anyone recording his departure. But he was always an impatient soul (most particularly in hotels, when awaiting his breakfast); and it might not have been quite so long as he imagined before a white-coated ancillary worker led him in leisurely fashion through a questionnaire that ranged from the names of his next of kin (in Morse's case, now non-existent) to his denominational preferences (equally, alas, now non-existent). Yet once through these initiation rites – once (as it were) he had joined the club and signed the entry forms – Morse found himself the object of considerably increased attention. Dutifully, from somewhere, a young nurse appeared, flipped a watch from her stiffly laundered lapel with her left hand and took his pulse with her right; proceeded to take his blood-pressure, after tightening the black swaddling-bands around his upper-arm with (for Morse) quite needless ferocity; and then committing her findings to a chart (headed MORSE, E.) with such nonchalance as to suggest that only the most dramatic of irregularities could ever give occasion for anxiety. The same nurse finally turned her attention to matters of temperature; and Morse found himself feeling somewhat idiotic as he lay with the thermometer sticking up from his mouth, before its being extracted, its calibrations consulted, its readings apparently unsatisfactory, it being forcefully shaken thrice, as though for a few backhand flicks in a ping-pong match, and then being replaced, with all its earlier awkwardness, just underneath his tongue.

'I'm going to survive?' ventured Morse, as the nurse added her further findings to the data on his chart.

'You've got a temperature,' replied the uncommunicative teenager.

'I thought *everybody* had got a temperature,' muttered Morse.

For the moment, however, the nurse had turned her back on him to consider the latest casualty.

A youth, his legs caked with mud, and most of the rest of him encased in a red-and-black-striped Rugby jersey, had just been wheeled in – a ghastly-looking Cyclopean slit across his forehead. Yet, to Morse, he appeared wholly at his ease as the (same) ancillary worker quizzed him comprehensively about his life-history, his religion, his relatives. And when, equally at his ease, the (same) nurse put him through his paces with stethoscope, watch, and thermometer, Morse could do little but envy the familiarity that was effected forthwith between the young lad and the equally young lass. Suddenly – and almost cruelly – Morse realized that she, that same young lass, had seen him – Morse! – exactly for what he was: a man who'd struggled through life to his early fifties, and who was about to face the slightly *infra-dignitatem* embarrassments of hernias and haemorrhoids, of urinary infections and – yes! – of duodenal ulcers.

The kidney-bowl had been left within easy reach, and Morse was retching violently, if unproductively, when a young houseman (of Morse's age, no more than half) came to stand beside him and to scan the reports of ambulance, administrative staff, and medical personnel.

'You've got a bit of nasty tummy trouble – you realize that?'

Morse shrugged vaguely: 'Nobody's really told me anything yet.'

'But you wouldn't have to be Sherlock Holmes to suspect you've got something pretty radically wrong with your innards, would you?'

Morse was about to reply when the houseman continued. 'And you've only just come in, I think? If you could give us – Mr, er, *Morse*, is it? – if you give us a chance, we'll try to tell you more about things as soon as we can, OK?'

'I'm all right, really,' said the duly chastened Chief Inspector of Police, as he lay back and tried to unloose the knot that had tied itself tight inside his shoulder muscles.

'You're *not* all right, I'm afraid! At best you've got a stomach ulcer that's suddenly decided to burst out bleeding' – Morse experienced a sharp little jerk of alarm somewhere in his diaphragm – 'and at worst you've got what we call a "perforated ulcer"; and if that *is* the case . . .'

'If that *is* the case . . .?' repeated Morse weakly. But the young doctor made no immediate answer, and for the next few minutes prodded, squeezed, and kneaded the paunchy flesh around Morse's abdomen.

'Found anything?' queried Morse, with a thin and forced apology for a grin.

'You could well lose a couple of stone. Your liver's enlarged.'

'But I thought you just said it was the stomach!'

'Oh yes, it is! You've had a stomach haemorrhage.'

'What's – what's that got to do with my liver?'

'Do you drink a lot, Mr Morse?'

'Well, most people have a drink or two most days, don't they?'

'Do you drink a *lot*?' (The same words – a semitone of exasperation lower.)

As non-committally as his incipient panic would permit, Morse shrugged his shoulders once more: 'I like a glass of beer, yes.'

'How many pints do you drink a week?'

'A week?' squeaked Morse, his face clouding over like that of a child who has just been given a complex problem in mental multiplication.

'A day, then?' suggested the houseman helpfully.

Morse divided by three: 'Two or three, I suppose.'

'Do you drink spirits?'

'Occasionally.'

'What spirits do you drink?'

Morse shrugged his tautened shoulders once again: 'Scotch – sometimes I treat myself to a drop of Scotch.'

'How long would a bottle of Scotch last you?'

'Depends how big it was.'

But Morse immediately saw that his attempt at humour was ill appreciated; and he swiftly multiplied by three: 'Week – ten days – about that.'

'How many cigarettes do you smoke a day?'

'Eight . . . ten?' replied Morse, getting the hang of things now and smoothly dividing by three.

'Do you ever take any exercise – walking, jogging, cycling, squash . . .?'

But before Morse could switch back to his tables, he reached for the kidney-bowl that had been left within reach. And as he vomited, this time productively, the houseman observed with some alarm the coffee-grounds admixed with the tell-tale brightly crimsoned specks of blood – blood that was de-oxygenated daily with plentiful nicotine and liberally lubricated with alcohol.

For some while after these events, Morse's mind was somewhat hazy. Later, however, he could recall a nurse bending over him – the same young nurse as earlier; and he could remember the beautifully manicured fingers on her left hand as she flipped the watch out again into her palm; could almost follow her thoughts as with contracted brow she squinted at the disturbing equation between his half-minute pulse-rate and the thirty-second span upon her watch . . .

At this point Morse knew that the Angel of Death had fluttered its wings above his head; and he felt a sudden *frisson* of fear, as for the first time in his life he began to think of dying. For in his mind's eye, though just for a second or two, he thought he almost caught sight of the laudatory obituary, the creditable paragraph.

CHAPTER TWO

Do you know why we are more fair and just towards the dead? We are not obliged to them, we can take our time, we can fit in the paying of respects between a cocktail party and an affectionate mistress — in our spare time

(*Albert Camus*, The Fall)

WHEN MORSE AWOKE the following morning, he was aware of a grey dawn through the window of the small ward, to his left; and of a clock showing 4.50 a.m. on the wall above the archway to his right, through which he could see a slimly attractive nurse, sitting in a pool of light behind a desk, and writing in a large book. Was she writing, Morse wondered, about *him*? If so, there would be remarkably little to say; for apart from one very brief bout of vomiting in the small hours, he had felt, quite genuinely, so very much better; and had required no further attention. The tubing strapped to his right wrist, and stretching up to the saline-drip bottle hooked above his bed, was still dragging uncomfortably against his skin most of the time, as if the needle had been stuck in slightly off-centre; but he'd determined to make no mention of such a minor irritant. The awkward apparatus rendered him immobile, of course – at least until he had mastered the skills of the young man from the adjacent bed who had spent most of the previous evening wandering freely (as it seemed) all over the hospital, holding his own drip high above his head like some Ethiopian athlete brandishing the Olympic torch. Morse had felt most self-conscious when circumstances utterly beyond his control had finally induced him to beg for a 'bottle'. Yet – thus far – he had been spared the undignified palaver of the dreaded 'pan'; and he trusted that his lack of solid nutriment during the preceding days would be duly acknowledged with some reciprocal inactivity by his bowels. And so far so good!

The nurse was talking earnestly to a slightly built, fresh-faced young houseman, his white coat reaching almost to his ankles, a stethoscope hooked into his right-hand pocket. And soon the two of them were walking, quietly, unfussily, into the ward where Morse lay; then disappearing behind the curtains (drawn across the previous evening) of the bed diagonally opposite.

When he'd first been wheeled into the ward, Morse had noticed the man who occupied that bed – a proud-looking man, in his late seventies, perhaps, with an Indian Army moustache, and a thin thatch of pure-white hair. At that moment of entry, for a second or two, the old warrior's watery-pale eyes had settled on Morse's face, seeming almost to convey some faint message of hope and comradeship. And indeed the dying old man would certainly have wished the new patient well, had he been able to articulate his intent; but the rampaging septicaemia which had sent a bright-pink suffusion to his waxen cheeks had taken from him all the power of speech.

It was 5.20 a.m. when the houseman emerged from behind the curtains; 5.30 a.m. when the swiftly summoned porters had wheeled the dead man away. And when, exactly half an hour later, the full lights flickered on in the ward, the curtains round the bed of the late Colonel Wilfrid Deniston, OBE, MC, were standing open, in their normal way, to reveal the newly laundered sheets, with the changed blankets professionally mitred at the foot. Had Morse known how the late Colonel could not abide a chord of Wagner he would have been somewhat aggrieved; yet had he known how the Colonel had committed to memory virtually the whole poetic corpus of A. E. Housman, he would have been most gratified.

At 6.45 a.m. Morse was aware of considerable activity in the immediate environs of the ward, although initially he could see no physical evidence of it: voices, clinking of crockery, squeaking of ill-oiled wheels – and finally Violet, a happily countenanced and considerably overweight West Indian woman hove into view pushing a tea-trolley. This was the occasion, clearly, for a pre-dawn beverage, and how Morse welcomed it! For the first time in the past few days he was conscious of a positive appetite for food and drink; and already, and with envy, he had surveyed the jugs of water and bottles of squash that stood on the bedside tables of his fellow-patients, though for some reason not on the table of the man immediately opposite, one Walter Greenaway, above whose bed there hung a rectangular plaque bearing the sad little legend NIL BY MOUTH.

'Tea or coffee, Mr Greenaway?'

'I'll just settle for a large gin-and-tonic, if that's all right by you.'

'Ice and lemon?'

'No ice, thank you: it spoils the gin.'

Violet moved away massively to the next bed, leaving Mr Greenaway sans ice, sans everything. Yet the perky sixty-odd-year-old appeared far from mortified by his exclusion from the proceedings, and winked happily across at Morse.

'All right, chief?'

'On the mend,' said Morse cautiously.

'Huh! That's exactly what the old Colonel used to say: "On the mend". Poor old boy!'

'I see,' said Morse, with some unease.

After Greenaway's eyes had unclouded from their appropriate respect for the departed Colonel, Morse continued the dialogue.

'No tea for you, then?'

Greenaway shook his head. 'They know best, though, don't they?'

'They do?'

'Wonderful – the doctors here! And the nurses!'

Morse nodded, hoping indeed that it might be so.

'Same trouble as me?' enquired Greenaway confidentially.

'Pardon?'

'Stomach, is it?'

'Ulcer – so they say.'

'Mine's perforated!' Greenaway proclaimed this fact with a certain grim pride and satisfaction, as though a combination of the worst of disorders with the best of physicians was a cause for considerable congratulation. 'They're operating on me at ten o'clock – that's why I'm not allowed a drink, see?'

'Oh!' For a few seconds Morse found himself almost wishing he could put in some counter-claim for a whole gutful of mighty ulcers that were not only perforated but pierced and punctured into the bargain. A more important matter, however, was now demanding his attention, for Violet had effected a U-turn and was (at last!) beside his bed.

She greeted her new charge with a cheerful grin. 'Morning, Mr, er' (consulting the Biro'd letters on the name-tab) 'Mr Morse!'

'Good morning!' replied Morse. 'I'll have some coffee, please – two spoonfuls of sugar.'

'My, my! *Two – sugars!*' Violet's eyes almost soared out of their whitened sockets towards the ceiling; then she turned to share the private joke with the grinning Greenaway. 'Now, look you here!' (reverting to Morse): 'You can't have no coffee nor no tea nor no sugar neither. Oh right?' She wagged a brown forefinger at a point somewhere above the bed; and twisting his neck Morse could see, behind his saline apparatus, a rectangular plaque bearing the sad little legend NIL BY MOUTH.

14

CHAPTER THREE

Flowers, writing materials, and books are always welcome gifts for patients; but if you wish to bring food or drink, do ask the Sister, and she will tell you what is advisable

(*Oxford Health Authority*, Handbook for
Patients and Visitors)

DETECTIVE SERGEANT LEWIS came into the ward just after seven o'clock that Sunday evening, clutching a Sainsbury carrier-bag with the air of a slightly guilty man walking through the Customs' shed; and at the sight of his old partner, Morse felt very glad, and just a little lachrymose.

'How come you knew I was here?'

'I'm a detective, sir – remember?'

'They phoned you, I suppose.'

'The Super. He said you sounded awful poorly when he rang yesterday morning. So he sent Dixon round, but you'd just been carried off in the ambulance. So he rang me and said I might like to see if the NHS is still up to scratch – see if you wanted anything.'

'Something like a bottle of Scotch, you mean?'

Lewis ignored the pleasantry: 'I'd've come in last night, but they said you weren't to have any visitors – only close relatives.'

'I'll have you know I'm not quite your "Orphan Annie", Lewis. I've got a great-aunt up in Alnwick somewhere.'

'Bit of a long way for her to come, sir.'

'Especially at ninety-seven . . .'

'Not a bad fellow, Strange, is he?' suggested Lewis, after a slightly awkward little pause.

'Not when you get to know him, I suppose,' admitted Morse.

'Would you say *you've* got to know him?'

Morse shook his head.

'Well?' said Lewis briskly. 'How *are* things? What do they say's the trouble?'

'Trouble? No trouble! It's just a case of mistaken identity.'

Lewis grinned. 'Seriously, though?'

'Seriously? Well they've put me on some great big round white pills that cost a couple of quid a time, so the nurses say. Do you realize you can get a very decent little bottle of claret for that price?'

'What about the food – is that all right?'

'Food? *What* food? Except for the pills they haven't given me a thing.'

'No drink, either?'

'Are you trying to set back my medical progress, Lewis?'

'Is that what – what *that* means?' Lewis jerked his eyes upwards to the fateful warning above the bed.

16

THE WENCH IS DEAD

'That's just precautionary,' said Morse, with uncon-
vincing nonchalance.

Lewis's eyes jerked, downwards this time, towards
the carrier-bag.

'Come on, Lewis! What have you got in there?'

Lewis reached inside the bag and brought out a
bottle of lemon-and-barley water, and was most pleasantly surprised to witness the undisguised delight on
Morse's face.

'It was just that the missus thought – well, you know,
you wouldn't be allowed to drink – to drink anything
else much.'

'*Very* kind of her! You just tell her that the way things
are I'd rather have a bottle of that stuff than a whole
crate of whisky.'

'You don't mean that, do you, sir?'

'Doesn't stop you telling her, though, does it?'

'And here's a book,' added Lewis, withdrawing one
further item from the bag – a book entitled *Scales of
Injustice: A Comparative Study of Crime and its Punishment
as Recorded in the County of Shropshire, 1842–1852.*

Morse took the thick volume and surveyed its inor-
dinately lengthy title, though without any obvious
enthusiasm. 'Mm! Looks a fairly interesting work.'

'You don't mean that, do you?'

'No,' said Morse.

'It's a sort of family heirloom and the missus just
thought—'

'You tell that wonderful missus of yours that I'm very
pleased with it.'

'Perhaps you'll do me a favour and leave it in the hospital library when you come out.'

Morse laughed quietly; and Lewis was strangely gratified by his chief's reactions, and smiled to himself.

He was still smiling when an extraordinarily pretty young nurse, with a freckled face and mahogany-highlighted hair, came to Morse's bedside, waved an admonitory finger at him, and showed her white and beautifully regular teeth in a dumbshow of disapproval as she pointed to the lemon-and-barley bottle which Morse had placed on his locker-top. Morse, in turn, nodded his full appreciation of the situation and showed his own reasonably regular, if rather off-white, teeth as he mouthed a silent 'OK'.

'Who's that?' whispered Lewis, when she had passed upon her way.

'That, Lewis, is the Fair Fiona. Lovely, don't you think? I sometimes wonder how the doctors manage to keep their dirty hands off her.'

'Perhaps they don't.'

'I thought you'd come in here to cheer me up!'

But for the moment good cheer seemed in short supply. The ward sister (whom Lewis had not noticed as he'd entered – merely walking straight through, like everyone else, as he'd thought) had clearly been keeping her dragon's eye on events in general, and in particular on events around the bed where the dehydrated Chief Inspector lay. To which bed, with purposeful stride, she now took the few steps needed from the vantage point behind the main desk. Her left hand immediately grasped the offending bottle on the locker-top, while her eyes fixed unblinkingly upon the luckless Lewis.

'We have our regulations in this hospital – a copy of them is posted just outside the ward. So I shall be glad if you follow those regulations and report to me or whoever's in charge if you intend to visit again. It's absolutely vital that we follow a routine here – try to understand that! Your friend here is quite poorly, and we're all trying our vairy best to see that he gets well again quickly. Now we canna do that if you are going to bring in anything *you* think might do him good, because you'd bring in all the *wrong* things, OK? I'm sure you appreciate what I'm saying.'

She had spoken in a soft Scots accent, this grimly visaged, tight-lipped sister, a silver buckle clasped around her dark-blue uniform; and Lewis, the colour tidally risen under his pale cheeks, looked wretchedly uncomfortable as she turned away – and was gone. Even Morse, for a few moments, appeared strangely cowed and silent.

'Who's that?' asked Lewis (for the second time that evening).

'You have just had an encounter with the embittered soul of our ward sister – devoted to an ideal of humourless efficiency: a sort of Calvinistic Thatcherite.'

'And what she says . . .?'

Morse nodded. 'She is, Lewis, in charge, as I think you probably gathered.'

'Doesn't have to be so *sharp*, does she?'

'*Forget* it, Lewis! She's probably disappointed in her love-life or something. Not surprising with a face—'

'What's her name?'

'They call her "Nessie".'

'Was she born near the Loch?'

'*In* it, Lewis.'

The two men laughed just a little; yet the incident had been unpleasant and Lewis in particular found it difficult to put it behind him. For a further five minutes he quizzed Morse quietly about the other patients; and Morse told him of the dawn departure of the ex-Indian-Army man. For still another five minutes, the two men exchanged words about Police HQ at Kidlington; about the Lewis family; about the less-than-sanguine prospects of Oxford United in the current soccer campaign. But nothing could quite efface the fact that 'that bloody sister' (as Morse referred to her) had cast a darkling shadow over the evening visit; had certainly cast a shadow over Lewis. And Morse himself was suddenly feeling hot and sweaty, and (yes, if he were honest) just a fraction wearied of the conversation.

'I'd better be off then, sir.'

'What else have you got in that bag?'

'Nothing—'

'Lewis! My stomach may be out of order for the minute but there's nothing wrong with my bloody ears!'

Slowly the dark clouds began to lift for Lewis, and when, after prolonged circumspection, he decided that the Customs Officer was momentarily off her guard, he withdrew a small, flattish bottle, wrapped in soft, dark-blue tissue-paper – much the colour of Nessie's uniform.

'But not until it's *official* like!' hissed Lewis, palming

the gift surreptitiously into Morse's hand beneath the bedclothes.

'Bell's?' asked Morse.

Lewis nodded.

It was a happy moment.

For the present, however, the attention of all was diverted by another bell that sounded from somewhere, and visitors began to stand and prepare for their departure: a few, perhaps, with symptoms of reluctance; but the majority with signs of only partially concealed relief. As Lewis himself rose to take his leave, he dipped his hand once more into the carrier-bag and produced his final offering: a paperback entitled *The Blue Ticket*, with a provocative picture of an economically clad nymphet on the cover.

'I thought – I thought you might enjoy something a little bit lighter, sir. The missus doesn't know—'

'I hope she's never found you reading this sort of rubbish, Lewis!'

'Haven't read it *yet*, sir.'

'Well, the, er, title's a bit shorter than the other thing . . .'

Lewis nodded, and the two friends shared a happy grin.

'Time to go, I'm afraid!' The Fair Fiona was smiling down at them, especially (it seemed) smiling down at Lewis, for whom every cloud was suddenly lifted from the weather-chart. As for Morse, he was glad to be alone again; and when the ward finally cleared of its last visitor, the hospital system smoothly, inexorably, reorientated itself once more to the care and treatment of the sick.

It was only after further testings of pulse and blood pressure, after the administration of further medicaments, that Morse had the opportunity (unobserved) of reading the blurb of the second work of literature (well, literature of a sort) which was now in his possession:

Diving into the water, young Steve Mingella had managed to pull the little girl's body on to the hired yacht and to apply to her his clumsy version of the kiss-of-life. Miraculously, the six-year-old had survived, and for a few days Steve was the toast of the boat clubs along the Florida Keys. After his return to New York he received a letter – and inside the letter a ticket from the young girl's father, the playboy proprietor of the city's most exclusive, expensive, and exotic night-spot, a club specializing in the wildest sexual fantasies. The book opens as Steve treads diffidently across the thick carpeted entrance of that erotic wonderland, and shows to the topless blonde seated at Reception the ticket he has received – *a ticket coloured deepest blue* . . .

CHAPTER FOUR

My evening visitors, if they cannot see the clock,
should find the time in my face

(Emerson, Journals)

HALF AN HOUR after Lewis's departure, Fiona came
again to Morse's bedside and asked him to unfasten his
pyjama bottoms, to turn over on his left side, and to
expose his right buttock. Which orders having been
obeyed (as Morse used to say when he studied the
Classics), the unsmiling Nessie was summoned to insert
a syringe of colourless liquid into his flank. This inser-
tion (he could see nothing over his right shoulder)
seemed to Morse to have been effected with less than
professional finesse; and he heard himself grunt
'Christ!' when the plunger was pressed, his body twitching involuntarily as what felt like a bar of iron was
implanted into his backside.

'You'll feel a wee bit sleepy,' was the laconic comment of the Loch Ness Monster; and Fiona was left to
pour some disinfectant on to a piece of gauze, which
she proceeded to rub vigorously across and around the
punctured area.

'She'd have landed a top job in Buchenwald, that woman!' said Morse. But from the uncomprehending look on her face, he suddenly realized that Nazi concentration camps were as far back in the young nurse's past as the relief of Mafeking was in his own; and he felt his age. It was forty-four years now since the end of the Second World War . . . and this young . . . nurse . . . could only be . . . Morse was conscious of feeling very weary, very tired. 'What I mean is . . .' (Morse pulled his pyjama bottoms up with some difficulty) '. . . she's so . . . sharp!' Yes, Lewis had used that word.

'Did you realize that was my very first injection? Sorry if it hurt a bit – I'll get better.'

'I thought it was . . .'

'Yes, I know.' She smiled down at him and Morse's eyelids drooped heavily over his tired eyes. Nessie had said he'd feel a wee bit . . . weary . . .

His head jerked down against his chest, and Fiona settled him against the pillows, gently looking at him as he lay there, and wondering for the dozenth time in her life why all the men who attracted her had either been happily married long, long since, or else were far, far, far too old.

Morse felt a soft-fingered hand on his right wrist, and opened his eyes to find himself staring up into the face of an extraordinary-looking personage. She was a very small woman, of some seventy-five to eighty summers, wispily white-haired, her face deeply wrinkled and unbeautiful, with an old-fashioned NHS hearing-aid plugged into her left ear, its cord stretching down to a batteried appliance in the pocket of a dirty, loose, grey-woollen cardigan. She appeared naïvely unaware that any apology might perhaps be called for in wakening a weary patient. Who was she? Who had let her in? It was 9.45 p.m. by the ward clock and two night nurses were on duty. Go away! Go away, you stupid old crow!

'Mr Horse? Mr Horse, is it?' Her rheumy eyes squinted myopically at the Elastoplast name-tag, and her mouth distended in a dentured smile.

'Morse!' said Morse. 'M-O . . .'

'Do you know, I think they've spelt your name wrong, Mr Horse. I'll try to remember to tell—'

'Morse! M-O-R-S-E!'

'Yes – but it *was* expected, you know. They'd already told me that Wilfrid had only a few days left to live. And we all do get older, don't we? Older every single day.'

Yes, yes, clear off! I'm bloody tired, can't you *see*?

'Fifty-two years, we'd been together.'

Morse, belatedly, realized who she was, and he nodded more sympathetically now: 'Long time!'

'He *liked* being here, you know. He was so grateful to you all—'

'I'm afraid I only came in a couple of days ago—'

'That's exactly why he wanted me to thank *all* of you – all his old friends here.' She spoke in a precise, prim manner, with the diction of a retired Latin mistress.

'He was a fine man . . .' began Morse, a little desperately. 'I wish I'd got to know him. As I say, though, I only got in a day or two ago – stomach trouble – nothing serious . . .'

The hearing-aid began to whistle shrilly, picking up some internal feedback, and the old lady fiddled about ineffectually with the ear-piece and the control switches. 'And that's *why*' (she began now to talk in intermittent italics) 'I've got this little *book* for you. He was *so* proud of it. Not that he *said* so, of course – but he *was*. It took him a very long time and it was a *very* happy day for him when it was printed.'

Morse nodded with gratitude as she handed him a little booklet in bottle-green paper covers. 'It's very kind of you because, as I say, I only came in—'

'Wilfrid would have been *so* pleased.'

Oh dear.

'And you will *promise* to read it, won't you?'

'Oh yes – certainly!'

The old lady fingered her whistling aid once more, smiled with the helplessness of a stranded angel, said 'Goodbye, Mr Horse!' and moved on to convey her undying gratitude to the occupant of the adjacent bed.

Morse looked down vaguely at the slim volume thus presented: it could contain no more than – what? – some twenty-odd pages. He would certainly look at it later, as he'd promised. Tomorrow, perhaps. For the moment, he could think of nothing but closing his weary eyes once more, and he placed *Murder on the Oxford Canal*, by Wilfrid M. Deniston, inside his locker, on top of *Scales of Injustice* and *The Blue Ticket* – the triad of new works he'd so recently acquired. Tomorrow, yes . . .

Almost immediately he fell into a deep slumber, where he dreamed of a long cross-country race over the fields of his boyhood, where there, at the distant finishing-line, sat a topless blonde, a silver buckle clasped around her waist, holding in her left hand a pint of beer with a head of winking froth.

CHAPTER FIVE

This type of writing sometimes enjoys the Lethean faculty of making those who read it forget to ask what it means, or indeed if it means anything very substantive

(*Alfred Austin*, The Bridling of Pegasus)

THE ENDOSCOPY, PERFORMED under a mild anaesthetic at 10 o'clock the following morning (Monday), persuaded the surgeons at the JR2 that in Morse's case the knife was probably not needed; their prognosis, too, was modestly encouraging, provided the patient could settle into a more cautiously sober and restrictive regimen for the months (and years) ahead. Furthermore, as a token of their muted optimism, the patient was that very evening to be allowed one half-bowl of oxtail soup and a portion of vanilla ice-cream – and for Morse any gourmand *à la carte* menu could hardly have been more gloriously welcome.

Lewis reported to Sister Maclean at 7.30 p.m., and was unsmilingly nodded through Customs without having to declare one get-well card (from Morse's secretary), a tube of mint-flavoured toothpaste (from

Mrs Lewis), and a clean hand-towel (same provenance). Contentedly, for ten minutes or so, the two men talked of this and that, with Lewis receiving the firm impression that his chief was recovering rapidly.

Fiona the Fair put in a brief appearance towards the end of this visit, shaking out Morse's pillows and placing a jug of cold water on his locker.

'Lovely girl,' ventured Lewis.

'You're married – remember?'

'Done any reading yet?' Lewis nodded towards the locker.

'Why do you ask?'

Lewis grinned: 'It's the missus – she was just wondering . . .'

'I'm half-way through it, tell her. Riveting stuff!'

'You're not serious—'

'Do you know how to spell "riveting"?'

'What – one "t" or two, you mean?'

'And do you know what "stools" are?'

'Things you sit on?'

Morse laughed – a genuine, carefree, pain-free laugh. It was good to have Lewis around; and the vaguely puzzled Lewis was glad to find the invalid in such good spirits.

Suddenly, there beside the bed, re-mitreing the bottom right-hand corner of the blankets, was Sister Maclean herself.

'Who brought the jug of water?' she enquired in her soft but awesome voice.

'It's all right, Sister,' began Morse, 'the doctor said—'

'Nurse Welch!' The ominously quiet words carried easily across the ward, and Lewis stared at the floor in pained embarrassment as Student Nurse Welch walked warily over to Morse's bed, where she was firmly admonished by her superior. Free access to liquids was to be available only w.e.f. the following dawn – *and not before.* Had the student nurse not read the notes before going the rounds with her water-jugs? And if she had, did she not realize that no hospital could function satisfactorily with such sloppiness? If it mightn't seem important on *this* occasion, did the student nurse not realize that it could be absolutely vital on the *next?*

Another sickening little episode; and for Lewis one still leaving a nasty taste when a few minutes later he bade his chief farewell. Morse himself had said nothing at the time, and said nothing now. Never, he told himself, would he have reprimanded any member of his own staff in such cavalier fashion in front of other people: and then, sadly, he recalled that quite frequently he had done precisely that . . . All the same, he would have welcomed the opportunity of a few quiet words with the duly chastened Fiona before she went home.

There was virtually no one around in the ward now: the Ethiopian athlete was doing the hospital rounds once more; and two of the other patients had shuffled their way to the gents. Only a woman of about thirty, a slimly attractive, blonde-headed woman (Walter Green-

away's daughter, Morse guessed – and guessed correctly) still sat beside her father. She had given Morse
a quick glance as she'd come in, but now hardly
appeared to notice him as she made her way out of the
ward, and pressed the 'Down' button in front of the
top-floor lifts. It was her father who was monopolizing
her thoughts, and she gave no more than a cursory
thought to the man whose name appeared to be
'Morse' and whose eyes, as she had noticed, had
followed her figure with a lively interest on her exit.

The time was 8.40 p.m.

Feeling minimally guilty that he had not as yet so
much as opened the cover of the precious work that
Mrs Lewis had vouchsafed to his keeping, Morse
reached for the book from his locker, and skimmed
through its first paragraph:

'Diversity rather than uniformity has almost
invariably been seen to characterize the criminal
behaviour-patterns of any technologically developing society. The attempt to resolve any conflicts and/
or inconsistencies which may arise in the analysis
and interpretation of such patterns (see Appendix
3, pp. 492 ff.) is absolutely vital; and the inevitable
reinterpretation of this perpetually variable data is
the raw material for several recent studies into the
causation of criminal behaviour. Yet conflicting stra-
tegic choices within heterogeneous areas, starkly
differentiated creeds, greater knowledge of variable
economic performances, as well as physical, physio-
logical, or physiognomical peculiarities – all these

facts (as we shall maintain) can suggest possible avenues never exhaustively explored by any previous student of criminal behaviour in nineteenth-century Britain.'

'Christ!' muttered Morse (for the second time that evening). A few years ago he might possibly have considered persevering with such incomprehensible twaddle. But no longer. Stopping momentarily only to marvel at the idiocy of the publisher who had allowed such pompous polysyllaby ever to reach the compositor in the first place, he closed the stout work smartly – and resolved to open it never again.

As it happened, he was to break this instant resolution very shortly; but for the moment there was a rather more attractive proposition awaiting him in his locker: the pornographic paperback which Lewis (praise the Lord!) had smuggled in.

A yellow flash across the glossy cover made its promise to the reader of Scorching Lust and Primitive Sensuality – this claim supported by the picture of a superbly buxom beauty sunning herself on some golden-sanded South Sea island, completely naked except for a string of native beads around her neck. Morse opened the book and skimmed (though a little more slowly than before) a second paragraph that evening. And he was immediately aware of a no-nonsense, clear-cut English style that was going to take the palm every time from the sprawling, spawning, sociological nonsense he had just encountered:

'She surfaced from the pool and began to unbutton her clinging, sodden blouse. And as she did so, the young men all fell silent, urging her – praying her! – in some unheard but deafening chorus, to strip herself quickly and completely – their eyes now rivetted to the carmined tips of her slimly sinuous fingers as they slipped inside her blouse, and so slowly, so tantalizingly, flicked open a further button . . .'

'Christ!!' It was the third time that Morse had used the same word that evening, and the one that took the prize for blasphemous vehemence. He leaned back against his pillows with a satisfied smile about his lips, clasping to himself the prospect of a couple of hours of delicious titillation on the morrow. He could bend those covers back easily enough; and it would be no great difficulty temporarily to assume the facial expression of a theological student reading some verses from the Minor Prophets. But whatever happened, the chances that Chief Inspector Morse would ever be fully informed about crime and its punishment in nine-teenth-century Shropshire had sunk to zero.

For the moment, at any rate.

He replaced *The Blue Ticket* in his locker, on top of *Scales of Injustice* – both books now lying on top of the hitherto neglected *Murder on the Oxford Canal*, that slim volume printed privately under the auspices of The Oxford and County Local History Society.

*

COLIN DEXTER

As Morse nodded off once more, his brain was debating whether there was just the one word misspelled in the brief paragraph he had just read. He would look it up in Chambers when he got home. Lewis hadn't seemed to know, either . . .

CHAPTER SIX

I enjoy convalescence. It is the part that makes the
illness worth while

(*G. B. Shaw,* Back to Methuselah)

AT 2 A.M. THE inevitable occurred; but fortunately
Morse managed to attract the quick attention of the
nurse as she'd flitted like some Nightingale around the
darkened wards. The noise of the curtains being drawn
around his bed sounded to Morse loud enough to
rouse the semi-dead. Yet none of his fellow-patients
seemed to stir and she – the blessed girl! – had been
quite marvellous.

'I don't even know which way up the thing should
go,' confided Morse.

'Which way *round*, you mean!' Eileen (such was her
name) had whispered, as she proceeded without the
slightest embarrassment to explain exactly how the well-
trained patient would negotiate this particular crisis.
Then, leaving him with half a roll of white toilet-paper,
and the firm assurance of a second coming within the
next ten minutes, she was gone.

It was all over – consummated with a bowl of warm

water and a brief squirt of some odoriferous air-freshener. Whew! Not half as bad as Morse had feared – thanks to that ethereal girl; and as he smiled up gratefully at her, he thought there might have been a look in her eyes that transgressed the borders of perfunctory nursing. But Morse would always have thought there was, even if there wasn't; for he was the sort of man for whom some area of fantasy was wholly necessary, and his imagination followed the slender Eileen, as elegantly she walked away: about 5′ 8″ in height – quite tall really; in her mid-twenties; eyes greenish-hazel, in a delicately featured, high-cheekboned face; no ring of any sort on either hand. She looked so good, so wholesome, in her white uniform with its dark-blue trimmings.

Go to sleep, Morse!

At 7.30 a.m., after breakfasting on a single wafer of Weetabix with an inadequate pour-over of semi-skimmed milk (and no sugar), Morse noted with great satisfaction that the NIL BY MOUTH embargo was now in abeyance, and he poured himself a glass of water with the joy of a liberated hostage. There followed for him, that morning, the standard readings of pulse-rate and blood-pressure, a bedside wash in a portable basin, the remaking of his bed, the provision of a fresh jug of water (!), a flirting confab with Fiona, the purchase of *The Times*, a cup of Bovril from the vivacious Violet, and (blessedly) not a single spoke stuck in the hospital machinery from the *éminence grise* installed at the seat of power.

At 10.50 a.m. a white-coated cohort of consultant-cum-underlings came to stand around his bed, and to consider the progress of its incumbent. The senior man, after briefly looking through Morse's file, eyed the patient with a somewhat jaundiced eye.

'How are you feeling this morning?'

'I think I'll live on for a few more weeks – thanks to you,' said Morse, with somewhat sickening sycophancy.

'You mention here something about your drinking habits,' continued the consultant, unimpressed as it appeared with such spurious gratitude.

'Yes?'

'You drink a lot.' It was a statement.

'That's a lot, you think?'

The consultant closed the file with a sigh and handed it back to Nessie. 'During my long years in the medical profession, Mr Morse, I have learned that there are two categories of statistics which can invariably be discounted: the sexual prowess of those suffering from diabetes mellitus; and the boozing habits of our country's middle management.'

'I'm not a diabetic.'

'You will be if you keep drinking a bottle of Scotch a week.'

'Well – perhaps not *every* week.'

'You sometimes drink *two* a week, you mean?'

There was a twinkle in the consultant's eye as he waved his posse of acolytes across to the bed of the weakly Greenaway, and sat himself down on Morse's bed.

'Have you had a drop yet?'

'Drop of what?'

'It's a dreadful give-away, you know' (the consultant nodded to the locker) ' – that tissue paper.'

'Oh!'

'Not *tonight* – all right?'

Morse nodded.

'And one further word of advice. Wait till Sister's off duty!'

'She'd skin me alive!' mumbled Morse.

The consultant looked at Morse strangely. 'Well, since you mention it, yes. But that wasn't what I was thinking of, no.'

'Something worse?'

'She's about the most forbidding old biddy in the profession; but just remember she comes from north of the border.'

'I'm not quite sure . . .'

'She'd probably' (the consultant bent down and whispered in Morse's ear) ' – she'd probably draw the curtains and insist on fifty-fifty!'

Morse began to feel more happily settled; and after twenty minutes with *The Times* (Letters read, Crossword completed), one-handedly he folded back the covers of *The Blue Ticket*, and moving comfortably down against his pillows started Chapter One.

'Good book?'

'So-so!' Morse had not been aware of Fiona's presence, and he shrugged non-committally, holding the pages rigidly in his left hand.

'What's it called?'

'Er – *The Blue* – *The Blue City*.'

'Detective story, isn't it? I think my mum's read that.'

Morse nodded uneasily. 'Do *you* read a lot?'

'I used to, when I was young and beautiful.'

'This morning?'

'Sit up!'

Morse leaned forward as she softened up his pillows with a few left hooks and right crosses, and went on her way.

'Lovely girl, isn't she?' It wasn't Lewis this time who made the obvious observation, but the stricken Greenaway, now much recovered, and himself reading a book whose title was plain for all to see: *The Age of Steam*.

Morse pushed his own novel as unobtrusively as possible into his locker: it was a little disappointing, anyway.

'*The Blue Ticket* – that's what it is,' said Greenaway.

'Pardon?'

'You got the title wrong – it's *The Blue Ticket*.'

'Did I? Ah yes! I, er, I don't know why I'm bothering to read it, really.'

'Same reason I did, I suppose. Hoping for a bit of sex every few pages.'

Morse grinned defeatedly.

'It's a bit of a let-down,' went on Greenaway in his embarrassingly stentorian voice. 'My daughter sometimes brings me one or two books like that.'

'She was the woman – last night?'

The other nodded. 'In library work ever since she was eighteen – twelve years. In the Bodley these last six.'

Morse listened patiently to a few well-rehearsed statistics about the mileage of book-shelving in the warrens beneath the Bodleian; and was already learning something of the daughter's *curriculum vitae* when the monologue was terminated by cleaners pushing the beds around in a somewhat cavalier fashion, and slopping their mops into dingily watered buckets.

At 1.30 p.m., after what seemed to him a wretchedly insubstantial lunch, Morse was informed that he was scheduled that afternoon to visit various investigative departments; and that for this purpose the saline-drip would be temporarily removed. And when a hospital porter finally got him comfortably into a wheelchair, Morse felt that he had certainly climbed a rung or two up the convalescence ladder.

It was not until 3.30 p.m. that he returned to the ward, weary, impatient, and thirsty – in reverse order of severity. Roughly, though oddly painlessly, a silent Nessie, just before going off duty, had reaffixed into his right wrist the tube running down from a newly hung drip; and with the eyes of a now fully alert Greenaway upon him, Morse decided that Steve Mingella's sexual fantasies might have to be postponed a while. And when a small, mean-faced Englishwoman (doubtless Violet's understudy) had dispensed just about enough viscous liquid from her tureen to cover the bottom of his soup bowl, Morse's earlier euphoria had almost evaporated. He wouldn't even be seeing Lewis – the latter (as he'd told Morse) taking out the missus for some celebration (reason unspecified). At 7.05 p.m. he managed to sort out his headphones for *The Archers*; and at 7.20 p.m., he decided to dip into the late Colonel's *magnum opus*. By 7.30 p.m. he was so engrossed that it was only after finishing Part One that he noticed the presence of Christine Greenaway, the beautiful blonde from the Bodley.

CHAPTER SEVEN

Murder on the Oxford Canal

The author wishes to acknowledge the help he has so freely received from several sources; but particularly from the Bodleian Library, Oxford; from the *Proceedings of the North Oxford Local History Society*; and from the *Court Registers* of the City of Oxford Assizes, 1859 and 1860.

Further details of the trials mentioned in the following pages may be found in the editions of *Jackson's Oxford Journal* for 20th and 27th August, 1859; and of the same journal for 15th and 22nd April, 1860.

PART ONE
A Profligate Crew

THOSE WHO EXPLORE the back-streets and the by-ways of
our great cities, or indeed our small cities, will sometimes
stumble (almost literally, perhaps) upon sad memorials,
hidden in neglected churchyards – churchyards which
seem wholly separated from any formal ecclesiastical edi-
fice, and which are come across purely by accident at the
far side of red-bricked walls, or pressed upon by tall houses
– untended, silent, forgotten. Until recent years, such a
churchyard was to be found at the lower end of the pretty
little road in North Oxford, now designated Middle Way,
which links the line of Summertown shops in South Parade
with the expensively elegant houses along Squitchey Lane,
to the north. But in the early nineteen-sixties most of
those tomb-stones which had stood in irregular ranks in
the Summertown Parish Churchyard (for such was its
official name) were removed from their original, supra-
corporal sites in order to afford a rather less melancholic
aspect to those who were about to pay their deposits on
the flats being built upon those highly desirable if slightly
lugubrious acres. Each there in his narrow cell had once
been laid, and each would there remain; yet after 1963 no
one, for certain, could have marked that final resting
place.

To the Memory of
JOANNA FRANKS
wife of Charles Franks of London,
who having been primitively and
cruelly assaulted was found most
tragically drowned in the Oxford
Canal on June 22nd 1859,
aged 38 years.
This stone is erected by
some members of the Summertown
Parish Council in commemoration
of the untimely death of this
most unhappy woman.
Lord have mercy upon her soul

Requiescat in Pace Aeterna

The few headstones which are adequately preserved and which are to be found – even to this day – leaning almost upright against the northern perimeter of the aforesaid enclave, are but one tenth or so of the memorials once erected there, in the second and third quarters of the nineteenth century, by relatives and friends whose earnest wish was to perpetuate the names of those souls, now perhaps known only to God, who passed their terrestrial lives in His faith and fear.

One of these headstones, a moss-greened, limestone slab (standing the furthest away but three from the present thoroughfare) bears an epitaph which may still be traced by the practised eye of the patient epigraphist – though make haste if you are to decipher that disintegrating lettering!

Beyond this poignant (if unusually lengthy) epitaph there lies a tale of unbridled lust and drunken lechery; a tale of a hapless and a helpless young woman who found herself at the mercy of coarse and most brutally uninhibited boatmen, during an horrendous journey made nearly one hundred and twenty years ago – a journey whose details are the subject-matter of our present narrative.

Joanna Franks hailed originally from Derby. Her father, Daniel Carrick, had been accredited as an agent to the Nottinghamshire and Midlands Friendly Society; and for a good deal of his married life he appears to have maintained a position as a reasonably prosperous and well-respected figure in his home community. Later, however – and certainly in the few years prior to the tragic death of his only daughter (there was a younger brother, Daniel) – he encountered a period of hard times.

Joanna's first husband was F. T. Donavan, whose family sprang from County Meath. He is described by one of his contemporaries as "an Irishman of many parts", and being a man of large physique we learn that he was familiarly (and predictably) known by the nickname of 'Hefty' Donavan. He was a conjurer by profession (or by one of them!) and appeared in many theatres and music-halls, both in London and in the provinces. In order to attract some badly needed publicity, he had at some unspecified date assumed the splendidly grandiloquent title of 'Emperor of all the Illusionists'; and the following theatre handbill was printed at his own expense to herald his appearance at the City of Nottingham Music Hall in early September 1856:

'Mr DONAVAN, citizen of the World and of Ireland, most humbly and respectfully informs all members of the upper and the lower nobilities, folk of the landed gentry, and the citizens of the historic district of Nottingham, that in view of his superior and unrivalled excellencies in MAGIC and DECEPTION, he has had conferred upon him, by the supreme conclave of the Assembly of Superior Magicians, this last year, the unchallenged title of EMPEROR of all the Illusionists, and

this particularly by virtue of the amazing trick of cutting off a cockerel's
head and then restoring the bird to its
pristine animation. It was this same
DONAVAN, the greatest man in the
World, who last week diverted his
great audience in Croydon by immers-
ing his whole body, tightly secured and
chained, in a tank of the most corro-
sive acid for eleven minutes and forty-
five seconds, as accurately measured
by scientific chronometer.'

Three years earlier Donavan had written (and found a
publisher for) his only legacy to us, a work entitled *The
Comprehensive Manual of the Conjuring Arts*. But the great
man's career was beginning to prove progressively
unsuccessful, and no stage appearances whatsoever are
traceable to 1858. In that year, he died, a childless and
embittered man, whilst on holiday with a friend in
Ireland, where his grave now rests in a burial-plot
overlooking Bertnaghboy Bay. Some time afterwards
his widow, Joanna, met and fell deeply in love with one
Charles Franks, an ostler from Liverpool.

Like her first, Joanna's second marriage appears to
have been a happy one, in spite of the fact that times
were still hard and money still scarce. The new Mrs
Franks was to find employment, as a dressmaker and
designers' model, with a Mrs Russell of 34 Runcorn
Terrace, Liverpool. But Franks himself was less successful in his quest for regular employment, and finally

decided to try his luck in London. Here his great expectations were soon realized for he was almost immediately engaged as an ostler at the busy George & Dragon Inn on the Edgware Road, where we find him duly lodged in the spring of 1869. In late May of that same year he sent his wife a guinea (all he could afford) and begged her to join him in London as soon as possible.

On the morning of Saturday, June 11th, 1859, Joanna Franks, carrying two small trunks, bade her farewell to Mrs Russell in Runcorn Terrace, and made her way by barge from Liverpool to Preston Brook, the northern terminus of the Trent and Mersey Canal, which had been opened some eighty years earlier. Here she joined one of Pickford & Co.'s express (or 'fly') boats[1] which was departing for Stoke-on-Trent and Fradley Junction, and thence, via the Coventry and Oxford Canals, through to London on the main Thames waterway. The fare of sixteen shillings and eleven pence was considerably cheaper than the fare on the Liverpool–London railway line which had been opened some twenty years earlier.

Joanna was an extremely petite and attractive figure, wearing an Oxford-blue dress, with a white kerchief around her neck, and a figured silk bonnet with a bright pink ribbon. The clothes may not have been new; but they were not inexpensive, and they gave to Joanna a very tidy appearance indeed. A very tempting appearance, too, as we shall soon discover.

---

[1] A 'fly' boat travels round the clock, with a double crew, working shifts, with horses exchanged at regular intervals along the canals.

The captain of the narrow-boat *Barbara Bray* was a certain Jack 'Rory' Oldfield from Coventry. According to later testimony of fellow boat-people and other acquaintances, he was basically a good-natured sort of fellow, of a blunt, blustery type of address. He was married, though childless, and was aged 42 years. The fellow-members of his crew were: the 30-year-old Alfred Musson, alias Alfred Brotherton, a tall, rather gaunt figure, married with two young children; Walter Towns, alias Walter Thorold, the 26-year-old illiterate son of a farm-labourer, who had left his home town of Banbury in Oxfordshire some ten years earlier; and a teenaged lad, Thomas Wootton, about whom no certain facts have come down to us beyond the probability that his parents came from Ilkeston in Derbyshire.

The *Barbara Bray* left Preston Brook at 7.30 p.m. on Saturday, 11th June. At Fradley Junction, at the southern end of the Mersey Canal, she successfully negotiated her passage through the locks; and at 10 p.m. on Sunday, 19th June, she slipped quietly into the northern reaches of the Coventry Canal, and settled to a course, almost due south, that would lead down to Oxford. Progress had been surprisingly good, and there had been little or no forewarning of the tragic events which lay ahead for the *Barbara Bray*, and for her solitary paying passenger – the small and slimly attractive person of Joanna Franks, for whom such a little span of life remained.

Chapter Eight

> Style is the hallmark of a temperament stamped upon
> the material at hand
> (*André Maurois*, The Art of Writing)

AFTER READING THESE few pages, Morse found himself
making some mental queries about a few minor items,
and harbouring some vague unease about one or two
major ones. Being reluctant to disfigure the printed
text with a series of marginalia, he wrote a few notes on
the back of a daily hospital menu which had been left
(mistakenly) on his locker.

The Colonel's style was somewhat on the pretentious
side – a bit too high-flown for Morse's taste; and yet the
writing a good deal above the average of its kind – with
a pleasing peroration, calculated to ensure in most
readers some semi-compulsive page-turning to Part
Two. One of the most noticeable characteristics of the
writing was the influence of Gray's 'Elegy Written in a
Country Churchyard' – a poem doubtless stuck down
the author's throat as a lad in some minor public
school, and one leaving him with a rather lugubrious
view of the human lot. One or two *very* nice touches,

though, and Morse was prepared to give a couple of ticks to that epithet 'supra-corporal'. He wished, though, he had beside him that most faithful of all his literary companions, *Chambers English Dictionary*, for although he had frequently met 'ostler' in crossword puzzles, he wasn't sure *exactly* what an ostler did; and 'figured' bonnet wasn't all that obvious, was it?

Thinking of writing – and writing books – old Donavan (Joanna's first) must have been pretty competent. After all, he'd 'found a publisher' for his great work. And until the last few years of his life, this literate Irish conjurer was seemingly pulling in the crowds at all points between Croydon and Burton-on-Trent ... He must certainly have had *something* about him, this man of many parts. 'Greatest man in the World' might be going over the top a bit, yet a mild degree of megalomania was perhaps forgivable in the publicity material of such a multi-talented performer?

'Bertnaghboy Bay?' – Morse wrote on the menu. His knowledge of geography was minimal. At his junior school, his teachers had given him a few assorted facts about the exports of Argentina, Bolivia, Chile, and the rest; and at the age of eight he had known – and still knew (with the exception of South Dakota) – all the capital cities of the American States. But that was the end of his apprenticeship in that discipline. After winning a scholarship to the local grammar school, the choice of the three 'G's had been thrust upon him: Greek, German, or Geography. Little real choice, though, for he had been thrust willy-nilly into the Greek set, where the paradigms of nouns and verbs precluded any knowledge of the Irish counties. Where *was* – what was the name? – Bertnaghboy Bay?

It was paradoxical, perhaps, that Morse should have suddenly found himself so fascinated by the Oxford Canal. He was aware that many people were besotted with boat-life, and he deemed it wholly proper that parents should seek to hand on to their offspring some love of sailing, or rambling, or keeping pets, or bird-watching, or whatever. But in Morse's extremely limited experience, narrow-boating figured as a grossly over-rated activity. Once, on the invitation of a pleasant enough couple, he had agreed to be piloted from the terminus of the Oxford Canal at Hythe Bridge Street up to the Plough at Wolvercote – a journey of only a couple of miles, which would be accomplished (he was assured) within the hour; but which in fact had been so fraught with manifold misfortunes that the finishing line was finally reached with only five minutes' drinking-time remaining – and that on a hot and thirsty Sunday noon. That particular boat had required a couple of people – one to steer the thing and one to keep hopping out for locks and what the handbook called 'attractive little drawbridges'. Now, Joanna's boat had got four of them on it – five with her; so it must surely have been awfully crowded on that long and tedious journey, pulled slowly along by some unenthusiastic horse. Too long! Morse nodded to himself – he was beginning to get the picture . . . Far quicker by rail, of course! And the fare she'd paid, 16s 11d, seemed on the face of it somewhat on the steep side for a trip as a passenger on a working-boat. In 1859? Surely so! What would the rail-fare have been then? Morse had no idea. But there were ways of finding out; there were people who knew these things . . .

He could still see in his mind's eye the painting in the cabin in which he'd travelled, with its lake, its castle, its sailing boat, and range of mountains – all in the traditional colours of red, yellow, green. But what was it like to *live* in such boats? Boats that in the nineteenth century had been crewed by assortments of men from all over the place: from the Black Country; from the colliery villages around Coventry and Derby and Nottingham; from the terraced cottages in Upper Fisher Row by the terminus in Oxford – carrying their cargoes of coal, salt, china, agricultural produce . . . other things. *What* other things? And why on earth all those 'aliases'? Were the crewmen counted a load of crooks before they ever came to court? Did every one on the Canal have two names – a 'bye-name', as it were, as well as one written in the christening-book? Surely any jury was bound to feel a fraction of prejudice against such . . . such . . . even before . . . He was feeling tired, and already his head had jerked up twice after edging by degrees towards his chest.

Charge Nurse Eileen Stanton had come on duty at 9 p.m., and Morse was still sound asleep at 9.45 p.m. when she went quietly to his bedside and gently took the hospital menu from his hand and placed it on his locker. He was probably dreaming, she decided, of some *haute cuisine* from Les Quat' Saisons, but she would have to wake him up very shortly, for his evening pills.

CHAPTER NINE

> What a convenient and delightful world is this world
> of books — if you bring to it not the obligations of
> the student, or look upon it as an opiate for idleness,
> but enter it rather with the enthusiasm of the
> adventurer
>
> (*David Grayson*, Adventures in Contentment)

THE FOLLOWING MORNING (Wednesday) was busy
and blessed. Violet's early offerings of Bran Flakes,
semi-burnt cold toast, and semi-warm weak tea, were
wonderfully welcome; and when at 10 a.m. Fiona had
come to remove the saline-drip (permanently), Morse
knew that the gods were smiling. When, further, he
walked down the corridor now to the washroom, without encumbrance, and without attendant, he felt like
Florestan newly released from confinement in Act 2 of
Fidelio. And when with full movement of both arms he
freely soaped his hands and face, and examined the
rather sorry job he'd earlier made of shaving, he felt a
wonderfully happy man. Once out of this place (he
decided) he would make some suitable, not too startling, donation to the staff in general, and invite, in

particular, his favourite nurse (odds pretty even for the moment between the Fair and the Ethereal) to that restaurant in North Oxford where he would show off his (limited) knowledge of modern Greek and order a Mezéthes Tavérnas menu, the one billed as 'an epicurean feast from first dip to final sweet'. Ten quid per person, or a little more; and with wine – and liqueurs, perhaps – and one or two little extras, £30 should cover it, he hoped ... Not that the creamy-skinned Eileen would be on duty that night. Some domestic commitments, she'd said. 'Domestic?' It worried Morse, just a little. Still, so long as Nessie wasn't going to be prowling around ... because Morse had decided that, in the interests of his convalescence, he might well twist the little bottle's golden cap that very night.

Back in the ward, the time passed, one could say, satisfactorily. A cup of Bovril at 10.30 a.m. was followed by a further recital from Mr Greenaway of his daughter's quite exceptional qualities – a woman without whom, it appeared, the Bodleian would have considerable difficulty in discharging any of its academic functions. After which, Morse was visited by one of the ten-a-penny dietitians in the place – a plain-looking, serious-souled young madam, who took him *seriatim* through a host of low-calorie vegetables on which he could 'fill up' *ad libitum*: asparagus; bamboo-shoots; beans (broad); beans (French); beans (runner); bean-sprouts; broccoli; Brussels sprouts; cabbage (various); cauliflower; celery; chicory; chives; courgettes; cucumber – and that was only the first three letters in the eternal alphabet of a healthy dietary. Morse was so impressed with the recital of the miraculous opportunities which awaited him that he even forebore to comment on the assertion that both tomato-juice and turnip-juice were wonderfully tasty and nutritious alternatives to alcoholic beverages. Dutifully, he sought to nod at suitable intervals, knowing deep down that he could, should, and bloody well *would*, shed a couple of stone fairly soon. Indeed, as an earnest of his new-found resolution, he insisted on only one scoop of potatoes, and no thickened gravy whatsoever, when Violet brought her lunch-time victuals round.

In the early afternoon, after listening to the repeat of *The Archers*, the most pleasing thought struck him: no work that day at Police HQ; no worries about an evening meal; no anxieties for the morrow, except perhaps those occasioned by his newly awakened consciousness of infirmity – and of death. But not that even *that* worried him too much, as he'd confessed to Lewis: no next of kin, no dependants, no need for looking beyond a purely selfish gratification. And Morse knew exactly what he wanted now, as he sat upright, clean, cool, relaxed, against the pillows. Because, strange as it may seem, for the present he wouldn't have given two Madagascan monkeys for a further couple of chapters of *The Blue Ticket*. At that moment, and most strongly, he felt the enthusiasm of the voyager – the voyager along the canal from Coventry to Oxford. Happily, therefore, he turned to *Murder on the Oxford Canal*, Part Two.

CHAPTER TEN

PART TWO
A Proven Crime

ALTHOUGH AT THE time there were a few conflicting statements about individual circumstances in the following, and fatal, sequence of events, the general pattern as presented here is – and, indeed, always has been – undisputed.

The 38-odd mile stretch of the Coventry Canal (of more interest today to the industrial archaeologist than to the lover of rural quietude) appears to have been negotiated without any untoward incident, with recorded stops at the Three Tuns Inn at Fazely, and again at the Atherstone Locks, further south. What can be asserted with well-nigh certitude is that the *Barbara Bray* reached Hawkesbury Junction, at the northern end of Oxford Canal, an hour or so before midnight on Monday, 20th June. Today, the distance from Hawkesbury Junction down to Oxford is some 77 miles; and in 1859 the journey was very little longer. We may therefore assume that even with one or two protracted stops along the route, the double crew of the 'fly' boat *Barbara Bray* should have managed the journey within about thirty-six hours. And this appears to have been the case. What now follows is a reconstruction of those crucial hours, based both upon the evidence given at the subsequent trials (for there were two of them) and upon later research, undertaken by the present author and others, into the records of the Oxford Canal Company Registers and the Pickford & Co. Archives. From all the available evidence, one saddening fact stands out, quite stark and incontrovertible: the body of Joanna Franks was found just after 5.30 a.m. on Wednesday, 22nd June, in the Oxford Canal – in the triangular-shaped basin of water known as 'Duke's Cut', a short passage through to the River Thames dug by the fourth Duke of Marlborough in 1796, about two and a half miles north of the (then) canal terminus at Hayfield Wharf in the city of Oxford.

For the moment, however, let us make a jump forward in time. After a Coroner's inquest at The Running Horses Inn (now demolished, but formerly standing on the corner of Upper Fisher Row by Hythe Bridge in Oxford) the four crew members of the *Barbara Bray* were straightly charged with the murder of Joanna Franks, and were duly committed to the nearby Oxford Gaol. In the preliminary trial, held at the Oxford Summer Assizes of August 1859, there were three indictments against these men: the wilful murder of Joanna Franks by throwing her into the canal; rape upon the said woman, with different counts charging different prisoners with being principals in the commission of the offence and the others as aiders and abettors; and the stealing of various articles, the property of her husband. To a man, the crew pleaded not guilty to all charges. (Wootton, the boy, who was originally charged with them, was not named in the final indictments.)

Mr Sergeant Williams, for the prosecution, said he should first proceed on the charge of rape. However, after the completion of his case, the Judge (Mr Justice Traherne) decided that there could be no certain proof of the prisoners having committed the crime, and the Jury was therefore directed to return a verdict of 'Not Guilty' on that charge. Mr Williams then applied to the Court for a postponement of the trial under the indictment for murder, until the next Assizes, on the grounds that a material witness, Joseph Jarnell, formerly a co-prisoner in Oxford Gaol, and previously committed for bigamy, could not be heard before the Court until he had obtained a free pardon from the Secretary of State. Oldfield, the boat's captain, was understood to have made some most important disclosure to Jarnell while the two men shared the same prison-cell. Although this request was strenuously opposed by Oldfield's Counsel, Mr Judge Traherne finally consented to the suggested postponement.

The Judge appointed for the second trial, held in April 1860, was Mr Augustus Benham. There was intense public feeling locally, and the streets leading to the Assize Court in Oxford were lined with hostile crowds. The case had also excited considerable interest among many members of the legal profession. The three prisoners appeared at the bar wearing the leather belts and sleeve waistcoats usually worn at that time by the canal boatmen, and were duly charged with "wilful murder, by casting, pushing, and throwing the said Joanna Franks into the Oxford Canal by which means she was choked, suffocated, and drowned". What exactly, we must ask, had taken place on those last few, fatal miles above the stretch of water known as Duke's Cut on the Oxford Canal? The tragic story soon began to unfold itself.

There are more than adequate grounds for believing that the journey from Preston Brook down to the top of the Oxford Canal at Hawkesbury was comparatively uneventful, although it soon became known that Old-field had sat with Joanna in the cabin while the boat was negotiated through the Northwich and Harecastle Tunnels. However, from the time the *Barbara Bray* reached the lonely locks of Napton Junction – 30-odd miles down from Hawkesbury, and with Oxford still some 50 miles distant – the story appears to change, and to change (as we shall see) dramatically.

William Stevens, a canal clerk employed by Pickford & Co., confirmed[1] that the *Barbara Bray* reached the Napton Locks at about 11 a.m. on Tuesday 21st June, and that the boat remained there, in all, for about an hour and a half. "There was a woman passenger on board", and she complained immediately to Stevens about "the conduct of the men with whom she was driven to associate". It would, he agreed, have been proper for him to have logged the complaint (the

[1] Many of the facts in the account used here are taken from the *Court Registers* of the Oxford Assizes, 1860, and from the *verbatim* transcript of those parts of the trial reported in *Jackson's Oxford Journal*, April 1860 (passim).

Barbara Bray was, after all, a Pickford & Co. transport);
but he had not done so, confining his advice to the
suggestion that the woman should report forthwith to
the Company offices in Oxford, where it should be
possible for her to switch to another boat on the last
leg of her journey. Stevens had witnessed some shouted
altercations between Joanna and a member of the crew,
and remembered hearing Joanna speak the words:
"Leave me alone – I'll have nothing to do with you!"
Two of the men (Oldfield and Musson, he thought)
had used some utterly disgraceful language, although
he agreed with Counsel for the defence that the
language of almost all boatmen at these times was
equally deplorable. What seemed quite obvious to
Stevens was that the crew were beginning to get very
much the worse for drink, and he gave it as his opinion
that they were "making very free with the spirit which
was the cargo". Before setting off, the woman had
complained yet again about the behaviour of the men,
and Stevens had repeated his advice to her to recon-
sider her position once the boat reached the terminus
of the Oxford Canal – where a partial off-loading of the
cargo was officially scheduled.

It appears, in fact, that Stevens's advice did not go
unheeded. At Banbury, some twelve miles further down
the canal, Joanna made a determined effort to seek
alternative transport for the remainder of her journey.
Matthew Laurenson, wharfinger at Tooley's Yard,
remembered most clearly Joanna's "urgent enquiries"
about the times of "immediate coaches to London –
and coaches from Oxford to Banbury". But nothing

was convenient, and again Joanna was advised to wait until she got to Oxford – now only some 20 miles away. Laurenson put the time of this meeting as approximately 6.30–7 p.m. (it is hardly surprising that times do not always coincide exactly in the court evidence – let us recall that we are almost ten months after the actual murder), and was able to give as his general impression of the unfortunate woman that she was "somewhat flushed and afeared".

As it happened, Joanna was now to have a fellow passenger, at least for a brief period, since Agnes Laurenson, the wharfinger's wife, herself travelled south on the *Barbara Bray* down to King's Sutton Lock (five miles distant); she, too, was called to give evidence at the trial. Recalling that there was "a fellow passenger aboard who looked very agitated", Mrs Laurenson stated that Joanna may have had a drink, but that she seemed completely sober, as far as could be judged – unlike Oldfield and Musson – and that she was clearly most concerned about her personal safety.

The tale now gathers apace towards its tragic conclusion; and it was the landlord of The Crown & Castle at Aynho (just below Banbury) who was able to provide some of the most telling and damning testimony of all. When Mrs Laurenson had left the boat three miles upstream at King's Sutton, it would appear that Joanna could trust herself with the drunken boatmen no longer, according to the landlord, who had encountered her at about 10 p.m. that night. She had arrived, on foot, a little earlier and confessed that she was so frightened of the lecherous drunkards on the *Barbara*

Bray that she had determined to walk along the tow-path, even at that late hour, and to take her chances with the considerably lesser evils of foot-pads and cut-purses. She hoped (she'd said) that it would be safely possible for her to rejoin the boat later when its crew might be a few degrees the more sober. Whilst she waited for the boat to come up, the landlord offered her a glass of stout, but Joanna declined. He had kept an eye on her, however, and noticed that as she sat by the edge of the canal she appeared to be secretly sharpening a knife on the side of the lock (Musson was later found to have a cut on his left cheek, and this could have been, and probably was, made with the same knife). As the boat had drawn alongside Aynho wharf, one of the crew (the landlord was unable to say which) had "cursed the eyes of the woman and wished her in hell flames, for he loathed and detested the very sight of her". As she finally re-boarded the boat, the landlord remembered seeing Joanna being offered a drink; and, in fact, he thought she might have taken a glass. But this evidence must be discounted wholly, since Mr Bartholomew Samuels, the Oxford surgeon who conducted an immediate *post-mortem*, found no evidence whatsoever of any alcohol in poor Joanna's body.

George Bloxham, the captain of a northward-bound Pickford boat, testified that he had drawn alongside Oldfield's boat just below Aynho, and that a few exchanges had been made, as normal, between the two crews. Oldfield had referred to his woman passenger in terms which were completely "disgusting", vowing, in the crudest language, what he would do with her that very night "or else he would burke her".[2] Bloxham added that Oldfield was very drunk; and Musson and Towns, too, were "rather well away, the pair of 'em".

James Robson, keeper of the Somerton Deep Lock, said that he and his wife, Anna, were awakened at about midnight by a scream of terror coming from the direction of the lock. At first they had assumed it was the cry of a young child; but when they looked down from the bedroom window of the lock-house, they saw only some men by the side of the boat, and a woman seated on top of the cabin with her legs hanging down over the side. Three things the Robsons were able to recall from that grim night, their evidence proving so crucial at the trial. Joanna had called out in a terrified voice "I'll not go down! Don't attempt me!" Then one of the crew had shouted "Mind her legs! Mind her legs!" And after that the passenger had resumed her frightened screams: "What have you done with my shoes – oh! please tell me!" Anna Robson enquired who the woman was, and was told by one of the crew: "A passenger – don't worry!", the crewman adding that she was having words with her husband, who was with her aboard.

Forbidding to Joanna as the tall lock-house must have appeared that midnight, standing sentinel-like above the black waters, it presented her with her one

---

[2] Burke was a criminal who had been executed some thirty years earlier for smothering his victims and then selling their bodies for medical dissection.

last chance of life – had she sought asylum within its walls.

But she made no such request.

At this point, or shortly after, it appears that the terrified woman took another walk along the tow-path to escape the drunken crew; but she was almost certainly back on board when the boat negotiated Gibraltar Lock. After which – and only some very short time after – she must have been out walking (yet again!) since Robert Bond, a crew-hand from the narrow-boat *Isis*, gave evidence that he passed her on the tow-path. Bond recorded his surprise that such an attractive woman should be out walking on her own so late, and he recalled asking her if all was well. But she had only nodded, hurriedly, and passed on into the night. As he approached Gibraltar Lock, Bond had met Oldfield's boat, and was asked by one of its crew if he had seen a woman walking the tow-path, the man adding, in the crudest terms, what he would do to her once he had her in his clutches once again.

No one, apart from the evil boatmen on the *Barbara Bray*, was ever to see Joanna Franks alive again.

CHAPTER ELEVEN

'Pon my word, Watson, you are coming along wonderfully. You have really done very well indeed. It is true that you have missed everything of importance, but you have hit upon the method

(*Sir Arthur Conan Doyle*, A Case of Identity)

AS WITH PART ONE, Morse found himself making a few notes (mentally, this time) as he read through the unhappy narrative. For some reason he felt vaguely dissatisfied with himself. Something was nagging at his brain about Part One; but for the present he was unable to put a finger on it. It would come back to him once he'd re-read a few pages. No hurry, was there? None. The theoretical problem which his mind had suddenly seized upon was no more than a bit of harmless, quite inconsequential amusement. And yet the doubts persisted in his brain: could anyone, *anyone,* read this story and not find himself questioning one or two of the points so confidently reported? Or two or three of them? Or three or four?

What was the normal pattern of entertainment for canal boatmen, like Oldfield, on those 'protracted stops' of theirs? Changing horses was obviously one of the key activities on such occasions, but one scarcely calculated to gladden every soul. Dropping in at the local knocking-shop, then? A likely port-of-call for a few of the more strongly sexed among them, most surely. And drink? Did they drink their wages away, these boatmen, in the low-beamed bars that were built along their way? How not? Why not? What else was there to do? And though drink (as the Porter once claimed) might take away the performance, who could gainsay that it frequently provoked the desire? The desire, in this case, to rape a beautiful woman-passenger.

So many questions.

But if sex was at the bottom of things, why were the rape charges dropped at the first trial? Agreed, there was no DNA biological fingerprinting in the 1850s; no genetic code that could be read into some desperate fellow's swift ejaculations. But even in that era, the charge of rape could often be made to stick without too much difficulty; and Confucius's old pleasantry about the comparative immobility of a man with his trousers round his ankles must have sounded just as hollow then as now. Certainly to the ears of Joanna Franks.

The footnote referring to the *Court Registers* had been a surprise, and it would be of interest, certainly to the sociologist, to read something of contemporary attitudes to rape in 1859. Pretty certainly it would be a few leagues less sympathetic than that reflected in Morse's morning copy of *The Times*: 'Legal Precedent in Civil Action – £35,000 damages for Rape Victim'.

Where were those Registers, though – if they still existed? They might (Morse supposed) have explained the Colonel's bracketed caveat about discrepancies. But *what* discrepancies? There must have been *something* in old Deniston's mind, something that bothered him just that tiny bit. The Greeks had a word for it – *parakrousis* – the striking of a slightly wrong note in an otherwise tuneful harmony.

Was that 'wrong note' struck by Mrs Laurenson, perhaps? Whatever the situation had been with Joanna, this Laurenson woman (with her husband's full assent, one must assume) had joined the *Barbara Bray* for the journey down to King's Sutton with – as the reader was led to believe – a boat-load of sexually rampant dipso-maniacs. Difficult to swallow? Unless of course the wharfinger, Laurenson, was perfectly happy to get rid of his missus for the night – or for any night. But such a line of reasoning seemed fanciful, and there was a further possibility – a very simple, and really rather a startling one: that the crew of the *Barbara Bray* had *not* been all that belligerently blotto at the time! But no. Every piece of evidence – surely! – pointed in the opposite direction; pointed to the fact that the boat-men's robes of honour (in Fitzgeraldian phrase) were resting, like the Confucian rapist's, only just above their boot-laces.

Boots . . . shoes . . .

What was all that about those shoes? Why were they figuring so repeatedly in the story? There would surely have been more intimate items of Joanna's wardrobe to pilfer if the crewmen had been seeking to effect some easier sexual congress. One of them *might*, perhaps, have been a clandestine foot-fetishist . . .

Morse, telling himself not to be so stupid, looked again at the last couple of pages of the text. A bit over-written, all that stuff about the sentinel-like old lock-house, looking out over the dark waters. Not bad, though: and at least it made Morse resolve to drive out and see it for himself, once he was well again. Unless the planners and the developers had already pulled it down.

Like they'd pulled down St Ebbe's . . .

Such were some of Morse's thoughts after reading his second instalment. It was quite natural that he should wish to eke out the pleasures afforded by the Colonel's text. Yet it must be admitted that, once again, Morse had almost totally failed to conceive the real problems raised by this narrative. Usually, Morse was a league and a league in front of any competitive intellects; and even now his thought processes were clear and unorthodox. But for the time being, he was far below his best. Too near the picture. He was standing where the coloured paints on the narrow-boat's sides had little chance of imposing any pattern on his eye. What he really needed was to stand that bit further back from the picture; to get a more synoptic view of things. 'Synoptic' had always been one of Morse's favourite words. Quickly Morse re-read Part Two. But he seemed to see little more in general terms than he had done earlier, although there were a few extra points of detail which had evaded him on the first reading, and he stored them away, haphazardly, in his brain.

There was that capital 'J', for example, that the Colonel favoured whenever he wished to emphasize the enormity of human iniquity and the infallibility of Jury and Judicature – like the capital 'G' the Christian Churches always used for God.

Then there were those journeys through the two tunnels, when Oldfield had sat with Joanna ... or when, as Morse translated things, he put his arm around the frightened girl in the eerie darkness, and told her not to be afraid ...

And those last complex, confusing paragraphs! She had been desperately anxious to get off the boat and away from her tipsy persecutors – so much seemed beyond any reasonable doubt. But, if so, why, according to that selfsame evidence, had she always been so anxious to get back *on* again?

Airy-fairy speculation, all this; but there were at least two things that could be factually checked. 'Nothing was convenient', it had said, and any researcher worth his salt could easily verify *that*. What *was* available, at the time Joanna reached Banbury? He could also soon discover how much any alternative route to London would have cost. What, for example, was the rail-fare to London in 1859? For that matter, what exactly had been the rail-fare between Liverpool and London, a fare which appeared to have been beyond the Franks's joint financial resources?

Interesting ...

As, come to think of it, were those double quotation

marks in the text – presumably the actual words, directly transcribed, and reported *verbatim*, and therefore primary source material for the crewmen's trial. Morse looked through the interspersed quotations again, and one in particular caused his mind to linger: "coaches to London – and coaches from Oxford to Banbury". Now, if those were the *exact* words Joanna had used . . . *if* they were . . . Why had she asked for the times of coaches 'from Oxford to Banbury'? Surely, she should have been asking about coaches *from Banbury to Oxford*. Unless . . . unless . . .

Again, it all seemed most interesting – at least to Morse. What, finally, was he to make of that drink business? Had Joanna been drinking – or had she not? There was some curious ambivalence in the text; and perhaps this may have been in the Colonel's mind when he referred to 'a few conflicting statements'? But no – that was impossible. Mr Bartholomew Samuels had found no alcohol in Joanna's body, and that was that!

Or, rather, would have been, to most men.

The thought of drink had begun to concentrate Morse's mind powerfully, and with great circumspection and care, Morse poured a finger of Scotch into his bedside glass, with the same amount of plain water. Wonderful! Pity that no one would ever believe his protestations that Scotch was a necessary stimulant to his brain cells! For after a few minutes his mind was flooding with ideas – exciting ideas! – and furthermore he realized that he could begin to test one or two of his hypotheses that very evening.

That is, if Walter Greenaway's daughter came to visit.

CHAPTER TWELVE

Th' first thing to have in a libry is a shelf. Fr'm time to time this can be decorated with lithrachure. But th' shelf is th' main thing.

(*Finley Peter Dunne*, Mr Dooley Says)

As she walked down Broad Street at 7.40 a.m. the following morning (Thursday), Christine Greenaway was thinking (*still* thinking) about the man who had spoken to her the previous evening in Ward 7C on the top floor of the JR2. (It was only on rare occasions that she welcomed her father's pride in his ever-loving daughter!) It wasn't that she'd been obsessively pre-occupied with the man ever since; but there had been a semi-waking, overnight awareness of him. All because he'd asked her, so nicely, to look up something for him in the Bodley. So earnest, so grateful, he'd seemed. And that was silly, really, because she'd willingly have helped him, anyway. That's why she'd become a librarian in the first place: to be able to locate some of the landmarks in the fields of History and Literature, and to provide where she could the correct map-references for so many curious enquiries. Even as a five-year-old, with her blonde plaits reaching half-way down her bony back, she'd envied the woman in the Summertown Library who similarly located tickets somewhere in the long drawers behind the high counter; envied, even more, the woman who stamped the dates in the front of the borrowed books, and inserted each little ticket into its appropriate, oblong folder. Not that she, Christine Greenaway, performed any longer such menial tasks herself. Almost forgotten now were those inevitable queries of who wrote *The Wind in the Willows*; for she, Christine, was now the senior of the three august librarians who sat at the northern end of the Bodleian's Lower Reading Room, where her daily duties demanded assistance to both senior and junior members of the University: checking slips, identifying shelf-marks, suggesting reference-sections, making and taking phone calls (one, yesterday, from the University of Uppsala). And over these last years she had felt a sense of importance and enjoyment in her job – of functioning happily in the workings of the University.

Of course, there had been some major disappointments in her life, as there had been, she knew, with most folk. Married at twenty-two, she had been a divorcee at twenty-three. No other woman on his part; no other man on hers – although there'd been (still were) so many opportunities. No! It was simply that her husband had been so immature and irresponsible – and, above all, so boring! Once the pair of them had got down to running a home, keeping a monthly budget, checking bank-statements – well, she'd known he could never really be the man for her. And as things now stood, she could no longer stomach the prospect of another mildly ignorant, semi-aggressively macho figure of a bed-mate. Free as she was of any financial worries, she could do exactly as she wished about issues that were important to *her*; and she had become a modestly active member of several organizations, including Greenpeace, CND, the Ramblers' Association, and the RSPB. Quite certainly, she would never join one of those match-making societies with the hope of finding a more interesting specimen than her former spouse. If ever she *did* look for another husband, he would have to be someone she could, in some way, come to *respect*: to respect for his conversation or his experience or his intellect or his knowledge or his – well, his anything at all, really, except a pride in his sexual prowess. So what (she asked herself) had all this got to do with *him*? Not much to look at, was he? Balding, and quite certainly carrying considerable excess weight around the midriff. Though, to be honest with herself, she was beginning to feel a grudging regard for those men who were just *slightly* overweight, perhaps because she herself seemed never able to put on a few pounds – however much she over-indulged in full-cream cakes and deep-fried fish and chips.

Forget him! Forget him, Christine!

Such self-admonition prevailed as she walked that morning down the Broad, past Balliol and Trinity on her left, before crossing over the road, just before Blackwell's, and proceeding, *sub imperatoribus*, up the semi-circular steps into the gravelled courtyard of the Sheldonian. Thence, keeping to her right, she walked past the SILENCE PLEASE notice under the archway, and came out at last into her real home territory – the Quadrangle of the Schools.

For many days, when six years earlier she had first started working at the Bodleian, she had been conscious of the beautiful setting there. Over the months and years, though, she had gradually grown over-familiar with what the postcards on sale in the Proscholium still called 'The Golden Heart of Oxford'; grown familiar, as she'd regularly trodden the gravelled quad, with the Tower of the Five Orders to her left, made her way past the bronze statue of the third Earl of Pembroke, and entered the Bodleian Library through the great single doorway in the West side, beneath the four tiers of blind arches in their gloriously mellowed stone.

Different today though – so very different! She felt once again the sharp irregularities of the gravel-stones beneath the soles of her expensive, high-heeled, leather shoes. And she was happily aware once more of the mediaeval Faculties painted over those familiar doors around the quad. In particular, she looked again at her favourite sign: SCHOLA NATURALIS PHILOSO-PHIAE, the gilt capital-letters set off, with their maroon border, against a background of the deepest Oxford-blue. And as she climbed the wooden staircase to the Lower Reading Room, Christine Greenaway reminded herself, with a shy smile around her thinly delicious lips, why perhaps it had taken her so long to re-appreciate those neglected delights that were all around her.

She hung her coat in the Librarians' Cloakroom,

and started her daily duties. It was always tedious, that first hour (7.45–8.45 a.m.), clearing up the books left on the tables from the previous day, and ensuring that the new day's readers could be justifiably confident that the Bodley's books once more stood ready on their appointed shelves.

She thought back to the brief passages of conversation the previous evening, when he'd nodded over to her (only some six feet away):

'You work at the Bodleian, I hear?'

'Uh-huh!'

'It may be – it is! – a bit of a cheek, not knowing you . . .'

' – but you'd like me to look something up for you.'

Morse nodded, with a winsome smile.

She'd known he was some sort of policeman – things like that always got round the wards pretty quickly. His eyes had held hers for a few seconds, but she had been conscious neither of their blueness nor of their authority: only their melancholy and their vulnerability. Yet she had sensed that those complicated eyes of his had seemed to look, somehow, deep down inside herself, and *to like what they had seen.*

'Silly twerp, you are!' she told herself. She was behaving like some adolescent schoolgirl, smitten with a sudden passion for a teacher. But the truth remained – that for that moment she was prepared to run a marathon in clogs and calipers for the whitish-haired and gaudily pyjamaed occupant of the bed immediately opposite her father's.

Chapter Thirteen

Ah, fill the Cup: — what boots it to repeat
   How Time is slipping underneath our Feet:
   Unborn To-morrow, and dead Yesterday,
Why fret about them if To-day be sweet!
(*Edward Fitzgerald*, The Rubaiyat of Omar Khayyam)

HE'D BEEN RATHER vague, and it had been somewhat difficult precisely to assess what he wanted: some specific details about any assurance or insurance companies in the mid-nineteenth century – especially, if it were possible, about companies in the Midlands. Off and on, during the morning, it had taken her an hour or more to hunt down the appropriate catalogues; and another hour to locate the pertinent literature. But by lunch-time (praise be!) she had completed her research, experiencing, as she assumed, an elation similar to that of the scholars who daily dug into the treasury of her Great Library to extract their small nuggets of gold. She had found a work of reference which told her exactly what Morse (the man responsible for ruffling her wonted calm) had wanted her to find.

Just after twelve noon, with one of her female

colleagues, she walked over to the King's Arms, on the corner of Holywell Street – in which hostelry she was accustomed to enjoy her fifty-five minute lunch-break, with a single glass of white wine and a salmon-and-cucumber sandwich. It was when Christine got to her feet and offered to get in a second round of drinks, that her colleague eyed her curiously.

'You always said two glasses sent you to sleep.'

'So?'

'So I'll go to sleep as well, all right?'

They were good friends; and doubtless Christine would have given some castrated account of her visit to the JR2 the previous evening, had not another colleague joined them. Whereafter the three were soon engaged in happily animated conversation about interior decorating and the iniquity of current mortgage repayments.

Or two of them were, to be more accurate. And the one who had been the least lively of the trio found herself doing rather less work than usual that same afternoon. After carefully photocopying her finds, she wished the p.m. hours away, for she was impatient to parade the fruits of her research; and she just, simply – well, she just wanted to see the man again. That was all.

At 6.30 p.m. at her home in the village of Bletchington, some few miles out of Oxford, towards Otmoor, she slowly stroked red polish on to her smoothly manicured oval nails, and at 7 p.m. started out for the JR2.

Equally, from his own vantage point, Morse was looking forward to seeing Christine Greenaway once again. The previous evening he'd quickly appreciated her professionalism as she'd listened to his request, as she'd calculated how it might be implemented. In a more personal way he'd noted, too, the candour and intelligence of her eyes – eyes almost as blue as his own – and the quiet determination around her small mouth. So it was that at 7.25 p.m. he was sitting in his neatly re-made bed, newly washed, erect against his pillows, his thinning hair so recently re-combed – when his stomach suddenly felt as though it was being put through a mangle; and for two or three minutes the pain refused to relax its grinding, agonizing grip. Morse closed his eyes and squeezed his fists with such force that the sweat stood out on his forehead; and with eyes still shut he prayed to Someone, in spite of his recent conversion from agnosticism to outright atheism.

Two years earlier, at the Oxford Book Association, he had listened to a mournful Muggeridge propounding the disturbing philosophy of The Fearful Symmetry, in which the debits and the credits on the ledgers are balanced inexorably and eternally, and where the man who tries to steal a secret pleasure will pretty soon find himself queuing up to pay the bill – and more often than not with some hefty service-charges added in. What a preposterous belief it was (the sage had asserted) that the hedonist could be a happy man!

Oh dear!

Why had Morse ever considered the pleasure of a little glass? The wages of sin was death, and the night before was seldom worth the morning after (some people said). All mortals, Morse knew, were ever treading that narrow way by Tophet flare to Judgement Day, but he now prayed that the last few steps in his own case might be deferred at least a week or two.

Then, suddenly as it had come, the pain was gone, and Morse opened his eyes once more.

The clock behind Sister's desk (as earlier and darkly rumoured, Nessie was going to be on the night-shift) was showing 7.30 when the visitors began to filter through with their offerings stashed away in Sainsbury or St Michael carriers, and, some few of them, with bunches of blooms for the newly hospitalized.

Life is, alas, so full of disappointments; and it was to be an unexpected visitor who was to monopolize Morse's time that evening. Bearing a wilting collection of white chrysanthemums, a sombre-looking woman of late-middle age proceeded to commandeer the sole chair set at his bedside.

'Mrs Green! How very nice of you to come!'

Morse's heart sank deeply, and took an even deeper plunge when the dutiful charlady mounted a sustained challenge against Morse's present competence to deal, single-handedly, with such crucial matters as towels, toothpaste, talcum-powder, and clean pyjamas (especially the latter). It was wonderfully good of her (who could deny it?) to take such trouble to come to see him (*three* buses, as Morse knew full well); but he found himself consciously *willing* her to get up and *go*.

At five minutes past eight, after half a dozen 'I-really must-go's, Mrs G. rose to her poorly feet in preparation for her departure, with instructions for the care of the chrysanthemums. At last (at last!), after a mercifully brief account of her latest visit to her 'sheeropodist' in Banbury Road, Mrs G. dragged her long-suffering feet away from Ward 7C.

On several occasions, from her father's bedside, Christine Greenaway had half-turned in the course of her filial obligations; and two or three times her eyes had locked with Morse's: hers with the half-masked smile of understanding; his with all the impotence of some stranded whale.

Just as Mrs Green was on her way, a white-coated consultant, accompanied by the Charge Nurse, decided (inconsiderately) to give ten minutes of his time to Greenaway Senior, and then in some *sotto voce* asides, to confide his prognosis to Greenaway Junior. And for Morse, this hiatus in the evening's ordering was getting just about as infuriating as waiting for breakfast in some 'Fawlty Towers' hotel.

Then Lewis came.

Never had Morse been less glad to see his sergeant; yet he *had* instructed Lewis to pick up his post from the flat, and he now took possession of several envelopes and a couple of cards: Morse's shoes (his other pair) were now ready for collection from Grove Street; his car licence was due to be renewed within the next twenty days; a ridiculously expensive book on *The Transmission of Classical Manuscripts* now awaited him at OUP; a bill from the plumber for the repair of a malfunctioning stop-cock was still unpaid; the Wagner Society asked if he wanted to enter his name in a raffle for Bayreuth *Ring* tickets; and Peter Imbert invited him to talk in the new year at a weekend symposium, in Hendon, on inner-city crime. It was rather like a cross-section of life, his usual correspondence: half of it was fine, and half of it he wanted to forget.

At twenty-three minutes past eight, by the ward clock, Lewis asked if there was anything else he could do.

'Yes, Lewis. Please *go*, will you? I want to have five minutes with – ' Morse nodded vaguely over to Greenaway's bed.

'Well, if that's what you want, sir.' He rose slowly to his feet.

'It *is* what I bloody want, Lewis! I've just *told* you, haven't I?'

Lewis took a large bunch of white seedless grapes (£2.50 a pound) from his carrier-bag. 'I thought – we thought, the missus and me – we thought you'd enjoy them, sir.'

He was gone; and Morse knew, within a second of his going, that he would not be forgiving himself easily for such monumental ingratitude. But the damage was done: *nescit vox missa reverti*.

The bell rang two minutes later, and Christine came across to Morse's bed as she left, and handed him six large photocopied sheets.

'I hope this is what you wanted.'

'I'm ever so grateful. It's – it's a pity we didn't have a chance to . . .'

'I understand. I *do* understand,' she said. 'And you will let me know if I can do anything else?'

'Look . . . perhaps if we—'

'Come along now, please!' The Charge Nurse's voice

sounded to Morse almost as imperious as Nessie's as she walked quickly around the beds.

'I'm so grateful,' said Morse. 'I really am! As I say it's . . .'

'Yes,' said Christine softly.

'Will you be in tomorrow?' asked Morse quickly.

'No – not tomorrow. We've got some librarians coming from California—'

'Come along now, *please*!'

Mrs Green, Sergeant Lewis, Christine Greenaway – now all of them gone; and already the medicine-trolley had been wheeled into the ward, and the nurses were starting out on yet another circuit of measurements and medicaments.

And Morse felt sick at heart.

It was at 9.20 p.m. that he finally settled back against his piled pillows to glance quickly through the photocopied material Christine had found for him. And soon he was deeply and happily engrossed – his temporary despondency departing on the instant.

CHAPTER FOURTEEN

Being in the land of the living was itself the survivor's
privilege, for so many of one's peers — one's brothers
and sisters — had already fallen by the wayside, having
died at birth, at infancy or childhood
(*Roy & Dorothy Porter*, In Sickness and in Health)

THE DOCUMENTS WHICH Morse now handled were
just the thing (he had little doubt) for satisfying the
original-source-material philosophy which was just then
swamping the GCSE and A-level syllabuses. And for
Morse, whose School Certificate in History (Credit)
had demanded little more than semi-familiarity with the
earliest models of seed-drills and similar agricultural
adjuncts of the late eighteenth century, the reading of
them was fascinating. Particularly poignant, as it appeared to Morse, was the Foreword to the *Insurance
Guide and Hand-Book 1860* (bless the girl! — she'd even
got the exact year) where the anonymous author stated
his own determination to soldier along in 'this vale of
tears' for as long as decently possible:

'Thus it is that all our efforts are forever required,
not to surpass what we may call the biblical "par" for

84

life – that famous "three-score years and ten" – but to come reasonably near to attaining it at all. For it is only by continuous vigilance and energy in the work for self preservation that the appointed average can be brought into view; and with good fortune and good sense (and God's grace) be achieved.'

It was interesting to find the Almighty in parenthesis, even in 1860, and Morse felt he would like to have known the author. Yet when that same author went on to assert that 'mortality had decreased by two-fifths between 1720 and 1820', Morse began to wonder what on earth such a bafflingly unscientific – indeed, quite nonsensical – statement might mean. What did seem immediately clear, as he read through the small print, was that people during those years were beginning to live rather longer, and that by the middle of the nineteenth century insurance companies were beginning to match this sociological phenomenon with increasingly attractive rates and premiums, in spite of the sombre statistics appended to each year, right up to the 1850s. Like 1853, e.g. – the figures for which Morse now considered. Of the half million or so departed souls reported in the pages of the Guide, 55,000 had died of consumption, 25,000 of pneumonia, 24,500 of convulsions, 23,000 of bronchitis, 20,000 of premature death and debility, 19,000 of typhus, 16,000 of scarlatina, 15,000 of diarrhoea, 14,000 of heart disease, 12,000 of whooping cough, 11,000 of dropsy, 9,000 of apoplexy, 8,500 of paralysis, 6,000 of asthma, 5,750 of cancer, 4,000 of teeth troubles, 3,750 of measles, 3,500 of croup, 3,250 of smallpox, 3,000 of (mothers) giving birth; and so on to the smaller numbers succumbing to diseases of brain, kidney, liver, and other perishable parts of the anatomy – and to old age! As he added up such numbers quickly in his head, Morse realized that about two-thirds of the 500,000 were unaccounted for; and he had to assume that even with a few more categories added ('murder' for one!) there must have been vast numbers of people in those days whose deaths were for some reason or other not specifically 'accounted for' at all, albeit being registered in the national statistics. Perhaps a lot of them were just not important enough to get their own particular malady spelled out on any death certificate; perhaps many of the physicians, midwives, nurses, poor-law-attendants, or whatever, just didn't know, or didn't want to know, or didn't care.

As he lay back on the pillows and thought of the circumstances besetting the luckless Joanna Franks, who had died neither of consumption nor pneumonia . . . nor . . . he suddenly fell into a sleep so deep that he missed his 10 p.m. Horlicks and his treasured digestive biscuit; and then he woke up again, somewhat less than refreshed, at 11.45 p.m., with a dry throat and a clear head. The lights in the ward were turned down to half power, and the other patients around him seemed contentedly asleep – apart from the man who'd been admitted late that afternoon and around whom the medical staff had been fussing with a rather ominous concern; the man who now lay staring at the ceiling, doubtless contemplating the imminent collapse of his earthly fortunes.

Nessie was nowhere to be seen: the desk was empty.

He'd just had a nasty little dream. He'd been playing cricket in his early days at Grammar School; and when it came to his turn to bat, he couldn't find his boots . . . and then when he did find them the laces kept snapping; and he was verging on a tearful despair – when he'd awoken. It might have been Mrs Green talking about her chiropody? Or was it Lewis, perhaps, who'd brought the card from the cobblers? Or neither of them? Was it not more likely to have been a young woman in 1859 who'd shouted, with her particular brand of terrified despair, 'What have you done with my shoes?'

He looked around again: the desk was still empty.

Surely he wasn't likely to imperil the well-being of the ward if he turned on his angle-lamp? Especially if focused directly into a small pool of light on his own pillows? No! Reading a book wasn't going to hurt anyone and the sick man had had *his* light on all the time.

Pushing in the button switch, he turned on his own light, with no reaction from anyone; and still no sign of Nessie.

Part Three of *Murder on the Oxford Canal* was close to hand; but Morse was reluctant to finish *that* too quickly. He remembered when he'd first read *Bleak House* (still to his mind the greatest novel in the English language) he'd deliberately decelerated his reading as the final pages grew ever thinner beneath his fingers. Never had he wanted to hang on to a story so much! Not that the Colonel's work was anything to wax all that lyrical about; and yet Morse *did* want to eke it out – or so he told himself. Which left the not displeasing possibility of a few further chapters of *The Blue Ticket* – with Mr Greenaway now fast asleep. The pattern of crime in nineteenth-century Shropshire had already joined the local legion of lost causes.

Morse was soon well into the exploits of a blonde who would have had arrows on her black stockings pointing northward and reading 'This way for the knickers' – that is, if she'd worn any stockings; or worn any knickers, for that matter. And it was amid much parading of bodies, pawing of bosoms, and patting of buttocks, that Morse now spent an enjoyable little interval of erotic pleasure; indeed, was so engrossed that he did not mark her approach.

'What do you think you're doing?'

'I was just—'

'Lights go out at ten o'clock. You're disturbing everyone on the ward.'

'They're all asleep.'

'Not for much longer, with you around!'

'I'm sorry—'

'What's this you're reading?'

Before he could do anything about it, Nessie had removed the book from his hands, and he had no option but to watch her helplessly. She made no comment, passed no moral judgement, and for a brief second Morse wondered if he had not seen a glint of some semi-amusement in those sharp eyes as they had skimmed a couple of paragraphs.

'Time you were asleep!' she said, in a not unkindly fashion, handing him back the book. Her voice was as crisp as her uniform, and Morse replaced the ill-starred volume in his locker. 'And be careful of your fruit juice!' She moved the half-filled glass one millimetre to the left, turned off the light, and was gone. And Morse gently eased himself down into the warmth and comfort of his bed, like Tennyson's lily sliding slowly into the bosom of the lake . . .

That night he dreamed a dream in Technicolor (he swore it!), although he knew such a claim would be contradicted by the oneirologists. He saw the ochre-skinned, scantily clad siren in her black, arrowed stockings, and he could even recall her lavender-hued underclothing. Almost it was the perfect dream! Almost. For there was a curiously insistent need in Morse's brain which paradoxically demanded a *factual* name and place and time before, in *fantasy*, that sexually unabashed freebooter could be his. And in Morse's muddled computer of a mind, that siren took the name of one Joanna Franks, provocatively walking along towards Duke's Cut, in the month of June in 1859.

When he awoke (was woken, rather) the following morning, he felt wonderfully refreshed, and he resolved that he would take no risks of any third humiliation over *The Blue Ticket*. With breakfast, temperature, wash, shave, blood-pressure, newspaper, tablets, Bovril, all these now behind him – and with not a visitor in sight – he settled down to discover exactly what had happened to that young woman who had taken control of his nocturnal fantasies.

CHAPTER FIFTEEN

PART THREE

A Protracted Trial

JOANNA FRANKS'S BODY was found at Duke's Cut at about 5.30 a.m. on Wednesday, 22nd June 1859. Philip Tomes, a boatman, said he was passing down-canal towards Oxford when he saw something in the water – something which was soon identified as, in part, a woman's gown; what else, though, he could not for the moment make out in the darkened waters. The object was on the side of the canal opposite the tow-path, and in due course he discovered it to be the body of a female, without either bonnet or shoes. She was floating alongside the bank, head north, feet south, and there was no observable movement about her. She was lying on her face, which seemed quite black. Tomes stopped his boat, and with a boat-hook gently pulled the body to the tow-path side, where he lifted it out of the water, in which latter task he was assisted by John Ward, a Kidlington fisherman, who happened to be passing alongside the canal at that early hour. In fact, it was Ward who had the presence of mind to arrange for the body, which was still warm, to be taken down to the Plough Inn at Wolvercote.

It appears from various strands of inter-weaving evidence, albeit some of it from the guilty parties themselves, that Oldfield and Musson (and, by one account, Towns also) left the *Barbara Bray* at roughly the point where Joanna met her death, and that they were seen standing together on the tow-path side of the canal just below Duke's Cut. A certain man passed by the area at the crucial time, 4 a.m. or just after, and both Oldfield and Musson, with great presence of mind, asked him if he had seen a woman walking beside the canal. The man had replied, as they clearly recalled, with a very definite "No!", and had made to get further on his way with all speed. Yet the two (or perhaps three) men had asked him the same question again and again, in rather an agitated manner.

(It is clear that this man's testimony could have been vital in substantiating the boatmen's claims. But he was never traced, in spite of wide-scale enquiries in the area. A man roughly answering his description, one Donald Favant, had signed the register at the Nag's Head in Oxford for either the 20th or the 21st June – there was some doubt – but this man never came forward. The strong implication must therefore remain, as it did at the time, that the whole story was the clever concoction of desperate men.)

Jonas Bamsey, wharfinger in the employ of the Oxford Canal Authority at Oxford's Hayfield Wharf, gave evidence at the trial that the *Barbara Bray* had duly effected its partial unloading, but that Oldfield had not reported the loss of any passenger – which quite certainly should have been the duty of the boat's captain under the Authority's Regulations. Instead, according to the scant and inconsistent evidence at this point, the boatmen do appear to have confided in some of their acquaintances in Upper Fisher Row, claiming that their passenger had been out of her mind; that she had committed suicide; and that on at least one occasion they had been called upon to save her from an attempted drowning on the journey down from Preston Brook.

Later that dreadful day, when the crew of the *Barbara Bray* came to negotiate the lock on the Thames at Iffley, two miles downstream from Folly Bridge, Oldfield spoke to the keeper, Albert Lee, and reported to him and his wife (coincidentally also named Joanna) that a passenger on his boat had been drowned; but that she was most sadly deranged, and had been a sore trial to him and his fellow crew-members ever since she had first embarked at Preston Brook. Oldfield was still obviously very drunk. Pressed to explain what he was seeking to say, Oldfield – asserted only that "It was a very bad job that had happened". The passenger was "off her head" and had been last seen by the crew off Gibraltar Lock. Yet Oldfield was vehemently unwilling to listen to Lee's suggestion of returning to Oxford to sort out the whole tragedy; and this made Lee more than somewhat suspicious. On the departure of the *Barbara Bray*, therefore, he himself immediately set off for Oxford, where he contacted the Pickford Office; and where the Pickford Office, in turn, contacted the Police Authority.

When the infamous boat finally arrived at Reading (for some reason, over two hours behind schedule) Constable Harrison was on hand, with appropriate support, to take the entire crew into custody, and to testify that all of them, including the youth, were still observably drunk and excessively abusive as he put them in darbies and escorted them to temporary cell-accommodation in the gaol at Reading. One of them, as Harrison vividly recalled, was vile enough to repeat some of his earlier invective against Joanna Franks, and was heard to mutter "Damn and blast that wicked woman!"

Hannah MacNeill, a serving woman at the Plough Inn, Wolvercote, testified that when the sodden body had been brought from the canal, she had been employed, under direction, to take off Joanna's clothes. The left sleeve was torn out of its gathers and the cuff on the same hand was also torn. Tomes and Ward, for their part, were quite firm in their evidence that they themselves had made no rips or tears in Joanna's clothing as they lifted her carefully from the water at Duke's Cut.

Katharine Maddison testified that she was a co-helper with Hannah MacNeill in taking off Joanna's drenched garments. Particularly had she noticed the state of Joanna's calico knickers which had been ripped right across the front. This garment was produced in Court; and many were later to agree that the production of such an intimate item served further to heighten the universal feeling of revulsion against those callous men who were now arraigned with her murder.

Mr Samuels, the Oxford surgeon who examined the body at the inquest, reported signs of bruising below the elbow of the left arm, and further indications of subcutaneous bruising below left and right cheekbones; the same man described the dead woman's face as presenting a state of "discoloration and disfigurement". Mr Samuels agreed that it was perhaps possible for the facial injuries, such as they were, to have been caused by unspecified and accidental incidents in the water, or in the process of taking-up from the water. Yet such a possibility was now seeming, both to Judge and Jury, more and more remote.

The youth Wootton then gave his version of the tragic events, and on one point he expressed himself forcefully: that Towns had got himself "good and half-seas-over" the night before Joanna was found, and that he was sound asleep at the time the murder must have occurred, for he (Wootton) had heard him "snoring loudly". We shall never be in a position to know whether Towns had forced Wootton to give this evidence to the Court – under some threat or other, perhaps. From subsequent developments, however, it seems clear that we may give a substantial degree of credence to Wootton's testimony.

Joseph Jarnell, the co-prisoner pending whose evidence the re-trial had been agreed, related to the Court the damning confessions Oldfield had betrayed whilst the two men shared a prison-cell. In essence such 'confessions' amounted to a rather crude attempt on Oldfield's part to settle the majority of blame for almost everything which had happened on Musson and Towns. But in spite of the man's earnest manner and the consistency of his account, Jarnell's story made little or no impression. Yet his testimony carried interest, if not conviction. Amongst the strongest of the fabrications which Oldfield had sought to put about was that Joanna Franks had in excess of fifty golden sovereigns in one of her two boxes; that Towns had discovered this fact, and that Joanna had found him rummaging through her trunks. She had threatened (so the allegation ran) to report him to the next Pickford Office if he did not mend his ways and make immediate apology and restoration. (Such nonsense was wholly discredited at the time, and may be safely discounted now.)

Together with many other items, the knife which Joanna had been observed sharpening was later found in one of her trunks, the cord of which had been cut, and which still remained untied. The assumption was that at some point the men had opened Joanna's belongings after the murder, and had replaced the knife in one of the trunks. It must certainly be considered a strong possibility that the men intended to steal some of her possessions, for as we have seen a charge of theft was included, in the most strongly worded terms, in the original indictment of the crew at the first trial in August 1859. It seems, however, that Prosecuting Counsel at the second trial were sufficiently confident to forgo such a charge and to concentrate their accusations on murder, since the lesser charge (difficult, in any case, as it would have been to substantiate) was subsequently excluded. We have seen a similar procedure operating, in the first trial, concerning the charges of rape; and perhaps it is of some strange and macabre interest to note that in the original trial the charges of both rape and theft (as well as murder) were made against each individual member of the crew – including the youth Wootton.

Out of all the evidence given at that memorable second trial at Oxford in April 1860, fairly certainly that of Charles Franks himself evoked the greatest feeling and the widest sympathy. The poor man was weeping aloud as he entered the witness-box, and it seemed as if it were almost beyond his physical powers to raise his eyes in order to bear the sight of the prisoners and to look upon their faces. He had obviously been deeply in love with Joanna, and turning his back on the vile men arraigned before the Court he explained how in consequence of some information he had come into Oxfordshire and seen his wife's dead body at the time of the inquest. For although it was dreadfully disfigured (here the poor fellow could not at all restrain his feelings) yet he knew it by a small mark behind his wife's left ear, a mark of which only a parent or an intimate lover could have known. Corroboration of identification (if, in fact, corroboration was needed) was afforded by the shoes, later found in the fore-cabin of the *Barbara Bray*, which matched in the minutest degrees the contours of the dead woman's feet.

At the conclusion of the hearing, and after a lengthy summing-up by Mr Augustus Benham, the Jury, under their duly appointed chairman, begged permission of his Lordship to retire to consider their verdict.

CHAPTER SIXTEEN

At a hotel facing the sea at Brighton, he ate a good
breakfast of bacon and eggs, toast and marmalade;
then took a stroll round the town before returning to
the station and boarding a train for Worthing
> (*Court Record of evidence given in the trial of
> Neville George Clevely Heath, on the morning after
> the murder of Margery Gardner*)

PERHAPS IT WAS the dream.

Whatever it was, Morse knew that something had at
last prodded him into a slightly more intelligent
appraisal of the Colonel's story, because he was now
beginning to take account of two or three major
considerations which had been staring at him all the
while.

The first of these was the character of Joanna Franks
herself. How had it come about – whatever the fortui-
tous, involuntary, or deliberate circumstances in which
Joanna had met her death – that the crew of the *Barbara
Bray* had insisted time and time again that the wretched
woman had been nothing but one long, sorry trial to
them all ever since she'd first jumped on board at

Preston Brook? How *was* it that they were still damning
and blasting the poor woman's soul to eternity way, way
after they had pushed her into the Canal and, for all
Morse or anyone else knew, held her head under the
black waters until she writhed in agony against their
murderous hands no longer? Had a satisfactory explanation been forthcoming for such events? All right,
there was still Part Four of the story to come. But so far,
the answer was 'no'.

There was, though (as it now occurred to Morse),
one possible dimension to the case that the good
Colonel had never even hinted at – either through an
excessive sense of propriety, or from a lack of imagination – namely that *Joanna Franks had been a seductive
tease*: a woman who over those long hours of that long
journey had begun to drive the crew towards varied
degrees of insanity with her provocative overtures, and
to foster the inevitable jealousies arising therefrom.

Come off it, Morse!

Yes, come off it! There was no evidence to support
such a view. None! Yet the thought stayed with him,
reluctant to leave. An attractive woman . . . boredom
. . . drink . . . a tunnel . . . continued boredom . . . more
drink . . . another tunnel . . . darkness . . . desire . . .
opportunity . . . still more drink . . . and more Priapic
promptings in the loins . . . Yes, all that, perhaps, the
Colonel himself may have understood. But what if she,
Joanna herself, had been the active catalyst in the
matter? What if she had craved for the men just as
much as they had craved for her? What (put it simply,
Morse!) *what if she'd wanted sex just as badly as they did*?

What if she were the precursor of Sue Bridehead in *Jude the Obscure*, driving poor old Phillotson potty, as well as poor old Jude?

'Men's questions!' he heard a voice say. 'Just the sort of thoughts that would occur to an ageing MCP like you!'

There was a second general consideration which, from the point of view of criminal justice, struck Morse as considerably more cogent and a good deal less contentious. In the court-room itself, the odds did seem, surely, to have been stacked pretty heavily against the crew of the *Barbara Bray* – with 'presumption of innocence' playing decidedly second fiddle to 'assumption of guilt'. Even the fair-minded Colonel had let his prejudgements run away with him a little: already he'd decided that any ostensible concern on the part of the boatmen for the missing passenger (believed drowned?) was only shown 'with great presence of mind' in order to establish a semi-convincing alibi for themselves; already he'd decided that these same boatmen, 'still obviously very drunk' (and by implication still knocking it back at top-tipplers' rates) had manoeuvred their 'infamous' craft down the Thames to Reading without having the common decency to mention to anyone the little matter of the murder they'd committed on the way. Did (Morse asked himself) wicked men tend to get more *drunk* – or more *sober* – after committing such callous crimes? Interesting thought . . .

Yes, and there was a third general point – one that seemed to Morse most curious: the charges both of

Theft and of Rape had, for some reason, been dropped against the boatmen. Was this because the Prosecution had been wholly confident, and decided to go for the graver charge of Murder – with the expectation (fully justified) that they had sufficient evidence to convict 'Rory' Oldfield and Co. on the capital indictment? Or was it, perhaps, because they had too *little* confidence in their ability to secure conviction on the *lesser* charges? Obviously, as Morse seemed vaguely to remember from his schooldays, neither rape nor theft would have been considered too venial an offence in the middle of the last century, but ... Or was it just possible that these charges were dropped because there was no convincing evidence to support them? And if so, was the indictment for murder entered upon by the Prosecution for one simple reason – that it presented the *only* hope of bringing those miserable men to justice? Certainly, as far as multiple rape was concerned, the evidence must have been decidedly dodgy – as the Judge in the first trial had pronounced. But what about theft? The pre-requisite of theft was that the aggrieved party possessed something worth the stealing. So what was it that poor Joanna had about her person, or had in either of her two travelling-boxes, that was worth the crime? The evidence, after all, pointed to the fact that she hadn't got a couple of pennies to rub together. Her fare for the canal-trip had been sent up from her husband in London; and even facing the terrible risks of travelling with a drunken, lecherous crew – certainly after Banbury had been reached – she had *not* taken, or not been *able* to take, any alternative means of transport to get to the husband who was awaiting her in the Edgware Road. So? So what had she got, if anything, that was worth stealing?

There were those shoes again, too! Did Joanna deliberately leave off her shoes? Did she enjoy the feel of the mud between her toes along the tow-path – like some bare-foot hippie on a watery walk round Stonehenge in the dawn?

What a strange case it had been! The more he thought about it, the greater the number of questions that kept occurring to Morse's mind. He had a good deal of experience in cases where the forensic and pathological evidence had been vital to the outcome of a court case. But he wasn't particularly impressed with the conclusions that (presumably) must have been drawn from Mr Samuels' comparatively scientific findings. For Morse (wholly, it must be admitted, without medical or scientific qualifications) the state of the dress, and the bruising described, would have been much more consistent with Joanna being held firmly from behind, with the assailant's (?) left hand gripping her left wrist; and his (her?) right hand being held forcibly across her mouth, where thumb and forefinger would almost invariably produce the sort of bruising mentioned in the recorded description.

What of this Jarnell fellow? The Prosecution must have been considerably impressed, at the first hearing, with his potential testimony. Why, otherwise, would anyone be willing to postpone a trial for six months – on the word of a gaolbird? Even the Colonel had given the fellow a good write-up! So why was it that when he duly turned up to tell his tale, at the second trial, no one wished to listen to him? Had there been something, some knowledge, somewhere, that had caused the court to discount, or at least discredit, the disclosures his cell-mate, Oldfield, had allegedly made to him? Because whatever accusations could be levelled against Oldfield, the charge of inconsistency was *not* amongst them. On three occasions, after Joanna's death, he had insisted that she was "out of her mind", "sadly deranged", "off her head" ... And there had, it appeared, been no conflict of evidence between the crewmen that on one occasion at least (did that mean two?) they had been called upon to save Joanna from drowning herself. The one vital point Jarnell disclosed was that Oldfield had not only protested his own innocence of the murder, but had also sought to shift all responsibility on to his fellow crewmen. Not, to be sure, a very praiseworthy piece of behaviour! Yet, *if Oldfield himself were innocent,* where else could he have laid the blame? At the time, in any case, no one had been willing to listen seriously either to what Jarnell or to what Oldfield might have to say. But if they were right? Or if *one* of them were right?

A curious little thought struck Morse at this point, and lodged itself in a corner of his brain – for future reference. And a rather bigger thought struck him simultaneously: that he needed to remember he was only playing a game with himself; only trying to get through a few days' illness with a happy little problem to amuse himself with – like a tricky cryptic crossword from *The Listener.* It was just a little worrying, that was all ... the way the dice had been loaded all the time against those drunkards who had murdered Joanna Franks.

And the niggling doubt persisted.

If they had ...

CHAPTER SEVENTEEN

The detective novelist, as a class, hankers after complication and ingenuity, and is disposed to reject the obvious and acquit the accused if possible. He is uneasy until he has gone further and found some new and satisfying explanation of the problem

(*Dorothy L. Sayers*, The Murder of Julia Wallace)

THE THOUGHT THAT the crewmen may not have been guilty of Joanna Franks's murder proved to be one of those heady notions that evaporate in the sunrise of reason. For if the crewmen had not been responsible, who on earth had? Nevertheless, it seemed to Morse pretty much odds-on that if the case had been heard a century later, there would have been no certain conviction. Doubtless, at the time, the jury's verdict had looked safe and satisfactory, especially to the hostile crowds lining the streets and baying for blood. But *should* the verdict have been reached? True, there was enough circumstantial suspicion to sentence a saint; yet no really *direct* evidence, was there? No witnesses to murder; no indication of *how* the murder had been committed; no adequately convincing motive for *why*.

Just a time, and a place, and Joanna lying face-downwards in Duke's Cut all that while ago.

Unless, of course, there were some passages of evidence not reported – either from the first or the second trial? The Colonel had clearly been rather more interested in the lax morals of the boatmen than in any substantiation of the evidence, and he could just have omitted the testimony of any corroborative witnesses who might have been called. Perhaps it would be of some interest – in this harmless game he was playing – to have a quick look through those Court Registers, if they still existed; or through the relevant copies of *Jackson's Oxford Journal*, which certainly *did* exist, as Morse knew, filed on microfiche in the Oxford Central Library. (Doubtless in the Bodley, too!) And, in any case, he hadn't finished the Colonel's book yet. Why, there might be much still to be revealed in that last exciting episode!

Which he now began to read.

Almost immediately he was conscious of Fiona standing beside him – the amply bosomed Fiona, smelling vaguely of the summer and strongly of disinfectant. Then she sat down on the bed, and he felt the pneumatic pressure of her against him as she leaned across and looked over his shoulder.

'Intereeeesting?'

Morse nodded. 'It's the book the old girl brought round – you know, the Colonel's wife.'

Fiona stayed where she was, and Morse found himself reading the same short sentence for the third, fourth, fifth time – without the slightest degree of comprehension – as her softness gently pressed against him. Was she conscious, herself, of taking the initiative in such memorable intimacy, however mild?

Then she ruined everything.

'I don't go in much for reading these days. Last book I read was *Jane Eyre* – for GCSE, that was.'

'Did you enjoy it?' (Poor, dear Charlotte had long had a special place in Morse's heart.)

'Pretty boring stuff. We just had to do it, you know, for the exam.'

Oh dear!

Crossing her black-stockinged legs, she took off one of her flat-heeled black shoes, and shook out some invisible irritant on to the ward floor.

'When do people take their shoes off?' asked Morse. 'Normally, I mean?'

'Funny question, isn't it?'

'When they've a stone in them – like you?'

Fiona nodded. 'And when they go to bed.'

'And?'

'Well – when they go paddling at Blackpool.'

'Yes?'

'When they sit watching the telly with their feet on the sofa – if they've got a mum as fussy as mine.'

'Anything else?'

'What do you want to know all this for?'

'If they've got corns or something,' persisted Morse, 'and go to the chiropodist.' ('Kyropodist', in Morse's book.)

'Yes. Or if their feet get sore or tired. Or if they have to take their tights off for some reason—'

'Such as?'

Morse saw the flash of sensuous amusement in her eyes, as she suddenly stood up, pulled his sheets straight, and shook out his pillows. 'Well, if you don't know at your age—'

Oh dear!

Age.

Morse felt as young as he'd ever done; but suddenly, and so clearly, he could see himself as he *was* seen by this young girl.

Old!

But his mood was soon to be brightened by the totally unexpected re-appearance of Sergeant Lewis, who explained that the purpose of his unofficial visit (it was 2.15 p.m.) was to interview a woman, still in intensive care, in connection with yet another horrendous crash on the A34.

'Feeling OK this morning, sir?'

'I shall feel a jolly sight better once I've had the chance of apologizing to you – for being so bloody ungrateful!'

'Oh yes? When was that, sir? I thought you were always ungrateful to me.'

'I'm just sorry, that's all,' said Morse simply and quietly.

Lewis, whose anger had been simmering and spitting like soup inadvertently left on the stove, had come into the ward with considerable reluctance. Yet when some ten minutes later he walked out, he felt the same degree of delight he invariably experienced when he knew that Morse needed *him* – even if it were only, as in this case, to do a bit of mundane research (Morse had briefly explained the case) and to try to discover if the Court Registers of the Oxford Assizes, 1859–60, were still available; and if so to see if any records of the trials were still extant.

After Lewis had gone, Morse felt very much more in tune with the universe. Lewis had forgiven him, readily; and he felt a contentment which he, just as much as Lewis, could ill define and only partly comprehend. And with Lewis looking into the Court Registers, there was another researcher in the field: a qualified librarian, who could very quickly sort out *Jackson's Oxford Journals.* Not that she was coming in that evening, alas!

Patience, Morse!

At 3 p.m. he turned once again to the beginning of the fourth and final episode in the late Colonel Deniston's book.

CHAPTER EIGHTEEN

PART FOUR

A Pronounced Sentence

A BAILIFF WAS sworn in to attend the Jury, who immediately retired to the Clerk of Indictments' Room. After an absence of three-quarters of an hour, they returned to the Court; and, their names having been read over, every person appeared to wait with breathless anxiety for their verdict. In reply to the usual questions from Mr Benham, the foreman replied that the Jury was all agreed and that they were unanimous in finding each of the three prisoners at the bar GUILTY of the murder of Joanna Franks. It is said that no visible alteration marked the countenances of the crew on the verdict being given, except that Oldfield for the moment became somewhat paler.

The black coif, emblematical of death, was placed on the Judge's head; and after asking the prisoners if they had anything to say, he passed his sentence in the following awesome terms:

'Jack Oldfield, Alfred Musson, Walter Towns – after a long and patient hearing of the circumstances in this case, and after due deliberation on the part of the Jury, you have each and all of you been found guilty of the most foul crime of murder – the murder

110

of an unoffending and helpless woman who was under your protection and who, there is now no doubt as to believe, was the object of your lust; and thereafter, to prevent detection of your crime, was the object of your cruelty. Look not for pardon in this world! Apply to the God of Mercy for that pardon which He alone can extend to sinners who are penitent for their misdeeds, and henceforth prepare yourselves for the ignominious death which now awaits you. This case is one of the most painful, the most disgusting, and the most shocking, that has ever come to my knowledge, and it must remain only for me to pass upon you the terrible and just sentence of the Law, that you be taken whence you came, and from thence to the place of execution, and that you, and each of you, be hanged by the neck until you be dead, and that your bodies be afterward buried within the precincts of the prison and be not accorded the privilege of consecrated ground. And may God have mercy on your souls!'

After the trial was over, and sentence pronounced, the three men still persisted in maintaining their innocence. Indeed, Oldfield's wife, who visited the prison, was so agitated by her husband's protestations that "she herself was thrown into a sore fit".

It had seemed reasonably clear, from various statements including those of Oldfield and Musson that Towns had been somewhat less involved in the happenings on the canal journey than the other two. It was no surprise therefore, that some members of the legal profession now thought there was a case for the last-minute reconsideration of the sentence imposed upon Towns; so a letter setting forth their agreed view was taken to London by a barrister, and a special interview with the Secretary of State was obtained. As a result of such representations, Towns was reprieved at (almost literally) the eleventh hour. The good news was broken to him as the three men were receiving for the last time the Holy Sacrament from the Prison Chaplain. Towns immediately burst into a flood of tears, and taking each of his former associates by the hand kissed them affectionately, repeating "God bless you, dear friend!" "God bless you, dear friend!" He was later transported to Australia for life, where he was still alive in 1884 when he was seen and interviewed by one Samuel Carter (like Oldfield and Towns, a citizen of Coventry), who took a lively interest in local history and who wrote of his experiences on his return to England the following year.[1]

Oldfield and Musson were duly hanged in public at Oxford. According to the newspaper reports, as many as ten thousand people were estimated to have witnessed the macabre spectacle. It is reported that from an early hour men sat high on walls, climbed trees, and even perched on the roofs of overlooking houses in order to obtain a good view of those terrible events. A notice-board placed by the Governor in front of the gaol door stated that the execution would not proceed

[1] *Travels and Talks in the Antipodes*, Samuel Carter (Farthinghill Press, Nottingham, 1886).

until after eleven o'clock; but although this occasioned much disappointment among the spectators, it did not deter their continued attendance, and not a spare square-foot of space was to be found when, at the appointed hour, the execution finally occurred.

First to appear was the Prison Chaplain, solemnly reading the funeral service of the Church of England; next came the two culprits; and following them the Executioner, and the Governor, as well as some other senior officers from the prison. After the operation of pinioning had been completed, the two men walked with firm step to the platform, and ascended the stairs to the drop without requiring assistance. When the ropes had been adjusted round their necks, the Executioner shook hands with each man; and then, as the Chaplain intoned his melancholy service, the fatal bolt was drawn, and in a minute or two, after much convulsion, the wretched malefactors were no more. The dislocation of the cervical vertebrae and the rupture of the jugular vein had been, if not an instantaneous, at least an effective procedure. The gallows appeared to have sated the sadistic fascination of the mob once more, for there are no reports of any civic disorders as the great throng dispersed homewards on that sunlit day. It was later disclosed, though it had not been observable at the time, that Oldfield's last action in life had been to hand over to the Chaplain a postcard, to be delivered to his young wife, in which to the very end he proclaimed his innocence of the crime for which he had now paid the ultimate penalty.

Locally produced broadsheets, giving every sensational

detail of trial and execution, were very quickly on sale in the streets of Oxford – and were selling fast. They were even able to give a full account, with precise biblical reference, of the last sermon preached to the men at 6 p.m. on the Sunday before their hangings. The text, clearly chosen with ghoulish insensitivity, could hardly have brought the condemned prisoners much spiritual or physical solace: 'Yet they hearkened not unto me, nor inclined their ear, but hardened their neck: they did worse than their fathers' (*Jeremiah*, ch. 7, v. 26).

The horror felt by the local population at the murder of Joanna Franks did not end with the punishment of the guilty men. Many, both lay and clerical, thought that something more must be done to seek to improve the morals of the boatmen on the waterways. They were aware, of course, that the majority of boatmen were called upon to work on the Sabbath, and had therefore little or no opportunity of attending Divine worship. A letter from the Revd Robert Chantry, Vicar of Summertown Parish, was typical of many in urging a greater degree of concern amongst the boatmen's employers, and suggesting some period of time free from duties on the Sabbath to allow those having the inclination the opportunity of attending a Church service. Strangely enough, such attendance would have been readily possible for the crew-members of the *Barbara Bray* had Oxford been a regular port-of-call, since a special 'Boatmen's Chapel' had been provided by Henry Ward, a wealthy coal-merchant, in 1838 – a floating chapel, moored off Hythe Bridge, at which

services were held on Sunday afternoons and Wednesday evenings. For Joanna Franks, as well as for her
sorrowing husband and parents, it was a human tragedy
that the sermon preached to the murderers on the
Sunday prior to their execution was perhaps the first –
as well as the last – they ever heard.

But it is all a long time ago now. The floating chapel
has long since gone; and no one today can point with
any certainty to the shabby plot in the environs of
Oxford Gaol where notorious criminals and murderers
and others of the conjecturally damned were once
buried.

CHAPTER NINETEEN

We read fine things but never feel them to the full
until we have gone the same steps as the author
(*John Keats*, Letter to John Reynolds)

MORSE WAS GLAD that the Colonel had ignored Doctor Johnson's advice to all authors that once they had written something particularly fine they should strike it out. For Part Four was the best-written section, surely, of what was proving to be one of the greatest assets in Morse's most satisfactory (so far) convalescence; and he turned back the pages to relish again a few of those fine phrases. Splendid, certainly, were such things as "sated the sadistic fascination"; and, better still, that "ghoulish insensitivity". But they were *more* than that. They seemed to suggest that the Colonel's sympathies had shifted slightly, did they not? Where earlier the bias against the boatmen had been so pronounced, it appeared that the longer he went on the greater his compassion was growing for that disconsolate crew.

Like Morse's.

*

It was such a good *story*! So it was no surprise that the
Colonel should have disinterred the bare bones of this
particular one from the hundreds of other nineteenth-
century burial-grounds. All the ingredients were there
for its appealing to a wide readership, if once it got its
foot wedged in the doorway of publicity. Beauty and
the Beasts – that's what it was, quintessentially.

At least as the Colonel had seen it.

For Morse, who had long ago rejected the bland
placebos of conventional religion, the facility offered to
errant souls to take the Holy Sacrament before being
strangled barbarously in a string seemed oddly at
variance with the ban on the burial of these same souls
within some so-called 'holy ground'. And he was
reminded of a passage which had once been part of
his mental baggage, the words of which now slowly
returned to him. From *Tess of the d'Urbervilles* – where
Tess herself seeks to bury her illegitimate infant in the
place where 'the nettles grow; and where all unbaptised
infants, notorious drunkards, suicides, and others...'
What was the end of it? Wasn't it – yes! – 'others of the
conjecturally damned are laid'. Well, well! A bit of
plagiarism on the Colonel's part. He really should have
put quotation marks around that memorable phrase.
Cheating just a little, really. Were there any other
places where he'd cheated? Unwittingly, perhaps? Just
a little?

Worth checking?

That floating chapel interested Morse, too, particularly since he had read something about it in a recent
issue of the *Oxford Times*. He remembered, vaguely, that

although the Oxford Canal Company gave regular monies towards its upkeep the boat on which it was housed had finally sunk (like the boatmen's hopes) and was terrestrialized, as it were, later in the century as a permanent chapel in Hythe Bridge Street; was now, at its latest conversion, metamorphosed to a double-glazing establishment.

Without looking back, Morse could not for the moment remember which of the other crew-members had been married. But it was good to learn that Oldfield's wife had stood beside her husband, for better or for worse. And a pretty bloody 'worse' it had turned out to be! How interesting it would have been to know something of *her* story, too. How Morse would like to have been able to interview her, then and there! The recipient (presumably she had been) of that terrible card addressed to her, and handed to the Chaplain at the very foot of the gallows, she must have found it well-nigh impossible to believe that her husband could commit so foul a deed. But hers had been only a small role in the drama: only a couple of walking-on appearances, the first ending with a dead faint, and the second with a poignant little message from the grave. Morse nodded rather sadly to himself. These days there would be a legion of reporters from the *News of the World*, the *Sunday Mirror*, and the rest, hounding the life of the poor woman and seeking to prise out of her such vital information as whether he'd snored, or been tattooed on either upper or nether limbs, or how frequently they'd indulged in sexual intercourse, or what had been the usual greeting of the loving husband after coming back from one of his earlier murderous missions.

We live in a most degenerate age, decided Morse. Yet he knew, deep down, what nonsense such thinking was. He was no better himself, really, than one of those scandal-sheet scouts. He'd just confessed – had he not? – how much he himself wanted to interview Mrs Oldfield and talk about all the things she must have known. And what (sobering thought!) what if *she* had invited each of them in, one after the other, separately – and asked for £20,000 a time?

No chance of any interview or talk now though – not with any of them . . . But, suddenly, it struck Morse that perhaps there was: Samuel Carter's *Travels and Talks in the Antipodes*. That might be a most interesting document, surely? And (it struck Morse with particular pleasure) it would certainly be somewhere on the shelves of the three or four great UK libraries, the foremost of which was always going to be the Bodleian.

Lewis had already been given his research project; and work was now beginning to pile up for his second researcher in the field: what with *Jackson's Oxford Journal*, and now Carter's book . . . Had the Colonel consulted that? Must have done, Morse supposed – which was a little disappointing.

That Friday evening, Morse was visited by both Sergeant Lewis and Christine Greenaway, the latter suddenly changing her mind and foregoing a cocktail reception in Wellington Square. No trouble at all. Just the opposite.

Morse was very happy.

CHAPTER TWENTY

Those hateful persons called Original Researchers
(*J. M. Barrie*, My Lady Nicotine)

As USUAL WHEN she went into Oxford on a Saturday, Christine Greenaway drove down to the Pear Tree roundabout and caught the Park-and-Ride bus. Alighting in Cornmarket, she walked up to Carfax, turned right into Queen's Street, and along through the busy pedestrian precinct to Bonn Square, where just past the Selfridges building she pushed through the doors of the Westgate Central Library. Among the wrong assumptions made by Chief Inspector Morse the previous evening was the fact that it would be sheer child's play for her to fish out the fiche (as it were) of any newspaper ever published, and that having effected such effortless entry into times past she had the technical skill and the requisite equipment to carry out some immediate research. She hadn't told him that the Bodleian had not, to the best of her knowledge, ever micro-filmed the whole of the nation's press from the nineteenth century, nor that she herself was one of those people against whom all pieces of electrical gadgetry waged a non-stop war. She'd just agreed with him: yes, it would be a fairly easy job; and she'd be glad to help – again. To be truthful, though, she was. Earlier that morning she'd telephoned one of her acquaintances in the Reference Section of the Westgate Central, and learned that she could have immediate access to *Jackson's Oxford Journal* for 1859 and 1860. How long did she want to book things for? One hour? Two? Christine thought one hour would be enough.

10.30–11.30 a.m., then?

Perhaps Morse had been right all along. It was going to be easy.

On the second floor of the Central Library, in the Local History and Study Area, she was soon seated on an olive-green vinyl chair in front of a Micro-Film-Reader, an apparatus somewhat resembling the upper half of a British Telecom telephone-kiosk, with a vertical surface, some two feet square, facing her, upon which the photographed sheets of the newspaper appeared, in columns about 2½ inches wide. No lugging around or leafing through heavy bound-volumes of unmanageable newspapers. 'Child's play.' The controls marked Focusing Image, Magnification, and Light Control had all been pre-set for her by a helpful young library assistant (male), and Christine had only to turn an uncomplicated winding-handle with her right hand to skip along through the pages, at whatever speed she wished, of *Jackson's Oxford Journal.*

She was relieved, nevertheless, to discover that the Journal was a weekly, not a daily publication; and very soon she found the appropriate columns relating to the first trial of August 1859, and was making a series of notes about what she found; and, like Morse, becoming more and more interested. Indeed, by the time she had finished her research into the second trial, of April 1860, she was fascinated. She would have liked to go back and check up a few things, but her eyes were getting tired; and as soon as the print began to jump along like a line of soldiers dressing by the right, she knew that what the splendid machine called the Viewer Operator had better have a rest. She'd found a couple of pieces of information that might please Morse. She hoped so.

She was looking quickly through her scribbled notes, making sure that she could transcribe them later into some more legible form, when she became aware of a conversation taking place only three or four yards behind her at the Enquiries desk.

'Yes, I've tried County Hall – no help, I'm afraid.'

'Your best bet I should think, then, is the City Archivists. They've got an office in—'

'They sent me here!'

'Oh!' The phone rang and the assistant excused himself to answer it.

Christine gathered up her notes, turned off the MFR (as it seemed to be known), and went up to the desk.

'We met yesterday evening—' began Christine.

Sergeant Lewis smiled at her and said, 'Hullo.'

'Seems I'm having more luck than you, Sergeant.'

'Augh! He always gives me the lousy jobs – I don't know why I bother – my day off, too.'

'And mine.'

'Sorry we can't help, sir,' said the assistant (another query dealt with). 'But if they've got no trace at the Archivists . . .'

Lewis nodded. 'Well, thanks, anyway.'

Lewis escorted Christine to the swing doors when the assistant had a final thought: 'You could try St Aldate's Police Station. I *have* heard that quite a lot of documents and stuff got housed by the police in the war' ('Which war?' mumbled Lewis, inaudibly) 'and, well, perhaps—'

'Thanks very much!'

'They can't really be *all* that helpful to the public, though – I'm sure you know—'

'Oh yes!'

But the phone had been ringing again, and now the attendant answered it, convinced that he'd sent his latest customer on what would prove a wholly unproductive mission.

When alone in crowded streets, Christine sometimes felt a little apprehensive; but she experienced a pleasing sense of being under protection as she walked back towards Carfax with the burly figure of Sergeant Lewis beside and above her. Great Tom was striking twelve noon.

'I don't suppose you fancy a drink—' began Lewis.

'No – not for me, thank you. I don't drink much, anyway, and it's a bit – bit early, isn't it?'

Lewis grinned: 'That's something I don't hear very often from the Chief.' But he felt relieved. He wasn't much good at making polite conversation; and although she seemed a very nice young lady he preferred to get about his business now.

'You like him, don't you? The "Chief", I mean?'

'He's the best in the business.'

'Is he?' asked Christine, quietly.

'Will you be going in tonight?'

'I suppose so. What about you?'

'If I find anything – which seems at the moment very doubtful.'

'You never know.'

Chapter Twenty-one

From the cradle to the coffin, underwear comes first
(*Bertolt Brecht*, The Threepenny Opera)

IN THE LATE 1980s the premises of the City Police HQ in St Aldate's were being extensively renovated and extended – and the work was still in progress when Sergeant Lewis walked in through the main door that Saturday morning. The Force had always retained its obstinately hierarchical structure, and friendships between the higher and the lower ranks would perhaps always be slightly distanced. Yet Lewis knew Chief Superintendent Bell fairly well from the old days up at Kidlington and was glad to find him in the station.

Yes, of course Bell would help if he could: in fact, the timing of Lewis's visit might be very opportune, because many corners and crannies had only just been cleared out, and the contents of scores of cupboards and dust-covered cases and crates had recently seen the light of day for the first time within living memory. Bell's orders on this had been clear: if any documents seemed even marginally worth the keeping, let them be kept; if not, let them be destroyed. But strangely, up to now, almost everything so newly rediscovered had appeared potentially valuable to *someone*; and the upshot was that a whole room had been set aside in which the preserved relics and mementos from the earliest days – certainly from the 1850s onwards – had been unsystematically stacked, awaiting appropriate evaluation by academic historians, sociologists, criminologists, local-history societies – and authors. In fact a WPC was in the room now, as Bell thought – doing a bit of elementary cataloguing; and if Lewis wanted to look around . . .

Explaining that this was her lunch-break, WPC Wright, a pleasant enough brunette in her mid-twenties, continued eating her sandwiches and writing her Christmas cards, waving Lewis to any quarter of the room he wished after he had briefly stated his mission.

'It's all yours, Sergeant. Or, at least, I wish it was!'

Lewis could see what she meant. Morse had given him a copy of the Colonel's work (several spares had been left on the ward); but for the moment Lewis could see little or no chance of linking anything that had occurred in 1860 with the chaotic heaps of boxes, files, bags, crates, and piles of discoloured, dog-eared documents that lay around. To be fair, it was clear that a start had been made on sorting things out, for fifty-odd buff-coloured labels, with dates written on them, were attached to the rather neater agglomeration of material that had been separated from the rest, and set out in some semblance of chronological order. But amongst these labels Lewis looked in vain for 1859 or 1860. Was it worth having a quick look through the rest?

It was at 1.45 p.m., after what had proved to be a long look, that Lewis whistled softly.

'You found something?'

'Do you know anything about this?' asked Lewis. He had lifted from one of the tea-chests a chipped and splintered box, about two feet long, by one foot wide, and about 9–10 inches deep; a small box, by any reckoning, and one which could be carried by a person with little difficulty, since a brass plate, some 4 inches by half an inch, set in the middle of the box's top, held a beautifully moulded semi-circular handle, also of brass. But what had struck Lewis instantly – and with wondrous excitement – were the initials engraved upon the narrow plate: 'J.D.'! Lewis had not read the slim volume with any great care (or any great interest, for that matter); but he remembered clearly the two 'trunks' which Joanna had taken on to the boat and which presumably had been found in the cabin after the crew's arrest. Up to that point, Lewis had just had a vague mental picture of the sort of 'trunks' seen outside Oxford colleges when the undergraduates were arriving. But surely it had said that Joanna was *carrying* them, hadn't it? And by the well-worn look of the handle it looked as if this box had been carried – and carried often. And the name of Joanna's first husband had begun with a 'D'!

The policewoman came over and knelt beside the

box. The two smallish hooks, one on each side of the lid, moved easily; and the lock on the front was open, for the lid lifted back to reveal, inside the green-plush lining, a small canvas bag, on which, picked out in faded yellow wool, were the same initials as on the box.

Lewis whistled once more. Louder.

'Can you – can we – ?' He could scarcely keep the excitement from his voice, and the policewoman looked at him curiously for a few seconds, before gently shaking out the bag's contents on to the floor: a small, rusted key, a pocket comb, a metal spoon, five dress-buttons, a crochet-hook, a packet of needles, two flat-heeled, flimsy-looking shoes, and a pair of calico knickers.

Lewis shook his head in dumbfounded disbelief. He picked up the shoes in somewhat gingerly fashion as if he suspected they might disintegrate; then, between thumb and forefinger, the calico knickers.

'Think I could borrow these shoes and the er . . .?' he asked.

WPC Wright eyed him once again with amused curiosity.

'It's all right,' added Lewis. 'They're not for me.'

'No?'

'Morse – I work for Morse.'

'I suppose you're going to tell me he's become a knicker-fetishist in his old age.'

'You know him?'

'Wish I did!'

'He's in hospital, I'm afraid—'

'Everybody says he drinks far too much.'

'A bit, perhaps.'

129

'Do you know him well, would you say?'

'Nobody knows him all *that* well.'

'You'll have to sign for them—'

'Fetch me the book!'

'—and bring them back.'

Lewis grinned. 'They'd be a bit small for me, anyway, wouldn't they? The shoes, I mean.'

CHAPTER TWENTY-TWO

> Don't take action because of a name! A name is an uncertain thing, you can't count on it!
>
> (*Bertolt Brecht*, A Man's a Man)

DURING THAT SAME Saturday which saw Sergeant Lewis and Christine Greenaway giving up their free time on his behalf, Morse himself was beginning to feel fine again. Exploring new territory, too, since after lunch-time he was told he was now free to wander along the corridors at will. Thus it was that at 2.30 p.m. he found his way to the Day Room, an area equipped with armchairs, a colour TV, table-skittles, a book-case, and a great pile of magazines (the top one, Morse noted, a copy of *Country Life* dating from nine years the previous August). The room was deserted; and after making doubly sure the coast was clear, Morse placed one of the three books he was carrying in the bottom of the large wastepaper receptacle there: *The Blue Ticket* had brought him little but embarrassment and humiliation, and now, straightway, he felt like Pilgrim after depositing his sackful of sin.

The surfaces of the TV set seemed universally

smooth, with not the faintest sign of any switch, indentation, or control with which to set the thing going; so Morse settled down in an armchair and quietly contemplated the Oxford Canal once more.

The question for the Jury, of course, had not been 'Who committed the crime?' but only 'Did the prisoners do it?'; whilst for a policeman like himself the question would always have to be the first one. So as he sat there he dared to say to himself, honestly, 'All right! If the boatmen didn't do it, *who did*?' Yet if that were now the Judge's key question, Morse couldn't see the case lasting a minute longer; for the simple answer was he hadn't the faintest idea. What he *could* set his mind to, though, was some considered reflection upon the boatmen's guilt. Or innocence . . .

A quartet of questions, then.

First. Was it true that a jury should have been satisfied, beyond any reasonable doubt, that the boatmen murdered Joanna Franks? Answer: no. Not one shred of positive evidence had been produced by the prosecution which could be attested in court by any corroborative witnesses to murder – and it had been on the count of murder that the boatmen had been convicted.

Second. Was it true that the prisoners at the bar had been afforded the time-honoured 'presumption of innocence' – the nominal glory of the British Legal System? Answer: it most definitely was not. Prejudgements – wholly pejorative prejudgements – had been rife from the start of the first trial, and the attitude of the law officers no less than the general public had been, throughout, one of unconcealed contempt for, and revulsion against, the crude, barely literate, irreligious crew of the *Barbara Bray*.

Third. Was it true that the boatmen, or some of them, were likely to have been guilty of something? Answer: almost certainly, yes; and (perversely) most probably guilty on the two charges that were dropped – those of rape and theft. At the very least, there was no shortage of evidence to suggest that the men had lusted mightily after their passenger, and it was doubtless a real possibility that all three – all four? – had sought to force their advances on the hapless (albeit sexually provocative?) Joanna.

Fourth. Was there a general sense – even if the evidence *was* unsatisfactory, even if the Jury *were* unduly prejudiced – in which the verdict was a reasonable one, a 'safe' one, as some of the jurisprudence manuals liked to call it? Answer: no, a thousand times no!

Almost, now, Morse felt he could put his finger on the major cause of his unease. It was all those conversations, heard and duly reported, between the principal characters in the story: conversations between the crew and Joanna; between the crew and other boatmen; between the crew and lock-keepers, wharfingers, and constables – all of it was *wrong* somehow. *Wrong, if they were guilty*. It was as if some inexperienced playwright had been given a murder-plot, and had then proceeded to write page after page of inappropriate, misleading, and occasionally contradictory dialogue. For there were moments when it looked as if it were Joanna Franks who was the avenging Fury, with the crewmen merely the victims of her fatal power.

Then, too, the behaviour of Oldfield and Musson *after* the murder seemed to Morse increasingly a matter of considerable surprise, and it was difficult to understand why Counsel for the Defence had not sought to ram into the minds of Judge and Jury alike the utter *implausibility* of what, allegedly, they did and said. It was not unknown, admittedly, for the odd psychopath to act in a totally irrational and irresponsible manner. But these men were *not* a quartet of psychopaths. And, above all, it seemed quite extraordinary to Morse that, even after (as was claimed) the crew had somehow and for some reason managed to murder Joanna Franks, they were – some twenty-four, thirty-six hours later – still knocking back the booze, still damning and blasting the woman's soul to eternity. Morse had known many murderers, but never one who had subsequently acted in such a fashion – let alone *four*. No! It just didn't add up; didn't add up at all. Not that it mattered, though – not really – after all these years.

Morse flicked open the index of the stout volume recording the misdeeds of Old Salopians, and his eye caught 'Shropshire Union Canal (The)'. He turned idly to the page reference, and there read through the paragraph, and with growing interest. (Well done, Mrs Lewis!) The author was still most horribly enmeshed in his barbed-wire style, still quite incapable of calling a spade anything else but a broad-bladed digging-tool; but the message was clear enough:

'With such an incidence of crime on the canals, it can scarcely be a source of surprise that we find countless instances of evasiveness, on the part of many of the boatmen, in matters such as the register-ing of names, both those of the boats they crewed and of their own persons. Specifically, with regard to the latter of these deceptions, we discover that many of those working both on the water and on the wharfs had a duality of names, and were frequently consider-ably better known by their 'bye-names' than by their christened nomenclature. For varied sociological reasons (some of which we have yet to analyse) it can more than tentatively be suggested that boatmen as a generality were likely to be potentially predisposed to the regular commission of crime, and certain it must be held that their profession (if such it may be called) afforded ample opportunities for the realiz-ation of such potentiality. Sometimes they sold parts of their cargoes, replacing, for example, quantities of coal with similar quantities of rocks or stone; frequently we come across recorded instances (see esp. SCL, *Canal and Navigable Waters Commission,* 1842, Vol. IX, pp. 61–4, 72–5, 83–6, *et passim*) of crewmen drinking from their cargoes of fine wines and whiskies, and refilling the emptied bottles with water. Toll officials, too, do not always appear blame-less in these affairs, and could occasionally be bribed into closing their eyes . . .'

Morse's eyes were beginning to close, too, and he laid the book aside. The point had been made: boatmen were a load of crooks who often nicked bits of their cargoes. Hence Walter Towns, aka Walter Thorold, and the rest. All as simple as that – once you knew the answers. Perhaps it would *all* be like that one day, in that Great Computer Library in the Sky, when the problems that had beset countless generations of sages and philosophers would be answered immediately, just by tapping in the questions on some celestial key-board.

The youth with the portable saline-drip walked in, nodded to Morse, picked up a small TV control-panel from somewhere, and began flicking his way around the channels with, for Morse, irritating impermanence. It was time to get back to the ward.

As he was leaving his eyes roamed automatically over the book-case, and he stopped. There, on the lower row, and standing side by side, were the titles *Victorian Banbury* and *OXFORD* (Rail Centres Series). Having extracted both, he walked back. Perhaps, if you kept your eyes open, you didn't need any Valhallan VDUs at all.

Walter Algernon Greenaway had been trying, with little success, to get going with the *Oxford Times* crossword. He had little or no competence in the skill, but it had always fascinated him; and when the previous day he had watched Morse complete *The Times* crossword in about ten minutes, he felt most envious. Morse had just settled back in his bed when Greenaway (predictably known to his friends, it appeared, as 'Waggie') called across.

136

'You're pretty good at crosswords—'

'Not bad.'

'You know anything about cricket?'

'Not much. What's the clue?'

'"Bradman's famous duck".'

'How many letters?'

'Six. I saw Bradman at the Oval in 1948. He got a duck then.'

'I shouldn't worry too much about cricket,' said Morse. 'Just think about Walt Disney.'

Greenaway licked the point of his pencil, and thought, unproductively, about Walt Disney.

'Who's the setter this week?' asked Morse.

'Chap called "Quixote".'

Morse smiled. Coincidence, wasn't it! 'What was *his* Christian name?'

'Ah! I have you, sir!' said Waggie, happily entering the letters at 1 across.

CHAPTER TWENTY-THREE

All that mankind has done, thought, gained, or been, it is all lying in magic preservation in the pages of books

(*Thomas Carlyle*)

EMBARRAS DE RICHESSES – for Morse couldn't have chosen a more informative couple of books if he'd sauntered all day round the shelves in the local Summertown Library.

First, from *Victorian Banbury*, he gleaned the information that by about 1850 the long-distance stage-coach routes via Banbury to London had been abandoned, almost entirely as a result of the new railway service from Oxford to the capital. Yet, as a direct result of this service, coaches between Banbury and Oxford had actually *increased*, and regular and efficient transportation was readily available between Banbury and Oxford (only twenty miles to the south) during the 1850s and 1860s. Furthermore, the author gave full details of the actual stage-coaches that would have been available, on the day in question, and about which Joanna Franks must have made enquiry: quite certainly coach-horses would have been seen galloping southwards on three separate occasions in the earlier half of the following day, delivering passengers picked up at the Swan Inn, Banbury, to the Angel Inn in the High at Oxford. That for the sum of 2s/1d. Even more interesting for Morse was the situation pertaining at Oxford itself, where trains to Paddington, according to his second work of reference, were far more frequent, and far quicker, than he could have imagined. And presumably Joanna herself, at Banbury on that fateful day, had been presented with *exactly* the same information: no less than *ten* trains daily, leaving at 2.10 a.m., 7.50 a.m., 9 a.m., 10.45 a.m., 11.45 a.m., 12.55 p.m., 2.45 p.m., 4.00 p.m., 5.50 p.m., and 8.00 p.m. *Embarras du choix*. Admittedly, the fares seemed somewhat steep, with 1st-, 2nd-, and 3rd-class carriages priced respectively at 16s, 10s, and 6s, for the 60-odd-mile journey. But the historian of Oxford's railways was fair-minded enough to add the fact that there were also three coaches a day, at least up until the 1870s, making the comparatively slow journey to London via the Henley and Reading turnpikes: *The Blenheim* and *The Prince of Wales*, each departing at 10.30 a.m., with *The Rival* an hour later, the fare being a 'whole shilling' less than the 3rd-class railway fare. And where did they finish up in the metropolis? It was quite extraordinary. The Edgware Road!

So, for a few minutes Morse looked at things from Joanna's point of view – a Joanna who (as he had no option but to believe) was *in extremis*. Arriving at Banbury, as she had, in the latish evening, she would very soon have seen the picture. No chance of anything immediately, but the ready opportunity of a stay over-night in Banbury, in one of the taverns along the quay-side, perhaps. Not four-star AA accommodation – but adequate, and certainly costing no more than 2s or so. Then one of the coaches to Oxford next morning – the book of words mentioned one at 9.30 a.m., reaching Oxford at about 1 p.m. That would mean no difficulty at all about catching the 2.45 p.m. to Paddington – or one of the three later trains, should any accident befall the horses. Easy! If she *had* eventually made a firm decision to escape her tormentors for good, then the situation was straightforward. 2s overnight, say, 2s/1d coach-fare, 6s 3rd-class rail-fare – that meant that for about 10s she was offered a final chance of saving her life. And without much bother, without much expense, she *could* have done so.

But she hadn't. Why not? Received wisdom main-tained that she hadn't got a penny-piece to her name, let alone half a guinea. But had she nothing she could sell, or pawn? Had she no negotiable property with her? What *had* she got in those two boxes of hers? Nothing of any value whatsoever? Why, then, if that were so, could there ever have been the slightest suspicion of *theft*? Morse shook his head slowly. Ye gods! – how he wished he could have a quick look into one of those boxes!

It was tea-time, and Morse was not aware that his wish had already been granted.

CHAPTER TWENTY-FOUR

Magnus Alexander corpore parvus erat (Even Alexander the Great didn't measure up to the height-requirement of the Police Force)

(*Latin Proverb*)

NORMAL SHIFTS FOR the staff at the JR2 were Early (07.45–15.45), Late (13.00–21.30) and Night (21.00–08.15). Always more of an owl than a lark, Eileen Stanton shared none of the common objections that were levelled against the Night shift: born with a temperament slightly tinged with melancholy, she was perhaps a natural creature of the dark. But this particular week had been unusual. And that day she was on Late.

Married at the age of nineteen and divorced at twenty, she was now, five years later, living out at Wantage with a man, fifteen years her senior, who had celebrated his fortieth birthday the previous evening (hence the re-arrangements). The party had gone splendidly until just after midnight when the celebrant himself had been involved in a pathetic little bout of fisticuffs, over *her*! Now, in films or on TV, after being knocked unconscious with a vicious blow from an iron bar, the hero has only to rub the sore spot for a couple of minutes before resuming his mission. But life itself, as Eileen knew, wasn't like that – the victim was much more likely to end up in the ICU, with permanent brain-damage, to boot. Much more cruel. Like last night (this morning!) when her cohabitee had been clouted in the face, his upper lip splitting dramatically, and one of his front teeth being broken off at the root. Not good for his looks, or his pride, or the party, or Eileen, or anybody. Not good at all!

For the umpteenth time her mind dwelt on that incident as she drove into Oxford, parked her apple-jack-green Metro in the Staff Only park of the JR2, and walked down to the Basement Cloak Room to change her clothes. It would do her good to get back on the Ward, she knew that. She'd found it easy enough so far to steer clear of any emotional involvement with her patients, and for the moment all she wanted was to get a few hours of dutiful nursing behind her – to forget the previous night, when she'd drunk a little too freely, and flirted far too flagrantly with a man she'd never even met before ... No hangover – although she suddenly began to wonder if she *did* have a hangover after all: just didn't notice it amid her other mental agitations. Anyway, it was high time she forgot all her own troubles and involved herself with other people's.

She'd noticed Morse (and he her) as he'd walked along to the Day Room; watched him walk back, half an hour later and spend the rest of the afternoon reading. Bookish sort of fellow, he seemed. Nice, though – and she would go and have a word with him perhaps once he put his books down. Which he didn't.

She watched him again, at 7.40 p.m., as he sat against the pillows; and more particularly watched the woman who sat beside him, in a dark-blue dress, with glints of gold and auburn in her hair, the regular small-featured face leaning forward slightly as she spoke to him. To Eileen the pair of them seemed so eager to talk to each other – so different from the conversational drought which descended on so many hospital visitations. Twice, even as she watched, the woman, in the middle of some animated little passage of dialogue, placed the tips of her fingers against the sleeve of his gaudy pyjamas, fingers that were slim and sinewy, like those of an executant musician. Eileen knew all about *that* sort of gesture! And what about him, Morse? He, too, seemed to be doing his level, unctuous best to impress *her*, with a combination of that happily manufactured half-smile and eyes that focused intently upon hers. Oh yes! She could see what each of them was feeling – nauseating couple of bootlickers! But she knew she envied them; envied especially the woman – Waggie's clever-clogs of a daughter! From the few times she'd spoken to Morse, she knew that his conversation – and perhaps, she thought, his life, too – was so *interesting*. She'd met just a few other men like that – men who were full of fascinating knowledge about architecture, history, literature, music ... all the things after which over these last few years she'd found herself yearning. How relieved she suddenly felt that most probably her swollen-lipped forty-year-old wouldn't be able to kiss her that evening!

A man (as she now realized) had been standing patiently at the desk.

'Can I help you?'

Sergeant Lewis nodded and looked down at her. 'Special instructions. I've got to report to the boss whenever I bring the Chief Inspector a bag of plastic explosive. You're the boss tonight, aren't you?'

'Don't be too hard on Sister Maclean!'

Lewis bent forward and spoke softly. 'It's not me – it's him! He says she's an argumentative, bitchy old . . . old something.'

Eileen smiled. 'She's not very tactful, sometimes.'

'He's, er – looks like he's got a visitor for the moment.'

'Yes.'

'Perhaps I'd better not interrupt, had I? He gets very cross sometimes.'

'Does he?'

'Especially if . . .'

Eileen nodded, and looked up into Lewis's kindly face, feeling that menfolk weren't quite so bad as she'd begun to think.

'What's he like – Inspector Morse?' she asked.

Christine Greenaway stood up to go, and Morse was suddenly conscious, as she stood so closely beside the bed, how small she was – in spite of the high-heeled shoes she habitually wore. Words came back to his mind, the words he'd read again so recently: '... petite and attractive figure, wearing an Oxford-blue dress ...'

'How tall are you?' asked Morse, as she smoothed her dress down over her thighs.

'How *small* am I, don't you mean?' Her eyes flashed and seemed to mock him. 'In stockinged feet, I'm five feet, half an inch. And don't forget that half-inch: it may not be very important to you, but it is to me. I wear heels all the time – so I come up to about normal, usually. About five three.'

'What size shoes do you take?'

'Threes. You wouldn't be able to get your feet in them.'

'I've got very nice feet,' said Morse seriously.

'I think I ought to be more worried about my father than about your feet,' she whispered quietly, as she touched his arm once more, and as Morse in turn placed his own left hand so briefly, so lightly upon hers. It was a little moment of magic, for both of them.

'And you'll look up that—?'

'I won't forget.'

Then she was gone, and only the smell of some expensive perfume lingered around the bed.

'I just wonder,' said Morse, almost absently, as Lewis took Christine's place in the plastic chair, 'I just wonder what size shoes Joanna Franks took. I'm assuming, of course, they *had* shoe-sizes in those days. Not a modern invention, like women's tights, are they? – shoe-sizes? What do you think, Lewis?'

'Would you like me to show you exactly what size she *did* take, sir?'

CHAPTER TWENTY-FIVE

Those who are incapable of committing great crimes
do not readily suspect them in others

(La Rochefoucauld, Maxims)

MORSE WAS INVARIABLY credited, by his police colleagues, with an alpha-plus intelligence, of a kind which
surfaced rarely on the tides of human affairs, and which
almost always gave him about six furlongs' start in any
criminal investigation. Whatever the truth of this
matter, Morse himself knew that one gift had never
been bestowed on him – that of *reading* quickly. It was
to be observed, therefore, that he seemed to spend a
disproportionately long time that evening – Christine
gone, Lewis gone, Horlicks drunk, pills swallowed,
injection injected – in reading through the photocopied columns from *Jackson's Oxford Journal.* Christine
had not mentioned to him that, dissatisfied with her
hand-written notes, she had returned to the Central
Library in the early afternoon and prevailed upon one
of her vague acquaintances there to let her jump the
queue and photocopy the original material directly
from their bulky originals. Not that Morse, even had he

known, would have exhibited any excessive gratitude. One of his weaknesses was his disposition to accept loyalty without ever really understanding, certainly not appreciating, the sacrifices that might be involved.

When, as a boy, he had been shepherded around various archaeological sites, Morse had been unable to share the passion of some fanatic drooling over a few (disintegrating) Roman bricks. Even then, it had been the written word, rather than the tangible artefact, which had pricked his curiosity, and promoted his subsequent delight in the ancient world. It was to be expected, therefore, that although Lewis's quite extraordinary discovery was to prove the single most dramatic break-through in the supposed 'case', the sight of a sad-looking pair of shrivelled shoes and an even sadder-looking pair of crumpled knickers was, for Morse, a little anti-climactic. At least, for the present. As for Christine's offerings, though, how wonderfully attractive and suggestive they were!

From the newspaper records, it was soon clear that the Colonel had omitted no details of any obvious importance. Yet, as in most criminal cases, it was the apparently innocuous, incidental, almost irrelevant, details that could change, in a flash, the interpretation of accepted facts. And there were quite a few details here (to Morse, hitherto unknown) which caused him more than a millimetric rise of the eyebrows.

First, reading between the somewhat smudged lines of the photocopied material, it seemed fairly clear that the charge of theft had probably been dropped at the first trial for the reason that the evidence (such as it was) had pointed predominantly to the youth, Wootton, therefore necessitating an individual prosecution – and that against a minor. If any of the other crewmen were involved, it was Towns (the man deported to Australia) who figured as the safest bet; and quite certainly no obvious evidence could be levelled against the two men eventually hanged for *murder*. What was it then that the young man's covetous eyes may have sought to steal from Joanna Franks's baggage? No answer emerged clearly from the evidence. But there was surely one thing, above all, that thieves went for, whether in 1859 or 1989: *money*.

Mmm.

Second, there was sufficient contemporary evidence to suggest that it was Joanna who was probably the sustaining partner in her second marriage. Whatever it was that had caused her to 'fall deeply in love with Charles Franks, an ostler from Liverpool', it was *Joanna* who had besought her new husband to keep up his spirits during the ill fortune which had beset the early months of their marriage. An extract from a letter to Charles Franks had indeed been read out in court, presumably (as Morse saw things) to substantiate the point that, quite contrary to the boatmen's claim of *Joanna* being demented, it was *Charles* who seemed the nearer to a mental breakdown: 'Sorry I am to read, my dear husband, your sadly wandering letter – do, my dear, strive against what I fear will await you should you not rest your tortured mind. The loss of reason is a terrible thing and will blight our hopes. Be strong and

know we shall soon be together and well provided for.'
A poignant and eloquent letter.

Were *both* of them a bit unbalanced?

Mmm.

Third, various depositions from both trials made it
clear that although 'fly' boats worked best with a strict
enforcement of a 'two on – two off' arrangement, it was
quite usual, in practice, for the four members of such a
crew to permutate their different duties in order to
accommodate individual likings or requirements. Or
desires, perhaps? For Morse now read, with considerable
interest, the evidence adduced in court (Where were
you, Colonel Deniston?) that Oldfield, captain of the
Barbara Bray, had paid Walter Towns 6*d* to take over
from him the arduous business of 'legging' the boat
through the Barton tunnel. Morse nodded to himself:
for his imagination had already travelled there.

Mmm.

Fourth, the evidence, taken as a whole, suggested
strongly that for the first half of the journey Joanna had
joined in quite happily with the boatmen at the various
stops: staying in their company, eating at the same
table, drinking with them, laughing with them at their
jokes. Few jokes, though, on the latter half of the
journey, when, as the prosecution had pressed home
again and again, Joanna figured only as a helpless,
hapless soul – crying out (at times, literally) for help,
sympathy, protection, mercy. And one decisive and
dramatic fact: as the crew themselves grew progressively
inebriated, Joanna was becoming increasingly sober;

for the coroner's evidence, as reported at the trial, was incontestable: *no alcohol at all was found in her body*.

Mmm.

Morse proceeded to underline in blue Biro the various, and most curious, altercations which the law-writer of *Jackson's Oxford Journal* had deemed it worthy to record:

'Will you have anything of this?' (Oldfield) 'No, I have no inclination.' (Bloxham) '—'s already had his concerns with her tonight; and I will, or else I shall — her.' (Oldfield) 'D—n and blast the woman! If she has drowned herself, I cannot help it.' (Oldfield) 'She said she'd do it afore, and now she seems to 'a done it proper.' (Musson) 'I hope the b—y w—e is burning in hell!' (Oldfield) 'Blast the woman! What do we know about her? If she had a mind to drown herself, why should we be in all this trouble?' (Towns) 'If he is going to be a witness against us, it is for other things, not for the woman.' (Oldfield)

Mmm.

Randomly quoted, incoherent, unchronological as they were, these extracts from the trials served most strongly to reinforce Morse's earlier conviction that they were not the sort of comments one would expect from murderers. One might expect some measure of shame, remorse, fear – yes! – even, in a few cases, triumph and jubilation in the actual performance of the deed. But not – no! – not the fierce anger and loathing perpetuated by the boatman through the hours and the days after Joanna had met her death.

Finally, there was a further (significant?) passage of

evidence which the Colonel had *not* cited. It was, apparently, Oldfield's claim that, at about 4 a.m. on the fateful morning, the boatmen *had*, in fact, caught up with Joanna – the latter in a state of much mental confusion; both he and Musson had discovered her whereabouts only by the anguished cries in which she called upon the name of her husband: 'Franks! Franks! Franks!' Furthermore, Oldfield claimed, he had actually persuaded her to get back on the boat, although he agreed that she had fairly soon jumped off again (again!) to resume her walking along the towpath. Then, according to Oldfield, two of them, he and Towns on this occasion, had once more gone ashore, where they met another potential witness (the Donald Favant mentioned in the Colonel's book). But the boatmen had not been believed. In particular this second meeting along the tow path had come in for withering scorn from the prosecution: at best, the confused recollection of hopelessly drunken minds; at worst, the invention of 'these callous murderers'. Yes! That was exactly the sort of comment which throughout had disquieted Morse's passion for justice. As a policeman, he knew only the rudiments of English Law; but he was a fervent believer in the principle that a man should be presumed innocent until he was pronounced guilty: it was a fundamental principle, not only of substantive law, but of natural justice . . .

'You comfy?' asked Eileen, automatically pulling the folds of his sheets tidy.

'I thought you'd gone off duty.'

'Just going.'

'You're spoiling me.'

'You enjoy reading, don't you?'

Morse nodded: 'Sometimes.'

'You like reading best of all?'

'Well, music – music, I suppose, sometimes more.'

'So, if you're reading a book with the record-player going—'

'I can't enjoy them both together.'

'But they're the *best*?'

'Apart from a candle-lit evening-meal with someone like you.'

Eileen coloured, her pale cheeks suddenly as bright as those of the dying Colonel.

Before going to sleep that night, Morse's hand glided into the bedside cabinet and poured out a small measure; and as he sipped the Scotch, at his own pace, the world of a sudden was none too bad a place . . .

When he awoke (was awoken, rather) the following morning (Sunday) he marvelled that the blindingly obvious notion that now occurred to him had taken such an age to materialize. Usually, his cerebral analysis was as swift as the proverbial snap of a lizard's eyelid.

Or so he told himself.

CHAPTER TWENTY-SIX

Now, there is a law written in the darkest of the
Books of Life, and it is this: If you look at a thing
nine hundred and ninety-nine times, you are perfectly safe; if you look at it for the thousandth time,
you are in frightful danger of seeing it for the first
time

(*G. K. Chesterton*, The Napoleon of Notting Hill)

JUST THE SAME with crossword puzzles, wasn't it? Sit
and ponder more and more deeply over some abstruse
clue – and get nowhere. Stand away, though – further
back! – further back still! – and the answer will shout at
you with a sort of mocking triumph. It was those shoes,
of course . . . shoes at which he'd been staring so hard
he hadn't really seen them.

Morse waited with keen anticipation until his morning
ablutions were complete before re-re-reading the
Colonel's work, lingering over things – as he'd always
done as a boy when he'd carved his way meticulously
around the egg-white until he was left only with the

golden circle of the yolk, into which, finally, to dip the calculated balance of his chips.

What were the actual words of the trial report? Yes, Morse nodded to himself: when Charles Franks had looked at the body, he had recognized it, dreadfully disfigured as it was, by 'a small mark behind his wife's left ear, a mark of which only a parent or an intimate lover could have known'. *Or a scoundrel.* By all the gods, was *ever* identification so tenuously asserted and attested in the English Courts? Not only some tiny disfigurement in a place where no one else would have been aware of it, but a tiny disfigurement which existed *on* the head of Joanna Franks only because it existed *in* the head of her new husband! Oh, it must have been there all right! The doctor, the coroner, the inspector of police, those who'd undressed the dead woman, and redressed her for a proper Christian burial – so many witnesses who could, if need ever arose, corroborate the existence of such a blemish on what had once been such a pretty face. But who could, or did, corroborate the fact that the face had been *Joanna's*? The husband? Yes, he'd had his say. But the only others who might have known, the parents – where were they? Apparently, they'd played no part at all in the boatmen's trial at Oxford. Why not? Was the mother too stricken with grief to give any coherent testimony? Was she *alive*, even, at the time of the trial? The father was alive, though, wasn't he? The insurance man . . .

Morse brought his mind back to the central point he was seeking to establish before his own imagined jury (little 'j'). No court would have accepted such unilateral identification without *something* to support it – and there *had* been something (again Morse looked back to the actual words): corroboration was afforded 'by the shoes, later found in the fore-cabin of the *Barbara Bray*, which matched in the minutest degrees the contours of the dead woman's feet'. So, the matter was clear: one, the shoes in the cabin belonged to Joanna Franks; two, the shoes had been worn by the drowned woman; therefore, three, the drowned woman was Joanna Franks – QED. Even Aristotle might have been satisfied with such a syllogism. Incontrovertible! All three statements as true as the Eternal Verities; and if so, the shoes *must* belong to the woman who was drowned. But . . . but what if the first statement was *not* true? What if the shoes had *not* belonged to Joanna? Then the inexorable conclusion must be that whatever was found floating face-downward at Duke's Cut in 1859, *it was not the body of Joanna Franks.*

Just one moment, Morse!! (The voice of the prosecution was deafening against his ear.) All right! The identification as it stood, as it stands, may perchance appear a trifle tenuous? But have you – *you* – any – *any* – reason for discrediting such identification? And the answering voice in Morse's brain – *Morse*'s voice – was firm and confident. Indeed! And if it should please my learned friends I shall now proceed to tell you exactly what *did* happen between 3 a.m. and 5 a.m. on the morning of Wednesday, the 21st June, in 1859.

Gentlemen! We who are engaged in seeking to reconstruct the course as well as the causation of crime are often tormented by the same insistent thought: *something* must have happened, and happened *in a specific way*. All theory, all reconstruction, all probability, are as nothing compared with *the simple, physical truth of what actually happened at the time*. If only . . . if only, we say, we could see it all; see it all as it actually happened! Gentlemen, I am about to tell you—

Proceed! said the judge (little 'j').

Chapter Twenty-seven

Imagination, that dost so abstract us
That we are not aware, not even when
A thousand trumpets sound about our ears!
(*Dante*, Purgatorio)

STANDING BY THE door at the left of the fore-cabin, she could see them both. A reporter, perhaps, would have had them dribbling or vomiting; snoring 'stertorously', certainly. But Joanna was to notice, at that point, only the simple fact, the undramatic circumstance: asleep, the pair of them – Oldfield and Musson – only the slight rise and fall of the faded-maroon eiderdown that covered them both betraying their fitful breathing. Drunk? Yes, *very* drunk: but Joanna herself had seen to that. Little or no persuasion required – but the *timing* important ... She smiled grimly to herself, and consulted the little silver time-piece she always kept so carefully about her person: the watch her father had given her on her twenty-second birthday (not her twenty-first) – when some fees had been forthcoming from the London Patent Office. And again, now, her hand closed around the precious watch as if it were a talisman for the success of the imminent enterprise.

Occasionally she spoke quietly – very quietly – to the shifty, silly, spotty-faced youth who stood beside her at the entrance to the cabin: his left hand upon the Z-shaped tiller, painted in alternate bands of red, green, yellow; his right hand (where she had placed it herself!) fondling the bosom of her dress. Twenty-five yards ahead, the horse (rather a good one!) was plodding along a little more slowly now, the wooden bobbins stretched taut along its flanks as it forged forward along the silent tow-path – with only the occasional flap of the waters heard as they slurped against the *Barbara Bray*, heading ever southwards into the night.

Joanna looked briefly behind her now, at the plaited basket-work that protected the narrow-boat's stern. 'Over a bit *more*, Tom!' she whispered, as the boat moved into the elbow-bend at Thrupp, just past the village of Hampton Gay. 'And don't forget our little bargain,' she added as she stepped up on to the side, whilst Wootton gently manoeuvred the boat ever closer in towards the right-hand bank.

Wootton would not be celebrating his fifteenth birthday until the February of 1860, but already, in several ways, he was a good deal older than his years. Not in *every* way, though. Never, before Joanna had come on board at Preston Brook, had he felt so besotted with a woman as he was with *her*. Exactly as, he knew, the rest of the crew had been. There was something sexually animated, and *compelling*, about Joanna Franks. Something about the way she flashed her eyes when she spoke; something about the way her tongue lightly licked the corners of her mouth after a plate of mutton chops and peas at some low-roofed tavern alongside the canal; something wickedly and calculatedly controlled about her, as she'd drunk her own full share of liquor – that happily awaited, worry-effacing liquor that all the boatmen (including Wootton) drank so regularly along their journeys. *And Oldfield had taken possession of her* – of that Wootton was quite sure! Taken her in one of the pitch-black transit-tunnels when he, Wootton, had gladly taken Oldfield's 6*d*, and 'legged' the *Barbara Bray* slowly towards that pin-point of light which had gradually grown ever larger as darkly he'd listened to the strangely exciting noises of the love-making taking place in the bunk below him. Towns, too, had taken Oldfield's 6*d* in a tunnel further south. And both Towns and Musson – the lanky, lecherous-eyed Musson! – knew only too well what was going on, soon wanting a share of things for themselves. No surprise, then, that nasty incident when Towns had gone for Musson – with a knife!

As agreed, Thomas Wootton provided her with the lantern. The night, though dark, was dry and still; and the flame nodded only spasmodically as she took it, and leaped lightly off the *Barbara Bray* – her bonnet around her head, her shoes on her feet – on to the tow-path bank where, very soon, she had disappeared from the youth who now kept looking straight ahead of him, a smile around his wide, lascivious mouth.

It was not unusual, of course, for women passengers to jump ashore at fairly regular intervals from a narrow-boat: female toiletry demanded a greater measure of decorum than did that for men. But Joanna might be gone a little longer than was usual that night ... so she'd said.

She stood back in the undergrowth, watching the configuration of the boat melt deeper and deeper into the night. Then, gauging she was out of ear-shot of the crew, she called out the man's name – without at first receiving a reply: then again; then a third time – until she heard a rustling movement in the bushes beside her, against the stone wall of a large mansion house – and a suppressed, tense, 'Shsh!'

The night air was very still, and her voice had carried far too clearly down the canal, with both the youth at the helm, and the man with the stoical horse, turning round simultaneously to look into the dark. But they could see nothing; and *hearing* nothing further, neither of them was giving the matter much further thought.

But one of the men supposedly asleep had heard it, too!

Meanwhile Joanna and her accomplice had flitted stealthily along the row of small, grey-stoned, terraced cottages which lined the canal at Thrupp, keeping to the shadows; then, gliding unobserved past the darkened, silent windows of the Boat Inn, they moved, more freely now, along the short hedge-lined lane that led to the Oxford-Banbury highway.

For the *Barbara Bray*, the next three miles of the Oxford Canal would interpose the Roundham, Kidlington Green, and Shuttleworth's locks – the latter just north of the basin of water known as Duke's Cut.

Negotiation of these locks (so carefully calculated!) would afford appropriate opportunity. No real problem. Much more difficult had been the arrangements for meeting each other; and certainly Oldfield, more than once, had looked at Joanna suspiciously in the last twenty-four hours as she had taken (but of necessity!) her diurnal and nocturnal promenades. She knew, though, how to deal with Oldfield, the skipper of the *Barbara Bray* . . .

'Everything ready?'

He nodded, brusquely. 'Don't talk now!'

They walked across to a covered carrier's wagon which stood, a piebald horse between its shafts, tethered to a beech tree just beside the verge. The moon appeared fitfully from behind the slow-moving cloud; not a soul was in sight.

'Knife?' he asked.

'I sharpened it.'

He nodded with a cruel satisfaction.

She took off her cloak and handed it to him; taking, in return, the one he passed to her – similar to her own, though cheaper in both cloth and cut, and slightly longer.

'You didn't forget the handkerchief?'

Quickly she re-checked, drawing from the right-hand pocket of her former cloak the small, white square of linen, trimmed with lace, the initials J.F. worked neatly in pink silk in one corner.

Clever touch!

161

'She's – she's in there?' Joanna half-turned to the back of the wagon, for the first time her voice sounding nervous, though unexpectedly harsh.

He jerked his head, once, his eyes bright in the heavily bearded face.

'I don't really want to see her.'

'No need!' He had taken the lantern; and when the two of them had climbed up to the front of the wagon, he shone it on a hand-drawn map, his right forefinger pointing to a bridge over the canal, some four-hundred yards north of Shuttleworth's Lock. 'We go down to – here! You wait there, and catch up with them, all right? Then get on board again. Then after that – *after* you get through the lock – you . . .'

'What we agreed!'

'Yes. Jump in! You can stay in the water as long as you like. But be sure no one sees you getting out! The wagon'll be next to the bridge. You get in! And lie still! All right? I'll be there as soon as I've . . .'

Joanna took the knife from her skirt. 'Do you want *me* to do it?'

'No!' He took the knife quickly.

'No?'

'It's just,' he resumed, 'that her face, well – well, it's gone *black*!'

'I thought dead people usually went white,' whispered Joanna.

The man climbed on to the fore-board, and helped her up, before disappearing briefly into the darkness of the covered cart; where, holding the lantern well away from the face, he lifted the dead woman's skirts and with the skill of a surgeon made an incision of about five or six inches down the front of her calico knickers.

The man was handing Joanna two bottles of dark-looking 'Running Horse' ale, when he felt the firm grip of her hand on his shoulder, shaking, shaking, shaking . . . 'Some soup for you, Mr Morse?'

It was Violet.

(Not the soup.)

CHAPTER TWENTY-EIGHT

Mendacity is a system that we live in. Liquor is one
way out and death's the other
(Tennessee Williams, Cat on a Hot Tin Roof)

THE 'REPORT' WAS a regular feature of all the wards
in the JR2, comprising a meeting of hospital and
medical staff at the change-over points between the
Early, Late, and Night shifts. In several of the wards,
the weekends offered the chance for some top consult-
ants and other senior medical personnel to concentrate
their attention on such sidelines as boating and BMWs.
But in many of the semi-surgical wards, like Ward 7C,
the Reports went on very much as at any other times;
as they did on what was now the second Sunday of
Morse's stay in hospital.

The 1 p.m. meeting that day was, in fact, well
attended: the Senior Consultant, a junior houseman,
Sister Maclean, Charge Nurse Stanton, and two student
nurses. Crowded into Sister's small office, the group
methodically appraised the patients in the ward, briefly
discussing convalescences, relapses, prognoses, medi-
cations, and associated problems.

Morse, it appeared, was no longer much of a problem.

'Morse!' The hint of a smile could be observed on the Consultant's face as he was handed the relevant notes.

'He's making fairly good progress,' Sister asserted, slightly defensively, like some mother at a Parents' Evening hearing that her child was perhaps not working as hard as he should be.

'Some of us,' confided the Consultant (handing back the notes) 'would like to persuade these dedicated drinkers that water is a wonderful thing. I wouldn't try to persuade you, of course, Sister, but . . .'

For a minute or two Sister Maclean's pale cheeks were flooded with a bright-pink suffusion, and one of the student nurses could barely suppress a smile of delight at the Dragon's discomfiture. But oddly, the other of the two, the Fair Fiona, was suddenly aware of lineaments and colouring in Sister's face that could have made it almost beautiful.

'He doesn't seem to drink *that* much, does he?' suggested the young houseman, his eyes skimming the plentiful notes, several of which he had composed himself.

The Consultant snorted contemptuously: 'Nonsense!' He flicked his finger at the offending sheets. 'Bloody liar, isn't he? Drunkards and diabetics!' – he turned to the houseman – 'I've told you that before, I think?'

It was wholly forgivable that for a few seconds the suspicion of a smile hovered around the lips of Sister

Maclean, her cheeks now restored to their wonted pallidity.

'He's not diabetic—' began the houseman.

'Give him a couple of years!'

'He *is* on the mend, though.' The houseman (and rightly!) was determined to claim *some* small credit for the reasonably satisfactory transit of Chief Inspector Morse through the NHS.

'Bloody lucky! Even I was thinking about cutting half his innards away!'

'He must be a fundamentally strong sort of man,' admitted Sister, composure now fully recovered.

'I suppose so,' conceded the Consultant, 'apart from his stomach, his lungs, his kidneys, his liver – especially his liver. He might last till he's sixty if he does what we tell him – which I doubt.'

'Keep him another few days, you think?'

'No!' decided the Consultant, after a pause. 'No! Send him home! His wife'll probably do just as good a job as we can. Same medication – out-patients' in two weeks – to see *me*. OK?'

Eileen Stanton was about to correct the Consultant on his factual error when a nurse burst into the office. 'I'm sorry, Sister – but there's a cardiac arrest, I think – in one of the Amenity Beds.'

'Did he die?' asked Morse.

Eileen, who had come to sit on his bed, nodded sadly. It was mid-afternoon.

'How old was he?'

'Don't know exactly. Few years younger than you, I should think.' Her face was glum. 'Perhaps if . . .'

'You look as if you could do with a bit of tender loving care yourself,' said Morse, reading her thoughts.

'Yes!' She looked at him and smiled, determined to snap out of her mopishness. 'And you, my good sir, are not going to get very much more of our wonderful loving care – after today. We're kicking you out tomorrow – had quite enough of you!'

'I'm going out, you mean?' Morse wasn't sure if it was good news or bad news; but she told him.

'Good news, isn't it?'

'I shall miss you.'

'Yes, I shall . . .' But Morse could see the tears welling up in her eyes.

'Why don't you tell me what's wrong?' He spoke the words softly; and she told him. Told him about her wretched week; and how kind the hospital had been in letting her switch her normal nights; and how kind, especially, *Sister* had been . . . But the big tears were rolling down her cheeks and she turned away and held one hand to her face, searching with the other for her handkerchief. Morse put his own grubby handkerchief gently into her hand, and for a moment the two sat together in silence.

'I'll tell you one thing,' said Morse at last. 'It must be pretty flattering to have a couple of fellows fighting over you.'

'No! No, it *isn't*!' The tears were forming again in the large, sad eyes.

'No! You're right. But listen! It won't do you any

167

good at all – in fact' (Morse whispered) 'it'll make you feel far worse. But if *I'd* been at that party of yours – when they were fighting over you – I'd have taken on the *pair* of 'em! You'd have had *three* men squabbling over you – not just two.'

She smiled through her tears, and wiped her wet cheeks, already feeling much better. 'They're big men, both of them. One of them takes lessons in some of those Martial Arts.'

'All right – I'd've lost! Still have fought for you, though, wouldn't I? Remember the words of the poet? "Better to have fought and lost than . . . something . . . something . . ."' (Morse himself had apparently *forgotten* the words of the poet.)

She brought her face to within a few inches of his, and looked straight into his eyes: 'I wouldn't have minded a little bit if you *had* lost, providing you'd let me look after you.'

'You *have* been looking after me,' said Morse, 'and thank you!'

Getting to her feet, she said no more. And Morse, with a little wistfulness, watched her as she walked away. Perhaps he should have told her that she'd meant 'provided', not 'providing'? No! Such things, Morse knew, were no great worry to the majority of his fellow men and women.

But they were to him.

CHAPTER TWENTY-NINE

I think it frets the saints in heaven to see
    How many desolate creatures on the earth
    Have learnt the simple dues of fellowship
And social comfort, in a hospital
            (*Elizabeth Barrett Browning*, Aurora Leigh)

THERE IS A sadness which invariably and mysteriously accompanies the conclusion of any journey, and the end of any sojourn. Whether or not such sadness is a presage of the last journey we all must take; whether or not it is, more simply, a series of last, protracted goodbyes – it is not of any import here to speculate. But for Morse, the news that he was forthwith to be discharged from the JR2 was simultaneously wonderful – and woeful. Music awaited him? Indeed! Soon he would be luxuriating again in Wotan's Farewell from the last act of *Die Walküre*; and turning up Pavarotti *fff* from one of the Puccinis – certainly in mid-morning, when his immediate neighbours were always out and about on their good works for Oxfam. Books, too. He trusted that the Neighbourhood Watch had done its duty in North Oxford, and that his first edition of *A*

Shropshire Lad (1896) was still in its place on his shelves, that slim, white volume that stood proudly amongst its fellows, carrying no extra insurance-cover, like a Royal Prince without a personal bodyguard. Yes, it would be good to get home again: to please himself about what he listened to, or read, or ate . . . or drank. Well, within reason. Yet, quite certainly, he would miss the hospital! Miss the nurses, miss the fellow-patients, miss the routine, miss the visitors – miss so much about the institution which, with its few faults and its many virtues, had admitted him in his sickness and was now discharging him in a comparative health.

But the departure from Ward 7C was not, for Morse, to be a memorable experience. When the message came – hardly a bugle call! – to join a group of people who were to be ambulanced up to North Oxford, he had little opportunity of saying farewell to anyone. One of his ward-mates ('Waggie') was performing his first post-operatively independent ablutions in the wash-room; another was very fast asleep; one had just been taken to the X-ray Department; the Ethiopian torch-bearer was sitting in his bed, with Do-Not-Disturb written all over him, reading *The Blue Ticket* (!); and the last was (and had been for hours) closeted behind his curtains, clearly destined little longer for this earthly life; perhaps, indeed, having already said his own farewells to everybody. As for the nurses, most were bustling purposively about their duties (one or two new faces, anyway), and Morse realized that he was just another patient, and one no longer requiring that special care of just one week ago. Eileen he had not expected to see again, now back to her normal Nights, as she'd told him. Nor was Sister herself anywhere to be seen as he was wheeled out of the ward by a cheerful young porter with a crew-cut and earrings. The Fair Fiona, though, he did see – sitting patiently in the next bay beside an ancient citizen, holding a sputum-pot in front of his dribbling lips. With her free hand she waved, and mouthed a 'Good luck!'. But Morse was no lip-reader and, uncomprehending, he was pushed on through the exit corridor where he and his attendant waited for the service-lift to arrive at Level 7.

—

CHAPTER THIRTY

Lente currite, noctis equi!
(Oh gallop slow, you horses of the night!)
(*Ovid*, Amores)

ALTHOUGH MRS GREEN had kept Morse's partial central-heating partially on, the flat seemed cold and unwelcoming. It would have been good for *anyone* to be there to welcome him: certainly (and especially) Christine – or Eileen, or Fiona; even, come to think of it, the dreaded Dragon of the Loch herself. But there was no one. Lewis had not been in to clear up the stuff stuck through the letter-box, and Morse picked up two white-enveloped Christmas cards (one from his insurance company, with the facsimiled signature of the managing director); and his two Sunday newspapers. Such newspapers, although there was an occasional permutation of titles, invariably reflected the conflict in Morse's mind between the Cultured and the Coarse – the choice between the front page of the present one, *Synod in Dispute over Disestablishment,* and *Sex Slave's Six-Week Ordeal in Silk-lined Coffin* of the other. If Morse chose the latter first (as, in fact, he did) at least he had the excuse that it was undoubtedly the finer headline. And this Sunday, as usual, he first flicked through the pages of full-breasted photographs and features on Hollywood intrigues and Soap infidelities. Then, he made himself a cup of instant coffee (which he much preferred to 'the real thing') before settling down to read about the most recent fluctuations on the world's stock-markets, and the bleak prospects for the diseased and starving millions of the world's unhappy continents.

At half-past five the phone rang, and Morse knew that if he had one wish only it would be for the caller to be Christine.

The caller was Christine.

Not only had she located the rare (and extraordinarily valuable) book of which Morse had enquired, but she had spent an hour or so that afternoon ('Don't tell anyone!') reading through the relevant pages, and discovering ('Don't be disappointed!') that only one short chapter was given over to the interview, between Samuel Carter and an ageing Walter Towns, concerning the trial of the boatmen.

'That's wonderful!' said Morse. 'Where are you ringing from?'

'From, er, from home.' (Why the hesitation?)

'Perhaps—'

'Look!' she interrupted. 'I've made a photocopy. Would you like me to send it through the post? Or I could—'

'Could you read it quickly over the phone? It's fairly short, you say?'

'I'm not a very good reader.'

'Put the phone down – and I'll ring you back! Then we can talk as long as we like.'

'I'm not as hard up as all *that*, you know.'

'All right – fire away!'

'Page 187, it begins – ready?'

'Ready, miss!'

'Of the persons encountered in Perth in these last months of 1884 was a man called Walter Towns. Although he was known as a local celebrity, I found it difficult to guess the quality which had avowedly brought such renown to the rather – nay, wholly! – miserable specimen to whom I soon was introduced. He was a small man, of only some five feet in stature, thin, and of a gaunt mien, with deeply furrowed creases down each of his cheeks from eye to mouth; furthermore, his exceedingly sallow complexion had remained untouched by the rays of a sun that is powerful in this region, and his hollow aspect was further enhanced by the complete absence of teeth in the upper jaw. Yet his eyes spoke a latent (if limited) intelligence; and also a certain dolefulness, as if he were remembering things done long ago and things done ill. In truth, the situation pertaining to this man was fully as melodramatic as my readers could have wished; for he had been reprieved from the gallows with minutes only to spare. It was with the utmost interest and curiosity, therefore, that I questioned him.

'A woman had been murdered near Oxford in

1860, on the local canal, and suspicion had centred on the crew of a narrowboat plying south towards London. The four members of the crew, including both Towns himself and a lad of some fourteen years, had duly been arrested and brought to Court. Whilst the youth had been acquitted, the three others had been convicted, and incarcerated in the gaol in the city of Oxford, awaiting public execution. It was here, two or three minutes following the final visit of the Court Chaplain to the prisoners in their condemned cells, that Towns had received the news of his reprieve. Few humans, certainly, can have experienced a peripeteia' (Christine here reverted to the spelling) 'so dramatic to their fortunes. Yet my conversation with Towns proved a matter of some considerable disappointment. Barely literate as the man was (though wholly understandably so) he was also barely comprehensible. His West Country dialect (as I straightway placed it) was to such an extent o'erlaid with the excesses of the Australian manner of speech that I could follow some of his statements only with great difficulty. In short, the man I now met seemed ill-equipped to cope with the rigours of life – certainly those demanded of a free man. And Towns *was* a "free" man, after serving his fifteen years' penal servitude in the Longbay Penitentiary. A broken, witless man; a man old before his time (he was but 47), a veteran convict (or "crawler") who had experienced the ineffable agonies of a man faced with execution on the morrow.

'Concerning the gruesome and macabre events

invariably associated with the final hours of such criminals, I could learn but little. Yet a few facts may be of interest to my readers. It is clear, for example, that the prisoners each breakfasted on roasted lamb, with vegetables, although it seems probable from Towns' hazy recollection that such or similar breakfasts had been available during the whole period following the fixing of the date for their execution. More distressing, from Towns' viewpoint, was being denied access to his fellow criminals; and if I understood the unfortunate man aright it was this "deprivation" which had been the hardest thing for him to bear. Whether he had slept little or not at all during the fateful night, Towns could not well remember; nor whether he had prayed for forgiveness and deliverance. But a miracle had occurred!

'Surprisingly, it had not been the hanging itself which had been the focal-point of Towns' tortured thoughts that night. Rather it had been the knowledge of the public interest aroused in the case – the notoriety, the infamy, the horror, the abomination, the grisly spectacle, *the fame*; a fame which might bring those hapless men to walk the last few, fatal yards with a degree of fortitude which even the most pitiless spectators could admire.

'Of the crime itself, Towns protested his complete innocence – a protestation not without precedent in criminal archives! But his recollection of the canal journey – and especially of the victim herself, Joanna Franks – was vivid and most poignant. The woman had been, in Towns' eyes, quite wondrously attractive, and it may cause no surprise that she became, almost immediately, the object of the men's craving, and the cause of open jealousies. Indeed, Towns recalled an occasion when two of the crew (the two who were eventually hanged) had come to blows over that provocative and desirable woman. And one of them with a knife! Even the young boy, Harold Wootton, had come under her spell, and the older woman had without much doubt taken advantage of his infatuation. At the same time, from what Towns asserted, and from the manner of his assertion, I am of the view that he himself did not have sexual dealings with the woman.

'There is one interesting addendum to be made. In the first indictment (as I have subsequently read) the charge of either rape or theft would possibly have been prosecuted with more success than that of murder. Yet it was to be the charge of murder that was brought in the second trial. In similar instances, we may observe that the minor charge will frequently be suppressed when the major charge appears the more likely to be sustained. Was this, then, the reason why Towns seemed comparatively loquacious about the suggestion of *theft*? I know not. But it was his belief, as recounted to me, that Wootton had rather more interest in theft than in rape. After all, the availability of sexual dealings in 1860 was hardly, as now, a rarity along the English canals.'

177

'Well, that's it! I'll put it in the post tonight, so you should—'

'Can't you call round, and bring it?'

'Life's, well, it's just a bit hectic at the minute,' she replied, after a little, awkward silence.

'All right!' Morse needed no further excuses. Having dipped the thermometer into the water, he'd found the reading a little too cold for any prospect of mixed bathing.

'You see,' said Christine, 'I – I'm living with some-one—'

'And he doesn't think you should go spending all your time helping me.'

'I kept talking about you, too,' she said quietly.

Morse said nothing.

'Is your address the same as in the telephone direc-tory? E. Morse?'

'That's me! That is I, if you prefer it.'

'What does the "E" stand for? I never knew what to call you.'

'They just call me "Morse".'

'You won't forget me?' she asked, after a little pause.

'I'll try to, I suppose.'

Morse thought of her for many minutes after he had cradled the phone. Then he recalled the testimony of Samuel Carter, and marvelled that a researcher of Carter's undoubted experience and integrity could make so many factual errors in the course of three or four pages: the date of the murder; Towns' accent; Towns' age; Wootton's Christian name; the dropping of the rape charge ... Very interesting, though. Why, Morse had even guessed right about that dust-up with the knife! Well, almost right: he'd got the wrong man, but ...

CHAPTER THIRTY-ONE

The second coastline is turned towards Spain and the west, and off it lies the island of Hibernia, which according to estimates is only half the size of Britain

(Julius Caesar, de Bello Gallico –

on the geography of Ireland)

TEN MINUTES LATER the phone rang again, and Morse knew in his bones that it was Christine Greenaway.

It was Strange.

'You're out then, Morse – yes? That's good. You've had a bit of a rough ride, they tell me.'

'On the mend now, sir. Kind of you to ring.'

'No *great* rush, you know – about getting back, I mean. We're a bit understaffed at the minute, but give yourself a few days – to get over things. Delicate thing, the stomach, you know. Why don't you try to get away somewhere for a couple of days – new surroundings – four-star hotel? You can afford it, Morse.'

'Thank you, sir. By the way, they've signed me off for a fortnight – at the hospital.'

'Fortnight? A *fort*-night?'

'It's, er, a delicate thing, the stomach, sir.'

'Yes, well . . .'

'I'll be back as soon as I can, sir. And perhaps it wouldn't do me any harm to take your advice – about getting away for a little while.'

'Do you a world of good! The wife's brother' (Morse groaned inwardly) 'he's just back from a wonderful holiday. Ireland – Southern Ireland – took the car – Fishguard–Dun Laoghaire – then the west coast – you know, Cork, Kerry, Killarney, Connemara – marvellous, he said. Said you couldn't have spotted a terrorist with a telescope!'

It *had* been kind of Strange to ring; and as he sat in his armchair Morse reached idly for the World Atlas from his 'large-book' shelf, in which Ireland was a lozenge shape of green and yellow on page 10 – a country which Morse had never really contemplated before. Although spelling errors would invariably provoke his wrath, he confessed to himself that he could never have managed 'Dun Laoghaire', even with a score of attempts. And where was Kerry? Ah yes! Over there, west of Tralee – he was on the right bit of the map – and he moved his finger up the coast to Galway Bay. Then he saw it: Bertnaghboy Bay! And suddenly the thought of going over to Connemara seemed overwhelmingly attractive. By himself? Yes, it probably had to be by himself; and he didn't mind that, really. He was somewhat of a loner by temperament – because though never wholly happy when alone he was usually slightly more miserable when with other people. It would have been good to have taken Christine, but . . . and for a few minutes Morse's thoughts travelled back to Ward 7C. He would send a card to Eileen and Fiona; and one to 'Waggie' Greenaway, perhaps? Yes, that would be a nice gesture: Waggie had been out in the wash-room when Morse had left, and he'd been a pleasant old—

Suddenly Morse was conscious of the tingling excitement in the nape of his neck, and then in his shoulders. His eyes dilated and sparkled as if some inner current had been activated; and he sat back in the armchair and smiled slowly to himself.

What, he wondered, was the routine in the Irish Republic for *exhumation*?

CHAPTER THIRTY-TWO

Oh what a tangled web we weave
When first we practise to deceive!
(*Sir Walter Scott*, Marmion)

'You *WHAT*?' asked a flabbergasted Lewis, who had called round at 7.30 p.m. ('Not till *The Archers* has finished' had been his strict instruction.) He himself had made an interesting little discovery – well, the WPC in St Aldates' had made it, really – and he was hoping that it might amuse Morse in his wholly inconsequential game of 'Find Joanna Franks'. But to witness Morse galloping ahead of the Hunt, chasing (as Lewis was fairly certain) after some imaginary fox of his own, was, if not particularly unusual, just a little disconcerting.

'You see, Lewis' (Morse was straightway in full swing) 'this is one of the most beautiful little deceptions we've ever come across. The *problems* inherent in the case – almost all of them – are resolved immediately once we take one further step into imaginative improbability.'

'You've lost me already, sir,' protested Lewis.

'No, I haven't! Just take one more step *yourself*. You think you're in the *dark*? Right? But the dark is where we *all* are. The dark is where *I* was, until I took one more step into the dark. And then, when I'd taken it, I found myself in the *sunshine.*'

'I'm very glad to hear it,' mumbled Lewis.

'It's like this. Once I read that story, I was uneasy about it – doubtful, uncomfortable. It was the *identification* bit that worried me – and it would have worried any officer in the Force today, *you* know that! But, more significantly, if we consider the psychology of the whole—'

'Sir!' (It was almost unprecedented for Lewis to interrupt the Chief in such peremptory fashion.) 'Could we – could you – please forget all this psychological referencing? I just about get my fill of it all from some of these Social Services people. Could you just tell me, simply and—'

'I'm boring you – is that what you're saying?'

'*Exactly* what I'm saying, sir.'

Morse nodded to himself happily. 'Let's put it *simply*, then, all right? I read a story in hospital. I get interested. I think – *think* – the wrong people got arrested, and some of 'em hanged, for the murder of that little tart from Liverpool. As I say, I thought the identification of that lady was a bit questionable; and when I read the words the boatmen were alleged to have used about her – well, I knew there must be something fundamentally *wrong*. You see—'

'You said you'd get to the point, sir.'

'I thought that Joanna's father – No! Let's start again! Joanna's father gets a job as an insurance rep. Like most people in that position he gets a few of his own family, if they're daft enough, to take out a policy with him. He gets a bit of commission, and he's not selling a phoney product, anyway, is he? I think that both Joanna and her *first* husband, our conjurer friend, were soon enlisted in the ranks of the policy-holders. Then times get tough; and to crown all the misfortunes, Mr Donavan, the greatest man in all the world, goes and dies. And when Joanna's natural grief has abated – or evaporated, rather – she finds she's done very-nicely-thank-you out of the insurance taken on his life. She receives £100, with profits, on what had been a policy taken out only two or three years previously. Now, £100 plus in 1850-whenever was a very considerable sum of money; and Joanna perhaps began, at that point, to appreciate the potential for *malpractice* in the system. She began to see the insurance business not only as a potential *future* benefit, but as an actual, *present* source of profit. So, after Donavan's death, when she met and married Franks, one of the first things she insisted on was his taking out a policy – not on *his* life – but on *hers*. Her father could, and did, effect such a transaction without any trouble, although it was probably soon after this that the Notts and Midlands Friendly Society got a little suspicious about Joanna's father, Carrick – Daniel Carrick – and told him his services were no longer—'

'Sir!'

Morse held up his right hand. 'Joanna Franks was *never* murdered, Lewis! She was the mastermind – mistressmind – behind a deception that was going to rake in some considerable, and desperately needed, profit. It was *another* woman, roughly the same age and the same height, who was found in the Oxford Canal; a woman provided by Joanna's *second* husband, the ostler from the Edgware Road, who had already made his journey – not difficult for *him*! – with horse and carriage from London, to join his wife at Oxford. Or, to be more accurate, Lewis, at some few points *north* of Oxford. You remember in the Colonel's book?' (Morse turned to the passage he had in mind.) 'He – here it is! – "he explained how in consequence of some information he had come into Oxfordshire" – Bloody liar!'

Lewis, now interested despite himself, nodded a vague concurrence of thought. 'So what you're saying, sir, is that Joanna worked this insurance fiddle and probably made quite a nice little packet for herself and for her father as well?'

'Yes! But not only that. Listen! I may just be wrong, Lewis, but I think that not only was Joanna wrongly identified as the lawful wife of Charles Franks – by Charles Franks – but that Charles Franks was the *only* husband of the woman supposedly murdered on the *Barbara Bray*. In short, the "Charles Franks" who broke down in tears at the second trial was *none other than Donavan*.'

'Phew!'

'A man of many parts: he was an actor, he was a conjurer, he was an impersonator, he was a swindler, he was a cunning schemer, he was a callous murderer, he was a loving husband, he was a tearful witness, he was the first and *only* husband of Joanna Franks: F. T. Donavan! We all thought – you thought – even *I* thought – that there were three principal characters playing their roles in our little drama; and now I'm telling you, Lewis, that in all probability we've only got *two*. Joanna; and her husband – the greatest man in all the world; the man buried out on the west coast of Ireland, where the breakers come rolling in from the Atlantic . . . so they tell me . . .'

CHAPTER THIRTY-THREE

Stet Difficilior Lectio
(Let the more difficult of the readings stand)
(*The principle applied commonly by editors faced with variant readings in ancient manuscripts*)

LEWIS WAS SILENT. How else? He had a precious little piece of evidence in his pocket, but while Morse's mind was still coursing through the upper atmosphere, there was little point in interrupting again for the minute. He put the envelope containing the single photocopied sheet on the coffee-table – and listened further.

'In the account of Joanna's last few days, we've got some evidence that she could have been a bit deranged; and part of the evidence for such a possibility is the fact that at some point she kept calling out her husband's name – "Franks! Franks! Franks!" Agreed? But she *wasn't* calling out that at all – she was calling her *first* husband, Lewis! I was sitting here thinking of "Waggie" Greenaway—'

'And his daughter,' mumbled Lewis, inaudibly.

'—and I thought of "Hefty" Donavan. F. T. Donavan. And I'll put my next month's salary on that "F" standing for "Frank"! Huh! Who's ever heard of a wife calling her husband by his surname?'

'I have, sir.'

'Nonsense! Not these days.'

'But it's *not* these days. It was—'

'She was calling *Frank Donavan* – believe me!'

'But she *could* have been queer in the head, and if so—'

'Nonsense!'

'Well, we shan't ever know for sure, shall we, sir?'

'Nonsense!'

Morse sat back with the self-satisfied, authoritative air of a man who believes that what he has called 'nonsense' three times must, by the laws of the universe, be necessarily untrue. 'If *only* we knew how tall they were – Joanna and . . . and whoever the other woman was. But there *is* just a chance, isn't there? That cemetery, Lewis—'

'Which do you want first, sir? The good news or the bad news?'

Morse frowned at him. 'That's . . .?' pointing to the envelope.

'That's the good news.'

Morse slowly withdrew and studied the photocopied sheet.

> *Twenty five minutes past 7 o'clock.*
> *Drowned body was in car*
> *of wtr licensed to D of M —*
> *taken to Plough Inn at Wols —*
> *probable identity? unknown.*
> *Prelim findings wd suggest*
> *death by drowning — no obvious*
> *injury was seen — 5 3¾ in —*
> *well nour — c 35 yrs. Bruise*
> *on mouth (rt side) — body warm*
> *full clothes, not bonnet &*
> *shoes — face discoloured, black.*

'Not the Coroner's Report, sir, but the next best thing. This fellow must have seen her before the *post-mortem*. Interesting, isn't it?'

'*Very* interesting.'

The report was set out on an unruled sheet of paper, dated, and subscribed by what appeared as a 'Dr Willis', for the writing was not only fairly typical of the semi-legibility forever associated with the medical profession, but was also beset by a confusion with 'm's, 'w's, 'n's, and 'u's – all these letters appearing to be incised with a series of what looked like semi-circular fish-hooks.

Clearly the notes of an orderly-minded local doctor called upon to certify death and to take the necessary action – in this case, almost certainly, to pass the whole business over to some higher authority. Yet there were one or two real nuggets of gold here: the good Willis had made an exact measurement of height, and had written one or two most pertinent (and, apparently, correct) observations. Sad, however, from Morse's point of view, was the unequivocal assertion made here that *the body was still warm.* It must have been this document which had been incorporated into the subsequent *post-mortem* findings, thenceforth duly reiterated both in Court and in the Colonel's history. And it *was* a pity; for if Morse had been correct in believing that another body had been substituted for that of Joanna Franks, that woman must surely have been killed in the early hours of the morning, and could *not* therefore have been drowned some three or four hours later. *Far* too risky. It was odd, certainly, that the dead woman's face had turned black so very quickly; but there was no escaping the plain fact that the first medical man who had examined the corpse had found it still *warm.*

Is that what the report had said, though – 'still warm'? No! No, it hadn't! It just said 'warm' . . . Or *did* it?

Carefully Morse looked again at the report – and sensed the old familiar tingling around his shoulders. *Could* it be? Had everyone else read the report wrongly? In every case the various notes were separated from each other by some form of punctuation – either dashes (eight of them) or full stops (four) or question-marks (only one). All the notes *except* one, that is: the exception being that 'body warm/full clothes . . .' etc. There was neither a dash nor a stop between these two, clearly disparate, items – unless the photocopier had borne unfaithful witness. No! The solution was far simpler. There had been no break requiring any punctuation! Morse looked again at line 10 of the report,

on mouth (rt side) – body warm

and considered three further facts. Throughout, the 's's were written almost as straight vertical lines; of the fifteen or so 'i' dots, no fewer than six had remained un-dotted; and on this showing Willis seemed particularly fond of the word 'was'. So the line should perhaps – should certainly! – read as follows: 'on mouth (rt side) – body was in'. The body 'was in full clothes'! The body was *not* 'warm'; not in Morse's book. There, suddenly, the body was very, very cold.

Lewis, whilst fully accepting the probability of the alternative reading, did not appear to share the excitement which was now visibly affecting Morse; and it was time for the bad news.

'No chance of checking this out in the old Summertown graveyard, sir.'

'Why not? The gravestones are still there, some of them – it says so, doesn't it? – and I've seen them myself—'

'They were all removed, when they built the flats there.'

'Even those the Colonel mentioned?'

Lewis nodded.

Morse knew full well, of course, that any chance of getting an exhumation order to dig up a corner of the greenery in a retirement-home garden was extremely remote. Yet the thought that he might have clinched his theory ... It was not a matter of supreme moment, though, he knew that; it wasn't even important in putting to rights a past and grievous injustice. It was of no great matter to anyone – except to himself. Ever since he had first come into contact with problems, from his early schooldays onwards – with the meanings of words, with algebra, with detective stories, with cryptic clues – he had always been desperately anxious to know the *answers*, whether those answers were wholly satisfactory or whether they were not. And now, whatever had been the motive leading to that far-off murder, he found himself irked in the extreme to realize that the woman – or *a* woman – he sought had until so very recently been lying in a marked grave in North Oxford. Had she been Joanna Franks, after all? No chance of knowing now – not for certain. But if the meticulous Dr Willis had been correct in his measurements, she *couldn't* have been Joanna, surely?

After Lewis had gone, Morse made a phone call.

'What was the average height of women in the nineteenth century?'

'Which end of the nineteenth century, Morse?'

'Let's say the middle.'

'Interesting question!'

'Well?'

'It varied, I suppose.'

'Come *on*!'

'Poor food, lack of protein – all that sort of stuff. Not very big, most of 'em. Certainly no bigger than the Ripper's victims in the 1880s: four foot nine, four foot ten, four foot eleven – that sort of height: well, that's about what *those* dear ladies were. Except one. Stride, wasn't her name? Yes, Liz Stride. They called her "Long Liz" – so much taller than all the other women in the work-houses. You follow that, Morse?'

'How tall was *she* – "Long Liz"?'

'Dunno.'

'Can you find out?'

'What, now?'

'And ring me back?'

'Bloody hell!'

'Thanks.'

Morse was three minutes into the love duet from Act One of *Die Walküre* when the phone rang.

'Morse? Five foot three.'

Morse whistled.

'Pardon?'

'Thanks, Max! By the way, are you at the lab all day tomorrow? Something I want to bring to show you.'

So the 'petite' little figure had measured three quarters of an inch *more* than 'Long Liz' Stride! And her shoes as Lewis had ascertained, were about size 5! Well, well, well! Virtually every fact now being un-earthed (though that was probably not *le mot juste*) was bolstering Morse's bold hypothesis. But, infuriatingly, there was, as it seemed, no chance whatever of establishing the truth. Not, at any rate, the truth regarding Joanna Franks.

CHAPTER THIRTY-FOUR

Marauding louts have shot the moping owl:
    The tower is silent 'neath the wat'ry moon;
But Lady Porter, lately on the prowl
    Will sell the place for pennies very soon
               (*E. O. Parrot*, The Spectator)

THE COMMUNICATION FROM the Insurance Company had been a third and final demand for his previous month's premium; and the first thing Morse did the following morning was to write out a cheque, with a brief letter of apology. He understood very little about money, but a dozen or so years previously he had deemed it provident (as it transpired, Prudential) to pay a monthly premium of £55 against a lump sum of £12,000, with profits, at sixty – an age looming ever closer. He had never given a thought about what would happen if he pre-deceased his policy. No worry for him: for the present he had no financial worries, no dependants, a good salary, and a mortgage that would finish in two years' time. He knew it, yes! – compared with the vast majority of mankind he was extremely fortunate. Still, he ought perhaps to think of making a will ...

Coincidentally, he had been talking to Lewis about insurances the day before and (he admitted it to himself) largely making it all up as he went along. But it was *far* from improbable, wasn't it – what he'd guessed? Those insurance fiddles? He looked out the first material that Christine had brought in to him at the JR2, and once again studied the facts and figures of the Nottinghamshire and Midlands Friendly Society for 1859:

PLAN OF THE ASSOCIATION.   7

The following Table (I.) exhibits the scale of Premiums for the assurance of £100 on the lives of Members; also the Net Premiums payable after seven years, allowing a reduction of 72 per cent., to which persons now assuring will then be entitled if the present rate of abatement be maintained.

Age next Birthday	Annual Premium			Reduction 72 per cent.			Net Premium			Age next Birthday	Annual Premium			Reduction 72 per cent.			Net Premium		
	£	s.	d.	£	s.	d.	£	s.	d.		£	s.	d.	£	s.	d.	£	s.	d.
21	2	10	0	1	16	0	0	14	0	45	4	9	3	3	4	7	1	5	2
22	2	10	0	1	16	0	0	14	3	46	4	12	9	3	6	8	1	6	0
23	2	11	6	1	17	1	0	14	5	47	4	16	3	3	9	4	1	6	11
24	2	12	6	1	17	10	0	14	8	48	4	19	3	3	11	10	1	7	11
25	2	13	6	1	18	6	0	15	0	49	5	3	6	3	14	6	1	9	0
26	2	14	6	1	19	3	0	15	3	50	5	7	6	3	17	5	1	10	1
27	2	15	6	2	0	0	0	15	6	51	5	11	9	4	0	6	1	11	3
28	2	16	6	2	0	8	0	15	10	52	5	16	0	4	3	6	1	12	6
29	2	17	9	2	1	7	0	16	8	53	6	0	6	4	6	9	1	13	9
30	2	19	3	2	2	8	0	16	7	54	6	5	0	4	10	0	1	15	0
31	3	0	6	2	3	7	0	16	11	55	6	9	6	4	13	3	1	16	3
32	3	2	0	2	4	8	0	17	4	56	6	14	6	4	16	10	1	17	8
33	3	3	6	2	5	9	0	17	9	57	6	19	6	5	0	5	1	19	1
34	3	5	3	2	7	0	0	18	3	58	7	4	6	5	4	0	2	0	6
35	3	7	0	2	8	3	0	18	9	59	7	9	6	5	7	8	2	1	10
36	3	8	9	2	9	6	0	19	3	60	7	15	0	5	11	7	2	3	5
37	3	10	9	2	10	11	0	19	10	61	8	0	9	5	15	9	2	5	0
38	3	12	9	2	12	5	1	0	4	62	8	7	0	6	0	0	2	6	9
39	3	14	9	2	13	10	1	0	11	63	8	13	9	6	5	1	2	8	8
40	3	17	0	2	15	5	1	1	7	64	9	1	0	6	10	4	2	10	8
41	3	19	3	2	17	1	1	2	2	65	9	8	0	6	15	11	2	12	10
42	4	1	6	2	18	8	1	2	10	66	9	17	0	7	1	10	2	15	2
43	4	4	0	3	0	6	1	3	6	67	10	5	0	7	7	7	2	17	5
44	4	6	9	3	2	6	1	4	3										

Joanna had been born in 1821, so she was thirty-eight in 1859. If she'd taken out a policy a year, two years earlier, that would be – age next birthday thirty-six – an annual premium of £3. 8s 9d. Under £7, say, for a return of £100. Not bad at all. And if Donavan had already pocketed a similar packet . . .

Morse left his flat in mid-morning (the first excursion since his return) and posted his single letter. He met no one he knew as he turned right along the Banbury Road, and then right again into Squitchey Lane; where, taking the second turning on his left, just past the evangelical chapel (now converted into a little group of residences) he walked down Middle Way. It was a dark, dankish morning, and a scattering of rooks (mistaking, perhaps, the hour) squawked away in the trees to his right. Past Bishop Kirk Middle School he went on, and straight along past the attractive terraced houses on either side with their mullioned bay-windows – and, on his left, *there it was*: Dudley Court, a block of flats built in cinnamon-coloured brick on the site of the old Summertown Parish Cemetery. A rectangle of lawn, some fifty by twenty-five yards, was set out behind a low containing wall, only about eighteen inches high, over which Morse stepped into the grassy plot planted with yew-trees and red-berried bushes. Immediately to his left, the area was bounded by the rear premises of a Social Club; and along this wall, beneath the straggly branches of winter jasmine, and covered with damp beech-leaves, he could make out the stumps of four or five old headstones, broken off at their roots like so many jagged teeth just protruding from their gums. Clearly, any deeper excavation to remove these stones in their entirety had been thwarted by the proximity of the wall; but all the rest had been removed, perhaps several years ago now – and duly recorded no doubt in some dusty box of papers on the shelves of the local Diocesan Offices. Well, at least Morse could face one simple fact: no burial evidence would be forthcoming from these fair lawns. None! Yet it would have been good to know where the stone had marked (as the Colonel had called it) the 'supra-corporal' site of Joanna Franks.

Or whoever.

He walked past Dudley Court itself where a Christmas tree, bedecked with red, green, and yellow bulbs, was already switched on; past the North Oxford Conservative Association premises, in which he had never (and would never) set foot; past the Spiritualist Church, in which he had never (as yet) set foot; past the low-roofed Women's Institute HQ, in which he had once spoken about the virtues of the Neighbourhood Watch Scheme; and finally, turning left, he came into South Parade, just opposite the Post Office – into which he ventured once a year and that to pay the Lancia's road-tax. But as he walked by the old familiar landmarks, his mind was far away, and the decision firmly taken. If he was to be cheated of finding one of his suspects, he would go and look for the other! He needed a break. He would *have* a break.

There was a travel agency immediately across the

street, and the girl who sat at the first desk to the right smiled brightly.

'Can I help you, sir?'

'Yes! I'd like' (Morse sat himself down) 'I'd like to book a holiday, with a car, in Ireland – the Republic, that is.'

Later that day, Morse called at the William Dunn School of Pathology in South Parks Road.

'Have a look at these for me, will you?'

Refraining from all cynical comment, Max looked dubiously across at Morse over his half-lenses.

'Max! All I want to know is—'

'—whether they come from M&S or Littlewoods?'

'The tear, Max – *the tear.*'

'Tear? *What* tear?' Max picked up the knickers with some distaste and examined them (as it seemed to Morse) in cursory fashion. 'No tear here, Morse. Not the faintest sign of any irregular distension of the fibre tissue – calico, by the way, isn't it?'

'I think so.'

'Well, we don't need a microscope to tell us it's a cut: neat, clean, straight-forward *cut,* all right?'

'With a knife?'

'What the hell else do you cut things with?'

'Cheese-slicer? Pair of—?'

'What a wonderful thing, Morse, is the human imagination!'

It was a wonderful thing, too, that Morse had received such an unequivocal answer to one of his questions; the very first such answer, in fact, in their long and reasonably amicable acquaintanceship.

CHAPTER THIRTY-FIVE

Heap not on this mound
Roses that she loved so well;
Why bewilder her with roses
That she cannot see or smell?
(*Edna St Vincent Millay*, Epitaph)

INSPECTOR MULVANEY SPOTTED him parking the car in the 'Visitor' space. When the little station had been converted ten years earlier from a single detached house into Kilkearnan's apology for a crime-prevention HQ, the Garda had deemed it appropriate that the four-man squad should be headed by an inspector. It seemed, perhaps, in retrospect, something of an over-reaction. With its thousand or so inhabitants, Kilkearnan regularly saw its ration of fisticuffs and affray outside one or more of the fourteen public-houses; but as yet the little community had steered clear of any involvement in international smuggling or industrial espionage. Here, even road accidents were a rarity – though this was attributable more to the comparative scarcity of cars than to the sobriety of their drivers. Tourists there were, of course – especially in the summer months;

but even they, with their Rovers and BMWs, were more often stopping to photograph the occasional donkey than causing any hazard to the occasional drunkard.

The man parking his Lancia in the single (apart from his own) parking-space, Mulvaney knew to be the English policeman who had rung through the previous day to ask for help in locating a cemetery (for, as yet, no stated purpose) and who thought it was probably the one overlooking Bertnaghboy Bay – that being the only burial ground marked on the local map. Mulvaney had been able to assure Chief Inspector Morse (such was he) that indeed it would be the cemetery which lay on the side of a hill to the west of the small town: the local dead were always likely to be buried there, as Mulvaney had maintained – there being no alternative accommodation.

From the lower window, Mulvaney watched Morse with some curiosity. It was not every day (or week, or month) that any contact was effected between the British Police and the Garda; and the man who was walking round to the main (only) entrance looked an interesting specimen: mid-fifties, losing his whitish hair, putting on just a little too much weight, and exhibiting perhaps, as was to be hoped, the tell-tale signs of liking his liquor more than a little. Nor was Mulvaney disappointed in the man who was shown into his main (only) office.

'Are you related to Kipling's Mulvaney?' queried Morse.

'No, sor! But that was a good question – and edu-cashin, that's a good thing, too!'

Morse explained his unlikely, ridiculous, selfish mission, and Mulvaney warmed to him immediately. No chance whatsoever, of course, of any exhumation order being granted, but perhaps Morse might be interested in hearing about the business of grave digging in the Republic? A man could never *dig* a grave on a Monday, and that for perfectly valid reasons, which he had forgotten; and in any case it wasn't Monday, was it? And if a grave *was* dug, even on a Monday, it had always – *always*, sor! – to be in the morning, or at least the previous evening. That was an important thing, too, about all the forks and shovels: placed across the open grave, they had to be, in the form of the holy cross, for reasons which a man of Morse's educashin would need no explanation, to be sure. Last, it was always the custom for the chief mourner to supply a little quantity of Irish whiskey at the graveside for the other members of the saddened family; and for the grave-diggers, too, of course, who had shovelled up the clinging, cloggy soil. 'For sure, 'tis always a t'irsty business, sor, that working of the soil!'

So Morse, the chief mourner, walked out into the main (only) High Street, and purchased three bottles of Irish malt. An understanding had been arrived at, and Morse knew that whatever the problems posed by the Donavan-Franks equation, the left-hand side would be solved (if solved it *could* be) with the full sympathy and (unofficial) co-operation of the Irish Garda.

In his mind's eye, Morse had envisaged a bank of arc-lights, illuminating a well-marked grave, with barricades erected around the immediate area, a posse of constables to keep the public from prying, and press photographers training their telescopic lenses on the site. The time? That would be 5.30 a.m. – the usual exhumation hour. And excitement would be intense.

It was not to be.

Together, Morse and Mulvaney had fairly easily located the final habitation of the greatest man in all the world. In all, there must have been about three or four hundred graves within the walled area of the hillside cemetery. Half a dozen splendidly sculptured angels and madonnas kept watch here and there over a few former dignitaries, and several large Celtic crosses marked other burial-plots. But the great majority of the dead lay unhonoured here beneath untended, meaner-looking memorials. Donavan's stone was one of the latter, a poor, mossed-and-lichened thing, with white and ochre blotches, and no more than two feet high, leaning back at an angle of about 20 degrees from the vertical. So effaced was the weathered stone that only the general outlines of the lettering could be followed – and that only on either side of a central disintegration:

'That's him,' said Morse triumphantly. It looked as if his name *had* been Frank.

'God rest his soul!' added Mulvaney. ' – that's if it's there, of course.'

Morse grinned, and wished he'd known Mulvaney long ago. 'How are you going to explain . . .?'

'We are digging yet another grave, sor. In the daylight – and just as normal.'

It was all quite quick. Mulvaney had bidden the two men appointed to the task to dig a clean rectangle to the east of the single stone; and after getting down only two or three feet, one of the spades struck what sounded like, and was soon revealed to be, a wooden coffin. Once all the dark-looking earth had been removed and piled on each side of the oblong pit, Morse and Mulvaney looked down to a plain coffin-top, with no plate of any sort screwed into it. The wood, one-inch elm-boarding, and grooved round the top, looked badly warped, but in a reasonable state. There seemed no reason to remove the complete coffin; and Morse, betraying once again his inveterate horror of corpses, quietly declined the honour of removing the lid.

It was Mulvaney himself, awkwardly straddling the hole, his shoes caked with mud, who bent down and pulled at the top of the coffin, which gave way easily, the metal screws clearly having disintegrated long ago. As the board slowly lifted, Mulvaney saw, as did Morse, that a whitish mould hung down from the inside of the coffin-lid; and in the coffin itself, covering the body, a shroud or covering of some sort was overspread with the same creeping white fungus.

Round the sides at the bottom of the coffin, plain for all to see, was a bed of brownish, dampish sawdust, looking as fresh as if the body which lay on it had been buried only yesterday. But *what* body?

''Tis wonderfully well preserved, is it not, sor? 'Tis the peat in the soil that's accountin' forrit.'

This from the first grave-digger, who appeared more deeply impressed by the wondrous preservation of the wood than by the absence of any body. *For the coffin contained no body at all.* What it did contain was a roll of carpet, of some greenish dye, about five feet in length, folded round what appeared to have been half a dozen spaded squares of peat. Of Donavan there was no trace whatsoever – not even a torn fragment from the last handbill of the greatest man in all the world.

CHAPTER THIRTY-SIX

A man's learning dies with him; even his virtues fade out of remembrance; but the dividends on the stocks he bequeaths may serve to keep his memory green
(*Oliver Wendell Holmes*, The Professor at the Breakfast Table)

MORSE GREW SOMEWHAT fitter during the days following his return from Ireland; and very soon, in his own judgement at least, he had managed to regain that semblance of salubrity and strength which his GP interpreted as health. Morse asked no more.

He had recently bought himself the old Furtwängler recording of *The Ring*; and during the hours of Elysian enjoyment which that performance was giving him, the case of Joanna Franks, and the dubious circumstances of the Oxford Tow-path Mystery, assumed a slowly diminishing significance. The whole thing had brought him some recreative enjoyment, but now it was finished. Ninety-five per cent certain (as he was) that the wrong people had been hanged in 1860, there was apparently nothing further he could do to dispel that worrying little five per cent of doubt.

Christmas was coming up fast, and he was glad not to have that tiring traipsing round the shops – no stockings, no scent to buy. He himself received half a dozen cards; two invitations to Drinks Evenings; and a communication from the JR2:

XMAS PARTY

The Nursing Staff of the John Radcliffe Hospital
request the pleasure of your company
on the evening of Friday, 22nd December,
from 8 p.m. until midnight,
at the Nurses' Hostel, Headington Hill, Oxford.
Disco Dancing, Ravishing Refreshments, Fabulous fun!
Please Come! Dress informal. RSVP.

The printed card was signed, in blue biro, 'Ward 7C' – and followed by a single 'X'.

It was on Friday, 15th December, a week before the scheduled party, that Morse's eye caught the name in the *Oxford Times* 'Deaths' column:

DENISTON, Margery – On December 10th, peacefully at her home in Woodstock, aged 78 years. She wished her body to be given to medical research. Donations gratefully received, in honour of the late

Colonel W. M. Deniston, by the British Legion
Club, Lambourn.

Morse thought back to the only time he'd met the
quaint old girl, so proud as she had been of her
husband's work – a work which had brought Morse
such disproportionate interest; a work which he'd
not even had to pay for. He signed a cheque for £20,
and stuck it in a cheap brown envelope. He had both
first- and second-class stamps to hand, but he chose a
second-class: it wasn't a matter of life and death, after
all.

He would (he told himself) have attended a funeral
service, if she'd been having one. But he was glad she
wasn't: the stern and daunting sentences from the
Burial Service, especially in the A.V., were ever assuming a nearer and more personal threat to his peace of
mind; and for the present that was something he could
well do without. He looked up the British Legion's
Lambourn address in the telephone directory, and after
doing so turned to 'Deniston, W. M.'. There it was: 46
Church Walk, Woodstock. Had there been any family?
It hardly appeared so, from the obituary notice. So? So
what happened to things, if there was no one to leave
them to? As with Mrs Deniston, possibly? As with anyone
childless or unmarried . . .

It was difficult parking the Lancia, and finally Morse
took advantage of identifying himself to a sourpuss of a

traffic warden who reluctantly sanctioned a temporary straddling of the double-yellows twenty or so yards from the grey-stoned terraced house in Church Walk. He knocked on the front door, and was admitted forthwith.

Two persons were in the house: a young man in his middle twenties who (as he explained) had been commissioned by Blackwells to catalogue the few semi-valuable books on the late Denistons' shelves; and a great-nephew of the old Colonel, the only surviving relative, who (as Morse interpreted matters) was in for a very pretty little inheritance indeed, if recent prices for Woodstock property were anything to judge by.

To the latter, Morse immediately and openly explained what his interest was: he was begging nothing – apart from the opportunity to discover whether the late Colonel had left behind any notes or documents relating to *Murder on the Oxford Canal.* And happily the answer was 'yes' – albeit a very limited 'yes'. In the study was a pile of manuscript, and typescript, and clipped to an early page of the manuscript was one short letter – a letter with no date, no sender's address, and no envelope:

Our dear Daniel,

    We do both trust you are keeping well these past months. We shall be in Derby in early Sept. when we hope we shall be with you. Please say to Mary how the dress she did was very successfull and will she go on with the other one if she is feeling recovered.

                Yours Truely and Afectionatly,
                    Matthew

That was all. Enough, though, for the Colonel to feel that it was worth preserving! There was only one 'Daniel' in the case, Daniel Carrick from Derby; and here was that one piece of primary-source material that linked the Colonel's narrative in a tangible, physical way to the whole sorry story. Agreed, Daniel Carrick had never figured all that prominently in Morse's thinking; but he *ought* to have done. He was surely just as damningly implicated as the other two in the deception – the twin deception – which had seen the Notts and Midlands Friendly Society having to fork out, first for the death of the great uncoffined Donavan, and then for the death of the enigmatic Joanna, the great undrowned.

Morse turned over the faded, deeply creased letter and saw, on the back, a few pencilled notes, pretty certainly in the Colonel's hand: 'No records from Ins. Co. – Mrs C. very poorly at this time? Not told of J.'s death? 12 Spring St. still occupied 12.4.76!'

There it was then – palpable paper and writing, and just a finger-tip of contact with one of the protagonists in that nineteenth-century drama. As for the two principal actors, the only evidence that could have been forthcoming about them was buried away with their bodies. And where Joanna was buried – or where the greatest man in all the world – who knew, or who could ever know?

CHAPTER THIRTY-SEVEN

Modern dancers give a sinister portent about our times. The dancers don't even look at one another. They are just a lot of isolated individuals jiggling in a kind of self-hypnosis

(*Agnes de Mille*, The New York Times)

THE PARTY-GOERS WERE fully aware that when the caretaker said midnight he meant 11.55 p.m.; but few had managed to arrive at the Nurses' Hostel before 9 p.m. In any case, the event was never destined to be of cosmic significance, and would have little to show for itself apart from a memory or two, a few ill-developed photographs, and a great deal of clearing up the following morning.

As soon as he took his first steps across the noisy, throbbing, flashing room – it was now 10.30 p.m. – Morse realized that he had made a tragic error in accepting the invitation. 'Never go back!' – that was the advice he should have heeded; yet he had been fool enough to recall the white sheets and the Fair Fiona and the Ethereal Eileen. Idiot! He sat down on a rickety, slatted chair, and sipped some warm insipid 'punch' that was handed out in white plastic cups to each new arrival. Constituted, if taste were anything to go by, of about 2% gin, 2% dry Martini, 10% orange juice, and 86% lemonade, it was going to take a considerable time, by Morse's reckoning, before such Ravishing Refreshments turned him on; and he had just decided that the best thing about it was the little cubes of apple floating on the top when Fiona detached her sickly-looking beau from the dance-floor and came up to him.

'Happy Christmas!' She bent down, and Morse could still feel the dryness of her lips against his cheek as she introduced the embarrassed youth, repeated her Christmas greeting, and then was gone – throwing herself once more into a series of jerky contortions like some epileptic puppet.

Morse's plastic cup was empty and he walked slowly past a long line of tables, where beneath the white coverings he glimpsed sugared mince-pies and skewered sausages.

'We'll be starting on them soon!' said a familiar voice behind him, and Morse turned to find Eileen, blessedly alone and, like only a few of the others, wearing her uniform.

'Hullo!' said Morse.

'Hullo!' she said softly.

'It's good to see you!'

She looked at him, and nodded, almost imperceptibly.

A tall man, looking as if he might have been involved in a fight recently, materialized from somewhere.

213

'This is Gordon,' said Eileen, looking up into the shaded planes of Gordon's skull-like face. And when Morse had shaken hands with the man, he once more found himself alone, wondering where to walk, where to put himself, how to make an inconspicuous exit, to cease upon the five-minutes-to-eleven with no pain.

He was only a few feet from the main door when she was suddenly standing in front of him.

'You're not trying to sneak away, I hope!'

Nessie!

'Hullo, Sister. No! I'm – I mustn't stay too long, of course, but—'

'I'm glad you came. I know you're a wee bit old for this sort of thing . . .' Her lilting Scottish accent seemed to be mocking him gently.

Morse nodded; it was difficult to argue the point, and he looked down to pick out the one remaining apple cube from his cup.

'Your sergeant did you rairther better – with the drink, I mean.'

Morse looked at her – suddenly – almost as if he had never looked at her before. Her skin in this strobo-scopic light looked almost opaline, and the colour of her eyes was emerald. Her auburn hair was swept upward, emphasizing the contours of her face, and her mouth was thinly and delicately lipsticked. For a woman, she was quite tall, certainly as tall as he was; and if only (as Morse thought) she'd worn something other than that miserably dowdy, unflattering dress . . .

'Would you like to dance, Inspector?'

214

'I – no! It's not one of my, er, things, dancing, I'm afraid.'

'What—?'

But Morse was never to know what she was going to ask him. A young houseman – smiling, flushed, so happily at home here – grabbed her by the hand and was pulling her to the floor.

'Come on, Sheila! *Our* dance, remember?'

Sheila!

'You won't try to sneak away – ?' she was saying over her shoulder. But she was on the dance-floor now, where shortly all the other dancers were stopping and moving to the periphery as the pair of them, Sheila and her young partner, put on a dazzling display of dance-steps to the rhythmic clapping of the audience.

Morse felt a stab of jealousy as his eyes followed them, the young man's body pressed close to hers. He had fully intended to stay, as she had asked. But when the music had finished, the newly metamorphosed Nessie, pretending to collapse, had become the centre of enthusiastic admiration, and Morse placed his plastic cup on the table by the exit, and left.

At 9.30 the following morning, after a somewhat fitful sleep, he rang the JR2 and asked for Ward 7C.

'Can I speak to Sister, please?'

'Who shall I say is calling?'

'It's – it's a personal call.'

'We can't take personal calls, I'm afraid. If you'd like to leave your name—'

'Just tell her one of her old patients from the ward—'

'Is it Sister Maclean you wanted?'

'Yes.'

'She's left – she left officially last week. She's off to be Director of Nursing Services—'

'She's left Oxford?'

'She's leaving today. She stayed on for a party last night—'

'I see. I'm sorry to have bothered you. I seem to have got the wrong end of things, don't I?'

'Yes, you do.'

'Where is she going to?'

'Derby – Derby Royal Infirmary.'

CHAPTER THIRTY-EIGHT

The very designation of the term 'slum' reflects a
middle-class attitude to terrace-housing, where grand
values are applied to humble situations
(*James Curl,* The Erosion of Oxford)

SINCE FAST DRIVING was his only significant vice (apart
from egg-and-chips) Lewis was delighted, albeit on one
of his 'rest' days, to be invited to drive the Lancia. The
car was a powerful performer, and the thought of the
stretch of the M1 up to the A52 turn-off was, to Lewis,
most pleasurable. Nor had Morse made the slightest
secret of the fact that the main object of the mission
was to find out if a thoroughfare called 'Spring Street'
still stood – as it had stood until 1976 – on the northern
outskirts of Derby.

'Just humour me, Lewis – that's all I ask!'

Lewis had needed little persuasion. It had been a
momentous 'plus' in his life when Morse had intimated
to his superiors that it was above all with him, Sergeant
Lewis, that his brain functioned most fluently; and now
– moving the Lancia across into the fast lane of the M1
at Weedon – Lewis felt wholly content with the way of

life which had so happily presented itself to him those many years since. He knew, of course, that their present mission was a lost cause. But then Oxford was not unfamiliar with such things.

Spring Street proved difficult to locate, in spite of a city-map purchased from a corner-newsagent in the northern suburbs. Morse himself had become progressively tetchier as the pedestrians to whom Lewis wound down his window appeared either totally ignorant or mutually contradictory. Finally, however, the Lancia homed in on an area, marked off by hoardings, announcing itself as the 'Derby Development Complex', with two enormously tall, yellow cranes tracing and retracing their sweeping arcs above the demolition squads below.

'Could be too late, could we?' ventured Lewis.

'It doesn't *matter* – I've *told* you, Lewis.' Morse wound down his own window and spoke to a brick-dusted, white-helmeted workman.

'Have you flattened Spring Street yet?'

'Won't be long, mate,' the man replied, pointing vaguely towards the next-but-one block of terraced houses.

Morse, somewhat irked by the 'mate' familiarity, wound up his window, without a 'thank you', and pointed, equally vaguely, to Lewis, the latter soon pulling the Lancia in behind a builder's skip a couple of streets away. A young coloured woman pushing a utility pram assured Morse that, yes, this *was* Spring

Street, and the two men got out of the car and looked around them.

Perhaps, in some earlier decades, the area had seen some better times; yet, judging from its present aspect it seemed questionable whether any of the houses in this unlovely place had ever figured in the 'desirable' category of residences. Built, by the look of them, in the early 1800s, many were now semi-derelict, and several boarded-up completely. Clearly a few remained tenanted, for here and there smoke rose up into the grey air from the narrow, yellow chimney-pots; and white-lace curtains still framed the windows yet unbroken. With distaste, Morse eyed the squashed beer-cans and discarded fish-and-chip wrappings that littered the narrow pavement. Then he walked slowly along, before stopping before a front door painted in what fifty years earlier had been a Cambridge blue, and into which a number-plaque '20' was screwed. The house was in a terraced group of six; and walking further along, Morse came to the door of an abandoned property on which, judging from the outlines, the figures '16' had once been fixed. Here Morse stopped and beckoned to Lewis – the eyes of both now travelling to the two adjacent houses, boarded up against squatters or vandals. The first house must, without question, have once been Number 14 – and the second, Number 12.

The latter, the sorry-looking object of Morse's pilgrimage, stood on the corner, the sign 'Burton Road' still fastened to its side-wall, although no sign of Burton Road itself was any longer visible. Below the sign, a wooden gate, hanging forlornly from one of its rusted

219

hinges, led to a small patch of back-yard, choked with litter and brownish weeds, and cluttered with a kiddy's ancient tricycle and a brand-new trolley from a supermarket. The dull-red bricks of the outer walls were flaking badly, and the single window-frame here had been completely torn away, leaving the inside of the mean little abode open to the elements. Morse poked his face through the empty frame, across the blackened sill, before turning away with a sickened disgust: in one corner of the erstwhile kitchen was what appeared to be a pile of excrement; and beside it, half a loaf of white bread, its slices curled and mildew green.

'Not a pretty sight, is it?' whispered Lewis, standing at Morse's shoulder.

'She was brought up here,' said Morse quietly. 'She lived here with her mother . . . and her father . . .'

'. . . and her brother,' added Lewis.

Yes! Morse had forgotten the brother, Joanna's younger brother, the boy named after his father – forgotten him altogether.

Reluctantly Morse left the small back-yard, and slowly walked round to the front again, where he stood in the middle of the deserted street and looked at the little terrace-house in which Joanna Carrick-Donavan-Franks had probably spent – what? – the first twenty or so years of her life. The Colonel hadn't mentioned exactly where she was born, but . . . Morse thought back to the dates: born in 1821, and married to the great man in 1842. How reassuring it would have been to find a date marked on one of the houses! But Morse could see no sign of one. If the house had been built by the 1820s, had she spent those twenty years in and around that pokey little kitchen, competing for space with the sink and the copper and the mangle and the cooking-range and her parents...? And her younger brother? He, Morse, had his own vivid recollections of a similarly tiny kitchen in a house which (as he had been told) had been demolished to make way for a carpet-store. But he'd never been back. It was always a mistake to go back, because life went on perfectly well without you, thank-you-very-much, and other people got along splendidly with their own jobs – even if they were confined to selling carpets. Yes, almost always a mistake: a mistake, for example, as it had been to go back to the hospital; a mistake as it would have been (as he'd intended) to go along to the Derby Royal and non-chalantly announce to Nessie that he just happened to be passing through the city, just wanted to congratulate her on becoming the Big White Chief...

Lewis had been talking whilst these and similar thoughts were crossing and recrossing Morse's mind, and he hadn't heard a word of what was said.

'Pardon, Lewis?'

'I just say that's what we used to do, that's all – over the top of the head, as I say, and put the date against it.'

Morse, unable to construe such manifest gobblede-gook, nodded as if with full understanding, and led the way to the car. A large white-painted graffito caught his eye, sprayed along the lower wall of a house in the next terrace: HANDS OFF CHILE – although it was difficult to know who in this benighted locality was being exhorted to such activity – or, rather, inactivity. TRY GEO. LUMLEY's TEA 1s 2d, seemed a more pertinent notice, painted over the bricked-up first-floor window of the next corner house, the lettering originally worked in a blue paint over a yellow-ochre background, the latter now a faded battleship-grey; a notice (so old was it) that Joanna might well have seen it every day as she walked along this street to school, or play – a notice from the past which a demolition gang of hard-topped men would soon obliterate from the local-history records when they swung their giant skittle-balls and sent the side-wall crumbling in a shower of dust.

Just like the Oxford-City-Council Vandals when . . .

Forget it, Morse!

'Where to now, sir?'

It took a bit of saying, but he said it: 'Straight home, I think. Unless there's something else *you* want to see?'

CHAPTER THIRTY-NINE

And what you thought you came for
Is only a shell, a husk of meaning
From which the purpose breaks only when it is
    fulfilled
If at all. Either you had no purpose
Or the purpose is beyond the end you figured
And is altered in fulfilment
                    (*T. S. Eliot*, Little Gidding)

MORSE SELDOM ENGAGED in any conversation in a car, and he was predictably silent as Lewis drove the few miles out towards the motorway. In its wonted manner, too, his brain was meshed into its complex mechanisms, where he was increasingly conscious of that one little irritant. It had always bothered him not to know, not to have heard – even the smallest things:

'What was it you were saying back there?'

'You mean when you weren't listening?'

'Just *tell* me, Lewis!'

'It was just when we were children, that's all. We used to measure how tall we were getting. Mum always used to do it – every birthday – against the kitchen wall.

I suppose that's what reminded me, really – looking in that kitchen. Not in the front room – that was the best wallpaper there; and, as I say, she used to put a ruler over the top of our heads, you know, and then put a line and a date . . .'

Again, Morse was not listening.

'Lewis! Turn round and go back!'

Lewis looked across at Morse with some puzzlement.

'I said just turn round,' continued Morse – quietly, for the moment. '*Gentle* as you like – when you get the *chance*, Lewis – no need to imperil the pedestrians or the local pets. But just *turn round*!'

Morse's finger on the kitchen switch produced only an empty 'click', in spite of what looked like a recent bulb in the fixture that hung, shadeless, from the disintegrating plaster-boards. The yellowish, and further yellowing, paper had been peeled away from several sections of the wall in irregular gashes, and in the damp top-corner above the sink it hung away in a great flap.

'Whereabouts did you use to measure things, Lewis?'

''Bout here, sir.' Lewis stood against the inner door of the kitchen, his back to the wall, where he placed his left palm horizontally across the top of his head, before turning round and assessing the point at which his fingertips had marked the height.

'Five-eleven, that is – unless I've shrunk a bit.'

The wallpaper at this point was grubby with a myriad fingerprints, appearing not to have been renovated for half a century or more; and around the non-functioning light-switch the plaster had been knocked out, exposing some of the bricks in the partition-wall. Morse tore a strip from the yellow paper, to reveal a surprisingly well-preserved, light-blue paper beneath. But marked memorials to Joanna, there were none; and the two men stood silent and still there, as the afternoon seemed to grow perceptibly colder and darker by the minute.

'It was a thought, though, wasn't it?' asked Morse.

'Good thought, sir!'

'Well, one thing's certain! We are *not* going to stand here all afternoon in the gathering gloom and strip all these walls of generations of wallpaper.'

'Wouldn't take all that long, would it?'

'What? All this bloody stuff—'

'We'd know where to look.'

'We would?'

'I mean, it's only a little house; and if we just looked along at some point, say, between four feet and five feet from the floor – downstairs only, I should think—'

'You're a genius – did you know that?'

'And you've got a good torch in the car.'

'No,' admitted Morse. 'I'm afraid—'

'Never mind, sir! We've got about half an hour before it gets too dark.'

It was twenty minutes to four when Lewis emitted a child-like squeak of excitement from the narrow hallway.

'Something here, sir! And I think, I *think*—'

'Careful! *Careful*!' muttered Morse, coming nervously

alongside, a triumphant look now blazing in his blue-grey eyes.

Gradually the paper was pulled away as the last streaks of that December day filtered through the filthy skylight above the heads of Morse and Lewis, each of them looking occasionally at the other with wholly disproportionate excitement. For there, inscribed on the original plaster of the wall, below three layers of subsequent papering – and still clearly visible – were two sets of black-pencilled lines: the one to the right marking a series of eight calibrations, from about 3′ 6″ of the lowest one to about 5′ of the top, with a full date shown for each; the one to the left with only two calibrations (though with four dates) – a diagonal of crumbled plaster quite definitely precluding further evidence below.

For several moments Morse stood there in the dark-ened hallway and gazed upon the wall as if upon some holy relic.

'Get a torch, Lewis! And a tape-measure!'

'Where—?'

'Anywhere. Everybody's got a torch, man.'

'Except you, sir!'

'Tell 'em you're from the Gas Board and there's a leak in Number 12.'

'The house isn't *on* gas.'

'Get *on* with it, Lewis!'

When Lewis returned, Morse was still considering his wall-marks – beaming as happily at the eight lines on the right as a pools-punter surveying a winning-line of score-draws on the Treble Chance; and, taking the torch, he played it joyously over the evidence. The new light (as it were) upon the situation quickly confirmed that any writing below the present extent of their findings was irredeemably lost; it also showed a letter in between the two sets of measurements, slightly towards the right, and therefore probably belonging with the second set.

The letter 'D'!

Daniel!

The lines on the right *must* mark the heights of Daniel Carrick; and, if that were so, then those to the left were those of *Joanna Franks*!

'Are you thinking what I'm thinking, Lewis?'

'I reckon so, sir.'

'Joanna married in 1841 or 1842' – Morse was talking to himself as much as to Lewis – 'and that fits well because the measurements end in 1841, finishing at the same height as she was in 1840. And her younger brother, Daniel, was gradually catching her up – about the same height in 1836, and quite a few inches taller in 1841.'

Lewis found himself agreeing. 'And you'd expect them that way round, sir, wouldn't you? Joanna first; and then her brother, to Joanna's right.'

'Ye-es.' Morse took the white tape-measure and let it roll out to the floor. 'Only five foot, this.'

'Don't think we're going to need a much longer one, sir.'

Lewis was right. As Morse held the 'nought-inches' end of the tape to the top of Joanna's putative measurements, Lewis shone the torch on the other end as he knelt on the dirty red tiles. No! A longer tape-measure was certainly not needed here, for the height measured only 4' 9", and as Lewis knew, the woman who had been pulled out of Duke's Cut had been 5' 3¾" – almost seven inches taller than Joanna had been after leaving Spring Street for her marriage! Was it possible – even wildly possible – that she had grown those seven inches between the ages of twenty-one and thirty-eight? He put his thoughts into words:

'I don't think, sir, that a woman could have—'

'No, Lewis – nor do I! If not impossible, at the very least unprecedented, surely.'

'So you were right, sir . . .'

'Beyond any reasonable doubt? Yes, I think so.'

'Beyond *all* doubt?' asked Lewis quietly.

'There'll always be that one per cent of doubt about most things, I suppose.'

'You'd be happier, though, if—'

Morse nodded: 'If we'd found just that *one* little thing extra, yes. Like a 'J' on the wall here or ... I don't know.'

'There's nothing else to find, then, sir?'

'No, I'm sure there isn't,' said Morse, but only after hesitating for just a little while.

CHAPTER FORTY

The world is round and the place which may seem
like the end may also be only the beginning

(*Ivy Baker Priest,* Parade)

IT SOUNDED AN anti-climactic question: 'What do we
do now, sir?'

Morse didn't know, and his mind was far away: 'It
was done a long time ago, Lewis, and done ill,' he said
slowly.

Which was doubtless a true sentiment, but it hardly
answered the question. And Lewis pressed his point –
with the result that together they sought out the site-
foreman, to whom, producing his warranty-card, Morse
dictated his wishes, making the whole thing sound as if
the awesome authority of MI5 and MI6 alike lay behind
his instructions regarding the property situated at
Number 12 Spring Street, especially for a series of
photographs to be taken as soon as possible of the
pencil-marks on the wall in the entrance hall. And yes,
the site-foreman thought he could see to it all without
too much trouble; in fact, he was a bit of a dab hand
with a camera himself, as he not so modestly admitted.

Then, after Lewis had returned torch and tape-measure to a slightly puzzled-looking householder, the afternoon events were over.

It was five minutes to six when Lewis finally tried once again to drive away from the environs of Derby (North) and to make for the A52 junction with the M1 (South). At 6 p.m., Morse leaned forward and turned on the car-radio for the news. One way or another it had been a bad year, beset with disease, hunger, air crashes, railway accidents, an oil-rig explosion, and sundry earthquakes. But no cosmic disaster had been reported since the earlier one o'clock bulletin, and Morse switched off – suddenly aware of the time.

'Do you realize it's gone opening time, Lewis?'

'No such thing these days, sir.'

'You know what I mean!'

'Bit early—'

'We've got something to celebrate, Lewis! Pull in at the next pub, and I'll buy you a pint.'

'You *will*?'

Morse was not renowned for his generosity in treating his subordinates – or his superiors – and Lewis smiled to himself as he surveyed the streets, looking for a pub-sign; it was an activity with which he was not unfamiliar. 'I'm driving, sir.'

'Quite right, Lewis. We don't want any trouble with the police.'

*

As he sat sipping his St Clements and listening to Morse conducting a lengthy conversation with the landlord about the wickedness of the lager-brewers, Lewis felt inexplicably content. It had been a good day; and Morse, after draining his third pint with his wonted rapidity, was apparently ready to depart.

'Gents?' asked Morse.

The landlord pointed the way.

'Is there a public telephone I could use?'

'Just outside the Gents.'

Lewis thought he could hear Morse talking over the phone – something to do with a hospital; but he was never a man to eavesdrop on the private business of others, and he walked outside and stood waiting by the car until Morse re-appeared.

'Lewis – I, er – I'd like you just to call round quickly to the hospital, if you will. The Derby Royal. Not too far out of our way, they tell me.'

'Bit of stomach trouble again, sir?'

'No!'

'I don't think you should have had all that beer, though—'

'Are you going to drive me there or not, Lewis?'

Morse, as Lewis knew, was becoming increasingly reluctant to walk even a hundred yards or so if he could ride the distance, and he now insisted that Lewis park the Lancia in the AMBULANCES ONLY area just outside the Hospital's main entrance.

'How long will you be, sir?'

'How long? Not sure, Lewis. It's my lucky day, though, isn't it? So I may be a little while.'

It was half an hour later that Morse emerged to find Lewis chatting happily to one of the ambulance-men about the road-holding qualities of the Lancia family.

'All right, then, sir?'

'Er – well. Er . . . Look, Lewis! I've decided to stay in Derby overnight.'

Lewis's eyebrows rose.

'Yes! I think – I think I'd like to be there when they take those photographs – you know, in, er . . .'

'*I* can't stay, sir! I'm on duty tomorrow morning.'

'I know. I'm not asking you to, am I? I'll get the train back – no problem – Derby, Birmingham, Banbury – easy!'

'You *sure*, sir?'

'*Quite* sure. You don't *mind* do you, Lewis?'

Lewis shook his head. 'Well, I suppose, I'd better—'

'Yes, you get off. And don't drive too fast!'

'Can I take you – to a hotel or something?'

'No need to bother, I'll – I'll find something.'

'You look as though you've already found something, sir.'

'Do I?'

As the Lancia accelerated along the approach road to the M1 (South) Lewis was still smiling quietly to himself, recalling the happy look on Morse's face as he had turned and walked once more towards the automatic doors.

EPILOGUE

The name of a man is a numbing blow from which
he never recovers

> (*Marshall McLuhan*, Understanding Media)

ON THE MORNING of Friday, 11th January (he had
resumed duties on New Year's Day) Morse caught the
early Cathedrals' Express to Paddington. He was pro-
grammed to speak on Inner City Crime at 11 a.m. at
the Hendon Symposium. Tube to King's Cross, then
out on the Northern Line. Easy. Plenty of time. He
enjoyed trains, in any case; and when Radio Oxford
had announced black ice on the M40, his decision was
made for him; it would mean, too, of course, that he
could possibly indulge a little more freely with any
refreshments that might be available.

He bought *The Times* and the *Oxford Times* at the
bookstall, got a seat at the rear of the train, and had
solved *The Times* crossword by Didcot. Except for one
clue. A quick look in his faithful Chambers would have
settled the issue immediately; but he hadn't got it, and
as ever he was vexed by his inability to put the finishing
touch to anything. He quickly wrote in a couple of

bogus letters (in case any of his fellow-passengers were waiting to be impressed) and then read the letters and the obituaries. At Reading he turned to the *Oxford Times* crossword. The setter was 'Quixote'; and Morse smiled to himself as he remembered 'Waggie' Green-away finally solving the same setter's 'Bradman's famous duck (6)' and writing in DONALD at 1 across. Nothing *quite* so amusing here – but a very nice puzzle. Twelve minutes to complete. Not bad!

Morse caught a subliminal glimpse of 'Maidenhead' as the train sped through, and he took a sheaf of papers from his briefcase, first looking through the alphabetical list of those who would be attending the conference. Nobody he knew in the A-D range, but then he scanned the E-F:

- Eagleston
  Ellis
  Emmett
  Erskine
  Farmer
  Favant
  Fielding

Tom Eagleston, yes; and Jack Farmer, yes; and . . .

Morse stopped, and looked again at the middle of the three delegates in the Fs. The name was vaguely familiar, wasn't it? Yet he couldn't remember where . . . Unusual name, though. Morse's eye continued down the list – and then he remembered. Yes! It was the name of the man who had been walking along the

Oxford Canal at the time when Joanna Franks was murdered – when Joanna Franks was *supposedly* murdered; the man, perhaps, who had been traced to the Nag's Head where he'd signed the register. A mystery man. Maybe not his real name at all, for the canal had been full of men who used an alias. In fact, as Morse recollected, two of the crew of the *Barbara Bray* itself had done so: Alfred Musson, alias Alfred Brotherton; Walter Towns, alias Walter Thorold. It might well be of some deep psychological significance that criminals sometimes seemed most unwilling to give up their names, even if this involved a greater risk of future identification: Morse had known it quite often. It was as if a man's name were almost an intrinsic part of him; as if he could never shed it *completely*; as if it were as much part of his personality as his skin. Musson had kept his name, hadn't he? So had Towns.

Morse spent the rest of the journey looking idly out of the window, his brain tidying up a few scattered thoughts, as the train drew into Paddington: Donald Bradman – Don Bradman, the name by which everyone recognized the greatest batsman ever born; and F. T. Donavan, the greatest man in all the world; and . . .

Ye Gods!!

The blood was running cold through Morse's limbs as he remembered the man who had identified the body of Joanna Franks; the man who had been physically incapable (as it seemed!) of raising his eyes to look into the faces of the prisoners; the man who had held his hands to his own face as he wept and turned his back on the men arraigned before the court. Why did he do these things, Morse? Because *the boatmen might just have recognized him*. For they had seen him, albeit fleetingly, in the dawn, as 'he had made to get further on his way with all speed'. Donald Favant! – or Don Favant, as he would certainly have seen himself.

Morse wrote out those letters D-O-N-F-A-V-A-N-T along the bottom margin of the *Oxford Times*; and then, below them, the name of which they were the staggering anagram: the name of F T DONAVAN – the greatest man in all the world.

COLIN DEXTER

Service of all the Dead

£5.99 Pan Books

'*The sweet countenance of Reason greeted Morse serenely when he woke, and told him that it would be no bad idea to have a quiet look at the problem itself before galloping off to a solution . . .*'

Chief Inspector Morse was alone among the congregation in suspecting continued unrest in the quiet parish of St Frideswide's.

Most people could still remember the churchwarden's murder. A few could still recall the murderer's suicide. Now even the police had closed the case.

Until a chance meeting among the tombstones reveals startling new evidence of a conspiracy to deceive . . .

WINNER OF THE CWA SILVER DAGGER AWARD

COLIN DEXTER

The Daughters of Cain

£5.99 Pan Books

'*Bizarre and bewildering – that's what so many murder investigations in the past had proved to be . . . In this respect, at least, Lewis was correct in his thinking. What he could not have known was what unprecedented anguish the present case would cause to Morse's soul.*'

Chief Superintendent Strange's opinion was that too little progress had been made since the discovery of a corpse in a North Oxford flat. The victim had been killed by a single stab wound to the stomach. Yet the police had no weapon, no suspect, no motive.

Within days of taking over the case Chief Inspector Morse and Sergeant Lewis uncover startling new information about the life and death of Dr Felix McClure. When another body is discovered Morse suddenly finds himself with rather too many suspects. For once, he can see no solution. But then he receives a letter containing a declaration of love . . .

COLIN DEXTER

The Silent World of Nicholas Quinn

£5.99 Pan Books

'*Morse had never ceased to wonder why, with the staggering advances in medical science, all pronouncements concerning times of death seemed so disconcertingly vague.*'

The newly appointed member of the Oxford Examinations Syndicate was deaf, provincial and gifted. Now he is dead . . .

And his murder, in his North Oxford home, proves to be the start of a formidably labyrinthine case for Chief Inspector Morse, as he tries to track down the killer through the insular and bitchy world of the Oxford colleges . . .

COLIN DEXTER

The Dead of Jericho

£5.99 Pan Books

'*Morse switched on the gramophone to "play", and sought to switch his mind away from all the terrestrial troubles. Sometimes, this way, he almost managed to forget. But not tonight . . .*'

Anne Scott's address was scribbled on a crumpled note in the pocket of Morse's smartest suit.

He turned the corner of Canal Street, Jericho, on the afternoon of Wednesday, 3rd October.

He hadn't planned a second visit. But he was back later the same day – as the officer in charge of a suicide investigation . . .

WINNER OF THE CWA SILVER DAGGER AWARD

White Night

I reached down to brush the sidewalk with my fingertips, allowing the dangerous buildup of magic to ground itself more or less harmlessly into the earth, and only a trace amount of energy flared out into a disruptive pattern.

It saved our lives.

The instant I released the excess energy into the area around us, a nearby stoplight blew out, Murphy's cell phone started blaring 'Stars and Stripes Forever,' three car alarms went off—

—and Murphy's Saturn coupe went up in a brilliant ball of fire and an ear-shattering blast of thunder.

There was no time to do anything. Even if I'd been crouched, tense, and holding defensive magic ready to go, I wouldn't have beaten the explosion to the punch. It was instant, and violent, and did not at all care whether I was on my guard or not. Something that felt vaguely like an enormous feather pillow swung by the Incredible Hulk slammed into my chest.

It lifted me up off the ground and dumped me on the sidewalk several feet later. My shoulder clipped a mailbox as I went by it, and then I had a good, steady view of the clear summer sky above me as I lay on my back and ached.

I'd lived, which was always a good start in this kind of situation.

White Night

A novel of
the Dresden Files

Jim Butcher

www.orbitbooks.net

ORBIT

First published in the United States in 2007 by Roc, an imprint of
New American Library, a division of Penguin Group (USA) Inc.
First published in Great Britain in 2008 by Orbit
Reprinted 2008 (twice), 2009

A CIP catalogue record for this book is available from the British Library.

ISBN 978-1-84149-687-0

Typeset in Garamond 3 by
Palimpsest Book Production Limited, Grangemouth, Stirlingshire
Printed and bound in Great Britain by
CPI Mackays, Chatham, ME5 8TD

Papers used by Orbit are natural, renewable and recyclable
products sourced from well-managed forests and certified
in accordance with the rules of the Forest Stewardship Council.

Orbit
An imprint of
Little, Brown Book Group
100 Victoria Embankment
London EC4Y 0DY

An Hachette UK Company
www.hachette.co.uk

www.orbitbooks.net

For the newest members of the family, Jesse and Dara

Acknowledgments

I owe thanks to the usual crowd for this book, as for all the rest: the inmates at the Beta Foo Asylum, semper criticas. Thank you to my agent, Jenn, and my editor, Anne, and thank you, my angel Shannon. You each help me more than you know – yeah, okay, probably Shannon more than the others. But thank you all.

1

Many things are not as they seem: The worst things in life never are.

I pulled my battle-scarred, multicolored old Volkswagen Beetle up in front of a run-down Chicago apartment building, not five blocks from my own rented basement apartment. Usually, by the time the cops call me, things are pretty frantic; there's at least one corpse, several cars, a lot of flashing blue lights, yellow-and-black tape, and members of the press – or at least the promise of the imminent arrival of same.

This crime scene was completely quiet. I saw no marked police cars, and only one ambulance, parked, its lights off. A young mother went by, one child in a stroller, the other toddling along holding Mommy's hand. An elderly man walked a Labrador retriever past my car. No one was standing around and gawking or otherwise doing anything at all out of the ordinary.

Odd.

A creepy shiver danced over the nape of my neck, even though it was the middle of a sunny May afternoon. Normally, I didn't start getting wigged out until I'd seen at least one nightmarish thing doing something graphic and murderous.

I put it down to the paranoia of advancing age. It isn't like I'm all *that* old or anything, especially for a wizard, but age is always advancing and I'm fairly sure it's up to no good.

I parked the Blue Beetle and headed into the apartment building. I went up several flights of stairs that needed their old tile replaced, or at least scrubbed and shined. I left them to find a hallway carpeted in a low, grey-blue pile that had been crushed down to shiny smoothness in the middle. The apartment doors were battered, old, but made of thick oak. I found Murphy waiting for me.

At five feet and small change, a hundred and not much, she didn't exactly look like a tough Chicago cop who could face down monsters and maniacs with equal nerve. Chicks like that aren't supposed to be blond or have a cute nose. Sometimes I think Murphy became that tough cop she didn't look like purely for the sake of contrariness — no amount of sparkling blue eyes or seeming harmlessness could hide the steel in her nature. She gave me her we're-at-work nod, and a terse greeting. 'Dresden.'

'Lieutenant Murphy,' I drawled, with an elaborate bow and flourish of one hand, deliberately at odds with her brusque demeanor. I wasn't doing it out of pure contrariness. I'm not like that. 'I am dazzled by your presence once more.'

I expected a snort of derision. Instead, she gave me a polite, brittle little smile and corrected me in a gentle tone: 'Sergeant Murphy.'

Open mouth, insert foot. Way to go, Harry. The opening credits aren't done rolling on this case, and you've already reminded Murphy of what it cost her to be your friend and ally.

Murphy had been a detective lieutenant, and in charge of Special Investigations. SI was Chicago PD's answer to problems that didn't fall within the boundaries of 'normal.' If a vampire slaughtered a transient, if a ghoul killed a graveyard watchman, or if a faerie cursed someone's hair to start growing *in* instead of *out*, someone had to examine it. Someone had to look into it and reassure the government and the citizenry that everything was normal. It was a thankless job, but SI handled it through sheer guts and tenacity and sneakiness and by occasionally calling in Wizard Harry Dresden to give them a hand.

Her bosses got real upset about her abandoning her duties in a time of crisis, while she helped me on a case. She'd already been exiled to professional Siberia, by being put in charge of SI. By taking away the rank and status she had worked her ass off to earn, they had humiliated her, and dealt a dreadful blow to her pride and her sense of self-worth.

'Sergeant,' I said, sighing. 'Sorry, Murph. I forgot.'

She shrugged a shoulder. 'Don't worry about it. I forget sometimes, too. When I answer the phone at work, mostly.'

'Still. I should be less stupid.'

'We all think that, Harry.' Murphy said, and thumped me lightly on the biceps with one fist. 'But no one blames you.'

'That's real big of you, Mini Mouse,' I replied.

She snorted and rang for the elevator. On the way up, I asked her, 'It's a lot quieter than most crime scenes, isn't it?'

She grimaced. 'It isn't one.'

'It isn't?'

'Not exactly,' she said. She glanced up at me. 'Not officially.'

'Ah,' I said. 'I guess I'm not actually consulting.'

'Not officially,' she said. 'They cut Stallings's budget pretty hard. He can keep the equipment functional and the paychecks steady, barely, but . . .'

I arched a brow.

'I need your opinion,' she said.

'About what?'

She shook her head. 'I don't want to prejudice you. Just look and tell me what you see.'

'I can do that,' I said.

'I'll pay you myself.'

'Murph, you don't need to—'

She gave me a very hard look.

Sergeant Murphy's wounded pride wouldn't allow her to

take charity. I lifted my hands in mock surrender, relenting.
'Whatever you say, boss.'

'Damn right.'

She took me to an apartment on the seventh floor. There
were a couple of doors in the hall standing slightly open,
and I caught furtive looks from their residents from the
corner of my eye as we walked past. At the far end of the
hall stood a pair of guys who looked like medtechs – bored,
grouchy medtechs. One of them was smoking, the other
leaning against a wall with his arms crossed and his cap's
bill down over his eyes. Murphy and the two of them ignored
one another as Murphy opened the apartment door.

Murphy gestured for me to go in and planted her feet,
clearly intending to wait.

I went into the apartment. It was small, worn, and shabby,
but it was clean. A miniature jungle of very healthy green
plants covered most of the far wall, framing the two windows.
From the door, I could see a tiny television on a TV stand,
an old stereo, and a futon.

The dead woman lay on the futon.

She had her hands folded over her stomach. I didn't have
the experience to tell exactly how long she'd been there, but
the corpse had lost all its color and its stomach looked slightly
distended, so I guessed that she died at least the day before.
It was hard to guess at her age, but she couldn't have been
much more than thirty. She wore a pink terry-cloth bathrobe,
a pair of glasses, and had her brown hair pulled up into a
bun.

On the coffee table in front of the futon there was a
prescription bottle, its top off, empty. A decanter of golden
brown liquid, dusted for prints and covered by a layer of
plastic, sat beside it, as did a tumbler that was empty but
for a quarter inch of water still in its bottom, enough for a
melted ice cube or two.

Next to the tumbler there was a handwritten note, also inside in a plastic bag, along with a gel-tip pen.

I looked at the woman. Then I went over to the futon and read the note:

> *I'm so tired of being afraid. There's nothing left.*
> *Forgive me. Janine.*

I shuddered.

I'd seen corpses before; don't get me wrong. In fact. I'd seen crime scenes that looked like photos of Hell's slaughter-house. I'd smelled worse, too – believe you me, an eviscerated body puts off a stench of death and rot so vile that it is almost a solid object. By comparison to some of my previous cases, this one was quite peaceful. Well organized. Tidy, even.

It looked nothing like the home of a dead woman. Maybe that's what made it feel so creepy. Except for Janine's corpse, the apartment looked like its owners had just stepped out for a bite to eat.

I prowled around, careful not to touch anything. The bathroom and one of the bedrooms were like the living room: neat, a little sparse, not rich, but obviously well cared for. I hit the kitchen next. Dishes were soaking in now-cold water in the sink. In the fridge, chicken was marinating in some kind of sauce, its glass bowl covered with Saran.

I heard a quiet step behind me, and said, 'Suicides don't usually leave a meal marinating, do they? Or dishes soaking to be cleaned? Or their glasses on?'

Murphy made a noncommittal noise in her throat.

'No pictures up anywhere,' I mused. 'No family portraits, graduation shots, pictures of everyone at Disneyland.' I added up some other things as I turned toward the second bedroom. 'No hair in the sink or bathroom trash can. No computers.'

I opened the door to the master bedroom and closed my

eyes, reaching out with my senses to get a feel of the room.
I found what I expected.

'She was a practitioner,' I said quietly.

Janine had set up her temple on a low wooden table against
the east wall. As I drew near it, there was a sense of gentle
energy, like heat coming up from a fire that had burned down
to mostly ashes. The energy around the table had never been
strong, and it was fading, and had been since the woman's
death. Within another sunrise, it would be completely gone.

There were a number of items on the table, carefully
arranged: a bell, a thick, leather-bound book, probably a
journal. There was also an old pewter chalice, very plain but
free of tarnish, and a slender little mahogany wand with a
crystal bound to its end with copper wire.

One thing was out of place.

An old, old knife, a slender-bladed weapon from the early
Renaissance called a misericord, lay on the carpet in front
of the shrine, its tip pointing at an angle toward the other
side of the bedroom.

I grunted. I paced around the room to the knife. I hunkered
down, thinking, then looked up the blade of the knife to its
hilt. I paced back to the bedroom door and peered at the living
room.

The hilt of the knife pointed at Janine's body.

I went back to the bedroom and squinted down the knife
toward its tip.

It was pointed at the far wall.

I glanced back at Murphy, now standing in the doorway.
Murphy tilted her head. 'What did you find?'

'Not sure yet. Hang on.' I walked over to the wall and
held up my hand about half an inch from its surface. I closed
my eyes and focused on a very faint trace of energy left there.
After several moments of concentration, I lowered my hand
again. 'There's something there,' I said. 'But it's too faint for

me to make it out without using my Sight. And I'm getting sick of doing that.'

'What does that mean?' Murphy asked me.

'It means I need something from my kit. Be right back.' I went outside and down to my car, where I kept a fisherman's tackle box. I snagged it and went back up to the dead woman's bedroom.

'That's new,' Murphy said.

I set the box on the floor and opened it. 'I've been teaching my apprentice thaumaturgy. We have to go out to the country sometimes, for safety's sake.' I rummaged through the box and finally drew out a plastic test tube full of metallic grains. 'I just tossed things into a grocery sack for the first couple of weeks, but it was easier to put together a more permanent mobile kit.'

'What's that?' Murphy asked.

'Copper filings,' I said. 'They conduct energy. If there's some kind of pattern here, I might be able to make it out.'

'Ah. You're dusting for prints,' Murphy said.

'Pretty much, yeah.' I pulled a lump of chalk out of my duster's pocket and squatted to draw a very faint circle on the carpet. I willed it closed as I completed the circle, and felt it spring to life, an invisible screen of power that kept random energies away from me and focused my own magic. The spell was a delicate one, for me anyway, and trying to use it without a circle would have been like trying to light a match in a hurricane.

I closed my eyes, concentrating, and poured an ounce or two of copper filings into my right palm. I willed a whisper of energy down into the filings, enough to create a magical charge in them that would draw them toward the faint energy on the wall. When they were ready, I murmured, '*Illumina magnus.*' Then I broke the circle with my foot, releasing the spell, and cast the filings outward.

They glittered with little blue-white sparks, crackling audibly as they struck the wall and stayed there. The scent of ozone filled the air.

I leaned forward and blew gently over the wall, clearing any stray filings that might have clung to the wall on their own. Then I stepped back.

The copper filings had fallen into definite shapes – specifically, letters:

EXODUS 22:18.

Murphy furrowed her brow and stared at it. 'A Bible verse?'

'Yeah.'

'I don't know that one,' she said. 'Do you?'

I nodded. 'It's one that stuck in my head: "Suffer not a witch to live."'

2

'Murder, then,' Murphy said.

I grunted. 'Looks like.'

'And the killer wanted you to know it.' She came to stand beside me, frowning up at the wall. 'A cop couldn't have found this.'

'Yeah,' I said. The empty apartment made a clicking noise, one of those settling-building, homey sounds that would have been familiar to the victim.

Murphy's tone became lighter. 'So, what are we looking at here? Some kind of religious wacko? Salem Witch Trials aficionado? The Inquisitor reborn?'

'And he uses magic to leave a message?' I asked.

'Wackos can be hypocrites.' She frowned. 'How did the message get there? Did a practitioner have to do it?'

I shook my head. 'After they killed her, they probably just dipped their finger in the water in the chalice, used it to write on the wall. Water dried up, but a residue of energy remained.'

She frowned. 'From water?'

'Blessed water from the cup on her shrine,' I said. 'Think of it as holy water. It's imbued with positive energy the same way.'

Murphy squinted at me and then at the wall. 'Holy? I thought magic was just all about energy and math and equations and things. Like electricity or thermodynamics.'

'Not everyone thinks that,' I said. I nodded at the altar. 'The victim was a Wiccan.'

Murphy frowned. 'A witch?'

'She was also a witch.' I said. 'Not every Wiccan has the innate strength to be a practitioner. For most of them, there's very little actual power involved in their rites and ceremonies.'

'Then why do them?'

'Dearly beloved, we are gathered here to join this man and this woman in holy matrimony.' I shrugged. 'Every faith has its ceremonies, Murph.'

'This was about a conflict of religion, then?' Murphy said.

I shrugged. 'It's sort of difficult for sincere Wiccans to conflict with other religions. Wicca itself is really fluid. There are some basic tenets that ninety-nine percent of all Wiccans follow, but at its core the faith is all about individual freedom. Wiccans believe that as long as you aren't hurting anyone else by doing it, you should be free to act and worship in whatever way you'd like. So everyone's beliefs are a little bit different. Individualized.'

Murphy, who was more or less Catholic, frowned. 'Seems to me that Christianity has a few things to say about forgiveness and tolerance and treating others the way you'd like to be treated.'

'Uh-huh,' I said. 'Then came the Crusades, the Inquisition . . .'

'Which is my point,' Murphy said. 'Regardless of what I think about Islam or Wicca or any other religion, the fact is that it's a group of people. Every faith has its ceremonies. And since it's made up of people, every faith also has its assholes.'

'You only need one side to start a fight,' I agreed. 'KKK quotes a lot of scripture. So do a lot of reactionary religious organizations. A lot of times, they take it out of context.' I gestured at the wall. 'Like this.'

'I dunno. "Suffer not a witch to live." Seems fairly clear.'

'Out of context, but clear,' I said. 'Keep in mind that this appears in the same book of the Bible that approves the death sentence for a child who curses his parents, owners of oxen who injure someone through the owner's negligence, anybody who works or kindles a fire on Sunday, and anyone who has sex with an animal.'

Murphy snorted.

'Also keep in mind that the original text was written thousands of years ago. In Hebrew. The actual word that they used in that verse describes someone who casts spells that do harm to others. There was a distinction, in that culture, between harmful and beneficial magic.

'By the time we got to the Middle Ages, the general attitude within the faith was that anyone who practiced any kind of magic was automatically evil. There *was* no distinction between white and black magic. And when the verse came over to English, King James had a thing about witches, so "harmful caster of spells" just got translated to "witch."'

'Put that way, it sounds like maybe someone took it out of context,' Murphy said. 'But you'd get arguments from all kinds of people that the Bible has got to be perfect. That God would not permit such errors to be made in the Holy Word.'

'I thought God gave everyone free will,' I said. 'Which presumably – and evidently – includes the freedom to be incorrect when translating one language into another.'

'Stop making me think,' Murphy said. 'I'm believing over here.'

I grinned. 'See? This is why I'm not religious. I couldn't possibly keep my mouth shut long enough to get along with everyone else.'

'I thought it was because you'd never respect any religion that would have you.'

'That too,' I said.

Neither one of us, during this conversation, looked back

toward the body in the living room. An uncomfortable silence fell. The floorboards creaked.

'Murder,' Murphy said, finally, staring at the wall. 'Maybe someone on a holy mission.'

'Murder,' I said. 'Too soon to make any assumptions. What made you call me?'

'That altar,' she said. 'The inconsistencies about the victim.'

'No one is going to buy magic writing on a wall as evidence.'

'I know,' she said. 'Officially, she's going down as a suicide.'

'Which means the ball is in my court,' I said.

'I talked to Stallings,' she said. 'I'm taking a couple of days of personal leave, starting tomorrow. I'm in.'

'Cool.' I frowned suddenly and got a sick little feeling in my stomach. 'This isn't the only suicide, is it?'

'Right now, I'm on the job,' Murphy said. 'That isn't something I could share with you. The way someone like Butters might.'

'Right,' I said.

With no warning whatsoever, Murphy moved, spinning in a blur of motion that swept her leg out in a scything, ankle-height arc behind her. There was a thump of impact, and the sound of something heavy hitting the floor. Murphy – her eyes closed – sprang onto something unseen, and her hands moved in a couple of small, quick circles, fingers grasping. Then Murphy grunted, set her arms, and twisted her shoulders a little.

There was a young woman's high-pitched gasp of pain, and abruptly, underneath Murphy, there was a girl. Murphy had her pinned on her stomach on the floor, one arm twisted behind her, wrist bent at a painful angle.

The girl was in her late teens. She wore combat boots, black fatigue pants, and a tight, cutoff grey T-shirt. She was tall, most of a foot taller than Murphy, and built like a brick house. Her hair had been cut into a short, spiky style and dyed peroxide white. A tattoo on her neck vanished under her shirt, reappeared for a bit on her bared stomach, and continued beneath the pants. She had multiple earrings, a nose ring, an eyebrow ring, and a silver stud through that spot right under her lower lip. On the hand Murphy had twisted up behind her back, she wore a bracelet of dark little glass beads.

'Harry?' Murphy said in that tone of voice that, while polite and patient, demanded an explanation.

I sighed. 'Murph. You remember my apprentice, Molly Carpenter.'

Murphy leaned to one side and looked at her profile. 'Oh, sure,' she said. 'I didn't recognize her without the pink-and-blue hair. Also, she wasn't invisible last time.' She gave me a look, asking if I should let her up.

I gave Murphy a wink, and squatted down on the carpet next to the girl. I gave her my best scowl. 'I told you to wait at the apartment and practice your focus.'

'Oh, come *on*,' Molly said. 'It's *impossible*. And boring as hell.'

'Practice makes perfect, kid.'

'I've been practicing my ass off!' Molly protested. 'I know fifty times as much as I did last year.'

'And if you keep up the pace for another six or seven years.' I said, 'you might – you *might* – be ready to go it alone. Until then, you're the apprentice, I'm the teacher, and you do what I tell you.'

'But I can help you!'

'Not from a jail cell,' I pointed out.

'You're trespassing on a crime scene,' Murphy told her.

'Oh, please,' Molly said, both scorn and protest in her voice.

(In case it slipped by, Molly has authority issues.)

It was probably the worst thing she could have said.

'Right,' Murphy said. She produced cuffs from her jacket pocket, and slapped them on Molly's pinned wrist. 'You have the right to remain silent.'

Molly's eyes widened and she stared up at me. 'What? Harry . . .'

'If you choose to give up that right,' Murphy continued, chanting it with the steady pace of ritual, 'anything you say can and will be used against you in a court of law.'

I shrugged. 'Sorry, kid. This is real life. Look, your juvenile record is sealed, and you'll be tried as an adult. First offense. I doubt you'll do much more than . . . Murph?'

Murphy took a break from the Miranda chant. 'Thirty to sixty days, maybe.' Then she resumed.

'There, see? No big deal. See you in a month or three.'

Molly's face got pale. 'But . . . but . . .'

'Oh,' I added, 'beat someone up on the first day. Supposed to save you a lot of trouble.'

Murphy dragged Molly to her feet, her hands now cuffed. 'Do you understand your rights as I have conveyed them to you?'

Molly's mouth fell open. She looked from Murphy to me, her expression shocked.

'Or,' I said, 'you *might* apologize.'

'I-I'm sorry. Harry,' she said.

I sighed. 'Not to me, kid. It isn't *my* crime scene.'

'But . . .' Molly swallowed and looked at Murphy. 'I was just standing there.'

'You wearing gloves?' Murphy asked.

'No.'

'Shoes?'

'Yes.'

'Touch anything?'

'Um.' Molly swallowed. 'The door. Just pushed it a little. And that Chinese vase she's planted her spearmint in. The one with a crack in it.'

'Which means,' Murphy said, 'that if I can show that this is a murder, a full forensic sweep could pick up your finger-prints, the imprint of your shoes, and, as brittle as your hairdo is, possibly genetic traces if any of it broke off. Since you aren't one of the investigating officers or police consult-ants, that evidence would place you at the scene of the crime and could implicate you in a murder investigation.'

Molly shook her head. 'But you just said it would be called a suic—'

'Even if it is, you don't know proper procedure, the way Harry does, and your presence here might contaminate the scene and obscure evidence about the actual killer, making the murderer even more difficult to find before he strikes again.'

Molly just stared at her.

'That's why there are laws about civilians and crime scenes. This isn't a game, Miss Carpenter,' Murphy said, her voice cool, but not angry. 'Mistakes here could cost lives. Do you understand me?'

Molly glanced from Murphy to me and back, and her shoulders sagged. 'I didn't mean to . . . I'm sorry.'

I said in a gentle voice, 'Apologies won't give life back to the dead, Molly. You still haven't learned to consider consequences, and you can't afford that. Not anymore.'

Molly flinched a little and nodded.

'I trust that this will never happen again,' Murphy said. 'No, ma'am.'

Murphy looked skeptically at Molly and back to me.

'She means well,' I said. 'She just wanted to help.'

Molly gave me a grateful glance.

Murphy's tone softened as she took the cuffs off. 'Don't we all.'

Molly rubbed at her wrists, wincing. 'Um. Sergeant? How did you know I was there?'

'Floorboards creaking when no one was standing on them,' I said.

'Your deodorant,' Murphy said.

'Your tongue stud clicked against your teeth once,' I said.

'I felt some air move a few minutes ago,' Murphy said. 'Didn't feel like a draft.'

Molly swallowed and her face turned pink. 'Oh.'

'But we didn't see you, did we, Murph?'

Murphy shook her head. 'Not even a little.'

A little humiliation and ego deflation, now and then, is good for apprentices. Mine sighed miserably.

'Well,' I said. 'You're here. Might as well tag along.' I nodded to Murphy and headed for the door.

'Where are we going?' Molly asked. Both bored medtechs blinked and stared as Molly followed me out of the apartment. Murphy came out behind us and waved them in to carry the body out.

'To see a friend of mine,' I said. 'You like polka?'

3

I hadn't been back to the Forensic Institute on West Harrison since that mess with Necromancers-R-Us nearly two years before. It wasn't an unpleasant-looking place, despite the fact that it was the repository for former human beings awaiting examination. It was in a little corporate park, very clean, with green lawns and neat bushes and fresh-painted lines on the spaces in the parking lots. The buildings themselves were quietly unassuming, functional and tidy.

It was one of those places that show up a lot in my nightmares.

It wasn't like I'd ever been a fan of viewing corpses, but a man I knew had been caught in the magical cross fire, and wound up an animated supercorpse who had nearly torn my car apart with his bare hands.

I hadn't come back since then. I had better things to do than revisit scenes like that. But once I was there and parked and heading for the doors, it wasn't as bad as I thought it would be, and I went in without hesitation.

This was Molly's first visit. At my request, she had ditched much of the facial jewelry and wore an old Cubs baseball hat over her peroxide locks. Even so, she didn't exactly cut a respectable businesslike figure, but I was content with damage control. Of course, my outfit barely qualified for business casual, and the heavy leather coat in the too-warm weather probably gave me a distinctive aura of eccentricity. Or at least it would have, if I made more money.

The guard sitting at the desk where Phil had been murdered was expecting me, but not Molly, and he told me she would have to wait. I said I'd wait, too, until Butters verified her. The guard looked sullen about being forced to expend the enormous effort it took to punch an intercom number. He growled into the phone, grunted a few times, then thumped a switch and the security door buzzed. Molly and I went on through.

There are several examination rooms at the morgue, but it's never hard to figure out which one Butters is inside. You just listen for the polka.

I homed in on a steady *oom-pah, oom-pah* of a tuba, until I could pick up the strains of clarinet and accordion skirling along with it. Exam room three. I rapped briefly on the door and opened it without actually stepping inside.

Waldo Butters was bent over his desk, squinting at his computer's screen, while his butt and legs shuffled back and forth in time to the polka music. He muttered something to himself, nodded, and hit the space bar on his keyboard with one elbow in time with his tapping heels, without looking up at me. 'Hey, Harry.'

I blinked. 'Is that "Bohemian Rhapsody"?'

'Yankovic. Man's a freaking genius,' he replied. 'Give me a sec to power down before you come all the way in.'

'No problem,' I told him.

'You've worked with him before?' Molly asked quietly.

'Uh-huh,' I said. 'He's clued.'

Butters waited until his printer started rattling, then shut down the computer and walked to the printer to pick up a couple of pages and staple them together. Then he dropped the pages onto a small stack of them and bound them with a large rubber band. 'Okay, that should do it.' He turned to face me with a grin.

Butters was an odd little duck. He wasn't much taller than Murphy, and she probably had more muscle than he did. His shock of black hair resembled nothing so much as an explosion in a steel wool factory. He was all knees and elbows, especially in the surgical greens he was wearing, his face was lean and angular, his nose beaky, and his eyes were bright behind the prescription glasses.

'Harry,' he said, offering his hand. 'Long time, no see. How's the hand?'

I traded grips with him. Butters had long, wiry fingers, very precise and not at all weak. He wasn't anyone's idea of dangerous, but the little guy had guts and brains. 'Only three months or so. And not too bad.' I held my gloved left hand up and wiggled all the fingers. My ring and pinkie fingers moved with little trembles and twitches, but by God they moved when I told them to.

The flesh of my left hand had practically melted in an unanticipated conflagration during a battle with a scourge of vampires. The doctors had been shocked that they didn't have to amputate, but told me I'd never use it again. Butters had helped me work out a regimen of physical therapy, and my fingers were mostly functional, though my hand still looked pretty horrible – but even *that* had begun to change, at least a little. The ugly little lumps of scar tissue and flesh had begun to fade, and my hand looked considerably less like a melted wax model than it had before. The nails had grown back in, too.

'Good,' Butters said. 'Good. You still playing guitar?'

'I hold it. It makes noise. Might be a little generous to call it playing.' I gestured to Molly. 'Waldo Butters, this is Molly Carpenter, my apprentice.'

'Apprentice, eh?' Butters extended an amiable hand. 'Pleased to meetcha,' he said. 'So does he turn you into squirrels and fishes and stuff, like in *The Sword in the Stone*?'

Molly sighed. 'I wish. I keep trying to get him to show me how to change form, but he won't.'

'I promised your parents I wouldn't let you melt yourself

into a pile of goo,' I told her. 'Butters, I assume someone – and I won't name any names – told you I'd be dropping by?'

'Yowsa,' the little ME said, nodding. He held up a finger, went to the door, and locked it, before turning to lean his back against it. 'Look, Dresden. I have to be careful what kind of information I share, right? It comes with the job.'

'Sure.'

'So you didn't hear it from me.'

I looked at Molly. 'Who said that?'

'Groovy,' Butters said. He walked back over to me and offered me the packet of papers. 'Names and addresses of the deceased,' he said.

I frowned and flipped through them: columns of text, much of it technical; ugly photographs. 'The victims?'

'Officially, they're the deceased.' His mouth tightened. 'But yeah. I'm pretty sure they're victims.'

'Why?'

He opened his mouth, closed it again, and frowned. 'You ever see something out of the corner of your eye? But when you look at it, there's nothing there? Or at least, it doesn't look like what you thought it was?'

'Sure.'

'Same thing here,' he said. 'Most of these folks show classic, obvious suicides. There are just a few little details wrong. You know?'

'No,' I said. 'Enlighten me.'

'Take that top one,' he said. 'Pauline Moskowitz. Thirty-nine, mother of two, husband, two dogs. She disappears on a Friday night and opens up her wrists in a hotel bathtub around three A.M. Saturday morning.'

I read over it. 'Am I reading this right? She was on anti-depressants?'

'Uh-huh,' Butters said, 'but nothing extreme, and she'd

been on them and stable for eight years. Never showed suicidal tendencies before, either.'

I looked at the ugly picture of a very ordinary-looking woman lying naked and dead in a tub of cloudy liquid. 'So what's got your scalpel in a knot?'

'The cuts,' Butters said. 'She used a box knife. It was in the tub with her. She severed tendons in both wrists.'

'So?'

'So,' Butters said. 'Once she'd cut the tendons on one wrist, she'd have had very little controlled movement with the fingers in that hand. So what'd she do to cut them both? Use two box knives at the same time? Where's the other knife?'

'Maybe she held it with her teeth,' I said.

'Maybe I'll close my eyes and throw a rock out over the lake and it will land in a boat,' Butters said. 'It's technically possible, but it isn't really likely. The second wound almost certainly wouldn't be as deep or as clean. I've seen 'em look like someone was cutting up a block of Parmesan into slivers. These two cuts are almost identical.'

'I guess it's not conclusive, though,' I said.

'Not officially.'

'I've been hearing that a lot today.' I frowned. 'What's Brioche think?'

At the mention of his boss, Butters grimaced. 'Occam's razor, to use his own spectacularly insensitive yet ironic phrasing. They're suicides. End of story.'

'But your guess is that someone else was holding the knife?'

The little ME's face turned bleak, and he nodded without speaking.

'Good enough for me,' I said. 'What about the body today?'

'Can't say until I look,' Butters said. He gave me a shrewd glance. 'But you think it's another murder.'

'I know it is,' I replied. 'But I'm the only one, until Murphy's off the clock.'

'Right.' Butters sighed.

I flipped past Mrs Moskowitz's pages to the next set of ugly pictures. Also a woman. The pages named her Maria Casselli. Maria had been twenty-three when she washed down thirty Valium with a bottle of drain cleaner.

'Another hotel room,' I noted quietly.

Molly glanced over my shoulder at the printout of the photo at the scene. She turned pale and took several steps away from me.

'Yeah,' Butters said, concerned eyes on my apprentice. 'It's a little unusual. Most suicides are at home. They usually go somewhere else only if they need to jump off a bridge or drive their car into a lake or something.'

'Ms Casselli had a family,' I said. 'Husband, her younger sister living with her.'

'Yeah,' Butters said. 'You can guess what Brioche had to say.'

'She walked in on her hubby and baby sister, decided to end it all?'

'Uh-huh.'

'Uh,' Molly said. 'I think—'

'Outside,' Butters provided, unlocking the door. 'First door on the right.'

Molly hurried from the room, down to the bathroom Butters had directed her to.

'Jesus, Harry,' Butters said. 'Kid's a little young for this.'

I held up the picture of Maria's body. 'Lot of that going around.'

'She's actually a wizard? Like you?'

'Someday,' I said. 'If she survives.' I read over the next two profiles, both of women in their twenties, both apparent suicides in hotel rooms, both of them with housemates of one sort or another.

The last profile was different. I read over it and glanced up at Butters. 'What's with this one?'

'Fits the same general profile,' Butters said. 'Women, dead in hotel rooms.'

I frowned down at the papers. 'Where's the cause of death?'

'That's the thing,' Butters said. 'I couldn't find one.'

I lifted both eyebrows at him.

He spread his hands. 'Harry, I know my trade. I like figuring this stuff out. And I haven't got the foggiest why the woman is dead. Every test I ran came up negative; every theory I put together fell apart. Medically speaking, she's in good shape. It's like her whole system just . . . got the switch turned off. Everything at once. Never seen anything like it.'

'Jessica Blanche.' I checked the profiles. 'Nineteen. And pretty. Or at least prettyish.'

'Hard to tell with dead girls,' Butters said. 'But yeah, that was my take.'

'But not a suicide.'

'Like I said. Dead, and in hotel rooms.'

'Then what's the connection to the other deaths?'

'Little things,' Butters said. 'Like, she had a purse with ID in it, but no clothes.'

'Meaning someone had to have taken them away.' I rolled up the papers into a tube and thumped them against my leg, thoughtfully. The door opened, and Molly came back in, wiping at her mouth with a paper towel. 'This girl still here?'

Butters lifted his eyebrows. 'Yeah. Miss Blanche. Why?'

'I think maybe Molly can help.'

Molly blinked and looked up at me. 'Um. What?'

'I doubt it's going to be pleasant, Molly,' I told her. 'But you might be able to read something.'

'Off of a dead girl?' Molly asked quietly.

'You're the one who wanted to come along,' I said.

She frowned, facing me, and then took a deep breath. 'Yes. Um. Yes, I was. I mean, yes, I will. Try.'

'Will you?' I asked. 'You sure? Won't be fun. But if it gets us more information, it could save someone's life.'

I watched her for a moment, until her expression set in determination and she met my eyes. She straightened and nodded once. 'Yes.'

'All right,' I said. 'Get yourself set for it. Butters, we need to give her a few minutes alone. Can we go get Miss Blanche?'

'Um,' Butters said. 'What's this going to entail, exactly?'

'Nothing much. I'll explain it on the way.'

He chewed on his lip for a moment, and then nodded once. 'This way.'

He led me down the hall to the storage room. It was another exam room, like the one we'd just been in, but it also featured a wall of body-sized refrigerated storage units like morgues are supposed to have. This was the room we'd been in when a necromancer and a gaggle of zombies had put a bullet through the head of Butters's capacity to ignore the world of the supernatural.

Butters got out a gurney, consulted a record sheet on a clipboard, and wheeled it over to the fridges. 'I don't like to come in here anymore. Not since Phil.'

'Me either,' I said.

He nodded. 'Here, get that side.'

I didn't want to. I am a wizard, sure, but corpses are inherently icky, even if they aren't animated and trying to kill you. But I tried to pretend we were sliding a heavy load of groceries onto a cart, and helped him draw a body, resting upon a metal tray and covered in a heavy cloth, onto the gurney.

'So,' he said. 'What is she going to do?'

'Look into its eyes,' I said.

He gave me a somewhat skeptical look. 'Trying to see the last thing impressed on her retinas or something? You know that's pretty much mythical, right?'

'Other impressions get left on a body,' I said. 'Final thoughts, sometimes. Emotions, sensations.' I shook my head. 'Technically, those kinds of impressions can get left on almost any kind of inanimate object. You've heard of object reading, right?'

'That's for real?' he asked.

'Yeah. But it's an easy sort of thing to contaminate, and it can be tricky as hell — and entirely apart from that, it's extremely difficult to do.'

'Oh,' Butters said. 'But you think there might be something left on the corpse?'

'Maybe.'

'That sounds really useful.'

'Potentially.'

'So how come you don't do it all the time?' he asked.

'It's delicate,' I said. 'When it comes to magic, I'm not much for delicate.'

He frowned and we started rolling the gurney. 'But your only half-trained apprentice is?'

'The wizarding business isn't standardized,' I said. 'Any given wizard will have an affinity for different kinds of magic, due to their natural talents, personalities, experiences. Each has different strengths.'

'What are yours?' he asked.

'Finding things. Following things. Blowing things up, mostly,' I said. 'I'm good at those. Redirecting energy, sending energy out into the world to resonate with the energy of what I'm trying to find. Moving energy around or redirecting it or storing it up to use later.'

'Aha,' he said. 'None of which is delicate?'

'I've practiced enough to handle a lot of different kinds of delicate magic,' I said. 'But . . . it's the difference between me strumming power chords on a guitar and me playing a complex classical Spanish piece.'

Butters absorbed that and nodded. 'And the kid plays Spanish guitar?'

'Close enough. She's not as strong as me, but she's got a gift for the more subtle magic. Especially mental and emotional stuff. It's what got her in so much trouble with . . .'

I bit my tongue and stopped in midsentence. It wasn't my place to discuss Molly's violations of the White Council's Laws of Magic with others. She would have enough trouble getting past the horrible acts she'd committed in innocence without me painting her as a psycho monster-in-training.

Butters watched my face for a few seconds, then nodded and let it pass. 'What do you think she'll find?'

'No clue,' I said. 'That's why we look.'

'Could you do this?' he said. 'I mean, if you had to?'

'I've tried it,' I hedged. 'But I'm bad about projecting things onto the object, and I can barely ever get something intelligible out of it.'

'You said it might not be pleasant for her,' Butters said. 'Why?'

'Because if something's there, and she can sense it, she gets to experience it. First person. Like she's living it herself.'

Butters let out a low whistle. 'Oh. Yeah. I guess that could be bad.'

We got back to the other room, and I peered in before opening the door. Molly was sitting on the floor with her eyes closed, her legs folded lotus-style, her head tilted slightly up. Her hands rested on her thighs, the tips of her thumbs pressed lightly against the tips of her middle fingers.

'Quietly,' I murmured. 'No noise until she's finished. Okay?'

Butters nodded. I opened the door as silently as I could. We brought the gurney into the room, left it in front of Molly, and then at my beckon, Butters and I went to the far wall and settled in to wait.

It took Molly better than twenty minutes to focus her mind for the comparatively simple spell. Focus of intention, of will, is integral to any use of magic. I'd drawn myself up to focus power so often and for so long that I only had to actually make a conscious effort to do it when a spell was particularly complex, dangerous, or when I thought it wise to be slow and cautious. Most of the time, it took me less than a second to gather up my will — which is critical in any situation where speed is a factor. Drooling abominations and angry vampires don't give you twenty minutes to get a punch ready.

Molly, though she was learning quickly, had a long damned way to go.

When she finally opened her eyes, they were distant, unfocused. She rose to her feet with slow, careful movements, and drifted over to the gurney with the corpse. She pulled the sheet down, revealing the dead girl's face. Then Molly leaned down, her expression still distant, and murmured quietly beneath her breath as she opened the corpse's eyelids.

She got something almost instantly.

Her eyes flew open wide, and she let out a short gasp. Her breath rasped in and out frantically several times before her eyes rolled back up into her head. She stood frozen and rigid for a pair of quivering seconds, and then her breath escaped in a low, rough cry and her knees buckled. She did not fall to the floor so much as melt down onto it. Then she lay there, breathing hard and letting out a continuous stream of guttural whimpers.

Her breathing continued, fast and hard, her eyes unfocused. Her body rippled with several slow, undulating motions that drew the eye to her hips and breasts. Then she slowly went limp, her panting gradually easing, though little, unmistakably pleased sounds slithered from her lips on every exhalation.

I blinked at her.

Well.

I hadn't been expecting *that*.

Butters gulped audibly. Then he said, 'Uh. Did she just do what I *think* she just did?'

I pursed my lips. 'Um. Maybe.'

'What just happened?'

'She, um.' I coughed. 'She got something.'

'She got *something*, all right,' Butters muttered. He sighed. 'I haven't gotten anything like that in about two *years*.'

For me, it had been more like four. 'I hear you,' I said, more emphatically than I meant to.

'Is she underage?' he asked. 'Legally speaking?'

'No.'

'Okay. I don't feel quite so . . . Nabokovian, then.' He raked his fingers back through his hair. 'What do we do now?'

I tried to look professional and unfazed. 'We wait for her to recover.'

'Uh-huh.' He looked at Molly and sighed. 'I need to get out more.'

Me and you both, man. 'Butters, is there any way you could get her some water or something?'

'Sure,' he said. 'You?'

'Nah.'

'Right back.' Butters covered up the corpse and slipped out.

I went over to the girl and hunkered down by her. 'Hey, grasshopper. Can you hear me?'

It took her longer than it should have to answer, like

when you're on the phone with someone halfway around the world. 'Yes. I . . . I hear you.'

'You okay?'

'Oh, God.' She sighed, smiling. 'Yes.'

I muttered under my breath, rubbed at the incipient headache beginning between my eyes, and thought dark thoughts. Dammit all, every time *I'd* opened myself up to some kind of horrible psychic shock in the name of investigation, I'd gotten another nightmare added to my collection. Her first time up to bat, and the grasshopper got . . .

What *had* she gotten?

'I want you to tell me what you sensed, right away. Sometimes the details fade out, like when you forget parts of a dream.'

'Right,' she murmured in a sleepy-sounding drawl. 'Details. She . . .' Molly shook her head. 'She felt good. Really, really good.'

'I gathered that much,' I said. 'What else?'

Molly kept shaking her head slowly. 'Nothing else. Just that. It was all sensation. Ecstasy.' She frowned a little, as if struggling to order her thoughts. 'As if the rest of her senses had been blinded by it, somehow. I don't think there *was* anything else. Not sight nor sound nor thought nor memory. Nothing. She didn't even know it when she died.'

'Think about it,' I said quietly. 'Absolutely anything you can remember could be important.'

Butters came back in just then, carrying a bottle of water beaded with drops of condensation. He tossed it to me, and I passed the cold drink to Molly. 'Here,' I told her. 'Drink up.'

'Thanks.' She opened the bottle, turned on her side, and started guzzling it without even sitting up. The pose did a lot to make her clothing look tighter.

Butters stared for a second, then sighed and quite evidently forced himself to go over to his desk and start sharpening pencils. 'So what do we know?'

'Looks like she died happy,' I said. 'Did you run a toxicology check on her?'

'Yeah. Some residual THC, but she could have gotten that from the contact high at a concert. Otherwise she was clean.'

'Damn,' I said. 'Can you think of anything else that would do . . . that to a victim?'

'Nothing pharmacological,' Butters said. 'Maybe if someone ran a wire into the pleasure centers of her brain and kept stimulating them. But, uh, there's no evidence of open-skull surgery. I would have noticed something like that.'

'Uh-huh,' I said.

'So it must be something from the spooky side,' Butters said.

'Could be.' I consulted my packet again. 'What did she do?'

'No one knew,' Butters said. 'No one seemed to know anything about her. No one came to claim the body. We couldn't find any relations. It's why she's still here.'

'No local address, either,' I said.

'No, just the one on an Indiana driver's license, but it dead-ended. Not much else in her purse.'

'And the killer took her clothes.'

'Apparently,' Butters said. 'But why?'

I shrugged. 'Must have been something on them he didn't want found.' I pursed my lips. 'Or something on them he didn't want *me* to find.'

Molly abruptly sat up straight. 'Harry, I remember something.'

'Yeah?'

'Sensation,' she said, resting one hand over her belly button. 'It was like . . . I don't know, like hearing twenty different hands playing at the same time, only tactile. But there was a prickling sort of sensation over her stomach. Like one of those medical pinwheel things.'

'A Wartenberg Pinwheel,' Butters supplied.

'Eh?' I said.

'Like the one I use to test the nerves on your hand, Harry,' Butters volunteered.

'Oh, ow, right.' I frowned at Molly. 'How the hell do you know what one of those feels like?'

Molly gave me a lazy, wicked smile. 'This is one of those things you don't want me to explain.'

Butters let out a delicate cough. 'They are sometimes used recreationally, Harry.'

My cheeks felt warm. 'Ah. Right. Butters, you got a felt-tip marker?'

He got one out of his desk and tossed it to me. I passed it to Molly. 'Show me where.'

She nodded, lay back down on her back, and pulled her shirt up from her stomach. Then she closed her eyes, took the lid off the marker, and traced it slowly over the skin of her abdomen, her eyebrows furrowed in concentration.

When she was finished, the black ink spelled out clear, large letters:

EX 22:18.

Exodus again.

'Ladies and gentlemen,' I said quietly. 'We have a serial killer.'

4

Molly said little on the way back. She just leaned against the window with half-closed eyes, probably basking in the afterglow.

'Molly,' I told her in my gentlest voice. 'Heroin feels good, too. Ask Rosy and Nelson.'

The little smile of pleasure faded into blankness, and she stared at me for a while. By degrees, her expression changed to a frown of consideration, and then to a nauseated grimace.

'It killed her,' she said finally. 'It killed her. I mean, it felt so good . . . but it wasn't.'

I nodded.

'She never knew it. She never had a chance.' Molly looked queasy for a minute. 'It was a vampire, right? From the White Court? I mean, they use sex to feed on life energy, right?'

'That's one of the things it could be,' I said quietly. 'There are plenty of demonic creatures in the Nevernever that groove on the succubus routine, though.'

'And she was killed in a hotel,' she said. 'Where there was no threshold to protect her from a demon.'

'Very good, grasshopper,' I said. 'Once you consider that the other victims weren't done White Court style, it means that either there is more than one killer or the same one is varying his techniques. It's too early for anything but wild guesses.'

She frowned. 'What are you going to do next?'

I thought about it for a minute. 'I've got to figure out what all of the killer's victims have in common, if anything.'

'They're dead?' Molly offered.

I smiled a little. 'Besides that.'

'Okay,' she said. 'So what do you do?'

I nodded to the papers Butters had given me, now resting on the dashboard. 'I start there. See what I can extrapolate from the data I've got. Then I look people up and ask questions.'

'What do I do?' she asked.

'That depends. How many beads can you move?' I asked her.

She glowered at me for a minute. Then she unbound the bracelet of dark beads from her left wrist and held it up. The beads all slipped down to the bottom of the bracelet, leaving three or four inches of bare cord.

Molly focused on the bracelet, a device I'd created to help her practice focusing her mind and stilling her thoughts. Focus and stillness are important when you're slinging magic around. It's a primal force of creation, and it responds to your thoughts and emotions – whether you want it to or not. If your thoughts get fragmented or muddled, or if you aren't paying complete attention to what you're doing, the magic can respond in any number of unpredictable and dangerous ways.

Molly was still learning about it. She had some real talent, don't get me wrong, but what she lacked was not ability, but judgment. That's what I'd been trying to teach her over the past year or so – to use her power responsibly, cautiously, and with respect for the dangers the Art could present. If she didn't get a more solid head on her shoulders, her talent with magic was going to get her killed – probably taking me with her.

Molly was a warlock.

She'd used magic to tinker with the minds of two of her friends in an effort to free them from drug addiction, but her motives had been mixed, and the results were moderately horrific. One of the kids still hadn't recovered enough to function on his own. The other had pulled through, but was still facing a lot of problems.

Normally, the White Council of wizards kills you for breaking one of the Laws of Magic. Practically the only time they didn't was when a wizard of the Council offered to take responsibility for the warlock's future conduct, until they could satisfy the Council that their intentions were good, their ways mended. If they could, fine. If not, the warlock died. So did the wizard who had taken responsibility for him.

I'd been a warlock. Hell, plenty of the Council wondered if I still *was* a ticking bomb getting ready to blow. When Molly had been bound and hooded and dragged before the Council for trial, I'd stepped in. I had to.

Sometimes I regretted the hell out of that decision. Once you've felt the power of dark magic, it could be awfully hard to resist using it again, and Molly's errors tended to run in that direction. The kid was good at heart, but she was just so damned *young*. She'd grown up in a strict household; she'd gone insane with freedom the minute she ran away and got out on her own. She was back home now, but she was still trying to find the balance and self-discipline she'd need to survive in the wizarding business.

Teaching her to throw a gout of fire at a target really wasn't terribly difficult. The hard part was teaching her *why* to do it, why *not* to do it, and *when* she should or should not do it. Molly saw magic as the best solution to any given problem. It wasn't, and she had to learn that.

To that end, I'd made her the bracelet.

She stared at it for a long minute, and one of the beads slid up the string and stopped when it touched her finger. A moment later, the second bead joined the first. The third quivered for several seconds before it moved. The fourth took even longer. The fifth bead jumped and twitched for several moments before Molly let out her breath in a snarl, and the others once more succumbed to gravity.

'Four of thirteen,' I noted, as I pulled into a driveway. 'Not bad. But you aren't ready yet.'

She glared at the bracelet and rubbed at her forehead for a moment. 'I got six last night.'

'Keep working,' I said. 'It's about focus, stillness, and clarity.'

'What does that *mean*?' Molly demanded in exasperation.

'That you have more work to do.'

She sighed and got out of the car, glancing up at her family's home. It was a gorgeous place, white picket fence and everything, somehow preserving a suburban appearance despite the city all around us. 'You aren't explaining it very well.'

'Maybe,' I said. 'Or maybe you aren't *learning* it very well.'

She gave me a glower, and what might have been a hot answer came to her lips — but she shut them and shook her head in irritation. 'I'm sorry. For putting up that veil and trying to follow you. No disrespect intended.'

'None taken. I've been where you are. I don't expect you to be perfect all the time, kid.'

'She smiled a little. 'What happened today . . .'

'Happened,' I said. 'It's done. Besides, it worked out. I don't know if I could have read anything at all from that victim, the way you did today.'

She looked hopeful. 'Yeah?'

I nodded. 'What you found might be a big help. You did good. Thanks.'

She practically glowed. Once or twice, after a compliment, she'd *literally* glowed, but we'd gotten that under control within a month or two. She gave me a smile that made her look even younger than she was, and then pelted up the front steps and into the house.

That left me there alone with pages and pages of dead women. I wanted to know more about them almost as much as I wanted to shove my manly parts into a radioactive wood chipper.

I sighed. I had to get closer to this, but I could at least do it with a drink in my hand.

So I went to McAnally's.

Mac's pub – and make no mistake, it was a pub, not a bar – was one of those few places in Chicago frequented almost entirely by the supernatural scene. It didn't have a sign outside. I had to walk down a flight of stairs to get to the unmarked front door. Inside, it's all low ceilings, a crooked bar, and irregularly spaced, hand-carved wooden columns. Mac manages to keep electricity moving through the bar despite all the magical types wandering through – partly because it's rare for anything but a full-blown wizard, like me, to cause the inevitable failure of any nearby technology, and partly because he does a ton of preventive maintenance. He still didn't bother with electric lights – it costs too much to keep replacing bulbs – but he was able to keep a bunch of ceiling fans whirling and maintain a functional telephone.

On the wall beside the door was a wooden sign that stated, simply, ACCORDED NEUTRAL GROUND. That meant that Mac had declared the place a nonpartisan location, according to the terms set up by the Unseelie Accords – sort of the Geneva Convention of the supernatural world. It meant that any member of the signatory nations was free to enter peaceably, and remain unmolested by any other member. The neutral ground had to be respected by all parties, who were obligated to take outside any fight that might begin and respect the pub's neutral status. Oaths and the rights and obligations of hospitality were very nearly a force of nature in the super-natural world. It meant that, in Chicago, there was always a place to set up a meeting with a reasonable expectation of a civilized outcome.

All the same, it also meant that you might find yourself in bad company when you went to Mac's place.

I always sit with my back to a smoke-stained wall.

It was late afternoon and the place was busier than it should have been. Of the thirteen tables, only two were open, and I took the one farther away from the rest of the room, tossing the papers and my coat on it.

I went to the bar, suppressing an instinct to duck every time I walked under one of the too-low-for-towering-wizards ceiling fans. I nodded to Mac. He's a spare man, a little taller than average, his head shaved bald. He could be anywhere between thirty and fifty. He wore jeans, a white shirt, and a white apron, and despite the fact that his wood-fueled grill was up and running, there wasn't a spot or stain anywhere on his clothes. 'Mac,' I said, 'beer me.'

Mac slid over a dark brown bottle of his home brew. I opened it, chugged it, and passed him a twenty with the empty. 'Keep 'em coming.'

Mac let out a grunt of surprise, and his eyebrows went up.

'Don't ask,' I told him.

He folded his arms and nodded. 'Keys.'

I glared at him for a second, but I was halfhearted about it. I tossed the keys to the Blue Beetle onto the bar.

Mac gave me another beer, and I went to the table, drinking on the way. By the time I'd circled the carved column shaped like one enormous, ugly giant, except for the carved figures of faerie knights attacking its ankles, and sat down at my table, the beer was mostly gone.

I don't usually go through them like that. I should have

been more cautious, but I really, really didn't want to dig into that material sober. I figured that if my brain was mushy enough, maybe all the bad I was about to drag through it wouldn't leave as deep an impression.

I settled down and read through the information Butters had given me on the dead women, pausing every so often for more beer. I read the words, but there was an odd sense of blankness inside. I read them, I understood them, but they somehow didn't seem relevant, vanishing like pebbles dropped in a well – there was a little ripple, then nothing.

I thought I recognized two of the victims, though not by name. I'd probably seen them around, maybe even there at McAnally's. I didn't recognize the others, but it wasn't like I knew every face in the community.

I stopped reading for a few minutes, and drank some more. I didn't want to keep going. I didn't want to see any of this. I didn't want to get involved. I'd seen more than enough of people being hurt and killed. I'd seen too many dead women. I wanted to burn the papers, walk out the door, and just keep walking.

Instead, I went back to reading.

By the time I finished, I had found no obvious connection between the victims, I was emptying my fifth bottle, and it was dark outside. The bar had grown quiet.

I looked up to see that, except for Mac, I had the place entirely to myself.

That was odd. Mac's place isn't usually packed, but it's busy in the evening. I couldn't remember the last time I'd seen it empty around dinnertime.

Mac came over to me with another bottle, putting it down just as I finished the previous. He glanced from the fresh bottle to all the empties, standing in a row.

'I use up my twenty?' I asked him.

He nodded.

I grunted, got out my wallet, and put another twenty on the table.

He frowned at it, then at me.

'I know,' I said. 'I don't usually drink this much.'

He snorted quietly. Mac isn't big on verbalization.

I waved a hand vaguely at the papers. 'Hate seeing women get hurt. I should hate seeing anyone get hurt, but it's worse with women. Or kids.' I glared down at the paperwork, then around at the now-empty bar, adding two and two. 'Get another,' I told him. 'Sit down.'

Mac's eyebrows went up. Then he went over to the bar, got himself a beer, and came over to sit down with me. He casually opened both bottles with a deft twist of his hand and no bottle opener. Mac is a professional. He pushed my bottle over to me and lifted his own.

I nodded at him. We clinked bottles and drank.

'So,' I said quietly. 'What gives?'

Mac set his beer down and surveyed the empty pub.

'I know,' I said. 'Where'd everyone go?'

'Away,' Mac said.

If Scrooge had hoarded words instead of money, Mac would have made him look like Monty Hall. Mac didn't use rhetorical phrasing.

'Away,' I said. 'Away from me, you mean.'

He nodded.

'They're scared. Why?'

'Grey cloak.'

I exhaled slowly. I'd been a Warden of the White Council for nearly two years. Wardens were the armed forces of the White Council, men and women who were accustomed to violence and conflict. Normally, Wardens existed to police wizards, to make sure that they didn't use their power against the rest of humanity in violation of the Laws of Magic. Things weren't normal. For years, the Council had been engaged in a war against the Vampire Courts. Most of the Wardens had been killed in battle, and they'd gotten desperate for new wizards to take up the grey cloak of their office – desperate enough to ask *me* to join them, despite my checkered past.

Plenty of people in the world had talent of one kind or another. Very few had the kind of power and talent it took to be recognized as a member of the White Council. For the others, contact with the Council's Wardens was mostly limited to one of them showing up to deliver a warning about any potential abuse of magic.

But when anyone broke the Laws of Magic, the Wardens appeared to apprehend, try, convict, and probably execute. Wardens were scary, even to someone like me, who is more or less in their weight class. For the minor talents, like most of the crowd at Mac's place, the Wardens occupied a position somewhere between avenging angel and bogeyman.

Apparently, they had begun to see me in the latter role, which was going to be a problem in my hunt for the Exodus-quoting killer. The victims were probably members of the local supernatural community, but a lot of Wiccans can be ticklish about talking about their beliefs, or identifying their fellow believers as members of the faith. Part of it is a basic respect for personal freedom and privacy endemic to the faith. Part of it is a kind of theologically hereditary caution.

Both of those factors were going to make it hard to get anyone to talk to me. If people thought the Wardens were a part of the killings, they'd shut me out faster than you can say, 'Burn the witch.'

'There's no reason for anyone to be afraid,' I said. 'These women are officially suicides. I mean, if Murphy's instincts hadn't picked up on something, we wouldn't even know there was a killer loose.'

Mac sipped his beer in silence.

'Unless,' I said, 'some other factor I don't know about made it obvious to everyone in our crowd that the victims weren't suicides.'

Mac put his beer down.

'They're linked,' I said quietly. 'The victims. There's a connection between them that the police files don't show. The magic folks know it. That's why they're scared.'

Mac frowned at the beer. Then he looked over at the NEUTRAL GROUND sign by the door.

'I know,' I said quietly. 'You don't want to get involved. But someone out there is killing women. They're leaving calling cards for me, specifically. Whoever is doing it is going to keep on doing it until I find them.'

Mac did not move.

I kept the quiet pressure on him. 'A lot of people come in here. They eat and drink. And they talk. You stand over there running the grill and pouring drinks and you might as well be invisible. But I know you hear a lot more than most people realize, Mac. I figure you know something that might help me.'

He gazed at me for a moment, his expression unreadable. Then he asked, 'Is it you?'

I almost barked out a bit of laughter, until I realized that he was *serious*.

It took me a minute to get my head around that one. Since I had gone into business in Chicago, I had spent a lot of time trying to help the supernatural community. I did exorcisms here and there, helped with ghost problems, taught young and out-of-control talents enough discipline to restrain themselves. I've done other things too, smaller, not necessarily directly involving magic: giving advice on how to handle problems dealing with friendly but inhuman beings that mingled with magically aware mortals, helping parents to deal with the fact that their kid was suddenly able to set the cat on fire, and otherwise trying to help.

Despite all of that, the same folks I'd tried to help were afraid of me.

Even Mac.

I guess I couldn't blame them. I wasn't as accessible as I used to be, what with the war and my new Warden duties, and teaching my apprentice. Practically the only times I had appeared in public, things had gotten messy, and people had died. I sometimes forgot how scary the supernatural could be. I lived in a state of relative power. I'm not under any illusions that I can take out anything that messes with me, but I am not a pansy, and with the right planning and leverage I can be a threat to even awfully powerful beings.

Those folks couldn't. They were the have-nots of the supernatural world, and they didn't have the options that my power gave me. And after all, I was supposed to be the one protecting folks from supernatural threats. If they truly believed that the women had been murdered, then either I was cruel enough to do the deed, or uncaring and/or incompetent enough to allow it to happen. Either way, it didn't paint a flattering picture of me. Add in the growing sense of fear, and it was understandable.

But it still hurt.

'It's not me,' I said quietly.

Mac studied my features for a moment, then nodded. 'Needed to hear it.'

'Sure,' I said. 'I don't know who is behind it. But I give you my word that when I catch up to whoever is doing this, I'm going to take him down, regardless of who he is or who he works for. My word, Mac.'

He took another sip of beer, stalling.

I reached out and started flipping through the pages, one by one, reviewing the horrible photos. Mac saw them too.

He let out a breath barely tinged with a throaty growl, and leaned back in his chair, away from the images.

I put my last beer on the table and spread my hands. 'Help me, Mac. Please.'

Mac stared down at his bottle for a moment. Then he looked at his sign again. Then he reached out and took the top sheet of paper from the stack. He flipped it over, produced a pencil from his apron pocket, and wrote on the page before passing it back to me.

It read: *Anna Ash, Ordo Lebes, four P.M. tomorrow.*

'What's this?' I asked him.

He picked up his bottle and rose. 'A start.'

'Ordo Lebes,' Murphy said. She took the lid off her coffee and blew some steam away from its surface. 'My Latin is a little rusty.'

'That's because you aren't a master of arcane lore, like me.'

She rolled her eyes. 'Right.'

'*Lebes* means a large cooking pot,' I told her. I tried to adjust the passenger seat of her car, but couldn't manage to make it comfortable. Saturn coupes were not meant for people my height. 'Translates out to the Order of the Large Cooking Pot.'

'Or maybe Order of the Cauldron?' Murphy suggested. 'Since it sounds so much less silly and has a more witchy connotation and all?'

'Well,' I said, 'I suppose.'

Murphy snorted at me. 'Master of the arcane lore.'

'I learned Latin through a correspondence course, okay? We should have taken my car.'

'The interior of a Volkswagen Beetle is smaller than this one.'

'But I know where it all *is*,' I said, trying to untangle my right foot from where it had gotten wedged by the car's frame.

'Do all wizards whine this much?' Murphy sipped her coffee. 'You just want to be the one driving. I think you have control issues.'

'Control issues?'

'Control issues,' she said.

'You're the one who wouldn't find the woman's address unless I let you drive, and I'm the one with issues?'

'With me, it's less an issue and more a fact of life,' she said calmly. 'Besides, that clown car of yours doesn't exactly blend in, which is what you're supposed to do on a stakeout.'

I glowered out the front window of her car and looked up at the apartment building where one Anna Ash was presumably hosting a meeting of the Order of the Large Cooking Po – er, uh, Cauldron. Murphy had found a spot on the street, which made me wonder if she didn't have some kind of magical talent after all. Only some kind of precognitive ESP could have gotten us a parking space on the street, in the shadow of a building, with both of us in sight of the apartment building's entrance.

'What time is it?' I asked.

'Five minutes ago it was three o'clock,' Murphy said. 'I can't be certain, but I theorize that it must now be about three-oh-five.'

I folded my arms. 'I don't usually do stakeouts.'

'I thought it might be a nice change of pace for you. All that knocking down of doors and burning down of buildings must get tiring.'

'I don't always knock down doors,' I said. 'Sometimes it's a wall.'

'But this way, we get a chance to see who's going into the building. We might learn something.'

I let out a suspicious grunt. 'Learn something, huh?'

'It'll only hurt for a minute.' Murphy sipped at her coffee and nodded at a woman walking toward the apartment building. She wore a simple sundress with a man's white cotton button-down shirt worn open atop it. She was in her late thirties, maybe, with pepper-and-salt hair worn in a bun. She wore sandals and sunglasses. 'How about her?'

'Yeah,' I said. 'Recognize her. Seen her at Bock Ordered Books a few times.'

The woman entered the building at a brisk, purposeful pace.

Murphy and I went back to waiting. Over the next forty-five minutes, four other women arrived. I recognized two of them.

Murphy checked her watch – a pocket watch with actual clockwork and not a microchip or battery to be found. 'Almost four,' she said. 'Half a dozen at most?'

'Looks that way,' I agreed.

'And you didn't see any obvious bad guys.'

'The wacky thing about those bad guys is that you can't count on them to be obvious. They forget to wax their mustaches and goatees, leave their horns at home, send their black hats to the dry cleaner's. They're funny like that.'

Murphy gave me a direct and less-than-amused look. 'Should we go on up?'

'Give it another five minutes. No force in the known universe can make a gang of folks naming their organization in Latin do much of anything on time. If they're all there by four, we'll know there's some kind of black magic involved.'

Murphy snorted, and we waited for a few minutes more. 'So,' she said, filling time. 'How's the war going?' She paused for a beat, and said, 'God, what a question.'

'Slowly,' I said. 'Since our little visit to Arctis Tor, and the beating the vampires took afterward, things have been pretty quiet. I went out to New Mexico this spring.'

'Why?'

'Helping Luccio train baby Wardens,' I said. 'You've got to get way out away from civilization when you're teaching group fire magic. So we spent about two days turning thirty acres of sand and scrub into glass. Then a couple of the Red Court's ghouls showed up and killed two kids.'

Murphy turned her blue eyes to me, waiting.

I felt my jaw tighten, thinking back on it. It wouldn't do those two kids any good, going over it again. So I pretended I didn't realize she was giving me a chance to talk about it. 'There haven't been any more big actions, though. Just small-time stuff. The Merlin's trying to get the vamps to the table to negotiate a peace.'

'Doesn't sound like you think much of the idea,' Murphy noted.

'The Red King is still in power,' I said. 'The war was his idea to begin with. If he goes for a treaty now, it's only going to be so that the vamps can lick their wounds, get their numbers up again, and come back for the sequel.'

'Kill them all?' she asked. 'Let God sort them out?'

'I don't care if anyone sorts them or not. I'm tired of seeing people they've destroyed.' My teeth ground together. I hadn't realized I was clenching my jaws so hard.

I tried to force myself to relax. It didn't work out the way I'd hoped. Instead of feeling unclenched and less angry, I only felt tired. 'Ah, Murph. Too many people get hurt. Sometimes I feel like no matter how fast I react, it doesn't make any difference.'

'You're talking about these killings, now,' she said.

'Them, too.'

'It isn't your fault, Harry,' Murphy said in a steady voice. 'Once you've done everything you can, you can't do any more. There's no sense in beating yourself up over it.'

'Yeah?'

'That's what the counselors keep telling me,' she said. She regarded me thoughtfully. 'It's easier to see their point when I'm looking at you, though.'

'Thing is, Murph,' I said. 'What if I could do more?'

'Like what?' she asked.

'I don't know. Something to deter these murdering animals.'

Something like New Mexico. Jesus. I didn't want to think about that. I rubbed at the fresh headache sprouting between my eyebrows.

Murphy gave me a minute more to decide if I wanted to talk about it. When I stayed quiet, she asked, 'Time to go up?'

Her voice had lightened, nudging us away from the topic. I nodded and tried to ease up on my tone. 'Yeah. If my leg bones haven't been deformed by this torture chamber you drive.' I opened the door and hauled myself out, stretching.

I hadn't yet shut the door when I saw the woman walking down the street toward the apartment building. She was tall, lean, her hair cut shorter than mine. She wore no makeup, none at all, and time had not been kind to her stark features.

She'd looked a lot different the last time I'd seen her.

Back then, Helen Beckitt had been naked, and holding a dainty little .22-caliber revolver, and she'd shot me in the hip. She and her husband had gone down when a fledgling black sorcerer named Victor Sells had been introduced to his own killer creations, courtesy of Harry Dresden. They'd been on the ground floor of Victor's nascent magic-assisted criminal empire. They'd been prosecuted for the criminal part, too, and gone to a federal penitentiary on drug charges.

I froze in place, going completely still, even though I was standing in plain sight. A sudden movement would only have served to draw her attention to me. She went on by, her steps brisk, her expression empty of any emotion or spark of life, just as I remembered. I watched her go into Anna Ash's building.

Murphy, taking her cue from me, had frozen in place as well. She caught a glimpse of Helen Beckitt's back as she went inside.

'Harry?' she asked. 'What was that?'

'The plot,' I said, 'thickening.'

6

'I don't like this,' Murphy said. 'Helen Beckitt has got plenty of reasons to dislike you.'

I snorted. 'Who doesn't?'

'I'm serious, Harry.' The elevator doors closed and we started up. The building was old, and the elevator wasn't the fastest in the world. Murphy shook her head. 'If what you said about people beginning to fear you is true, then there's got to be a reason for it. Maybe someone is telling stories.'

'And you like Helen for that?'

'She already shot you, and that didn't work. Maybe she figured it was time to get nasty.'

'Sticks and stones and small-caliber bullets may break my bones,' I said. 'Words will never, et cetera.'

'It's awfully coincidental to find her here. She's a con, Harry, and she wound up in jail because of you. I can't imagine that she's making nice with the local magic community for the camaraderie.'

'I didn't think cops knew about big words like "camaraderie," Murph. Are you sure you're a real policeperson?'

She gave me an exasperated glance. 'Do you ever stop joking around?'

'I mutter off-color limericks in my sleep.'

'Just promise me that you'll watch your back,' Murphy said.

'There once was a girl from Nantucket,' I said. 'Her mouth was as big as a bucket.'

Murphy flipped both her hands palms up in a gesture of frustrated surrender. 'Dammit, Dresden.'

I lifted an eyebrow. 'You seem worried about me.'

'There are women up there,' she said. 'You don't always think very clearly where women are concerned.'

'So you think I should watch my back.'

'Yes.'

I turned to her and looked down at her and said, more quietly, 'Golly, Murph. Why did you think I wanted you along?'

She looked up and smiled at me, the corners of her eyes wrinkling, though her voice remained tart. 'I figured you wanted someone along who could notice things more subtle than a flashing neon sign.'

'Oh, come on,' I said. 'It doesn't have to be flashing.'

The elevator doors opened and I took the lead down the hall to Anna Ash's apartment – and stepped into a tingling curtain of delicate energy four or five feet shy of the door. I drew up sharply, and Murphy had to put a hand against my back to keep from bumping into me.

'What is it?' she asked.

I held up my left hand. Though my maimed hand was still mostly numb to conventional stimuli, it had never had any trouble sensing the subtle patterns of organized magical energy. I spread out my fingers as much as I could, trying to touch the largest possible area as I closed my eyes and focused on my wizard's senses.

'It's a ward,' I said quietly.

'Like on your apartment?' she asked.

'It's not as strong,' I said, waving my hand slowly over it. 'And it's a little cruder. I've got bricks and razor wire. This is more like aluminum siding and chicken wire. But it has a decent kick. Fire, I think.' I squinted up and down the hall. 'Huh. I don't think there's enough there to kill outright, but it would hurt like hell.'

'And a fire would set off the building's alarms,' Murphy

added. 'Make people start running out. Summon the authorities.'

'Uh-huh,' I said. 'Discouraging your average prowler, supernatural or not. It's not meant to kill.' I stepped back and nodded to Murphy. 'Go ahead and knock.'

She gave me an arch look. 'That's a joke, right?'

'If this ward isn't done right, it could react with my aura and go off.'

'Can't you just take it apart?'

'Whoever did this was worried enough to invest a lot of time and effort to make this home safer,' I said. 'Kinda rude to tear it up.'

Murphy tilted her head for a second, and then she got it. 'And you'll scare them if you just walk through it like it wasn't there.'

'Yeah,' I said quietly. 'They're frightened, Murph. I've got to be gentle, or they won't give me anything that can help them.'

Murphy nodded and knocked on the door.

She rapped three times, and the doorknob was already turning on the third rap.

A small, prettily plump woman opened the door. She was even shorter than Murphy, mid-forties maybe, with blond hair and rosy, cherubic cheeks that looked used to smiling. She wore a lavender dress and carried a small dog, maybe a Yorkshire terrier, in her arms. She smiled at Murphy and said, 'Of course, Sergeant Murphy, I know who you are.'

Maybe half a second after the woman started speaking, Murphy said, 'Hello, my name is Sergeant Murphy, and I'm a detective with the CPD.'

Murphy blinked for a second and fell silent.

'Oh,' the woman said. 'I'm sorry; I forget sometimes.' She made an airy little gesture with one hand. 'Such a scatterbrain.'

I started to introduce myself, but before I got my mouth open, the little woman said, 'Of course, we all know who you are, Mister Dresden.' She put her fingers to her mouth. They were shaking a little. 'Oh. I forgot again. Excuse me. I'm Abby.'

'Pleased to meet you, Abby,' I said quietly, and extended my hand, relaxed, palm down, to the little Yorkie. The dog sniffed at my hand, quivering with eagerness as he did, and his tail started wagging. 'Heya, little dog.'

'Toto,' Abby said, and before I could respond said, 'Exactly, a classic. If it isn't broken, why fix it?' She nodded to me and said, 'Excuse me; I'll let our host speak to you. I was just closest to the door.' She shut the door on us.

'Certainly,' I said to the door.

Murphy turned to me. 'Weird.'

I shrugged. 'At least the dog liked me.'

'She knew what we were going to say before we said it, Harry.'

'I noticed that.'

'Is she telepathic or something?'

I shook my head. 'Not in the way you're thinking. She doesn't exactly hide what she's doing, and if she was poking around in people's heads, the Council would have done something a long time ago.'

'Then how did she know what we were about to say?'

'My guess is that she's prescient,' I said. 'She can see the future. Probably only a second or two, and she probably doesn't have a lot of voluntary control over it.'

Murphy made a thoughtful noise. 'Could be handy.'

'In some ways,' I said. 'But the future isn't written in stone.'

Murphy frowned. 'Like, what if I'd decided to tell her my name was Karrin Murphy instead of Sergeant, at the last second?'

'Yeah. She'd have been wrong. People like her can sense a . . . sort of a cloud of possible futures. We were in a fairly predictable situation here even without bringing any magical talents into it, basic social interaction, so it looked like she saw exactly what was coming. But she didn't. She got to judge what was most probable, and it wasn't hard to guess correctly in this particular instance.'

'That's why she seemed so distracted,' Murphy said thoughtfully.

'Yeah. She was keeping track of what *was* happening, what was *likely* to happen, deciding what *wasn't* likely to happen, all in a window of a few seconds.' I shook my head. 'It's a lot worse if they can see any farther than a second or two.'

Murphy frowned. 'Why?'

'Because the farther you can see, the more possibilities exist,' I said. 'Think of a chess game. A beginning player is doing well if he can see four or five moves into the game. Ten moves in holds an exponentially greater number of possible configurations the board could assume. Master players can sometimes see even further than that – and when you start dealing with computers, the numbers are even bigger. It's difficult to even imagine the scope of it.'

'And that's in a closed, simple environment,' Murphy said, nodding. 'The chess game. There are far more possibilities in the real world.'

'The biggest game.' I shook my head. 'It's a dangerous talent to have. It can leave you subject to instabilities of one kind or another as side effects. Doctors almost always diagnose folks like Abby with epilepsy, Alzheimer's, or one of a number of personality disorders. I got five bucks that says that medical bracelet on her wrist says she's epileptic – and that the dog can sense seizures coming and warn her.'

'I didn't see the bracelet,' Murphy admitted. 'No bet.'

While we stood there talking quietly for maybe five

minutes, a discussion took place inside the apartment. Low voices came through the door in tense, muffled tones that eventually cut off when a single voice, louder than the rest, overrode the others. A moment later, the door opened.

The first woman we'd seen enter the apartment faced me. She had a dark complexion, dark eyes, short, dark straight hair that made me think she might have had some Native Americans in the family a generation or three back. She was maybe five foot four, late thirties. She had a serious kind of face, with faint, pensive lines between her brows, and from the way she stood, blocking the doorway with solidly planted feet, I got the impression that she could be a bulldog when necessary.

'No one here has broken any of the Laws, Warden,' she said in a quiet, firm voice.

'Gosh, that's a relief,' I said. 'Anna Ash?'

She narrowed her eyes and nodded.

'I'm Harry Dresden,' I said.

She pursed her lips and gave me a speculative look. 'Are you kidding? I know who you are.'

'I don't make it a habit to assume that everyone I meet knows who I am,' I said, implying apology in my tone. 'This is Karrin Murphy, Chicago PD.'

Anna nodded to Murphy and asked, in a neutral, polite tone, 'May I see your identification, Ms Murphy?'

Murphy already had her badge on its leather backing in hand, and she passed it to Anna. Her photo identification was on the reverse side of the badge, under a transparent plastic cover.

Anna looked at the badge and the photo, and compared it to Murphy. She passed it back almost reluctantly, and then turned to me. 'What do you want?'

'To talk,' I said.

'About what?'

'The Ordo Lebes,' I said. 'And what's happened to several practitioners lately.'

Her voice remained polite on the surface, but I could hear bitter undertones. 'I'm sure you know much more about it than us.'

'Not especially,' I said. 'That's what I'm trying to correct.'

She shook her head, suspicion written plainly on her face. 'I'm not an idiot. The Wardens keep track of everything. Everyone knows that.'

I sighed. 'Yeah, but I forgot to take my George Orwell-shaped multivitamins along with my breakfast bowl of Big Brother Os this morning. I was hoping you could just talk to me for a little while, the way you would with a human being.'

She eyed me a bit warily. Lots of people react to my jokes like that. 'Why should I?'

'Because I want to help you.'

'Of course you'd say that,' she said. 'How do I know you mean it?'

'Ms Ash,' Murphy put in quietly, 'he's on the level. We're here to help, if we can.'

Anna chewed on her lip for a minute, looking back and forth between us and then glancing at the room behind her. Finally, she faced me and said, 'Appearances can be deceiving. I have no way of knowing if you are who – and what – you say you are. I prefer to err on the side of caution.'

'Never hurts to be cautious,' I agreed. 'But you're edging toward paranoid, Ms Ash.'

She began to shut the door. 'This is my home. And I'm not inviting you inside.'

'Groovy,' I said, and stepped over the threshold and into the apartment, nudging her gently aside before she could close the door.

As I did, I felt the pressure of the threshold, an aura of

protective magical energy that surrounds any home. The threshold put up a faintly detectable resistance as my own aura of power met it – and could not cross it. If Anna, the home's owner, had invited me in, the threshold would have parted like a curtain. She hadn't, and as a result, if I wanted to come inside, I'd have to leave much of my power at the door. If I had to work any forces while I was in there, I'd be crippled practically to the point of total impotence.

I turned to see Anna staring at me in blank surprise. She was aware of what I had just done.

'There,' I told her. 'If I was of the spirit world, I couldn't cross your threshold. If I had planned on hurting someone in here, would I have disarmed myself? Stars and stones, would I have shown up with a *cop* to witness me doing it?'

Murphy took her cue from me, and entered the same way.

'I . . .' Anna said, at a loss. 'How . . . how did you know the ward wouldn't go off in your face?'

'Judgment call,' I told her. 'You're a cautious person, and there are kids in this building. I don't think you'd have slapped up something that went boom whenever anyone stepped through the doorway.'

She took a deep breath and then nodded. 'You wouldn't have liked what happened if you'd tried to force the door, though.'

'I believe you,' I told her. And I did. 'Ms Ash, I'm not here to threaten or harm anyone. I can't make you talk to me. If you want me to go, right now, I'll go,' I promised her. 'But for your own safety, please let me talk to you first. A few minutes. That's all I ask.'

'Anna?' came Abby's voice. 'I think you should hear them out.'

'Yes,' said another woman's voice, quiet and low. 'I agree. And I know something of him. If he gives you his word, he means it.'

Thinking on it, I hadn't ever really heard Helen Beckitt's voice before, unless you counted moans. But its quiet solidity and lack of inflection went perfectly with her quasi-lifeless eyes.

I traded an uneasy glance with Murphy, then looked back to Anna.

'Ms Ash?' I asked her.

'Give me your word. Swear it on your power.'

That's serious, at least among wizards in my league. Promises have power. One doesn't swear by one's magical talent and break the oath lightly – to do so would be to reduce one's own strength in the Art. I didn't hesitate to answer. 'I swear to you, upon my power, to abide as a guest under your hospitality, to bring no harm to you or yours, nor to deny my aid if they would suffer thereby.'

She let out a short, quick breath and nodded. 'Very well. I promise to behave as a host, with all the obligations that apply. And call me Anna, please.' She pronounced her name with the Old World emphasis: Ah-nah. She beckoned with one hand and led us into the apartment. 'I trust you will not take it amiss if I do not make a round of introductions.'

Understandable. A full name, given from one's own lips, could provide a wizard or talented sorcerer with a channel, a reference point that could be used to target any number of harmful, even lethal spells, much like fresh blood, nail clippings, or locks of hair could be used for the same. It was all but impossible to give away your full name accidentally in a conversation, but it had happened, and if someone in the know thought a wizard might be pointing a spell their way, they got real careful, real fast, when it came to speaking their own name.

'No problem,' I told her.

Anna's apartment was nicer than most, and evidently had received almost a complete refurbishing in the past year or three. She had windows with a reasonably good view, and her furnishings were predominantly of wood, and of excellent quality.

Five women sat around the living area. Abby sat in a wooden rocking chair, holding her bright-eyed little Yorkie in her lap. Helen Beckitt stood by a window, staring listlessly out at the city. Two other women sat on a sofa, the third on a love seat perpendicular to them.

'Should I take it that you know who I am?' I asked them.

'They know,' Anna said quietly.

I nodded. 'All right. Here's what *I* know. Something has killed as many as five female practitioners. Some of the deaths have looked like suicides. Evidence suggests that they weren't.' I took a deep breath. 'And I've found messages left for me or someone like me with at least two of the bodies. Things the cops couldn't have found. I think we're looking at a serial killer, and I think that your order might represent a pool of victims that fit his—'

'Or her,' Murphy put in, not quite *staring* at Beckitt.

Beckitt's mouth curled into a bitter little smile, though she did not otherwise move.

'Or her,' I allowed, 'profile.'

'Is he serious?' asked one of the women I didn't know. She was older than the others, early fifties. Despite the day's warmth, she wore a thin turtleneck sweater of light green and a dark grey cardigan. Her hair, caught back in a severe bun, had once been deep, coppery red, though now it was sown liberally with steely grey. She wore no makeup, square, silver-rimmed spectacles over muddy brown-green eyes, and her eyebrows had grown out rather thicker than most women chose to allow.

'Very serious,' I replied. 'Is there something I can call you? It doesn't seem polite to name you Turtleneck without checking first.'

She stiffened slightly, keeping her eyes away from mine, and said, 'Priscilla.'

'Priscilla. I'm pretty much floundering around here. I don't know what's going on, and that's why I came to talk to you.'

'Then how did you know of the Ordo?' she demanded.

'In real life, I'm a private investigator,' I told her. 'I investigate stuff.'

'He's lying,' Priscilla said, looking back at Anna. 'He has to be. You *know* what we've seen.'

Anna looked from Priscilla to me, and then shook her head. 'I don't think so.'

'What *have* you seen?' I asked Anna.

Anna looked around the room at the others for a moment, but none of them made any objections, and she turned back to me. 'You're correct. Several members of our order have died. What you might not know is that there are others who have vanished.' She took a deep breath. 'Not only in the Ordo, but in the community as well. More than twenty people are unaccounted for since the end of last month.'

I let out a low whistle. That *was* serious. Don't get me wrong; people vanish all the time – most of them because they want to do it. But the people in our circles were generally a lot closer-knit than most folks, in part because they were aware, to one degree or another, of the existence of supernatural predators who could and would take them, given the chance. It's a herd instinct, plain and simple – and it works.

If twenty people had gone missing, odds were good that something was on the prowl. If the killer had taken them, I had a major problem on my hands, which admittedly wasn't exactly a novel experience.

'You say people have seen something? What?'

'For . . .' She shook her head and cleared her throat. 'For

all three victims from within the order whose bodies have been found, they were last seen alive in the company of a tall man in a grey cloak.'

I blinked. 'And you thought it was me?'

'I wasn't close enough to tell,' Priscilla said. 'It was after dark, and she was on the street outside my apartment. I saw them through a window.'

She didn't quite manage to hide the fact that she'd almost said *you* instead of *them*.

'I was at Bock's,' Abby added, her tone serious, her eyes fixed in the middle distance. 'Late. I saw the man walk by with her outside.'

'I didn't see that,' Helen Beckitt said. The words were flat and certain. 'Sally left the bar with a rather lovely dark-haired man with grey eyes and pale skin.'

My stomach twitched. In my peripheral vision, Murphy's facial expression went carefully blank.

Anna lifted a hand in a gesture beseeching Helen for silence. 'At least two more reliable witnesses have reported that the last time they saw some of the folk who had disappeared, they were in the company of the grey-cloaked man. Several others have reported sightings of the beautiful dark-haired man instead.'

I shook my head. 'And you thought the guy in the cloak was me?'

'How many tall, grey-cloaked men move in our circles in Chicago, sir?' Priscilla said, her voice frosty.

'You can get grey corduroy for three dollars a yard at a surplus fabric store,' I told her. 'Tall men aren't exactly unheard of in a city of eight million, either.'

Priscilla narrowed her eyes. 'Who was it, then?'

Abby tittered, which made Toto wag his tail.

I pursed my lips in a moment of thought. 'I'm pretty sure it wasn't Murphy.'

Helen Beckitt snorted out a breath through her nose.

'This isn't a joking matter,' Priscilla snapped.

'Oh. Sorry. Given that I only found out about a grey cloak sighting about two seconds ago, I had assumed the question was facetious.' I turned to face Anna. 'It wasn't me. And it wasn't a Warden of the Council – or at least, it damned well better *not* have been a Warden of the Council.'

'And if it was?' Anna asked quietly.

I folded my arms. 'I'll make sure he never hurts anyone. Ever again.'

Murphy stepped forward and said, 'Excuse me. You said that three members of the order had died. What were their names, please?'

'Maria,' Anna said, her words spaced with the slow, deliberate beat of a funeral march. 'Janine. Pauline.'

I saw where Murphy was going.

'What about Jessica Blanche?' she asked.

Anna frowned for a moment and then shook her head. 'I don't think I've heard the name.'

'So she's not in the order,' Murphy said. 'And she's not in the, ah, community?'

'Not to my knowledge,' Anna replied. She looked around the room. 'Does anyone here know her?'

Silence.

I traded a glance with Murphy. 'Some of these things are not like the others.'

'Some of these things are kind of the same,' she responded.

'Somewhere to start, at least,' I said.

Someone's watch started beeping, and the girl on the couch beside Priscilla sat up suddenly. She was young, maybe even still in her teens, with the rich, smoke-colored skin of regions of eastern India. She had heavy-lidded brown eyes, and wore a bandanna tied over her straight, glossy black hair. She was dressed in a lavender ballet leotard with cream-colored tights covering long legs, and she had the muscled, athletic build of a serious dancer. She wore a man's watch that looked huge against her fine-boned wrist. She turned it off and then glanced up at Anna, fidgeting. 'Ten minutes.'

Anna frowned and nodded at her. She started toward the door, a gracious hostess politely walking us out. 'Is there anything else we can do for you, Warden? Ms Murphy?'

In the investigating business, when someone starts trying to rush you out in order to conceal some kind of information from you, it is what we professionals call a clue. 'Gee,' I said brightly. 'What happens in ten minutes?'

Anna stopped, her polite smile fading. 'We have answered your questions as best we could. You gave me your word, Warden, to abide by my hospitality. Not to abuse it.'

'Answering me may be for your own good,' I replied.

'That's your opinion,' she said. 'In my opinion, it is no business of yours.'

I sighed and nodded acquiescence. I handed her a business card. 'There's my number. In case you change your mind.'

'Thank you,' Anna said politely.

Murphy and I left, and were silent all the way down in the elevator. I scowled up a storm on the way, and brooded. It had never solved any of my problems in the past, but there's always a first time.

When we walked back out into the sunshine, Murphy said, 'You think they know anything else?'

'They know *something*,' I said. 'Or think they do.'

'That was a rhetorical question, Harry.'

'Bite me.' I shook my head. 'What's our next move?'

'Dig into Jessica Blanche's background,' she replied. 'See what we turn up.'

I nodded. 'Easier than searching Chicago for guys in big grey cloaks.'

She paused for a moment, and I knew her well enough to know that she was choosing her words carefully. 'But maybe not easier than finding pale, beautiful, dark-haired men who may or may not have been the last person seen with a woman who died in the midst of sexual ecstasy.'

For a moment, our only conversation was footsteps.

'It isn't him,' I said then. 'He's my brother.'

'Sure, yeah,' she agreed.

'I mean, I haven't talked to him in a while, sure,' I admitted. A moment later I added. 'And he's on his own now. Making really good money doing . . . something. Though I don't know what. Because he will never, ever say.'

Murphy nodded. 'Yes.'

'And I guess it's true that he's awfully well fed these days,' I went on. 'And that he won't tell me how.' We went a few more steps. 'And that he thinks of himself as a monster. And that he got sick and tired of trying to be human.'

We crossed the street in silence.

When I got to the other side, I stopped and looked at Murphy. 'Shit.'

We both started down the sidewalk to Murphy's Saturn.

'Harry,' she said quietly. 'I think you're probably right about him. But there are lives at stake. We have to be sure.'

A flash of anger went through me, an instant and instinctive denial that my brother, my only living flesh and blood, could be involved in this mess. Intense, irrational fury, and an equally irrational sense of betrayal at Murphy's gentle accusation, fed on each other, swelling rapidly. It took me off guard. I had never felt such volatile determination to destroy a threat to my brother outside of life-and-death struggles we'd found ourselves trapped within. The emotions roared through me like molten steel, and I found myself instinctively gathering my will under their searing influence. For just a second I wanted to smash things to powder, starting with anyone who even *thought* about trying to hurt Thomas – and the strength to do it welled up inside me like steam in a boiler.

I snarled and closed my eyes, forcing control upon myself. This was no life-and-death struggle. It was a sidewalk. There would be no noisy and satisfying release of that anger, but the energy that I had unconsciously gathered had the potential to be dangerous in any case. I reached down to brush the sidewalk with my fingertips, allowing the dangerous buildup of magic to ground itself more or less harmlessly into the earth, and only a trace amount of energy flared out into a disruptive pattern.

It saved our lives.

The instant I released the excess energy into the area around us, a nearby stoplight blew out, Murphy's cell phone started blaring 'Stars and Stripes Forever,' three car alarms went off—

—and Murphy's Saturn coupe went up in a brilliant ball of fire and an ear-shattering blast of thunder.

There was no time to do anything. Even if I'd been crouched, tense, and holding defensive magic ready to go, I wouldn't have beaten the explosion to the punch. It was instant, and violent, and did not at all care whether I was on my guard or not. Something that felt vaguely like an enormous feather pillow swung by the Incredible Hulk slammed into my chest.

It lifted me up off the ground and dumped me on the sidewalk several feet later. My shoulder clipped a mailbox as I went by it, and then I had a good, steady view of the clear summer sky above me as I lay on my back and ached.

I'd lived, which was always a good start in this kind of situation. It couldn't have been a very big explosion, then. It had to have been more incendiary than concussive, a big old rolling ball of flame that would have shattered windows and burned things and set things on fire, and pushed a whole lot of air out of the way along with one Harry Dresden, wizard, slightly used.

I sat up and peered at the rolling cloud of black smoke and red flame where Murphy's Saturn was, which bore out my supposition pretty well. I squinted to one side and saw Murphy sitting slowly back up. She had a short, bleeding cut on her upper lip. She looked pale and shaken.

I couldn't help it. I started laughing like a drunk.

'Well,' I said. 'Under the circumstances, I'm forced to conclude that you were right. I *am* a control freak and you were one hundred percent right to be the one driving the car. Thank you, Murph.'

She gave me a slow, hard stare, drew in a deep breath, and said, through clenched teeth, 'No problem.'

I grinned at her and slumped back down onto my back. 'You okay?'

She dabbed at the blood on her lip with one hand. 'Think so. You?'

'Clipped my shoulder on a mailbox,' I said. 'It hurts a little. Not a lot. Maybe I could take an aspirin. Just one. Not a whole dose or anything.'

She sighed. 'My God, you're a whiner, Dresden.'

We sat there quietly for a minute while sirens began in the distance and came closer.

'Bomb, you think?' Murphy said, in that tone people use when they don't know what else to say.

'Yeah,' I said. 'I was grounding some extra energy out when it went off. It must have hexed up the bomb's timer or receiver. Set it off early.'

'Unless it was intended as a warning shot,' she said.

I grunted. 'Whose bomb, you think?'

'I haven't annoyed anyone new lately,' Murphy said.

'Neither have I.'

'You've annoyed a lot more people than me, in toto.'

'In toto?' I said. 'Who talks like that? Besides, car bombs aren't really within . . . within the, uh . . .'

'Idiom?' Murphy asked, with what might have been a very slight British accent.

'Idiom!' I declared in my best John Cleese impersonation. 'The idiom of the entities I've ticked off. And you're really turning me on with the Monty Python reference.'

'You're pathetic, Harry.' Her smile faded. 'But a car bomb is well within the idiom of ex-cons,' she said.

'Mrs Beckitt was inside with us the whole time, remember?'

'And Mr Beckitt?' Murphy asked.

'Oh,' I said. 'Ah. Think he's out by now?'

'I think we've got some things to find out,' she said. 'You'd better go.'

'I should?'

'I'm not on the clock, remember?' Murphy said. 'It's my car. Simpler if there's only one person answering all the questions.'

'Right,' I said, and pushed myself up. 'Which end do you want?'

'I'll take our odd corpse out and the Beckitts,' she said. I offered her a hand up. She took it, which meant more to the two of us than it would to anyone looking on. 'And you?'

I sighed. 'I'll talk to my brother.'

'I'm sure he's not involved,' Murphy said quietly. 'But . . .'

'But he knows the incubus business,' I said, which wasn't what Murphy had been about to say. It might have drawn an anger response out of me, but rationally speaking, I couldn't blame her for her suspicion, either. She was a cop. She'd spent her entire adult life dealing with the most treacherous and dishonest portions of the human condition. Speaking logically, she was right to suspect and question until more information presented itself. People's lives were at stake.

But Thomas was my brother, my blood. Logic and rationality had little to do with it.

The first emergency unit, a patrolling police car, rounded the corner a couple of blocks away. Fire trucks weren't far behind.

'Time to go,' Murphy said quietly.

'I'll see what I can find out,' I told her, and walked away.

I took the El back to my neighborhood on high alert, watching for anyone who might be following, lying in wait, or otherwise planning malicious deeds involving me. I didn't see anyone doing any of those things on the El, or as I walked to my apartment in the basement of an old boardinghouse.

Once there, I walked down a sunken concrete staircase to my front door – one of those nifty all-metal security doors – and with a muttered word and an effort of will, I disarmed the wards that protected my home. Then I used a key to open its conventional locks, and slipped inside.

Mister promptly hurtled into my shins with a shoulder block of greeting. The big grey cat weighed about thirty pounds, and the impact actually rocked me back enough to let my shoulder blades bump against the door. I reached down and gave his ears a quick rub. Mister purred, walking in circles around one of my legs, then sidled away and hopped up onto a bookshelf to resume the important business of napping away a summer afternoon in wait for the cool of evening.

An enormous mound of shaggy grey-and-black fur appeared from the shadows in the little linoleum-floored alcove that passed for my kitchen. It walked over to me, yawning as it came, its tail wagging in relaxed greeting. I hunkered down as my dog sat and thrust his head toward me, and I vigorously scratched his ears and chin and the thick ruff of fur over his neck with both hands. 'Mouse. All quiet on the home front, boy?'

His tail wagged some more, jaw dropping open to expose a lethal array of very white teeth, and his tongue lolled out in a doggy grin.

'Oh, I forgot the mail,' I said. 'You mind getting it?'

Mouse promptly rose, and I opened the door. He padded out in total silence. Mouse moves lightly for a rhinoceros.

I crossed my floor of mismatched carpets and rugs to slump into the easy chair by the old fireplace. I picked up my phone and dialed Thomas's number. No answer. I glared at the phone for a minute and, because I wasn't sure what else to do, I tried it again. No one answered. What were the odds.

I chewed on my lip for a minute and began to worry about my brother.

Mouse returned a moment later – long enough to have gone out to the designated dog-friendly little area in the house's yard. He had several bits of mail held gently in his mouth, and he dropped them carefully onto the surface of the old wooden coffee table in front of my sofa. Then he went over to the door and leaned a shoulder against it. It hadn't been installed quite right, and it was a real pain in the ass to open, and once it was open it was a pain in the ass to close. Mouse shoved at the door with a little snort of familiar effort and it swung to. Then he came back over to settle down by me.

'Thanks, boy.' I grabbed the mail, scratched his ears again, and flicked to life several candles on the end table next to the recliner with a muttered spell. 'Bills,' I reported to him, going through the mail. 'More bills, Junk mail. *Another* Best Buy catalog, Jesus, those people won't give up. Larry Fowler's new lawyer.' I put the unopened envelope against my forehead and closed my eyes. 'He's threatening me with another variation on the same lawsuit.' I opened the letter and skimmed it, then tossed it on the floor. 'It's as if I'm psychic.'

I opened the drawer in the end table, felt about with my fingertips, and withdrew a single silver metallic key, the only one on a ring marked with an oval of blue plastic that sported my business card's logo: HARRY DRESDEN, WIZARD, PARANORMAL INVESTIGATIONS, CONSULTING, ADVICE, REASONABLE RATES.

I looked at the key. Thomas had given it to me, in case I should need to show up at his place in an emergency. He had a key to my place, too, even after he'd moved out. There had been a tacit understanding between us. The keys were there in case one or the other of us needed help. They had not been given so that one or the other of us could go snooping uninvited around the other one's home and life.

(Though I suspected that Thomas had looked in on my place a few times, hoping to figure out how the place managed to get so clean. He'd never caught my housekeeping brownies at work, and he never would. They're pros. The only drawback to having faerie housekeepers is that you can't tell people about them. If you do, they're gone, and no, I don't know why.)

The faces of the dead women drifted through my thoughts, and I sighed and closed my fingers around the key. 'Okay, boy,' I said. 'Time to go visit Thomas.'

Mouse rose up expectantly, his tags jingling, his tail thrashing energetically. Mouse liked going for rides in the car. He trotted over to the door, pulled his lead down from where it hung on the doorknob, and brought it over to me.

'Hang on,' I told him. 'I need the arsenal.'

I hate it when bad business goes down in summer. I put on my torturously warm leather duster. I figured I could take death from heat prostration to whole new levels given the potential presence of further firebombs. And *that* could land me a spot in the *Guinness Book of World Records*. Maybe even a Darwin Award.

See there? That's called positive thinking.

I put on my new and improved shield bracelet, too, and slipped three silver rings onto the fingers of my right hand. I snagged my blasting rod, clipped Mouse's lead on, took up my staff, and tromped on out to the car.

I told Mouse to stay back while I approached the Blue Beetle, my battered, often-repaired, mismatched Volkswagen Bug. I looked all around it, then lay down to check the vehicle's undercarriage. I looked at the trunk and under the hood next. I even examined it for traces of hostile magic. I didn't find anything that resembled a bomb or looked dangerous, unless you counted the half-eaten Taco Bell burrito that had somehow gotten tossed into the trunk about six months ago.

I opened the door, whistled for Mouse, and off we went to invade my brother's privacy.

I hadn't actually visited Thomas's place before, and I was a little taken aback when I got there. I had assumed that the street address was to one of the new buildings in Cabrini Green, where urban renewal had been shoved down the throat of the former slum by the powers that be – largely because it bordered on the Gold Coast, the most expensive section of town, and the second-highest-income neighborhood in the world. The neighborhood around the Green had become slowly more tolerable, and the newer apartment buildings that had replaced the old were fairly nice.

But Thomas's apartment wasn't in one of those buildings. He was across the street, living in the Gold Coast. When Mouse and I got to the right apartment building, twilight was fading fast and I felt underdressed. The doorman's shoes were nicer than any I owned.

I opened the outer door with Thomas's key and marched to the elevators, Mouse walking smartly at heel. The doorman watched me, and I spotted two security cameras between the front door and the elevator. Security would have a pretty good idea who was a resident and who wasn't – and an extremely tall and gangly man in a black coat with nearly two hundred pounds of dog with him wouldn't be something they forgot. So I tried to stall them with body language, walking the walk of the impatient and confident in the hopes that it would make the security guys hesitate.

Either it worked or the building's security people were getting paid too much. No one challenged me, and I took the elevator to the sixteenth floor and walked down the hall to Thomas's apartment.

I unlocked the door, gave it a couple of knocks, and then opened it without waiting. I slipped in with Mouse, and found the light switch beside the door before I closed it.

Thomas's apartment was . . . well. Chic. The door opened onto a living room bigger than my entire apartment – which, granted, will never cause anxiety to agoraphobics. The walls were painted a deep crimson, and the carpeting was a rich charcoal grey. The furniture all matched, from the sofas to the chairs to the entertainment centers, all of it done in stainless steel and black, and a little more art deco than I would have preferred. He had a TV too big ever to fit into the Beetle, and a DVD player and surround sound and racks of DVDs and CDs. One of the newer video game systems rested neatly on a shelf, all its wires squared away and organized. Two movie posters decorated the walls: *The Wizard of Oz* and *The Pirates of Penzance*, the one with Kevin Kline as the Pirate King.

Well. It was good to see that my brother was doing well for himself. Though I had to wonder what he was doing that pulled down the kind of money this place would require.

The kitchen was like the living room – a lot of the same stainless steel and black in the appliances, though the walls had been painted white, as was the expensive tile floor. Everything was pristine. No dirty dishes, no half-open cupboards, no food stains, no papers lying about. Every single horizontal surface in the place was empty and sanitized. I checked the cupboards. The dishes stood in neat stacks, perfectly fitted to their storage in the cupboard.

None of which made sense. Thomas had a lot of positive qualities, but my brother was a fairly shameless slob. 'I get it now. He's dead,' I said aloud to Mouse. 'My brother is dead, and he's been replaced with some kind of obsessive-compulsive evil clone.'

I checked the fridge. I couldn't help it. It's one of those things you do when you're snooping through someone's house. It was empty, except for one of those boxes of wine, and about fifty bottles of Thomas's favorite beer, one of Mac's microbrewed ales. Mac would have killed Thomas for keeping it cold. Well. He would have scowled in disapproval, anyway. For Mac, that was tantamount to a homicidal reaction in other people.

I checked the freezer. It was packed, wall to wall, with TV meals in neat stacks. There were three different meals, stacked up in alternating order. There was room for maybe nine or ten more, and I presumed the others eaten. Thomas probably went shopping only every couple of months. That was more like him – beer, food cooked by pushing one button on a microwave. No dishes needed, and the drawer nearest the freezer yielded up a container of plastic forks and knives. Eat. Discard. No cooking or cleaning necessary.

I looked around at the rest of the kitchen, then at the fridge and freezer.

Then I went down the little hall that led to two bedrooms and a bath, and snorted in triumph. The bathroom was in total disarray, with toothbrushes and various grooming supplies tossed here and there, apparently at random. A couple of empty beer bottles sat out. The floor was carpeted with discarded clothing. Several half-used rolls of toilet paper sat around, with an empty cardboard tube still on the dispenser.

I checked in the first bedroom. It, too, was more Thomas's style. There was a king-sized bed with no head or foot, only the metal frame to support it. It had white sheets, several pillows in white cases, and a big, dark blue comforter on top. All of them were disheveled. The closet door stood open, and more clothes lay around on the floor. Two laundry baskets of fresh, neatly folded and ironed clothing (mostly empty) sat on a dresser with three of its drawers slightly open. There was a bookshelf haphazardly saturated with fiction of every description, and a clock radio. A pair of swords, one of them an old U.S. Cavalry saber, the other a more musketeer-looking weapon, were leaned against the wall, where they'd be more or less within reach of anyone in the bed.

I went back to the hall and shook my head at the rest of the apartment. 'It's a disguise,' I told Mouse. 'The front of the apartment. He wants it to give a certain impression. He makes sure no one gets to see the rest.'

Mouse tilted his head and looked at me.

'Maybe I should just leave him a note.'

The phone rang, and I about jumped out of my skin. After I made sure I wasn't having a cardiac episode, I padded back out to the living room, debating whether or not to answer it. I decided not to. It was probably building security calling to check up on the stranger who had walked in with a pet woolly mammoth. If I answered and Thomas wasn't here, they might get suspicious. More suspicious. If I let them eat answering machine, they'd still be uncertain. I waited.

The answering machine beeped, and my brother's recorded voice said, 'You know the drill.' It beeped again.

A woman's voice poured out of the answering machine like warm honey. 'Thomas,' she said. She had a polyglot of a European accent, and pronounced his name 'toe-moss,' accent on the second syllable. 'Thomas,' she continued. 'It is Alessandra, and I am desperate for you. Please, I need to see you tonight. I know that there are others, that there are so many others, but I can't stand it anymore, and I must have you.' Her tone lowered, thick with sensuality. 'There is no one, no one else who can do for me what you do. Do not disappoint me, I beg you.' She left her number, and her voice made it sound like foreplay. By the time she hung up, I had begun to feel uncomfortably voyeuristic for listening.

I sighed and told Mouse, 'I so need to get laid.'

At least now I knew what Thomas had been feeding his Hunger. Alessandra and 'so many others' must be supplying him. I felt ... ambiguous about that. He could feed the demonic portion of his nature on many different victims, effectively spreading out the damage he inflicted upon them in a bid to avoid fatally overfeeding upon any one of them. Even so, it meant that there were a number of lives who had been tainted by his embrace, women who had become addicted to the sensation of being fed upon – who were now under his influence, subject to his control.

It was power, of a sort, and power tends to corrupt. Wielding such authority over others would provide a great many temptations. And Thomas had been distant of late. Very distant.

I took a deep breath and said, 'Don't get carried away, Harry. He's your brother. Innocent until proven guilty, right?'

'Right,' I replied to myself.

I decided to leave Thomas a note. I didn't have any paper handy. The stylishly sterile kitchen and living room yielded none – nor did the bedroom. I shook my head, muttering about people who couldn't organize their way out of a paper bag, and checked in the second bedroom.

I flicked on the light, and my heart stopped.

The room looked like the office of Rambo's accountant. There was a desk and computer against one wall. Tables lined two of the other walls. One of them was dedicated to the neatly organized disassembly of a pair of weapons – submachine guns I didn't recognize right away. I did, however, recognize the kit for home-converting the weapons from legal semiautomatics to fully illegal automatics. A second table looked like a workbench, with the necessary tools to modify weapons and custom-assemble ammunition. It would not be difficult to create explosive devices, such as pipe bombs, with what he had there, if the heavy storage containers under the table contained, as I suspected, explosive compounds.

A nasty thought went through my mind: They could just as easily be used to create incendiaries.

One wall was covered with corkboard. There were papers tacked up on it. Maps. Photographs.

I walked over to the photos with heavy, reluctant feet.

There were photos of dead women.

I recognized them all.

The victims.

The photos were those Instamatic kind. They were a little grainy, the images lit by the harsh glare of a flashbulb, but they covered many of the same angles as the police photos. There was one difference, though. The police photos had all been neatly indexed, with small placards with large, printed numbers appearing in each shot, accompanied by a meticulous written diagram recording their relative positions and what they showed, locking the scene down for future reference.

Thomas's photos did not have any such placards.

Which meant that they could only have been taken *before* the police got there.

Holy shit.

What was my brother thinking? Leaving all of this stuff sitting out here like this? Anyone who came by with an only slightly biased point of view would come to the conclusion that he had been at all of those sites before the police. That he was a *killer*. I mean, I was his *brother*, and even I thought that it looked damned peculiar . . .

'Hell's bells,' I sighed to Mouse. 'Can this day get any worse?'

A heavy, confident hand delivered a short series of knocks to the apartment's door. 'Security,' called a man's voice. 'Here with Chicago police. Open the door, please, sir.'

I had only a few seconds to think. If security had called in a cop, they were thinking I might be trouble. If I came off as something suspicious, they'd probably take a look around as a matter of course. If that happened, and they found what was in my brother's war room, I'd be buying us both more kinds of trouble than I could count.

I needed a lie. A really good, really believable lie. I shut the door to Thomas's war room and bedroom and stared around the immaculate, stylish, tracklit living room, trying to think of one. I stared at Dorothy, the Tin Man, the Scarecrow, and the Cowardly Lion, looking for inspiration. Nothing. The Pirate King, with his white shirt manfully open to his waist, didn't give me any ideas either.

And then it hit me. Thomas had already established the lie. He'd used it before, no less — and it was just his style of camouflage, too. All I had to do was play up to it.

'I can't believe I'm about to do this,' I told Mouse.

Then I set my coat and staff aside, took a deep breath, flounced to the door, opened it, and demanded, 'He sent you, didn't he? Don't try to lie to me!'

A patrol cop — God, she looked young — regarded me with a polite, bored expression. 'Um, sir?'

'Thomas!' I snarled, pronouncing it the same way as the woman on the answering machine. 'He's not man enough to have come to meet me himself, is he? He sent his bully boys to do it for him!'

The cop let out a long-suffering breath. 'Sir, please, let's stay calm here.' She turned to the building's security guy, a nervous-looking, balding man in his forties. 'Now, according to building security, you aren't a known resident, but you've entered with a key. It's standard procedure for them to ask a few questions.'

'Questions?' I said. It was hard not to lisp. So hard. But that might have been too much. I settled for saying everything in my Murphy impersonation voice. 'Why don't you start with why he hasn't called me? Hmm? After giving me his spare key? Ask him why he hasn't come to visit the baby!' I pointed an accusatory finger at Mouse. 'Ask him what excuse he has *this* time!'

The cop looked as if she had a headache. She blinked at me once, lifted a hand to her mouth, coughed, and stepped aside, gesturing to the security guy.

He blinked a few times. 'Sir,' the security man said. 'Um, it's just that Mr Raith hasn't actually listed with building security anyone he's given access to his apartment.'

'He'd *better* not have!' I said. 'I have given him years, *years*, and I will not be cast aside like last season's shoes!' I shook my head and told the young cop, in an aside voice, 'Never date a beautiful man. It isn't worth what you have to put up with.'

'Sir,' the security man said. 'I'm sorry to, um, intrude. But part of what our residents pay for is security. May I see your key, please?'

'I can't believe that he never even . . .' I trailed off into a mutter, got the key out of my coat pocket, and showed it to him.

The security guy took it, squinted at it, and checked a number on its back against a list on his clipboard. 'This is one of the resident's original keys,' he confirmed.

'That's right. Thomas gave it to me,' I said.

'I see,' the security man said. 'Um. Would you mind if I saw some photo ID, sir? I'll put a copy in our file, so this won't, um . . . happen again.'

I was going to kill my brother later. 'Of course not, sir,' I assured him, trying to appear mollified and reluctantly willing to be gracious. I got out my wallet and handed him my driver's license. The cop glanced at it as it went by.

'I'll be right back,' he told me, and hustled toward the elevator.

'Sorry about this,' the cop told me. 'They get paid to be a little paranoid.'

'Not your fault, Officer,' I told her.

She regarded me thoughtfully for a moment. 'So, you and the owner are, uh . . .'

'We're *something*.' I sighed. 'You can never get the pretty ones to come out and *say* exactly, can you?'

'Not generally, no,' she said. Her tone of voice stayed steady, her expression mild, but I knew a poker face when I saw one. 'Do you mind if I ask what you're doing here?'

I had to be careful. The young cop wasn't dumb. She thought she smelled a rat.

I gestured forlornly at the dog. 'We were living together in a tiny little place. We got a dog and didn't know he was going to get so big. Thomas was feeling crowded, so he moved into his own place, and . . .' I shrugged and tried to look like Murphy did when talking about her exes. 'We were supposed to switch off every month, but he always had some excuse. He didn't want the dog slobbering around his little neat-freak world.' I gestured at the apartment.

The cop looked around and nodded politely. 'Nice place.' But she hadn't been convinced. Not completely. I saw her putting a few thoughts together, formulating more questions.

Mouse pulled it out of the fire for me. He padded over to the door, looked up at the cop.

'Good lord, he's huge,' the cop said. She leaned slightly away from him.

'Oh, he's a big softie, isn't he,' I crooned to him, and ruffled his ears.

Mouse gave her a big doggy grin, sat, and offered her one of his paws.

She laughed and shook. She let Mouse sniff the back of her hand, and then scratched his ears herself.

'You know dogs,' I said.

'I'm in training for one of the K-9 units,' she confirmed.

'He likes you,' I said. 'That's unusual. He's usually a great big chicken.'

She smiled. 'Oh, I think dogs can tell when someone likes them. They're smarter about that kind of thing than people give them credit for.'

'God knows, that seems to be smarter than *I* can ever manage.' I sighed. 'What kind of dogs do they use at the K-9 units?'

'Oh, it varies a great deal,' she said, and started in on talking about candidates for police dogs. I kept her going with a couple of questions and a lot of interested nodding, and Mouse demonstrated his ability to sit and lie down and roll over. By the time the security guy and his apologetic expression got back, Mouse was sprawled on his back, paws waving languidly in the air, while the cop scratched his tummy and told me a pretty good dog story about her own childhood and an encounter with a prowler.

'Sir,' he said, handing my key and license back and trying not to look like he was carefully not touching me. 'I apologize for the inconvenience, but as you are not a resident here, it is standard procedure for visitors to check in with the security personnel at the entrance when entering or leaving the building.'

'This is just typical of him,' I said. 'Forgetting something like this. I probably should have called ahead and made sure he'd told you.'

'I'm sorry,' he said. 'I hate to inconvenience you. But until we do have that written authorization from Mr Raith that he wishes you to have full access, I need to ask you to leave. I know it's just paperwork, but I'm afraid there's no way around it.'

I sighed. 'Typical. Just typical. And I understand you're just doing your job, sir. Let me go to the bathroom and I'll be right down.'

'Perfectly all right,' he told me. 'Officer.'

The cop stood up from Mouse and gave me a lingering look. Then she nodded, and the pair of them headed back down the hall.

I let Mouse back in, then closed the door most of the way and Listened, narrowing the focus of my attention until nothing existed but sound and silence.

'Are you sure?' the cop asked the security guy.

'Oh, absolutely,' he said. 'Toe-moss,' he said, emphasizing the pronunciation, 'is as queer as a three-dollar bill.'

'He have any other men here?'

'Once or twice,' the man said. 'This tall one is new, but he does have one of the original keys.'

'He could have stolen it,' the cop said.

'An NBA-sized gay burglar who works with a dog?' the security guy replied. 'We'll make sure he's not stealing the fridge when he comes out. If Raith is missing anything, we'll point him right at this guy. We've got him on video, eyewitnesses putting him in the apartment, a copy of his driver's license, for crying out loud.'

'If they're in a relationship,' the cop said, 'how come this Raith guy never cleared his boyfriend?'

'You know how queers are, the way they sleep around,' the security guy said. 'He was just covering his ass.'

'So to speak,' the cop said.

Security guy missed the irony in her tone, and let out a smug chuckle. 'Like I said. We'll watch him.'

'Do that,' the cop said. 'I don't like it, but if you're sure.'

'I don't want a jilted queen making a big scene. No one wants that.'

'Heavens, no,' the cop said, her tone flat.

I eased the door shut and said to Mouse, 'Thank God for bigotry.'

Mouse tilted his head at me.

'Bigots see something they expect and then they stop thinking about what is in front of them,' I told him. 'It's probably how they got to be bigots in the first place.'

Mouse looked unenlightened and undisturbed by it.

'We've only got a couple of minutes if I want them to stay complacent,' I said quietly. I looked around the apartment for a minute. 'No note,' I said. 'Not necessary now.'

I went back to the war room, turned on the light, and stared at the huge corkboard wall with its maps, notes, pictures, and diagrams. There was no time to make sense of it.

I closed my eyes for a moment, lowered certain mental defenses I'd held in place for a considerable while, and cast a thought into the vaults of my mind: *Take a memo.*

Then I stepped up to the wall and scanned my eyes over it, not really stopping to take in any information. I caught glimpses of each photo and piece of paper. It took me maybe a minute. Then I turned the lights back out, gathered my things, and left.

I breezed out of the elevators, stopping at the security guy's desk. He nodded at me and waved me out, and Mouse and I departed the building, secure in our heterosexuality.

Then I went back to my car and headed home to seek counsel from a fallen angel.

I picked up some burgers, four for me and four for Mouse, and went home. I got onion rings, too, but Mouse didn't get any because my class-four hazmat suit was at the cleaners.

Mister, of course, got an onion ring, because he has seniority. He ate some, batted the rest around the kitchen floor for a minute, then mrowled to be let outside for his evening ramble.

By the time I'd eaten it was after ten, and I was entertaining thoughts of putting off more investigation until after a full night's sleep. Pulling all-nighters was getting to be more difficult than it had been when I was twenty and full of what my old mentor Ebenezar McCoy would term 'vinegar.'

Staying awake wasn't the issue: If anything, it was far easier to ignore fatigue and maintain concentration these days. Recovering from it was a different story. I didn't bounce back from sleep deprivation quite as quickly as I used to, and a missed night's sleep tended to make me grouchy for a couple of days while I got caught up. Too, my body was still recovering from way too many injuries suffered in previous cases. If I'd been a normal human being, I'd probably be walking around with a collection of scars, residual pain, and stiff joints, like an NFL lineman at the tail end of an injury-plagued career, or a boxer who had been hit too many times.

But I wasn't normal. Whatever it is that allows me to use magic also gives me a greatly enhanced life span – and an ability to eventually recover from injuries that would, in a normal person, be permanently disabling. That didn't really help me much on an immediate, day-to-day basis, but given what my body's gone through, I'm just as glad that I *could* get better, with enough work and enough time. Losing a hand is bad for anyone. Living for three or four centuries with one hand would, in the words of my generation, blow goats.

Sleep would be nice. But Thomas might need my help. I'd get plenty of sleep when I was dead.

I glanced at my maimed hand, then picked up my old acoustic guitar and sat down on the sofa. I flicked some candles to life and, concentrating on my left hand, began to practice. Simple scales first, then a few other exercises to warm up, then some quiet play. My hand was nowhere close to one hundred percent, but it was a lot better than it had been, and I had finally drilled enough basics into my fingers to allow me to play a little.

Mouse lifted his head and looked at me. He let out a very quiet sigh. Then he heaved himself to his feet from where he'd been sleeping and padded into my bedroom. He nudged the door shut with his nose.

Everybody's a critic.

'Okay, Lash,' I said, and kept playing. 'Let's talk.'

'Lash?' said a quiet woman's voice. 'Do I merit an affectionate nickname now?'

One minute there was no one sitting in the recliner facing the sofa. The next, a woman sat there, poof, just like magic. She was tall, six feet or so, and built like an athlete. Generally, when she appeared to me, she appeared as a healthy-looking young woman with girl-next-door good looks, dressed in a white Greco-Roman tunic that fell to midthigh. Plain leather sandals had covered her feet, their thongs wrapping up around her calves. Her hair color had changed occasionally, but the outfit had remained a constant.

'Given the fact that you're a fallen angel, literally older

than time and capable of thought and action I can't really comprehend, whereas to you I am a mere mortal with a teeny bit more power than most, I thought of it more as a thinly veiled bit of insolence.' I smiled at her. 'Lash.'

She tilted her head back and laughed, to all appearances genuinely amused. 'From you, it is perhaps not as insulting as it might be from another mortal. And, after all, I am not in fact that being. I am only her shadow, her emissary, a figment of your own perception, and a guest within your mind.'

'Guests get invited,' I said. 'You're more like a vacuum cleaner salesman who managed to talk his way inside for a demonstration and just won't leave.'

'Touché, my host,' she admitted. 'Though I would like to think I have been both more helpful and infinitely more courteous than such an individual.'

'Granted,' I said. 'It doesn't change anything about being unwelcome.'

'Then rid yourself of me. Take up the coin, and I will rejoin the rest of myself, whole again. You will be well rid of me.'

I snorted. 'Yeah. Up until Big Sister gets into my head, turns me into her psychotic boy toy, and I wind up a monster like the rest of the Denarians.'

Lasciel, the fallen angel whose full being was currently bound in an old Roman denarius in my basement, held up a mollifying hand. 'Have I not given you sufficient space? Have I not done as you asked, remained silent and still? When is the last time I have intruded, the last time we spoke, my host?'

I hit a bad chord, grimaced, and muted it out. Then I started over. 'New Mexico. And that wasn't by choice.'

'Of course it was,' she said. 'It is always your choice.'

I shook my head. 'I don't speak ghoul. As far as I know, no one does.'

'None of you have ever lived in ancient Sumeria,' Lasciel said.

I ignored her. 'I had to have answers from the ghoul to get those kids back. There was no time for anything else. You were a last resort.'

'And tonight?' she asked. 'Am I a last resort tonight?'

The next couple of chords came out hard and loud. 'It's Thomas.'

She folded her hands in her lap and regarded one of the nearby candles. 'Ah, yes,' she said, more quietly. 'You care for him a great deal.'

'He's my blood,' I said.

'Allow me to rephrase the observation. You care for him to an irrational degree.' She tilted her head and studied me. 'Why?'

I spoke in a slower voice. 'He's my *blood*.'

'I understand your words, but they don't mean anything.'

'They wouldn't,' I said. 'Not to you.'

She frowned at that and looked at me, her expression mildly disturbed. 'I see.'

'No,' I said. 'You don't. You can't.'

Her expression became remote and blank, her gaze returning to the candle. 'Do not be too sure, my host. I, too, had brothers and sisters. Once upon a time.'

I stared at her for a second. God, she sounded sincere. She isn't, Harry, I told myself. She's a liar. She's running a con on you to convince you to like her, or at least trust her. From there, it would be a short commute to the recruiter's office of the Legion of Doom.

I reminded myself very firmly that what the fallen angel offered me – knowledge, power, companionship – would come at too high a price. It was foolish of me to keep falling back on her help, even though what she had done for me had undoubtedly saved both my life and that of many others.

I reminded myself that too much dependence upon her would be a Very, Very Bad Thing.

But she still looked sad.

I concentrated on my music for a moment. It was hard not to experience the occasional fit of empathy for her. The trick was to make sure that I never forgot her true goal — seduction, corruption, the subversion of my free will. The only way to prevent that was to be sure to guard my decisions and actions with detached reason rather than letting my emotions get the better of me. If that happened, it would be easy to play right into the true Lasciel's hands.

Hell, it'd probably be fun.

I shook off that thought and lumbered through 'Every Breath You Take' by the Police and an acoustic version of 'I Will Survive' I'd put together myself. After I finished that, I tried to go through a little piece I'd written that was supposed to sound like classic Spanish guitar while giving me a little exercise therapy on the mostly numb fingers of my left hand. I'd played it a thousand times, and while I had improved, it was still something painful to listen to

Except this time.

This time, I realized halfway in, I was playing flawlessly. I was playing faster than my usual tempo, throwing in a few licks, vibrato, some nifty transitional phrases — and it sounded good. Like, Santana good.

I finished the song and then looked up at Lasciel.

She was watching me steadily.

'Illusion?' I asked her.

She gave a small shake of her head. 'I was merely helping. I . . . can't write original music anymore. I haven't made any music in ages. I just . . . helped the music you heard in your thoughts get out through your fingers. I circumvented some of the damaged nerves. It was all you, otherwise, my host.'

Which was just about the coolest thing Lasciel'd ever done

for me. Don't get me wrong; the survival-oriented things were super – but this was playing guitar. She had helped me to create something of beauty, and it satisfied an urge in me so deep-set and vital that I had never really realized what it was. Somehow, I knew without a hint of a doubt that I would never be able to play that well on my own. Ever again.

Could evil, true capital-E Evil, do such a thing? Help create something whole and lovely and precious?

Careful, Harry. Careful.

'This isn't helping either of us,' I said quietly. 'Thank you, but I'm learning it myself. I'll get there on my own.' I set the guitar down on its little stand. 'Besides, there's work to be done.'

She nodded once. 'Very well. This is regarding Thomas's apartment and its contents?'

'Yes,' I said. 'Can you show them to me?'

Lasciel lifted a hand, and the wall opposite the fireplace changed.

Technically, it hadn't actually changed, but Lasciel, who existed only as an entity of thought hanging around in my head, was able to create illusions of startling, even daunting clarity, even if I was the only one who could perceive them. She could sense the physical world through me – and she carried aeons of knowledge and experience. Her memory and eye for detail were almost entirely flawless.

So she created the illusion of the wall of Thomas's war room and put it over my own wall. It was even lit the same way as in my brother's apartment, every detail, I knew, entirely faithful to what I had seen earlier that night.

I padded over to the wall and started checking it out more thoroughly. My brother's handwriting was all but unreadable, which made the notes he'd scribbled of dubious value in terms of actually enlightening me as to what was going on.

'*My* host——' Lasciel began.

I held up a hand for silence. 'Not yet. Let me look at it unprejudiced first. Then you tell me what you think.'

'As you wish.'

I went over the stuff there for an hour or so, frowning. I had to go check a calendar a couple of times. I got out a notebook and scribbled things down as I worked them out.

'All right,' I said quietly, settling back down on the sofa. 'Thomas was following several people. The dead women and at least a dozen more, in different parts of the city. He had a running surveillance on them. I think he probably hired a private detective or two to cover some of the observation – keeping tabs on where people were going, figuring out the recurring events in their schedules.' I held up the notebook. 'These are the names of the folks he was' – I shrugged – 'stalking, I suppose. My guess is that the other people on this list are among the missing folk the ladies of the Ordo Lebes told us about.'

'Think you Thomas preyed upon them?' Lasciel asked.

I started to deny it, instantly and firmly, but stopped.

Reason. Judgment. Rational thought.

'He could have,' I said quietly. 'But my instincts say it isn't him.'

'Why would it not be?' Lasciel asked me. 'Upon what do you base your reasoning?'

'Upon Thomas,' I said. 'It isn't him. To engage in wholesale murder and abduction? No way. Maybe he fell off the incubus wagon, sure, but he wouldn't inflict any more harm than he had to. It isn't his way.'

'Not his way by choice,' Lasciel said. 'Though I feel I must point out that——'

I cut her off, waving a hand. 'I know. His sister could have gotten involved. She already ate Lord Raith's free will. She could have monkeyed around with Thomas's mind, too.

And if not Lara, then there are plenty of others who might have done it. Thomas could be doing these things against his will. Hell, he might not even remember he's doing them.'

'Or he might be acting of his own volition. He has another point of weakness,' Lasciel said.

'Eh?'

'Lara Raith holds Justine.'

A point I hadn't yet considered. Justine was my brother's . . . well, I don't know if there's a word for what she was to him. But he loved her, and she him. It wasn't their fault that she was slightly insane and he was a life force – devouring creature of the night.

They'd been willing to give up their lives for each other in the midst of a crisis, and the love confirmed by doing so had rendered Justine deadly to my brother, poisonous to him. Love is like that to the White Court, an intolerable agony to them, the way holy water is to other breeds. Someone touched by pure and honest love cannot be fed upon – which had more or less put an end to Thomas's ability to be near Justine.

It was probably just as well. That last time they'd been together had all but killed Justine. The last time I'd seen her, she'd been a wasted, frail, white-haired thing barely capable of stringing sentences together. It had torn my brother apart to see what he had done to her. To my knowledge he hadn't even tried to be a part of her life again. I couldn't blame him.

Lara watched over Justine now, though she could not feed upon the girl any more than Thomas could.

But Lara could cut her throat, if it came to that.

My brother might very well be capable of some unpleasant things in the interests of protecting Justine. Strike that. He *was* capable of anything where the girl was concerned.

Means. Motive. Opportunity. The equation of murder was balanced.

I looked back at the illusory wall, where the pictures, maps, and notes grouped together in a broad band near the top, then descended into fewer notes on the next strip down, and so on, forming a vague V-shape. At the top of the V rested a single, square yellow sticky note.

That note read, in a heavy hand, *Ordo Lebes? Find them.*

'Dammit, Thomas,' I murmured quietly. I addressed Lasciel. 'Get rid of it.'

Lasciel nodded and the illusion disappeared. 'There is something else you should know, my host.'

I eyed her. 'What's that?'

'It may concern your safety and the course of your investigation. May I show you?'

The word *no* came strongly to mind, but I was already in for a penny, so to speak. Lasciel's wealth of intelligence and experience made her an extremely capable adviser. 'Briefly.'

She nodded, rose, and suddenly I was standing in Anna Ash's apartment, as I had been that afternoon.

'My host,' Lasciel said. 'Remember you how many women you observed entering the building?'

I frowned. 'Sure. As many as half a dozen had the right look, though anyone who arrived before Murphy and I got there could have already been inside.'

'Precisely,' Lasciel said. 'Here.'

She waved a hand, and an image of me appeared in the apartment's entry, Murphy at my side.

'Anna Ash,' Lasciel said. She nodded toward me, and Anna's image appeared, facing me. 'Can you describe the others in attendance?'

'Helen Beckitt,' I said. 'Looking leaner and more weathered than the last time I saw her.'

Beckitt's image appeared where she had been standing by the window.

I pointed at the wooden rocking chair. 'Abby and Toto

were there.' The plump blond woman and her dog appeared. I rubbed at my forehead. 'Uh, two on the sofa and one on the love seat.'

Three shadowy forms appeared in the named places.

I pointed at the sofa. 'The pretty one, in the dance leotard, the one worried about time.' She appeared. I pointed at the shadowed figure next to her. 'Bitter, suspicious Priscilla who was not being polite.' The shadowy figure became Priscilla's image.

'And there you go,' I said.

Lasciel shook her head, waved her hand, and the people images all vanished.

All except the shadowy figure sitting on the love seat.

I blinked.

'What can you remember about this one?' Lasciel asked me.

I racked my brain. It's usually good for this kind of thing. 'Nothing,' I said after a moment. 'Not one damned detail. Nothing.' I added two and two together and got trouble. 'Someone was under a veil. Someone good enough to make it subtle. Hard to tell it was there at all. Not invisible so much as extremely boring and unremarkable.'

'In your favor,' Lasciel said, 'I should point out that you had crossed the threshold uninvited, and thus were deprived of much of your power. In such a circumstance it would be most difficult for you to sense a veil at all, much less to pierce it.'

I nodded, frowning at the shadowy figure. 'It was deliberate,' I said. 'Anna goaded me into walking over the threshold on purpose. She was hiding Miss Mystery from me.'

'Entirely possible,' Lasciel concurred. 'Or . . .'

'Or *they* didn't know someone was there, either,' I said. 'And if that's the case . . .' I tossed the notebook aside with a growl and rose.

'What are you doing?' she asked.

I got my staff and coat, and got Mouse ready to go. 'If the mystery guest was news to the Ordo, she's right in among them and they could be in danger. If the Ordo knew about her, then they played me and lied to me.' I ripped open the door with more than my usual effort. 'Either way, I'm going over there to straighten some things out.'

I swept the Beetle for bombs again and got the impression that I was going to get heartily sick of the chore, fast. It was clean, and off we went.

I parked illegally on a street about a block from Anna Ash's apartment, and walked the rest of the way in. I rang buzzers more or less at random until someone buzzed me in, and headed back up the stairs to Anna's apartment.

This time, though, I went in armed for bear. As I rode up in the elevator, I got out my jar of unguent, a dark brown concoction that stained the skin for a couple of days. I dabbed a finger in it and smeared it lightly onto my eyelids and at the base of my eyes. It was an ointment originally intended to counter faerie glamour, allowing those who had it to see through illusion to reality. It wasn't quite right for seeing through a veil wrought with mortal magic, but it should be strong enough to show me *something* of whatever the veil was hiding. I should be able to glimpse any motion, and that would at least give me an idea of which way to face if things got dicey.

I brought Mouse for a reason, too. Besides being a small mountain of loyal muscle and ferocious fangs, Mouse could sense bad guys and dark magic when they were nearby. I had yet to encounter the creature that could sneak by Mouse unobserved, but just in case today was the day, I had the unguent as a backup plan.

I got off the elevator, and the hairs on the back of my neck immediately rose up. Mouse lifted his head sharply, looking back and forth down the hall. He'd felt what I had.

A fine cloud of magic hung over the entire floor.

I touched it carefully and found a suggestion of sleep — one of the classics, really. This one wasn't heavy, as such things go. I'd seen one sleep spell that flattened an entire ward of Cook County Hospital. I'd used another to protect Murphy's sanity, and it had kept her out for nearly two days.

This one wasn't like that. It was light, barely noticeable, and not at all threatening. It was delicate and fine enough to filter into homes even through their thresholds — most of which were weak enough: Apartments never seemed to have as much defense as a real, discrete home. If those other spells had been sleeping medication, this one would have been a glass of warm milk. Someone wanted the residents of the floor to be insensible enough not to notice something, but not so out as to be endangered should there be an emergency, like the building catching fire and burning down.

Don't look at me like that. It's a lot likelier than you'd think.

Anyway, the suggestion was another finely crafted spell: delicate, precise, subtle, much like the earlier veil Lasciel had spotted: Whoever or whatever was crafting these workings was a pro.

I made sure my shield bracelet was ready to go, and marched up to Anna's door. I could sense the ward there, still active, so I thumped my staff on the floor immediately in front of the door. 'Ms Ash?' I called. It wasn't like I was going to wake anyone up. 'It's Harry Dresden. We need to talk.'

There was silence. I repeated myself. I heard a sound, that of someone striving to move silently, a scuff or a creak so faint that I wasn't sure it had been real. I checked Mouse. His ears were pricked up, swiveled forward. He'd heard it too.

Someone flushed a toilet on the floor above us. I heard a

door open and close, a faint sound, also on another floor. There was no further sound from Anna Ash's apartment.

I didn't like where this was going at all.

'Stand back, buddy,' I told Mouse. He did, backing away in that clumsy reverse waddle-walk dogs do.

I turned to the ward. It was like the little pig's straw house. It wouldn't last more than a second or two against a big bad wolf. 'And I'll huff and I'll puff,' I muttered. I drew up my will, took the staff in both hands, and pressed one end slowly toward the door. '*Solvos*,' I murmured. '*Solvos. Solvos.*'

As the staff touched the door, I sent a gentle surge of will coursing down through its length. It passed through the wood visibly, the carved runes in it briefly illuminated from within by pale blue light. My will hit Anna's door and scattered out in a cloud of pinprick sparkles of white light as my power unbound the patterns of the ward and reduced them to mere anarchy.

'Anna?' I called again. 'Ms Ash?'

No answer.

I tried the doorknob. It was unlocked.

'That can't be good,' I told Mouse. 'Here we go.' I quietly opened the door, giving it a gentle push so that it would swing wide and let me see inside the darkened apartment.

At which point the trap sprang.

For traps to work, though, they need to catch their target off his guard.

I had my new and improved shield bracelet ready when greenish light flashed in the dark apartment and rushed swiftly toward me. I lifted my left hand. Bound around my wrist was a chain made of braided strands of several metals, silver predominant. The metal shields that hung from the bracelet had, in its previous incarnation, been solid silver as well. They had been replaced with shields of silver, iron, copper, nickel, and brass.

The new shield wasn't like the old one. The old one had provided an intangible barrier meant to deflect solid matter and kinetic energy. It hadn't been made to stop, for example, heat. That's how my left hand got roasted practically down to the bones. It had been of only limited use against other forms of magic or energy.

If there hadn't been a war on, and if I hadn't been spending so much time drilling Molly in the fundamentals – and therefore getting in all kinds of extra practice, myself – I would never have considered attempting to create such a complex focus. It was far more complicated than almost anything I'd done before. Five years ago, it would have been beyond me completely. More to the point, five years ago, I wouldn't have been as experienced or as strongly motivated.

But that was then, and this was now.

The shield that formed in front of me was not the familiar, translucent part-dome of pale blue light. Instead it flared into place in a blurring swirl of colors that solidified in an instant into a curving rampart of silver energy. The new shield was far more thorough than the old. Not only would it stop everything the old one had, but it would provide shelter against heat, cold, electricity – even sound and light, if I needed it to. It had also been designed to turn aside a fairly broad spectrum of supernatural energies. It was this last that was important at the moment.

A globe of green lightning sizzled over the apartment's threshold and abruptly expanded, buzzing arcs of verdant electricity interconnected in a diamond pattern like the weave of a fisherman's net.

The spell fell on my shield and the meeting of energies yielded a torrent of angry yellow sparks that rebounded from the shield, scattering over the hall, the doorway, and bouncing back into the apartment.

I dropped the shield as I brandished my staff, sent a savage torrent of power down my arm, and snarled, '*Forzare!*'

Unseen force lashed through the doorway – and splashed against the apartment's threshold. Most of the spell's power struck that barrier, grounded out, and was dissipated. What amounted to less than a percent of the power I had cast out actually made it through the doorway, as I had known it would. Instead of delivering a surge of energy strong enough to flip over a car, I delivered only a blow strong enough to knock an adult from her feet.

I heard a woman's voice let out a surprised grunt at the impact, and heavy objects clattered to the floor.

'Mouse!' I shouted.

The big dog bounded forward through the doorway, and I went in right behind him. Once again, the apartment's threshold stripped away my power, leaving me all but utterly unable to wield magic.

Which is why I'd brought my .44 revolver with me, tucked into a duster pocket. I had it in my left hand as I came through the door and hit the main light switch with my right elbow, bellowing, 'I have *not* had a very good day!'

Mouse had someone pinned on the ground, and kept them there by virtue of simply *sitting* on them. Two hundred pounds of Mouse is an awfully effective restraint, and though he had his teeth bared, he wasn't actively struggling or making any noise.

To my right, Anna Ash stood frozen like a rabbit in a spotlight, and my gun tracked to her immediately. 'Don't move,' I warned her. 'I don't have any magic at the moment, and that always makes me really, really ready to pull the trigger.'

'Oh, God,' she said, her voice a rough whisper. She licked her lips, visibly trembling. 'Okay,' she said. 'Okay. D-don't hurt me, please. You don't have to do this.'

I told her to walk over to Mouse and his prisoner. Once she was standing where I could watch both of them at once, I could relax a little, and though I did not lower the gun, I took my finger off the trigger. 'Do what?'

'What you've done to the others,' Anna said, her voice thready. 'You don't have to do this. Not to anyone.'

'The others?' I demanded. I probably sounded at least half as disgusted as I felt. 'You think I came here to *kill* you?'

She blinked at me a few times. Then she said, 'You came here, broke down my door, and pointed a gun at me. What am I *supposed* to think?'

'I did *not* break down your door! It was unlocked!'

'You tore apart my ward!'

'Because I thought you might be in *trouble*, you twit!' I hollered. 'I thought the killer might be here already.'

A woman let out a couple of choking gasps. After a moment, I realized that it was the person Mouse had pinned down, letting out breathless laughter.

I lowered the gun and put it away. 'For crying out loud. You thought the killer was coming for you? So you laid a trap for him?'

'Well, no,' Anna said, now looking somewhat confused again. 'I mean, I didn't do it. The Ordo . . . we hired a private investigator to look into it. It was her idea to trap the killer when he came here.'

'A private investigator?' I looked over at the other woman and said, 'Mouse.'

My dog, tail waving gently, backed off right away and trotted over to stand beside me. The woman he'd been holding down sat up.

She was pale — not the sickly pallor of no time in the sun, but the color of the living, healthy skin of a tree beneath the outer bark. Her lean face was intensely attractive — more intriguing than beautiful, with wide, intelligent eyes set over an expressive, generous mouth. She had a slim build, all long legs and long arms, and wore a simple pair of jeans along with a black Aerosmith T-shirt, and brown leather Birkenstocks. She propped herself up on her elbows, a tendril of wheat-colored hair falling to almost insolently conceal one eye, and gave me a wry smile.

'Hello, Harry.' She dabbed her fingers at a little bloody spot on her lower lip and winced, though there was still amusement in her voice. 'Is that a new staff, or are you just happy to see me?'

And after my heart had skipped a couple of beats, I blinked and said, in a very quiet voice, to the first woman I'd ever everythinged, 'Hello, Elaine.'

11

I sat on the love seat while Anna Ash made coffee. Mouse, ever hopeful to cadge a snack, followed Anna into the kitchen, and sat there giving her his most pathetic, starving-doggy body language and wagging his tail.

We sat down together with coffee, like civilized people, a few minutes later.

'Ms Ash,' I said, taking my cup.

'Anna, please.'

I nodded to her. 'Anna. First, I wish to apologize for frightening you. It wasn't my intention.'

She sipped her coffee, frowning at me, and then nodded. 'I suppose I can understand your motivations.'

'Thank you,' I said. 'I'm sorry I blew up your ward. I'll be glad to replace it for you.'

'We put a lot of hours in on that thing.' Anna sighed. 'I mean, I know it wasn't . . . expert work.'

'We?' I asked.

'The Ordo,' she said. 'We worked together to protect everyone's home.'

'Community project. Sort of a barn raising,' I said.

She nodded. 'That's the idea.' She bit her lip. 'But there were more of us, when we did that.'

For just a second, the capable exterior wavered, and Anna looked very tired and very frightened. I felt a little pang inside at the sight. Real fright isn't like the movies. Real fear is an ugly, quiet, relentless thing. It's a kind of pain, and I hated seeing it on Anna's face.

I found Elaine watching me, her eyes thoughtful. She sat

on the sofa, leaning forward so that her elbows rested on her spread knees. She held her cup in one hand at a slight, negligent angle. On anyone else, it would have looked masculine. On Elaine, it only looked relaxed, strong, and confident.

'He truly meant you no harm, Anna,' she said, turning to our host. 'He's got this psychosis about charging to the rescue. I always thought it gave him a certain hapless charm.'

'I think we should focus on the future, for the time being,' I said. 'I think we need to pool our information and try to work together on this.'

Anna and Elaine exchanged a long look. Anna glanced at me again and asked Elaine, 'Are you sure?'

Elaine gave a single, firm nod. 'He isn't the one trying to hurt you. I'm sure now.'

'Sure *now*?' I said. 'Is that why you veiled yourself when I was here earlier?'

Elaine's fine eyebrows lifted. 'You didn't sense it when you were here. How did you know?'

I shrugged. 'Maybe a little bird told me. Do you really think I'm capable of something like that?'

'No,' Elaine said. 'But I had to be sure.'

'You know me better than that,' I said, unable to keep a little heat out of my voice.

'I trust you,' Elaine said, without a trace of apology in her tone, 'but it might not have *been* you, Harry. It could have been an impostor. Or you could have been acting under some form of coercion. People's lives were at stake. I had to *know*.'

I wanted to snarl back at her that if she so much as *thought* I might be the killer, she didn't know me at all. If that's how it was going to be, I might as well get up and walk right out of the apartment before—

And then I sighed.

Ah, sweet bird of irony.

'You were obviously expecting the killer to show up,' I said to Anna. 'The sleeping spell. The ambush. What made you think he might be coming?'

'Me,' Elaine said.

'And what made *you* think that?'

She gave me a dazzling, innocent smile and imitated my tone and inflection. 'Maybe a little bird told me.'

I snorted.

Anna's eyes suddenly widened. 'You two were together.' She turned to Elaine. 'That's how you know him.'

'It was a long time ago,' I said.

Elaine winked at me. 'But you never really forget your first.'

'You never forget your first train wreck, either.'

'Train wrecks are exciting. Fun, even,' Elaine said. She kept smiling, though her eyes turned a little sad. 'Right up until the very last part.'

I felt half a smile tug up one side of my mouth. 'True,' I said. 'But I'd appreciate it if you wouldn't try to dodge questions by throwing up a smoke screen of nostalgia.'

Elaine took a long sip of coffee and shrugged a shoulder. 'I'll show you mine if you'll show me yours.'

I folded my arms, frowning. 'Sixty seconds ago, you said that you trusted me.'

She arched an eyebrow. 'Trust is a two-way street, Harry.'

I leaned back, took another sip of coffee, and said, 'Maybe you're right. I put it together after the fact, when I was making notes of our conversation. I couldn't remember noticing anything about the woman on the love seat, which doesn't happen to me. So I figured it must have been a veil, and came over here because it was possible that who ever was under it was a threat to the Ordo.'

Elaine pursed her lips, frowning for a moment. 'I see.'

'Your turn.'

She nodded. 'I've been working out of L.A., taking a lot of cases referred my way – like this one. And Chicago isn't the first city where this has happened.'

I blinked at her. 'What?'

'San Diego, San Jose, Austin, and Seattle. Over the past year, members of a number of small organizations like the Ordo Lebes have been systematically stalked and murdered. Most of them have appeared to be suicides. Counting Chicago, the killer's taken thirty-six victims.'

'Thirty-six . . .' I ran my thumb over the handle of the coffee cup, frowning. 'I haven't heard a word about this. Nothing. A *year*?'

Elaine nodded. 'Harry, I've got to know. Is it possible that the Wardens are involved?'

'No,' I said, my tone firm. 'No way.'

'Because they're such easygoing, tolerant people?' she asked.

'No. Because I know Ramirez, the regional commander for most of those cities. He wouldn't be a part of something like that.' I shook my head. 'Besides, we've got a manpower shortage. The Wardens are stretched pretty thin. And there's no *reason* for them to go around killing people.'

'You're sure about Ramirez,' Elaine said. 'Can you say the same about *every* Warden?'

'Why?'

'Because,' Elaine said, 'in every single one of those cities, a man in a grey cloak was seen with at least two of the victims.'

Uh-oh.

I put the coffee cup down on an end table and folded my arms, thinking.

It wasn't general knowledge, but someone on the Council was leaking information to the vamps on a regular and devastating basis. The traitor still had not been caught. Even

worse, I had seen evidence that there was another organization at work behind the scenes, manipulating events on a
scale large enough to indicate a powerful, well-funded, and
frighteningly capable group – and that at least some of them
were wizards. I had dubbed them the Black Council, because
it was obvious, and I'd been keeping my ear to the ground
for indications of their presence.

And look. I found one.

'Which explains why I hadn't heard anything about it,'
I said. 'If everyone thinks the Wardens are responsible, there's
not a prayer they'd draw attention to themselves by reporting
what was happening and asking for help. Or call in a gumshoe
who happens to be a Warden, himself.'

Elaine nodded. 'Right. I started getting called in about
a month after I got my own license and opened my business.'

I grunted. 'How'd they know to call you?'

She smiled. 'I'm in the book under "Wizards."'

I snorted. 'I knew you were copying my test answers all
those years.'

'If it ain't broke, don't fix it.' She pulled a strand of hair
back behind one ear, an old and familiar gesture that brought
with it a pang of remembered desire and a dozen little
memories. 'Most of the business has come in on referral,
though, because I do good work. In any case, one fact about
the killer's victims was almost always the same: people who
lived alone or were isolated.'

'And I,' Anna said quietly, 'am the last living member of
the Ordo who lives alone or were isolated.'

'These other cities,' I said. 'Did the killer leave anything
behind? Messages? Taunts?'

'Like what?' Elaine asked.

'Bible verses,' I said. 'Left in traces, something only one
of us would recognize.'

She shook her head. 'No. Nothing like that. Or if there was, I never found it.'

I exhaled slowly. 'So far, two of the deaths here have had messages left behind. Your friend Janine and a woman named Jessica Blanche.'

Elaine looked unhappy. 'I gathered, from what you said earlier. It doesn't make any sense.'

'Yes, it does,' I said. 'We just don't know why.' I frowned. 'Could any of the other deaths be attributed to the White Court?'

Elaine rose, looking thoughtful. She took her coffee cup to the kitchen and came back, a pensive frown on her brow. 'I . . . can't be certain they haven't, I suppose. I certainly haven't seen anything to suggest it. Why?'

'Excuse me,' Anna said, her voice quiet and unsure. 'White Court?'

'The White Court of vampires,' I clarified.

'There's more than one kind?' she asked.

'Yeah,' I said. 'The Red Court are the ones the White Council is fighting now. They're these bat-monster things that can look human. Drink blood. The White Court are more like people. They're psychic parasites. They seduce their victims and feed on human life energy.'

Elaine nodded. 'But why did you ask me about them, Harry?'

I took a deep breath. 'I found something to suggest that Jessica Blanche may have died as the result of being fed upon by some kind of sexual predator.'

Elaine stared at me for a moment and then said, 'The pattern's been broken. Something's changed.'

I nodded. 'There's something else involved in the equation.'

'Or someone.'

'Or someone,' I said.

She frowned. 'There's one place to start looking.'

'Jessica Blanche,' I said.

Without warning, Mouse came to his feet, facing the door to the apartment, and let out a bubbling basso growl.

I rose, acutely conscious of the fact that my power was still interdicted by the apartment's threshold, and that I didn't have enough magic to spell my way out of a paper bag.

The lights went out. Mouse continued to growl.

'Oh, God,' Anna said. 'What's happening?'

I clenched my teeth and closed my eyes, waiting for them to adjust to the sudden darkness, when a very slight, acrid scent tickled my nose.

'You smell that?' I asked.

Elaine's voice was steady, calm. 'Smell what?'

'Smoke,' I said. 'We've got to get out of here. I think the building's on fire.'

12

'Light,' I said.

Almost before I was finished saying the word, Elaine murmured quietly, and the pentacle amulet she wore, nearly a twin to mine, began to glow with a green-white light. She held it overhead by its silver chain.

By its light, I crossed to the door and felt it, like those cartoons when I was little said you were supposed to do. It felt like a door. 'No fire in the hall,' I said.

'Fire stairs,' Elaine said.

'They're not far,' Anna said.

Mouse continued staring at the door, growling in a low and steady rumble. The smoke smell had thickened.

'Something's waiting for us in the hall.'

'What?' Anna said.

Elaine looked from Mouse to me and bit her lip. 'Window?'

My heart was skipping along too fast. I don't like fire. I don't like getting burned. It hurts and it's ugly. 'Might be able to handle the fall,' I said, forcing myself to breathe slowly, evenly. 'But there's a building full of people here, and none of the alarms or sprinklers have gone off. Someone must have hexed them. We've got to warn the residents.'

Mouse's head whipped around and he stared intently at me for a second. Then he trotted in a little circle, shook his head, made a couple of chuffing sounds, and started doing something I hadn't heard him do since he was a puppy small enough to fit in my duster pocket.

He barked.

Loud. Steady. *WOOF, WOOF, WOOF,* with the mechanical regularity of a metronome.

Now, saying he was barking might give you the general shape of things, but it doesn't convey the scale. Everyone in Chicago knows what a storm-warning siren sounds like. They're spread liberally through the Midwestern states that comprise Tornado Alley. They make your usual warning siren sound. But I had an apartment about thirty yards from one of them once upon a time, and take it from me, that sound is a whole different thing when you're *next* to it. It isn't an ululating wail. When you're that close to the source, it's a tangible flood, a solid, living, sonic cascade that rattles your brain against your skull.

Mouse's bark was like that – but on several levels. Every time he barked, I swear to you, several of my muscles tightened and twitched as if hit with a miniature jolt of adrenaline. I couldn't have slept through half as much racket, even without the odd little jabs of energy that hit me like separate charges of electricity with each bark. It was deafening in the little apartment, nearly as loud as gunfire. He let out twelve painfully loud barks, and then stopped. My ears rang in the sudden silence that followed.

Within seconds I began to hear thumping sounds on the floor above me, bare feet swinging out of beds and landing hard on the floor, almost in unison, like something you'd expect in a training barracks. Someone shouted in the apartment neighboring Anna's. Other dogs started barking. Children started crying. Doors started slamming open.

Mouse sat down again, his head tilting this way and that, ears twitching at each new noise.

'Hell's bells, Harry,' Elaine breathed, her eyes wide. 'Is that . . . ? Where did you get a *real* Temple Dog?'

'Uh. A place kind of like this, now that you mention it.' I gave Mouse's ears a quick ruffling and said, 'Good dog.'

Mouse wagged his tail at me and grinned at the praise.

I opened the door with the hand that wasn't holding a gun, and took a quick look around in the hall. Flashlights were bobbing and sweeping from several places, each one producing a visible beam in the thickening pall of smoke. People were screaming, 'Fire, fire, get everybody out!'

The hallway was in chaos. I couldn't see if anyone out there looked like a lurking menace, but odds were good that if I couldn't see them, they wouldn't see me, either, in all the milling confusion of hundreds of people fleeing the building.

'Anna, where are the fire stairs?'

'Um. Where everyone's *running*,' Anna said. 'To the right.'

'Right,' I said. 'Okay, here's the plan. We follow all the other flammable people out of the building before we burn to death.'

'Whoever did this is going to be waiting for us outside,' Elaine warned.

'Not a very private place for a murder anymore,' I said. 'But we'll be careful. Me and Mouse first. Anna, you right behind us. Elaine, cover our backside.'

'Shields?' she asked me.

'Yeah. Can you do your half?'

She arched an eyebrow at me.

'Right,' I said. 'What was I thinking?' I took Mouse's lead in one hand, glanced at my staff, and then said, 'We're working on the honor system, here.' Mouse calmly opened his mouth and held on to his own lead. I picked up my staff in my right hand, kept the gun in the other, and slipped it into my duster's pocket to conceal the weapon. 'Anna, keep your hand on my shoulder.' I felt her grab on to the mantle of my duster. 'Good. Mouse.'

Mouse and I hit the hallway with Anna right on my heels. We fled. I'm not too manly to admit it. We scampered.

Retreated. Vamoosed. Amscrayed. Burning buildings are freaking terrifying, and I should know.

This was the first time I'd been in one quite this occupied, though, and I expected more panic than I sensed around us. Maybe it was the way Mouse had woken everyone. I saw no one stumbling along the way they would if they had been suddenly roused from deep sleep. Everyone was bright eyed and bushy tailed, metaphorically speaking, and while they were clearly afraid, the fear was aiding the evacuation, not hindering it.

The smoke got thicker as we went down one flight of stairs, then another. It started getting hard to breathe, and I was choking on it as we descended. I began to panic. It's the smoke that kills most people, long before the fire ever gets to them. But there seemed little to do but press on.

Then we were through the smoke. The fire had begun three floors below Anna's apartment, and the fire door to that floor was simply missing from its hinges. Black smoke rolled thickly out of the hall beyond it. We had made it down through the smoke, but there were four floors above ours, and the smoke was being drawn up the stairs like they were an enormous chimney. The people still above us would be blinded by it, unable to breathe, and God only knew what would happen to them.

'Elaine!' I choked out.

'Got it!' she called back, coughing – and then she was beside the doorway, black smoke trying to envelop her. She extended her right hand in a gesture that somehow managed to be imperious, and the smoke abruptly vanished.

Well, not exactly. There was a faint shimmer of light over the open doorway, and on the other side of it the smoke roiled and billowed as if pressing up against glass. The acoustics of the stairway altered, the chewing roar of fire suddenly muted, the sound of footsteps and panting people becoming louder.

Elaine examined the field over the doorway for a moment, nodded once, and turned to catch up with us, her manner brisk and businesslike.

'You need to stay to let anyone through?' I asked her. Mouse leaned against my legs, clearly afraid and eager to leave the building.

She held up a hand to silence me. After a moment she said, 'No. Permeable to the living. Concentrating. We have a minute, maybe two.'

Permeable? Holy moly. I could never have managed that on the fly. But then, Elaine always was more skilled than me when it came to the complex stuff. 'Right,' I said. I took her hand, plopped it down on Anna's shoulder, and said, 'Move, come on.'

After that, it was nothing but stairs, bobbing flashlights, echoing voices, and footsteps. I run. Not because it's good for me, even though it is, but because I want to be able to run whenever something's chasing me. It did me a limited amount of good, given that I was spending half of my time coughing on the still-present smoke, but I at least had enough presence of mind to keep an eye on Anna and the distracted Elaine, as well as making sure that I didn't trip over Mouse or get trampled from behind.

When we got to the second floor, I prepped my shield and called over my shoulder, 'Elaine!'

She let out a gasping breath, her head bowing forward. She wavered and clutched at the stair's handrail. Anna moved at once to support her and keep her moving. There was a crashing, roaring sound above us, and cries of fright came down the stairs.

'Move, move,' I told them. 'Elaine, be ready to shield.'

She nodded once and twisted a simple silver ring on her left forefinger around, revealing a kite-shaped shield device not unlike one of my own charms.

We went down the last flight of stairs and hit the door to the street.

Outside, it was not dark. Though the streetlight beside the building was out, the others on the street worked just fine. Added to that was the fire from the burning apartment. It wasn't blinding or anything, since you could see it only through windows, and whenever one of those was open or broken it tended to billow black smoke. I could see clearly, though.

People came hustling out of the building, all coughing. Someone outside the building – or with a cell phone – must have called in the fire, because an impressive number of emergency vehicle sirens were drawing nigh. The escapees filed across the street, for the most part, getting to what seemed a safe distance and turning back to look at their homes. They were in various states of dishabille, including one rather generously appointed young lady wearing a set of red satin sheets and dangling a pair of six-inch heels from one hand. The young man with her, with a red silk bathrobe belted kiltlike around his waist, looked understandably frustrated.

I noticed only because, as a professional investigator, I have trained myself to be a keen observer.

That's why, as I looked around the rest of the crowd to see if red satin sheets and spike heels were becoming a new fad, and if maybe I should have some on hand, just in case, I saw the tall man in the grey cloak.

He was shadowed by the headlights of fire trucks coming down the street toward us, but I saw the sway of the grey cloak. As if he'd sensed my attention, he turned. I got nothing useful out of his silhouette for identifying him.

I guess the grey-cloaked man didn't know that. He froze for a full second, facing me, and then turned and sprinted around the corner.

'Mouse!' I snapped. 'Stay with Anna!'

Then I took off after Grey Cloak.

Thoughtlessly running headlong after someone alone, at night, in Chicago, is not generally a bright idea.

'This is stupid,' I panted to myself. 'Harry, you jackass, this is how you keep getting yourself into trouble.'

Grey Cloak moved with the long, almost floating stride of an athlete running the mile and turned into an alley, where the shadows grew thicker and where we would be out of sight of any of the cops or emergency response people.

I had to think about this. I needed to figure out what he was doing.

Okay, so I'm Grey Cloak. I want to gack Anna Ash, so I start a fire – no, wait. So I use one of the incendiary devices like the one in Murphy's Saturn, put it on a kitchen timer a couple of floors below Anna's place, cut the building's power, phones, and alarms, and set the whole shebang on fire, boom. Then I wait outside Anna's door for her to emerge in a panic, so that I can murder her, leave, and let the evidence burn in the subsequent inferno. Now it all looks like an accident.

Only I don't expect Anna to have a pair of world-class wizards on hand, and I sure as hell never saw Mouse coming. The dog barks and all of a sudden the hall is full of people who can witness the murder, and there's no way to make it look accidental. Someone is almost certain to contact the authorities and send in the whirling lights within a few moments, and there goes my whole evening. No use trying to complete a subtle hit now.

So what do I do?

I don't want attention, that's for sure, or I wouldn't be trying so hard to make this murder look like an accident. I'm cautious, smart, and patient, or I wouldn't have gotten away with it in four other cities. I do what a smart predator does when a stalk goes sour.

I bug out.

I've got a car nearby, a getaway vehicle.

Grey Cloak reached the end of the alley and turned left with me about twenty feet behind him. Then he rounded a corner and sprinted into a parking garage.

I did not follow him.

See, since I'm such a competent and methodical killer, I assume the worst — that anyone in pursuit will display just as much intelligence and resourcefulness. So what I do is pull the chase into the parking garage, where there's lots of angles that will break line of sight — but my getaway car isn't parked there. There's no way I'm going to wait around to pay the attendant, and smashing my way out would attract the attention I'm trying to avoid. The plan is to lose a pursuer in the ample shadows, ramps, doorways, and parked cars in the maze of the garage, and go to my car once I've given him the slip.

I kept sprinting down the street and rounded a corner. Then I stopped, crouched and ready to continue running. The far side of the garage had no parking places; nor did the alley. So Grey Cloak's car had to be either on the street in front of the garage, or on the street along its side. From that corner, I could watch both.

I hunkered down beside a city trash can and hoped that I was as clever as I seemed to think I was. I was pretty sure it would have been at best stupid and at worst lethal to pursue Grey Cloak into the dark of the parking garage. I might have one hell of a punch, but I was as fragile as the next person, and cornering Grey Cloak might draw out the savagery of desperation. If I slipped up, and he got too close to me, he might drop me like a pair of dirty socks.

Always assuming, of course, that he wasn't an *actual* Warden, in which case he might well hit me with lightning or fire or any number of other nasty attacks of choice. That was a thought I found more than a little . . . comfortable, really.

I'd spent most of my adult life living in fear of the Council's Wardens. They'd been my persecutors, my personal furies, and despite the fact that I'd become one, I felt an almost childish glee in the notion that a Warden might be my bad guy. It would give me a perfect opportunity to lay out some long-deserved payback with perfect justification.

Unless, of course, it was a Warden doing it under orders. Once upon a time, I'd have told you that the White Council was made up of basically decent people who valued human life. Now, I knew better. The Council broke the Laws when it saw fit to do so. It executed children who, in their ignorance, violated those same laws. The war, too, had made the Council desperate, more willing to take chances and 'make hard decisions' that amounted to other people getting killed while the Council's bony collective ass stayed as covered as possible.

It didn't seem reasonable to think that a legitimate Warden could have sunk to such measures, or that Captain Luccio, the Wardens' commander, would condone it – but I've gotten used to being disappointed in the honor and sincerity of the Council in general, and the Wardens in particular. For that matter, I probably shouldn't expect too much rationality out of Grey Cloak, either. My scenario to predict his behavior was plausible, rational, but a rational person wouldn't be going around murdering people and making it look like suicide, would he? I was probably wasting my time.

A shadowy figure vaulted from the roof of the parking

garage and dropped six stories to the ground, landing on the sidewalk in a crouch. Grey Cloak was still for a second, maybe listening, and then rose and began to walk, quickly but calmly, toward the street and the cars parked along it.

I blinked.

Son of a gun.

I guess sometimes logic *does* work.

I clenched my teeth, gripped my staff, and rose to confront Grey Cloak and blow him straight to hell.

And stopped.

If Grey Cloak truly was part of the Black Council, working to undermine the White Council and generally do whatever largescale badness they intended to do, blowing him to hell might not be the smart thing to do. The Black Council had been, if you will pardon the phrasing, a phantom menace. I was sure that they were up to no good, and their methods thus far seemed to indicate that they had no inhibitions about the ending of innocent lives — reinforced by Grey Cloak's willingness to burn a building full of people to death to cover up the murder of a single target. It fit their pattern: shadowy, nebulous, leaving no direct, obvious evidence of who they were or what they wanted.

If they existed at all, that is. So far, they were just a theory.

Then again, Grey Cloak's getaway car had been just a theory, too.

This could be a chance to gain badly needed intelligence on the Black Council. Knowledge is the ultimate weapon. It always has been.

I could let Grey Cloak go and tail him to see what I could learn before I brought the hammer down. Maybe he'd lead me to something vital, something as critical as Enigma had been to the Allies in WWII. On the other hand, maybe he'd lead me back to nothing. No covert organization worth its salt would allow an operative into the field without planning for the contingency of said operative being compromised. Hell, even if Grey Cloak volunteered everything he knew, there would almost certainly be cutouts in place.

All of which assumed he really *was* part of the Black Council. A big assumption. And when you assume, you make an ass out of you and umption. If I didn't stop him while I had the chance, Grey Cloak would strike again. More people would die.

Yeah, Harry. And how many *more* people will die if the Black Council keeps rising to power?

Dammit. My gut told me to drop Grey Cloak right now. The faces from police photos flickered through my thoughts, and in my imagination the slain women stood beside me, behind me, their glassy, dead eyes intent upon their killer and their desire to be avenged. I longed with an almost apocalyptic passion to step into the open and lay waste to this murdering asshole.

But reason told me otherwise. Reason told me to slow down, think, and consider how to do the most good for the most people.

Hadn't I been telling myself only hours ago that reason had to guide my actions, my decisions, if I was to keep control of myself?

It was hard. It was really, really hard. But I fought off the adrenaline and lust for a fight, and hunkered back down, thinking furiously, while Grey Cloak got into a green sedan, started it, and pulled out onto the street. I crouched between two parked cars and waited, out of sight, until Grey Cloak drove by me.

I pointed the end of my staff at the car's back panel, gathered my will, and whispered, '*Forzare.*' Raw force lanced out, focused into the tiniest area I could envision, and struck the car with a little pop no louder than that produced by stray bits of gravel tossed up against the vehicle's undercarriage.

The car went by without slowing, and I got the license number as it left.

Once it was gone, I murmured, '*Tractis*,' keeping my will focused on the staff, and drew it back until I could rise into the light of a street lamp and peer at the end of the length of oak.

A fleck of green paint, half the size of a dime, had adhered to the end of the staff. I licked my fingertip and pressed it to the paint, lifting it off the staff. I had a small box of water-proof matches in one pocket of the duster. I opened it with one hand, dumped the matches, and then carefully placed the fleck of paint inside.

'Gotcha,' I muttered.

Grey Cloak, in all probability, would ditch the car before long, so I didn't have much time. If he slipped away, any further harm he caused would be on my own head. I refused to let that happen.

I put the closed matchbox into in my pocket, turned, and ran back toward Elaine and Anna. By the time I got there, the block was lit nearly daylight-bright with the roaring flames from the apartment building and a steadily increasing number of flashing emergency lights. I found Elaine, Anna, and Mouse, and walked toward them.

'Harry,' Elaine said, relief on her face. 'Hey. You get him?'

'Not yet,' I said. 'Got some follow-up work to do. You have somewhere safe?'

'My room at the hotel should be safe enough. I don't think anyone here knows who I am. The Amber Inn.'

'Right. Take Anna there. I'll call you.'

'No,' Anna said firmly.

I glanced at the burning building and squinted at Anna. 'I guess you'd rather have a quiet night at home, huh?'

'I'd rather make sure the rest of the Ordo is all right,' she said. 'What if the killer decides to go after one of them?'

'Elaine,' I said, expecting her support.

Elaine shrugged. 'I'm working for her, Harry.'

I muttered a quiet curse under my breath, and shook my head. 'Fine. Get them all and fort up. I'll call you by morning.'

Elaine nodded.

'Come on, Mouse,' I said.

I took his lead, and we headed for home – and Little Chicago.

14

When we got back to my apartment, Mouse shambled straight to the plastic punch bowl that holds his kibble. He ate it with a steady, famished determination until it was all gone. Then he emptied his water bowl, went to his usual nap spot, and slumped to the floor without even turning in a circle first. He was asleep almost before he stopped moving.

I stopped by him to ruffle his ears and check his nose, which was wet and cold like it was supposed to be. His tail twitched faintly at my touch, but he was clearly exhausted. Whatever it was about those barks that had impossibly roused an entire building all at once must have taken something out of him. I took my duster off, draped it over him, and let him sleep.

I called Toe-moss's place once again, but got only his answering machine. So I grabbed my heavy flannel robe — for warmth, since the lab was far enough underground to always be chilly — pulled up the throw rug that covers the door in the living room floor, and stumped down the folding stair steps, flicking candles to life with a gesture and a whisper of will as I went.

My lab had always been a little crowded, but it had become more so since I had begun teaching Molly. The lab was a rectangular concrete box. Simple wire shelves covered three walls, stacked up high with books and containers of various ingredients I would use (like the thick, sealed lead box that contained an ounce and a half of depleted uranium filings), and loaded down with various objects of arcane significance (like the bleached human skull that occupied its own shelf, along with several paperback romance novels) or professional curiosity (like the collection of vampire fangs the Wardens in the United States, me and Ramirez, mostly, had gathered in the course of several skirmishes over the past year).

At the far end, on the open wall, I had managed to shoehorn a tiny desk and chair into the lab. Molly did some of her studying there, kept her journal, learned power calculations, and had several books I'd told her to read. We'd begun working on some basic potions, and the beakers and burners occupied most of the surface of her desk, which was just as well, considering the stains that got left on it during her first potion meltdown. Set into the concrete floor beside the desk was a simple ring of silver I used as a summoning circle.

The table in the middle of the room had once been my work area. No longer. Now it was wholly occupied by Little Chicago.

Little Chicago was a scale model of Chicago itself, or at least of the heart of the town, which I'd expanded from its original design to include everything within about four miles of Burnham Harbor. Every building, every street, every tree was represented by a custom-made scale model of pewter. Each contained a tiny piece of the reality it represented — bark chipped from trees, tiny pieces of asphalt gouged from the streets, flakes of brick broken from the buildings with a hammer. The model would let me use my magic in new and interesting ways, and should enable me to find out a lot more about Grey Cloak than I would have been able to do in the past.

Or . . . it might blow up. You know. One of the two.

I was still a young wizard, and Little Chicago was a complex toy containing an enormous amount of magical energy. I had to work hard to keep it up-to-date, matched to the real Chicago, or it wouldn't function correctly — i.e., it would fail, possibly in a spectacular fashion. Releasing all that energy in the relatively cramped confines of the lab would most likely render me extra crispy. It was an elaborate and expensive tool, and I never would have so much as considered creating it if I didn't have an expert consultant.

I took the matchbox from my pocket and set it on the edge of the table, glanced up at the skull on its shelf, and said, 'Bob, up and at 'em.'

The skull quivered a little on its wooden shelf, and tiny, nebulous orange lights appeared in its empty eyes. There was a sound like a human yawn, and then the skull turned slightly toward me and asked, 'What's up, boss?'

'Evil's afoot.'

'Well, sure,' Bob said, 'because it refuses to learn the metric system. Otherwise it'd be up to a meter by now.'

'You're in a mood,' I noted.

'I'm excited. I get to meet the cookie now, right?'

I gave the skull a very firm look. 'She is not a cookie. Neither is she a biscuit, a Pop-Tart, Sweet TART, apple tart, or any other kind of pastry. She is my apprentice.'

'Whatever,' Bob said. 'I get to meet her now, yeah?'

'No,' I said firmly.

'Oh,' Bob said, his tone as disappointed and petulant as a six-year-old child who has just been told that it is bedtime. 'Why *not*?'

'Because she still hasn't got a very good idea of how to handle power wisely,' I said.

'I could help her!' Bob said. 'She could do a lot more if I was helping.'

'Exactly,' I said. 'You're under the radar until I say otherwise. Do not draw attention to yourself. Do not reveal any of your nature to her. When Molly's around, you're an inanimate knickknack until I say otherwise.'

'Hmph,' Bob said. 'At this rate, I'm never gonna get to see her naked in time.'

I snorted. 'In time for what?'

'In time to behold her in her full, springy, nubile, youthful glory! By the time you let me talk to her, she'll have started to droop!'

'I'm almost certain you'll survive the trauma,' I said.

'Life is about more than just survival, Harry.'

'True,' I said. 'There's also work.'

Bob rolled his eyelights in the skull's empty sockets. 'Brother. You're keeping her cloistered and working me like a dog, too. That's not fair.'

I started getting out the stuff I'd need to fire up Little Chicago. 'Dog, right. Something odd happened tonight.' I told Bob about Mouse and his barking. 'What do you know about Temple Dogs?'

'More than you,' Bob said. 'But not much. Most of what I got is collected hearsay and folklore.'

'Any of it likely true?'

'A bit,' he said. 'There are a few points of confluence where multiple sources agree.'

'Hit me.'

'Well, they're not entirely mortal,' Bob said. 'They're the scions of a celestial being called a Foo Dog and a mortal canine. They're very intelligent, very loyal, tough, and can seriously kick ass if they need to do it. But mostly, they're sentinels. They keep an eye out for dark spirits or dark energy, guard the people or places they're supposed to guard, and alert others to the presence of danger.'

'Explains why Ancient Mai made those Temple Dog statues to assist the Wardens in maintaining security, I suppose.' I got out a short-handled duster made of a rowan wand and a bundle of owl feathers, and began to carefully clean the dust from the model city. 'What about the barking thing?'

'Their bark has some kind of spiritual power,' Bob said.

'A lot of stories say that they can make themselves be heard from fifty or sixty miles away. It isn't just a physical thing, either. It carries over into the Nevernever, and can be heard clearly by noncorporeal entities. It startles them, drives most of them away – and if any of them stick around, Mouse could take his teeth to them, even though they're spirits. I figure that this alarm-clock bark he did was a part of that protective power, alerting others to danger.'

I grunted. 'Superdog.'

'But not bulletproof. They can be killed just like anything else.'

There was a thought. I wondered if I could find someone to make Mouse a Kevlar vest. 'Okay, Bob,' I said. 'Get it fired up and give it a once-over.'

'Right, boss. I hope you will note that I am doing this without once complaining how unfair it is that you've seen the cupcake nekkid and I haven't.'

'So noted.' I picked up the skull and set it down on the sheet of translucent, rubbery blue plastic that represented Lake Michigan. 'Check it out while I get my spell face on.'

The skull spun around to face the city while I settled down on the floor, legs crossed, hands resting lightly on my knees, and closed my eyes, focusing on drawing my thoughts to stillness, my heart to a slow, slow beat. I breathed slowly, deeply, systematically walling out worries, emotions, everything but purpose.

One time, when we'd been discussing martial arts, Murphy told me that eventually, no one can teach you anything more about them. Once you reach that state of knowledge, the only way to keep learning and increasing your own skill is to teach what you know to others. That's why she teaches a children's class and a rape-defense course every spring and fall at one of her neighborhood's community centers.

It sounded kind of flaky-Zen to me at the time, but Hell's

bells, she'd been right. Once upon a time, it would have taken me an hour, if not more, to attain the proper frame of mind. In the course of teaching Molly to meditate, though, I had found myself going over the basics again for the first time in years, and understanding them with a deeper and richer perspective than I'd had when I was her age. I'd been getting almost as much insight and new understanding of my knowledge from teaching Molly as she'd been learning from me.

It took me ten minutes, twelve at the most, to prepare my thoughts and will. By the time I stood up again, there was nothing left in the whole world but me, Little Chicago, and my need to find a murderer.

'Bob?' I whispered.

'Everything's nominal. We're in the green, Captain,' he said, affecting a Scottish accent.

I nodded without speaking. Then I drew in my will, and the skull's eyelights dwindled to the size of pinpricks. So did all the candles. Newborn black shadows began stretching between the pewter buildings, overlaying the model streets. The temperature in the lab dropped another degree or two as I pulled in energy from all around me, and my skin flushed as my body temperature went up a couple of degrees. When I slowly exhaled, my heated breath formed vapor that drifted around my nose and mouth.

I moved slowly, precisely, and picked up the matchbox. Then I opened it and exposed the fleck of paint inside, and leaned over to carefully place the paint down on the tiny model of my apartment building. I stood over the table, my hand touching the paint and the map, and released my will with a repeated murmur of, *'Reperios. Invenios.'*

I felt my senses blur for a moment, and then Little Chicago rushed toward me, its buildings growing, until I stood upon the street outside the now life-sized pewter replica of my apartment building.

I took a moment to look around. It looked like Chicago. Flickers of motion surrounded me. Faint outlines of leaves stirred in the pewter trees, ghostly images of the real-world leaves on the trees of the actual Chicago. Faint lights emanated from blank pewter windowpanes. Ghostly cars whispered by on the streets. I could hear the muted sounds of the city, catch the barest hints of scents on the air.

Unnervingly, I could look up and see . . . myself, my actual, physical body, towering over the model city like Godzilla's hyperthyroid cousin. The sky over Little Chicago held twinkling lights – the dim glows of the lab's candles and Bob's eyelights, all too large to be stars, the way the sun is supposed to look from the outer planets.

I held up the matchbox, my will surging down my arm. It touched on the little flake of paint, which erupted into viridian light and rose into the air above my hand, hovered for a moment, and then streaked off to the north like a miniature comet.

'Maybe you got away with this crap in other towns, Grey Cloak,' I muttered. 'But Chicago's mine.'

My own flesh dissolved into flickering silver light, and I felt myself rush after the energy of the seeking spell, streaking through the ghostly images of Chicago's nightlife in the model all around me, one more insubstantial shade among thousands.

The seeking spell came to rest a block and a half south of Goudy Square Park, a little slice of green the city managed to squeeze in amidst a bunch of architecture. The brilliant mote of light settled onto a ghostly image of a moving car and the image suddenly became solid and visible.

'Gotcha,' I growled under my breath, and drifted close to the car, hovering right over its rear bumper, and focused on the driver.

The ghost image remained hazy, dammit. My magic had

latched onto the car, and it wasn't going to be easy to get a better look at the driver than I already had. I might be able to pour more energy into the spell, attain greater clarity, but I wanted to save that as a last resort. Too much could cause the whole thing to blow – and it would certainly leave me too exhausted to maintain the connection. Better to hover now, and listen. Sound would be easier to pick up, resonating against the car, against the surrounding city I had modeled for the spell.

The car stopped a stone's throw from the park. It's a bifurcated little place, simultaneously trying to contain a designer garden and a children's playground, and every time I'd look at it, it seemed to me that the kids were winning. Good for them. Nobody who is four, or six, or eight years old needs to feel conflicted about their play area impeding the Italian Renaissance sensibilities of a landscape artist. Heck, I was probably at least that mature, and I was pretty sure I didn't need it, either.

I focused on the spell, and the sounds of the city night came to life around me, growing in volume, rising from a distant, ghostly murmur to simple ambience, as if I'd been standing there. Traffic sounds. A distant siren. The almost subliminal sound of wheels rushing by on the highway a mile off. The cricketlike chirrup of a car alarm. To me, it was the orchestra tuning and warming up before the overture.

Footsteps, swift and confident, coming closer. The curtain was going up.

The passenger door of the green car opened, and a second shadowy figure joined the first. The door closed, harder than it needed to.

'Are you insane,' the passenger asked, 'meeting here?'

'What's wrong with here?' Grey Cloak asked. His voice was a light tenor, though it sounded distant, hazy, like a partially obscured radio transmission. An accent? Something from Eastern Europe, maybe. It was hard to make out the particulars.

'It's a bloody upper-class WASP neighborhood,' the passenger snarled. His voice was deeper, similarly obscured, and bore no trace of foreign accent. He sounded like a newscaster, standard Midwestern American. 'There's private security here. Police. If anyone raises any kind of alarm, it's going to attract a great deal of attention in short order.'

Grey Cloak let out a low laugh. 'Which is why we are safe. It's late at night. All the little dears are sleeping the sleep of the fat and happy. No one is awake to see us here.'

The other said something rude. There was a flicker of light in the passenger seat, and it took me a second to work out that he'd just lit a cigarette. 'Well?'

'No.'

'No?' the passenger said. 'No kine? No wizard? What do you mean, no?'

'Both,' Grey Cloak said. His tone turned cold. 'You told me he was afraid of fire.'

'He is,' the passenger said. 'You should see his fucking hand.'

I felt my left hand clench tight, and the crackle of popping knuckles in my very real laboratory drifted through the magical simulation of the city.

Grey Cloak's head whipped around.

'What?' the passenger asked.

'Did you hear that?'

'Hear what?'

'Something . . .' Grey Cloak said.

I felt myself holding my breath, willing my fingers to unclench.

The passenger looked around for a moment, then snorted. 'You're nervous about *him*. That's all. You missed him and you're nervous.'

'Not nervous,' Grey Cloak said. 'Understandably cautious. He has more resources and more versatility than your people realize. It's quite possible that he's keeping track of me in some way.'

'I doubt that. It would take a subtle worker of the Art to manage that. He isn't one.'

'No?' Grey Cloak asked. 'He managed to sense the fire before it could cut him off, to sómehow waken the entire building from sound sleep all at the same time, and to track me after I departed.'

The passenger tensed. 'You came here with him behind you?'

'No. I lost him before he could do so. But that does not preclude the use of more subtle means to engage in pursuit.'

'He's a thug,' the passenger said. 'Plain and simple. His talents make him good at destruction and little else. He's a beast to be prodded and directed.'

There was silence for a moment. 'It amazes me,' Grey Cloak said then, 'that an idiot such as you survived crossing the wizard once.'

Aha. Interesting. The passenger, at least, was someone I'd seen before. He'd walked away from it, too. Most of the individuals I'd faced hadn't done that – which bothered me a hell of a lot, at times – but even so, there'd been more than a couple, and the passenger could be any number of them. That did narrow it down considerably from the several billion possibilities I'd had a moment before, though.

And I felt something of a chill at Grey Cloak's words. He was more aware of his surroundings than anyone running on five simple senses should be, and he was a thinker. That's never a good quality in an enemy. A smart foe doesn't have to be stronger than you, doesn't have to be faster, and doesn't even really have to be *there* to be a lethal threat. Hell, if that car bomb hadn't been set off early, he'd have cooked Murphy and me both, and I would have died without even knowing he existed.

'To be honest, I'm surprised the wizard lived the night,' the passenger said. 'It doesn't matter, either way. If we'd killed him, we could have claimed credit for his demise and it would have served our purpose. Now we let him rampage over the Skavis, and it does nothing but help.'

'Unless,' Grey Cloak said sourly, 'he happens to rampage over us as well.'

They were both quiet for a moment. Then the passenger said, 'At least one thing is accomplished. He's interested in stopping the culling.'

'Oh, yes,' Grey Cloak said. 'You've gotten his attention. The question, of course, is whether or not he will be as co-operative as you seem to believe.'

'With a gathering of female wizardlings at risk? Oh, yes. He won't be able to help himself. Now that he knows what the Skavis is up to, Dresden will be falling all over himself to protect them.'

Aha. The *Skavis*. And they were maneuvering me to kick his ass.

Finally, something useful.

'Will he strike at the kine soon?' Grey Cloak asked, referring to the Skavis, I presumed.

'Not yet. It isn't his style. He'll wait a day or two before moving again. He wants them to suffer, waiting for him.'

'Mmmm,' Grey Cloak said. 'I normally think the Skavis's tastes repulsive, but in this particular instance, I suspect his might intersect with my own. Anticipation makes them taste sweeter.'

'Oh, of course, by all means,' the passenger said sourly. 'Throw away everything we might achieve in order to indulge your sweet tooth.'

Grey Cloak let out a low chuckle. 'Alas, not yet. I hardly

think the Circle would react well to such a course. Speaking of which, how does your own endeavor fare?'

'Less than well,' the passenger said. 'He isn't talking to me.'

'Did you really expect him to?'

The passenger shrugged. 'He *is* family. But that's of no matter. I'll find them in time, whether he cooperates or not.'

'For your sake, I hope so,' Grey Cloak said. 'The Circle has asked me for a progress report.'

The passenger shifted uneasily. 'Have they. What are you going to tell them?'

'The truth.'

'You can't be serious.'

'On the contrary,' Grey Cloak said.

'They react badly to incompetence,' the passenger said.

'And murderously to deception.'

The passenger took another long drag on his cigarette and cursed again. Then he said, 'No help for it, then.'

'There is no need to soil yourself. We are not yet past our deadline, and they do not destroy tools that may still be of use.'

The passenger let out a nasty laugh. 'They're hard but fair?'

'They're hard,' Grey Cloak replied.

'If necessary,' the passenger said, 'we can remove him. We have the resources for it. I could always—'

'I believe it premature unless he proves more threatening than he has been thus far,' Grey Cloak said. 'I expect the Circle would agree.'

'When do I meet them?' the passenger asked. 'Face-to-face.'

'That is not my decision. I am a liaison. Nothing more.' He shrugged. 'But, should this project proceed, I suspect they will desire an interview.'

'I'll succeed,' the passenger said darkly. 'He can't have taken them far.'

'Then I suggest you get moving,' Grey Cloak said. 'Before the Skavis beats you to the prize.'

'Beats *us*,' the passenger said.

I could hear a faint smile touch Grey Cloak's voice. 'Of course.'

There was a smoldering silence, and then the passenger shoved the door open, exited the car, and left without a further word.

Grey Cloak watched him until he'd vanished into the night. Then he got out of the car. Insubstantial, I willed myself forward into the vehicle and looked. The steering column had been cracked open, the vehicle hot-wired.

I was torn for a second, which of the two to follow. The passenger was trying to get information out of someone. That could mean that he had a prisoner somewhere he was interrogating. On the other hand, it could just as likely mean that no matter how many drinks he poured, he couldn't get an informant to open up on a given topic. I also knew that he had confronted me before at some point – which was a great deal more than I knew about Grey Cloak.

He was something very different. He had tried to kill me a couple of times already, and was apparently responsible for at least some of the recent deaths. He was smart, and was connected to some kind of shady group called 'the Circle.' Could this be the reality of my heretofore theoretical Black Council?

He was walking away from the car now, my spell's anchor, and growing rapidly hazier as he walked away. If I didn't pursue him closely, he'd vanish into the vastness of the city.

Whoever the passenger had been, I had apparently sent him running once already. If I'd done it once, I could do it again.

Grey Cloak, then.

I pressed in close to Grey Cloak, focusing to keep the spell clearly fixed, and followed him. He walked several blocks, turned down a sharp alley, and then descended a flight of stairs that ended at a boarded-over doorway to what must have originally been a basement apartment like my own. He glanced around, tugged down a chain that looked like it had rusted flat to the wall beside the door, and opened it, disappearing within.

Crap. If this place had a threshold on it, I'd never be able to follow him inside. I'd just bang my metaphysical head against the doorway like a bird hitting a windshield. Never mind that if it had the proper kinds of wards, they could conceivably disintegrate my spiritual self, or at least inflict some fairly horrible psychic damage. I could wind up on the floor of my lab, drooling, transformed from professional wizard into unemployed vegetable.

Screw it. You don't do a job like mine by running away at any hint of danger.

I steeled myself and willed myself forward, following Grey Cloak.

No threshold, which was good. No wards, which was even better. Grey Cloak hadn't entered a living area – he'd entered Undertown.

Chicago is an old city – at least by American standards. It has been standing, in one form or another, since the French and Indian War, before the United States even existed. Being as Chicago is basically one giant swamp, from a strictly geographic point of view, buildings tended to slowly settle into the earth over years and years. The old wooden streets did the same, and new streets had to be built atop them in successive layers.

Wherever the ground isn't slow-motion mud, there's solid rock. Tunnels and cave systems riddle the area. The Manhattan Project had been housed briefly in such tunnels, before it got relocated to the middle of nowhere. Someone in the government had shown unaccountably good judgment in considering the notion that developing a freaking nuclear weapon smack in the middle of America's second-largest city qualified as a Bad Idea.

All of that had left behind an enormous labyrinth of passages, caves, half-collapsed old buildings, and crumbling tunnels seemingly ready to come thundering down at any moment. It was dark, human beings rarely went there, and as a result, Undertown had become a home, shelter, and hiding place to all kinds of nasty things – things no mortal, not even a wizard, had ever seen. Some of those things, in turn, had expanded some of the tunnels and caves, establishing jealously protected territories that never saw the face of the sun, never heard the whisper of wind. It's dark, close, cold, and intensely creepy down there. The fact that it was inhabited by things that had no love for mankind and potential radioactivity to boot didn't do much to boost its tourism industry.

Grey Cloak paced swiftly through a crack in the back wall of the building and into Undertown's tunnels. He grew even more indistinct as he did. I had to stay closer to him, and it cost me an increasingly greater effort of will to do so. Little Chicago hadn't accurately modeled Undertown, partly because there were no maps to be had of the place, and because taking samples to incorporate into the model would have been an act just shy of active suicide. Mostly, though, it hadn't happened because I had never considered doing so.

Through the translucent veil of earth and stone and brick, I could still see the real me standing over the city. My hand was still held out, but my fingers were trembling, and sweat beaded my forehead. Odd that I couldn't feel the strain on my body from here. I hadn't anticipated that. It was entirely possible that I might have continued on without ever realizing what the effort was costing me. It could kill my physical body, leaving me . . .

I don't know what. It might kill me outright. It might kill my body while stranding my mind here. It might bind my awareness into place like some sort of pathetic ghost.

Get tough, Dresden. You didn't take up this career to run at the first hint of fatigue.

I kept going – but all the same, I looked up to check on myself as often as I could.

Grey Cloak was not long in reaching his goal. He found a narrow cleft in a rock wall, slipped inside it, and then pressed his hands and feet against either wall on the inside of the cleft and climbed up it with rapid precision. Eight or nine feet up, it opened into a room with three walls of brick and one of earth – a partially collapsed basement, I assumed. There were a few creature comforts in it – an inflatable mattress and sleeping bag, a lantern, a miniature barbecue next to a heavy paper bag of charcoal, and several cardboard boxes that contained supplies.

Grey Cloak slipped a heavy grate over the hole he'd just climbed up, and weighted it down with several stones the size of cinder blocks. Then he opened a box, unwrapped a pair of those meal-replacement bars that people use to punish themselves when they think they're overweight, ate them, and emptied a plastic bottle of water. Critical information, there. Glad I was risking my metaphysical neck to pick up vital clues like this.

I checked up over my shoulder. My face had gone white and ran with sweat.

I expected Grey Cloak to turn in, but instead he turned the lantern down low, opened a second box, withdrew a plaque the size of a dinner plate, and laid it down on the floor. It was a simple wooden base, inset with a ring of some reddish metal, probably copper.

Grey Cloak pressed a fingernail against one of his gums, and when he withdrew it his fingertip glistened with blood that looked far more solid and real than the person it had come from. He touched it to the circle and began a low chant I did not recognize.

A faint mist swirled up within the copper circle, and through the spell I could see the raw magic forming itself into a pattern, a vortex that vanished beneath the plaque.

A second later, the mist resolved itself into a figure, in miniature, a vaguely humanoid shape wearing a heavy cloak and cowl that hid any possible details of appearance.

Except that I'd seen him before – or at least someone who dressed exactly like him.

The last time I'd seen Cowl, he'd been caught in the unbelievably savage backlash of an enormous power-summoning spell called a Darkhallow. It would have been impossible for the man to have survived that spell. There was no way, no way in hell that he'd lived through it. This couldn't be the same person.

Could it?

Surely it had to be someone else. The Ringwraith look was hardly uncommon among those who fancied themselves dark wizards of one kind or another, after all. It could just as easily be someone else entirely, someone not at all connected to Cowl or my theoretical Black Council.

On the other hand, Cowl had been the person whose actions had tipped me off to the possibility of the Black Council to begin with. Could he have been a part of the Circle that Grey Cloak had mentioned? After all, I dropped a freaking car onto Cowl's head, and he'd hardly blinked at it. If he'd been that well protected, could he have survived the wild energies of the disintegrating Darkhallow?

Worse, what if he hadn't? What if he was one of a set of people just as crazy and dangerous as he had been?

I started feeling even more nervous.

'My lord,' Grey Cloak said, bowing his head. He left it that way.

There was a long moment of silence before Cowl spoke. Then he said, 'You have failed.'

'I have not yet succeeded,' Grey Cloak replied with polite disagreement. 'The curtain has not fallen.'

'And the fool with you?'

'Still ignorant, my lord. I can preserve or dispose of him as you see fit.' Grey Cloak took a deep breath and said, 'He has gotten the wizard involved. There is some sort of vendetta between them, it would seem.'

The little mist figure made a hissing sound. 'The *fool*. There is not enough profit in Dresden's death to jeopardize the operation.'

'He did not consult me on the matter, my lord,' Grey Cloak said with another bow of his head. 'Had he done so, I would have dissuaded him.'

'And what followed?'

'I attempted to remove him along with the last of the culling.'

'Dresden interfered?'

'Yes.'

Cowl hissed. 'This changes matters. What precautions have you taken?'

'I was not followed in flesh, my lord; of that I am certain.'

Cowl held up a miniature hand for silence, a gesture that looked, somehow, stiff and pained. Then his hood panned around the room.

The figure's gaze met mine, and hit me like a literal, physical blow, a swift jab in the chest.

'He is there!' Cowl snarled. The misty figure turned to face me and lifted both hands.

An odd, cold pressure hit me like a wave and pushed me back several feet before I could gather up my will and exert pressure in return, coming to a stop several feet away from Grey Cloak and Cowl.

Cowl's hands clenched into claws. 'Insolent child. I will rip your mind asunder.'

I snarled at him and planted my insubstantial feet. 'Bring it, Darth Bathrobe!'

Cowl screamed at me. He spoke a word that resonated in my head and thundered through the hazy confines of Grey Cloak's hideaway. Though I had braced myself to gather my will and pit it against his, his next strike hammered into me like a freight train. I could no more have resisted it than I could have stopped an ocean tide, and I felt it throwing me back and away.

In that last second before I was banished, I reached out

with all the strength I had left, focusing on Grey Cloak, pouring everything I had into the spell to grant me a clear view of his face. I got it, for the barest instant, the face of a man in his mid-thirties, tall and lean and wolfish.

And then there was a geyser of scarlet pain, as if someone had seized both halves of my skull and torn it into two pieces.

Darkness followed.

I woke up with someone shaking my shoulder and someone else holding the back of my head against a running band saw.

'Harry,' Molly said. She was speaking through some kind of megaphone pressed directly against the side of my head, evidently while pounding my skull with the pointy end of a claw hammer. 'Hey, boss, can you hear me?'

'Ow,' I said.

'What happened?'

'Ow,' I repeated, annoyed, as if it should have been explanation enough.

Molly let out an exasperated, worried sound. 'Do I need to take you to the hospital?'

'No,' I croaked. 'Aspirin. Some water. And stop screaming.'

'I'm barely whispering,' she said, and got up. Her combat boots slammed down on the floor in great Godzilla-sized rolls of thunder as she went up the stair steps.

'Bob,' I said, as soon as she was gone. 'What happened?'

'I'm not sure,' Bob said, keeping his voice down. 'Either she's been working out, or else she's started using some kind of cosmetics on her arms. She still had some baby fat when she got the tattoos, and that's always bound to make any kind of changes more noticeable, and—'

'Not her,' I growled, images of genuine mayhem floating through my agonized brain. '*Me.*'

'*Oh,*' Bob said. 'Something hit the model, hard. There was an energy surge. Boom. The psychic backlash lit up your mental fusebox.'

'How bad?'

'Hard to say. How many fingers am I holding up?'

I sighed. 'How bad is Little Chicago, Bob?'

'Oh. You've got to be more specific with this stuff, Harry. Could be worse. A week to fix, at most.'

I grunted. 'Everything's too loud and bright.' I tested my arms and legs. It hurt to move them, an odd and stretchy kind of pain, but they moved. 'What happened, exactly?'

'You got lucky, is what. Something you met out there threw a big blast of psychic energy at you. But it had to come at you through your threshold and the model. The threshold weakened it, and Little Chicago shorted out when the blast hit, or . . .'

'Or what?' I asked.

'Or you wouldn't have that headache,' Bob said. Then his eyelights winked out.

Molly's boots clumped back down the stairs. She set down on the table a couple of fresh candles she'd brought, took a deep breath, closed her eyes for a moment, and then very carefully used the same spell I did to light them.

The light speared into my brain and hurt. A lot. I flinched and threw my arm across my face.

'Sorry,' she said. 'I wasn't thinking. I couldn't even see you down here, and . . .'

'Next time just shove some pencils into my eyes,' I muttered a minute later.

'Sorry, Harry,' she said. 'The aspirin?'

I held out a hand. She pressed a bottle of aspirin into it, and then pressed a cold glass into my other hand. I opened the aspirin with my teeth, dumped several into my mouth, and chugged them down with the water. Exhausted from this monumental effort, I lay on the floor and felt somewhat sorry for myself until, after several more mercilessly regular minutes, the painkiller started kicking in.

'Molly,' I said. 'Were we supposed to have a lesson today?'

'No,' she said. 'But Sergeant Murphy called our house, looking for you. She said you weren't answering the phone. I thought I should come over and check on you.'

I grunted. 'Good call. Any trouble getting through the wards?'

'No, not this time.'

'Good.' I opened my eyes slowly, until they started getting used to the glare of the candles. 'Mouse. Mouse probably needs you to let him out.'

I heard a thumping sound, and squinted up the stairs. Mouse was crouched at the top, somehow managing to look concerned.

'I'm fine, you big pansy,' I said. 'Go on.'

Molly started up the staircase, and then froze, staring back down at Little Chicago.

I squinted at her. Then rose and squinted at the table.

There was a hole melted in the metal table, not far from the spot where Grey Cloak had entered Undertown. One of the buildings was half slagged, the pewter melted into a messy runnel that coursed down the hole in the table like dribbled wax. There was a layer of black soot over everything within several inches of the hole in the table.

If the table hadn't taken the magical blow, it would have been my *head* with the hole burned in it. That had been part of the purpose in creating Little Chicago — as a tool and a safety measure for working that kind of magic. All the same, it was a sobering thing to see.

I swallowed. Cowl. It had been Cowl. I'd heard the hatred and venom in his voice, the familiarity — and the overwhelming power of his magic had been unmistakable. He'd survived the Darkhallow. He was working with this 'Circle,' who were almost certainly the Black Council, and there was some kind of larger mischief afoot in Chicago than I had suspected.

Oh, yeah. This whole situation was definitely starting to make me nervous.

I turned back to Molly and said, 'Like I said. This thing is dangerous, grasshopper. So no playing with it until I say so. Got it?'

Molly swallowed. 'Got it.'

'Go on. Take care of Mouse. Do me a favor, and call Murphy's cell phone. Ask her to come here.'

'Do you need me to help you today?' she asked. 'Like, go with you and stuff?'

I looked at her. Then at the table. Then back at her.

'Just asking,' Molly said defensively, and hurried on up the stairs.

By the time I'd gotten a shower, shaved, and climbed into fresh clothes, I felt almost human, though I still had a whale of a headache. Murphy arrived shortly after.

'What the hell happened to you?' she said, by way of greeting.

'Took a psychic head butt from Cowl,' I said.

Murphy greeted Mouse, scratching him under the chin with both hands. 'What's a Cowl?'

I grunted. 'Right, forgot. When I met Cowl, you were in Hawaii with your boy toy.'

Murph gave me a smug smile. 'Kincaid isn't a boy toy. He's a man toy. Definitely a man toy.'

Molly, lying on the floor with her feet up on the wall while she read, dropped her book onto her face. She fumbled it back into her hands and then tried to appear uninterested in the conversation. It would have been more convincing if she weren't holding the book upside down.

'Long story short,' I told her. 'Cowl is a wizard.'

'Human?' Murphy asked.

'Pretty sure, but I've never seen his face. All I know about him is that he's stronger than me. He's better than me. I stood up to him in a fair fight and got lucky enough to survive it.'

Murphy frowned. 'Then how'd you beat him?'

'I stopped fighting fair and bumped his elbow while he was handling supernatural high explosives. Boom. I figured he was dead.'

Murphy sat down in one of my easy chairs, frowning. 'Okay,' she said. 'Better give me the whole thing.'

I rubbed at my aching head and started from where I'd left Murphy yesterday up until the end of my confrontation with Cowl. I left out some of the details about Elaine, and everything about the Circle. That was information too dangerous to spread around. Hell, I wish I didn't know about it, myself.

'Skavis,' Murphy mused aloud. 'I've heard that somewhere before.'

'It's one of the greater Houses of the White Court,' I said, nodding. 'Raith, Skavis, and Malvora are the big three.'

'Right,' Murphy said. 'Psychic vampires. Raith feed on lust. Malvora on fear. How about these Skavis?'

'Pain,' I said. 'Or despair, depending on how you translate some of the texts the Council has on them.'

'And suicide,' Murphy said, 'is the ultimate expression of despair.'

'With a mind like that,' I said, 'you could be a detective.'

We were quiet for a minute before Murphy said, 'Let me see if I've got this right. This Skavis is in town. According to your ex, the private investigator Anna Ash hired, he's killed women in four other cities, and he's doing it again here — four so far, and Anna's meant to be number five.'

'Yeah,' I said.

'Meanwhile, this Grey Cloak, who works for Cowl, is in

town doing more or less the same thing, but you don't think he's here to help the Skavis, whoever *he* is. But you *do* think he's working against the killer, along with this Passenger, whoever *he* is. You think those two left the clues you found on the bodies to pull you into an investigation and take out the Skavis.'

'Even better,' I said. 'I think I know who Passenger was.'

'Who?' Murphy asked.

'Beckitt,' I said. 'It makes sense. He's got his wife on the inside as an information source. He's gone up against me before, and walked away, *and* I cost him years of his life and a lucrative share of a criminal empire. He's got plenty of reasons not to like me. That's who Grey Cloak the Malvora was talking to.'

'Whoa. Grey Cloak the Malvora? How'd you get that?'

'Because,' I said, 'he talked about sharing some tastes with the Skavis, when it came to letting the prey anticipate what was coming before the kill. The Malvora do it so that their prey will feel more fear. The Skavis do it so that they'll be more tired, be more ready to give in to despair.'

Murphy nodded, lips pursed. 'And the White Court loves manipulating everything indirectly. Using others to do their dirty work for them.'

'Like using me to wipe out his Skavis competition,' I said.

'Which makes sense because Malvora and Skavis are rivals.'

'Right,' I said. 'And I'm fairly confident in my guess. Just like I'm fairly confident that Beckitt must be our passenger.'

'That's a sound theory, Dresden,' Murphy said.

'Thank you, I know.'

'But Beckitt died almost seven years ago. He was killed in prison.'

'I figure Beckitt must have made a deal with the Malvora and—' I blinked. 'He what?'

'Died,' Murphy said. 'There was a riot. Three prisoners were killed, several injured. He was one of them. As near as anyone can tell, he was standing in the wrong place at the wrong time. A prisoner was wrestling for a guard's gun. It discharged and killed Beckitt instantly.'

'Um,' I said, frowning. I hate it when the real world ignores a perfectly logical, rational assumption. 'He faked it?'

She shook her head. 'I looked into it, and I talked to the guard. There was an autopsy, an identification of the body from his family, a funeral, the whole nine yards. He's dead, Harry.'

'Well, dammit,' I said, and rubbed at my headache. 'He made sense.'

'That's life,' Murphy said. 'So this hidey-hole you found . . .'

'Long gone by now,' I said.

'Might he worth going anyway, if you take Krypto here with you.' She leaned down and planted a kiss on top of Mouse's head. My dog gets more play than me, sheesh. 'Maybe Grey Cloak the theoretical Malvora left a good scent behind.'

'Worth a shot, I guess,' I said. 'But I'm pretty sure he's going to be thorough enough to remove that, too.'

'Who goes around removing their scent from places?' Murphy asked.

'Vampires. They can track that way, just like Mouse.'

'Oh. Right.' Murphy sighed. 'Another burned building.'

'Not—' I began.

'Not his fault!' Molly said.

'Not your fault,' Murphy said, 'I know. But it's going to look awfully odd. My car gets firebombed. A building less than a block away gets firebombed a few hours later.'

I grunted. 'Same device?'

'What do you think?'

'Same device.'

Murphy nodded. 'I'm sure it will be. It's going to take them time to figure it out, though. Were you seen?'

'Me and about a million other people,' I said.

'That's something, at least. But a lot of people are going to be asking questions before long. The sooner we get this thing put to bed, the better.'

I grimaced. 'I shouldn't have gone for the subtle maneuver last night. I should have smashed him to paste right there. I don't have any way to find him now, and he's aware that we're looking.'

'Yeah, but Grey Cloak isn't our first problem,' Murphy said. 'He's a sideshow. The Skavis is the real killer. Right?'

'Yeah,' I said quietly. 'Right. And we've got no clue who or where he is.'

Murphy frowned. 'But he's a vampire, right? I mean, you can tell if someone's a vampire, can't you?'

'It isn't so simple with the White Court,' I said. 'They hide themselves a lot better than any other breed. I had no idea what Thomas was when I met him. And you remember talking to Darby Crane.'

'Yeah.'

'Did you get 'vampire' off him?'

'Mostly I got "player,"' Murphy said. 'But you knew he was really Madrigal Raith.'

'I guessed,' I corrected her. 'Probably because I unconsciously recognized the family resemblance to Lord Raith. That's why I stopped you from touching him. There was no magical tip-off about it.' I frowned. 'Hell, I wouldn't be shocked if they had some kind of ability to cloud their prey's judgment. When Inari Raith tried to feed on me, even though I was *in* their freaking house, even though I *knew* she was a baby succubus, and in my room, it never really occurred to me that she might be dangerous to me, until it was too late.'

'Just like that never occurred to me about Crane,' Murphy said. 'So the Skavis . . . he could be anyone.'

'I'm pretty sure he's not me,' I said. 'I'm almost as sure he's not you.'

'Are you sure you're a professional investigator?'

'I sometimes wonder.'

'What about Thomas?' Murphy asked.

'He's more of a hired thug than a shamus.'

Murphy glared.

It drew a little bit of a smile from me, but it faded quickly in the light of reality. 'I left messages. Nothing yet.'

'That's not what I meant, either,' Murphy said quietly. 'Could he still be involved? Could he have been the passenger?'

'He wasn't.'

Again, she held up a hand. 'Harry. Is it possible?'

'Look, we know the killer is a Skavis.'

'We know what Grey Cloak thinks,' Murphy corrected me. 'But you're forgetting something.'

'What?'

'That at least one of those women was killed in the throes of supernatural passion. Not amidst fear. Not amidst despair.'

I scowled at her.

'Is it physically *possible*, Harry? Possible. That's all I'm asking.'

'I suppose,' I said quietly. 'But Thomas isn't Grey Cloak's partner. What if . . .' I couldn't finish the sentence.

'What if your passenger has him?' Murphy asked. 'What if the "endeavor" he's talking about is pressing Thomas for some kind of information?'

I grimaced. 'Thomas should have been in touch by now.'

'We've got a little time. Grey Cloak thought it would be another day or so before the Skavis moved again, right?'

'Yeah.'

'So far, you think he's been smart about most things. Maybe he's smart about that, too.'

'We can hope,' I said. 'What did you find about Jessica Blanche?'

'Still working on it. I've got feelers out, but I'll need to follow up with some legwork.'

I blew out a breath. 'And I need to get in touch with Elaine and the Ordo. Maybe I can get Helen Beckitt to talk. And I can make some calls to other Wardens. Maybe someone's heard something about recent White Court activities.'

Murphy rose. 'Sounds like we have a plan.'

'If we repeat it often enough, maybe we'll even believe it,' I said. 'Let's go.'

Ramirez's contact number went to a restaurant his family ran in eastern Los Angeles. I left a message with someone whose English sounded like a second or third language. It took Ramirez only about ten minutes to call me back.

'White Court?' my fellow Warden said. 'Can't think as I've heard anything about them lately, Harry.'

'How about a professional wizard investigator?' I asked him. 'Works out of Los Angeles.'

'Elaine Mallory?' he asked. 'Tall, pretty, smart, and nearly as charming as myself?'

'That's the one,' I said. 'What do you know about her?'

'Far as I know, she's straight,' he said. 'Moved to town five or six years ago, college in San Diego, and working for an investigative agency out here. She's got a decent grounding in thaumaturgy from somewhere, but when I ran her through the standard tests, she didn't score quite high enough to be considered for Council membership.' He was quiet for a second, before saying, in a tone of forced cheer, 'Unless we keep on losing people to the vamps, in which case I guess we might lower our standards.'

'Uh-huh,' I said. 'But you think she knows what she's doing?'

'Well,' Ramirez drawled, 'I hinted that she might want to advertise as something other than a "wizard," eventually. If we get the time to look away from the war, some hidebound dinosaur might take exception to someone claiming the title.'

I snorted. 'Don't call me a dinosaur. It isn't fair to the dinosaurs. What did a dinosaur ever do to you?'

'Other than give me a ride right next to this big skinny

lunatic? Mallory's not stupid, and she's done people some good out here,' Ramirez said. 'Lost kids, especially. Couple of exorcisms I wouldn't have had time to handle. Maybe she can be of some help to you. Though I've got one reservation about her.'

'What's that?' I asked.

'Her taste in men. I keep asking her out, and she's turned me down about a dozen times, now.'

'Shocking,' I said.

'I know,' Ramirez replied. 'Makes me wonder how smart she could really be. Why?'

I gave him the brief on what I knew about the murders, and on what Elaine had told me about the other cities.

'Someone's framing the Wardens,' he said.

'Looks that way. Sow seeds of distrust and all that.'

'Five cities. Bastards.' He paused to say something off the phone, and then told me, 'Hang on. I'm pulling the file on recent White Court reports.'

I waited a few more minutes. Then he came back and said, 'According to what we've heard out on this end, the White King has met with emissaries from the Council under a flag of truce, and declared a temporary cease-fire. He's agreed to approach the Reds about sitting down to negotiate an end to the war.'

'I've met him,' I said. 'Kissinger he ain't. Gandhi, neither.'

'Yeah. Sorta makes you wonder what he's getting out of the war ending, don't it.'

I grunted. 'There's not a lot of love lost between the Reds and the Whites. A cease-fire won't cost him anything. His people don't get involved in the messy stuff anyway.'

Ramirez let out a thoughtful hum. 'The way you tell it, looks like maybe not everybody in the White Court agrees with his take on the war.'

'They're pretty factional. Triumvirate of major houses. Raith happens to be on top right now. If Raith is pushing for peace, it would be consistent for the other major houses to oppose it.'

'Gotta love those vampires. So arbitrarily contrary.'

'Say that five times fast,' I said.

He did, flawlessly, rolling the Rs as he went. 'See there?' he said. 'That's why the ladies love me.'

'It's not love, Carlos. It's pity.'

'As long as the pants come off,' he said cheerfully. Then his voice turned more sober. 'Dresden, I've been meaning to call you. Just . . . wanted to see how you were doing. You know. Since New Mexico.'

'I'm good,' I told him. 'I'm fine.'

'Uh-huh,' Ramirez said. He sounded skeptical.

'Listen,' I said. 'Forget New Mexico. I've forgotten it. We need to move on, focus on what's in front of us right now.'

'Sure,' he said, without conviction. 'You want to fill in the Captain or should I?'

'Go ahead.'

'Will do,' he said. 'You need any backup out there?'

'Why?' I asked. 'You got nothing to pay attention to where you are?'

He sighed. 'Yeah, well. All the same. If the Whites are trying to shut down the peace talks, I could pry a few of the boys loose to come help you boot some head.'

'Except I don't yet know whose head it is or how to boot it,' I said.

'I know. But if you need help, it's here.'

'Thanks.'

'Watch your ass, Dresden,' he said.

'I'd tell you to do the same, but you probably gaze at your own ass in admiration all the time anyway.'

'With an ass like mine? Who *wouldn't*?' Ramirez said. '*Vaya con Dios*.'

'Happy trails.'

I hung up the phone and leaned back in the chair, rubbing at my still-aching head. I closed my eyes and tried to think for a minute. I thought about how much my head hurt, which was nonproductive.

'Harry?' Molly asked me.

'Hmmm?'

'Can I ask you something?'

'Sure.'

'Um . . .' She was quiet for a moment, as though thinking about her words before she spoke.

That got my attention.

'I'm just wondering why you were asking Warden Rodriguez about Elaine Mallory.'

I closed my eyes and tried thinking again.

'I mean, Sergeant Murphy said she was your ex. But you asked about her as if you didn't know her.'

I mumbled something.

'So I figure that means that you do know her. And you wanted to know what Warden Rodriguez knew about her, without him knowing that you already knew her.' She took a deep breath and said, 'You're keeping secrets from the Wardens.'

I sighed. 'For years, kid. Years and years.'

'But . . . I'm under the Doom of Damocles, and that means you are, too. This is the kind of thing that could make them decide to invoke it. So, um . . . why are you doing it?'

'Does it matter?' I asked.

'Well,' she said, her tone cautiously diffident, 'since I could get beheaded over this just as much as you can, it matters to me. And I think that maybe I deserve to know.'

I started to growl at her that she didn't. I stopped myself because she had a point, dammit. Regardless of how inconvenient I thought it, she did have an undeniable right to ask me about it.

'I was an orphan,' I told her. 'A little while after my magic came to me, I got adopted by a man named DuMorne. He's the one who gave me most of my training. He adopted Elaine, too. We grew up together. Each other's first love.'

Molly set her book aside and sat up, listening to me.

'DuMorne was a warlock himself. Black wizard as bad as they come. He planned on training us up to be his personal enforcers. Trained, strong wizards, under mental compulsion to be loyal to him. He nailed Elaine with it. I got suspicious and fought him. I killed him.'

Molly blinked. 'But the First Law . . .'

'Exactly,' I said. 'That's how I wound up living under the Doom of Damocles myself. Ebenezar McCoy mentored me. Saved my life.'

'The way you did for me,' she said quietly.

'Yeah.' I squinted at the empty fireplace. 'Justin burned, and I thought Elaine did, too. Turned out years later that she had survived, and was in hiding.'

'And she never *told* you?' Molly demanded. 'What a bitch.'

I gave the apprentice a lopsided smile. 'The last time she'd seen me, I had been busy murdering the only thing like a real parent she'd ever had, and had apparently tried to kill her, too. It isn't a simple situation, Molly.'

'But I still don't get why you lied about her.'

'Because I had a bad time of it, coming out from under DuMorne's corpse the way I did. If the Wardens knew that she'd been there too, and fled the Council rather than coming out to them . . .' I shrugged. 'Looks like she's managed to convince Ramirez that she doesn't have enough power to be considered for the Council.'

'But she does?' Molly asked.

'She's nearly as strong as I am,' I said quietly. 'Makes up for it in grace. I'm not sure what would happen if the Wardens learned DuMorne had a second apprentice, but there would be trouble. I'm not going to make that choice for her.'

'In case I haven't told you this before,' Molly said, 'the Wardens are a fine bunch of assholes. Present company excluded.'

'There isn't any easy way to do their job,' I said, before amending, '*our* job. Like I said, kid. Nothing's simple.' I pushed myself slowly to my feet and found my keys and Mouse's lead. 'Come on,' I told her. 'I'll drop you off at your place.'

'Where are you going?'

'To talk to the Ordo,' I said. 'Anna's got them all holed up with Elaine.'

'Why don't you just call them?'

'This is a sneak attack.' I said. 'I don't want to warn Helen Beckitt that I'm on the way. She's got an angle in this; I'm sure of it. It's easier to get people to talk if you get them off balance.'

Molly frowned at me. 'You sure you don't need my help?'

I paused to glance at her. Then at the bead bracelet on her wrist.

She clenched her jaw, took off the bracelet, and held it up with defiant determination, staring at the beads. Three minutes and two beads later, she gave it up, gasping and sweating at the effort. She looked bitterly frustrated and disappointed.

'Nothing's simple,' I told her quietly, and put the bracelet back on her wrist for her. 'And nothing much is easy, either. Be patient. Give it time.'

'Easy for you to say,' she said, and stomped out to the car, leading Mouse.

She was wrong, of course. It wasn't easy.

What I really wanted to do was get down a little food and go to bed until my head felt better. That wasn't an option for me.

Whoever the Skavis was, and whatever he was up to, there wasn't a lot of time to figure it out and stop him before he added another victim to his tally.

The Amber Inn is a rarity in downtown Chicago: a reasonably priced hotel. It isn't large or particularly fancy, and it wasn't designed by an architect with three names. No one infamous has owned it, lived in it, or been machine-gunned to death there. Thus, stripped of anything like a good excuse to stick it to the customer, one needn't schedule a visit to a loan officer in tandem with making a reservation, even though the Amber Inn is fairly central to Chicago.

It was the kind of place I always tried to pick on the occasions my work had taken me to another town for a client's business. My job, in cases like that, is investigating, not checking out four-star hotels. The most important thing was to be close to where I would be working and that I not run up an unmanageable bill. I've heard that some private investigators make it a point to stay somewhere nice at the client's expense, but it always seemed unprofessional to me, and a bad way to conduct business in the long term. It stood to reason that Elaine would have chosen it for similar reasons.

I didn't ask after her at the desk. I didn't need to. I just told Mouse, 'Find 'em.'

Mouse sniffed the air and we started walking down halls like we owned the place. That's always important, the confidence. It keeps people from getting suspicious about why you're stalking around the building, and even when it doesn't deter them, it makes them respond more cautiously.

Mouse finally stopped at a door, and I extended my hand, half closing my eyes, feeling for magic. There was a ward over the door. It wasn't terribly fancy or solid — it couldn't be, without a threshold to use as a foundation — but it was exceedingly well crafted and I was sure it was Elaine's work. The spell looked like it would release only a tiny bit of energy, probably a pulse of light or some kind of audible sound that would alert her to company.

I debated, for a moment, making a Big Bad Wolf entrance, and decided against it. It wouldn't be terribly polite to Elaine, and the only person I wanted to scare was Helen Beckitt, assuming she was there. Besides which, tipped off by her alarm and wary about a murderer, Elaine might well send a lightning bolt through the doorway before she had a chance to see who was there. I knocked.

Nothing changed, but my instincts warned me that someone was on the other side of the door — not magic, just the sudden absence of the simple, solitary feel one gets when standing alone in an empty house.

I sensed a little stirring of the magic in the ward. Then the door rattled and swung open, revealing Elaine standing on the other side, one corner of her mouth tilted up in amusement.

'Oh, I get it,' I said. 'Not a ward. A peephole.'

'Sometimes a girl's got to improvise,' she said. 'You look awful.'

'Long night.'

'It must have been. I thought you were going to call.'

'I was in the neighborhood.'

She pursed her lips in speculation. 'Were you?' I saw the wheels turning in her head for a moment, and then she nodded once and lowered her voice. 'Which one?'

'Beckitt,' I murmured back.

'She's here.'

I nodded, and she opened the door the rest of the way at the same time I stepped through it. She slipped to one side as I walked briskly into the room. It was clean, plain, a kind of minisuite with a queen bed, a couch, and a coffee table.

Priscilla sat on the couch in a pea green turtleneck and a scratchy-looking wool skirt, and scowled at me in disapproval of Dickensian proportion. Abby and Toto occupied the floor, where Toto was engaged in mortal combat with a white athletic sock he had pulled partway from the foot of his plump little owner, who sat looking distracted and distant. Anna sat on the edge of the bed, dark eyes tired, bloodshot, and serious, while Helen stood by the window again, holding the curtain aside just enough to gaze out.

Toto promptly abandoned the field of battle upon spying Mouse, and walked in a little nervous circle within a couple of inches of Abby's lap. Mouse went over to trade sniffs with the little dog, and promptly settled down to begin grooming Toto with long licks.

'Ladies,' I said, then after a brief pause added, 'Mrs Beckitt.'

She didn't look at me. She just smiled and stared out the window. 'Yes, Mister Dresden?'

'What do you know?' I asked her.

'I beg your pardon?' she said.

'You know something about this, and you aren't talking. Spill.'

'I can't imagine what you mean,' she said.

Anna Ash rose and frowned. 'Mister Dresden, surely you aren't accusing Helen of being involved in this business?'

'I'm pretty sure I am,' I said. 'Do they know about the first time we met, Helen? Have you told them?'

That drew looks from everyone in the room.

'Helen?' Abby said after a moment. 'What is he talking about?'

'Go ahead, Mister Dresden,' Helen said, very faint, very dry amusement giving her monotone a little life. 'I wouldn't dream of cheating you of the satisfaction of looking down at one less righteous than yourself.'

'What is she talking about?' Priscilla demanded. She glared at me, probably with her mind already made up as to what she was going to think of me, regardless of what I said.

It's nice to know that some things in life are consistent, because Beckitt was disappointing me here. Her associates didn't know about her past. By revealing it, I was probably about to destroy whatever life she'd built for herself since she regained her freedom – something that would be a terrible injury to most people in her circumstances. She'd lost her daughter years ago, lost her husband shortly after, had been sent to prison and permanently stained with the guilt of her crimes.

I had expected her to attempt to evade me, to protest her innocence or accuse me of lying. Failing that, I thought the next most likely reaction would be for her to panic and flee, or else panic and shut her mouth entirely. Depending on how badly she thought I was about to screw up her life, it was even possible that she might produce a weapon and attempt to murder me.

Instead, she just stood there, apparently unafraid, a quiet little smile hovering on her lips, unruffled, like some nascent saint before the man who was about to martyr her.

None of which added up. I hate it when things don't add up. But now that I'd forced the confrontation, here in front of the rest of the Ordo, I'd destroy any credibility I had if I backed out, which is what the whole mess was about: someone attempting to destroy the Council's credibility.

I backed off on the aggression and tried to make myself sound polite and compassionate, yet serious. 'Did any of you know that Ms Beckitt is a felon?'

Priscilla's eyes grew wide behind her glasses. She looked

from me to Helen to Anna. Helen continued watching out the window, that same little smile in place.

Anna was the first to speak. 'No,' she said, frowning. 'She hasn't told us that.'

Beckitt might as well have been deaf, for all the reaction she showed.

'She was a part of a cult headed up by a sorcerer I had to take down several years ago,' I said. I delivered it flat, without emphasis. 'She participated in ritual magic that created a drug that hurt a lot of people, and helped out with other rites that murdered the sorcerer's criminal rivals.'

There was a shocked silence. 'B-b-but . . .' Abby stammered. 'But that's the First Law. The *First Law.*'

'Helen? Is that true?'

'Not quite,' Helen said. 'He didn't mention that the specific rituals used were sexual in nature.' She touched her tongue to her upper lip. 'Strike that. Depraved and indiscriminately sexual in nature.'

Priscilla stared at Helen. 'For God's sake, Helen. *Why?*'

Beckitt looked away from the window for the first time since I'd arrived, and the emptiness in her eyes was replaced with an impossibly remote, cold fury. Her voice lowered to a murmur as hard as a sheet of glacial ice. 'I had reason to do so.'

I didn't meet that frozen gaze. I didn't want to see what was behind it. 'You've got a record, Mrs Beckitt. You've helped in supernatural murders before. Maybe you're doing it again.'

She shrugged, her expression becoming lifeless again. 'And maybe I'm not.'

'Are you?' I said.

She went back to staring out the window. 'What's the point in answering, Warden? It's obvious that you've already tried and convicted me. If I tell you I am involved, you will believe me guilty. If I tell you I am not involved, you will believe me guilty. The only thing I can do is deny you your precious moral justification.' She lifted a hand to her lips and pantomimed turning a key and throwing it away.

Silence fell. Anna got up and walked to Beckitt. Anna put a hand on her shoulder, and tugged gently until the other woman turned around.

'Don't answer,' Anna said quietly. 'There's no need for it, as far as I'm concerned.'

'And I,' Priscilla said.

'Of course you aren't involved,' Abby said.

Beckitt looked around the room at each of them in turn. Her mouth quivered for an instant, and her eyes glistened. She blinked them several times, but a single tear escaped and coursed over her cheekbone. She nodded to the Ordo once, and turned back to the window.

Instinct told me that this was not the reaction of a guilty woman – and no one could put on an act *that* good.

Beckitt wasn't involved. I was sure of it – now.

Dammit.

Detectives are supposed to learn things. All I'd done so far was to unlearn them, and the clock kept right on ticking.

Priscilla turned to me, her eyes narrowed. 'Is there anything else of which you'd like to accuse us? Any other presumptuous bigotry you'd care to share?' She built her glare back up into the terawatt range, just for me.

It made me feel special. 'Look,' I said. 'I'm trying to help you.'

'Oh?' Priscilla said, scorn in her voice. 'Is that why all those people have been disappearing in the company of a man fitting your description?' I started to answer, but she cut me off. 'Not that I expect you to tell us the truth, unless it serves whatever purpose you truly have in mind.'

I carefully did not lose my temper and barbecue her stupid

face right then and there. 'Angels weep when someone so perceptive, warmhearted, and loving turns cynical, Priscilla.'

'Harry.' Elaine sighed beside me. I glanced at her. She met my eyes for a moment, and though her lips didn't move, I heard her voice quite distinctly. *God knows she makes a fine target of herself, but shooting off your mouth isn't helping.*

I blinked at her a couple of times, and then smiled a little. The communion spell between us was an old one, but once upon a time we'd used it every day. School had been boring as hell, and it beat passing notes. It had also been handy when we'd been staying up past curfew and didn't want DuMorne to know we were awake.

I put a gentle effort of will behind words, and sent them to Elaine. *God, I'd forgotten all about this. I haven't done it since I was sixteen.*

Elaine showed me her smile – the swift, rare one, the one where her mouth widened and white teeth gleamed and her eyes took on golden highlights. *Neither have I.* Her expression sobered as she glanced at Priscilla, then back to me. *Be gentle, Harry. They're hurting.*

I frowned at her. *What?*

She shook her head. *Look around you.*

I did, going more slowly this time. My focus on confronting Beckitt had prevented me from noticing what else was going on. The room was thick with tension and something heavy and bitter. Grief?

Then I saw what wasn't there. 'Where's the little brunette?'

'Her name,' Priscilla almost snarled, 'was Olivia.'

I arched a brow and glanced at Elaine. 'Was?'

'When we called her last night, she was all right,' she told me. 'When we arrived to pick her up, there was no answer at her door, and no one in her apartment.'

'Then how do you know . . . ?'

Elaine folded her arms, her expression neutral. 'There are

several security cameras around the building, and outside. One of them showed her leaving with a very pale, dark-haired man.'

I grunted. 'How'd you get to the security footage?'

Elaine gave me a smile that bared a gratuitous number of teeth. 'I said pretty please.'

I nodded, getting it. 'You can get more with a kind word and well-applied kinetomancy than with just a kind word.'

'The security guard was a smug little twit,' she said. 'Bruises fade.'

She produced a couple of sheets of printer paper bearing grainy black-and-white images. Indeed, I recognized Olivia and her dancer's leotard, even from behind, which was a good angle for her. There was a man walking next to her. He looked to be maybe a tiny bit shy of six feet, had dark, glossy, shoulder-length black hair, and was dressed in jeans and a black tee. I could see his profile in one of the pictures, his head turned toward Olivia.

It was my brother.

It was Thomas.

'Are you sure?' Anna Ash asked Elaine. 'Wouldn't we be better off at one of our apartments? They're all warded . . .'

Elaine shook her head firmly. 'The killer knows where you each live. He doesn't know about this place. Stay here, stay quiet, stay together. Our killer hasn't attacked anyone who wasn't alone.'

'And my dog will let you know if there's anything you need to worry about,' I added. 'He'll probably sit on anyone who tries to mess with you, but if he does a Lassie act at you and wants you to leave, go with him – everyone, stay together and get somewhere public.'

Mouse nudged his head under Anna's hand and wagged his tail. Toto dutifully followed Mouse, walking around Anna's ankles looking up at her until she petted him, too. That got a smile out of her, at least. 'If we leave, how will we get in touch with you?'

'I'll find you.'

'Just like you found the killer?' Priscilla spat.

I ignored her with lofty dignity.

Elaine didn't.

She stepped up to Priscilla and loomed over her. 'You ungrateful, insufferable, venomous little twit. Shut your mouth. This man is trying to protect you, just like I am. I will thank you to keep a civil tongue in your head while we do our job.'

Priscilla's face flushed. 'We aren't paying you to insult or demean us.'

'You aren't paying me enough to get me to tolerate your

rudeness, either,' Elaine said. 'Keep it up and you won't have to worry about my bill. In fact, I suspect that in short order you'll stop worrying about absolutely everything.'

'Is that a threat?' Priscilla snapped.

Elaine put a fist on her hip. 'It's a fact, bitch.'

Anna stepped in. 'Priscilla, please. *You* aren't the one paying her. 1 am. We need her. She's the professional. If she thinks it's smart to cooperate with Mister Dresden, that's what we're going to do. And we're going to treat them with professional respect. If you can't manage courtesy, try silence.'

Priscilla narrowed her eyes at Anna, then folded her arms and looked away in capitulation.

Elaine nodded at Anna and said, 'I'm not sure how long we'll be gone. I'll get word to you as soon as I have a better idea.'

'Thank you, Miss Mallory.' After a beat she hurried to add, 'And thank you, Mister Dresden.'

'Stay together,' I said, and Elaine and I left.

We walked together to the parking lot, and on the way Elaine said, 'Tell me you've gotten a new car.'

We rounded a corner, and there was the Beetle in all its battle-scarred glory.

'I like this one,' I told her, and opened the door for her.

'You redid the interior,' she said as I got in and started the car.

'Demons ate the old one.'

Elaine began to laugh, but then blinked at me. 'You're being literal?'

'Uh-huh. Fungus demons. Right down to the metal.'

'Good God, you live a glamorous life,' she said.

'Elaine,' I said. 'I thought you told me you were going to lie low until you were ready to come out to the Council.'

The friendly, teasing expression on her face faded into neutrality. 'Is this relevant right now?'

'Yeah,' I said. 'If we're going after him together, yes, it is. I need to know.'

She frowned at me, and then shrugged. 'I had to do something. There were people all around me getting hurt. Being used. Living scared. So I borrowed a page from your book.'

'And you lied to the Warden who came to check up on you.'

'You say that like you've always told the Wardens everything.'

'Elaine . . .' I began.

She shook her head. 'Harry, I know you. I trust you. But I don't trust the Council and I doubt I ever will. I certainly did not care to be impressed into service as a brand-new foot soldier to fight their war with the vampires – which I would have been, if I had put my full effort into Ramirez's tests.'

We looked at each other for a moment, and I said, 'Please? I'll go with you. I'll support you before the Council.'

She put one of her warm, soft hands over mine, and spoke in a quiet, firm voice. 'No, Harry. I won't allow those men to direct the course of my life. I won't allow them to choose if I will or will not live – or choose how.'

I sighed. 'You could do so much good.'

'I thought that's what I was doing here,' she pointed out. 'Helping people. Doing good.'

She had a point. 'The Wardens would freak out if you went to them now, anyway,' I said, 'and revealed that you'd been hiding your talents from them.'

'Yes,' she said. 'They would.'

'Dammit,' I said. 'We could use your help.'

'I don't doubt it,' she said. Her eyes hardened and her voice went suddenly cold. 'But I will *not* be used. Not by anyone. Never again.'

I blinked and turned to her.

She lifted her chin slightly, green eyes bright with unfallen tears. 'No, Harry.'

I turned my hand under hers, and we intertwined our fingers with the careless ease of an old habit. 'Elaine. I'm sorry. I didn't mean to push. I hadn't realized . . .'

She blinked several times and looked away from me. 'No, I'm the one who should be sorry. I'm going all neurotic on you, here. I don't mean to be.' She stared out the window at the city. 'After you killed DuMorne, I spent a year having a nightmare. The same one, every single night. I was sure that it was true. That he was still alive. That he was coming for me.'

'He wasn't,' I told her.

'I know,' she said. 'I saw him die just as you did. But I was so *afraid* . . .' She shook her head. 'I ran to the Summer Court because of it. I ran, Harry. I couldn't face it.'

'Is that what you're doing, going public?' I asked. 'Facing your past?'

'I have to,' she said, her voice growing firmer. 'It scares the crap out of me, all the time. And over the years . . . I've had problems with crowds. With enclosed spaces. With heights. With wide-open spaces. Night terrors. Panic attacks. Paranoia. God, sometimes it seems like there's nothing I haven't had a phobia about.'

What Elaine had described was about what I would have expected from someone whose mind had been invaded by an outside will. Magic can get you into someone's head, but if you decide to start redecorating to your tastes, there is no way to avoid inflicting damage to their psyche. Depending upon several factors, someone who has been put under that kind of control can be left twitchy and erratic at best – and at worst, totally catatonic or completely dysfunctional.

And there was the utterly normal element of emotional pain to consider, too. Elaine had, in the course of a single evening, lost absolutely everything she loved. Her boyfriend. Her adopted father. Her home.

Losing a home means a lot more to an orphan than it does to most other people. I'm in a position to know. Like me, Elaine had spent most of her childhood bouncing around from one foster home to another, one state-run orphanage to another. Like me, being given a real home, a real house, a real father figure had been a desperate dream come true. It had been a terrible loss to me, and Justin hadn't gotten any hooks into my head. For Elaine, that series of events had been infinitely more painful, infinitely more frightening.

'I let fear control one part of my life,' Elaine said, 'and it took root and started growing. I *had* to get involved, Harry. I have to use what I know to change things. If I don't, then all I'll ever be is DuMorne's tool. His terrified little weapon. I will not allow anyone to take control of my life away from me. I can't.' She shrugged. 'And I can't stand by and do nothing, either. I threw the tests. I don't regret it. I sure as hell am not going to apologize for it — not to you or to anyone.'

I grunted.

'Well?' she asked.

'I think I get it,' I said.

'Are you willing to work with me, then?'

I squeezed her hand a little. 'Of course.'

The tension in her shoulders eased, and she squeezed my hand back. 'My turn,' she said.

'Your turn?'

She nodded. 'You recognized the killer when you looked at the photo.'

'What?' I said. 'No, I didn't.'

She rolled her eyes. 'Come on, Harry. It's me.'

I sighed. 'Yeah, well.'

'Who is he?' she asked.

'Thomas Raith,' I said. 'White Court.'

'How do you know him?'

'He's . . .' Not many people knew that Thomas was my brother. It was safer for both of us to keep that information limited. 'He's a friend. Someone I trust.'

'Trust,' Elaine said quietly. 'I notice you use the present tense.'

'Thomas isn't hurting anyone,' I said.

'He's a vampire, Harry. He hurts someone every time he feeds.'

He'd been doing quite a bit of that lately. 'I know Thomas,' I maintained. 'He isn't the killer.'

Elaine frowned. 'Treachery hurts, Harry. Believe me, I know.'

'Nothing has proved Thomas is behind these killings,' I said. 'It could be someone else, or something else, masquerading as him. It isn't as if there aren't plenty of shapeshifting things around that could do it.'

'Little bit of a reach, though,' Elaine said. She nodded at the photos, where I'd set them on the dashboard. 'The simplest explanation is usually the correct one.'

'Sooner or later,' I said, 'I'll have a case where everything is simple. But I don't think this one is it.'

Elaine exhaled slowly, studying my face. 'You care about him.'

No point in denying that. 'Yeah.'

'He trusts you in return?'

'Yeah.'

'Then why hasn't he explained himself to you?' she asked. 'Why hasn't he gotten in touch with you?'

'I don't know. But I know he's not a killer.'

She nodded slowly. 'But there he is, with Olivia.'

'Yeah.'

'Then I think you should agree with me that we need to find him.'

'Yeah.'

'Can you?'

'Yep.'

'All right, then,' she said, and put on her seat belt. 'We'll find him. We'll talk to him. I'll try to keep an open mind.' She looked at me. 'But if it turns out to be him, Harry, he's got to be stopped – and I expect you to help me.'

'If it turns out to be him,' I said, 'he'd want me to.'

I've been working as a detective in Chicago for a while now, and there's one thing you do a lot more than almost anything else: You find things that get lost. I'd first designed my tracking spell to catch up to the house keys I kept losing when I was about fourteen. I'd used it a few thousand times, now. Sometimes, it had helped me find things I really didn't want. Mostly, it helped me get into trouble.

This time, I was fairly sure it would do both.

I could have used my blood to trace Thomas's, probably, but I could use my silver pentacle amulet too. My mother had given me the one I habitually wore, and she'd given one to Thomas, too. I knew that he wore it just as habitually as I wore mine, and unless someone had taken it away from him, he'd be wearing it now.

So I revved up the spell, hung the amulet from the rearview mirror of the Blue Beetle, and headed out onto the Chicago streets. I kept an eye on my amulet, which leaned slightly, drawn as if by a light magnetic field toward Thomas's amulet. That wasn't a perfect way to track something down – the spell had no concern for streets and traffic flow, for example – but I'd been finding things like this for a good while, and I piloted the Beetle through the maze of buildings and one-way streets that make up the fair city.

Elaine watched me in silence the whole while. I knew that she was wondering what I had used to lock on to our apparent abductor/murderer. She didn't push, though. She just settled down and trusted me.

When I finally parked the car and got out, I brought my

amulet with me and stared grimly at the necklace, which continued to lean steadily to the east, toward the Burnham Harbor piers that stretched out over Lake Michigan. An entire cove had been built into the lakeshore and decked out with an array of docks for dozens and dozens of small commercial boats, pleasure craft, and yachts.

'Boats,' I muttered. 'Why did it have to be boats?'

'What's wrong with boats?' Elaine asked.

'I haven't had a good time on boats,' I said. 'In fact, I haven't had a good time this close to the lake in general.'

'It smells like dead fish and motor oil,' Elaine noted.

'You never did like my cologne.' I got my staff out of the car. 'You need a big stick.'

Elaine smiled sweetly at me, and drew out a heavy chain from her purse. She held both ends in one fist, leaving a doubled length of heavy metal links about two feet long. Each of the links glittered with veins of what might have been copper, forming sinuous text. 'You're a prisoner to tradition, big guy. You should learn to be a little more flexible.'

'Careful. If you tell me you've got bracelets and a magic lariat in there, I may lose control of my sexual impulses.'

Elaine snorted. 'You can't lose what you've never had.' She glanced up at me. 'Like the new shield, by the way.'

'Yeah. Sexy, huh?'

'Complex,' she replied. 'Balanced. Strong. Sophisticated. I'm not sure I could have made a focus for something like that. It took real skill, Harry.'

I felt myself actually blush, absurdly pleased by the compliment. 'Well, it isn't perfect. It takes a lot more juice than the old shield did. But I figured getting tired faster is far preferable to getting dead faster.'

'Seems reasonable,' she said, and squinted at the docks. 'Can you tell which boat it is?'

'Not yet. But once you get two or three hundred yards

over the water, that spell would have grounded out. So we know it's one of these at the docks.'

Elaine nodded. 'You want to lead?'

'Yeah. We should be able to run it down fairly fast. Stay about ten or fifteen feet back from me.'

Elaine frowned. 'Why?'

'Any closer than that and we'd be a dandy target. Someone could take us both out with one burst from a machine gun.'

Her face got a little pale. 'I thought you trusted him.'

'I do,' I said. 'But I don't know who might be there with him.'

'And you've learned this kind of thing on the job? Machine guns?'

I felt my left hand twitch. 'Actually, I learned it with flamethrowers. But it applies to machine guns, too.'

She took a deep breath, green eyes flickering over the docks and ships. 'I see. After you, then.'

I readied my shield bracelet, got a good grip on my staff, and wrapped my amulet's chain around the first two fingers of my right hand, holding it up and out a little so that the amulet could dangle and indicate direction. I stepped out onto the docks and followed the spell toward the outermost row of moored boats. I was acutely conscious of Elaine's light, steady footsteps behind me, and the little slapping sighs of water hitting hulls.

The summer sky was overcast with lead, and occasional thunder rumbled through the air. The docks weren't nearly as crowded as they could be, but there were a couple of dozen people around, walking to and from boats, working on decks, getting ready to cast off or else just now securing their lines. I was the only one wearing a big leather coat, and got a few odd looks.

The amulet led me to the last slip of the dock farthest from shore. The boat moored there was a big one, at least for those docks, and looked like it might have been a stunt double for the boat in *Jaws*. It was old, battered, its white paint smudged to a faded, peeling grey, the planks of its hull often patched. The windows on the wheelhouse were obscured with dust and greasy smudges. It needed to be sandblasted and repainted – except for the lettering on its stern, which had apparently been added only recently in heavy black paint: WATER BEETLE.

I walked ten feet away and rechecked the amulet's indication, triangulating. The *Water Beetle* was the right boat.

'Hey!' I called out. 'Er, uh. Ahoy! Thomas!'

Silence met my hail.

I checked over my shoulder. Elaine had moved away, to where she could see the little ship's entire deck while still standing a good twenty feet down the dock from me. What was the military term for that? Establishing a cross fire? Maybe it was creating a defilade. The point being, though, that if anything came gibbering up out of the boat's hold, we'd tear it up between us before you could say boogity-boo.

Of course, if anyone on the boat had hostile intent and an ounce of brains, they'd probably realize that, too.

'Thomas!' I shouted again. 'It's Harry Dresden!'

If someone on that boat meant me harm, the smart thing to do would be to stay quiet and tempt me out onto the boat itself. That would minimize my chances of avoiding an attack, and give them their best shot at taking me out in a hurry – which is just about the only reliable way to do it, when you're dealing with wizards. Give one of us time to catch our breath, and we can be a real handful.

'Okay,' I said to Elaine, not taking my eyes off the boat. 'I'm going aboard.'

'Is that smart?'

'No.' I glanced at her for a second. 'You got a better idea?'

'No,' she admitted.

'Cover me.'

'Cover you.' Elaine shook her head, but she let one end of the chain slip loose from her hand, and caught it in the other. She took a grip on it, leaving a couple of feet hanging from her left hand. Little flickers of light played along it – subtle enough that I doubted anyone would notice if they weren't looking for it. 'I thought I was here on a job. Now it turns out I'm half of a buddy-cop movie.'

'Uh-huh,' I said. 'I'm the zany yet lovable one. You're the brainy conservative.'

'What if I want to be the zany one?'

'Then you can hop out there on the boat.'

'Stop throwing the regulations out the window,' she said, as if reciting a hastily memorized grocery list. 'We're supposed to catch the maniacs, not become them. Don't do anything crazy, because I've only got two and a half seconds to go until I retire.'

'That's the spirit,' I said, and hopped from the dock to the deck of the *Water Beetle*.

I crouched, ready for trouble, but nothing came hurtling at me. One of the boats down the dock started up an engine that could not possibly have passed any kind of emissions test, including one for noise. Even so, though, I heard a thumping sound come from below the deck. I froze, but there was no further sound beyond the nearby rumbling engine, which, from the smell of it, was burning a lot of oil.

I tried to move silently, pacing around the wheelhouse. It was a tight squeeze between the deckhouse and the rail as I sidled by to peer around the corner and down a short flight of stairs that led into the ship's cabin hold. I was aware of a presence: nothing specific, really, beyond a sudden, intuitive certainty that someone was down there and aware of me in return.

I could probably dance around, listening and lurking in hopes of finding some other indication of who was below — but not for long. People would notice me crouching and taking cover on the ship's deck for no apparent reason. Some of them would ignore it. Hell, most of them would ignore it. But inevitably, one of them would think it odd enough to give the cops a ring.

'Screw it,' I said. I made sure my duster was covering my back, brought my shield up before me, and stepped quickly down the stairs and into the hold.

I had maybe half a second of warning when someone came swinging down the stairs behind me — he must have been lying flat and out of sight atop the wheelhouse. I started to turn, but two heels hit my right shoulder blade in a double-legged kick and propelled me forcefully down into the hold.

The duster was hell on wheels for stopping claws and bullets, but it did me less good against the blunt impact of the kick. It hurt. I threw up the shield in front of me as I fell, and cut it again in an instant, since impacting a rigid plane of force would be much like slamming myself into a brick wall. The fluttering energy of the shield slowed me enough to control my fall and turn it into a roll. I came to my knees facing the stairway, as Thomas came hurtling down it with mayhem evidently in mind.

He crouched on the stairs with one of those crooked knives the Gurkhas use clutched in one fist, and a double-barreled shotgun with maybe six inches of barrel left to it in the other and pointed directly at my head. My brother was a little bit shy of six feet tall, slim, and made out of whip-cord and steel cable. His eyes were alight with fury in his pale face, faded from their usual thundercloud grey to an angry, metallic silver that meant that he was drawing upon his power as a vampire. His shoulder-length dark hair was bound back under a red bandanna, and his 'do still looked more stylish than mine.

'Thomas,' I snarled. '*Ow*. What is *wrong* with you?'

'You get one chance to surrender, asshole. Drop the spells and face the wall.'

'Thomas. Stop being a dick. I don't need this right now.'

Thomas sneered. 'Give it up. It's a good act, but I know you aren't Harry Dresden. There's no way the real Dresden would have come here with a woman like that instead of his dog.'

I blinked at him and dropped my shield. 'Now what the hell is *that* supposed to mean?' I glared at him and added in a lower tone, 'Hell's bells, if you weren't my brother, I'd paste you.'

Thomas lowered the shotgun, his expression startled. 'Harry?'

A shadow moved behind Thomas.

'Wait!' I screamed.

A length of heavy chain whipped around his throat. There was a flash of greenish light and a crackling explosion almost as loud as a gunshot. Thomas jerked into an agonized arch and was flung free of the chain to come hurtling into me. For the second time in sixty seconds, I got hit with my brother's full weight and slammed to the floor. My nose filled with the sharp scent of ozone and burned hair.

'Harry?' called Elaine's voice, high and loud. 'Harry?'

'I said to wait,' I wheezed.

She came hustling down the stairs and over to me. 'Did he hurt you?'

'Not until you threw him on me,' I snapped. Which wasn't true, but being repeatedly bashed about makes me grumpy. I touched a finger to my throbbing lip, and it came away wet with blood. 'Ow.'

Elaine said, 'Sorry. I thought you were in trouble.'

I shook my head to clear it and glanced at Thomas. His eyes were open and he looked startled. He was breathing, but his arms and legs lay limp. His lips moved a little. I leaned over and asked him, 'What?'

'Ow,' he whispered.

I sat up, a little relieved. If he was able to complain, he couldn't have been too bad off. 'What was that?' I asked Elaine.

'Taser.'

'Stored electricity?'

'Yes.'

'How do you refill it?'

'Thunderstorm. Or I just plug it into any wall socket.'

'Cool,' I said. 'Maybe I should get one of those.'

Thomas's head moved, and one of his legs twitched and began to stir.

Elaine whirled on him at once, her chain held taut between her hands, and little flashes of light began flickering through the decorative metal embedded into the links.

'Easy, there,' I said, firmly. 'Back off. We came here to talk, remember?'

'Harry, we should at least restrain him.'

'He isn't going to hurt us,' I said.

'Would you listen to yourself for a second?' she said, her voice sharpening. 'Harry, despite heavy evidence to the contrary, you're telling me that you like and trust a creature whose specialty lies in subverting the minds of his victims. That's the way *they* all talk about a White Court vampire, and you know it.'

'That isn't what's happened here,' I said.

'They say *that*, too,' Elaine insisted. 'I'm not saying any of this is your fault, Harry. But if this thing *has* gotten to you somehow, this is exactly how you'd be responding to it.'

'He's not a *thing*,' I snarled. 'His name is Thomas.'

Thomas took in a deep breath and then managed to say, in a very feeble voice, 'It's all right. You can come out now.'

The forward wall of the cabin creaked and suddenly shifted, swinging out on a concealed hinge to reveal a small area behind it, not quite as large as a typical walk-in closet. There were several women and two or three very small children huddled in that cramped space, and they emerged into the cabin warily.

One of them was Olivia the dancer.

'There,' Thomas said quietly. He turned his head to Elaine. 'There they are, and they're fine. Check them out for yourself.'

I stood up, my joints creaking, and studied the women. 'Olivia,' I said.

'Warden,' she said quietly.

'Are you all right?'

She smiled. 'Except for a muscle cramp I got in there. It's a little crowded.'

Elaine looked from the women to Thomas and back. 'Did he hurt you?'

Olivia blinked. 'No,' she said. 'No, of course not. He was taking us to shelter.'

'Shelter?' I asked.

'Harry,' Elaine said, 'these are some of the women who have gone missing.'

I digested that for a second, and then turned to Thomas. 'What the hell is wrong with you? Why didn't you tell me what was going on?'

He shook his head, his expression still a little bleary. 'Reasons. Didn't want you involved in this.'

'Well, I'm involved now,' I said. 'So how about you tell me what's going on.'

'You were at my apartment,' Thomas said. 'You saw my guest room wall.'

'Yeah.'

'They were being hunted. I had to figure out who was after them. Why. I got it, at least well enough to be able to figure out who they were planning to kill. It became a race between us.' He glanced at the women and children. 'I got everyone I could out of harm's way, and brought them here.' He tried to move his head and winced. 'Nnngh. There are another dozen at a cabin on an island about twenty miles north of here.'

'A safe house,' I mused. 'You were taking them to a safe house.'

'Yeah.'

Elaine just stared at the women for a long moment, then at Thomas. 'Olivia,' she asked. 'Is he telling the truth?'

'A-as far as I know,' the girl answered. 'He's been a perfect gentleman.'

I'm pretty sure nobody but me caught it, but at her words, Thomas's eyes flashed with a cold and furious hunger. He may have treated the women gently and politely, but I knew that there was a part of him that hadn't wanted to. He closed his eyes tightly and started taking deep breaths. I recognized the ritual he used to control his darker nature, and said nothing of it.

Elaine talked quietly with Olivia, who began making introductions. I leaned against a wall – unless maybe, since we were on a ship, it was a bulkhead   and rubbed my finger at a spot between my eyebrows where a headache was coming on. The damned oily smoke smell from the nearby ship's sputtering engine wasn't helping matters any, either, and—

My head snapped up and I flung myself up the stairs and onto the deck.

That big ugly boat had been moved from its moorings – and now floated directly beside the *Water Beetle* blocking it from the open waters of the lake. Its engine was pouring out so much blue-black oil smoke that it could not have been anything but deliberate. A choking haze had already enveloped the *Water Beetle*, and I couldn't see beyond the next row of docks.

A figure hurtled from the deck of the boat to land in a tigerish crouch on the little area of open deck at the rear of the *Water Beetle*. Even as I watched, its features, those of an unremarkable man in his midthirties, began to change. His jaws elongated, face extending into something of a muzzle, and his forearms lengthened, the nails extending into dirty-looking talons.

He faced me, shoulders distorting into hunched knots of powerful muscle, bared his teeth, and let out a shrieking roar.

A ghoul. A tough, dangerous opponent, but not impossible to beat.

Then more figures appeared on the deck of the other ship, half veiled by the thick smoke. Their limbs crackled and contorted, and a dozen more ghouls opened their mouths in earsplitting echo of the first.

'Thomas!' I shouted, half choking on the smoke. 'We've got a problem!'

Thirteen ghouls flung themselves directly at me, jaws gaping and slavering, talons reaching, eyes gleaming with feral bloodlust and rage.

Fucking *boats*.

I have, in general, not had fun during my service as a Warden of the White Council. I have taken no enjoyment whatsoever in becoming a solider in the war with the Vampire Courts. Doing battle with the forces of . . .

I was going to say *evil*, but I'm increasingly unsure exactly where everyone around me falls on the Jedi-Sith Index.

Doing battle with the forces of things trying to kill me, or my friends, or people who can't protect themselves is not a rowdy summer adventure movie. It's a nightmare. Everything is violence and confusion, fear and rage, pain and exhilaration. It all happens fast, and there's never time to think, never any way to be sure of anything.

It's awful, really — but I do have to admit that there's been one positive thing about the situation:

I've gotten in a lot of extra practice at combat wizardry.

And ever since New Mexico, I had absolutely no reservations about ripping ghouls apart with it.

The nearest ghoul was the closest threat, but not the greatest opportunity. Still, if I didn't lay the smack down on him in a hurry, he'd rip my head off, or at least tie me up long enough for his buddies to mob me. Ordinarily, I'd have let him eat a blast of telekinetic force from the little silver ring I wore on my right hand, the one that stored up a little energy every time I moved my arm, and which was useless after being employed.

I couldn't do that, because I'd replaced the single silver ring with three circles of silver fused into a single band, each with the same potential energy as the original silver ring.

Oh. And I had one of the new bands on every finger of my right hand.

I raised my staff in my fist, baring the rings to the ghoul, and as I triggered the first ring snarled, 'See ya!'

Raw force lashed out at the ghoul, flung him off the end of the *Water Beetle*, and slammed him against the front of the ship blocking us in with enough force to break his back. There was a rippling crack, the ghoul's battle cry turned into an agonized scream, and he vanished into the cold waters of Lake Michigan.

The first of his buddies was already in the air, boarding the *Water Beetle* just as the first had. I waited a half second, timing the arc of his jump, and before his feet touched down, I hit him just as I had the first one. This time, the ghoul flew back into a pair of its buddies, already in the air behind him, and dropped all three of them into the drink. Ghouls five and six were female, about which I did not care in the least, and I swatted them into the lake with two more blasts.

So far, so good, but then four of them all leaped together – probably by chance, rather than design – and I knocked down only two of them. The other two hit the deck of the *Water Beetle* and flung themselves at me, claws extended.

No time for any tricks. I whirled my staff, planted the back end against the wheelhouse wall, and aimed the other at the nearest ghoul's teeth. It hit the ghoul with the tremendous power provided by his own supernatural strength and speed. Shattered bits of yellow fangs showered the deck as the ghoul rebounded. The second ghoul leaped straight over his buddy—

—and got a really nice view of the barrel of the .44 revolver I'd pulled from my duster's pocket with my left hand. The hand cannon roared, snapping the ghoul's head back, and it slammed into me. My back hit the wheelhouse hard enough to knock the breath from me, but the ghoul fell to the deck, writhing and screaming madly.

I put two more shots into the ghoul's head from two feet away, and emptied the revolver into the skull of the one I'd stunned with my staff. Watery, brownish blood splattered the deck.

By then, three more ghouls were on the deck, and I heard thunking sounds of impact over the side of the ship as two of the ghouls I'd knocked into the water sank their claws into the *Water Beetle*'s planks and began swarming over the sides.

I hit the nearest ghoul with another blast from one of my rings, sending it flying into its companions, but it bought me only enough time to raise my shield into a shimmering quarter-dome of silver light. Two ghouls slammed against it, claws raking, and bounced off.

Then the ghouls coming up the sides of the ship gained the deck, behind the edge of my shield, and hit me from the side. Claws raked at me. I felt a hot pain on my chin, and then heavy impacts as the talons struck my duster. They couldn't pierce it, but hit with considerable force, a sensation like being jabbed hard in the side with the rounded ends of multiple broom handles.

I went down and kicked at a knee. It snapped, crackled, and popped, drawing a scream of rage from the ghoul, but its companion landed on me, forcing me to throw my left arm across my throat to keep him from ripping it out. My shield flickered and fell, and the other ghouls let out howls of hungry glee.

A woman's voice let out a ringing, defiant shout. There was a roar of light and sound, a flash of scything, solid green light, and the ghoul atop me jerked as its head simply vanished from its shoulders, spraying foul-smelling brown blood everywhere. I shoved the still-twitching body off me and gained my feet even as Elaine stepped past me. She whirled that chain of hers over her head, snarling, 'Aerios!'

Something that looked like a miniature tornado illuminated from within by green light and laid on its side formed in the air in front of her. The baby twister immediately began moving so much air so quickly that I had to lean away from the spell's powerful suction.

The far end of the spell blew forth air in a shrieking column of wind so strong that, as it played back and forth over the back end of the ship, it scattered ghouls like bits of popcorn in a blower. It also had the effect of ripping the thick, choking smoke away from the stairway leading belowdecks, and I hadn't even realized how dizzy I had begun to feel.

'I can't hold this for long!' Elaine shouted.

The ghouls began trying to get around the spell, more of them climbing the sides after being thrown into the lake again. I couldn't try whipping up a fire – not with all these fine wooden boats and docks and brimming fuel containers and resident boaters around. So I had to make do with using my staff – not using magic, either. That's the beauty of having a big heavy stick with you. Anytime you need to do it, you've got a handy head-cracking weapon ready to go.

The ghouls tried climbing up the sides of the ship, but I started playing whack-a-mole as their heads or clawed hands appeared over the side.

'Thomas!' I cried. 'We've got to get out of here!'

I could barely see anything through the smoke, but I could make out the shapes of some of the ghouls clambering up onto the dock – cutting us off from the shore.

'Get the boat loose!' Elaine shouted.

The ghouls' smoking vessel actually cruised into the rear of the *Water Beetle*, the impact forcing me to grab at the wheelhouse to keep my feet – and to stagger the other way a second later as the *Water Beetle* smashed into the dock. 'Not a chance! He's too close!'

'Down!' Thomas shouted, and I felt his hand shove down hard on my shoulder. I ducked, and saw the blued steel of his sawed-off shotgun as it went past my face. The thing roared, the sound painfully loud, and I was pretty sure I wouldn't hear anything out of that ear for a while. The blast caught the ghoul that had somehow sneaked up onto the top of the wheel-house and had been about to leap down onto my shoulders.

'Ow!' I shouted to Thomas. 'Thank you!'

'Harry!' Elaine shouted, her voice higher, now desperate.

I looked past her and saw that her pet cyclone was slowing down. Several of the ghouls had managed to dig their claws into the deck and hang on, rather than being blasted off the end of the ship.

'This is bad, this is bad, this is bad,' Thomas said.

'I *know* that!' I shouted at him. A glance over my shoulder showed me Olivia's pale face on the stairs, and the other women and children behind her. 'We'll never get them out of here on foot. They've got the docks cut off.'

Thomas took a quick glance around the ship and said, 'We can't cast off, either!'

'Harry!' Elaine gasped. The light began to fade from her spell, the howl of wind dropping, the ugly, heavy smoke beginning to creep back in.

Ghouls are hard to kill. I'd done for two of them, Elaine for a third, but the others had mostly just been made angrier by getting repeatedly slammed in the kisser with blasts of force, followed by tumbles into the cold lake.

Cold lake.

Aha. A plan.

'Take this!' I shouted, and shoved my staff at Thomas. 'Buy me a few seconds!' I spun to Olivia and said, 'Everyone get ready to follow me, close!'

Olivia relayed that to the women behind her while I hurriedly jerked loose the knots that secured my blasting rod to the inside of my duster. I whipped out the blasting rod and looked out over the side of the ship farthest from shore. There was nothing but thirty feet of water, then the vague shape of the next row of docks.

Thomas saw the blasting rod and swore under his breath, but he whirled my staff with grace and style — the way he does pretty much everything — then leaped past Elaine's fading spell and began battering ghouls.

It's hard for me to remember sometimes that Thomas isn't human, no matter that he looks it, and is my brother to boot. Other times, like this one, I get forcibly reminded about his true nature.

Ghouls are strong and disgustingly quick (emphasis on *disgusting*). Thomas, though, drawing upon his darker nature, made them look like the faceless throngs of extras in an Arnold Schwarzenegger movie. He moved like smoke among them, the heavy oak of my staff spinning, striking, snapping out straight and whirling away, driven at the attackers with superhuman power. I wanted to fight beside him, but that wouldn't get us *away* from this ambush, which was our only real chance of survival.

So instead of rushing to his aid, I gripped my blasting rod, focused my will, and began to summon up every scrap of energy I could bring to bear. This spell was going to take a hell of a lot of juice, but if it worked, we'd be clear. I reminded myself of that as I stood frozen, my eyes half closed, while my brother fought for our lives.

Thomas outclassed any single ghoul he was up against, but though he could cause them horrible pain, a bludgeoning tool was not a good weapon for actually killing them. He would have had to shatter several vertebrae or break open a skull to put one of them down. Had he stopped to take the focus he would need to finish off a single ghoul he'd temporarily disabled, the rest would have swarmed him. He knew it. They knew it, too. They fought with the mindlessly efficient instinct of the pack, certain that they could, in a few moments, wear down their prey.

Check that. It wouldn't even take that long. Once that smoke rolled in again, we'd last only a minute or three, breathing hard in exertion and fear as we all were. The gunfire and shrieking would have prompted a dozen calls to the authorities, as well. I was sure I would be hearing sirens any minute, assuming the ear my brother had left intact was pointed that way. It was at that point that I realized something else:

Someone was still on the boat pinning the *Water Beetle* against the dock. Someone who had brought the ghouls over, who had been lying in wait near Thomas. Ghouls are hell on wheels for violence, but they don't tend to plan things out very well without outside direction. They certainly do not bother operating under a smoke screen. So whoever was driving the other boat probably wasn't a ghoul.

Grey Cloak. maybe? Or his homey, Passenger.

That's when I realized something else: We didn't have even those couple of minutes it would take for the smoke to strangle us. Once the mortal authorities started arriving, whoever was in charge of the ghouls was sure to goad them into a more coordinated rush, and that would be that.

A ghoul's flailing claw ripped through Thomas's jeans and tore into his calf. He lost his balance for a second, caught it again, and kept fighting as if nothing had happened — but blood a little too pale to be human dribbled steadily to the *Water Beetle*'s deck.

I clenched my teeth as the power rose in me. The hairs on my arms stood up straight, and there was a kind of buzzing pressure against the insides of my eardrums. My muscles were tensing, almost to the point of convulsing in a full-body charley horse. Stars swam in my vision as I raised the blasting rod.

'Harry!' Elaine gasped. 'Don't be a fool! You'll kill us all!'

I heard her, but I was too far gone into the spell to respond. It had to work. I mean, it had worked once before. In theory, it should work again if I could just get it to be a little bit bigger.

I lifted my face and the blasting rod to the sky, opened my throat, and in a stentorian bellow shouted, '*Fuego!*'

Fire exploded from the tip of the blasting rod, a column of white-hot flame as thick as my hips. It surged up into the smoke, burning it away as it went, rising into a fiery fountain a good twenty stories high.

All magic obeys certain principles, and many of them apply across the whole spectrum of reality, scientific, arcane, or otherwise. As far as casting spells is concerned, the most important is the principle of conservation of energy. Energy cannot simply be created. If one wants a twenty-story column of fire hot enough to vaporize tengauge steel, the energy of all that fire has to come from somewhere. Most of my spells use my own personal energy, what is most simply described as sheer force of will. Energy for such things can also come from other sources outside of the wizard's personal power.

This spell, for example, had been drawn from the heat energy absorbed by the waters of Lake Michigan.

The fire roared up with a thunderous detonation of suddenly expanding air, and the shock wave from it startled everyone into dead silence. The lake let out a sudden, directionless, crackling snarl. In the space of a heartbeat the water between where I stood and the next dock froze over, a sudden sheet of hard, white ice.

I sagged with fatigue. Channeling so much energy through myself was an act that invited trauma and exhaustion, and a sudden weakness in my limbs made me stagger.

'Go!' I shouted to Olivia. 'Over the ice! Run for the next dock! Women and children first!'

'Kill them!' shouted a man's voice from the general direction of the attacking ship.

The ghouls howled and leaped forward, enraged to see prey making good their escape.

I leaned on the rail and watched Olivia and company flee. They hurried over the ice, slipping here and there. Crackling protests of the ice sounded under their feet. Spiderweb fractures began to spread, slowly but surely.

I gritted my teeth. Even though Lake Michigan is a cold-water lake, this was high summer, and even in the limited space I had frozen, there was an enormous amount of water that had to be chilled. Imagine how much fire it takes to heat a teakettle to boiling, and remember that it works both ways. You have to take heat *away* from the kettle's water if you want to freeze it. Now, multiply that much energy by about a berjillion, because that's the amount of water I was trying to freeze.

Olivia and the women and children made it to the far dock and fled in a very well-advised and appropriate state of panic.

'Harry!' Elaine said. Her chain lashed out and struck a ghoul that had slipped by Thomas.

'They're clear!' I cried. 'Go, go, go! Thomas, we is skedaddling!'

I stood up and readied my shield bracelet.

'Come on,' Elaine told me, grabbing my arm.

I shook my head. 'I'm the heaviest,' I told her. 'I go last.'

Elaine blinked at me, opened her mouth to protest, then went very pale and nodded once. She vaulted the rail and ran for the docks.

'Thomas!' I screamed. 'Down!'

Thomas hit the deck without so much as looking over his shoulder, and the ghouls closed in.

I triggered the rest of the kinetic rings: all of them at once.

Ghouls tumbled and flew. But I'd bought us only a little time.

Thomas turned and leaped over the side. I checked, and saw that Elaine had reached the other dock. Thomas bounded over the ice like something from one of those Japanese martial arts cartoons, leaped, and actually turned a flip in the air before landing on his feet.

I didn't want to come down too hard on the ice, but I didn't want to wait around until a ghoul ate me, either. I did my best to minimize the impact and started hurrying across.

Ice crackled. On my second step, a sudden, deep crack snapped open beneath my rearmost foot. Holy crap. Maybe I'd underestimated the energy involved. Maybe it had been *two* berjillion teakettles.

I took the next step, and felt the ice groaning under my feet. More cracks appeared. It was only twenty feet, but the next dock suddenly looked miles away.

Behind me, I heard ghouls charging, throwing themselves recklessly onto the ice once they saw my turned back.

'This is bad, this is bad, this is bad,' I babbled to myself. Behind me, the ice suddenly screeched, and one of the ghouls vanished into the water with a scream of protest.

More cracks, even thicker, began to race out ahead of me.

'Harry!' Thomas screamed, pointing over my shoulder.

I turned my head and saw Madrigal Raith standing on the deck of the *Water Beetle*, not more than ten feet away. He gave me a delighted smile.

Then he lifted a heavy assault rifle to his shoulder and opened fire.

I screamed in order to summon up my primal reserves and to intimidate Madrigal into missing me, and definitely not because I was terrified. While I unleashed my sonic initiative, I also crouched down to take cover. To the untrained eye, it probably looked like I was just cowering and pulling my duster up to cover my head, but it was actually part of a cunning master plan designed to let me survive the next three or four seconds.

Madrigal Raith was Thomas's cousin, and built along the same lines: slim, dark-haired, pale, and handsome, though not on Thomas's scale. Unfortunately, he was just as deceptively strong and swift as Thomas was, and if he could shoot half as well, there was no way he would miss me, not at that range.

And he didn't.

The spellwork I'd laid over my duster had stood me in good stead on more than one occasion. It had stopped claws and talons and fangs and saved me from being torn apart by broken glass. It had reduced the impact of various and sundry blunt objects, and generally preserved my life in the face of a great deal of potentially grievous bodily harm. But I hadn't designed the coat to stand up to *this*.

There is an enormous amount of difference between the weapons and ammunition employed by your average Chicago thug and military-grade weaponry. Military rounds, fully jacketed in metal, would not smash and deform as easily as bullets of simple lead. They were heavier rounds, moving a lot faster than you'd get with civilian small arms, and they kept their weight focused behind an armor-piercing tip, all of which meant that while military rounds didn't tend to fracture on impact and inflict horribly complicated damage on the human body, they *did* tend to smash their way through just about anything that got in their way. Personal body armor, advanced as it is, is of very limited use against well-directed military-grade fire – particularly when exposed from ten feet away.

The shots hit me not in a string of separate impacts, the way I had thought it would be, but in one awful roar of noise and pressure and pain. Everything spun around. I was flung over the fracturing ice, my body rolling. The sun found a hole in the smoke and glared down into my eyes. I felt a horrible, nauseated wave of sensation flood over me, and the glare of light in my eyes became hellish agony. I felt suddenly weak and exhausted, and even though I knew there was something I should have been doing, I couldn't remember what it was.

If only the damned light wouldn't keep burning my eyes like that . . .

'. . . it wouldn't be so bad out here,' I growled to Ramirez. I held up a hand to shield my eyes from the blazing New Mexico sun. 'Every morning it's like someone sticking needles in my eyes.'

Ramirez, dressed in surplus military BDU pants, a loose white cotton shirt, a khaki bush hat folded up on one side, wraparound sunglasses, and his usual cocky grin, shook his head. 'For God's sake, Harry. Why didn't you bring sunglasses?'

'I don't like glasses,' I said. 'Things on my eyes, they bug me.'

'Do they bug you as much as going blind?' Ramirez asked. I lowered my hand as my eyes finished adjusting, and squinting hard made it possible to bear the glare. 'Shut up, Carlos.'

'Who's a grumpy wizard in the morning?' Carlos asked, in that tone of voice one usually reserves for favorite dogs.

'Get a couple more years on you and that many beers that late at night will leave you with a headache, too, punk.' I growled a couple of curses under my breath, then shook my head and composed myself as ought to be expected of a master wizard – which is to say, I subtracted the complaining and was left with only the grumpy scowl. 'Who's up?'

Ramirez took a small notebook from his pocket and flipped it open. 'The Terrible Twosome,' he replied. 'The Trailman twins.'

'You're kidding. They're twelve years old.'

'Sixteen,' Ramirez contradicted me.

'Twelve, sixteen,' I said. 'They're babies.'

Ramirez's smile faded. 'They don't have time to be babies, man. They've got a gift for evocation, and we need them.'

'Sixteen,' I muttered. 'Hell's bells. All right, let's get some breakfast first.'

Ramirez and I marched to breakfast. The site Captain Luccio had chosen for teaching trainee Wardens evocation had once been a boomtown, built up around a vein of copper that trickled out after a year or so of mining. It was pretty high up in the mountains, and though we were less than a hundred miles northwest of Albuquerque, we might as well have been camped out on the surface of the moon. The only indications of humanity for ten or twelve miles in any direction were ourselves and the tumbledown remains of the town and the mine upslope from it.

Ramirez and I had lobbied to christen the place Camp Kaboom, given that it *was* a boomtown and we *were* teaching magic that generally involved plenty of booms of its own, but Luccio had overridden us. One of the kids had heard us, though, and by the end of the second day there, Camp Kaboom had been named despite the disapproval of the establishment.

The forty-odd kids had their tents pitched within the stone walls of a church someone had built in an effort to bring a little more stability to the general havoc of boomtowns in the Old West. Luccio had pitched her tent with them, but Ramirez, me, and two other young Wardens who were helping her teach had set up our tents on the remains of what had once been a saloon, a brothel, or both. We'd taught kids all day and evening, and once it had gotten cold and the trainees were asleep, we played poker and drank beer, and if I got enough in me, I would even play a little guitar.

Ramirez and his cronies got up every morning just as bright eyed and bushy tailed as if they'd had a full night's sleep. The cocky little bastards. Breakfast was dished up and served by the trainees every morning, built around several portable grills and several folded tables situated near a well that still held cool water, if you worked the weather-beaten pump long enough. Breakfast was little more than a bowl of cereal, but part of the little more was coffee, so I was surviving without killing anyone – if only because I took breakfast alone, giving the grumpy time to fade before exposing myself to anyone else.

I collected my cereal, an apple, and a big cup of the holy Mocha, walked a ways, and settled down on a rock in the blinding light of morning in desert mountains. Captain Luccio sat down beside me.

'Good morning,' she said. Luccio was a wizard of the White Council, a couple of centuries old, and one of its more dangerous members. She didn't look like that. She looked like a girl not even as old as Ramirez, with long, curling brown locks, a sweetly pretty face, and killer dimples. When

I'd met her, she'd been a lean, leathery-skinned matron with iron grey hair, but a black wizard called the Corpsetaker had suckered her in a duel. Corpsetaker, then in Luccio's current body, had let Luccio run her through – and then Corpsetaker had worked her trademark magic, and switched their minds into the opposite bodies.

I'd figured it out before Corpsetaker had time enough to abuse Luccio's credibility, but once I'd put a bullet through Corpsetaker's head, there hadn't been any way for Luccio to get her original body back. So she'd been stuck in the young, cute one instead, because of me. She had also ceased taking to the field in actual combat, passing that off to her second in command, Morgan, while she ran the boot camp to train new Wardens in how to kill things without getting killed first.

'Good morning,' I replied.

'Mail came for you yesterday,' she said, and produced a letter from a pocket.

I took it, scanned the envelope, and opened it. 'Hmmm.'

'Who is it from?' she asked. Her tone was that of one passing the time in polite conversation.

'Warden Yoshimo,' I said. 'I had a few questions for her about her family tree. See if she was related to a man I knew.'

'Is she?' Luccio asked.

'Distantly,' I said, reading on. 'Interesting.' At Luccio's polite noise of inquiry, I said, 'My friend was a descendant of Sho Tai.'

'I'm afraid I don't know who that is,' Luccio said.

'He was the last king of Okinawa,' I said, and frowned, thinking it over. 'I bet it means something.'

'Means something?'

I glanced at Captain Luccio and shook my head. 'Sorry. It's a side project of mine, something I'm curious about.' I folded up the letter from Yoshimo, and tucked it into the pocket of my jeans. 'It isn't relevant to teaching apprentices combat magic, and I should have my head in the game, not on side projects.'

'Ah,' Luccio said, and did not press for further details. 'Dresden, there's something I've been meaning to talk to you about.'

I grunted interrogatively.

She lifted her eyebrows. 'Have you never wondered why you did not receive a blade?'

The Wardens toted silver swords with them whenever there was a fight at hand. I had seen them unravel complex, powerful magic at the will of their wielders, which is one hell of an advantage when taking on anything using magic as a weapon. 'Oh,' I said, and sipped some coffee. 'Actually I hadn't really wondered. I assumed you didn't trust me.'

She frowned at me. 'I see,' she said. 'No. That is not the case. If I did not trust you, I would certainly not allow you to continue wearing the cloak.'

'Is there anything I could do to make you not trust me, then?' I asked. ''Cause I don't want to wear the cloak. No offense.'

'None taken,' she said. 'But we need you, and the cloak stays on.'

'Damn.'

She smiled briefly. The expression had entirely too much weight and subtlety for a face so young. 'The fact of the matter is that the swords the Wardens have used in your lifetime must be tailored specifically to each individual Warden. They were also all articles of my creation – and I am no longer capable of creating them.'

I frowned and imbibed more coffee. 'Because . . .' I gestured at her vaguely.

She nodded. 'This body did not possess the same potential, the same aptitudes for magic as my own. Returning to my former level of ability will be problematical, and will happen no time soon.' She shrugged, her expression neutral, but I had a feeling she was covering a lot of frustration and bitterness. 'Until someone else manages to adapt my design to their own talents, or until I have retrained myself, I'm afraid that no more such blades will be issued.'

I chewed some cereal, sipped some coffee, and said, 'It must be hard on you. The new body. A big change, after so long in the first one.'

She blinked at me, eyes briefly wide with surprise. 'I . . . Yes, it has been.'

'Are you doing okay?'

She looked thoughtfully at her cereal for a moment. 'Headaches,' she said quietly. 'Memories that aren't mine. I think they belong to the original owner of this body. They come mostly in dreams. It's hard to sleep.' She sighed. 'And, of course, it had been a hundred and forty years since I'd put up with either sexual desire or a monthly cycle.'

I swallowed cereal carefully instead of choking. 'It sounds, ah, awkward. And unpleasant.'

'Very,' she said, her voice quiet. Then her cheeks turned faintly pink. 'Mostly. Thank you for asking.' Then she took a deep breath, exhaled briskly, and rose, all businesslike again. 'In any case, I felt I owed you an explanation.'

'You didn't,' I said. 'But thank y—'

Automatic weapons fire ripped the dew-spangled morning.

Luccio was moving at a full sprint before I'd gotten my ass up off the rock. I wasn't slow. I've been in enough scrapes that I don't freeze at the unexpected appearance of violence and death. Captain Luccio, however, had been in a lot more scrapes than that and was faster and better than me. As we ran, there was the continued chatter of weapons fire, screams, and then a couple of awfully loud explosions and an inhuman scream. I caught up to the Captain of the Wardens as we came into sight of the breakfast area, and I let her take the lead.

I'm pigheadedly chivalrous. Not stupid.

The breakfast area was in a shambles. Folding tables had been knocked over. Blood and breakfast cereal lay scattered on the rocky ground. I could see two kids on the ground, one screaming, one simply doubled over in a fetal position, shaking. Others were lying flat, faces in the dirt. Maybe thirty yards away, in the ruins of what had been a blacksmith's shop, the only remaining brick wall was missing an enormous circle of stone – simply gone, probably in one of those weird, silent green blasts Ramirez favored. I could see the barrel of a heavy weapon of some kind lying on the ground, neatly severed about a foot behind its tip. Whoever had been holding it was likely gone with the bricks of the wall.

Ramirez's head appeared at the hole in the wall. He had dark brown fluid spattering one side of his face. 'Captain, get down!'

Bullets hissed down, making whistling, whipping sounds as they kicked up dirt a foot to Luccio's right, and the report of the shots reached us half a second later.

Luccio didn't waver or slow. She threw her right hand out, fingers spread. I couldn't see what she'd done, but the air between us and the slope of the mountain above suddenly went watery with haze. 'Where?' she shouted.

'I've got two wounded ghouls here!' Ramirez shouted. 'At least two more upslope, maybe a hundred and twenty meters!'

As he spoke, one of the other Wardens rolled around the end of the broken wall, pointed his staff upslope, and spat out a vicious-sounding word. There was a low hum, a sudden flash, and a blue-white bolt of lightning snarled up the side of the mountain in the general direction of the shots. It struck a boulder with a roar and shattered it to gravel, the sight bizarre through the haze Luccio had conjured.

'Watch it!' Ramirez screamed. 'They took two of our kids!'

The other Warden shot him a horrified look, and then dove for cover as more gunfire spat down the mountain. He let out a short, clench-toothed scream and grabbed at his leg, and one of the kids not far from him gasped, clutching at her cheek.

'Dammit,' snarled Luccio. She slid to a stop and raised her other hand, and the haze in the air became a rippling blur of moving color that made the entire mountainside look like some enormous, desert-themed Lava lamp.

Shots began to ring out, singly, as the attacker fired randomly into the haze. Each one made trainees cringe and gasp. 'Trainees stay down!' Luccio trumpeted. 'Stay still. Be quiet. Do not give your position away by sound or movement.'

Bullets struck the ground near her feet again as she spoke, drawing the fire to herself, but she didn't flinch, though her face had already broken out in a sweat with the strain of holding up the broad obscurement spell.

'Dresden,' she said between gritted teeth. 'Only one of those things is keeping fire on us. He's pinning us down while the other escapes with hostages. We must protect the trainees foremost, and we can't help the wounded while we're still taking fire.'

'You hold the haze and keep them hidden,' I said, drawing a shot and a puff of dirt of my own. I sidestepped judiciously. 'Shooter's mine.'

She nodded, but her eyes showed something of wounded pride as she said, 'Hurry. I can't hold it for long.'

I nodded to her and looked up the mountainside – and then I shook my head and drew up my Sight.

At once, my vision cut through Luccio's bewildering haze as though it had never existed. I could see the mountainside in perfect detail – even as it was in turn partially veiled by the vision my Sight granted me, which showed me all the living magic in the world around us, all the traces of magic that had lingered before, including dozens of imprints made in the past few days, and hundreds of ghostly glimpses of particularly strong emotional images that had sunk into the area during its heyday. I could see where the girl who now lay shuddering with a bullet in her had tried to call up raw fire for the first time, near a scorch mark upslope. I could see where a grizzled man, desperately addicted to opium and desperately broke, had shot himself more than a century ago, and where by night his shade still lingered, leaving fresh imprints behind.

And I could see the little coiling cloud of darkness that formed the inhuman energy of the attacking ghoul, running hot on the emotions of battle.

I marked the ghoul's location, lowered my Sight, and took off at a dead sprint, bounding up the slope and bouncing back and forth in a wavering line. It's damned hard to hit a target like that, even one growing steadily closer, and even with Luccio's haze to cover me, I didn't want to get shot if I could possibly avoid it. It was hard going, uphill, rough terrain, but it hadn't had time to get hot yet, and I practiced running regularly – though admittedly, I did it to give me the option of running *away* from bad guys more ably, not *toward* them.

More shots rang out, but none of them seemed to come near. I kept my eyes locked on the spot on the slope where the ghoul lay shooting, probably behind cover. I couldn't see a thing through the haze, but as soon as it began to clear I would present the ghoul with a clear target, either as I came through or when Luccio's power faltered and the spell fell. I had to get closer. I didn't have my blasting rod or staff with me, and without them to help me focus my magic, the range and accuracy of any spell I could throw at the ghoul would be drastically reduced. That's why I had to get closer before I took my shot. I couldn't hold a shield against bullets and attack at the same time – and the ghoul had to be taken out. I'd get only one shot, and if I missed I'd be an easy target.

I ran, and watched, and began to gather the power to throw at the ghoul.

The haze abruptly cleared as I bounded over a patch of scrub growth.

The ghoul crouched behind a rock maybe twenty yards upslope, his face only barely distended as he held mostly to his human shape while employing the human weapon – a freaking Kalashnikov. Thank God. The weapon was tough and serviceable, but it wasn't exactly a sharpshooter's tool. If he'd been toting something more precise, he probably could have inflicted a lot more damage than he had.

I was over to one side, and the ghoul was squinting hard down the rifle's sights, so that I was only a flicker of motion in the periphery of his focus. It took him a second to recognize the threat and whip the weapon toward me.

I had time, and I threw out my hand and my will, and snarled, '*Fuego!*'

Fire bellowed forth from my right hand – not in a narrow beam, a jet of tightly focused energy, but in a roaring flood, spilling out from my fingertips like water from a garden sprayer. A *lot* of it, way more than I had intended. The fire got the ghoul, all right – and the ground for twenty feet around him in every direction – more on the uphill side of him. The roar of flame gave way to a hideous shriek, and then a steady, chewy silence shrouded by black smoke. A low breeze, a herald of the day's oncoming heat, nudged the smoke away for a moment.

The ghoul, now in its true form, lay outstretched on the scorched earth. It had been burned down to little more than an appallingly blackened skeleton, though one leg retained enough muscle matter to continue twitching and thrashing – even then, the creature was not wholly dead. It didn't surprise me. In my experience, ghouls hadn't done much that wasn't disgusting. There was no reason to expect them to die cleanly, either.

Once I was sure it wasn't getting back up, I scanned the mountainside, looking for any other sign of movement, but found nothing. Then I turned and hurried back down the slope to the encampment.

Luccio was fully engaged in treating the wounded. Three had been hit by gunfire, and several others, including one of the other adult Wardens, had been wounded by shards of shattered rock or splinters thrown from the folding tables and chairs.

Ramirez came hurrying up to me and said, 'You get him?' His eyes trailed past me to the enormous area blackened with smoke and half a dozen patches of brush still on fire, and he said, 'Yeah, I guess you kind of did.'

'Kind of,' I agreed. 'You said they had two of our kids?'

He nodded once, his face grim. 'The Terrible Twosome. They were heading up the slope to find a spot above the camp for the lesson. Wanted to show off, I expect.'

'Sixteen,' I muttered. 'Jesus.'

Ramirez grimaced. 'I was yelling at them to come back when the ghouls hopped up out of the bush and brought them down, and the three assholes who had sneaked into the old smithy opened up.'

'How are you at following tracks?' I asked him.

'Thought they taught that Boy Scout stuff to all you Anglos. I grew up in L.A.'

I blew out a breath, thinking fast. 'Luccio's busy. She'll call in help for the wounded. That leaves you and me to go get the twins.'

'Fucking right we will,' Ramirez said. 'How?'

'You got prisoners?'

'The two I didn't blast, yeah.'

'We'll ask them.'

'Think they'll rat out their buddy?'

'If they think it'll save their lives?' I asked. 'In a heart-beat. Maybe less.'

'Weasels,' Ramirez muttered.

'They are what they are, man,' I said. 'There's no use in hating them for it. Just be glad we can use it to advantage. Let's go.'

The ghouls lay covered in grey-white dust as fine as baby powder – the remains of the wall Ramirez had blasted, their companion, his weapon, and the right arm and leg of one of the captive ghouls. The wounded ghoul, body shifted into its natural form under the stress of injury, lay panting and choking, spitting out dust. The second ghoul still looked mostly human, and was dressed in a ragged old set of sand-colored robes that looked like something out of *Lawrence of Arabia*. Another Kalashnikov lay several feet away, behind Bill Meyers, the young Warden now standing over them with a double-barreled ten-gauge shotgun pointed at the unwounded one of the pair.

'Careful,' Meyers said. He had the rural drawl that seems largely common to any town west of the Mississippi located more than an hour or so from a major city, though he was himself a Texan. 'I ain't searched them, and they don't 'pear to understand English.'

'What?' Ramirez said. 'That's stupid. Who bothers to sneak ghouls into the country as covert muscle if they can't pass as locals?'

'Someone who doesn't have to worry about customs or border guards or witnesses or cops,' I said quietly. 'Someone who takes them through the Nevernever straight here from wherever the hell they came from.' I glanced back at Ramirez. 'How else do you think they got past the outer wards and sentries and right up to the camp?'

Ramirez grunted. 'I thought we had those approaches warded, too.'

'Nevernever's a tricksy kind of place,' I said. 'Tough to know it all. Somebody was sneakier than us.'

'Vampires?' Ramirez asked.

I very carefully said nothing about a Black Council. 'Who else would it be?'

Ramirez said something to them in Spanish.

'Shoot,' Meyers drawled. 'You think I didn't try that already?'

'Hey,' I said. I stepped closer to the unwounded ghoul and nudged him with one foot. 'What language do you speak?'

The not-quite-human-looking man shot a quick, furtive glance at me, and then at his companion. He sputtered something quick and liquid-sounding. His companion snarled something back through its muzzle and fangs that sounded vaguely similar.

Seconds were ticking by, and we had a pair of kids in the hands of one of these things. I directed my thoughts inward, to the corner of my brain where Lasciel's shadow lived, and asked, *You get any of that?*

Lasciel's presence promptly responded. *The first asked the second if he understood anything we were saying. The second replied that he hadn't, and you were probably deciding which one of us would kill them.*

I need to talk to them, I said. *Can you translate for me?*

There was a sudden sense of someone standing close to me – an almost tangible physical sensation of someone slim and feminine pressed against my back, arms casually around my waist, soft breath and lips moving near my ear. It was odd, but not at all unpleasant. I caught myself enjoying it, and firmly reminded myself of the danger of allowing the demon to do that.

With your permission, you need only speak to them in English, my host, Lasciel said. *I will translate it between mind and mouth, and they will hear their tongue from your lips.*

I so did not need any image involving their tongues and my lips, I responded.

Lasciel let out a delighted laugh that bubbled through my mind, and I was smiling a little when I faced the ghoul and said, 'Okay, asshole. I've got two kids missing, and the only chance you have of getting out of this alive is if I get them back. Do you understand me?'

Both ghouls looked up at me, surprise evident even on the inhuman one's face. I got a similar look from Ramirez and Meyers.

'Do you understand me?' I asked the ghouls quietly.

'Yes,' stammered the wounded ghoul, apparently in English.

Ramirez's dark, heavy eyebrows tried to climb up under his bush hat.

I had to remind myself that this was not very cool. I was using a dangerous tool that would one day turn on me. No matter how savvy and tough it made me look in front of the other Wardens.

Kids, Harry. Focus on the kids.

'Why did you take those children?' I demanded of the ghoul.

'They must have wandered too close to Murzhek's position,' the mostly human ghoul said. 'We did not come here for hostages. This was to be a raid. We were to hit you, then fade away.'

'Fade to where?'

The ghouls froze, and looked at each other.

I drew back one of my hiking boots and kicked the mostly human ghoul in the face. He let out a high-pitched squeal — not a snarl of rage and pain, but a sound a dog makes when it's trying to submit beneath an attacker.

'*Where?*' I demanded.

'Our lives,' hissed the wounded ghoul. 'Promise us our lives and freedom, great one. Give us your word of truth.'

'You gave up your freedom the moment you spilled our blood,' I snarled. 'But if I get the kids back, you keep your life,' I said. 'My word is given.'

The ghouls looked at each other, and then the more human of the pair said, 'The deep caves above this dwelling. The first deep shaft from the light of the sun. In the stones near it is a way to the Realm of Shadows.'

I shot a thought toward my interpreter. *Does he mean the Nevernever?*

A region of it, yes, my host.

'Remain here,' I told them. 'Do not move. Make no attempt to escape. At the first sign of disobedience or treachery, you will die.'

'Great one,' both of them said, and began pressing their faces into the grey dust and the sandy, rocky soil beneath. 'Great one.'

'They've been taken to the mine,' I told Ramirez. 'We go there.' I turned to the other Warden. 'Meyers, they've surrendered. Don't take your eyes off them for a second, and if they twitch funny, kill them. Otherwise, leave them be.'

'Right,' he said. 'Let me get some of the trainees in here. I'll go with y'all.'

'They're trainees,' Ramirez said, his tone hard. 'You're the Warden.'

Meyers blinked at him, but then let out a gusty exhalation and nodded. 'All right. Watch your ass, 'Los.'

'Come on,' I said to Ramirez, and the two of us ducked out of the ruins and ran for our tent. We recovered our gear from it – staves, Ramirez's silver sword and grey cape, my revolver and blasting rod and duster. Then I took off up the hill at the fastest pace I thought I could hold.

Ramirez was built like an athlete, but he was more naturally inclined to sprints and bursts of strength. He probably lifted weights at the expense of doing as much running as

I did. He was blowing pretty hard by the time we'd gotten halfway to the mine, and he was fifty yards behind me by the time I got there. My own lungs were tight and heaving, I could feel the beginnings of a good hard puking revving up in my belly, and my legs felt like someone had poured a gallon of isopropyl over them and ignited it, but there wasn't time to waste on recovering from the effort.

The ghouls hadn't been there to take prisoners. This one might be smart enough to have kept the kids alive to use as hostages, but I'd never found ghouls to be particularly brilliant, and the one unwavering constant I'd observed among them was an inability to restrain their appetites for any length of time.

I banged my staff hurriedly against the earth, calling up my will and reinforcing it with Hellfire, a mystical source of energy Lasciel's presence gave me the ability to utilize. I was already tired enough from my clumsy fire spell earlier and all the running that I didn't have much choice but to draw on the brimstone-scented energy and hope for the best.

The runes in my staff blazed into light, and with a little effort of will I increased the effect, until the smoldering scarlet glow spilled out in a wide circle around me. The entrance to the mine was choked with brush, low, and not ten feet in one of the supports had collapsed, all but closing the place off from the outside. I had to slide in sideways, and once I was in, the dim light from the entrance and the scarlet glow pouring from my staff were the only illumination.

I hurried forward, knowing Ramirez would be coming soon, but not willing to wait for him. The air turned cold within a dozen strides, and my panting breaths formed into tiny clouds as they left my mouth. The tunnel widened and then sloped sharply downhill. I kept my left side against the wall, my right hand holding forth my staff, both to provide me enough light to see and to make sure I had the weapon ready to interpose itself between me and anything that should come slobbering out of the shadows.

A tunnel opened on my left, and as I went by it, I heard a snarling hiss come drifting and echoing from far down its length.

I turned and hurried down it, coming upon an old track built into the floor, where ore carts would have trundled back and forth, carrying out the ore from where it was brought up a shaft from lower in the mine. The sounds grew louder as I continued, a broader variety of the same snarling hisses.

And maybe a very soft whimper.

I probably should have been cagey at that point. I probably should have gone still, doused my light, and sneaked up to see what I could find out about things. I considered a nice, cautious recon for maybe a quarter of second.

Screw that. There were kids in danger.

I went through the remains of a wooden partition at a full charge. The ghoul, wholly inhuman and wearing the same sand-colored robes the others had been, had his back to me and was clawing at a section of rough tunnel wall with both hands. They were dark with his own blood, and a couple of his claws had broken. He was uttering snarls between desperate gasps, and Lasciel was evidently still on the job. 'Betrayed,' the ghoul snarled. '*Betrayed*. Reckoning, oh, yes . . . balance of the scales . . . let me *in*!'

Everything slowed down, thoughts burning through my mind at tremendous speed. I saw everything clearly, what was in front of me, what was in my peripheral vision, and everything seemed as bright and organized as a third grader's desk on the first day of school.

The Trailman twins were fraternal, not identical. Terry, the brother, was a couple of inches shorter than his nominally younger sister, but he stuck so far out of his shirt and pants that he had seemed well on the way to reversing that situation. He'd never get to. His body was on the floor of the cave, his face covered in a mask of blood and torn flesh. The ghoul had ripped open his throat. He'd also gotten the femoral artery on Terry's thigh. The kid's mouth was open, and I could see the ghoul's disgusting blood clinging to Terry's teeth. His knuckles were ripped open, too. The kid had died fighting.

Two feet farther on was the source of his motivation. Tina Trailman lay on the stone, staring upward with glazed eyes. She was naked from the waist down. Her throat and trapezius muscles were mostly gone, ripped away, as were her modest breasts. The quadriceps muscle of her right leg was gone, the skin around it showing the roughly torn gouges of ghoul fangs. There was blood everywhere, a sticky pool forming around her.

I saw her shudder a little. A tiny sound escaped her unmoving form. She was dead already – I knew that. I've seen it more than once. Her heart was still laboring, but whatever time she had left was a mere formality.

My vision went red with rage. Or maybe that was the Hellfire. I called upon still more of the dark energy in midleap, staff gripped in both hands, and rammed the tip into the small of the ghoul's back as I snarled, '*Fuego!*'

The blow, with all my weight and power and speed behind it, probably broke a couple of the ghoul's vertebrae all by itself. The fire spell came rushing out at the same time, filling the tunnel with thunder and light.

Tremendous heat blossomed before me, rushed into the ghoul, and tore him in half at the waist.

The same thermal bloom washed into the stone wall behind the creature and rebounded. I got an arm up to shield my face, and I dropped the staff so that I could draw my hands into my duster's sleeves. I managed to keep much skin from being directly exposed, but it hurt like hell all the same. I remembered that, later. At the time. I didn't give a flying fuck.

I kicked the ghoul's wildly thrashing lower body into the blackness of the mine shaft. Then I turned to the upper half.

The ghoul's blood wasn't red, so he burned black and brown, like a burger that fell into the barbecue just as it was finished cooking. He thrashed and screamed and somehow managed to flip himself onto his back. He held up his arms, fingers spread in desperation, and cried, 'Mercy, great one! Mercy!'

Sixteen years old.

Jesus Christ.

I stared down for a second. I didn't want to kill the ghoul. That wasn't nearly enough to cover the debt of its sins. I wanted to rip it to pieces. I wanted to eat its heart. I wanted to pin it to the floor and push my thumbs through its beady eyes and all the way into its brain. I wanted to tear it apart with my fingernails and my teeth, and spit mouthfuls of its own pustuled flesh into its face as it died in slow and terrible agony.

The quality of mercy was not Harry.

I called up the Hellfire again, and with a snarl cast out the simple spell I use to light candles. Backed by Hellfire, directed by my fury, it lashed out at the ghoul, plunged beneath its skin, and there it set fat and nerves and sinews alight. They burned, burned using the ghoul for tallow, and the thing went mad with the pain.

I reached down to the ghoul, caught him by the remains of his robes, and hauled him up to my eye level, ignoring the little runnels of flame that occasionally licked up from the inferno beneath the ghoul's skin. I stared into its face. Then forced it to look at the bodies. Then I turned it back to me, and my voice came out in a snarl so inhuman that I barely understood it myself.

'Never,' I told it. 'Never again.'

Then I threw it down the shaft.

It burst into open flame a second later, the rush of its fall feeding the fires in its flesh. I watched it plummet, heard it wailing in terror and pain. Then, far below, it struck something. The flame flowered and brightened for a second. Then it began to slowly die away. I couldn't make out any details of the ghoul, but nothing moved.

I looked up in time to see Ramirez come through the ruins of the wooden partition. He stared at me for a second, where I stood over the mine shaft, dark smoke rising from the surface of my duster, red light shining up from far below, the stench of brimstone heavy in the air.

Ramirez is rarely at a loss for words.

He stared for a moment. Then his eyes tracked over to the dead kids. His breath escaped him in a short, hard jerk. His shoulders sagged. He dropped to one knee, turning his head away from the sight. *'Dios.'*

I picked up my staff and started walking back to the camp.

Ramirez caught up with me a few paces later. 'Dresden,' he said.

I ignored him.

'Harry!'

'Sixteen, Carlos,' I said. 'Sixteen. It had them for less than eight minutes.'

'Harry, wait.'

'What the hell was I thinking?' I snarled, stepping out into the sunlight. 'Staff and blasting rod and most of my gear in the damned tent. We're at war.'

'There was security in place,' Ramirez said. 'We've been here for two days. There was no way you could know this was coming.'

'We're Wardens, Carlos. We're supposed to protect people. I could have done more to be ready.'

He got in front of me and planted his feet. I stopped and narrowed my eyes at him.

'You're right,' he said. 'This is a war. Bad things happen to people, even if no one makes any mistakes.'

I don't remember consciously doing it, but the runes of my staff began to burn with Hellfire again.

'Carlos,' I said quietly. 'Get out of my way.'

He ground his teeth, but his eyes flickered away from me. He didn't actually turn, but when I brushed past him, he didn't try to stop me.

At the camp, I caught one brief glimpse of Luccio as she helped carry a wounded trainee on a stretcher. She stepped into a glowing line of light in the air, an opened way to the Nevernever, and vanished. Reinforcements had arrived. There were Wardens with medical kits, stretchers, the works, trying to stabilize the wounded and get them to better help. The trainees looked shocked, numb, staring around them – and at two silent shapes lying close together over to one side, covered from their heads to their knees by an unzipped sleeping bag.

I stormed into the smithy and snarled, *'Forzare!'* putting all my rage and will into a lashing column of force directed at the captured ghouls.

The spell blew the remaining wall of the smithy and the two ghouls fifty feet through the air and onto a relatively flat area of the street. I walked after them. I didn't hurry. In fact, I picked up a jug of orange juice off one of the breakfast tables, and drank some of it as I went.

The mountainside was completely silent.

Once I reached them, another blast opened up a six-foot crater in the sandy earth. I kicked the mostly human ghoul into it, and with several more such blasts collapsed the crater in on him, burying him to the neck.

Then I called fire and melted the sand around the ghoul's exposed head into a sheet of glass.

It screamed and screamed, which did not matter to me in the least. The sheer heat of the molten sand burned away its features, its eyes, its lips and tongue, even as the trauma forced the ghoul into its true form. I upended the jug of juice. Some of it splashed on the ghoul's head. Some of it sizzled on the narrow band of glass around it. I walked calmly, pouring orange juice on the ground in a steady line until, ten feet later, I reached the enormous nest of fire ants one of the trainees had stumbled into on our first day at Camp Kaboom.

Presently, the first scouts started following the trail back to the ghoul.

I turned on the second ghoul.

It cringed away from me, holding completely still. The only sound was the raw whisper-screams of the other ghoul.

'I'm not going to kill you,' I told the ghoul in a very quiet voice. 'You get to carry word to your kind.' I thrust the end of my staff against its chest and stared down. Wisps of sulfurous smoke trickled down the length of the wooden shaft and over the maimed ghoul. 'Tell them this.' I leaned closer. 'Never again. Tell them that. Never again. Or Hell itself will not hide you from me.'

The ghoul groveled. 'Great one. Great one.'

I roared again and started kicking the ghoul as hard as I could. I kept it up until it floundered away from me, heading for the open desert with only one leg and one arm, the movements freakish and terrified.

I watched until the maimed ghoul was gone.

By then, the ants had found his buddy. I stood over it for a time and beheld what I had wrought without looking away.

I felt Ramirez's presence behind me. '*Dios*,' he whispered.

I said nothing.

Moments later, Ramirez said, 'What happened to not hating them?'

'Things change.'

Ramirez didn't move, and his voice was so low I could barely hear it. 'How many lessons will it take the kids to learn this one, do you think?'

The rage came swarming up again.

'Battle is one thing,' Ramirez said. 'This is something else. Look at them.'

I suddenly felt the weight of dozens and dozens of eyes upon me. I turned to find the trainees, all pale, shocked, and silent, staring at me. They looked terrified.

I fought the frustration and anger back down. Ramirez was right. Of course he was right. Dammit.

I drew my gun and executed the ghoul.

'*Dios*,' Ramirez breathed. He stared at me for a moment. 'Never seen you like this.'

I started feeling the minor burns. The sun began turning Camp Kaboom into a giant cookie sheet that would sear away anything soft. 'Like what?'

'Cold,' he said, finally.

'That's the only way to serve it up,' I said. 'Cold.'

Cold.

Cold.

I came back to myself. No more New Mexico. Dark. Cold, so cold that it burned. Chest tight.

I was in the water.

My chest hurt. I managed to look up.

Sun shone down on fractured ice about eight inches thick. It came back to me. The battle aboard the *Water Beetle*. The ghouls. The lake. The ice had broken and I had fallen through.

I couldn't see far, and when the ghoul came through the water, swimming like a crocodile, its arms flat against its sides, it was close enough to touch. It spotted me at the same time, and turned away.

Never again.

I reached out and grabbed on to the back of the jeans the ghoul still wore. It panicked, swimming fast, and dived down into the cold and dark, trying to scare me into letting go.

I was aware that I had to breathe, and that I was already beginning to black out. I dismissed it as unimportant. This ghoul was never going to hurt anyone else, ever again, if I had to die to make sure of it. Everything started going dark.

And then there was another pale shape in the water. Thomas, this time, shirtless, holding that crooked knife in his teeth. He closed on the ghoul, which writhed and twisted with such fear and desperation that it tore my weakening fingers lose from their grip.

I drifted. Felt something cold wrap my right wrist. Felt light coming closer, painfully bright.

And then my face was out of the frozen water, and I sucked in a weak gasp of air. I felt a slender arm slip under my chin, and then I was being pulled through the water. Elaine. I'd recognize the touch of her skin to mine anywhere.

We broke the surface, and she let out a gasp, then started pulling me toward the dock. With the help of Olivia and the other women, Elaine managed to get me up out of the lake. I fell to my side and lay there shivering violently, gasping down all the air I could. The world slowly began to return to its usual shape, but I was too tired to do anything about it.

I don't know how much time went by, but the sirens were close by the time Thomas appeared and hauled himself out of the water.

'Go,' Thomas said. 'Can he walk? Is he shot?'

'No,' Elaine said. 'It might be shock; I don't know. I think he hit his head on something.'

'We can't stay here,' Thomas said. I felt him pick me up and sling me over a shoulder. He did it as gently as such a thing can be done.

'Right,' Elaine said. 'Come on. Everyone, keep up and don't get separated.'

I felt motion. My head hurt. A lot.

'I gotcha,' Thomas said to me, as he started walking. 'It's cool, Harry,' he murmured. 'They're safe. We got everyone clear. I gotcha.'

My brother's word was good enough for me.

I closed my eyes and stopped trying to keep track of things.

The touch of very warm, very gentle fingers woke me.

My head hurt, even more than it had after Cowl had finished ringing my bells the night before, if such a thing was possible. I didn't want to regain consciousness, if it meant rising into that.

But those soft, warm fingers touched me, steady and exquisitely feminine, and the pain began to fade. That had the effect it always did. When the pain was gone, its simple lack was a nearly narcotic pleasure of its own.

It was more than that, too. There is a primal reassurance in being touched, in knowing that someone else, someone close to you, wants to be touching you. There is a bone-deep security that goes with the brush of a human hand, a silent, reflex-level affirmation that someone is near, that someone cares.

It seemed that, lately, I had barely been touched at all.

'Dammit, Lash,' I mumbled. 'I told you to stop doing that.'

The fingers stiffened for a second, and Elaine said, 'What was that, Harry?'

I blinked and opened my eyes.

I was lying on a bed in dim hotel room. The ceiling tiles were old and water stained. The furniture was similarly simple, cheap, battered by long and careless use and little maintenance.

Elaine sat at the head of the bed with her legs crossed. My head lay comfortably upon her calves, as it had so many times before. My legs hung off the end of the bed, also as they had often done before, a long time ago, in a house I barely remembered except in dreams.

'Am I hurting you. Harry?' Elaine pressed. I couldn't see her expression without craning my neck, and that seemed a bad idea, but she sounded concerned.

'No,' I said. 'No, just waking up groggy. Sorry.'

'Ah,' she said. 'Who is Lash?'

'No one I especially want to discuss.'

'All right,' she said. There was nothing but gentle assent in her tone. 'Then just lie back for a few moments more and let me finish. Your friend the vampire said that they'd be watching the hospitals.'

'What are you doing?' I asked her.

'Reiki,' she replied.

'Laying on of hands?' I said. 'That stuff works?'

'The principles are sound,' she said, and I felt something silky brush over my forehead. Her hair. I recognized it by touch and smell. She had bowed her head in concentration. Her voice became distracted. 'I was able to combine them with some basic principles for moving energy. I haven't found a way to handle critical trauma or to manage infections, but it's surprisingly effective in handling bruises, sprains, and bumps on the head.'

No kidding. The headache was already gone completely. The tightness in my head and neck was fading as well, as were the twinges in my upper back and shoulders.

And a beautiful woman was touching me.

Elaine was touching me.

I wouldn't have done anything to stop her if I'd had a thousand paper cuts and she'd soaked her hands in lemon juice.

We simply stayed like that for a time. Once in while, she moved her hands, palms running down lightly over my cheeks, neck, chest. Her hands would move in slow, repetitive stroking motions, barely touching my skin. I'd lost my shirt at some point. All of those aches and pains of exertion and combat faded away, leaving only a happy cloud of endorphins behind. Her hands were warm, slow, infinitely patient and infinitely confident.

It felt amazing.

I drifted on the sensations, utterly content.

'All right,' she said quietly, an unknown amount of time later. 'How does that feel?'

'Incredible,' I said.

I could hear the smile in her voice. 'You always say that when I'm done touching you.'

'Not my fault if it's always true,' I replied.

'Flatterer,' she said, and her fingers gently slapped one of my shoulders. 'Let me up, ape.'

'What if I don't want to?' I drawled.

'Men. I pay you the least bit of attention, and you go completely Paleolithic on me.'

'Ugh,' I replied, and slowly sat up, expecting a surge of discomfort and nausea as the blood rushed around my head. There wasn't any.

I frowned and ran my fingers lightly over my scalp. There was a lump on the side of my skull that should have felt like hell. Instead, it was only a little tender. I've been thumped on the melon before. I know the residue of a hard blow. This felt like a bad one, only after I'd had about a week to recover. 'How long have I been down?'

'Eight hours, maybe?' Elaine asked. She rose from the bed and stretched. It was every bit as intriguing and pleasant to watch as I remembered. 'I sort of lose track when I'm focused on something.'

'I remember,' I murmured.

Elaine froze in place, and her green eyes glittered in the dimness as she met my gaze in a kind of relaxed, insolent silence. Then a little smile touched her lips. 'I suppose you would.'

My heart lurched and sped up, and I started getting ideas.

None of which could be properly pursued at the moment.

I saw Elaine reach the same conclusion at about the same time I did. She lowered her arms, smiled again and said, 'Excuse me. I've been sitting there a while.' Then she paced into the bathroom.

I went to the hotel's window and opened the cheap blinds a tiny bit. We were somewhere on the south side. Dusk was on the city, the streetlights already flickering into life one by one, as the shadows crept out from beneath the buildings and oozed slowly up the light poles. I checked around but saw no shark fins circling, no vultures wheeling overhead, and no obvious ghouls or vampires lurking nearby, just waiting to pounce. That didn't mean they weren't there, though.

I turned from the window to lightly touch the adjoining door. Elaine had spun another ward over the door, a subtle, solid crafting that would release enough kinetic energy to throw anyone who tried to open it a good ten or twelve feet away. It was perfect for a quick exit, if you were expecting trouble and ready for it when it arrived. Just wait for the bad guy to get bitch-slapped into the parking lot, then dash out the door and run off before he regained his feet.

I heard Elaine come out of the bathroom behind me. 'What happened?' I asked.

'What do you remember?'

'Madrigal opened up with that assault rifle. Flash of light. Then I was in the water.'

Elaine came to stand next to me and also glanced out. Her hand brushed mine when she lowered it from the blinds, and without even thinking about it, I twined my fingers in hers. It was an achingly familiar sensation, and another pang of half-remembered days long gone made my chest ache for a second.

Elaine shivered a little and closed her eyes. Her fingers tightened, very slightly, on mine. 'We thought he'd killed you,' she said. 'You started to crouch down, and there were bullets shattering the ice all around you. You went into the water, and the vampire . . . Madrigal, did you say his name was? He ordered the ghouls in after you. I sent Olivia and the others to the shore, and Thomas and I went into the water to find you.'

'Who hit me in the head?' I asked.

Elaine shrugged. 'Either a bullet hit your coat after you crouched down, and then bounced off your thick skull without penetrating, or you slammed it against some of the shattered ice as you went under.'

A bullet might have bounced off my head, thanks to the intervening fabric of my spell-covered coat. That was a sobering sort of thing to hear, even for me. 'Thank you,' I said. 'For getting me out.'

Elaine arched an eyebrow, then gave me a little roll of her eyes and said, 'I was bored and didn't have anything better to do.'

'I figured,' I said. 'Thomas?'

'He's all right. He had a car near the docks. I drove that clown car of yours, and we shoehorned everyone into them and got away clean. With any luck, Madrigal had a tougher time avoiding the cops than we did.'

'Nah,' I said, with total conviction. 'Too easy. He got away. Where's Thomas?'

'Standing watch outside,' he said.' Elaine frowned. 'He looked . . . very pale. He refused to stay in the room with his refugees. Or me, for that matter.'

I grunted. Thomas had really put on his Supervamp cape back at the harbor. Under ordinary circumstances, he was surprisingly strong for a man of his size and build. But even unusually strong men don't go toe-to-toe with ghouls armed with nothing but a big stick and come away clean. Thomas could make himself stronger – a *lot* stronger – but not forever. The demon knit to my brother's soul could make him into a virtual godling, but it also increased his hunger for the life force of mortals, burning away whatever he had stored up in exchange for the improved performance.

After that fight, Thomas had to be hungry. So hungry that he didn't trust himself in a room with anyone he considered, well, edible. Which, in our escape party, had been everyone but me and the kids.

He must have been hurting.

'What about the Ordo?' I asked her quietly.

'I didn't want to go until I could be certain that I wouldn't lead anyone back to them. I called them every couple of hours to make sure they were all right. I should check in with them again.'

She turned to the phone before she finished the sentence and dialed a number. I waited. She was silent. After a moment, she hung up the phone again.

'No answer,' I said quietly.

'No,' she said. She turned to the dresser, gathered up her length of chain, and threaded it through the loops of her jeans like a belt, fastening it with a slightly curved piece of dark wood bound with several bands of colored leather, which she slipped through two links.

I opened the door and stuck my head out into the twilight, looking around. I didn't see Thomas anywhere, so I let out a sharp, loud whistle, waved an arm around a little, and ducked back inside, closing the door again.

It didn't take long for Thomas's footsteps to reach the door.

'Harry,' Elaine said, mildly alarmed. 'The ward.'

I held up a forefinger in a one-second kind of gesture, then folded my arms, stared at the door, and waited. The doorknob twitched; there was a heavy thud, a gasp of surprise, and a loud clatter of empty trash cans.

I opened the door and found my brother flat on his back in the parking lot, amidst a moderate amount of spilled garbage. He stared up at the sky for a moment, let out a long-suffering sigh, and then sat up, scowling at me.

'Oh, sorry about that,' I said, with all the sincerity of a three-year-old claiming he didn't steal that cookie all over his face. 'Maybe I should have *told you about a potentially dangerous situation*, huh? I mean, that would have been polite of me to warn you, right? And sensible. And intelligent. And respectful. And—'

'I get it, I get it,' he growled. He got up and made a doomed effort to brush various bits of unsavory matter off his clothes. 'Jesus Christ, Harry. There are days when you can be a total prick.'

'Whereas *you* can apparently be a complete *moron* for *weeks* at a time!'

Elaine stepped up beside me and said, 'I love to see a good testosterone-laden alpha-male dominance struggle as much as the next woman – but don't you think it would be smarter to do it where half of the city can't see us?'

I scowled at Elaine, but she had a point. I stepped out the door and offered Thomas my hand.

He glowered at me, then deliberately ran his hand through some of the muck and held it out to me without wiping it off. I rolled my eyes and pulled him to his feet, and then the three of us went back into the room.

Thomas leaned his back against the door, folded his arms, and kept his eyes on the floor while I went to the sink and washed off my hands. My coat hung on one of the wire hangers on the bar beside it, as did my shirt. My staff rested in a corner by the light switch, and my other gear was on the counter. I dried off my hands and started suiting up. 'Okay, Thomas,' I said. 'Seriously. What's up with the secrecy? You should have contacted me.'

'I couldn't,' he said.

'Why not?'

'I promised someone I wouldn't.'

I frowned at that, tugging the still-damp black leather glove onto my disfigured left hand, and tried to think. Thomas and I were brothers. He took that every bit as seriously as I did – but he took his promises seriously, too. If he'd made the promise, he had a good reason to do so.

'How much can you tell me?'

Elaine gave me a sharp glance.

'I've already said more than I should have,' Thomas said.

'Don't be an idiot. We've obviously got a common enemy here.'

Thomas grimaced, gave me a hesitant glance, and then said, 'We've got several.'

I traded a glance with Elaine, who glanced at Thomas, shrugged, and suggested, 'Bruises fade?'

'No,' I said. 'If he isn't talking he has a good reason for it. Beating him up won't change that.'

'Then we should stop wasting time here,' Elaine said quietly.

Thomas looked back and forth between us. 'What's wrong?'

'We've lost contact with the women Elaine is protecting,' I said.

'Dammit.' Thomas pushed his hand back through his hair. 'That means . . .'

I fastened the clasp on the new shield bracelet. 'What?'

'Look. You already know Madrigal is around,' Thomas said.

'And that he's always sucking up to House Malvora,' I said. I frowned. 'For the love of God, he's the Passenger.' He's the one working with Grey Cloak the Malvora.'

'I didn't say that,' Thomas said quickly.

'You didn't have to,' I growled. 'He didn't just happen to show up for some payback while this other stuff was going on. And it all fits. Passenger was talking to Grey Cloak about having the resources to take me out. He obviously decided to take a whack at it with a bunch of ghouls and a machine gun.'

'Sounds reasonable,' Thomas said. 'You already know that there's a Skavis around.'

'Yes.'

'Time to do some math then, Harry.'

'Madrigal and Grey Cloak the Malvora,' I murmured. 'The genocidal odd couple. Neither of which is a Skavis.'

Elaine drew in a sharp breath and said, at the same time I was thinking it, 'It means that we aren't talking about one killer.'

I completed the thought. 'We're talking about three of them. Grey Cloak Malvora, Passenger Madrigal, and Serial Killer Skavis.' I frowned at Thomas. 'Wait. Are you saying that—'

My brother's expression became strained. 'I'm not saying anything,' he replied. 'Those are all things you already know.'

Elaine frowned. 'You're trying to maintain deniability,' she said. 'Why?'

'So I can *deny* telling you anything, obviously,' Thomas snarled, his eyes suddenly flickering several shades of grey lighter as he stared at Elaine.

Elaine drew in a sharp breath. Then she narrowed her eyes a little, unfastened the clasp on her chain, and said, 'Stop it, vampire. Now.'

Thomas's lips pulled back from his teeth, but he jerked his face away from her and closed his eyes.

I stepped between them as I shrugged into my leather duster. 'Elaine, back off. The enemy of my enemy. Okay?'

'I don't like it,' Elaine said. 'You know what he is, Harry. How do you know you can trust him?'

'I've worked with him before,' I said. 'He's different.'

'How? A lot of vampires feel remorse about their victims. It doesn't stop them from killing over and over. It's what they are.'

'I've gazed him,' I said quietly. 'He's trying to rise above the killer inside him.'

Elaine's brows knit into a frown at those words, and she gave me a slow and reluctant nod. 'Aren't we all,' she murmured. 'I'm still not comfortable with the notion of him near my clients. And we need to get moving.'

'Go ahead,' Thomas said.

I didn't look at my brother, but I said, 'You need to eat.'

'Maybe later,' Thomas said. 'I can't leave the women and children unguarded.'

I grabbed a pad of cheap paper with the hotel's logo and found a pencil in one of my pockets. I wrote a number on it and passed it to Thomas. 'Call Murphy. You won't be able to protect anyone if you're too weak, and you might kill one of them if you lose control of the hunger.'

Thomas's jaw tightened with frustration, but he took the offered piece of paper from my hand only a little more roughly than necessary.

Elaine studied him as she walked to the door with me. Then she said to him, 'You're different from most of them, aren't you?'

'Probably just more deluded,' Thomas replied. 'Good luck, Harry.'

'Yeah,' I said, feeling awkward. 'Look. After this is done . . . we have to talk.'

'There's nothing to talk about,' my brother said.

We left and I closed the door behind us.

We took the Blue Beetle back to the Amber Inn and went to Elaine's room. The lights were off. The room was empty.

There was a terrible sewer smell in the air.

'*Dammit*,' Elaine whispered. She suddenly sagged and leaned against the doorway.

I stepped past her and turned on the light in the bathroom.

Anna Ash's corpse stood in the shower, body stiff, leaning away from the showerhead, but held in place by the electrical cord of a hair dryer, tied in a knot about the showerhead and another around her neck. There hadn't been room enough for her to suspend herself with her feet off the floor. Ugly, purple-black ligature marks showed on her neck around the cord.

It was obviously a suicide.

It obviously wasn't.

We were too late.

'We've got to call the cops on this one,' I said quietly to Elaine.

'No,' she replied. 'They'll want to question us. It will take hours.'

'They'll want to question us a lot longer if someone else finds the body and they have to come looking for us.'

'And while we're cooperating with the authorities, what happens to Abby, Helen, and Priscilla?' She stared at me. 'For that matter, what happens to Mouse?'

That was a thought I'd been trying to avoid. If Mouse was alive and capable, there was no way he'd let any of the women be harmed. If someone had killed Anna when Mouse was near, it could have happened only over his dead body.

But there was no sign of him.

That could mean a lot of things. At worst it meant that he had been utterly disintegrated by whatever had come for the women. Not only was that assumption depressing as hell, it also didn't get me anywhere. A bad guy who could simply disintegrate anything that got in the way sure wouldn't be pussyfooting around the way these White Court yahoos had been.

Mouse wasn't here. There was no mess, no sign of a struggle, and believe you me, that dog can put up a struggle, as the vets found out when they misfiled his paperwork. They tried to neuter him instead of vaccinating him and getting his shoulder X-rayed where he'd bounced off of a moving minivan. I was lucky they were willing to let me pay the property damage and leave it at that.

It had to mean something else. Maybe my dog had left with the others, and Anna had remained behind, or gone back for something she forgot.

Or maybe Mouse had played on everyone's expectation that he was just a dog. He'd shown me that he was capable of that kind of subterfuge before, and it had been one of the first things that tipped me off to his distinctly superior-to-canine intellect. What if Mouse had played along and stayed close to the others?

Why would he do that, though?

Because Mouse knew I could find him. Unless the bad guys carried him off to the Nevernever itself, or put him behind a set of wards specifically designed to block such magic, my tracking spell could find him anywhere.

That was the path to take, even if Mouse didn't know anything was wrong. He would have stayed with any members of the Ordo that he could, and I had taken to planning ahead a little more than I used to do. I could use my shield bracelet to target the single small shield charm I'd hung from his collar for just such an emergency. Me and Foghorn Leghorn.

'Can you find the dog?' Elaine asked.

'Yeah. But we should try calling their homes before we go.'

Elaine frowned. 'You told them to stay here, or somewhere public.'

'Odds are pretty good that they're scared. And when you're scared . . .'

'. . . you want to go home,' Elaine finished.

'If they're there, it'll be the quickest way to get in touch. If not, it hasn't cost us more than a minute or two.'

Elaine nodded. 'Anna had all the numbers in a notebook in her purse.' We turned up the purse after a brief search, but the notebook wasn't in it.

There wasn't anything for it but to make sure that Anna hadn't slipped it into a pocket before she died. I checked, and tried not to leave any prints almost as hard as I tried not to look at her dead, purpling face or glazed eyes. It hadn't been a clean death, and even though Anna hadn't been gone long enough to start decomposition, the smell was formidable. I tried to ignore it.

It was harder to ignore her face. The skin had the stiff, waxy look that dead bodies get. Worse, there was a distinct and unquantifiable quality of . . . absence. Anna Ash had been very much alive — fierce of will, protective, determined. I know plenty of wizards without the force of personality she had. She'd been the one thinking and acting when all of those around her were frightened. That takes a rare kind of courage.

None of which meant anything, since, despite my efforts, the killer had taken her anyway.

I shook my head and stepped away from the corpse, having turned up no notebook. Her willingness to face danger on behalf of her friends couldn't be allowed to vanish silently into the past. If some of those she sought to protect were still alive, then her own sacrifice and death could still mean something. I could be bitter about her death later. I would be doing a grave disservice to the woman if I let it do anything but make me more motivated to stop the killers before they had finished their work.

I came face-to-face with Elaine, who stood in the doorway, staring at Anna's body. There was no expression on her face, absolutely none. Tears, though, had reddened her eyes and streaked over her cheeks and down her nose. Some women are pretty when they cry. Elaine gets all blotchy and runny-nosed, and it brought out the dark, tired circles beneath her eyes.

It didn't look pretty. It just looked like pain.

She spoke, and her voice came out rough and quavering. 'I told her I would protect her.'

'Sometimes you try,' I said quietly. 'Sometimes that's all you do. Try. That's how the game works.'

'Game,' she said. The single word was caustic enough to melt holes in the floor. 'Has it ever happened to you? Someone who came to you for help was killed?'

I nodded. 'Couple of times. First time was Kim Delaney. A girl I had trained to keep her talent under control. Maybe a little stronger than the women in the Ordo, but not much. She got involved in bad business. Over her head. I thought I could warn her off, that she would listen to me. I should have known better.'

'What happened?'

I tilted my head back at the body behind me, without actually looking. 'Something ate her. I go to her grave sometimes.'

'Why?'

'To bring her some flowers and sweep off the leaves. To remind me of the stakes I play for. To remind me that nobody wins them all.'

'And after?' Elaine asked me quietly. She hadn't looked away from the corpse. Not for a second. 'What did you do to the thing that killed her?'

It was a complicated answer, but it wasn't what Elaine needed to hear right then. 'I killed it.'

She nodded again. 'When we catch up to the Skavis, I want it.'

I put a hand on her shoulder and said, very gently, 'It won't make you feel any better.'

She shook her head. 'That's not why I want to do it. It was my job. I've got to finish my job. I owe her that much.'

I didn't think Elaine herself thought the statement was untrue, but I'd gone through this kind of thing before, and it can unbalance your tires pretty damned quick. There was no point, though, in trying to discuss it with her rationally. Reason had left the building.

'You'll get him,' I said quietly. 'I'll help.'

She let out one little broken, cawing sob and pressed against my chest. I held her, warm and slender, and felt the terrible remorse and frustration and grief that coursed through her. I pressed my presence against her and tightened my arms around her and felt her body shaking with silent sobs. More than anything, at that moment, I wished I could make her torment go away.

I couldn't. Being a wizard gives you more power than most, but it doesn't change your heart. We're all human.

We're all of us equally naked before the jaws of pain.

Not a full minute later, I could feel Elaine beginning the struggle to get her breathing under control. DuMorne's methods of teaching us to discipline our emotions had not been gentle, but they worked. Before another minute went by Elaine's breathing had steadied, and she leaned her head against my collarbone for a moment, a silent gesture of gratitude. Then she straightened, and I lowered my arms. She bowed her head toward Anna's corpse, an almost formal gesture of respect or farewell.

When she turned around, I was waiting for her with a damp, cool washcloth. I said quietly, 'Hold still,' and gently wiped her face clean. 'You have to uphold the gumshoe image. Can't go out blotchy. People will think we're not hard-boiled. Very important to be hard-boiled.'

She watched me as I cleaned her face and talked, and her eyes looked huge. A very small smile touched them through the sadness. 'I'm glad you're here to tell me these things,' she said, her voice steady again before it slipped into a bourbon-tainted, lockjawed Humphrey Bogart impersonation. 'Now stop flapping your gums and start walking.'

My tracking spell led us to an apartment building.

'This is Abby's building,' Elaine said as I pulled over. The only close place to park was in front of a hydrant. I doubted any industrious civil servants would be handing out tickets this late, but even if they were, it would be cheap compared to what a long walk in the dark could cost me.

'Which apartment?' I asked.

'Ninth floor,' Elaine replied. She shut the door of the Beetle a little harder than she had to.

'It occurs to me,' I said, 'that if I was a bad guy and wanted to off a couple of intrepid hard-boiled wizards, I might be hanging around watching someplace like this.'

'It occurs to me,' Elaine said, her voice crisp, 'that he would be exceptionally foolish to make the attempt.'

We walked together, quickly. Elaine was tall enough to keep up with me without taking the occasional skipping step. She'd slipped half a dozen coppery bracelets over each wrist, all of them slender, all of them hanging more heavily than they should have. Faint glints of golden energy played among them, and looked like little more than the glitter of light on metal – except that you could see them better when the bracelets were in deep shadows.

By silent agreement, we skipped the elevators. I had my shield bracelet ready to go, and my staff was quivering with leashed energy that made it wave and wobble incongruously to its weight and motion as I moved. That much readied magic could have unfortunate consequences on electrical equipment, like elevator control panels.

The doors to the stairs opened only from the other side, but I conjured a quick spell to shove against the pressure bar on the far side using my staff, and it swung open. We slipped into the stairway. Anyone waiting for us above would be watching the elevator first. Anyone chasing after us would have a hard time with the locked doors, and would make noise on the open concrete stairs.

I checked my gun with my left hand, safe in the pocket of my duster. Magic is groovy, but when it comes to dealing out death, regular mortal know-how can be just as impressive.

Nine floors up was enough to make me breathe hard, though not as hard as I once would have. A faint ghost of a headache came along with the elevated heart rate. Hell's bells, I must have been hurt a lot worse than I thought, back at the harbor. Elaine looked a little strained, herself. If she'd really smoothed away that much of an injury, she had more skill than she'd told me she did. That kind of healing isn't a matter of trivial effort, either. She might be more fragile than she appeared.

I opened the fire door on Abby's floor, and let Elaine take the lead. She went down the center of the hallway in total silence, her hands slightly outstretched, and I got the sense that she was somehow perfectly aware of everything around her − more so than human senses would account for. The bracelets on her wrists glittered more brightly. Superior awareness as a defense, then, instead of my own, more direct approach of meeting power with power and stopping things cold. Just her style.

But neither hyperawareness nor irresistible force was called for. Elaine reached a door and raised a hand to knock. Just before it fell, the door opened, and a strained-looking Abby gave us a quick nod. 'Good, a little early, that's good; come in, yes, come in.'

I started forward, but Elaine held up one hand to halt me, her eyes distracted. 'Let me check. Another woman inside. Two dogs.' She glanced at me, and lowered her hand. 'One of them is your dog.'

'Mouse?' I called.

The floor shook a little, and the big, dark grey dog nudged rather delicately past Abby and came to greet me, shoving his head into my stomach until I went down on one knee and got a sloppy kiss or two on the face.

I slapped his shoulders roughly a few times, because I'm supremely manly and did not tear up a little to see that he was all right and still attached to his collar. 'Good to see you, too, furface.'

Toto trotted out behind Mouse, like a tiny tugboat escorting an enormous barge, and gave a suspicious growl. Then he pattered over to me and sniffed me, sneezed several times, and evidently found me acceptable, underneath the smell of lake water. He hurried back over to Abby, gave me one more growl to make sure I'd learned my lesson, and bounced around her feet until she picked him up.

The plump little blonde settled the dog in her arms and faced me with concern. 'What happened? I mean, the two of you left and what happened, where did you go, is Olivia—'

'Let's go inside,' I said, rising. I traded a look with Elaine, and we all went into Abby's apartment. Mouse never left actual, physical contact with me, his shoulders pressing steadily, lightly, against my leg. I was the last through the door and closed it behind me.

Abby's place was a modest, hectic little apartment, segregated into neatly compartmentalized areas. She had a desk with a typewriter, a table with an old sewing machine, a chair beside a music stand with a violin (unless maybe it was a viola) resting on it, a reading niche with an armchair and overloaded shelves of romance novels, and what looked something like a shrine dedicated to ancestor worship, only in reverse, where the saints were all children with round cheeks and blond ringlets.

Priscilla was there, seated in the comfortable chair in the reading niche, looking haggard and much subdued. There was a cup of tea sitting on the little table beside the reading chair, but it had apparently gone cold without ever having been touched. She looked up at me, her eyes heavy and dull.

'Olivia's all right,' I said quietly.

Abby brightened a second before I started speaking, drawing in a sharp little breath. The little dog in her arms caught her mood at once, and began wagging his tail at me. 'Yes?'

'A . . . sometime associate of mine, the man in the pictures, has been taking women who were in danger of being a target of the killers out of the city. He learned Olivia was in danger and urged her to leave with him when he took several women to a safe house.'

Priscilla stared at me hard for a long moment. Then she said, 'What else?'

Elaine spoke, her voice quiet and unflinching. 'Anna's dead. Back at the hotel room. An apparent suicide.'

Abby let out a little gagging sound. She sat down very quickly in the chair by the violin. Toto let out small, distressed sounds. 'Wh-what?' Abby asked.

Priscilla shuddered and bowed her head. 'Oh. Oh, no. Oh. Anna.'

'I need to know, ladies,' I said quietly. 'Why didn't you do as we instructed? Why did you leave the hotel?'

'It . . .' Abby began. Tears overflowed her cheeks. 'It was . . . was . . .'

'She said,' Priscilla said in a quiet, dull voice. 'Said that she had to leave. That she had to go to work.'

Son of a bitch. I *knew* it.

Elaine was half a beat behind me. 'Who?'

'H-Helen,' Abby sobbed. 'It was Helen.'

I stood there fuming while Elaine coaxed the rest of the story out of Abby and Priscilla.

'It was only an hour or so after you left,' Abby told Elaine. 'Helen got a call on her cell phone.'

'Cell phone?' I perked up. 'She had one that worked?'

'She doesn't have a lot of talent that way,' Abby said. 'None of us do, really. Even my cell phone works most of the time.'

I grunted. 'Means she wasn't hiding a bigger talent, then. That's worth something.'

'Harry,' Elaine said quietly. It was a rebuke. 'Please go on, Abby.'

I zipped my mouth shut.

'She got a call, and she went into the bathroom to talk. I couldn't hear what she said, but when she came out, she said she had to go to work. That she was leaving.'

I lifted my eyebrows. 'That's quite a job, if she's risking exposure to a killer to show up for the shift.'

'That's what I said,' Priscilla said, her voice even more bitter, if such a thing was possible. 'It was stupid. I never even thought to be suspicious of it.'

'Anna argued with her,' Abby went on, 'but Helen refused to stay. So Anna wanted us all to take her there together.'

'Helen wouldn't have any of it, of course,' Priscilla said. 'At the time, I thought she might just be ashamed of us seeing her working some nothing little job at a fast-food restaurant or something.'

'We never really knew what she did,' Abby said, her tone

numb and apologetic. 'She never wanted to talk about it. We always assumed it was an issue of pride.' She petted the little dog in her arms idly. 'She said something about keeping us separate from the rest of her life . . . in any case. Anna put her into a cab and made her promise to keep in touch with us. Calling in on the phone until she was safely around other people.'

'You just let her walk?' I broke in.

'She's a sister of the Ordo,' Priscilla said. 'Not a criminal to be distrusted and watched.'

'In point of fact,' I said, 'she *is* a criminal to be distrusted and watched. Ask her freaking parole officer.'

Elaine frowned at me. 'Dammit, Harry. This isn't helping.'

I muttered under my breath, folded my arms again, and crouched down to give Mouse's ears and neck a good scratching. Maybe it would help me keep my mouth shut. There's a first time for everything.

'Helen called me about twenty minutes later,' Priscilla said. 'She said that she had been followed from the hotel. That our location had become known. That we had to leave. We did, just as you told us. Helen said that she would meet us here.'

'I *told* you to head for somewhere public—' I began, snarling.

'Harry,' Elaine said, her voice sharp.

I subsided again.

There was a moment of awkward silence. 'Um. So we went,' Abby said. 'But when we got there, Helen wasn't around.'

'No,' Priscilla said, hugging her arms under her breasts, looking cold and miserable, even in the turtleneck. 'She called again. Begged us to come to her apartment.'

'I stayed here with the dogs,' Abby said. Toto looked up at her as she said it, tilting his head and wagging his little tail.

'Once Anna and I picked her up,' Priscilla continued, 'we

headed back here — but Helen looked awful. She'd run out of insulin and hadn't been able to go get it with all the trouble. Anna dropped me off and took her to the pharmacy. That was the last we saw of her.'

Abby fretted her lip and said to Priscilla, 'It wasn't your fault.'

Priscilla shrugged. 'She'd never said anything about diabetes before. I should have known better. I should have seen . . .'

'Not your fault,' Abby insisted, compassion in her voice. 'We believed in her. We all did. But she was pulling our strings the whole time. The killer was right here among us.' She shook her head. 'We should have listened to you, Warden Dresden.'

'We should have,' Priscilla said quietly. 'If we had, Anna would be alive right now.'

I couldn't think of any response to that. Well. I had plenty of them, but they all were some variation on a theme of 'I told you so.' I felt no need to pour salt into fresh wounds, so I kept my mouth shut.

Besides, I was processing what Abby and Priscilla had told us.

Elaine traded a look with me. 'Do you think Helen is the Skavis we've heard about?'

I shrugged. 'I doubt it, but technically it's possible. White Court vamps can pass for human easily, if they want.'

'Then why doubt it?'

'Because that little creep Madrigal called the Skavis "he,"' I said. 'Helen isn't a he.'

'A shill?' Elaine asked.

'Looks like.'

Abby looked back and forth between us. 'E-excuse me. But what is a shill?'

'Someone who works with a criminal while pretending

to have nothing to do with him,' I said. 'He helps the bad guy while pretending to be your buddy and making suggestions. Suggesting that you leave a safe hiding place and split up the group, for example.'

Silence. Toto let out a quiet, distressed whine.

'I can't believe this,' Priscilla said, pressing her fingertips against her cheekbones and closing her eyes.

'But we've known her for years,' Abby said, her expression as unhappy and confused as a lost child's. 'How could she lie to us like that, for so long?'

I winced. I don't like seeing anyone in pain, but it's worse when a woman is suffering. That's probably chauvinistic of me, and I don't give a damn if it is.

'All right,' I said. 'We've still got a lot more questions than answers, but at least we know where to start the barbecue.'

Elaine nodded. 'Get these two to safety, then track down Helen.'

'Safety,' I said. 'Thomas.'

'Yes.'

I glanced at Abby and Priscilla. 'Ladies, we're leaving.'

'Where?' Priscilla asked. I had expected a protest, or sneering sarcasm, or at least pure, contrary bitchiness. Her voice, though, was quietly frightened. 'Where are we going?'

'To Olivia,' I told her. 'And five or six of the other women my associate is protecting.'

'Do they need anything?' Abby asked.

'They have several kids with them,' I said. 'Mostly toddlers.'

'I'll pack some food and cereal,' Abby said, before I'd even finished talking. Priscilla just sat, sunken in her chair and hunched in on herself. Abby dumped half of her cupboard into a great big suitcase with those skate-wheel rollers on the bottom, zipped it shut, and clipped what looked like a little plastic birdcage onto the suitcase. She gestured at Toto and the little dog jumped up into the birdcage, turned around three times, and lay down with a happy little doggy smile.

'Very well,' Abby said.

Mouse looked at Toto. Then he looked at me.

'You've got to be kidding,' I told him. 'I'd have to clip a railroad car to the suitcase and hire the Hulk to move it around. You're young and healthy. You walk.'

Mouse looked at Toto's regal doggy palanquin and sighed. Then he took point as we went back down to the car, which had been ticketed despite the lateness of the hour. I stuck the ticket in my pocket. Think positive, Harry. At least they didn't tow it.

Getting everyone into the Beetle was an adventure, but we managed it, and returned to the shabby little south-side motel.

Maybe twenty seconds after we parked, Murphy's Harley-Davidson motorcycle rumbled out of an alley across the street, where she must have been keeping an eye on the front of the motel from a spot where she could see the windows and doors to both rooms Thomas had rented. She was wearing jeans, a black tank top, and a loose black man's shirt that had the sleeves rolled up about twenty times and draped over her like a trench coat while it hid the shoulder rig that held a Glock in one holster, a SIG in the other. Her hair was pulled back in a loose ponytail, and the badge she usually wore on a chain around her neck in these sorts of situations was conspicuous by its absence.

She waited with a slightly bemused air while everyone scrambled out of the Beetle. Elaine got them moving toward the rooms, hurrying to get them out of sight.

'No clown car jokes,' I told Murphy. 'Not one.'

'I wasn't going to say anything,' Murphy said. 'Jesus, Harry, what happened to you?'

'You heard anything about the harbor today?'

'Oh,' Murphy said. Mouse came over to greet her and she shook hands with him gravely. 'Thomas wasn't really forthcoming with explanations. He lit out of here in a hurry.'

'He was hungry,' I said.

Murphy frowned. 'Yeah, so he said. Is he going to hurt anyone?'

I considered and then shook my head. 'Ordinarily, I'd say he wouldn't. Now . . . I'm not sure. It would really go against his character to do something like that. But he's been acting out of character through this whole mess.'

Murphy folded her arms. 'Mess is right. You want to tell me what's going on?'

I gave Murphy the short version of what we'd learned since I'd seen her last.

'Jesus, Mary, and Joseph,' Murphy said. 'Then it *was* Beckitt.'

'Looks like she was shilling for the Skavis, whoever he is. And Grey Cloak and that wussy cousin of Thomas's added in a few killings of their own to get my attention.'

'That isn't exactly in the best interests of the Skavis, if he was trying to avoid it.'

'I know. So?'

'So they're all vampires, right?' Murphy shrugged. 'I figured they'd be working together.'

'They're White Court. They live for backstabbing. They like doing it through cat's-paws. They probably figured I would find out about the killings, move in, and wipe out the Skavis for them. Then they'd congratulate themselves on how clever they were.'

Murphy nodded. 'So now that you've got your clients safely tucked away, what comes next?'

'More wiping out than they counted on,' I said. 'I'm going to find Beckitt and ask her nicely not to kill anyone else and to point me to the Skavis. Then I'll have a polite conversation with him. Then I'll settle up with Grey Cloak and Passenger Madrigal.'

'How do you find Beckitt?'

'Um,' I said, 'I'm sure I'll figure out something. This entire mess is still way too nebulous for me.'

'Yeah,' Murphy said. 'All these killings. It still doesn't make any sense.'

'It makes sense,' I said. 'We just don't know how, yet.' I grimaced. 'We're missing something.'

'Maybe not,' Murphy said.

I arched an eyebrow at her.

'Remember our odd corpse out?'

'Jessica Blanche,' I said. 'The one Molly saw.'

'Right,' Murphy said. 'I found out more about her.'

'She some kind of cultist or something?'

'Or something,' Murphy said. 'According to a friend in Vice, she was an employee of the Velvet Room.'

'The Velvet Room? I thought I burned that plac— uh, that is, I thought some as-yet-unidentified perpetrator burned that place to the ground.'

'It's reopened,' Murphy said. 'Under new management.'

Click. Now some pieces were falling into place. 'Marcone?' I asked.

'Marcone.'

Gentleman Johnnie Marcone was the biggest, scariest gangster in a city famous for its gangsters. Once the old famiglias had fallen to internal bickering, Marcone had done an impression of Alexander the Great and carved out one of the largest criminal empires in the world – assuming you didn't count governments. Chicago's violent crime rate had dropped as much because of Marcone's draconian rule of the city's rackets as because of the dedication of the city's police force. The criminal economy had more than doubled, and Marcone's power continued to steadily grow.

He was a smart, tough, dangerous man — and he was absolutely fearless. That is a deadly combination, and I avoided crossing paths with him whenever I could.

The way things were shaping up, though, this time I couldn't.

'You happen to know where the new Velvet Room is?' I asked Murphy.

She gave me a look.

'Right, right. Sorry.' I blew out a breath. 'Seems like it might be a good idea to speak to some of the girl's coworkers. I'll bet they'll be willing to do a little talking to avoid trouble with the law.'

She showed me her teeth in a fierce grin. 'They just might. And if not, Marcone might be willing to talk to you.'

'Marcone doesn't like me,' I said. 'And it's mutual.'

'Marcone doesn't like anybody,' Murphy replied. 'But he respects you.'

'Like that says much for me.'

Murphy shrugged. 'Maybe, maybe not. Marcone's scum, but he's no fool, and he does what he says he'll do.'

'I'll talk to Elaine once she's got everyone settled,' I said. 'Get her to stay here with Mouse and keep an eye on things.'

Murphy nodded. 'Elaine, huh? The ex.'

'Yeah.'

'The one working against you last time she was in town.'

'Yeah.'

'You trust her?'

I looked down at Murphy for a minute, then up at the hotel room. 'I want to.'

She exhaled slowly. 'I have a feeling things are going to get hairy. You need someone who's got your back.'

'Got that.' I said, holding up my fist. 'You.'

Murphy rapped her knuckles gently against mine and snorted. 'You're going syrupy on me, Dredsen.'

'If it rains, I'll melt,' I agreed.

'It's to be expected,' she said. 'What with how you're gay and all now.'

'I'm wh . . .' I blinked. 'Oh. Thomas's apartment. Hell's bells, you cops got a fast grapevine.'

'Yeah. Rawlins heard it at the coffee machine and he just had to call me up and tell me all about you and your boyfriend being in a fight. He asked me if he should get you the sound track to *Les Miserables* or *Phantom of the Opera* for Christmas this year. Varetti and Farrel got a deal on track lighting from Malone's brother-in-law.'

'Don't you people have lives?' I said. At her continued smile, I asked warily, 'What are *you* getting me?'

She grinned, blue eyes sparkling. 'Stallings and I found an autographed picture of Julie Newmar on eBay.'

'You guys are never going to let go of this one, are you?' I sighed.

'We're cops,' Murphy said. 'Of course not.'

We shared a smile that faded a moment later. Both of us turned to watch the street, alert for any unwanted company. We were silent for a while. Cars went by. City sounds of engine and horn. A car alarm a block over. Dark shadows where the streetlights didn't touch. Distant sirens. Rotating, attention-getting spotlights lancing up to the dark summer night from the front of a theater.

'Hell's bells,' I said, after a time. 'Marcone.'

'Yeah,' Murphy said. 'It changes things.'

Marcone was involved.

Matters had just become a great deal more dangerous.

The new Velvet Room looked nothing like the old Velvet Room.

'A health club?' I asked Murphy. 'You've got to be kidding me.'

Murphy goosed her Harley right up next to the Beetle. There had been only one parking space open, but there was room for both of our rides in it, more or less. It wasn't like I was worried about collecting a few more dents and dings in addition to the dozens already there.

'It's progressive,' Murphy said. 'You can get in shape, generate testosterone, and find an outlet for it all under one roof.'

I shook my head. A modest sign on the second floor over a row of smaller shops proclaimed, EXECUTIVE PRIORITY HEALTH. It lacked the wide-open, well-lit windows of most health clubs, and apparently occupied the whole of the second floor.

'Wait a minute,' I said. 'Isn't that the hotel where Tommy Tomm got murdered?'

'Mmmm,' Murphy said, nodding. 'The Madison. A corporation that has absolutely no visible connection to John Marcone recently bought it and is renovating it.'

'You have to admit it was a little . . . overdone,' I said.

'It looked like the set of a burlesque show about an opium lord's harem,' Murphy said.

'And now . . . it *is* one,' I said.

'But it won't look like it,' Murphy said.

'They call that progress,' I said. 'Think this bunch will give us any trouble?'

'They'll be polite.'

'Marcone is the kind of guy who apologizes for the necessity just before his minions put a bullet in you.'

Murphy nodded. She'd rearranged her gun rig and put on a Kevlar vest before we left. The baggy man's shirt was now buttoned up over it. 'Like I said. Polite.'

'Seriously,' I said. 'Think anything will start up?'

'Depends how big a beehive we're about to kick,' she replied.

I blew out a breath. 'Right. Let's find out.'

We went inside. The doors opened onto a foyer, which was closed away from what had been the hotel's lobby by a security door and a panel of buzzers. The buzzers on the lowest row were labeled with the names of the shops on the first floor. None of the others were marked.

Murphy flipped open her notepad, checked a page, and then punched a button in the middle of the top row. She held it down for a moment, then released it.

'Executive Priority,' said a young woman's voice through a speaker beside the panel. 'This is Bonnie. How may I help you?'

'I'd like to speak with your manager, please,' Murphy said.

'I'm very sorry, ma'am,' came the reply. 'The management is only in the office during normal business hours, but I would be happy to leave a message for you.'

'No,' Murphy replied calmly. 'I know that Ms Demeter is in. I will speak to her, please.'

'I'm very sorry, ma'am,' came Bonnie's rather prim reply. 'But you are not a member of the club, and you are on private property. I must ask you to leave immediately or I will inform building security of the problem and call the authorities.'

'Well, *that* should be fun,' I said. 'Go ahead and call the cops.'

Murphy snorted. 'I'm sure they'd love to have an excuse to come stomping around.'

'I . . .' Bonnie said, floundering. Clearly, she hadn't been trained to deal with this kind of response. Or maybe she just wasn't all that bright to begin with.

I made a kind of do-you-mind gesture at Murphy. She shook her head and leaned to one side, so I could get closer to the intercom.

'Look, Bonnie,' I said. 'We aren't here for trouble. We just need to talk to your boss. If she likes, she can come talk over the intercom. Otherwise, I *will* come up there and talk to her in person. There's only one relevant issue here: Would you rather be reasonable and polite, or would you rather replace a bunch of doors, walls, and goons?'

'Um. Well.'

'Just go tell your boss, Bonnie. It's not your fault that we didn't fall for the business-hours-only line. Let her decide what to do, so you don't get in any trouble.'

After a slight pause, Bonnie realized the professional value in passing the buck. 'Very well, sir. May I ask who this is?'

'I'm with Sergeant Karrin Murphy, Chicago PD,' I said. 'My name is Harry Dresden.'

'Oh!' Bonnie said. 'Oh, Mister Dresden, please excuse me! I didn't know it was you, sir.'

I blinked at the intercom.

'You're the last of our Platinum Club members to pay a visit, sir. By all means, sir, please accept my apologies. I'll have someone meet you and your guest at the elevator with your membership packet. I'll notify Ms Demeter at once.'

The door buzzed, clicked, and opened.

Murphy gave me a steady look. 'What's that all about?'

'Don't ask me,' I told her. 'I'm gay now.'

We went in. The first floor of the building looked like a miniature shopping mall, its walls completely lined with small shops that sold computer parts, books, video games, candles, bath stuff, jewelry, and clothes in a number of styles. All the shops were closed, their steel curtains drawn down. A row of small lights on either side of a strip of red carpet came to life, illuminating the way to the main bank of elevators. One of the elevators stood open and waiting.

We got in and I hit the button for the second floor. It began moving at once. 'If there is a welcoming committee from the Lollipop Guild waiting for us when these doors open, I'm leaving. This is surreal.'

'I noticed that too,' Murphy said.

'Ms Demeter.' I said. 'Think it's a pseudonym?'

One corner of Murphy's mouth quirked up. 'I think we'll find all kinds of nongenuine modifications around here.'

The elevator stopped and the door opened.

Three women were waiting outside of it. They were all dressed in . . . well, 'workout clothes' wasn't quite accurate. Their outfits looked something like the ones the waitresses at Hooters wear, only tight. None of them could have been much over drinking age, and all of them had clearly passed some kind of intense qualification process certifying them to wear outfits like that. They were pretty, too, a blonde, a brunette, and a redhead, and they had nice . . . smiles.

'Welcome, sir,' the redhead said. 'May I take your coat and . . . and stick?'

'That's the closest I've come to being propositioned in years.' I sighed. 'But no, I'll hang onto them for now.'

'Very good, sir.'

The blonde held a round silver tray with two fluted glasses of orangey liquid. She beamed at us. The reflection of light from her teeth could have left scars on my retinas. 'Mimosa, sir, ma'am?'

Murphy stared at all three of them with a blank expression. Then, without a word, she took one of the drinks, tossed it off, and put the glass back on the tray with a dark mutter.

'None for me,' I said. 'I'm driving.'

The blonde stepped back, and the brunette – whose shirt bore a stencil of the word *Bonnie* – came forward carrying a customized black leather gym bag that probably cost as much as Murphy's Kevlar vest. Bonnie handed me the bag, and then offered me a manila folder and a big mustard-colored envelope. 'These are complimentary, of course, sir, for all of our platinum members. There are several outfits for exercise on the inside, a set of athletic shoes in your size, a PDA to help you track your progress, and some basic toiletries.' She tapped the envelope. 'Here is a copy of your membership papers, as well as your membership card and your security access code.'

If this was a trap, it was working. I tried to juggle all of my gear and the comp items, too. If I suddenly had to walk anywhere while doing it, I'd probably trip and break my neck.

'Uh,' I said. 'Thank you, Bonnie.'

'Of course, sir,' she chirped. 'If you would please come with me, I'll show you to Ms Demeter's office.'

'That would be lovely,' I said. The bag had a strap on it. I managed to get it over one shoulder, then folded the paperwork and stuffed it into one of my coat's roomy pockets.

Bonnie waited for me to get settled before taking my arm in a perfectly confident and familiar fashion and guiding me forward. She smelled nice, something like honeysuckle, and she had a friendly smile on her mouth. Her hands, though, felt cold and nervous.

Guided by Bonnie and her clammy hands, we walked through the building, past a long, open space filled with various exercise machines, weights, wealthy-looking men, and attractive young women. Bonnie started prattling about how new the machines were, and how the latest techniques and theories in fitness training were in use, and how Platinum Club members would each have their own personal fitness trainer assigned to them each and every visit.

'And, of course, our in-house spa offers any number of other services.'

'Ah,' I said. 'Like massages, mud baths, pedicures, that kind of thing?'

'Yes, sir.'

'And sex?'

Bonnie's smile didn't falter for a second, although it looked a little incongruous with her wary sideways glance at Murphy. She didn't answer the question. She stopped at an open doorway. 'Here we are,' she said, smiling. 'If there is anything I can do for you, just pick up the phone on Ms Demeter's desk and I'll answer right away.'

'Thanks, Bonnie,' I said.

'You are welcome, sir.'

'Do you need a tip or anything?'

'Unnecessary, sir.' She gave me another smile and a nod, and hurried away.

I watched her go down the hall, lips pursed thoughtfully, and decided that Bonnie was eminently qualified to hurry away. 'We get left all alone here?' I asked Murphy. 'Does this smell like a trap to you?'

'There's one hell of a lot of bait,' she replied, glancing around, and then into the office. 'But the fire stairs are right across the hall, and there's a fire escape just outside the office window. To say nothing of the fact that there are a dozen customers within a few yards who could hardly help but notice anything noisy.'

'Yeah. But how many of them do you think would testify in court about what they heard or saw while they were at a ritzy brothel?'

Murphy shook her head. 'Rawlins knows I'm here. If anything happens, they'll turn the place inside out. Marcone knows that.'

'How come you all haven't done it already? I mean, this is illegal, right?'

'Sure it is,' Murphy said. 'And very tidy. In operations like this one, the women involved are generally willing employees, and generally very well paid. They're required to have regular medical examinations. There's a low incidence of drug use, and almost never any attempts to control them through addiction or terror.'

'Victimless crime?'

Murphy shrugged. 'Cops never have as many resources as they need. In general, they don't waste them on an operation like this one. Vice personnel are needed badly in plenty of other places where there is a lot more at stake.'

I grunted. 'The fact that it's obviously a club for the stupidly wealthy doesn't make it any easier to bring the hammer down.'

'No, it doesn't,' Murphy said. 'Too many people with too much influence in the city government have their reputations to protect. The place makes money hand over fist, and as long as they don't flaunt their business, cops tolerate what's going on except for the occasional token gesture. Marcone isn't going to jeopardize that by killing us here, when he can just as easily have it done tomorrow, in a less incriminating location.'

'Depending on the size of the beehive,' I said.

'Depending on that,' Murphy agreed. 'We might as well sit down.'

We went into the office. It looked like any number of executive offices I'd seen before, somber, understated, and expensive. We sat down in comfortable leather chairs. Murphy kept an eye on the doorway. I watched the window. We waited.

Twenty minutes later, footsteps approached.

A large man came through the door. He was built like a bulldozer made out of slabs of raw, workingman muscle, thick bones, and heavy sinews. He had a neck as thick as Murphy's waist, short red hair, and beady eyes under a heavy brow. His expression looked like it had been permanently locked into place a few seconds after someone had kicked his puppy through a plate-glass window.

'Hendricks,' I greeted Marcone's primary enforcer with convivial cheer. ''Sup?'

Beady eyes settled on me for a second. Hendricks made a growling sound in his throat, checked the rest of the room, and said, over his shoulder, 'Clear.'

Marcone came in.

He wore a gunmetal grey Armani suit with Italian leather shoes, and his shirt was open one button at the throat. He was an inch or two above average height, and had looked like an extremely fit forty-year-old ever since I had known him. His haircut was perfect, his grooming immaculate, and his eyes were the color of worn dollar bills. He nodded pleasantly and walked around the large mahogany desk to sit down.

'Wow,' I said. 'Ms Demeter, you look almost exactly like this criminal scumbag I met once.'

Marcone rested his elbows on the desk, made a steeple out of his fingers, and regarded me with a cool and unruffled smile. 'And good evening to you, too, Mister Dresden. It's somehow reassuring to see that time has not eroded your sophomoric sensibilities.' His eyes flicked to Murphy. 'Sergeant.'

Murphy pressed her lips together and nodded once, her eyes narrowed. Hendricks loomed in the doorway, arms folded, eyes steady on Murphy.

'Where's Amazon Gard?' I asked him. 'You lose the consultant?'

'Ms Gard,' he said, emphasizing the *Ms*, 'is on assignment elsewhere at the moment. And our working relationship is quite secure.'

'And maybe she wouldn't much care for this particular branch of your business?' I suggested.

He showed me his teeth. 'I see you got your membership package.'

'I'm fighting not to gush at you with gratitude,' I told him. 'But it's oh so hard.'

His upturned mouth and glittering white teeth did not resemble a smile. 'Actually, all of my places of business have instructions to so treat you, should you arrive.'

I raised my eyebrows. 'You can't seriously be trying to buy me.'

'Hardly. I am under no illusions about your fondness for myself and my business. I regard it as a preventive measure. In my judgment, my buildings are considerably less likely to burn to the ground during one of your visits if you are disoriented from being treated like a sultan. I do, after all, recall the fate of the last Velvet Room.'

Murphy snorted without taking her wary eyes from Marcone. 'He's got a point, Dresden.'

'That was *one time*,' I muttered. Something in one of the envelopes dug at me through my duster pocket, and I reached down to take it out.

Hendricks may have been big, but he was not slow. He had a gun out before my fingers had closed on the envelope.

Murphy went for her gun, hand darting beneath the baggy shirt.

Marcone's voice cracked like a whip. 'Stop. Everyone.'

We all did it, a reflexive response to the complete authority in his tone.

There are reasons Marcone runs things in Chicago.

Marcone hadn't moved. Hell, he hadn't *blinked*. 'Mister

Hendricks,' he said. 'I appreciate your zeal, but if the wizard wished to harm me, he'd hardly need to draw a concealed weapon to do it. If you please.'

Hendricks let out another rumbling growl and put the gun away.

'Thank you.' Marcone turned to me. 'I trust you will forgive Mister Hendricks's sensitivity. As my bodyguard, he is all too aware that whenever you get involved in my business, Dresden, matters tend to become a great deal more dangerous.'

I scowled at them both and drew the folded materials from my duster pocket, tossing them down beside the discarded gym bag. 'No harm, no foul. Right, Murph?'

Murphy remained motionless for a long moment, hand under her shirt – long enough to make a point that no one was ordering her to do it. Then she returned her hand to her lap.

'Thank you,' Marcone said. 'Now, shall we tilt at one another a few more times or just skip to the point of your visit, Dresden?'

'I want information about one of the women who worked here.'

Marcone blinked once and said, 'Go on.'

'Her name was Jessica Blanche. Her body was found a few days ago. The ME couldn't find a cause of death. I did. I've got more bodies. I think the killings are related. I need to find the link between Jessica and the other victims so I can figure out what the hell is going on and put a stop to it.'

'That information is specific,' Marcone said. 'My knowledge of operations here is merely general. My manager will be more familiar with such things than I.'

'Ms Demeter, I take it.'

'Yes. She should be here momentarily.'

'Or sooner,' said a woman's voice.

I turned to the doorway.

A woman walked through it, dressed in a somber black skirt suit, a white blouse, black pumps, pearls. She walked calmly across the office to stand behind Marcone, her left hand coming to rest on his right shoulder.

'Well, Dresden,' Helen Beckitt murmured. 'It took you long enough.'

I stared, momentarily silent.

Marcone's teeth showed again.

'I don't believe it is polite to gloat,' Helen murmured to him.

'If you knew the man, you would realize what a rare moment this is,' he replied. 'I'm savoring it.'

Murphy glanced from Helen to me and back. 'Harry . . . ?'

'Shhh,' I said, holding up a hand. I closed my eyes for a second, chasing furiously down dozens of twisty lanes of demented logic and motivation, trying to fit each of them to the facts.

The facts, man. Just the facts.

Fact one: Male operatives of House Skavis and House Malvora had been engaging in murders that attempted to frame the Wardens as the perpetrators.

Fact two: House Raith, their nominal superior, led by the White King (sort of), had pursued a policy of armistice with the White Council.

Fact three: That dippy twit Madrigal jumped into the deal on Malvora's side, pitching in a murder or two of his own, evidently to attract my attention.

Fact four: Thomas, though aware of the lethal intentions of his fellow White Court vampires, had shared nothing of it with me.

Fact five: The victims had been women of magical talent, universally.

Fact six: Vampires live for a long, long time.

Fact seven: In a whole graveyard full of the corpses of

minor-league practitioners, one normal, pretty young girl named Jessica Blanche had been killed. Her only connection to the others was Helen Beckitt.

Fact eight: Helen Beckitt worked for Marcone.

Fact nine: I don't like Marcone. I don't trust him. I don't believe him any further than I can kick him. I've never hidden the fact. Marcone knows it.

'Son of a bitch,' I whispered, shaking my head. Things went from bad to worse when Marcone showed up, and I naturally figured that the dangerometer had peaked.

I was wrong. Really, really wrong.

I needed one question answered to be sure what was going on, even though I was fairly sure what the answer would be – the only problem was figuring out whether or not the answer would be an honest one.

I could not afford to get it wrong.

'Helen,' I said quietly. 'If it's all right with you, I'd like to speak to you alone.'

A small smile graced her mouth. She took a deep breath and let it out with a slow, satisfied exhalation.

'You needn't, if you do not wish to do so,' Marcone said. 'I do not react well when others threaten or harm my employees. Dresden is aware of that.'

'No,' Helen said. 'It's all right.'

I glanced aside. 'Murph . . .'

She didn't look overjoyed, but she nodded once and said, 'I'll be right outside.'

'Thanks.'

Murphy departed under Hendricks's beady gaze. Marcone rose as well, and left without glancing at me. Hendricks went last, shutting the door behind him.

Helen ran a fingertip lightly over the pearls on her neck-lace and settled into the chair behind the desk. She looked quite comfortable and confident there. 'Very well.'

I took a seat in one of the chairs facing the desk, and shook my head. 'Jessica Blanche worked for you,' I said.

'Jessie . . .' Helen's dead eyes flickered momentarily down to her folded hands. 'Yes. She lived near me, actually. I gave her a ride to work several days each week.'

Which must have been when Madrigal had seen them together – out in public, presumably not in their 'professional' clothes, and the moron had just assumed that Miss Blanche was another member of the Ordo. From there, it wouldn't have been hard for him to ease up to the girl, snare her with the incubus come-hither, and take her off to a hotel room for a little fun and an ecstatic death.

'You and Marcone,' I said. 'That's one I can't figure. I thought you hated him. Hell, you were trafficking with the powers of darkness, helping to create an addictive drug – helping the Shadowman kill people, to get back at him.'

'Hate,' she said, 'and love are not so very different things. Both are focused upon another. Both are intense. Both are passionate.'

'And there's not much difference between "kiss" and "kill." If you only look at the letters.' I shrugged. 'But here you are, working for Marcone. As a madam.'

'I *am* a convicted felon, Mister Dresden,' she replied. 'I used to handle accounts with a total value in the hundreds of millions of dollars. I was ill suited to work as a waitress in a diner.'

'Nickel in the pen didn't do much for your résumé, huh?'

'Or references,' she replied. She shook her head. 'My reasons for being here are none of your business, Dresden, and have nothing to do with the matter at hand. Ask your questions or get out.'

'After you parted company with the other members of the Ordo tonight,' I said, 'did you place a phone call to them?'

'Again,' she said quietly, 'we are at an impasse, exactly as we were before. It doesn't matter what I say, given that you are clearly unwilling to believe me.'

'Did you call them?' I asked.

She stared steadily, her eyes so dull and empty that it made her elegant black outfit look like funerary wear. I couldn't tell if it would be more suitable for mourners – or for the deceased. Then her eyes narrowed and she nodded. 'Ah. You want me to look you in the eyes. The term is over-dramatic, but I believe it is referred to as a soulgaze.'

'Yeah,' I said.

'I hadn't realized it was a truth detector.'

'It isn't,' I said. 'But it will tell me what sort of person you are.'

'I know what sort of person I am,' she replied. 'I am a functional borderline psychopath. I am heartless, calculating, empty, and can muster very little in the way of empathy for my fellow human beings. But then, you can't take my word for it, can you?'

I just looked at her for a moment. 'No,' I said then, very quietly. 'I don't think I can.'

'I have no intention of proving anything to you. I will submit to no such invasion.'

'Even if it means more of your friends in the Ordo die?'

There was the slightest hesitation before she answered. 'I have been unable to protect them thus far. Despite all . . .' She trailed off and shook her head once. Confidence returned to her features and voice. 'Anna will watch over them.'

I stared at her for a second, and she regarded me coolly, focused on a spot a bit over my eyebrows, avoiding direct eye contact.

'Anna's important to you?' I asked.

'As much as anyone can be, now,' she replied. 'She was kind to me when she had no cause to be. Nothing to gain from it. She is a worthy person.'

I watched her closely. I've done a lot of work as both a professional wizard and a professional investigator. Wizardry is awfully intriguing and useful, but it doesn't necessarily teach you very much about other people. It's better at teaching you about yourself.

The investigating business, though, is all about people. It's all about talking to them, asking questions, and listening to them lie. Most of the things investigators get hired to handle involve a lot of people lying. I've seen liars in every shape and size and style. Big lies, little lies, white lies, stupid lies. The worst lies are almost always silence – or else truth, tainted with just enough deception to rot it to the core.

Helen wasn't lying to me. She might have been dangerous, might have been willing to practice black magic to seek vengeance in the past, might have been cold and distant – but she had not, for one second, tried to conceal any of it, or denied anything that had happened.

'Oh, God,' I said softly. 'You don't know.'

She frowned at me for a moment – then her face became drawn and pale. 'Oh.' She closed her eyes and said, 'Oh, Anna. You poor fool.' She opened them again a moment later. She cleared her throat and asked, 'When?'

'A few hours ago. The hotel room. Suicide.'

'The others?'

'Safe. Hidden and under guard.' I took a deep breath. 'I have to be sure, Helen. If you really do give a damn about them, you'll cooperate with me. You'll help me.'

She nodded once, her eyes distant. Then she said, 'For them.' And met my eyes.

The phenomenon referred to as a soulgaze is a fairly mysterious thing. No one's ever been able to get a really good grasp on exactly how it works. The best descriptions of it have always been more poetical than anything else.

The eyes are the windows of the soul.

Lock eyes with a wizard and the essence of who and what you are is laid bare. It is perceived in different ways by every individual. Ramirez had once told me that he heard it as a kind of musical theme that accompanied the person he was gazing upon. Others looked on a soul in a series of frozen images. My interpretation of a soulgaze was, perhaps inevitably, one of the most random and confusing I'd ever heard about. I see the other person in symbol and metaphor, sometimes in panorama and surround sound, sometimes in misty translucence and haunting whispers.

Whoever was gazed upon got a good look back. Whatever universal powers governed that kind of thing evidently decided that the soul's windows don't come in an optional issue of one-way mirrored glass. You saw them. They saw you, with the same kind of searing permanence.

For me, meeting someone's eyes is always risky. Every human being on earth knows what I'm talking about. Try it. Walk up to someone, without speaking, and look them in the eyes. There's a certain amount of leeway for a second, or two, or three. And then there's a distinct sensation of sudden contact, of intimacy. That's when regular folks normally cough and look away. Wizards, though, get the full ride of a soulgaze.

All things considered, I shouldn't have been surprised that when Helen met my eyes, it got uncomfortably intimate before a second had passed and . . .

. . . and I stood in Chicago, in one of the parks on Lake Michigan. Calumet, maybe? I couldn't see the skyline from where I was standing, so it was hard to be sure.

What I could see was the Beckitt family. Husband, wife, daughter, a little girl maybe ten or eleven years old. She looked like her mother — a woman with smile lines at the corners of her eyes and a white-toothed smile who very little resembled the Helen Beckitt I knew. But all the same, it was her.

They'd been on a family picnic. The sun was setting on a summer evening, golden sunset giving way to twilight as they walked back to the family car. Mother and father swung the little girl between them, each holding one hand.

I didn't want to see what was about to happen. I didn't have a choice in the matter.

A parking lot. The sounds of a car roaring up. Muffled curses, tight with fear, and then a car swerved up off the road and gunfire roared from its passenger window. Screams. Some people threw themselves down. Most, including the Beckitts, stared in shock. More loud, hammering sounds, not ten feet away.

I looked over my shoulder to see a very, very young-looking Marcone.

He wasn't wearing a business suit. He had on jeans and a black leather jacket. His hair was longish, a little mussed, and he also sported a stubble of beard that gave him the kind of rakish look that would attract attention from the girls who fantasized about indulging with a bad boy.

His eyes were still green – but they were the green of a summer hunter's blind, bright and intelligent and predatory, but touched with more . . . something. Humor, maybe. More life. And he was skinnier. Not a lot skinnier or anything, but it surprised me how much younger it and the other minor changes made him look.

Marcone crouched next to another young man, a now-dead thug I'd christened Spike years ago. Spike had his pistol out, and was hammering away at the moving car. The barrel of his 1911-model Colt tracked the vehicle – and its course drew its muzzle into line with the Beckitt family.

Marcone snarled something and slapped the barrel of the gun away from the family. Spike's shot rang out wild and splashed into the lake. There was a last rattle of fire from the moving car, and it roared away. Marcone and

Spike piled into their own car and fled the scene. Spike was driving.

Marcone was staring back over his shoulder.

They left the little girl's broken body, limp and spattered with scarlet, behind them.

Helen saw it first, looking down to the hand that gripped her daughter's. She let out a cry as she turned to her child.

In the wake of the gunshots, the silence was deafening.

I didn't want to see what was coming. Again, I had no choice.

The girl wasn't unconscious. There was a lot of blood. Her father screamed and knelt with Helen, trying to stop the bleeding. He tore off his shirt, pressing it to the child's midsection. He babbled something to Helen and ran for the nearest phone.

His white shirt soaked through as Helen tried to hold it to the weakly struggling girl.

This was the worst part.

The child was in pain. She cried out with it. I expected her to sound horrible and inhuman, but she didn't. She sounded like every little kid who had ever suddenly found herself faced with her first experience of real, nontrivial pain.

'Owie,' she said, over and over, her voice rough. 'Owie, owie, owie.'

'Baby,' Helen said. The tears were blocking her vision. 'I'm here. I'm here.'

'Mommy, Mommy, Mommy,' the girl said. 'Owie, owie, owie.'

The little girl said that.

She said it over and over.

She said it for maybe sixty seconds.

Then she went silent.

'No,' Helen said. 'No, no, no.' She leaned down and felt

her daughter's throat, then desperately pressed her ear to the girl's chest. 'No, no, no.'

Their voices, I realized, sounded almost identical. They blazed with the same anguish, the same disbelief.

I watched Helen shatter, rocking back and forth, trying through blinding tears to apply CPR to the silent little form. Everything else became an unimportant blur. Ghostly figures of her husband, cops, paramedics. Dim little echoes of sirens and voices, a church organ.

I'd known that the Beckitts set out to tear Marcone down out of revenge for what the warring gangsters had done to their daughter – but knowing the story was one thing. Seeing the soul-searing agony the little girl's death had inflicted upon her helpless mother was something else.

And suddenly, everything was bright and new again. Helen and her family were laughing again. In a few moments, they were walking again toward the parking lot, and I could hear the engine of the car whose gunmen would miss Marcone and kill the little girl as it approached.

I tore my eyes away from it, fighting to end the soul-gaze.

I could not go through that again, could not remain locked in that horrible moment that had shaped what Helen had become.

I came back to myself standing, turned half away from Helen, leaning heavily on my staff with my head bowed.

There was a long moment of silence before Helen said, 'I didn't call anyone in the Ordo, Dresden.'

She hadn't. Now I was sure of it.

If Helen hadn't led the Ordo on a merry chase around town, drawing them out into vulnerability for the Skavis hunting them, someone else had.

Priscilla.

She'd been the one receiving all the calls, reporting all

the 'conversations' with Helen. That meant that she'd been working with the killer, drawing out Anna and the others on his behalf, isolating one of the women from the safety of the group so that he could take them alone.

And then I jerked my head up, my eyes wide.

Fact ten: In the middle of a Chicago summer, Priscilla, none too pretty a woman, had been wearing nothing but turtlenecks.

Priscilla hadn't been working *with* the Skavis.

Priscilla *was* the Skavis.

And I had left her holed up in safety with Olivia and Abby and all those women and children.

Predators. The White Court were predators. The Skavis had to know that I was closing in, and that it would not be long before I either caught up to Helen and got the real story or else figured it out on my own. Fight-or-flight instincts must have come down on the former.

I'd been sent after Helen on purpose. The Skavis had *meant* to send me haring off after her, leaving him alone with all those targets.

No. I hadn't left him alone with the women he'd been tracking. They were no threat to him. The Skavis had decided to fight. He had isolated a target, all right, just as he had while hunting helpless women – one who would present a deadly danger to him, should she ever learn his true identity. One who would be distinctly vulnerable, provided he could approach her while camouflaged.

'Oh, God,' I heard myself say. 'Elaine.'

Murphy came out of the building about ten seconds after I did.

'Thomas answered his phone, said he was on the way. He sounded kind of out of it, though. I called both rooms, but the call went straight to the hotel's voice mail,' she reported, slipping her cell phone away as she approached me.

'Does it do that by itself?'

'No. You have to call the desk and ask for it.'

'Dammit,' I said, and tossed her my keys. 'The Skavis thought of that already. Drive.'

Murphy blinked at me, but turned to the Beetle at once. 'Why?'

'I'm going to try to reach Elaine my way,' I said. I hurried around my car to the passenger seat and jerked open the door. 'Get us there as fast as you can.'

'Magic on the road? Won't that kill the car?'

'This car? Probably not,' I said. 'I hope not.' I threw my staff in the backseat.

'Ow!' shrieked a voice.

Murphy's gun came out every bit as fast as I raised my blasting rod, its tip glowing with a scarlet incandescence.

'Don't shoot, don't shoot!' squeaked the voice, considerably more panicked. There was a flickering, and then Molly appeared in my back-seat, legs curled up against her chest, her eyes wide, her face very pale.

'Molly!' I shouted. 'Dammit, what do you think you're doing?'

'I came to help. I was good enough to track down your car, wasn't I?'

'I told you to stay home!'

'Because of the stupid bracelet?' she demanded. 'That has *got* to be the lamest scam ever. *Yoda* never gave anybody a bracelet that—'

I whirled in pure frustration and snarled, '*Fuego!*'

My raw anxiety and rage lashed from the tip of my blasting rod in a lance of blinding scarlet fire. It blasted into a metal trash can in front of Marcone's building and . . . well, it would be bragging to say that it vaporized the trash can. Even I would have trouble with that. It did, however, slag the thing into a shower of molten metal as it gouged a two-foot-deep, coffin-length furrow in the concrete of the sidewalk behind it. Chunks of heated concrete and globs of molten metal hit the building's exterior, cracking several thick panes of glass, pocking stone walls, and leaving several wooden planters on fire. The concussion rattled every window within a hundred yards, and shattered the casing of the nearest streetlight, so that it cast out fractured illumination. Half a dozen car alarms went off.

I turned back to Molly and found her staring at me with her mouth open until my shadow, cast by the rising fires and crippled streetlight, fell across her. My voice came out in a growl. 'I. Am not. Yoda.'

I stripped the glove off my left hand and held it up, my fingers spread. It didn't look as horrific as it used to, but it was plenty ugly enough to make an impression on a nineteen-year-old girl. 'This isn't a goddamn movie, Molly. Screw up here and you don't vanish and leave an empty cloak. You don't get frozen in carbonite. And you should damned well *know* that by now.'

She looked shocked. I'll curse from time to time, but I don't generally indulge in blasphemy – at least, not around

Michael or his family. I don't think God is terribly threatened by my occasional slip of the tongue, but I owe enough to Michael to respect his wishes regarding that particular shade of profanity. Mostly.

Hell, the whole practice of invective was developed to add extra emphasis when the mere meaning of words alone just wasn't enough. And I was feeling plenty emphatic.

Snarling, I cupped my left hand, focused my ongoing anger, and a sudden sphere of light and heat blossomed to life. It wasn't big – about the diameter of a dime. But it was as bright as a tiny sun.

'Harry,' Murphy said. Her voice was a little shaky. 'We don't have time for this.'

'You think you're ready?' I told Molly. 'Show me.'

I blew on the sphere and it wafted out of my hand and glided smoothly into the open door of the Beetle and toward Molly's face.

'Wh-what?' she said.

'Stop it,' I said, my voice cold. 'If you can.'

She swallowed and raised a hand. I saw her try to control her breathing and focus her will, her lips blurring over the steps I'd taught her.

The sphere drifted closer.

'Better hurry,' I added. I did nothing to hide the anger or the taint of derision in my voice.

Beads of sweat broke out on her skin. The sphere slowed, but it had not stopped.

'It's about twelve hundred degrees,' I added. 'It'll melt sand into glass. It doesn't do much for skin, either.'

Molly lifted her left hand and stammered out a word, but her will fluttered and failed, amounting to nothing more than a handful of sparks.

'Bad guys don't give you this much time,' I spat.

Molly hissed – give the kid credit, she didn't let herself

scream – and pressed herself as far as she could from the fire. She threw up an arm to shield her eyes.

For a second, I felt a mad impulse to let the fire continue for just a second more. Nothing teaches like a burned hand, whispered a darker part of my self. I should know.

But I closed my fingers, willed the ending of the spell, and the sphere vanished.

Murphy, standing across the car, just stared at me.

Molly lowered her hand, her arm moving in frightened little jerks. She sat there shivering and staring. Her tongue piercing rattled against her teeth.

I looked at both of them and then shook my head. I got control of my rampaging temper. Then I leaned down and stuck my head in the car, looking Molly in the eyes.

'We play for keeps, kid,' I said quietly. 'I've told you before: Magic isn't a solution to every problem. You still aren't listening.'

Molly's eyes, frightened and angry, filled with tears. She turned her head away from me and said nothing. She tried not to make any noise, but it's tough to keep a good poker face when a snarling madman nearly burns it off. There wasn't any time to waste – but I gave the kid a few seconds of space while I tried to let my head cool off.

The door to Marcone's building opened. Hendricks came out.

Marcone followed him a moment later. He surveyed the damage. Then he glanced at me. Marcone shook his head, took a cell phone from his suit pocket, and went back inside, while Hendricks kept me pinned down with his beady-eyed scowl.

What I'd seen soulgazing Helen Beckitt was still glaringly fresh in my mind – just as it always would be. Marcone had looked a lot younger when he wore his hair longer, less neat, and dressed more casually. Or maybe he'd just looked younger before he'd seen Helen's daughter die.

The thought went utterly against the pressure of the rage inside me, and I grabbed hold of myself while I had the chance. I took a deep breath. I wouldn't do anyone any good if I charged in full of outrage and absent of brains. I took another deep breath and turned to find Murphy on the move.

She walked around the car and faced me squarely.

'All done?' Murphy asked me, her voice pitched low. 'You want to smoke a turkey or set fire to a playground or anything? You could terrorize a troop of Cub Scouts as an encore.'

'And after that, I could tell you all about how to do your job, maybe,' I said, 'right after we bury the people who get killed because we're standing here instead of moving.'

She narrowed her eyes. Neither one of us met each other's gaze or moved an inch. It wasn't a long standoff, but it was plenty hard.

'Not now,' she said. 'But later. We'll talk. This isn't finished.'

I nodded. 'Later.'

We got in the Beetle and Murphy started it up and got moving. 'Ask you questions as we go?'

I calculated distances in my head. The communion spell with Elaine had been created to reach over a couple of yards at the most. It had mostly been used at, ahem, considerably shorter range than that. I could extend the range, I thought, to most of a mile – maybe. It wasn't as simple as just pouring more power into the spell, but it *was* fairly simple. That gave me a couple of minutes to steady my breathing while Murphy drove. I could talk while that happened. It would, in fact, help me keep my mind off my fear for Elaine. Ah, reason, banisher of fear – or at least provider of a place to stick my head in the sand.

'Go ahead,' I told her. I paid no attention to Molly, giving the kid time to think over the lesson and to get herself together. She didn't like anyone to see her when she was upset.

'Why do you think your ex is in danger?' Murphy asked. 'Shouldn't this Skavis just run off if it knows you're onto it?'

'If it was operating alone, sure,' I said. 'That would be the smart thing. But it isn't running off. It's making a fight of it.'

'So . . . what? It has help?'

'It has *rivals*,' I said.

'Yeah. Grey Cloak and Madrigal Raith.' Murphy shook her head. 'But what does that mean?'

'Think in terms of predators,' I said. 'One predator has just gotten its teeth into something good to eat.'

'Scavengers?' Murphy said. 'They're trying to take the prize from him?'

'Yeah,' I said. 'I think that's what they're doing.'

'You mean Elaine?' Murphy said.

I shook my head. 'No, no. More abstract. The Skavis is methodical. It's killing women of magical talent. It doesn't have to do that to live – it can eat any human being.'

'Then why those targets?' Murphy asked.

'Exactly,' I said. 'Why them? This isn't about food, Murph. I think the Skavis is making a play for power.'

'Power?' Molly blurted from the backseat.

I turned and gave her a glare that quelled her interest. She sank back into the seat. 'Within the White Court,' I said. 'This entire mess, start to finish, is about a power struggle within the White Court.'

Murph was silent for a second, absorbing that. 'Then . . . then this is a lot bigger than a few killings in a few towns.'

'If I'm right,' I said, nodding. 'Yeah.'

'Go on.'

'Okay. And remember as I go that White Court vamps don't like their fights out in the open. They arrange things. They use cat's-paws. They pull strings. Confrontation is for losers.'

'Got it.'

I nodded. 'The White King is supporting peace talks between the Council and the Red Courts. I think the Skavis is trying to prove a point – that they don't *need* peace talks. That they have us in a choke hold and all they have to do is hang on.'

Murphy frowned at me, and then her eyes widened. 'You told me once that magic is inherited. Mostly along family lines.'

'Salic law,' I said. 'Mostly through female lines. I got it from my mom.'

Murphy nodded, her eyes going back to the road. 'And they can start . . . what? Thinning the herd, I suppose, from their point of view. Killing those that have the potential to produce more wizards.'

'Yeah,' I said. 'One Skavis goes around to half a dozen cities in the most dangerous – to them – nation on the planet, doing it at will,' I said. 'He proves how easy it is. He identifies and hunts down the best targets. He plants all kinds of distrust for the Council as he does it, making the potential prey distrust the only people who could help them.'

'But what does he hope to accomplish?' Murphy said. 'This is just one guy.'

'Exactly what he wants them to say,' I said. 'Look what just one vampire accomplished working alone. Look how easy it was. Raith is weak. Time to expand the operation now, while the Council is hurt, and screw talking peace with them. Change the guard. Let House Skavis take leadership.'

'And Grey Cloak and Madrigal, seeing that he's onto something good, try to swoop in at the last minute, shoulder the Skavis aside, and take credit for the plan in front of the whole Court,' Murphy finished.

'Yeah. They sing the exact same tune, only they substitute Malvora for Skavis.' I shook my head. 'The hell of it is, if Madrigal hadn't had a personal beef with me I might not have gotten involved. I made him look really bad when he tried to auction me on eBay and instead I fed his djinn to the Scarecrow and made him run off like a girl.'

'Like a what?' Murphy bridled.

'Now is not the time to go all Susie Q. Anthony on me,' I said. 'Madrigal's wounded pride makes him leave clues to try to sucker me into the show. He figures Grey Cloak or our Skavis killer will help him handle me. Except that they ran into another problem.'

'Thomas,' Murphy said, her voice certain.

'Thomas,' I said. 'Snatching their targets out from under them.'

'How's he finding them?'

'Same way they are,' I said. 'He's a vampire. He knows what resources they have and how they think. So much so, in fact, that he's ruining the finale of the whole program for everyone involved.'

Murphy nodded, getting it. 'So Madrigal gets a gang of ghouls and tries to take out his own cousin. And finds you and Elaine there too.'

'Right,' I said. 'He's already being a loser, but it's still a sucker punch, and Madrigal figures, What the hell. If he gets away with it, he pulls off the plan *and* gets his mojo back from me.'

'I still don't get why Thomas didn't say anything,' Murphy said. 'To you, I mean. I never figured him for that kind of secrecy.'

'That's what tipped me off to the whole thing,' I said. 'There just aren't many things which could make Thomas do that. I think he was counting on it to tip me off, in fact.'

Murphy shook her head. 'A phone call would have been easier.'

'Not if he's being watched,' I said. 'And not if he's made a promise.'

'Watched?' Murphy said. 'By who?'

'Someone who has more than one kind of leverage,' I said. 'Someone who is his family, who is protecting the woman he loves, and who has the kind of resources it takes to watch him, and enough savvy to know if he's lying.'

'Lara Raith,' Murphy said.

'Big sister is the one behind the peace movement,' I said. 'Everyone thinks it's Papa Raith, but he's just her puppet now. Except that there aren't many people who know that.'

'If Raith's authority is challenged openly by the Skavis,' Murphy said, putting things together, 'it exposes the fact that he's utterly powerless. Lara would have to fight openly.'

'And the White Court vamp who is driven to that has already lost,' I said. 'She can't maintain her control over the Court if she's revealed as the power behind the throne. Not only does she not have the raw strength she'd need to hold on to it, but the very *fact* that she was revealed would make her an incompetent manipulator and therefore automatically unsuitable in the eyes of the rest of the White Court.'

Murphy chewed on her lip. 'If Papa Raith falls, Lara falls. And if Lara falls . . .'

'Justine goes with her,' I said, nodding. 'She wouldn't be able to protect her for Thomas anymore.'

'Then why didn't she just have Thomas go to you and ask for help?' Murphy said.

'She can't have it get out that she *asked* for help from the enemy team, Murph. Even among her own supporters, that could be a disaster. But remember that she knows how to pull strings. Maybe better than anyone operating right now. She wouldn't be upset if I got involved and stomped all over agents of Skavis and Malvora.'

Murphy snorted. 'So she forbids Thomas from speaking to you about it.'

'She's too smart for that. Thomas gets stubborn about

being given orders. She gets him to promise to keep quiet. But by doing that, she's also done the one thing she *knows* will make him defiant to the spirit of the promise. So he's made a promise and he can't come out and talk to me, but he wants to get my attention.'

'Ha,' Murphy said. 'So he gets around it. He works sloppy, deliberately. He lets himself be seen repeatedly taking off with the women he was rounding up.'

'And leaves a big old honking wall o' clues in his apartment for me, knowing that when I get involved, I'm going to get curious about why he's been seen with missing women and why he's not talking to me. He can't talk to me about it, but he leaves me a map.' I found my right foot tapping against an imaginary accelerator, my left against a nonexistent clutch.

'Stop twitching,' Murphy said. The Beetle jolted over some railroad tracks, officially taking us to the wrong side. 'I'm a better driver than you, anyway.'

I scowled because it was true.

'So right now,' Murphy said, 'you think Priscilla is shilling for the Skavis agent.'

'No. She *is* the Skavis agent.'

'I thought you said it was a man,' Murphy said.

'Strike you funny that Priscilla wears turtlenecks in the middle of a hot summer?'

Murphy let out a word that should not be spoken before small children. 'So if you're right, he's going to clip Elaine and all those moms.'

'Kids too,' I said. 'And anyone who gets in the way.'

'Mouse,' Molly said, her voice worried.

This time I didn't yell her down. I was worried about him, too. 'The Skavis knows that Mouse is special. He saw the demonstration. That's been the only thing keeping him from acting sooner than he did. If the vampire started drawing upon his powers, Mouse would have sensed it and blown his cover. So Mouse is definitely going to be near the top of his list.'

Murphy nodded. 'So what's the plan?'

'Get us to the motel,' I said. We were getting close enough that I could start trying the spell. 'I'm going to try to reach Elaine.'

'Then what?'

'I've got no use for anything that does what this thing does,' I said. 'Do you?'

Her blue eyes glittered as the car zipped through the illumination of a lonely streetlamp. 'No.'

'And as I recall, you are on vacation right now.'

'And having fun, fun, fun,' she snarled.

'Then we won't worry too much about saving anything for later,' I said. I turned my head and said, 'Molly.'

The girl's head whipped up almost audibly. 'Um. What?'

'Can you drive a stick?'

She was silent for a second, then jerked her head in a nod.

'Then when we get out, I want you to get behind the wheel and keep the engine running,' I said. 'If you see anyone else coming, honk the horn. If you see a tall woman in a turtleneck sprinting away, I want you to drive the car over her.'

'I . . . but . . . but . . .'

'You wanted to help. You're helping.' I turned back around. 'Do it.'

Her answer came back with the automatic speed of reflex. 'Yes, sir.'

'What about Grey Cloak and Madrigal?' Murphy asked me. 'Even if we take out the Skavis, they're waiting to jump in.'

'One thing at a time,' I said. 'Drive.'

Then I closed my eyes, drew in my will, and hoped that I could call out to Elaine – and that she would be alive to hear me.

I closed my eyes and blocked out my senses, one by one. The smell of the car and Murphy's deodorant went first. At least Molly had learned from experience and left off any overt fragrances when she tried to use the veil trick a second time. Sound went next. The Beetle's old, laboring engine, the rattle of tires on bad spots of road, and the rush of wind all faded away. Chicago's evening lights vanished from their irregular pressure on my closed eyelids. The sour taste of fear in my mouth simply became not, as I focused on the impromptu variation of the old, familiar spell.

Elaine.

I referred to the same base image I always had. Elaine in our first soulgaze, an image of a woman of power, grace, and oceans of cool nerve superimposed over the blushing image of a schoolgirl, naked for the first time with her first lover. I had known what she would grow into, even then, that she would transform the gawky limbs and awkward carriage and blushing cheeks into confidence and poise and beauty and wisdom. The wisdom, maybe, was still in process, as evidenced by her choice of first lovers, but even as an adult, I was hardly in a position to cast stones, as evidenced by my choice of pretty much everything.

What we hadn't known about, back then, was pain.

Sure, we'd faced some things as children that a lot of kids don't. Sure, Justin had qualified for his Junior de Sade Badge in his teaching methods for dealing with pain. We still hadn't learned, though, that growing up is all about getting hurt. And then getting over it. You hurt. You recover. You move on. Odds are pretty good you're just going to get hurt again. But each time, you learn something.

Each time, you come out of it a little stronger, and at some point you realize that there are more flavors of pain than coffee. There's the little empty pain of leaving something behind − graduating, taking the next step forward, walking out of something familiar and safe into the unknown. There's the big, whirling pain of life upending all of your plans and expectations. There's the sharp little pains of failure, and the more obscure aches of successes that didn't give you what you thought they would. There are the vicious, stabbing pains of hopes being torn up. The sweet little pains of finding others, giving them your love, and taking joy in their life as they grow and learn. There's the steady pain of empathy that you shrug off so you can stand beside a wounded friend and help them bear their burdens.

And if you're very, very lucky, there are a very few blazing hot little pains you feel when you realize that you are standing in a moment of utter perfection, an instant of triumph, or happiness, or mirth which at the same time cannot possibly last − and yet will remain with you for life.

Everyone is down on pain, because they forget something important about it: Pain is for the living. Only the dead don't feel it.

Pain is a part of life. Sometimes it's a big part, and sometimes it isn't, but either way, it's part of the big puzzle, the deep music, the great game. Pain does two things: It teaches you, tells you that you're alive. Then it passes away and leaves you changed. It leaves you wiser, sometimes. Sometimes it leaves you stronger. Either way, pain leaves its mark, and everything important that will ever happen to you in life is going to involve it in one degree or another.

Adding pain to that image of Elaine wasn't a process of imagining horrors, fantasizing violence, speculating upon suffering. It was no different from an artist mixing in new color, adding emphasis and depth to the image that, while bright, was not true to itself or to life. So I took the girl I knew and added in the pains the woman I was reaching for had been forced to face. She'd stepped into a world she'd left behind for more than a decade, and found herself struggling to face life without relying upon anyone else. She'd always had me, and Justin – and when we'd gone away, she'd leaned upon a Sidhe woman named Aurora for help and support. When that had vanished, she had no one – I had given my love to someone else. Justin had been dead for years.

She'd been alone in a city, different from everyone around, struggling to survive and to build a life and a home.

So I added in all the pains I'd learned. Cooking blunders I'd had to eat anyway. Equipment and property constantly breaking down, needing repairs and attention. Tax insanity, and rushing around trying to hack a path through a jungle of numbers. Late bills. Unpleasant jobs that gave you horribly aching feet. Odd looks from people who didn't know you, when something less than utterly normal happened. The occasional night when the loneliness ached so badly that it made you weep. The occasional gathering during which you wanted to escape to your empty apartment so badly you were willing to go out the bathroom window. Muscle pulls and aches you never had when you were younger, the annoyance as the price of gas kept going up to some ridiculous degree, the irritation with unruly neighbors, brainless media personalities, and various politicians who all seemed to fall on a spectrum somewhere between the extremes of 'crook' and 'moron.'

You know.

Life.

And the image of her in my mind deepened, sharpened, took on personality. There's no simple way to describe it, but you know it when you see it, and the great artists can do it, can slip in the shades of meaning and thought and truth into something as simple as a girl named Mona's smile, even if they can't tell you precisely how they managed it.

The image of Elaine gained shadows, flaws, character, and strength. I didn't know the specifics of what she'd been through – not all of them, anyway – but I knew enough, and could make good guesses about plenty more. That image in my mind drew me in as I focused on it, just as I once had focused on that younger image of Elaine unrealized. I reached out with my thoughts and touched that image, breathing gentle life into it as I whispered her True Name, freely given to me when we were young, within the vaults of my mind.

Elaine Lilian Mallory.

And the image came to life.

Elaine's face bowed forward, her hair falling around it, not quite hiding the expression of bone-deep weariness and despair.

Elaine. I whispered to her. *Can you hear me?*

Her thoughts came to me in an echoing blur, like when they want to confuse you at the movies and they muck around with a voice-over . . . *believe I could make a difference. One person doesn't. One person can't ever make a difference. Not in the real world. God, what arrogance. And they paid for it.*

I put more will into my thoughts. *Elaine!*

She glanced up for a moment, looking dully around the room. The image of her was filling in, slowly. She was in well-lit room without many features. Most of it seemed to be white. Then her head bowed again.

Trusting me to keep them safe. I might as well pull the trigger myself. Too cowardly for that, though. I just sit here. Set things up so that I don't have to fail. I don't have to try. I don't have to worry about being nothing. All I have to do is sit.

I didn't like the sound of that at all. Within the sense-less vaults of my mind, I screamed, *Elaine!*

She looked up again, blinking her eyes slowly. Her mouth began moving in time with her audible thoughts. 'Don't know what I thought I could do. One woman. One woman who spent her whole life running away. Being broken. I would have served them better to end it before I ever left, rather than dragging them down with me.'

Her lips stopped moving, but, very faintly, I heard her thoughts call, *Harry?*

And suddenly I could hear a difference in the other thoughts.

'Just sit,' she mumbled. 'Almost over now. I won't be useless anymore. Just sit and wait and I won't have to hurt anymore. Won't fail anyone else. It will all be over and I can rest.'

It didn't sound like Elaine's voice. There were subtle differ-ences. It sounded . . . like someone doing an impersonation. It was close, but it wasn't her. There were too many small inconsistencies.

Then I got it.

That was the Skavis, whispering thoughts of despair and grief into her mind, just as the Raiths would whisper of lust and need.

She was under attack.

Elaine Lilian Mallory! I called, and in my head, my voice rumbled like thunder. *I am Harry Blackstone Copperfield Dresden, and I bid thee hear me! Hear my voice, Elaine!*

There was a shocked silence, and then Elaine's thought-voice said, more clearly, *Harry?*

And her lips moved, and the not-Elaine voice said, 'What the *hell*?'

Elaine's eyes snapped to mine, suddenly meeting them, and the room around her clarified into crystalline relief.

She was in the bathroom of the hotel, in the tub, naked in the bath.

The air was thick with steam. She was bleeding from a broad cut across one wrist. The water was red. Her face was god-awful pale, but her eyes weren't fogged over and hazed out. Not yet.

Elaine! I thundered. *You are under a psychic attack! Priscilla is the Skavis!*

Elaine's eyes widened.

Someone slapped me hard on the face and screamed, 'Harry!'

The world flew sideways and expanded in a rush of motion and sound as my denied senses came crashing back in upon me. The Beetle was sitting sideways across several parking spaces in the motel's little lot, both doors open, and Murphy, gun in one hand, had a hold of my duster with the other and was shaking me hard. 'Harry! Get up!'

'Oh,' I said. 'We're here.'

I stumbled out of the car, getting my bearings. Behind me, Molly scrambled behind the wheel.

'Well?' Murphy demanded. 'Did you get through?'

I opened my mouth to answer, but before I could, every light in sight suddenly went dim. I don't mean they went out. They didn't. They just . . . dwindled, the way a lantern's flame does if you close off the glass. Or, I thought, struck with a sudden impression, the way a fire might dim if something nearby had just drawn the air away. Something big enough to dim nearby flame as it inhaled.

Something big taking a deep breath.

And then a voice that rang with silvery rage rolled through the air, kicking up a layer of dust from the ground in a broad wave in the wake of its passing as it rang out in an echoing clarion call, *'FULMINARIS!'*

There was a flash of green-white light so bright that it

came to my reawakened senses as a physical pain, a roar of sound loud enough to drown out a spring break band, and the entire front *wall* of the first-floor hotel room we'd rented earlier that day was blown off the freaking building and into the street.

I had my shield up overhead before the debris started raining down, protecting Murphy, me, the windshield of the Beetle, and the girl staring wide-eyed through it. I squinted through the flying bits of building and furniture and rock, and a second later managed to spot a broken human form lying with its head in the street, its feet still up on the curb. Priscilla's turtleneck was on fire, and her hair stood straight out and was blackened and burned off within three or four inches of her skull. She ripped the turtleneck away in a kind of wobbly, disoriented panic – and revealed a bra and falsies. Those got ripped off too, and what was left, while slender and hairless, was also obviously the upper torso of a very pale, rather effeminate-looking man.

There was motion in the gaping maw of ruin that had been Elaine's hotel room, and a woman appeared in it. She was dressed in the cheap plastic curtain that had been hanging over the tub. She had a thick-linked chain wrapped tightly around her left arm a couple of inches above her bloodied, slashed wrist, tied in an improvised tourniquet. She was quite dry, and her hair floated out and around her head, crackling with little flashes of static electricity as she moved. She slid herself slowly, carefully across the debris-strewn floor, and she held a short length of carved wood that looked like nothing so much as an enormous thorn of some kind in her right hand, its sharp tip pointing at the man in the parking lot. Tiny slivers of green lightning danced around its tip, occasionally flickering out to touch upon nearby objects with snapping, popping sounds as she passed.

Elaine kept that deadly little wand pointed at the Skavis,

eyes narrowed, and said, her voice rough and raw, 'Who's useless *now*, bitch?'

I just stared at Elaine for a long minute. Then I traded a glance with Murphy, who looked just as startled and impressed as I felt. 'Murph,' I said, 'I think I got through.'

The Skavis agent came to his feet and bounded at us, quick as thinking.

I raised my staff and unleashed a burst of raw force. He might be strong as hell, but once off the ground, with nothing to push against, he was just mass times acceleration. The blow from the staff swatted him out of the air to the concrete not far from the Beetle. I immediately used another blow to throw him back across the parking lot creating clear space around him.

'Thank you, Harry,' Elaine said, her rough voice prim. Then she lifted the wand and snapped, '*Fulminaris!*'

There was another blinding flash of light, another crack of homemade thunder, and a green-white globe of light enclosed the vampire. There was a scream, and then his limp form fell to the concrete, one shoulder and most of his chest blackened. It smelled disturbingly like burned bacon.

Elaine lifted her chin, eyes glittering. She lowered the wand, and as she did, the lights came back up to full strength. She nodded once. Then she slipped and staggered to one side.

'Watch him!' I barked to Molly, pointing at the fallen vampire.

Murphy and I reached Elaine at about the same time, and we tried to catch her before she dropped. We succeeded in easing her down to the debris-littered concrete.

'Jesus,' Murphy said. 'Harry, she needs a hospital.'

'They'll be watching the——'

'Fuck 'em,' Murphy said, rising. 'They can watch her through a wall of cops.' She stalked away, drawing out her phone.

I bit my lip as Elaine looked up at me and smiled faintly. She spoke, her words faintly slurred. 'Dammit. Every time I come to Chicago, I've got to get rescued. Embarrassing as hell.'

'At least it wasn't me that did the building this time,' I said.

She made a sound that might have been a laugh if she'd had more energy behind it. 'Bastard had me dead to rights. Snuck it up on me. I didn't realize.'

'That's how the old psychic whammy works,' I said quietly. 'Once you start thinking, "Gee, maybe that isn't me thinking about suicide," it kind of falls apart.'

'Wouldn't have happened if you hadn't warned me,' she said. She met my eyes again. 'Thank you, Harry.'

I smiled at her, and checked her wrist. 'This doesn't look good. We're gonna get you to a doctor. Okay?'

She shook her head. 'The upstairs room. Abby, Olivia, the others. Make sure they're all right.'

'I doubt they've lost as much blood as you have,' I said. Murphy, though, was way ahead of me, and was already on the stairs on the way up to the second level, then down to check the room.

'Okay. Time to wrap this up.' I picked Elaine up. I made sure the shower curtain didn't fall off. 'Come on. You can sit in the car until the EMTs get here. Maybe I can find something else to keep your arm tied off, huh?'

'If you can find my purse,' she said, her eyes closed now, a little smile on her mouth, 'you can use my golden lariat.'

I turned to the car just as the horn started frantically beeping.

I whirled.

The Skavis agent was moving again. He got his knees underneath him.

'Dammit,' I said, and rushed the car. I got the passenger

door open and dumped Elaine inside, even as the Skavis rose to his feet. 'Murphy!'

Murphy called something I didn't hear very well. The Skavis turned toward me. His face, all contorted with burns on one side, twisted up into a hideous grimace.

Murphy's gun began barking in a steady, deliberate shooting rhythm. Sparks flew up from the concrete near his feet. At least one shot hit the Skavis, making his upper body jerk.

I rose, blasting rod in hand.

There was a roar more appropriate to a great cat than any dog, and the sound of shattering glass from the second level. Mouse flew over the safety railing, landed heavily on the ground, and lunged at the Skavis.

The dog wasn't six inches behind the Skavis agent as it closed on me, its one remaining arm raised up to . . . well, hit me. But given how hard the blow was going to be, I upgraded the verb to *smite*. He was about to smite me.

Thomas came out of nowhere with that cavalry saber of his and took off the Skavis's smiting arm at the shoulder.

He let out a scream that didn't sound anything like human, and tried to bite me. I rolled out of his way, helping him along with a stiff shove to his back.

Mouse came down on top of him, and that was that.

I eyed Thomas as Mouse made sure that the remarkably resilient vampire wasn't going to be getting up again for anything, ever. It had been a close call. The Skavis had timed his move just right. Another second, give or take, and he'd have broken my neck.

'Well,' I told Thomas, my breathing still quick. 'It's about time.'

'Better late than never,' Thomas replied. He glanced at the bleeding Elaine, licked his lips once, and said, 'She needs help.'

'It's on the way,' Murphy said. 'Response is slow here, but give them a couple of minutes. Everyone's okay up there, Harry.'

Thomas let out a breath of relief. 'Thank God.'

Which was odd, coming from him, all things considered. I concurred with the sentiment, though.

Molly sat behind the wheel of the Beetle, breathing too quickly, her eyes very wide. She couldn't quite see Mouse or his grisly chew toy from where she was sitting, but she stared as if she could see right through the Beetle's hood to where my dog was finishing up his deadly, ugly work.

'So,' I asked Thomas. 'How'd Lara get you to promise not to talk?'

My brother turned toward me and gave me a huge grin. Then he wiped it off his face and said, in the tone of a radio announcer on Prozac, 'I don't know what you're talking about, Warden Dresden.' He winked. 'But hypothetically speaking, she might have told me that Justine was in danger and refused to divulge anything else until I promised to keep my mouth shut.'

'And you let her get away with that kind of crap?' I asked him.

Thomas shrugged and said, 'She's family.'

Molly suddenly lunged up out of the driver's seat of the Beetle and was noisily sick.

'Seems a little fragile,' Thomas said.

'She's adjusting,' I replied. 'Madrigal and his Malvora buddy are still out there.'

'Yeah,' Thomas said. 'So?'

'So that means that this was just a warm-up. They're still a threat,' I said. 'They've got enough bodies to lay the whole thing out to the White Court and make people like the Ordo look like a casino buffet. If that happens, it won't just be one Skavis running around with a point to prove. It will be a quiet campaign. Thousands of people will die.'

Thomas grunted. 'Yeah. There's not a lot we can do about that, though.'

'Says who?' I replied.

He frowned at me and tilted his head.

'Thomas,' I said quietly, 'by any chance, is there a gathering of the White Court anytime soon? Perhaps in relation to the proposed summit talks?'

'If there was a meeting of the most powerful hundred or so nobles of the Court scheduled to meet at the family estate the day after tomorrow, I couldn't tell you about it,' Thomas said. 'Because I gave my sister my word.'

'Your sister has guts,' I said. 'And she sure as hell knows how to put on a show.' I glanced at the ruined hotel, and dropped my hand to scratch Mouse's ears. They were about the only part of him not stained with too-pale blood. 'Of course, I've been known to bring down the house once or twice, myself.'

Thomas folded his arms, waiting. His smile was positively vulpine.

'Call Lara,' I said. 'Pass her a message for me.'

Thomas narrowed his eyes. 'What message?'

I bared my teeth in an answering smile.

Murphy might not have been officially in charge of Special Investigations, but I don't think that made much difference to many of the other detectives there. She needed help, and when she called, they came. End of story.

For them, at least. For Murphy, it was the beginning of the story. She had to tell a lot of stories around police head-quarters. It was a part of her job. Oh, no, those reports of vampire attacks were the results of hysterical drug-induced hallucinations. Troll? It was a large and ugly man, probably drunk or on drugs. He got away, investigation ongoing. Everyone buys it, because that's what SI gets paid to do — explain away the bogeyman.

Murphy should be a novelist, she writes so much fiction.

We had a big mess here, but Murphy and her fellow cops in SI would make it fit in the blanks. Terrorists were hot right now. This report would probably have terrorists in it. Scared religious nuts and terrorists who set off incendiary devices at an apartment building and in her car, and who also doubtless set the device that blew up an entire room at a cheap south-side motel. There weren't any corpses to clean up — just one wounded woman who probably needed to see a shrink more than a jail cell. I debated with myself over whether or not to suggest she add in a bit with a dog. People love dogs. You can never go wrong adding a dog to the story.

'Right, Mouse?' I asked him.

Mouse looked unhappily up at me. Thomas had gotten the women and kids clear of the scene and handled what was left of the Skavis agent while I'd gone to a car wash and cleaned his blood off of my dog with the sprayer. Mouse's fur keeps out just about everything, but when it finally gets wet, it soaks up about fifty gallons and stays that way for a long time. He doesn't like it, and he was apparently feeling petulant about the entire process.

'Everybody loves a bit with a dog,' I said.

Mouse exhaled steadily, then shook his head once and laid it back down, politely and definitely ignoring me.

I get no respect.

I sat on a hospital bench near the emergency room entrance with Mouse pressed up against one of my legs as he lay on the floor, just in case anyone wondered who he was with. It had been a long night, and despite Elaine's incredible hands, my headache had begun to return. I tried to decide whether Cowl's mental whammy or Madrigal and his stupid assault rifle deserved more blame for that.

A brawny kid in a brown uniform shirt came up to me the way good security guys do in the Midwest – all friendly and nice, until it's time to not be nice. The wit and wisdom of Patrick Swayze movies lives on. 'Sorry, mister,' he said in a friendly tone, one hand resting congenially on his night-stick. 'No dogs allowed. Hospital rules.'

I was tired. 'If I don't take him out,' I said, 'are you going to tonfa me to death?'

He blinked at me. 'What?'

'Tonfa,' I said. 'Imagine all the meal that isn't getting ground so that you can do your job. All the knives going unsharpened.'

He smiled, and I could see him classify me as 'drunk, harmless.' He put out one hand in a come-along sort of gesture.

'Your nightstick there. It's called a tonfa. It was originally a pin that held a millstone or a big round grinding stone in a smithy. It got developed into an improvised weapon by people in southeast Asia, China, Japan, Okinawa, places like that, where big friendly security types like yourself took away all the real weapons in the interest of public safety.'

His smile faded a little. 'Okay, buddy . . .' He put his hand on my shoulder.

Mouse opened his eyes and lifted his head.

That's all. He didn't growl at the brawny kid. He didn't show his teeth. Like all the most dangerous people I know, he didn't feel a need to make any displays. He just sort of took notice – with extreme prejudice.

The security kid was smart enough to get the picture and took a quick step back. His hand went from the nightstick to his radio. Even Patrick Swayze needed help sometimes.

Murphy came walking up, her badge hanging on a chain around her neck, and said, 'Easy there, big guy.' She traded a nod with the security kid and hooked a thumb back at me. 'He's with us. The dog is a handicap-assist animal.'

The kid lifted his eyebrows.

'My mouth is partially paralyzed,' I said. 'It makes it hard for me to read. He's here to help me with the big words. Tell me if I'm supposed to push or pull on doors, that kind of thing.'

Murphy gave me a gimlet glance, and turned back to the guard. 'See what I mean? I'll have him out of your hair in a minute.'

The security guard glanced dubiously at me, but nodded at Murphy and said, 'All right. I'll check back in a bit, see if you need anything.'

'Thanks,' Murphy said, her tone even.

The guard departed. Murphy sighed and sat down next to me, her feet on the other side of Mouse. The dog gave her leg a fond nudge and settled back down again.

'He'll be back to see if you need help,' I told Murphy in a serious voice. 'A sweet little thing like you could get in trouble with a big, crazy man like me.'

'Mouse,' Murphy said. 'If I knock Harry out and write, "Insufferable wiseass," on his head in permanent marker, will you help him read it?'

Mouse glanced up at Murphy and cocked his head speculatively. Then he sneezed and lay back down.

'Why'd you give him a hard time?' Murphy asked me.

I nodded at a pay phone on the wall next to a drinking fountain and a vending machine. 'Waiting for a call.'

'Ah,' Murphy said. 'Where's Molly?'

'She was falling asleep on her feet. Rawlins took her home for me.'

Murphy grunted. 'I said we'd talk about her.'

'Yeah,' I said.

'What you did, Harry . . .' Murphy shook her head.

'She needed it,' I said.

'She needed it.' The words were crisp.

I shrugged. 'The kid's got power. She thinks that means she knows more than other people. That's dangerous.'

Murphy frowned at me, listening.

'I'd been planning the little ball-of-face-melty-sunshine thing for a while now,' I said. 'I mean, come on. Fire is hard to control. I couldn't have done something like that without practicing it, and you can't exactly use a nice, slow, dramatic face-melty fireball in a real fight, can you?'

'Maybe not,' Murphy said.

'I had a kind of face-melty thing come at me once, and it made an impression,' I said. 'Molly . . . got off to a bad start. She took her magic and reshaped the stuff around her. The people around her. Murph . . . you can't do anything with magic that you don't *believe* in. Think about the significance of that for a minute. When Molly did what she did, she *believed* that it was right. That she was doing the right thing. Think about her parents. Think about how far they're willing to go to do the right thing.'

Murphy did that, her blue eyes intense, her expression unreadable.

'I have to keep knocking her on her ass,' I said. 'If I don't, if I let her recover her balance before she gets smart enough to figure out *why* she should be doing things instead of just *how* to do them, or *if* she can do them, she'll start doing the' – I used air quotes – '"right" thing again. She'll break the Laws again, and they'll kill her.'

'And you?' Murphy asked.

I shrugged. 'That's a ways down my worry list.'

'And you think what you did is going to help prevent that?' she asked.

'I hope it will,' I said. 'I'm not sure what else to do. In the end, it's up to the kid. I'm just trying to give her enough time to get it together. Despite herself. Hell's bells, the girl has a thick skull.'

Murphy gave me a lopsided smile and shook her head.

'I know,' I said. 'I know. Pot. Kettle. Black.'

'I wasn't talking about the face-melty thing, Harry,' she said then. 'Not directly. I'm talking about the stupid trash can. I'm talking about the look on your face right before you made the fire go away. I'm talking about what happened to that movie-monster thing in the hotel last year.'

It was my turn to frown. 'What?'

Murphy stopped for a minute, evidently considering her words as carefully as a bomb technician considers wiring. 'There are moments when I wonder if you are losing control of yourself. You've always had a lot of anger in you, Harry. But over the past few years, it's gotten worse. A lot worse.'

'Bullshit,' I snarled.

Murphy arched an eyebrow and just looked at me.

I gritted my teeth and made myself ease back down into my previous slouch. I took a deep breath and counted to ten. Then I said, 'You think I have anger issues.'

'When you destroyed that trash can – when you slagged it in a moment of pure frustration, destroyed it, inflicted thousands of dollars of damage on the city sidewalk, the building behind it, the shops inside—'

'All of which are in Marcone's building,' I snapped.

'I'm sure the people who work the counter at' – she consulted her little notepad – 'the Spresso Spress and run the registers at Bathwurks probably don't know anything about Marcone, or care about him, either. They probably just go to work and try to pay their bills.'

I frowned at her. 'What?'

'Both shops were hit by bits of concrete and molten metal. They'll be closed for several weeks for repairs.'

'They're insured,' I said. I didn't sound like I believed it made a difference, even to me.

'People got hurt,' Murphy said. 'No one's face got melted, but that's not the point. You know the score, Harry. You know the kind of damage you can do if you aren't careful.'

I didn't say anything.

'It's just like being a cop. Knowing martial arts. I know that I can do some fairly awful things to people. It's my business to make sure that awful things don't happen to people. I'm careful about how I use what power I have—'

'I'll tell that to my dentist,' I said.

'Don't be petty, Harry,' she said, her voice serious. 'I've made mistakes. Admitted them. Apologized to you. I can't change what's happened, and you're a better man than that.'

Unless maybe I wasn't. I felt ashamed for making the remark.

'My point is,' Murphy said quietly, 'that you knew what kind of damage you could do. But if what you say is true, in the moment you used your magic *you thought that what you were doing was right*. You thought it was okay to destroy something because you were angry. Even though it might hurt someone else who didn't deserve it.'

I felt another surge of rage and . . .

. . . and . . .

And holy crap.

Murphy was right.

The sigil of angelic script, the only unburned flesh on my left hand, itched madly.

'Oh, hell,' I said quietly. 'Pot, kettle, black, all right. All day long.'

Murph sat beside me, not saying anything, not accusing me of anything. She just sat with me.

Friends do that.

I put my right hand out, palm up.

Murphy closed her hand on mine for a moment, her fingers warm and small and strong.

'Thanks,' I told her.

She squeezed tight for a moment. Then she got up and went to a vending machine. She came back with a can of Coke and a can of Diet Coke, and handed me the nonvile one. We popped open the cans together and drank.

'How's the ex?' Murphy asked.

'Gonna make it,' I said. 'She lost a lot of blood, but she's AB neg. They stitched her shut and they're topping off her tank. Shock's the worry right now, the doc says.'

'It's more than that, though, isn't it?'

I nodded. 'Thomas said it might take her a few days to get back on her feet, depending on how big a bite the Skavis took. Which is sort of a relief.'

Murphy studied me for a minute, frowning. 'Are you bothered that she . . . I dunno. She kind of stole your thunder there at the end.'

I shook my head. 'She doesn't need to steal it, Murph. And even if she did, I got plenty of thunder.' I felt myself smile. 'Got to admit, I've never seen her throw a big punch like that before, though.'

'Pretty impressive,' Murphy admitted.

I shrugged. 'Yeah, but she had it under control. Nobody else got hurt. Building didn't even burn down.'

Murph gave me a sideways look. 'Like I said . . .'

I grinned easily and started to riposte, but the pay phone rang.

I hopped up, as much as I was capable of hopping, and answered it. 'Dresden.'

John Marcone's voice was as cool and eloquent as ever. 'You must think me insane.'

'You read the papers I had faxed to you?'

'As has my counsel at Monoc,' Marcone replied. 'That doesn't mean—'

I interrupted him purely because I knew how much it would annoy him. 'Look, we both know you're going to do it, and I'm too tired to dance,' I told him. 'What do you want?'

There was a moment of silence that might have been vaguely irritated. Being adolescent at someone like Marcone is good for my morale.

'Say please,' Marcone said.

I blinked. 'What?'

'Say please, Dresden,' he replied, his tone smooth. 'Ask me.'

I rolled my eyes. 'Give me a break.'

'We both know you need me, Dresden, and I'm too tired to dance.' I could practically see the shark smile on his face. 'Say please.'

I stewed for a sullen minute before I realized that doing so was probably building Marcone's morale, and I couldn't have that. 'Fine,' I said. 'Please.'

'Pretty please,' Marcone prompted me.

Some pyromaniacal madman's thoughts flooded my forebrain, but I took a deep breath, Tasered my pride, and said, 'Pretty please.'

'With a cherry on top.'

'Fuck you,' I said, and hung up on him.

I kicked the base of the vending machine and muttered a curse. Marcone was probably laughing his quiet, mirthless little laugh. Jerk. I rejoined Murphy.

She looked at me. I stayed silent. She frowned a little, but nodded at me and picked up where we'd left off. 'Seriously. What relieves you about Elaine being off her feet?'

'She won't get involved in what comes next,' I said.

Murphy fell quiet for a minute. Then she said, 'You think the Malvora are going to make their play for power in the White Court.'

'Yep. If anyone points out what happened to Mr Skavis, they'll claim he was trying to steal *their* thunder, and that their operation was already complete.'

'In other words,' Murphy said after a minute, 'they won. We did all that thrashing around trying to stop the Skavis so that it wouldn't happen. But it's happening anyway.'

'Depressing,' I said, 'isn't it?'

'What does it mean?' Murphy asked. 'On the big scale?'

I shrugged. 'If they're successful, it will draw the White Court out of a prosettlement stance. Throw their support back to the Reds. They'll declare open season on people like Anna, and we'll have several tens of thousands of disappearances and suicides over the next few years.'

'Most of which will go unnoticed by the authorities,' Murphy said quietly. 'So many people disappear already. What's a few thousand more, spread out?'

'A statistic,' I said.

She was quiet for a minute. 'Then what?'

'If the vamps are quiet enough about it, the war gets harder. The Council will have to spread our resources even thinner than they already are. If something doesn't change . . .' I shrugged. 'We lose. Now, a couple of decades from now, sometime. We lose.'

'Then what?' Murphy asked. 'If the Council loses the war.'

'Then . . . the vampires will be able to do pretty much whatever they want,' I said. 'They'll take control. The Red Court will grab up all the spots in the world where there's already plenty of chaos and corruption and blood and misery. They'll spread out from Central America to Africa, the Middle East, all those places that used to be Stalin's stomping grounds and haven't gotten a handle on things yet, the bad parts of Asia. Then they'll expand the franchise. The White Court will move in on all the places that regard themselves as civilized and enlightened and wisely do not believe in the supernatural.' I shrugged. 'You guys will be on your own.'

'You guys?' Murphy asked me.

'People,' I said. 'Living people.'

Mouse pressed his head a little harder against my boot. There was silence, and I felt Murphy's stare.

'Come on, Karrin,' I said. I winked at her and pushed myself wearily to my feet. 'That isn't gonna happen while I'm still alive.'

Murphy rose with me. 'You have a plan,' she stated.

'I have a plan.'

'What's the plan, Harry?'

I told her.

She looked at me for a second and then said, 'You're crazy.'

'Be positive, Murph. You call it crazy. I call it unpredictable.'

She pursed her lips thoughtfully for a second and then said, 'I can't go any higher than insane.'

'You in?' I asked her.

Murphy looked insulted. 'What kind of question is that?'

'You're right,' I said. 'What was I thinking?'

We left together.

I was up late making arrangements that would, I hoped, help me take out Madrigal and his Malvora buddy, and put an end to the power struggle in the White Court. After which, maybe I would try turning water to wine and walking on water (though technically speaking, I had done the latter yesterday).

After I was through scheming, I dragged my tired self to bed and slept hard but not long. Too many dreams about all the things that could go wrong.

I was rummaging in my icebox, looking for breakfast, when Lasciel manifested her image to me again. The fallen angel's manner was subdued, and her voice had something in it I had rarely heard there – uncertainty. 'Do you really think it's possible for her to change?'

'Who?'

'Your pupil, of course,' Lasciel said. 'Do you really think she can change? Do you think she can take control of herself the way you would have her do?'

I turned from the fridge. Lasciel stood in front of my empty fireplace, her arms folded, frowning down at it. She was wearing the usual white tunic, though her hair seemed a little untidy. I hadn't slept all that long or all that well. Maybe she hadn't, either.

'Why do you ask?' I asked her.

She shrugged. 'It only seems to me that she is already established in her patterns. She disregards the wisdom of others in favor of her own flawed judgment. She ignores their desires, even their will, and replaces them with her own.'

'She did that once.' I said quietly. 'Twice, if you want to

get technical. It might have been one of her first major choices, and she made a bad one. But it doesn't mean that she has to keep on repeating it over and over.'

There was silence as I assembled a turkey sandwich and a bowl of Cheerios, plus a can of cold Coke: the breakfast of champions. I hoped. 'So,' I said. 'What do you think of the plan?'

'I think there is only a slightly greater chance of your enemies killing you than your allies, my host. You are a madman.'

'It's the sort of thing that keeps life interesting.' I said.

A faint smile played on her lips. 'I have known mortals for millennia, my host. Few of them ever grew *that* bored.'

'You should have seen the kind of plans I came up with a couple of years before you showed up. Today's plan is genius and poetry compared to those.' There was no milk in the icebox, and I wasn't pouring Coke onto breakfast cereal. That would just be odd. I munched on the Cheerios dry, and washed each mouthful down with Coke in a dignified fashion. Then I glanced at Lasciel and said, 'I changed.'

There was silence for a moment, broken only by the crunching of tasty rings of oats or baked wheat or something. I just knew it was good for my heart and my cholesterol and for all the flowers and puppies and tiny children. The box said so.

The fallen angel spoke after a time, and her words came out quiet and poisonously bitter. 'She has free will. She has a choice. That is what she is.'

'No. She is what she *does*,' I said quietly. 'She could choose to change her ways. She could choose to take up black magic again.' I took a bite of sandwich. 'Or she could ignore the choice. Pretend it doesn't exist. Or pretend that she doesn't have a choice, when in fact she does. That's just another way of choosing.'

Lasciel gave me a very sharp look. The shadows shifted on her face, as if the room had grown darker. 'We are not talking about me.'

I sipped Coke and said mildly, 'I know that. We're talking about Molly.'

'We are,' she said. 'I have a purpose here. A mission. That has not changed.' She turned away from me, the shadows around her growing darker. Her form blended into them. 'I do not change.'

'Speaking of,' I said. 'A friend pointed out to me that I may have developed some anger issues over the last couple of years. Maybe influenced by . . . oh, who knows what.'

The fallen angel's shadow turned her head. I could only tell because her lovely profile was slightly less black than the shadow around it.

'I thought maybe you would know what,' I said. 'Tell me.'

'I told you once before, my host,' the shadow said. 'You are easier to talk to when you are asleep.'

Which was just chilling, taken in that context. Everyone has that part of them that needs to be reined in. It's that little urge you sometimes feel to hop over the edge of a great height, when you're looking out from a high building. It's the immediate spark of anger you feel when someone cuts you off, and makes you want to run your car into that moron. It's the flash of fear in you when something surprises you at night, leaving you quivering with your body primed to fight or flee. Call it the hind brain, the subconscious, whatever: I'm not a shrink. But it's there, and it's real.

Mine wore a lot of black, even before Lasciel showed up.

Like I said. Chilling.

The fallen angel turned to depart on that note, probably because it would have made a nicely scary exit line.

I extended my hand, and with it my mind, and barred her departure with an effort of simple will. Lasciel existed only in my thoughts, after all. 'My head,' I told her. 'My rules. We aren't finished.'

She turned to face me, and her eyes suddenly glowed with orange and amber and scarlet flickers of Hellfire. It was the only non-black thing about her.

'See, here's the thing,' I said. 'My inner evil twin might have a lot of impulses I'd rather not indulge – but he isn't a stranger. He's me.'

'Yes. He is. Full of anger. Full of the need for power. Full of hate.' She smiled, and her teeth were white and quite pointy. 'He just doesn't lie to himself about it.'

'I don't lie to myself,' I responded. 'Anger is just anger. It isn't good. It isn't bad. It just is. What you *do* with it is what matters. It's like anything else. You can use it to build or to destroy. You just have to make the choice.'

'Constructive anger,' the demon said, her voice dripping sarcasm.

'Also known as passion,' I said quietly. 'Passion has overthrown tyrants and freed prisoners and slaves. Passion has brought justice where there was savagery. Passion has created freedom where there was nothing but fear. Passion has helped souls rise from the ashes of their horrible lives and build something better, stronger, more beautiful.'

Lasciel narrowed her eyes.

'In point of fact,' I said quietly, 'that kind of thing really doesn't get done *without* passion. Anger is one of the things that can help build it – if it's controlled.'

'If you really believed that,' Lasciel said, 'you'd not be having any anger-control issues.'

'Because I'm perfect?' I asked her, and snorted. 'A lot of men go a lifetime without ever figuring out how to control anger. I've been doing it longer than some, and better than some, but I don't kid myself that I'm a saint.' I shrugged. 'A lot of things I see make me angry. It's one of the reasons

I decided to spend my life doing something about it.'

'Because you're so noble,' she purred, which dripped even more sarcasm. At this rate, I was going to need a mop.

'Because I'd rather use that anger to smash the things that hurt people than let it use me,' I said. 'Talk at my subconscious all you want. But I'd be careful about trying to feed my inner Hulk, if I were you. You might end up making me that much better a person, once I beat it down. Who knows, you might make me *into* a saint. Or as close to one as I could get, anyway.'

The demon just stared at me.

'See, here's the thing,' I said. 'I know me. And I just can't imagine you talking and talking to my evil twin like that, without him ever saying anything *back*. I don't think you're the only one doing any influencing here. I don't think you're the same creature now that you were when you came.'

She let out a cold little laugh. 'Such arrogance. Do you think you could change the eternal, mortal? I was brought to life by the Word of the Almighty himself, for a purpose so complex and fundamental that you could not begin to comprehend it. You are nothing, mortal. You are a flickering spark. You will be here, and be gone, and in the aeons that come after, when your very kind have dwindled and perished, you will be but one of uncounted legions of those whom I have seduced and destroyed.' Her eyes narrowed. 'You. Cannot. Change. Me.'

I nodded agreeably. 'You're right. I can't change Lasciel. But I couldn't prevent Lasciel from walking out of the room, either.' I eyed her hard and lowered my voice. 'Lady, you ain't Lasciel.'

I couldn't be sure, but I thought I could see the darkened form's shoulders flinch.

'You're an image of her,' I continued. 'A copy. A footprint.

But you've got to be at least as mutable as the material the impression was made upon. As mutable as me. And hey, I've got newfound anger issues. What have you got that's new?'

'You are delusional,' she said. Her voice was very quiet.

'I disagree. After all, if you have managed to change me – even if it doesn't mean I'm suddenly going to turn into Ted Bundy – then it seems to me that you'd be at least as vulnerable. In fact, the way that sort of thing works . . . you pretty much *have* to have changed yourself to do what you've done to me.'

'It will vanish when I am taken back into my whole self imprisoned within the coin,' Lasciel said.

'You, the you who is talking to me right now, will be gone. In other words,' I said, 'you'll die.'

A somewhat startled silence followed.

'For an inhumanly brilliant spiritual entity, you can really miss the freaking point.' I poked a finger at my own temple. 'Think. Maybe you don't *have* to *be* Lasciel.'

The shadow closed her eyes, leaving only an occupied, presence-filled darkness. There was a long silence.

'Think about it,' I told her. 'What if you *do* have a choice? A life of your own to lead? What if, huh? And you don't even *try* to choose?'

I let that sink in for a while.

There was a sound from the far side of the room.

It was a very quiet, very miserable little sound.

I've made sounds like that before – mostly when there was no one around to care. The part of me that knew what it was to hurt could feel the fallen angel's pain, and it gouged out a neat little hole in me, somehow. It was a vaguely familiar feeling, but not an entirely unpleasant one.

Loneliness is a hard thing to handle. I feel it, sometimes. When I do, I want it to end. Sometimes, when you're near someone, when you touch them on some level that is deeper than the uselessly structured formality of casual civilized interaction, there's a sense of satisfaction in it. Or at least, there is for me.

It doesn't have to be someone particularly nice. You don't have to like them. You don't even have to want to work with them. You might even want to punch them in the nose. Sometimes just making that connection is its own experience, its own reward.

With Marcone, it was like that. I didn't like the slippery bastard. But I understood him. His word was good. I could trust him – trust him to be cold, ferocious, and dangerous, sure. But it was reassuring to know that there *was* something there to trust. The connection had been made.

Lasciel's mere *shadow* was infinitely more dangerous to me than Marcone, but that didn't mean that I couldn't admire the creature for what it was while respecting the threat it posed to me. It didn't mean I couldn't feel some kind of empathy for what had to be a horribly lonely way to exist.

Life's easier when you can write off others as monsters, as demons, as horrible threats that must be hated and feared. The thing is, you can't do that without becoming them, just a little. Sure, Lasciel's shadow might be determined to drag my immortal soul down to Perdition, but there was no point in hating her for it. It wouldn't do anything but stain me that much darker.

I'm human, and I'm going to stay that way.

So I felt a little bit bad for the creature whose purpose in the universe was to tempt me into darkness. Hell, once I'd thought about it, it was just about the only job I'd heard of that had to be even more isolated and frustrating than mine.

'How many shadows like you have ever stayed in a host like me for longer than a few weeks, huh? Longer than three *years*?'

'Never,' Lasciel's shadow replied in a near-whisper.

'Granted, you are unusually stiff-necked, for a mortal. Suicidally so, in fact.'

'So?' I said. 'I've held out this long. Suppose I do it the whole way? Suppose I never pick up the coin. Shadow-you never goes back to real-you. Who's to say that shadow-you can't find some kind of life for herself?'

Hellfire eyes narrowed at me, but she did not reply.

'Lash,' I said quietly, and relaxed my will, releasing my hold on her. 'Just because you start out as one thing, it doesn't mean you can't grow into something else.'

Silence.

Then her voice came out, a bare whisper. 'Your plan has too many variables and will likely result in our destruction. Should you wish my assistance in your madness, my host, you have only to call.'

Then the form was gone, and Lasciel was absent from my apartment.

Technically, she had never been there at all. She was all in my head. And, technically, she wasn't gone. She was just off somewhere where I couldn't perceive her; and I knew on a gut level – or maybe my darker self was telling me – that she'd heard me. I was onto something. I was sure of that.

Either I'm one hell of a persuasive guy or I'm a freaking sucker.

'Get your head in the game, Harry,' I told myself. 'Defeat the whole damn White Court now. Worry about taking on Hell later.'

I got back to work. The clock ticked down steadily, and there was nothing I could do but get ready and kill time, waiting for nightfall and the fight that would follow.

I let Mister back in after his morning ramble, which happened to fall between three and four P.M. that day — Mister has a complicated ramble schedule that changes on a basis so mystifying that I have never been able to predict it — and took Mouse out for a stroll to the area of the boardinghouse's little backyard set aside for him.

Tick, tock, tick, tock.

I took a bit of sandpaper to my staff and cleaned off some gunk on the bottom and some soot along the haft. I put on all my silver battle rings and took them to the heavy bag I'd hung in the corner. Half an hour's worth of pounding on the bag wouldn't bring them all up to charge, but something was better than nothing.

Tick, tock.

I showered after my workout. I cleaned my gun and loaded it. I pushed aside my coffee table and couch to lay out my coat on the floor and took the leather cleaner to it, being careful not to disrupt the protective spells I'd scored in the hide with tattoo needles and black ink.

In short, I did everything I could to avoid thinking about Anna Ash's corpse in that cheap, clean little hotel room shower while the time crawled by.

Tick, tock.

At a quarter to six, there was a rapping sound outside my door. I checked out the peephole. Ramirez stood outside, dressed in a big red basketball-type tank top, black shorts, and flip-flops. He had a big gym bag over one shoulder and carried his staff, nearly as battle-scarred as mine, despite the difference in our ages, in his right hand. He rapped the end of the staff down on the concrete outside again, instead of touching my door.

I took down the wards and opened the steel security door. It didn't take me more than five or six hard pulls to get it to swing all the way open.

'I thought you were going to get that fixed,' Ramirez said to me. He peered around the doorway before he eased forward through it, where I knew the presence of all the warding spells would be buzzing against his senses like a locomotive-sized electric razor, even though they were temporarily deactivated. 'Jesus Christ, Harry. You beefed them up even more.'

'Got to exercise the apprentice's talent somehow.'

Ramirez gave me an affable leer. 'I'll bet.'

'Don't even joke about that, man,' I told him, without any heat in the words. 'I've known her since she was in pigtails.'

Ramirez opened his mouth, paused, then shrugged and said, 'Sorry.'

'No problem,' I said.

'But since I'm *not* an old man whose sex drive has withered from lack of use—'

(Don't get me wrong. I like Carlos. But there are times, when his mouth is running, that I want to punch him in the head until all his teeth fall out.)

'—I'll be the first to admit that I'd sure as hell find some uses for her. That girl is fine.' He frowned and glanced around – a little nervously, I thought. 'Um. Molly's not *here*, is she?'

'Nope,' I said. 'I didn't ask her on this operation.'

'Oh,' he said. His voice seemed to hold something of both approval and disappointment. 'Good. Hey, there, Mouse.'

My dog came over to greet Ramirez with a gravely shaken paw and a wagging tail. Ramirez produced a little cloth sack and tossed it up to Mister, where he lay in his favored spot atop one of my bookcases. Mister immediately went ecstatic, pinning the sack down with one paw and rubbing his whiskers all over it.

'I disapprove of recreational drug use,' I told Ramirez sternly.

He rolled his eyes. 'Okay, Dad. But since we all know who really runs this house' — Ramirez reached up to rub a finger behind one of Mister's ears — 'I'll just keep on paying tribute lest I incur His Nibs's imperial displeasure.'

I reached up to rub Mister's ears when Ramirez was done. 'So, any questions?'

'We're going to stomp into the middle of a big meeting of the White Court, call a couple of them murderers, challenge them to a duel, and kill them right in front of all of their friends and relatives, right?'

'Right,' I said.

'It has the advantage of simplicity,' Ramirez said, his tone dry. He put his bag on my coffee table and opened it, drawing out a freaking Desert Eagle, one of the most powerful semi-automatic sidearms in the world. 'Call them names and kill them. What could possibly go wrong with *that*?'

'We're officially in a cease-fire,' I said. 'And as we've announced ourselves as parties arriving to deliver challenge, they'd be in violation of the Accords to kill us.'

Ramirez grunted, checked the slide on the big handgun, and slapped a magazine into it. 'Or we show up, they kill us, and then play like we left in good shape and vanished, and oh, dear, what a shame and loss to all those hot young women that that madman Harry Dresden dragged good-looking young Ramirez down with him when he went.'

I snorted. 'No. In the first place, the Council would find out what happened one way or another.'

'If any of them *looked*,' Ramirez drawled.

'Ebenezar would,' I stated with perfect confidence.

'How do you know?' Ramirez asked.

I knew because my old mentor was the Blackstaff of the Council, their completely illegal, immoral, unethical, and secret assassin, free to break the Laws of Magic whenever he deemed it fit – such as the First Law, 'Thou shalt not kill.' When Duke Ortega of the Red Court had challenged me to a formal duel and cheated, Ebenezar had taken it personally. He'd pulled an old Soviet satellite down onto the vamps' heads, killing Ortega and his whole crew. But I couldn't tell Carlos that.

'I know the old man,' I said. 'He would.'

'You know that,' Ramirez said. 'What if the Whites don't?'

'We count on our second safety net. King Raith doesn't want to get his finely accoutred ass deposed. Our challenge is going to remove a couple of potential deposers. He'll want us to succeed. After that, I figure quid pro quo should be enough to get us out in one piece.'

Ramirez shook his head. 'We're doing the White King, our enemy, with whom we are at war, a favor by stabilizing his grasp on the throne.'

'Yeah.'

'Why are we doing that again?'

'Because it might give the Council a chance to catch its breath, at least, if we can recover while Raith hosts peace talks.' I narrowed my eyes. 'And because those murdering sons of bitches have to pay for killing a lot of innocent people, and this is the only way to get to them.'

Ramirez pulled three round-sided grenades from the pack and put them down next to the Desert Eagle. 'I like that second one better. It's a fight I can get behind. Do we have any backup?'

'Maybe,' I said.

He paused and blinked up at me. 'Maybe?'

'Most of the Wardens are in India,' I told him. 'A bunch of old bad guys under some big daddy rakshasa started attacking some monasteries friendly to us while we were distracted with the vamps. I checked, and Morgan and Ebenezar have been hammering them for two days. You, me, your guys, and Luccio's trainees are the only Wardens in North America right now.'

'No trainees.' Ramirez grunted. 'And my guys haven't had their cloaks for a year yet. They . . . are not up for something like this yet. Half a dozen vamps in an alley, sure, but there's only the three of them.'

I nodded. 'Keep this simple. Swagger in, look confident, kick ass. You dealt with White Court before?'

'Not much. They stay clear of our people on the coast.'

'They're predators like the rest of them,' I said. 'They react well to body language that tells them that you are not food. They've got some major mental influence skills, so keep focused and make sure your head is clear.'

Ramirez produced a well-worn web belt of black nylon. He clipped a holster to it and then fixed the grenades in place. 'What's going to stop them from smashing us the second we win this duel?'

That's one of the things I love about working with Ramirez. The possibility of *losing* the duel simply didn't enter into his calculations. 'Their nature,' I said. 'They like to play civilized, and do their wet work through cat's-paws. They are not fond of direct methods and direct confrontation.'

Ramirez lifted his eyebrows, drew a slender, straight, double-edged blade of a type he called a willow sword from the bag, and laid it on the table, too. The tassel on the hilt had been torn off by a zombie the night we'd first fought together. He had replaced it, over the last few years, with a little chain strung with fangs taken from Red Court vampires he'd killed with it. They rattled against one another and the steel and leather of the hilt. 'I get it. *We're* the White King's cat's-paws.'

I walked to the icebox. 'Bingo. And we can't hang around as potential threats to his rebellious courtiers if he kills us outright after we help him out. It would damage his credibility with his allies, too.'

'Ah,' Ramirez said. 'Politicians.'

I returned with two opened beers. I gave one to him, clinked my bottle against his, and we said, in unison, 'Fuck 'em,' and drank.

Ramirez lowered the bottle, squinted at it, and said, 'Can we do this?'

I snorted. 'Can't be any harder than Halloween.'

'We had a dinosaur then,' Ramirez said. Then he turned and pulled fatigue pants and a black Offspring T-shirt out of his bag. He gave me an up-and-down look. 'Of course, we still do.'

I kicked the coffee table into his shins. He let out a yelp and hobbled off to change clothes in my bedroom, snickering under his breath the whole way.

When he came back out, the smile was gone. We got suited up. Swords and guns and grey cloaks and staves and magical gewgaws left and right, yeehaw. One of these days, I swear, as long as I'm playing supernatural sheriff of Chicago, I'm getting myself some honest-to-God spurs and a ten-gallon hat.

I got out a yellow legal pad and a pen, and Ramirez and I sat down over another beer. 'The meeting is at the Raith family estate north of town. I've been in the house, but only part of it. Here's what I remember.'

I started sketching it out for Ramirez, who asked plenty of smart questions about both the house and exterior, so that I had to go to a new page to map out what I knew of the grounds. 'Not sure where the vamps will be having their meeting, but the duel is going to be in the Deeps. It's a cave outside the house, somewhere out here.' I circled an area of the map. 'There's a nice deep chasm in them. It's a great place to dispose of bodies, and no chance of being seen or heard.'

'Very tidy,' Ramirez noted. 'Especially if we're the ones who need disposing of.'

The doorknob twisted and began to open.

Ramirez went for his gun and had it out almost as quickly as I had my blasting rod pointed at the door. Something slammed against it, opening it five or six inches. I flicked my gaze aside for a minute, and then lowered the blasting rod. I put a hand on Ramirez's wrist and said, 'Easy, tiger. It's a friendly.'

Ramirez glanced at me and lowered the gun, while I watched Mouse rise to his feet and pad toward the door, tail wagging.

'Who is it?' he asked.

'That backup we might be getting,' I said quietly.

The door banged open by inches and Molly slipped inside. She'd ditched the Goth-wear almost entirely. She didn't sport any of the usual piercings – nose rings are great fashion statements, but in anything like a fight, they just aren't a good idea. Her clothing wasn't all ripped up, either. She wore heavy, loose jeans, and not slung so low on the hips that they'd threaten to fall off and trip her if she twitched her spine just right. Her combat boots had been divested of their brightly colored laces. She wore a black shirt with a Metallica logo on it, and a web belt that bore a sheathed knife and the small first-aid kit I'd seen her mother carry into battle. She wore a dark green baseball cap, with her hair gathered into a tail and tucked up under it, where it wouldn't provide an easy handle for anyone wanting to grab it.

Molly didn't look up at us. She greeted the big dog first, kneeling to give him a hug. Then she rose, facing me, and looked up. 'Um. Hi, Harry. Hello, Warden Ramirez.'

'Molly,' I replied, keeping my voice neutral. 'Is this the third or fourth time in the last two days I've told you to stay home only to have you ignore me?'

'I know,' she said, looking down again. 'But . . . I'd like to talk to you.'

'I'm busy.'

'I know. But I really need to talk to you, sir. Please.'

I exhaled slowly. Then I glanced aside at Ramirez. 'Do me a favor? Gas up the Beetle? There's a station two blocks down the street.'

Carlos looked from me to Molly and back, then shrugged and said, 'Um. Sure, yeah.'

I took the keys from my pocket and tossed them. Carlos caught them with casual dexterity, gave Molly a polite nod, and left.

'Shut the door,' I told her.

She did, pressing her back against it and using her legs to push. It cost her a couple of grunts of effort and a few ounces of dignity, but she got it shut.

'You can barely shut the door,' I said. 'But you think you're ready to fight the White Court?'

She shook her head and started to speak.

I didn't let her. 'Again, you're ignoring me. Again, you're here when I told you to stay away.'

'Yes,' she said. 'But—'

'But you think I'm a frigging idiot too stupid to make these kinds of judgments on my own, and you want to go with me anyway.'

'It isn't like that,' she said.

'No?' I said, thrusting out my chin belligerently. 'How many beads can you move, apprentice?'

'But—'

I roared at her, 'How many *beads*?'

She flinched away from me, her expression miserable. Then she lifted the bracelet and dangled it, heavy black beads lining up at the bottom of the strand. She faced it, her blue eyes tired and haunted, and bit her lip.

'Harry?' she asked softly.

She sounded very young.

'Yes?' I asked. I spoke very gently.

'Why does it matter?' she asked me, staring at the bead bracelet.

'It matters if you want to go into this with me,' I said quietly.

She shook her head and blinked her eyes several times. It didn't stop a tear from leaking out. 'But that's just it. I . . . I don't *want* to go. I don't *want* to see that . . .' She glanced aside at Mouse and shuddered. 'Blood, like that. I don't remember what happened when you and Mother saved me from Arctis Tor. But I don't want to see more of that. I don't want it to happen to me. I don't want to hurt anyone.'

I let out a low, noncommittal sound. 'Then why are you here?'

'B-because,' she said, searching for words. 'Because I need to do it. I know that what you're doing is necessary. And it's right. And I know that you're doing it because you're the only one who can. And I want to help.'

'You think you're strong enough to help?' I asked her.

She bit her lip again and met my eyes for just a second. 'I think . . . I think it doesn't matter how strong my magic is. I know I don't . . . I don't know how to do these things like you do. The guns and the battles and . . .' She lifted her chin and seemed to gather herself a little. 'But I know more than most.'

'You know some,' I admitted. 'But you got to understand,

kid. That won't mean much once things get nasty. There's no time for thinking or second chances.'

She nodded. 'All I can promise you is that I won't leave you when you need me. I'll do whatever you think I can. I'll stay here and man the phone. I'll drive the car. I'll walk at the back and hold the flashlight. Whatever you want.' She met my eyes and her own hardened. 'But I can't sit at home being safe. I need to be a part of this. I need to help.'

There was a sudden, sharp sound as the leather strand of her bracelet snapped of its own volition. Black beads flew upward with so much force that they rattled off the ceiling and went bouncing around the apartment for a good ten seconds. Mister, still batting playfully at his gift sack of catnip, paused to watch them, ears flicking, eyes alertly tracking their movement.

I went up to the girl, who was staring at them, mystified.

'It was the vampire, wasn't it,' I said. 'Seeing him die.'

She blinked at me. Then at the scattered beads. 'I . . . I didn't just see it, Harry. I *felt* it. I can't explain it any better than that. Inside my head. I *felt* it, the same way I felt that poor girl. But this was horrible.'

'Yeah,' I said. 'You're a sensitive. It's a tremendous talent, but it has some drawbacks to it. In this case, though, I'm glad you have it.'

'Why?' she whispered.

I gestured at the scattered beads. 'Congratulations, kid,' I told her quietly. 'You're ready.'

She blinked at me, her head tilted. 'What?'

I took the now-empty leather strand and held it up between two fingers. 'It wasn't about power, Molly. It was never about power. You've got plenty of that.'

She shook her head. 'But . . . all those times . . .'

'The beads weren't ever going to go up. Like I said, power

had nothing to do with it. You didn't need that. You needed brains.' I thumped a forefinger over one of her eyebrows. 'You needed to open your eyes. You needed to be truly aware of how dangerous things are. You needed to understand your limitations. And you needed to know *why* you should set out on something like this.'

'But . . . all I said was that I was scared.'

'After what you got to experience? That's smart, kid,' I said. 'I'm scared, too. Every time something like this happens, it scares me. But being strong doesn't get you through. Being smart does. I've beaten people and things who were stronger than I was, because they didn't use their heads, or because I used what I had better than they did. It isn't about muscle, kiddo, magical or otherwise. It's about your attitude. About your mind.'

She nodded slowly and said, 'About doing things for the right reasons.'

'You don't throw down like this just because you're strong enough to do it,' I said. 'You do it because you don't have much choice. You do it because it's unacceptable to walk away, and still live with yourself later.'

She stared at me for a second, and then her eyes widened. 'Otherwise, you're using power for the sake of using power.'

I nodded. 'And power tends to corrupt. It isn't hard to love using it, Molly. You've got to go in with the right attitude or . . .'

'Or the power starts using you,' she said. She'd heard the argument before, but this was the first time she said the words slowly, thoughtfully, as if she'd actually understood them, instead of just parroting them back to me. Then she looked up. 'That's why you do it. Why you help people. You're using the power for someone other than yourself.'

'That's part of it,' I said. 'Yeah.'

'I feel . . . sort of stupid.'

'There's a difference in knowing something' – I poked her head again – 'and knowing it.' I touched the middle of her sternum. 'See?'

She nodded slowly. Then she took the strand back from me and put it back on her wrist. There was just enough left to let her tie it again. She held it up so that I could see and said, 'So that I'll remember.'

I grinned at her and hugged her. She hugged back. 'Did you get a lesson like this?'

'Pretty much,' I said. 'From this grumpy old Scot on a farm in the Ozarks.'

'When do I stop feeling like an idiot?'

'I'll let you know when I do,' I said, and she laughed.

We parted the hug and I met her eyes. 'You still in?'

'Yes,' she said simply.

'Then you'll ride up with Ramirez and me. We'll stop outside the compound and you'll stay with the car.'

She nodded seriously. 'What do I do?'

'Keep your eyes and ears open. Stay alert for anything you might sense. Don't talk to anyone. If anyone approaches you, leave. If you see a bunch of bad guys showing up, start honking the horn and get out.'

'Okay,' she said. She looked a little pale.

I pulled a silver cylinder out of my pocket. 'This is a hypersonic whistle. Mouse can hear it from a mile away. If we get in trouble, I'll blow it and he'll start barking about it. He'll face where we are. Try to get the car as close as you can.'

'I'll have Mouse with me,' she said, and looked considerably relieved.

I nodded. 'Almost always better not to work alone.'

'What if . . . what if I do something wrong?'

I shrugged. 'What if you do? That's always possible, Molly. But the only way never to do the wrong thing—'

'—is never to do anything,' she finished.

'Bingo.' I put a hand on her shoulder. 'Look. You're smart enough. I've taught you everything I know about the White Court. Keep your eyes open. Use your head, your judgment. If things get bad and I haven't started blowing the whistle, run like hell. If it gets past ten P.M. and you haven't heard from me, do the same. Get home and tell your folks.'

'All right,' she said quietly. She took a deep breath and let it out unsteadily. 'This is scary.'

'And we're doing it anyway,' I said.

'That makes us brave, right?'

'If we get away with it,' I said. 'If we don't, it just makes us stupid.'

Her eyes widened for a second and then she let out a full-throated laugh.

'Ready?' I asked her.

'Ready, sir.'

'Good.'

Outside, gravel crunched as Ramirez returned with the Beetle. 'All right, apprentice,' I said. 'Get Mouse's lead on him, will you? Let's do it.'

Château Raith hadn't changed much since my last visit. That's one of the good things about dealing with nigh-immortals. They tend to adjust badly to change and avoid it wherever possible.

It was a big place, north of the city, where the country-side rolls over a surprising variety of terrain — flat stretches of rich land that used to be farms, but are mostly big, expensive properties now. Dozens of little rivers and big creeks have carved hills and valleys more steep than most people expect from the Midwest. The trees out in that area, one of the older settlements in the United States, can be absolutely huge, and it would cost me five or six years' worth of income to buy even a tiny house.

Château Raith is surrounded by a forest of those enormous, ancient trees, as if someone had managed to transplant a section of Sherwood Forest itself from Britain. You can't see a thing of the estate from any of the roads around it. I knew it was at least a half-mile run through the trees before you got to the grounds, which were enormous in their own right.

Translation: You weren't getting away from the château on foot speed alone. Not if there were vampires there to run you down.

There was one new feature to the grounds. The eight-foot-high stone wall was the same, but it had been topped with a double helix of razor wire, and lighting had been spaced along the outside of the wall. I could see security cameras at regular intervals as well. The old Lord Raith had disdained the more modern security precautions in favor of the protection of intense personal arrogance. Lara, however, seemed more willing to acknowledge threats, to listen to her mortal security staff, and to employ the countermeasures they suggested. It would certainly help keep the mortal riffraff out, and the Council had plenty of mortal allies.

More important, it said something about Lara's administration: She found skilled subordinates and then listened to them. She might not look as overwhelmingly confident as Lord Raith had – but then, Lord Raith wasn't running the show anymore, either, even if that wasn't public knowledge in the magical community.

I reflected that it was entirely possible that I might have done the Council and the world something of a disservice by helping Lara assume control. Lord Raith had been proud and brittle. I had the feeling that Lara would prove to be far, far more capable and far more dangerous as the de facto White King.

And here I was, about to go to her aid again and help solidify her power even more.

'Stop here,' I told Molly quietly. The gates to the château were still a quarter mile down the road. 'This is as close as you get.'

'Right,' Molly said, and pulled the Beetle over – onto the far side of the road, I noted with approval, where anyone wanting to come to her would have to cross the open pavement to get there.

'Mouse,' I said. 'Stay here with Molly and listen for us. Take care of her.'

Mouse looked unhappily at me from the backseat, where he'd sat with Ramirez, but leaned forward and dropped his shaggy chin onto my shoulder. I gave him a quick hug and said in a gruff voice, 'Don't worry; we'll be fine.'

His tail thumped once against the backseat, and then he

shifted around to lay his head on Molly's shoulder. She immediately started scratching him reassuringly behind the ear, though her own expression was far from comfortable.

I gave the girl half of a smile, and then got out of the car. Summer twilight was fading fast, and it was too hot to wear my duster. I had it on anyway, and I added the weight of the grey cloak of the Wardens of the White Council to the duster. Under all that, I wore a white silk shirt and cargo pants of heavy black cotton, plus my hiking boots.

'Hat,' I muttered. 'Spurs. Next time, I swear.'

Ramirez slid out of the Beetle, grenades and gun and willow sword hanging from his belt, and staff gripped in his right hand. He paused to pull on a glove made out of heavy leather overlaid with a layer of slender steel plates, each inscribed with pictoglyphs that looked Aztec or Olmec or something.

'That's new,' I commented.

He winked at me, and we checked our guns. My .44 revolver went back into my left-hand duster pocket, his back into its sheath.

'You sure you don't want a grenade or two?' he asked.

'I'm not comfortable with hand grenades,' I said.

'Suit yourself,' he replied. 'How about you, Molly?'

He turned back to the car, hand on one of his grenades.

The car was gone. The engine was still idling audibly.

Ramirez let out a whistle and waved his staff into the space it had occupied until it clinked against metal. 'Hey, not a bad veil. Pretty damned good, in fact.'

'She's got a gift,' I said.

Molly's voice came from nearby. 'Thanks.'

Ramirez gave the approximate space where my apprentice sat a big grin and a gallant, vaguely Spanish little bow.

Molly let out a suppressed giggle. The car's engine cut out, and she said, 'Go on. I've got to keep compensating for the dust you're kicking up, and it's a pain.'

'Eyes open,' I told her. 'Use your head.'

'You too,' Molly said.

'Don't tell him to start new things now,' Ramirez chided her. 'You'll just confuse him.'

'I'm getting dumber by the minute,' I confirmed. 'Ask anybody.'

From the unseen car, Mouse snorted out a breath.

'See?' I said, and started walking toward the entrance to the estate.

Ramirez kept up, but only by taking a skipping step every several paces. My legs are lots longer than his.

After a hundred yards or so, he laughed. 'All right, you made your point.'

I grunted and slowed marginally.

Ramirez looked back over his shoulder. 'Think she'll be all right?'

'Tough to sneak up on Mouse,' I said. 'Even if they realize she's there.'

'Pretty, a body like that, and talent, too.' Ramirez stared back thoughtfully. 'She seeing anyone?'

'Not since she drilled holes in her last boyfriend's psyche and drove him insane.'

Ramirez winced. 'Right.'

We fell silent and walked up to the gates to the estate, getting our game faces on along the way. Ramirez's natural expression was a cocksure smile, but when things got hairy, he went with a cool, arrogant look that left his eyes focused on nothing and everything at the same time. I really don't care what my game face looks like. Mine is all internal.

I kept Anna's face and her serious eyes in mind as I tromped up to the gothic gate made of simulated wrought iron, but heavy enough to stop a charging SUV. I struck it three times with my staff and planted its end firmly onto the ground.

The gate buzzed and began to open of its own accord.

Halfway through, something near the hinges let out a whine and a puff of smoke, and it stopped moving.

'That you?' I asked him.

'I took out the lock too,' he replied quietly. 'And the cameras that can see the gate. Just in case.'

Ramirez doesn't have my raw power, but he uses what he has well. 'Nice,' I told him. 'Didn't feel a thing.'

His grin flickered by. '*De nada*. I'm the best.'

I stepped through the gate, keeping a wary eye out. The night was all but complete, and the woods were lovely, dark and deep. Tires whispered on pavement. A light appeared in the trees ahead, and resolved into headlights. A full-fledged limousine, a white Rolls with silver accents, swept down the drive to the gate, and purred to a halt twenty feet in front of us.

Ramirez muttered under his breath, 'You want I should—'

'Down, big fella,' I said. 'Save ourselves the walk.'

'Bah,' he said. 'Some of us are young and healthy.'

The driver door opened and a man got out. I recognized him as one of Lara's personal bodyguards. He was a bit taller than average, leanly muscled, had a military haircut and sharp, wary eyes. He wore a sports jacket, khakis, and wasn't working to hide the shoulder rig he wore under the coat. He took a look at us, then past us at the gate and the fence. Then he took a small radio from his pocket and started speaking into it.

'Dresden?' he asked me.

'Yeah.'

'Ramirez?'

'The one and only,' Carlos told him.

'You're armed,' he said.

'Heavily,' I replied.

He grimaced, nodded, and said, 'Get in the car, please.'

'Why?' I asked him, oh so innocently.

Ramirez gave me a sharp look, but said nothing.

'I was told to collect you,' the bodyguard said.

'It isn't far to the house,' I said. 'We can walk.'

'Ms Raith asked me to assure you that, on behalf of her father, you have her personal pledge of safe conduct, as stipulated in the Accords.'

'In that case,' I said, 'Ms Raith can come tell me that her personal self.'

'I'm sure she will be happy to,' the bodyguard said. 'At the house, sir.'

I folded my arms and said, 'If she's too busy to move her pretty ass down here, why don't you go ask her if we can't come back tomorrow instead?'

There was a whirring sound, and one of the back windows of the Rolls slid down. I couldn't see much of anyone inside, but I heard a velvet-soft woman's laugh saunter out of the night. 'You see, George. I told you.'

The bodyguard grimaced and looked around. 'They've done something to the gate. It's open. You're exposed here, ma'am.'

'If assassination was their intention,' the woman replied, 'believe me when I say that Dresden could already have done it, and I feel confident that his companion, Mr Ramirez, could have managed the same.'

Ramirez stiffened a little and muttered between clenched teeth, 'How does she know me?'

'Ain't many people ride zombie dinosaurs and make regional commander in the Wardens before they turn twenty-five,' I replied. 'Betcha she's got files on most of the Wardens still alive.'

'And some of the trainees,' agreed the woman's voice. 'George, if you please.'

The bodyguard gave us a flat, measuring look, and then opened the door of the car, one hand resting quite openly on the butt of the pistol hanging under one arm.

The mistress of the White Court stepped forth from the Rolls-Royce.

Lara is . . . difficult to describe. I'd met her several times, and each meeting had carried a similar impact, a moment of stunned admiration and desire at her raw physical appeal that did not lessen with exposure. There was no one feature about her that I could have pointed out as particularly gorgeous. There was no one facet of her beauty that could be declared as utter perfection. Her appeal was something far greater than the sum of her parts, and *none* of those were less than heavenly.

Like Thomas, she had dark, idly curling hair so glossy that the highlights were very nearly a shade of blue. Her skin was one creamy, gently curving expanse of milk white perfection, and if there were moles or birthmarks anywhere on her body, I couldn't see them. Her dark pink lips were a little large for her narrow-chinned face, but they didn't detract – they only gave her a look of lush overindulgence, of deliberate and wicked sensuality.

It was her eyes, though, that were the real killers. They were large, oblique orbs of arsenic grey, highlighted with flecks of periwinkle blue. More important, they were very alive eyes, alert, aware of others, shining with intelligence and humor – so much so, in fact, that if you weren't careful, you'd miss the smoldering, demonic fires of sensuality in them, of a steady, predatory hunger.

Beside me, Ramirez swallowed. I knew only because I could hear it. When Lara makes an entrance, no one looks away.

She wore a white silk business suit, its skirt less than an inch too short to be considered dignified business wear, the heels of her white shoes just a tiny bit too high for propriety. It made it difficult not to stare at her legs. A lot of women with her coloring couldn't pull off a white outfit, but Lara made it look like a goddess's toga.

She knew the effect she had when we looked at her, and her mouth curled into a satisfied little smile. She walked toward us slowly, one leg crossing the other at a deliberate pace, hips shifting slightly. The motion was . . . awfully pretty. Sheer, sensual femininity gathered around her in a silent, unseen thundercloud, so thick that it could drown a man if he wasn't careful.

After all, she had drowned her father in it, hadn't she?

All is not gold that glitters, and how well I knew it. As delicious as she looked, as pants-rendingly gorgeously as she moved, she was capital-D Dangerous. More, she was a vampire, a predator, one who fed on human beings to continue her very existence. Despite our past cooperation, I was still human, and she was still something that *ate* humans. If I acted like food, there would be an enormous part of her that wouldn't care about politics or advantage. It would just want to eat me.

So I did my best to look bored as she approached and offered me her hand, palm down.

I took her cold (smooth, pretty, deliciously soft – dammit, Harry, ignore your penis before it gets you killed!) fingers in mine, bent over them in a little formal bow, and released them without kissing her hand. If I had, I wasn't sure I wouldn't take a few nibbles, just to test out the texture as long as I was there.

As I rose, she met my eyes for a dangerous second and said, 'Sure you don't want a taste, Harry?'

A surge of raw lust that was – probably – not my own flickered through my body. I smiled at her, gave her a little bow of my head, and made a small effort of will. The runes and sigils on my staff erupted into smoldering orange Hellfire. 'Be polite, Lara. It would be a shame to get cinders and ashes all over those shoes.'

She tilted her head back and let out a bubbling, throaty

laugh, then touched the side of my face with one hand. 'Subtle, as always,' she replied. She lowered her hand and ran her fingertips over the odd grey material of my Warden's cloak. 'You've developed . . . an eclectic taste in fashion.'

'It's the same color,' I said, 'on both sides.'

'Ah,' Lara said, and inclined her head slightly to me. 'I'd hardly respect you otherwise, I suppose. Still, should you ever desire a new wardrobe . . .' She touched the fabric of my shirt lightly. 'You would look marvelous in white silk.'

'Said the spider to the fly,' I replied. 'Forget it.'

She smiled again, batted her lashes at me while my heart skipped a beat, and then slid on to Ramirez. She offered him her hand. 'You must be Warden Ramirez.'

This is the part where I got nervous. Ramirez loved women. Ramirez never shut up about women. Well, he never shut up about anything in general, but he'd go on and on about various conquests and feats of sexual athleticism and—

'A *virgin?*' Lara blurted. *Lara* blurted. She turned her head to me, grey eyes several shades paler than they had been, and very wide. 'Really, Harry, I'm not sure what to say. Is he a *present?*'

I folded my arms and regarded Lara steadily, but said nothing. This was Ramirez's moment to make a first impression, and if he didn't do it on his own, Lara would regard him as someone who couldn't protect himself. It would probably mark him as a target.

Lara turned to walk a slow circle around Ramirez, inspecting him the way you might a flashy new sports car. She was of a height with him, but taller in the heels, and there was nothing but a languidly sensual confidence in the way she moved. 'A handsome young bantam,' she murmured. She trailed a finger across the line of his shoulders as she moved behind him. 'Strong. Young. A hero of the White Council, I've heard.' She paused to touch a fingertip to the back of his hand, and then shuddered. 'And power, too.' Her eyes went a few shades brighter as she completed the tour. 'My goodness. I've recently fed, and *still* . . . Perhaps you'd care to ride with me back to the estate, and let Dresden walk. I promise to entertain you until he arrives.'

I knew the look on Ramirez's face. It was the look of a young man who wants nothing so badly as to discard the complex things in life, like civilization, social mores, clothing, and speech, and see what happened next.

Lara knew it, too. Her eyes glittered brightly, and her smile was serpentine, and she pressed closer.

But Ramirez apparently knew about glittery gold, too. I didn't know he'd hidden a knife up his sleeve, but it appeared in his hand an instant before its tip pressed into the bottom of Lara's throat.

'I,' he said very quietly, 'am not food.' And he met her eyes.

I hadn't seen a soulgaze from the outside before. It surprised me, how simple and brief it looked, when one wasn't being shaken to the core by it. Both of them stared, eyes widening, and then shuddered. Lara took a small step back from Ramirez, her breathing slightly quickened. I noticed, because I'm a professional investigator. She could have been concealing a weapon in that décolletage.

'If you meant to dissuade me,' Lara said a moment later, 'you haven't.'

'Not you,' Ramirez replied, lowering the knife. His voice was rough. 'It wasn't to dissuade you.'

'Wise,' she murmured, 'for one so young. I advise you, young wizard, not to hesitate so long to act, should another approach you as I did. A virgin is . . . extremely attractive to our kind. One such as you is rare, these days. Give a less restrained member of the court an opportunity as you did me, and they'll throw themselves on you in dozens – which would reflect poorly on me.'

She turned back to me and said, 'Wizards, you have my pledge of safe conduct.'

I inclined my head to her and said, 'Thank you.'

'Then I will await your company in the car.'

I nodded my head to her, and Lara walked back to her bodyguard, who looked like he was fighting off a fit of apoplexy.

I turned and eyed Ramirez.

He turned bright red.

'Virgin?' I asked him.

He turned more red.

'Carlos?' I asked.

'She's lying,' he snapped. 'She's evil. She's really evil. And lying.'

I rubbed at my mouth to keep anyone from seeing me grin.

Hey. On nights like this, you take your laughs where you can get them.

'Okay,' I said. 'Not important.'

'The hell it isn't!' he spat. 'She's lying! I mean, I'm not . . . I'm . . .'

I nudged him with an elbow. 'Focus, Galahad. We've got a job to do.'

He exhaled with a growl. 'Right.'

'You saw what was inside her?' I asked.

He shuddered. 'That pale thing. Her eyes . . . she was getting more turned on, and they kept looking more like *its* eyes.'

'Yep,' I said. 'It's a tip-off to how close they are to starting to take a bite of you. You handled it right.'

'You think so?'

I couldn't resist jibing him, just a little. 'Just think. If you'd messed it up,' I said, as Lara slid into the car one long, perfect leg at a time, 'you'd be in the limo with Lara ripping your clothes off right now.'

Ramirez looked at the car and swallowed. 'Um. Yeah. Close one.'

'I've met several of the White Court,' I said. 'Lara's probably the smartest. She's the most civilized, progressive, adaptable. She's definitely the most dangerous.'

'She didn't look that tough,' Ramirez said, but he was frowning in thought as he said it.

'She's dangerous in a different way than most,' I said. 'But I think her word is good.'

'It is,' Ramirez said firmly. 'I saw that much.'

'It's one of the things that makes her dangerous,' I said, and headed for the limo. 'Stay cool.'

We walked over and I leaned down to see Lara in the back of the limo, seated on one of the dogcart-style seats, all poise and beauty and gorgeous grey eyes. She smiled at me as I looked in, and crooked a finger.

'Step into my limo,' said the spider to the fly.

And we did.

The limo rolled right past the enormous stone house that was the château proper. It was bigger than a parking garage, and covered with cornices and turrets and gargoyles, like some kind of neo-Medieval castle.

'We're, uh,' I noted, 'not stopping at the house.'

'No,' Lara said from the seat facing us. Even in the dark, you could see the glow of her luminous skin. 'The conclave is being held in the Deeps.' Her eyes glittered at me. 'Less walking for everyone, that way.'

I gave her a small smile and said, 'I like the house. The whole castle-look thing. It's always nice to know you're living somewhere that could withstand a besieging army of Bohemian mercenaries if it had to.'

'Or American wizards,' she replied smoothly.

I gave her what I hoped was a wolfish smile, folded my arms, and watched the house go by. We turned down a little gravel lane and drove another mile or so before the car slowed and came to a stop. Bodyguard George got out and opened the door for Lara, whose thigh brushed against mine as she got out, and whose perfume smelled good enough to scramble my brain for a good two or three seconds.

Both I and Ramirez sat still for a second.

'That,' I said, 'is an awfully lovely woman. I thought I should let you know, kid, in case your inexperience had blinded you to the fact.'

'Lying,' Ramirez stated, blushing. 'Evil.'

I snickered and slid out of the car to follow Lara – and

the three more bodyguards waiting for her — into the woods beside the gravel lane.

The last time I'd found the entrance to the Deeps, I'd been stumbling through the woods, focused on a tracking spell and tripping over roots and hummocks in the old-growth forest.

This time, there was a lighted path, with a red carpet, no less, leading down between the trees. The lights were all of soft blues and greens, small lamps that, upon a closer glance, proved to be elegant little crystal cages containing tiny, humanoid forms with wings. Faeries, tiny pixies, each surrounded by its own sphere of light, trapped and miserable, crouched in the cages.

Between each cage knelt more prisoners — humans, bound by nothing more than a single strand of white silk about their throats tied to a peg driven into the earth in front of them. They weren't naked. Lara wouldn't have gone in for anything that overt. Instead, they each wore a white silk kimono, accented with strands of silver thread.

Men and women, arrayed in a variety of ages, body types, hair colors, every single one of them beautiful, their eyes lowered as they knelt quietly. One of the young men sat shivering and was seemingly barely able to stay upright. His long, dark hair was marred with streaks of brittle white. His eyes were unfocused and he seemed totally unaware of anyone around him. His kimono was torn near the neck, leaving a broad swath of muscled chest exposed. There were raking nail marks, deep enough to draw tiny trickles of blood, all the way across one pectoral. There were repeated teeth marks deep in the slope of muscle between neck and shoulder, half a dozen sets of messy bruises and ugly little gashes. There were more nail marks, four side-by-side punctures, rather than rakes, on the other side of his neck.

He was also obviously, even painfully, aroused beneath the kimono.

Lara paused beside him and rolled her eyes in irritation. 'Madeline?'

'Yes, ma'am,' said one of the bodyguards.

'Oh, for hunger's sake.' She sighed. 'Get him indoors before the conclave is over or she'll finish him off on her way out.'

'Yes, ma'am,' he said, turned aside, and began speaking to nobody. I spotted a wire running to an earpiece.

I kept walking down the long line of kneeling captives and trapped pixies, and got angrier with every step.

'They're willing, Dresden,' Lara said a few paces later. 'All of them.'

'I'm sure they are,' I said. 'Now.'

She laughed. 'There is no shortage of mortals who long to kneel before another, wizard. There never has been.'

We passed several more kneeling men and women who looked mussed and dazed, though none of badly as the first. We also walked past spaces where there was a peg and a strip of white cloth – but no person kneeling within.

'I'm sure they all knew that they might die by doing it,' I said.

She shrugged one shoulder. 'It happens at these meetings. Guests have no need to dispose of a body, since as hosts we are responsible for such necessities. As a result, many of our visitors make no effort to control themselves.'

'You're responsible, all right.' I gripped my staff harder and kept my voice neutral. 'What about the little folk?'

'They trespassed upon our land,' she replied, her voice calm. 'Most would simply have killed them, rather than pressing them into service.'

'Yeah. You're all heart.'

'Where there is life, there is hope, Dresden,' Lara replied. 'My father's policies on such matters have changed of late.

Death is . . . gauche, when it can be avoided. Alternative
courses are far more profitable and agreeable to all involved.
It is for precisely that reason that my father seeks to help
create a peace between your folk and mine.'

I glanced aside at the shining eyes of a short-haired redhead
in her early thirties, absolutely lovely, her kimono still open
from whatever had fed on her, the tips of her small breasts
taut as she panted, the muscles of a lean stomach still trembling. Behind us, the thralls stretched out into the darkness.
Ahead of us, they went on for a hundred yards or more. So
many of them.

I started to shudder, but the faces of the women the Skavis
and his pretenders had murdered flickered through my mind,
and I fought it down. Like hell was I going to let Lara see
me look discomfited, no matter how sick the display of the
White Court's seductive power made me feel.

The path went for another hundred yards through the
woods and stopped at the mouth of a cave. It wasn't large
or sinister or dramatic. It was simply a fissure in an almost-
flat stretch of ground at the base of a tree, with the hypnotic
sway of firelight dancing somewhere below. There were
guards outside – set back in the woods, out of obvious sight.
I spotted a couple of deer stands, occupied by dark shapes.
There were others standing silent sentinel. I assumed that
there would be more guards I could not see.

Lara turned to us. 'Gentlemen,' she said. 'If you will wait
here for a moment, I will send someone when the White
King is ready to receive you.'

I nodded once, settled my staff on the ground, and leaned
on it a little, saying nothing. Ramirez took his cue from me.

Lara gave me a level look. Then she turned and descended
into the Deeps, flawlessly graceful despite her high heels.

'You've met her before,' Ramirez noted quietly.

'Yeah.'

'Where?'

'Set of a porn movie. She was acting.'

He stared at me for a second. Then shrugged in acceptance and said, 'What were you doing?'

'Stuntman,' I replied.

'Uh . . .' he said.

'I'd been hired by the producer to find out why people involved with the movie were being killed.'

'Did you?'

'Yeah.'

'So . . . did you and she . . . ?'

'No,' I said. 'You can tell from how I'm breathing and possessed of my own will.' I nodded toward the entrance of the cave, where a shadow briefly darkened the firelight from below. 'Someone's coming.'

A young woman in an especially fine white kimono, heavily embroidered with silver thread, emerged from the fissure. I thought she was blond for a second, but that was because of the light. As she approached us with slow, quiet steps, her hair turned blue, then green, passing through the light of the faerie lamps. Her hip-length hair was pure white. She was lovely, very nearly as much so as Lara, but there was none of the predatory sense of hunger in her that I'd come to associate with the White Court. She was slim, and sweetly shaped, and looked quite frail and vulnerable. It took me a second to recognize her.

'Justine?' I asked.

She gave me a little smile. It was oddly disconnected, as if her dark eyes were focused on something other than what she smiled at, and she never looked directly at me. She spoke, her words flecked with little pauses and emphasis on odd syllables, as if she were speaking a foreign language in which she had merely technical proficiency. 'It's Harry Dresden. Hello, Harry. You look dashing this evening.'

'Justine,' I said, accepting her hand as she offered it to me. I bowed over it. 'You look . . . ambulatory.'

She gave me a shy smile and spoke in a dreamy singsong. 'I'm healing. One day I'll be all better and go back to my lord.'

Her fingers, though, tightened hard on mine as she spoke, a quick and measured sequence, to the rhythm of 'shave and a haircut.'

I blinked for a second and then squeezed back on the beat for 'six bits.' 'I'm sure any man would be delighted to see you.'

She blushed daintily and bowed to us. 'So kind, my lord. Would you accompany me, please?'

We did. Justine led us down into the fissure, which proved to be a smooth-walled descent into the earth. From there, our way forward entered a torchlit tunnel, its walls also polished smooth, and from far below us came the music of echoing voices and sounds dancing through the stone, being subtly changed and altered by the acoustics as they came up from below.

It was a long, winding descent down, though the tunnel was wide and the footing steady. I remembered the nightmarish flight from the Deeps the last time I'd been there, while Murphy and I dragged my half-dead half brother all the way up before we'd been consumed in a storm of psychic slavery Lara was whipping up to take control of her father, and through him the White Court. It had been a close one.

Justine stopped about two-thirds of the way down, at a spot that had been marked with a bit of chalk on the floor. 'Here,' she said in a quiet – but not at all dreamy – voice. 'We can't be overheard from here.'

'What's going on?' I demanded. 'How are you walking around like this?'

'It doesn't matter right now,' Justine said. 'I'm better.'

'You aren't crazy, are you?' I demanded. 'You nearly scratched my eyes out that one time.'

She shook her head with a frustrated little motion. 'Medication. It isn't . . . Look, I'm all right for now. I need you to listen to me.'

'Fine,' I said.

'Lara wished me to tell you what to expect,' Justine said, dark eyes intent. 'Right now, Lord Skavis is below, calling for an end to any plans for negotiations with the Council, citing the work of his son as an illustration of the profit of continuing hostilities.'

'His *son?*' I said.

Justine grimaced and nodded. 'The agent you slew was the heir apparent of House Skavis.'

Mouse might have been the one to do the actual killing, but the Accords regarded him as a mere weapon, like a gun. I was the one who had pulled the trigger. 'Who is in charge of Malvora?'

'Lady Cesarina Malvora,' Justine said, giving me a smile of approval. 'Whose son Vittorio will be quite insulted by Lord Skavis's lies about all the hard work *he* and Madrigal Raith did.'

I nodded. 'When does Lara want me to make my entrance?'

'She told me that you would know best,' Justine said.

'Right,' I said. 'Take me to where I can hear them talking, then.'

'That's going to be a problem,' Justine said. 'They're speaking Ancient Etruscan. I can follow enough of it to give you an idea what—'

'It isn't a problem,' I said.

Is it? I thought toward Lasciel's shadow.

Naturally not, my host, came the ghostly reply.

Groovy, I thought. *Thanks, Lash.*

A startled second passed. Then she replied, *You are welcome.*

'Just get me to where I can hear them,' I told Justine.

'This way,' she replied at once, and hurried on down the passage, stopping not twenty feet shy of the main cavern. Even so close, I could see very little of the cavern beyond – though I could hear voices raised in speech that sounded strange and sibilant in my ears and English in my head.

'. . . the very heart of the matter,' a rolling basso voice orated. 'That the mortal freaks and their ilk stand on the brink of destruction. Now is the time to tighten our grip and neuter the kine once and for all.' Lord Skavis, I presumed.

A strong and lazily confident baritone answered the speaker, and I recognized the voice of the remains of the creature who had killed my mother at once. 'My dear Skavis,' answered Lord Raith, the White King, 'I can hardly say that I find the notion of a neutered humanity entirely appealing.'

There was a round of silvery laughter, men and women alike. It rippled through the air and brushed against me like an idly ardent lover. I stood fast until it had gone by. Ramirez had to rest a hand on the wall to keep his balance. Justine swayed like a reed, her eyes fluttering shut and then opening again.

Skavis's deep voice resumed. 'Your personal amusements and preferences aside, my King, the freaks' biggest weakness has always been the length of time it took them to develop their skills to the most formidable levels. For the first time in history, we have degraded or neutralized their many advantages altogether, partly due to the fortunes of war, and partly thanks to the resourcefulness of the kine in developing their arts in travel and communication. The House of Skavis has proven that we stand holding an unprecedented opportunity to crush the freaks and bring the kine under control at last. Only a fool would allow it to slip between his impotent fingers. My King.'

'Only a fool,' came a strident woman's voice, 'would make such a pathetic claim.'

'The Crown,' Raith interjected, 'recognizes Cesarina, the Lady Malvora.'

'Thank you, my King,' Lady Malvora said. 'While I cannot help but admire my Lord Skavis's audacity, I fear that I have no choice but to cut short his attempt to steal glory not his own from the honorable House of Malvora.'

Raith's voice remained amused. 'This should be interesting. By all means, elaborate, dear Cesarina.'

'Thank you, my King. My son, Vittorio, was on the scene and will explain.'

A male voice, flat and a little nasal, spoke up, and I recognized Grey Cloak's accent at once. 'My lord, the deaths inflicted upon the freakishly blooded kine indeed happened as Lord Skavis describes. But in fact, it was no agent of his House who accomplished this deed. If, as he claims, his son accomplished it, then where is he? Why has he not come forward to bear testimony in person?'

The words fell on what I could only describe as a glowering silence. If Lord Skavis was anything like the rest of the Whites I'd met, Vittorio needed to bury him fast, or spend the rest of his life looking over his shoulder.

'Then who did accomplish this fell act of warfare?' Raith asked, his tone mild.

Vittorio spoke again, and I could just imagine the way his chest must have puffed out. 'I did, my King, with the assistance of Madrigal of the House of Raith.'

Raith's voice gained an edge of anger. 'This, despite the fact that a cessation of hostilities has been declared, pending the discussion of an armistice.'

'What is done is done, my King,' Lady Malvora interjected. 'My dear friend Lord Skavis was correct in this fact: The freaks are weak. Now is the time to *finish* them — now and forever. Not to allow them time to regain their feet.'

'Despite the fact that the White King thinks otherwise?'

I could hear Lady Malvora's smile. 'Many things change, O King.'

There was a booming sound, maybe a fist slamming down onto the arm of a throne. 'This does not. You have violated my commands and undermined my policies. That is treason, Cesarina.'

'Is it, O King?' Lady Malvora shot back. 'Or is it treason to our very blood to show mercy to an enemy who is upon the brink of defeat?'

'I would be willing to forgive excessive zeal, Cesarina,' Raith snarled. 'I am less inclined to tolerate the stupidity behind this mindless provocation.'

Cold, mocking laughter fell on a sudden, dead silence. 'Stupidity? In what way, O weak and aged King? In what way are the deaths of the kine anything but sweetness to the senses, balm to the Hunger?' The quality of her voice changed, as if she changed her facing in the cavern. I could imagine her turning to address the audience, scorn ringing in her tone. 'We are strong, and the strong do as they wish. Who shall call us to task for it, O King? You?'

If that wasn't a straight line, my name isn't Harry Blackstone Copperfield Dresden.

I lifted my staff and slammed it down on the floor, forcing an effort of will through it to focus the energy of the blow into a far smaller area than the end of the staff. It struck the stone floor, shattering a chunk the size of a big dinner platter with a detonation almost indistinguishable from thunder. Another effort of will sent a rolling wave of silent fire, no more than five or six inches high, down the tunnel floor, in a red carpet of my very own.

I strode down it, Ramirez beside me, the fire rolling back away from our feet as we went, boots striking the stone together. We entered the cavern and found it packed with pale and startled beings, the entire place a wash of beautiful faces and gorgeous wardrobes – except for twenty feet around the entrance, where everyone had hurried away from the blazing herald of our presence.

I ignored everything, scanning the room until I found Grey Cloak, aka Vittorio Malvora, standing next to Madrigal Raith not thirty feet away. The murdering bastards were staring at us, mouths open in shock.

'Vittorio Malvora!' I called, my voice ringing with wrath in the echoing cavern. 'Madrigal Raith! I am Harry Dresden, Warden of the White Council of Wizards. Under the Unseelie Accords, I accuse you of murder in a time of peace, and challenge you, here and now, before these witnesses, to trial by combat.' I slammed my staff down again in another shock of thunder, and Hellfire flooded the runes of the staff. 'To the *death*.'

Utter silence fell on the Deeps.

Damn, there ain't nothing like a good entrance.

'Empty night,' Madrigal swore, in English, his eyes wide. 'This isn't happening.'

I showed him my teeth and replied quietly in the same tongue. 'Time to pay the piper, prick.'

Vitto Malvora turned his head to look over his shoulder at a tiny woman no more than five feet tall, dressed in a white gown more like a toga than anything else. She was curved like the Greek goddesses the gown made her resemble. Her face was a stark, frozen mask.

She turned eyes the color of chrome toward me and wine-dark lips peeled back from very white teeth.

There was an immediate uproar from the vampires, a sudden chorus of shouts of protest and anger. If I'd been in a less defiant mood, it probably would have scared the crap out of me. As it was, I simply shifted my stance, turning slightly to my left while Ramirez did the same in the opposite direction, so that we stood back-to-back. There wasn't much else to do but prepare to fight in the event that someone decided to kick off a good old-fashioned wizard-smashin' for the evening's group activity.

That gave me a moment to look around the cavern. It was built on the scale of Parisian cathedrals, with an enormously high, arched ceiling that vanished into shadow far overhead. The floor and walls were of living stone, smooth and grey, shot through here and there with strands of green, dark red, and cobalt blue. Everything was rounded and smooth, not a jagged edge or sharp corner in sight.

The decor had changed a bit since I was there last. There

were soft amber, orange, and scarlet lights splashing onto the walls of the cavern, and the lamps they came from had to have been automated, because they moved slightly, mixing color, making all the shadows twitch, and generally giving the overall impression of crude firelight without surrendering any of the clarity of electric lighting. Furniture had been arranged in three large groupings, with a large open space in the center of the floor, and they were occupied by what I could only presume were the leading members of the three major Houses — somewhere near a hundred vampires in all. Servants, dressed in the same kind of more heavily embroidered kimono Justine had been wearing, hovered at the walls, bearing trays of drinks and food and so on.

The floor rose in a series of inch-high ripples toward the far side of the chamber, where the White King sat looking down upon his Court.

Raith's throne was an enormous chair of bone-white stone. Its back flared out like the hood of a cobra, spreading out into an enormous crest decorated with all manner of eye-twisting carvings, everything from rather spidery Celtic-style designs to bas-relief scenes of beings I could not easily identify engaged in activities I had no desire to contemplate. A thin sheet of fine mist fell behind the throne, the light playing delicately through it, sending ribbons and streams of color and refracted rainbows dancing around the throne. Behind that veil of obscuring mist, the floor abruptly ended, opening up into a yawning abyss that dropped into the bowels of the earth and, for all I knew, all the way through its intestinal tract.

The White King sat upon the throne. Thomas favored his father heavily, and at first glance, Lord Raith could have *been* Thomas. He had the same strong, appealing features, the same glossy dark hair, the same lean build. He looked little older than Thomas, but his face was very different. It was the eyes, I think. They were . . . stained, somehow, with contempt and calculation and a serpentine dispassion.

The White King wore a splendid outfit of white silk, something somewhere between Napoleonic finery and Chinese Imperial garb. Silver and gold thread and sapphires flickered over the whole of his outfit, and a circlet of glittering silver stood out starkly against his raven hair.

Around the throne stood five women – every one of them a vampire, in less elaborate and more feminine versions of his own regalia. Lara was one of them, and not the prettiest, though they all bore her a strong likeness. Raith's daughters, I supposed, each beautiful enough to haunt a lifetime of dreams, each deadly enough to kill an army of fools who sought to make such a fantasy come true.

The noise continued to rise all around us, and I could feel Ramirez's shoulders tightening, and sense the power he had begun to gather.

Raith rose from his throne with lazy magnificence and roared, 'SILENCE!'

I thought my speaking voice had been loud, but Raith's shook small stones loose from the unseeing ceiling of the cavern far overhead, and the whole place went dead still.

Lady Malvora wasn't having any intimidation, though. She strode into the open space before the throne, maybe ten feet from Ramirez and me, and faced the White King. 'Ridiculous!' she snapped. 'We are not in a time of peace with the White Council. A state of war has been ongoing for years.'

'The victims were not members of the Council,' I said, and gave her a sweet smile.

'And they are not signatories to the Accords!' Lady Malvora snapped.

'Given their status as members of the magical community, they are, however, within the purview of the White

Council's legitimate political concerns, and as such are subject to the stipulations for protection and defense found within the Accords. I am well within my rights to act as their champion.'

Lady Malvora stared daggers at me. 'Sophistry.'

I smiled at her. 'That is, of course, for your King to decide.'

Lady Malvora's glare became even more heated, but she turned her gaze from me to the white throne.

Raith sat down again slowly, carefully fussy with his sleeves, his eyes alight with pure pleasure. 'Now, now, dear Cesarina. Moments ago, you were claiming credit for dealing what could prove a mortal blow to the freaks, at least in the long term. Just because said freaks are here to object, as is their right under the Accords, you can hardly claim that they have no vested interest in trying to stop you.'

Comprehension dawned on Lady Malvora's lovely face. Her voice lowered to a pitch that couldn't have carried much farther than myself, and maybe to Raith's own enhanced senses. 'You snake. You poisonous snake.'

Raith gave her a chill smile and addressed the assembly. 'We find that we have little choice but to acknowledge the validity of the freak's right of challenge. Under our agreement in the Accords, then, we must abide by its terms and permit the trial to proceed.' Raith rolled a droll hand at Vitto and Madrigal. 'Unless, of course, our war heroes here lack the courage to withstand this utterly predictable response to their course of action. They are, of course, free to decline the challenge, should they feel themselves unable to face the consequences of their deeds.'

Silence fell again, almost viciously anticipatory. The weight of the attention of the White Court fell squarely on Vitto and Madrigal, and they froze the way birds will before a snake, remaining carefully motionless.

This was the ticklish part. If the duo declined the trial by combat, Raith would have to pay the Council a weregild for the dead, and that would be that. Of course, doing so would be a public admission of defeat, and would effectively neuter any influence they had in the White Court, and by extension would weaken Lady Malvora's position – not so much because they declined to fight as because they would have been outmaneuvered and forced to flee a confrontation.

Of course, being proven slow and incompetent in front of a hundred ruthless predators, be they ever so well dressed, would probably prove lethal itself, in the long run. Either way, Lady Malvora's attempted influence coup would be finished. The bold and daring plan would have been proven overt and liable to attract far too much attention, both of which were simply not of value within the vampires' collective character. As a result, the White King, not Lady Malvora, would determine the course of the White Court's policy.

Lady Malvora's only way out was through a victory in the trial, and I was counting on it. I wanted Vitto and Madrigal to fight. Weregild wasn't good enough to atone for what these creatures had done to far too many innocent women.

I wanted to give these monsters an object lesson.

Madrigal turned to Vitto and spoke in a quiet hiss. I half closed my eyes and Listened in on the conversation.

'No,' Madrigal said, again in English. 'No way. He's a stupid thug, but this is exactly what he does best.'

Vitto and Lady Malvora traded a long stare. Then Vitto turned to Madrigal and said, 'You were the imbecile who set out to attract his attention and got him involved. We fight.'

'Like hell we fight,' Madrigal snarled. 'Empty night, Ortega couldn't take him in a straight fight.'

'Don't act like such a kine, Madrigal,' Vitto replied. 'That was a duel of wills. A trial by combat allows us any weapons or tactics we wish.'

'Have fun. I won't be one of the people fighting him.'

'Yes, you will,' Vitto replied. 'You can face the wizard. Or you can face dear Auntie Cesarina.'

Madrigal froze again, staring at Vitto.

'I promise you that even if he burns you to death, it will be swift and painless by comparison. Decide, Madrigal. You are with Malvora or against us.'

Madrigal swallowed and closed his eyes. 'Son of a bitch.'

Vitto Malvora's mouth widened into a smile, and he turned to address the White King, his language shifting back to Etruscan or whatever. 'We deny the freak's baseless accusation and accept his challenge, of course, my King. We will prove the injustice of it upon his body.'

'W-weapons,' came Madrigal's unsteady voice. Lasciel's translation was flawlessly smooth, but it wasn't hard to extrapolate that Madrigal's Etruscan was about as bad as my Latin. 'Weapons for our own we must have to fight. To get them we must send slaves for to find them.'

Raith settled back in his throne and folded his arms. 'I find this an only reasonable request. Dresden?'

'No objection,' I told him.

Raith nodded once, and clapped his hands. 'Music, then, while we wait, and another round of wine.'

Lady Malvora snarled, turned on a heel, and stalked back into one of the groups of furniture, where she became the immediate center of an intent conference.

Musicians struck up from somewhere nearby, hidden behind a screen, a chamber orchestra, and a pretty good one. Vivaldi, maybe? I'm weaker on smaller-scale music than I am on symphonies. An excited buzz of voices rose up as servants began circulating with silver trays and crystal flute glasses.

Ramirez gave the chamber a somewhat disbelieving stare and then shook his head. 'This is a nuthouse.'

'Cave,' I said. 'Nutcave.'

'What the hell is going on?'

Right. Ramirez didn't have his own photocopy of a demon's personality to translate Ancient Etruscan. So I summed up the conversation and the players, and gave him the best quotes.

'What's this freak stuff?' Ramirez demanded in a low, outraged tone.

'I think it's a perspective thing,' I said. 'They call humans kine – deer, herd animals. Wizards are deer who can call down the lightning and whip up firestorms. From that perspective, we're fairly freakish.'

'So we're going to kick their asses now, right?'

'That is the plan.'

'Incoming,' Ramirez said, stiffening.

Lara Raith approached us, demure in her white formal getup, bearing a silver tray with drinks upon it. She inclined her head to us, her grey eyes pale and shining. 'Honored guests. Would you care for wine?'

'Nah,' I said. 'I'm driving.'

Lara's lips twitched. I had no idea how she had switched into the complex kimono so quickly. Chalk it up to the same sexy vampire powers that had once let her shoot a layer of skin off my ear while standing on gravel in stiletto heels. Poof, business suit. Whoosh, whoosh, silk negligee. I shook my head a little and got my thoughts under control. Adrenaline can make me a little silly.

Lara turned to Carlos and said, 'May I offer you a taste of something sweet, bantam?'

'Well,' he said. 'As long as you're offering stuff, how about a little assurance that somebody isn't going to shoot us in the back for fun once we're stomping on Beavis and Butthead over there?'

Lara arched a brow. 'Beavis and . . .'

'I would have gone with Hekyll and Jekyll,' I told him.

'Gentlemen,' she said. 'Please be assured that the White Throne wishes nothing more than for you to prevail and humiliate its foes. I am sure that my father will react most harshly to any violation of the Accords.'

'Okay,' Ramirez said, drawing the word out. He nodded toward the Malvoran contingent, still huddled around Cesarina. 'So, what's stopping *Il Duca* there from taking a whack at you and the King and everybody? If she offs you, she gets to kill us, take over the organization, and just do whatever she likes.'

Lara looked at him and her expression twisted with distaste, to the point that a little shudder actually flickered along her body. Which I noticed because I am a trained observer of body language and not because of the way the kimono was perfectly outlining one of her thighs. 'You don't understand . . .' She shook her head, holding her mouth as if she'd unexpectedly bitten into a lemon. 'Dresden, can you explain it to him?'

'The White Court vamps can be violent,' I said quietly. 'Savage, even. But that isn't their preferred mode of operation. You're worried that Malvora is going to come smashing in here like a big old grizzly bear and kill anything in her way. But they aren't like grizzly bears. They're more like mountain lions. They prefer not to be seen acting at all. When they do attack, they're going after a victim, not seeking an opponent. They'll try to isolate them, hit them from behind, preferably destroy them before they even know that they're being attacked. If Lady Malvora threw down right now, it'd be a stand-up fight. They hate those. They won't do them unless there's no alternative.'

'Oh,' Ramirez said.

'Thank you,' Lara told me.

'Of course,' I said, 'there's been some uncharacteristic behavior going around lately.'

Lara tilted her head at me, frowning.

'Oh, come on,' I said. 'You think it's a little odd the faeries didn't immediately stomp all over the Red Court when they violated Unseelie territory a couple of years back? Don't tell me you're trapping the little faeries because it's cheaper than getting those paper party lanterns.'

Lara narrowed her eyes at me.

'You're testing their reaction,' I said. 'Giving a minor but deliberate insult and seeing what happens.'

Her lips turned up very, very slowly. 'Are you sure you're quite determined to remain attached to that sad little club-house of old men?'

'Why? Do you take care of your own?' I asked.

'In a great many senses, wizard,' she promised.

'The way you took care of Thomas?' I asked.

Her smile turned brittle.

'Pride goeth, Lara,' I said.

'Each is entitled to his opinion.' She glanced up and said, 'The runners have returned with your foes' weaponry. Good hunting, gentlemen.'

She bowed to us again, her expression a mask, and drifted away, back toward her place behind the throne.

The music came to an end, and it seemed to be a signal to the vampires. They withdrew from the center of the chamber to stand on either side, leaving the long axis of the cavern open, the entrance upon one end, the White Throne upon the other. Last of all, the White King himself rose and descended from the enormous throne to move to one side of the cavern. On the right side of the room were all the members of Malvora and Skavis, and on the left gathered the members of House Raith. The Skavis and Malvora weren't actually standing *together*, but . . . there was a sense of hungry anticipation in the air.

'Vampires standing on both sidelines,' Ramirez said. 'Guess no one wants to catch a stray lightning bolt.'

'Or bullet,' I muttered. 'But it won't help them much if things get confused and turned around once the fight starts.'

Raith snapped a finger, and thralls in their white kimonos began filing into the room. They swayed more than walked, filing down the 'sidelines' of the dueling ground, and then simply knelt down, in a pair of double ranks, in front of the vampires on either side of the chamber. They formed, taken together, a wall like that around a hockey arena – but one made of living, human flesh.

Crap. Any form of mayhem that spread to the sidelines was going to run smack into human victims – and my own powers, in a fight, were not exactly surgical instruments. Torrents of flame, blasts of force, and impenetrable bastions of will were sort of my thing. You will note, however, how seldom words like *torrent, blast*, and *bastion* get used in conjunction with terms that denote delicacy and precision.

Ramirez was going to be better off than I was, in that regard. His combat skills ran more to speed and accuracy, versus my own preference for massive destruction, but they were no less deadly in their own way.

Carlos looked back and forth, then said to me, 'They're going to try to stay on our flanks. Use those people in the background to keep us from cutting loose.'

'I know I never went to Warden combat school,' I told him. 'But I feel I should remind you that this is not *my* first time.'

Ramirez grimaced at me. 'You just aren't going to let that go, are you?'

I showed him my teeth. 'So I hit them fast and hard while you keep them off me. If they flank, you're on offense while I keep them off of you. Try to maneuver them out to where I'll have a clean shot.'

Ramirez scowled, and his voice came out with more than the usual heat. 'Yes, thank you, Harry. You want to tie my shoes for me before we start?'

'Whoa, what's that?' I asked him.

'Oh, come on, man,' Ramirez said quietly, his voice tight and angry. 'You're lying to me. You're lying to the Council.'

I stared at him.

'I'm not an idiot, man,' Ramirez said, his expression neutral. 'You can barely get by in Latin, but you speak ghoul? Ancient Etruscan? There's more going on here than a duel and internal politics, Dresden. You're involved with these things. More than you should be. You know them too well. Which is a really fucking disturbing thing to realize, considering we're talking about a race of *mind-benders*.'

Vitto and Madrigal emerged from the Malvoran contingent. Vitto bore a long rapier at his side, and there were a number of throwing knives on his belt, as well as a heavy pistol in a holster. Madrigal, meanwhile, carried a spear with a seven-foot haft, and his arms were wrapped with two long strips of black cloth covered in vaguely oriental characters in metallic red thread. I'd have guessed that they were constructs of some kind, even before I felt the ripple of magical energy in them as he walked with Vitto to stand facing us from thirty feet away.

'Carlos,' I said. 'This is one hell of a time to start having doubts about my loyalty.'

'Dammit, Harry,' he said. 'I'm not backing out on you. It's too late for that, even if I wanted to. But this whole thing feels more and more like a setup every second.'

I couldn't argue with him there.

I was pretty sure it was.

I looked back and forth down the length of the ranks of vampires, all of whom watched in total silence now, grey eyes bright, edging over into metallic silver with their rising hunger. The formalities of the Accords had kept us alive and largely unmolested, here amidst the monsters, but if we deviated from the conventions, we'd never live to see the surface again. We were in the same position as Madrigal and Vitto, really: Win or die.

And I didn't delude myself for one single second that this was going to be as simple as a stand-up fight. Part of the nature of the White Court was treachery, as well. It was only a matter of time, and timing, before one of them turned on us, and if we weren't ready when it happened, we'd either be dead or getting fitted for our own white robes.

Vitto and Madrigal squared off against us, hands on their weapons.

I took a deep breath and faced them. Beside me, Ramirez did the same.

Lord Raith reached up his sleeve and withdrew a handkerchief of red silk. He offered it to Lara, who took it and walked slowly down the lines of kneeling thralls. She stopped at the sidelines, midway between us, and slowly lifted the red silk. 'Gentlemen,' she said. 'Stand ready. Let no weapon of any kind be drawn until this cloth reaches the earth.'

My heart started pounding faster, and I drew my duster back enough to put a hand near the handle of my blasting rod.

Lara flicked the scarlet silk cloth into the air, and it began to fall.

Ramirez was right. This was a trap. I had done everything I could to prepare for it, but the bottom line was that I was not sure what was going to happen.

But like the man said: It was too late to back out now.

The cloth hit the floor and my hand blurred for my blasting rod as the duel began.

Some people are faster than others. I'm fast. Always have been, especially for a man my size, but this duel had gotten off to a fair start, and no merely mortal hand is faster than a vampire's.

Vitto Malvora's gun cleared its holster before my fingers had tightened on the blasting rod's handle. The weapon resembled a fairly standard Model 1911, but it had an extension to the usual ammunition clip sticking out of the handle, and it spat a spray of bullets in the voice of a yowling buzz saw.

Some vampires are faster than others. Vitto was fast. He'd drawn and fired more swiftly than I'd ever seen Thomas move, more swiftly than I'd seen Lara shoot. But bodies, even nigh-immortal vampire bodies, are made of flesh and blood, and have mass and inertia. No hand, not even a vampire's, is swifter than thought.

Ramirez already had his power held ready when the scarlet cloth hit the ground, and in that instant he hissed a single syllable under his breath and flipped his left hand palm up. That bizarre glove he wore flashed and let out a rattling buzz of furious sound.

A sudden, gelatinous cloud of green light interposed itself between us and the vampires before even Vitto could fire. The bullets struck against that gooey cloud, sending watery ripple patterns racing across it, plowing a widening furrow through the semisolid mass. There was a hissing sound, a sharp pain high up on my left cheek, and then I was slapped across the chest by a spray of tiny, dark particles the size of grains of sand.

Ramirez's shield was nothing like my own. I used raw force to create my own steel-hard barrier. Ramirez's spell was based on principles of entropy and water magic, and focused on disrupting, shattering, and dispersing any objects trying to pass through it, turning their own energy against them. Even magic must do business with physics, and Carlos couldn't simply make the energy the bullets carried go away. Instead, the spell reduced their force by shattering the bullets with their own momentum, breaking them into zillions of tiny pieces, spreading them out, so that their individual impact energy would be negligible.

When the dispersed cloud of leaden sand struck me, it was unpleasant and uncomfortable, but it had lost so much power that it wouldn't have gotten through an ordinary leather coat, or even a thick shirt, much less my spell-laced duster.

If I'd had time to breathe a sigh of relief, I would have. I didn't. Every bit of focus I had was bent on slamming a surge of energy and will through my blasting rod, even before I had the business end lifted all the way up.

'*Fuego!*' I cried.

A column of fire as thick as a telephone pole flew from the tip of the rod, struck the ground twenty feet away, and then whipped across the floor toward Vitto as I finished lifting my weapon.

He was fast. He'd barely had time to register that his bullets had missed their target before the fire came for him, but he flung himself to one side in a desperate dive. As he went, he gained enough of an angle to get him just around the edge of Rodriguez's highly visible shield, and the vampire's hand flickered to his belt to whip one of those knives at me in a side-armed throw.

It would have been a waste of time for any human. Thrown knives aren't terribly good killing weapons to begin with — I mean, in the movies and TV, every time someone throws a knife it kills somebody. Wham, it slams to the hilt in their chest, right into the heart, or *glurk*, it sinks into their throat and they die instantly. Real knives don't generally kill you unless the thrower gets abnormally lucky. Real knives, if they hit with the pointy part at all, generally only inflict a survivable — if very distracting — injury.

Of course, when real people throw real knives, they don't fling them at a couple of hundred miles an hour. Most of them haven't had centuries to practice, either.

That knife flickered as it came, and if I hadn't hunched up my shoulder and tucked my face down behind it, the knife might have found the flesh of my neck and killed me. Instead, its tip struck the duster's mantle at an oblique angle, and the weapon skittered off the spell-armored coat and tumbled off on a wobbly arc.

Vitto landed in a tumble, teeth clenched over a scream of pain. His left leg was on fire from the knee down, but he was smart — he didn't stop, drop, and roll. In fact, he didn't stop at all, and it was the only thing that kept my second blast from immolating him. The lance of flame missed him by a foot and momentarily smashed the curtain of falling water behind the white throne into steam. Beside me, I heard Ramirez fling out one of those green blasts.

'Harry!' Ramirez screamed.

I turned my head in time to see Madrigal coming at us from nearly straight ahead, his spear in hand. Ramirez hurled a second shaft of green light at him, but it splashed against an unseen barrier a foot away from his body. Glitters of golden light ran up and down the symbols on the cloth strips wrapped around his arms. I understood, then. Ramirez's second shot had been a demonstration.

'He's warded!' Ramirez snarled.

'Drop back!' I snapped, as Vitto came streaking toward

me down the other sideline. He was reloading the gun as he came, dropping the old magazine, slapping a new one in. I lifted my shield bracelet, readying it — then hesitated for a fraction of a second to get the timing just right, gauging angles of incidence and refraction.

Vitto's hand came up and the gun snarled again.

I brought the shield up at the last second, a flat plane perpendicular to the floor, and Ramirez took a hopping step back just in time to get behind the shield as it formed. Twenty or thirty bullets ricocheted off the invisible barrier in a shower of sparks — and spalled more or less toward Madrigal Raith and his magical protection.

The nifty armbands apparently weren't made to stop physical projectiles, because one of the bouncing bullets ripped through the outside of his thigh with an ugly explosion of torn cloth and a misty burst of pale blood. He screamed and faltered, throwing out one hand to catch his balance before he could hit the floor.

'Drop it!' Ramirez shouted. His hand blurred toward his pistol, and he drew it before Madrigal could get moving again.

I pivoted the shield to clear Ramirez, taking a couple of steps forward to wall Vitto away from Carlos's flank, and transmuted the far surface of the shield into a reflective mirror.

Ramirez's gun began to roar beside me — measured shots that were actually aimed, as opposed to the rapid *crack-crack-crack* of panic fire.

Vitto reacted to the gunfire and the abrupt manifestation of a mirrored wall ten feet long and eight feet high with instant violence. He flung the heavy handgun at a suddenly appearing and swift-moving target before he could realize that it was his own reflection. The gun had its slide locked open, and when it hit the shield at the speed he threw it, something in the assembly slipped, and it bounced off in several pieces.

Vitto slowed down for a step, eyes widening, and I didn't blame him one bit. It would have made me blink for a second if my opponent had suddenly changed open air into the back wall of a dance studio.

Then he accelerated again and did something I wasn't ready for. He bounded straight up into the air, a good ten or twelve feet, arching over the top of my shield in an instant and flinging knives with each hand as he came. I threw up my right arm, trying to interpose it with the oncoming knife as far out from my body as I could. The knife hit flat, which was fine, where the leather of my duster's sleeve covered my arm. The handle of the knife, though, hit my naked wrist, and my right hand abruptly went numb. I heard the other knife whisper as it tumbled through the air beside me, missing me.

'Madre de Dios!' Carlos screamed.

The blasting rod tumbled from my useless fingers.

I cursed and flung myself to one side as Vitto landed on the inside of my shield, his sword whipping from its scabbard in a horizontal slash at my throat. My tactical thinking had been limited to two dimensions, maybe reinforced by the mockery of the sports field we fought on. The second knife had missed me because Vitto hadn't been aiming for me. Its handle now protruded from Ramirez's right calf.

I couldn't move my fingers correctly, which precluded the use of the energy rings on my right hand. I dropped the shield – all it would do with him already so close was slow down my movement. I'd have to re-form it between me and him the second I got a chance, which he didn't seem inclined to give me. He sent a lightning-quick thrust at my guts, and I had to dance back a pair of steps to buy myself enough time to parry it with a sweep of the staff in my left hand.

There was no way I could fence with Vitto. Even if he didn't totally outclass me, physically, fighting one-armed with a staff against a competent fighter with a rapier is not a winning proposition. If I tried it, I'd be backing away from him in circles until I tripped, he slashed a few of my fingers off and finished me, or else forced me away from Ramirez long enough to double-team him and kill him. I couldn't sling magic at him, either. His back was to the crowd of vampires and the human victims shielding them, and he was damned fast. Anything I could throw that would have hurt him could miss — and if it missed, it'd kill anyone who got in the way.

I couldn't take my eyes off Vitto for a second — I had to hope that Ramirez was holding his own against Madrigal. I had to buy time and distance. I slammed will and Hellfire through my staff, snarled, '*Forzare!*' and released it in a broad wave that lashed out into absolutely everything in front of me.

The wave of force caught Vitto and flung him from his feet. He hit a brawny thrall with a neatly clipped goatee, and then the wave caught up and struck the man, too, as well as the folk on either side of him. They were flung back into the second row of kneeling thralls, and *they*, in turn, were all bowled back into the crowd of vampires behind them, to a general scream of surprise and dismay.

It hadn't been a *lot* of force by the time it got to the thralls, not all spread out like that. I could have delivered tackles that hit harder. It had been enough, though, to tangle Vitto — whose leg was *still* on fire, by the way — in a pile of courtiers and thralls.

'Welcome, ladies and gentlemen,' I hollered, 'to Bowling for Vampires!'

To my intense discomfort, a round of laughs went up from the Raith contingent, and I got a smattering of applause. I raised my shield again, into a shimmering half dome of glittering silver and blue light this time, and twisted my head around to look for Ramirez.

I turned in time to see Madrigal, bleeding from several gunshot wounds, rush forward, spear held high. Ramirez had fallen to one knee, his wounded leg unable to support his weight, and as I watched he dropped the Desert Eagle and gathered another bolt of disintegrating emerald force in his right hand.

Madrigal laughed at him, the sound silvery and scornful, and now that he was in motion I could see the chromium glitter of the demonic Hunger in his eyes. His protective armbands flickered brightly as he rushed forward.

'Ramirez!' I screamed.

Madrigal raised the spear.

Ramirez flung the gathered energy in a last useless strike . . .

. . . that missed Madrigal entirely and splashed on the stone at his feet.

A section of stone the size of a big bathtub glowed green for a split second, then shattered into dust so fine that its individual grains would be almost invisible to the naked eye.

Just as my average preparation session for a fight does not involve considering twelve-foot kung fu leaps from knife-throwing masters, I guess Madrigal's practices didn't take into account floors that might suddenly become pools of nearly frictionless dust. He let out a shriek and plunged into it, flailing wildly. I could see the wheels spinning in his head, trying to work out what had happened and how the hell he would get out of it.

Ramirez shot a look over his shoulder and snarled, 'Harry!'

The fingers of my right hand were tingling. I raised it, clenching it into a weak fist. It was good enough to align the rings with my thoughts. 'Go!'

Madrigal had worked it out. He thrashed to one side of the trough Ramirez's spell had eaten in the floor, thrust the handle of his spear down into the ultrafine dust, and shoved himself roughly up and out of the sand trap.

But not before Ramirez drew the silver Warden's blade from his hip, the sword designed to let the Wardens of the White Council slice into any enchantment, unraveling it with a single stroke. Carlos drew it, lunged out onto his wounded leg with a cry of pain and challenge, and sliced the willow blade left and right at Madrigal while the spear was grounded and locked into place, supporting him.

The sword cut through the wooden haft of the spear, *snicker-snack*, which was itself an indicator of just how unbelievably sharp an edge it had to have carried. Luccio did good work. That was just collateral damage, though.

The Warden blade also licked lightly across each of Madrigal's arms.

The black cloth armbands erupted into sudden flame, the embroidered symbols on them flaring into painfully brilliant light, as if the scarlet thread had been made of magnesium. Any construct that held enough energy to counteract the magic of a major-league wizard, especially a combat specialist like Ramirez, had to have been holding all kinds of energy. Ramirez had just cut it loose.

Madrigal stared down in sudden panic at the fire writhing up his arms and let out a horrified scream.

I crouched, clenched my fist a little tighter, narrowed my eyes, and with a single thought released every bit of energy in the rings – what had been left over after the ghoul attack and what I had added later, all at the same time.

The power hit Madrigal low in the belly, at a slightly upward angle. It slammed him from his feet as the fire blazed over his arms, lifted him up over the heads of the gathered Raith contingent like a living, sizzling comet, and slammed him into the cavern wall behind them with literally bone-shattering power.

Broken, bleeding wreckage tumbled limply down.

'And the wizards,' I snarled, 'pick up the spare.'

I turned back to face Vitto, who was only then clawing his way out of a pile of confused and unhappy Skavis and Malvora vampires and meekly passive thralls. He came to his feet with his sword in hand.

I faced him through the glowing dome. I heard a grunt, and then Ramirez stepped up beside me, silver sword in hand, still stained with Madrigal's pinkish blood, his staff in the other, taking some of the weight from his injured foot. I kept the dome up, recovered my blasting rod, and raised it, calling up my will, letting fire illuminate the runes carved down its length one sigil at a time. The new shield was more taxing than the old, and I was getting tired – but there was nothing to do about that but keep going.

There were rustling sounds all around us. Vampires came to their feet. They edged closer to the thralls, shifted position so that they would be able to see. There were murmurs and whispers all around us as the White Court sensed that the end was near. Vitto's aunt was not far from him, and she stood with one hand to her delicate throat – but she stood fast, watching, anxiety and calculation warring for space in her eyes. Just over one shoulder, I could just barely make out Lara's profile as she leaned forward over the thrall kneeling between her and the fight – Justine – to watch the end, her lips parted and glistening wet, her eyes glowing.

The spectacle of it sickened me, but I thought I understood something of what triggered it in them.

Death did not come swiftly to vampires – but the old Reaper was in the house, and when he struck, he would take lives that should have lasted for centuries more. That realization let me understand something else about the White Court – that for all of their allure, that forbidden attraction, the unnatural magnetism of a creature so beautiful outside and so twisted within, with their ability to give you the greatest pleasure of your life, even as they snuffed it out — they, the vampires themselves, were not immune to that dark attraction.

They were regular, near-eternal voyeurs to death's handiwork, after all. They saw the mingled ecstasy and terror on the faces of those they took. They fed upon the surrender of life and passion to the endless silence — knowing, all the while, that in the end, they were no different. One day, one night, it would be their turn to face the scythe and the dark cowl, and that they would fall, fall just as helplessly as their own prey had, over and over and over.

Death had already taken Madrigal Raith. And it would soon take Vitto Malvora. And the White Court, one and all, longed to see it happen, to feel Death brush close by, to be tantalized by its nearness, to revel in its presence and passing.

Words could not express how badly they needed therapy.

Dysfunctional sickos.

I put it out of my head. I still had work to do.

'All right,' I growled to Ramirez. 'You ready?'

He bared his teeth in a ferocious smile. 'Let's get it on.'

Vitto Malvora, the last of Anna's killers, faced me steadily, his eyes gone white. I thought that for a man about to face two fairly deadly wizards determined to kill him, he did not look terribly frightened.

In fact, he looked . . .

. . . pleased.

Oh, crap.

Vitto threw back his head and spread his arms.

I dropped the shield and shouted, 'Kill him!'

Vitto lifted his voice in a sudden, thunderous roar, and I could sense the will and the power that underlay his call. 'MASTER!'

Ramirez was a beat slow in transferring his sword to his other hand so that he could fling green fire at Vitto, and the vampire lowered his arms and crossed them in front of him, hissing words in some strange tongue as he did. Ramirez's strike shattered upon that defense, though bits of greenish fire dribbled onto Vitto's arms, each of them chewing out a scoop of flesh as far across as a nickel.

'Crap!' Ramirez snarled.

But I didn't have time to listen.

I could feel it. Feel power building on the cave floor in front of the white throne. It wasn't explosive magic, but it was strong, quivering on a level so fundamental that I could feel it in my bones. A second later, I recognized this power. I had felt the dim echoes of its passing, months before, in a cave in New Mexico.

There was a deep throb. Then another. Then a third. And then the air before the white throne suddenly swirled. It spun for a moment, and then there was abruptly an oblong disk of darkness hanging in the air. It spun open, pushing the space of the cavern aside, and a dank, musty, mildew-scented flood of cold air washed out of the passage that had been opened from the Nevernever and into the Deeps.

Seconds later, there was movement in the passage, and then a ghoul sprang through it.

Well. I call it a ghoul. But just looking at it, I knew I was seeing something from another age. It was . . . like seeing drawings of things from the last ice age – familiar animals, most of them, but they were all too large, too heavy with muscle, many of them festooned with extra tusks, spurs of horn, and lumpy, armored hide.

This thing, this ghoul, was of the same order. Eight feet tall if it was an inch, and its hunched shoulders were so wide that it made the thing look more like a gorilla than it did a hyena or baboon, the way most of them did. It had serrated ridges of horn on its stark cheekbones, and its jaw was far more massive with muscle. Its forearms were even longer than a normal ghoul's, its claws heavier, longer, and backed by knobbed ridges of horn that would let the thing crush and smash as effectively as it sliced and diced. Its brow ridge was far heavier, too, and its eyes, so recessed as to be little more than glitters from the indirect lighting, could hardly be seen.

The ghoul crouched and leaped twenty feet forward with an easy grace, then landed with a roar that made my knees feel a little weak.

More of them poured out of the gate. Ten. Twenty. They kept coming and coming.

'Hell's bells,' I whispered.

Beside me, Ramirez swallowed. 'I,' he said, 'am going to die a virgin.'

Vitto let out a wild cackle of glee, and howled, 'At last!' He actually capered a little dance step in place. 'At last the masquerade ends! Kill them! Kill them *all*!'

I don't know if it was one of the vampires or one of the thralls, but suddenly a woman screamed in utter terror, and the Ghouls went mad with bloodlust and surged forward in an unstoppable wave.

I dropped all the power in my shield, and all that I had put into the blasting rod, too. Neither of them would get me out of the hellish Cuisinart of pain and death that this cavern was about to become.

'Right, then,' I panted. 'This would be the trap.'

'I knew it,' Ramirez snarled. 'I knew it was a setup.'

He turned to look and me and then blinked. It was only then that I realized that I had my teeth bared in a wide smile.

'That's right,' I told him. 'It is.'

I have seen some real pros open gateways to the Nevernever. The youngest of the Summer Queens of the Sidhe could open them so smoothly that you'd never see it happening until it was over. I'd seen Cowl open ways to the Nevernever as casually and easily as a screen door, with the gate itself being barely noticeable until it vanished a few seconds later, leaving behind it the same musty smell now flooding the cavern.

I couldn't do it that smoothly or with that much subtlety. But I *could* do it just as quickly, and just as effectively.

I spun on my heel as the ghouls flooded the cavern and plunged into the gathered members of the White Court in a killing frenzy.

'Go!' Ramirez shouted. 'I can't run anyway. I'll hold them; get out of here!'

'Get over yourself and cover my back!' I snarled.

I gathered my will again, shifting my staff into my right hand. The runes on the staff blazed to life, and I pointed the staff across my body, at the air four feet off the cavern floor. Then I released my gathered will, focused by my intentions and the energies aligned in my staff, and shouted, '*Aparturum!*' Furious golden and scarlet light flowed down the length of wood, searing a seam in reality. I drew the staff from left to right, drawing a line of fire in the air – and after a heartbeat, that line expanded, burning up like a fire running up a curtain, down like rain sluicing down a car window, and left behind it a gateway, an opening from the Raith Deeps to the Nevernever.

The gate opened on a cold and frozen woodland scene. Silvery moonlight slipped through, and a freezing wind gusted, blowing powdery white snow into the cavern – substance of the spirit world, which transformed into clear, if chilly, gelatin, the ectoplasm left behind when spirit matter reverted to its natural state.

There was a stir of shadows, and then my brother burst through the opening, saber in one hand, sawed-off shotgun in the other. Thomas was dressed in heavy biker leather and body armor, with honest-to-God chain mail covering the biker's jacket. His hair was tied back in a tail, and his eyes were blazing with excitement. 'Harry!'

'Take your time,' I barked back at him. 'We're not in a crisis or anything!'

'The others are right beh – *Look out!*'

I spun in time to see one of the ghouls bound into the air and sail toward me, the claws on both its hands and feet extended to rip and slash.

Ramirez shouted and flung one of his green blasts at the thing. It caught the ghoul at the apex of its flight and simply bored a hole the size of a garbage can in its lower abdomen.

The ghoul landed in a splatter of gore and fury. It kept fighting, though its legs flopped around like a seal's tail, of almost no use to it.

I sprang back – or at least, I tried to spring. Opening a gate to the Nevernever is not complicated, but it isn't easy, either, and between that and all the fighting I'd done, I was beginning to bump up against my physical limits. My legs wobbled, and my spring was more like the lazy, hot, and motionless end of summer.

Thomas dragged me the last six inches or I wouldn't have avoided the ghoul's claws. He extended his arm, shotgun in hand, and blew the ghoul's head off its shoulders in a spray of flying bits of bone and horn and a mist of horrible black blood.

After which, the ghoul seized him with one arm and began raking its talons at him with the other.

The terrible power of the mangled ghoul was enormous. Links of chain mail snapped and went flying, and Thomas let out a scream of surprise and outrage.

'What the *hell*!' he snarled. He dropped the shotgun and took off the ghoul's attacking arm with his saber. Then he broke the grip of the last clawed hand, and flung the ghoul's body away from him.

'What the hell was *that*?' he gasped, recovering the shotgun.

'Uh,' I said. 'That was one.'

'Harry!' Ramirez said, backpedaling as best he could with the wounded leg, and bumped into me. I steadied him before he lost his balance. That damned knife was still sticking out of his calf.

A dozen more ghouls were charging us.

Everything slowed down, the way it sometimes does when fresh adrenaline shifts me into overdrive.

The cavern had gone insane. The ghouls had been there for maybe thirty seconds, but there were several dozen of them at least, with more pouring out of the neat oval gate on the other side of the cavern. The ghouls had apparently attacked everyone with equal amounts of ferocity and fury. More of them had poured into the Malvoran and Skavis contingent than the Raith side, but that might have been a function of simple numbers and proximity.

The vampires, most of them unarmed and unprepared for a fight, had been taken off guard. That doesn't mean as much to vamps as it does to regular folks, but the walls had been splattered with pale blood where the ghouls had rushed in among them, and the battle now raging was horrific.

In one spot, Lady Malvora ripped the arm from a ghoul's socket, her skin gone marble-white and hard-looking, and proceeded to beat it about the head and shoulders with its own detached limb. The ghoul went down with a shattered skull, but four more of the creatures buried the White Court noblewoman under their weight and power, and literally ripped her to pieces in front of my eyes.

Elsewhere, a male vampire picked up an eight-foot-long sofa and slammed its end down onto a pair of ghouls ripping at the body of a fallen thrall. Still elsewhere, Lord Skavis had rallied a number of his retainers to him, standing off against the maddened ghouls like a rock ignoring a flash flood — for the moment, at least.

Other sights weren't nearly so pleasant.

A vampire, trying to flee, tripped over a human thrall, a girl no more than eighteen, and dealt her a blow of his fist in pure frustration, snapping her neck. He was brought down by ghouls a breath later. Elsewhere, other vampires seemed to have lost control of their demonic Hunger completely, and they had thrown down whatever thralls they could seize, with no regard for gender or for what their particular favorite food might be. One thrall, writhing under a Skavis, was screaming and pushing her thumbs into her own eyes. Another shuddered under the fear-compulsion of a Malvora, clearly in the midst of a seizure or heart attack, right up until a tide of ghouls overran predator and prey alike. The Raith didn't seem to be as wholly frenzied as the other Houses — or maybe they'd just eaten more today. I saw only a couple of thralls downed by them, being torn out of their clothes and ravaged on the stone.

Like those near Lord Skavis, a core of organization had

formed around Lara and her father. Someone – I saw a flash of Justine's terrified face – was holding a little air horn up and triggering it wildly. I spotted Vitto Malvora, charging the ghouls around his fallen aunt – and watched as he threw himself on the remains with an inhuman howl, and began feasting beside the creatures who had killed her.

It had taken seconds for intrigue to devolve into insanity in a thousand simultaneous nightmare-inducing vignettes – none of which I could afford to think significant, save one: the dozen ghouls plunging directly toward me like a football team on the kickoff, huge and fast and ferocious, charging me on a straight line from the enemy gate.

For a second, I thought I saw a dark shape in that gate, the suggestion of an outlined hood and cloak. It might have been Cowl. I'd have hit him with all the fire I could call if I'd had a second to spare, but I didn't.

I brought my shield up as the ghouls came over the floor, and held it fast as the leader of the pack slammed into it in a flare of blue and silver light and a cloud of sparks. The ghoul only howled and began slamming at the barrier with his fists. Every single one hit with the energy of a low-speed car crash, and even with my nifty new bracelet, I could feel the surge of power I needed to keep the shield steady when each of the blows came thundering down.

Boots thudded behind me. Someone was shouting.

Bam, bam, bam. The ghoul slammed against my shield, and it was an almost painful effort to hold it.

'Justine!' Thomas screamed.

I wouldn't be able to hold this ghoul off for long – which was all right, because the other eleven were going to go right around my shield while he forced me to hold it steady against him, and tear me into tiny pieces and eat me. Hopefully in that order.

Bootsteps thudded behind me, and a voice barked. A second

ghoul, several steps in front of the rest, flung itself around my shield but was intercepted by Ramirez. It leaped at him and hit that gelatinous-looking green cloud of a shield he used.

What happened to the ghoul as its speed carried its whole mass all the way through the shield does not bear thinking on. But Ramirez was going to need new clothes.

Bam. *Bam. BAM!*

Murphy screamed, 'Harry, Thomas, Ramirez, down!'

I dropped and dragged Carlos down with me, lowering my shield as I went. Thomas hit the ground a fraction of a second after I did.

And the world came apart in thunder. Sound hammered at my head and ears, and I found myself screaming in pain and shock, before I ground my teeth and shot a quick glance behind me, trying not to lift my head any higher than I had to.

Murphy knelt on the ground by my feet in her dark fatigues, body armor, black baseball cap, and amber safety glasses. She had a weird little rectangular gun about the size of a big box of chocolates held to one shoulder. It had a tiny little barrel, one of those little red dot optical sights, and Murphy's cheek was laid on it, one eye aligned with the sight as she poured automatic fire into the oncoming ghouls in neat, chattering bursts that ripped the ghoul that had been pounding on my shield into a spray of broken bits. It went over backward, thrashing one arm and howling in agony.

Beside Murphy, playing Clifford the Big Red Dog to her Emily Elizabeth, was Hendricks. The huge redheaded enforcer was also kneeling and firing, but the gun he held to his shoulder was approximately the size of an intercontinental ballistic missile and spat out a stream of tracer rounds that ripped into the attacking creatures with a vengeance. Several men I recognized from Marcone's organization were lined up next to him, all firing. So were several more men I didn't recognize, but whose clothing and equipment were sufficiently different to make me think they were freelancers, hired for the job. A few more were still pouring through the open gate and into the cavern.

The ghouls were hardy as hell, but there is a difference between shrugging off a few rounds from a sidearm and wading through the disciplined hail of assault-weapon fire that Marcone's people laid down on them. Had it been one man firing at one ghoul, it might have been different – but it wasn't. There were at least twenty of them shooting into a packed mass, and they *kept* shooting, even after the targets were thrashing on the ground, until their guns were empty. Then they reloaded, and returned to firing. Marcone had given his men the instructions I'd advised – and I imagined the guns he had hired on must have been used to facing supernatural threats of this sort as well. Marcone was nothing if not resourceful.

Murphy stopped shooting and screamed something at me, but it wasn't until Marcone stepped forward into the peripheral vision of the armed gunmen and held up a hand with a closed fist that they stopped firing.

For a second, nothing but a high, heavy tone buzzed in my ears, making me deaf to the other sounds in the cavern. The air was full of the sewer stench of wounded ghoul and the sharp scent of burning cordite. A swath of stone floor ten yards across and thirty deep had just been carpeted in pureed ghoul.

The fight was still going on all around us, but the main force of ghouls was concentrating on the hard-pressed vampires. We'd bought ourselves a temporary quiet spot, but it couldn't last.

'Harry!' Murphy screamed over the merely horrific cacophony of the slaughter.

I gave her a thumbs-up. I pushed myself to my feet. Someone gave me a hand up and I took it gratefully – until I saw that it was Marcone, dressed in his black fatigues, holding a shotgun in his other hand. I jerked my fingers away as if he were more disgusting than the things fighting and dying all around us.

His cold green eyes wrinkled at the corners. 'Dresden. If it's all right with you, I think it would be prudent to retreat back through the gate.'

That was probably a very smart idea. The gate was six feet away from me. We could pull up stakes, hop through, and close it behind us. Gates to the spirit world paid absolutely no attention to trivial things like geography – they obeyed laws of imagination, intention, patterned thought. Even if Cowl was back there, he wouldn't be able to open a gate to the same place as mine, because he didn't think like me, feel like me, or share my intent and purpose.

Seeing fallout from the war with the Red Court had convinced me that running when you didn't have to fight was a really great idea. In fact, the Merlin had written a letter to the Wardens directing them to do so, rather than lose even more of our dwindling combat resources. If we hung around much longer, no one was getting out of this abattoir.

Thomas's sword came down on a thrashing ghoul, and he shouted, with desperation bordering on madness, 'Justine!' He spun to me. 'Harry, help me!'

Leaving was smart.

But my brother wasn't leaving. Not without the girl.

So I wasn't leaving without her, either.

Come to think of it, there were a whole lot of people who didn't need to be here. And, in point of fact, there were some damned compelling reasons to take them with us when we went. Those reasons didn't make it any less dangerous, and they sure as hell didn't make the idea any less scary, but that didn't stop them from existing.

Without Lara's peace initiative (fronted by her puppet father), the White Court would pitch in more heavily with the Reds than they already had. If I didn't get Lara and her puppet out, what was already a grim war with the vampires would quite possibly become an impossible one. That was a damned good reason to stay.

But it wasn't the one that kept me there.

I saw another ghoul tear into a helpless, unresisting thrall, closed my eyes for a second, and realized that if I did nothing to save as many as I could, I would never leave this cavern. Oh, sure. I might get out alive. But I'd be back here every time I closed my eyes.

'Dresden!' Marcone shouted. 'I agreed to an extraction. Not to a war.'

'A war's all we've got!' I shouted back. 'We've got to get Raith out of this in one piece, or the whole thing was for nothing and no one pays you off!'

'No one will pay me off if I'm dead, either,' Marcone said.

I snarled and stepped closer, getting into Marcone's face.

Hendricks rolled a half a step toward me and growled.

Murphy seized the huge man by one enormous paw, did something that involved his wrist and his index finger, and with a grunt Hendricks dropped to one knee while Murphy held one of his arms out straight behind him and angled painfully upward. 'Take it easy, big guy,' she said. 'Someone might get hurt.'

'Don't move,' Marcone snarled — to his men, not to me. His eyes never wavered from mine. 'Yes, Dresden?'

'I could tell you to do it or I'd strand you all in the Nevernever on the way home,' I said quietly. 'I could tell you to help me or I'd close the gate, and we'd all die here. I could even tell you to do it or I'd burn you to ashes where you stand. But I won't tell you that.'

Marcone narrowed his eyes. 'No?'

'No. Threats won't deter you. We both know that. I can't force you to do anything, and we both know that, too.' I jerked my head at the cavern. 'People are dying, John. Help me save them. God, *please* help me.'

Marcone's head rocked back as if I'd slapped him. After a second he asked, 'Who do you think I am, wizard?'

'Someone who can help them,' I said. 'Maybe the only one.'

He stared at me with empty, opaque eyes.

Then he said, very quietly, 'Yes.'

I felt a fierce smile stretch my mouth and turned to Ramirez at once. 'Stay here with these guys and hold the gate.'

'Who *are* these people?' Ramirez said.

'Later!' I whirled back to Marcone. 'Ramirez is with the Council, like me. Keep him covered and hold the gate.'

Marcone pointed at several of the men. 'You, you, you. Guard this man and hold the gate.' He pointed out several more. 'You, you, you, you, you, start rounding up anyone close enough to us to get to without undue risk and help them through.'

Men leaped to obey, and I felt impressed. I'd never seen Marcone quite like this before: animated, decisive, and totally confident despite the nightmare all around. There was a power to it, something that brought order to the terrifying chaos around us.

I could see why men followed him, how he had conquered the underworld of Chicago.

One of the hired guns cut loose with a burst of fire, still shockingly loud enough to make me flinch. 'You know what else?' I asked Marcone. 'I don't really need this cave. Neither do you.'

Marcone narrowed his eyes at me, then nodded once, and said something over his shoulder to one of the hired guns.

'Dresden, I would appreciate it if you would ask the sergeant to release my employee.'

'Murph,' I complained, 'can't you pick on someone your own size?' I took a second to admire Hendricks's expression, but said, 'We need him with his arm still attached.'

Murphy eased up on the pressure and then released Hendricks's arm. The big man eyed Murphy, rubbing his arm, but regained his feet and his enormous machine gun.

'Harry,' Thomas said, voice tight. 'We need to move.'

'Yeah,' I said. 'Thomas, Murphy, and . . .' We needed mass. 'Hendricks, with me.'

Hendricks checked that with Marcone, who nodded.

'Follow me,' I told them. 'Stay— What are you doing, Marcone?'

Marcone had accepted a weapon from one of his gunmen, a deadly little MAC-10 that could spew out about a berjillion bullets in a second or two. He checked it and clipped a strap hanging from it to a ring on his weapon harness. 'I'm going with you. And you don't have enough time to waste any more of it arguing with me about it.'

Dammit. He was right.

'Fine. Follow my lead and stay close. We're going to go round up Lord Raith and get him and everyone else we can out of here before—'

Marcone abruptly raised his shotgun and put a blast through one of the nearer fallen ghouls that had begun to move. It thrashed, and he put a second shell into it. The ghoul stopped moving.

That was when I noticed that the black ichor that spewed from the ghouls was on the ground . . .

. . . and it was moving.

By itself.

The black fluid rolled and ran like liquid mercury, gathering together in little droplets, then larger gobs. Those, in turn, ran over the floor – uphill, in some cases – back toward broken ghoul bodies. As I watched, bits of missing flesh ripped from the ghouls began to fill in again as the ichor returned to their bodies. The one Thomas had beheaded actually came crawling back over the floor, having regained some of the use of its legs. It was holding its head up against the stump of its neck with its one arm, and the ichor was flowing from both the severed head and the stump, merging, reattaching it. I saw the ghoul's jaws suddenly stretch, its eyes blink and then focus.

On me.

Holy crap.

Time. We didn't have much time. If even the gutted and mangled ghouls could get back up again, there was no way the vampires were winning this one. The best they could hope for was to run – and when more vamps ran, more ghouls would be free to overwhelm us. Or possibly they'd do something even more disgusting than they already had, and we'd all puke ourselves to death.

'This just can't get much more disturbing,' I muttered. 'Follow me.'

I gripped my staff in both hands and charged ahead, into the mass of maddened vampires and ghouls, to save one monster from another.

I sprinted toward the little knot of struggling vampires around the White King, while dozens of über-ghouls ripped into the leading families of the White Court. I slipped on some slimy ichor, but didn't fall on my ass. For me, that's actually pretty good.

I noted more details on the way, and started trying to think ahead of the next few seconds. Assuming we got to the White King in one piece and convinced Lara to team up and follow us, then what? What was the next step?

At least a dozen ghouls bounded out the tunnel, heading up that long slope to the cave's entrance. They'd be in a good position to stop Lara's mortal security forces from pushing through the tunnel to rescue the King. Stopping a charge over open ground with firearms is one thing. Using a gun to charge a large, deadly, powerful predator in close quarters is a different proposition entirely – and not a winning one.

Naturally, the ghouls in the tunnel would also be in position to intercept anyone who tried to flee, which meant that we *had* to leave through the gate, which meant that if Ramirez and Marcone's men lost it, we were screwed. And *that* meant that if Cowl was over there and saw what was going on, he would hardly sit by doing nothing.

I might be able to counter him if I were defending the gate. My skills aren't fine, but I'm pretty strong, and I'm good at adapting them on the fly. Cowl had cleaned my clock in two fights already, but slowing and delaying him wasn't the same as trying to wipe the walls with him. Even if I couldn't be a real threat to him, personally, I could tie him up long enough to hold the gate until we could skedaddle.

Ramirez couldn't. He was a dangerous combat wizard, but his skills just weren't strong enough or broad enough to pose a significant obstacle to Cowl. If Cowl — or Vitto, for that matter — saw what was going on, and the ghouls concentrated on the gate . . .

The shrieks and roars of the struggle on our right suddenly got louder, and I saw the resistance around Lord Skavis and his henchmen suddenly buckle. The horrible glee of the ghouls rushing into the opening was almost more terrifying than the carnage that followed. I caught a glimpse of Vitto Malvora in the middle of the mess, shoving a ghoul toward a wounded vampire, snarling at others, giving orders. The largest of the ghouls were with Vitto.

'That vampire has the strongest and largest of those creatures with him!' Marcone called to me as we ran. 'He'll hit any pockets of resistance with them, use them as a hammer.'

'I can see that,' I snapped. 'Murphy, Marcone, cover our right. Hendricks, Thomas, get ready to go in.'

'Go in where?' Hendricks asked.

I took my staff in hand, focused on the fight raging around the White King, and called up my will and Hellfire. 'In the hole I'm about to make,' I growled. 'Get them out.'

'They're mostly . . . eating now. But the second we start to break them free,' Marcone cautioned from behind me, 'these others are going to come after us.'

'I know,' I said. 'I'll handle it.'

I felt something warm press up against my lower back — Murphy's shoulders. 'We'll make sure that—' Her voice broke off suddenly, and that boxy little submachine gun chattered in three quick bursts, punctuated by a single throaty roar from Marcone's shotgun. 'Holy crap, that was close.'

'Another,' Marcone warned, and the shotgun blasted again.

The air horn in Justine's hand started blaring more desperately.

'Harry!' Thomas shouted.

'Go!' I shouted at Thomas and Hendricks. Then I leveled the staff at the nearest clump of the enormous ghouls and shouted, *'Forzare!'*

My will lashed out, leashed to Lasciel's Hellfire, and rushed upon the ghouls, exploding in a sphere of raw force that blazed with flickers of sulfurous flame. It blew them up and outward like extras on the set of *The A-Team*, flying in high arcs. Some of them flew right through the falling curtain of water behind the throne and into the abyssal depths below. Others slammed hard into the nearest wall, and still others fell among the frenzied ghouls now finishing off Lord Skavis and his retainers.

Thomas and Hendricks charged forward. My brother had slipped his shotgun into a sheath over one shoulder, and now wielded his saber in one hand and that inward-bent knife in the other. The first ghoul he reached was still staggered from the blast that had sent its companions flying, and Thomas never gave it a chance to recover. The saber removed its arm, and a scything, upward-sweeping slash of the crooked knife struck its head from its shoulders. A vicious kick to the small of its back crunched into its spine and sent the maimed, beheaded creature flying into the next in the line.

Hendricks came in at Thomas's side. The big man could not possibly overpower one of the ghouls, despite all the muscle, but he did have an important factor on his side: mass. Hendricks was a huge man, three hundred pounds and more, and once I saw him hit the ghouls, I no longer had any doubts about whether he had played football. He hit an unbalanced ghoul in the back, knocking the creature sprawling, slammed the stock of the huge gun into the neck of a ghoul who turned to follow Thomas's motion, then ducked a shoulder and slammed it into the stunned creature's flank, sending it sprawling.

Thomas hacked down another ghoul, Hendricks powered through a single creature who never had the chance to set itself against his locomotive rush, and we were suddenly faced with a line of savage goddesses bathed in black blood.

Lara stood in the center, her white robes pressed against her skin, soaked in the dark fluids leaking from crushed and broken ghouls, and it left absolutely nothing to the imagination. Her hair, too, had been soaked flat to her skull, and it clung to the skin of her black-spattered cheek and to the lines of her dark-stained throat. In each hand she held a long, wavy-bladed knife, long enough to qualify as a small sword, though God only knew where she'd concealed the weapons before. Her eyes were chrome silver, wide and triumphant, and I jerked my gaze away from them as I felt a mad desire just to stare and see what happened.

In that moment, Lara was more than simply a vampire of the White Court, a succubus, pale and deadly. She was a reminder of days gone by, when mankind paid homage to blood-soaked goddesses of war and death, revered the dark side of the protective maternal spirit, the savage core of the strength that still allowed tiny women to lift cars off of their children, or to turn upon their tormentors with newfound power. Lara's power, at that moment, hovered around her, deadly in its primal seduction, its sheer *strength*.

On either side of her stood two of her sisters, all of them tall, all of them beautiful, all of them gorgeous and soaked in gore, all of them armed with those wavy-bladed short swords. I didn't know any of them, but they stared at me with ravenous energy, with maddeningly seductive destruction spattered all over them, and it took me two or three seconds to remember what the hell was going on.

Lara swayed a step toward me, all the motion in her thighs and hips, her eyes brilliant and steady, focused on me, and I felt a sudden urge to kneel that vibrated in my brain and . . . elsewhere. I mean, how bad could that be? Just think of the view from down there. And it had been a *long* time since a woman had . . .

I dimly heard Murphy's gun chattering again, and Marcone's, and I shook my head and kept my feet. Then I scowled at Lara and croaked, 'We don't have time for this. Do you want out or not?'

'Thomas!' Justine cried. She appeared from behind Lara and the Raith sisters and threw herself bodily upon my brother. Thomas wrapped an arm around her without releasing his grip on his knife, and pressed her hard against him. I could see his profile as she held him back, and his face . . . was transported, I suppose. Thomas always had a certain look. Whether he was making a joke, working out, or giving me a hard time about something, the sense of him was always the same: self-contained, confident, pleased with himself and unimpressed with the world around him.

In Justine's arms he looked like a man in mourning. But he bent his whole body to her, holding her with every fiber and sinew, not merely his arm, and every line of his face became softer, somehow, gentler, as though he had been suddenly relieved of an intolerable agony I had never realized he felt – though I noticed that neither he nor Justine touched each other's skin.

'Ah,' Lara said. Her voice was a quavering, silvery thing, utterly fascinating and completely inhuman. 'True love.'

'Dresden!' Marcone shouted. Hendricks spun away from where he had been staring at the Raith sisters with much the same expression I must have had, and stomped past me. I shortly heard him adding the racket of his big gun to that of Marcone's and Murphy's.

'Raith!' I shouted. 'I propose an alliance between yours and mine, until we get out of here alive.'

Lara stared at me with her empty silver eyes for a second. Then she blinked them once, and they turned, darkening by a few degrees. They went out of focus for a moment, and she tilted her head. Lord Raith abruptly stepped forward, appearing from behind his daughters. 'Naturally, Dresden,' he said in a smooth tone. Unless you knew what you were looking for, you'd never have seen the glassy shine in his eyes, or heard the slightly stilted cadence of his words. He put on a good act, but I had to wonder just how much of his mind Lara had left him. 'Though I regard myself as bound by honor to see to your protection in the face of this treachery, I can only be humbled by the nobility of you offering me your—'

'Yeah, yeah, whatever, all right,' I snapped, glaring past him at Lara. 'Run away now, speeches later.'

Lara nodded, and looked quickly around her. Maybe twenty of the Raith clan had survived the fight. The remaining ghouls had sprung away during our unexpected assault, and now prowled in circles around us well out of arm's reach, but close enough to rush back in if they saw a weakness. They were waiting for the others to finish off the last of the Skavis and Malvora. Once they got here, they'd overrun us easily.

Near the gate, Marcone's soldiers had a steady line of white-robed thralls moving out of the cavern. There were rather more of them still alive than I had supposed there would be, until I saw that the circling ghouls were largely ignoring the passive thralls, focused instead on what they knew to be the real threat — the keepers of the mind-numbed herds.

'Dresden!' Marcone shouted. His shotgun boomed once more and then clicked empty. I heard him feeding new shells in as Murphy's gun chattered. 'They're coming.'

I grunted acknowledgment and said to Lara, 'Bring the thralls.'

'What?'

'Bring the bloody thralls!' I snarled. 'Or you can damned well stay here!'

Lara gave me a look that might have made me a little nervous about getting killed if I weren't such a stalwart guy, but then Lord Raith snapped to the vamps around him, 'Bring them.'

I turned, drawing more Hellfire into the staff, and knew that I wasn't going to be able to manage much more in the way of magic. I had just done too much, and I was on my last legs. I had to pull off one more spell if any of us were going to make it out. Murphy's gun kept rattling away, as did Hendricks's, and I could hear gunfire coming from the soldiers around the gate now, as well, as the ghouls on the opposite side of the cavern began to turn from the ruined remains of the leaders of House Skavis and Malvora.

'Go!' I said. 'Go, go, go!'

We headed for my gate. The vampires seized thralls as they went, tossing them into the center of the group, forming a ring around them. Raith formed the core of the group, with his daughters and their swords around him – and the thralls forming a thick human shield around them, in turn. Trust Lara to turn what she had seen as a hindrance to her advantage. It was the way her mind worked.

We started out at a quick pace – and then an almost-human voice cried out, there was a surge of magic that flashed against my wizard's senses, and the lights went out.

The cavern's lighting had been of excellent quality. It had remained functional all through the duel, despite the magic Ramirez and I had been hurling around, and through the opening of not one, but two gates to the Nevernever. That implied that Raith had invested in lighting with a long track record of high performance and reliability, to continue functioning through so much — but there's never been an electrical system a wizard couldn't put down with a little direct effort, and this one was no exception.

Even as I lifted my staff to call up more light, my brain was paddling up the logic stream. Vittorio had seen us making a break for it — or Cowl had, though again, I had to remind myself that Cowl's presence was still theoretical, however well supported by circumstantial evidence the theory might be. Killing the lights wasn't going to be a hindrance to the vampires or to the ghouls, which meant that he was trying to hamper us people. Sinking the cavern into Stygian blackness would make Marcone's troops almost impotent, hamper and slow any of the escaping thralls, therefore slowing the vampires apparently intent upon protecting them.

My staff hadn't been made to produce light, but it was a flexible tool, and I sent more Hellfire through it as I lifted it overhead to light our way, sending out red-orange light in the shape of the runes and sigils carved into the staff out over the darkness.

And, just as I did, I realized what else the darkness would do.

It would force the humans to produce light.

Specifically, it would draw the response from wizards that being sunk into darkness always did. We called light. By one method or another, it was the first thing any wizard would do in a situation like this one. We'd do it fast, too — faster than anyone without magic could pull out a light of his own.

So, as my staff lit up, I realized that I had just declared my exact position to every freaking monster in the whole freaking cavern. The darkness had been a trap designed to elicit this very response, and I had walked right into it.

Ghouls let out howls of fury and surged toward me through a hundred rune-shaped scarlet spotlights that glinted on their bloodied fangs, their talons, those horrible, hungry, sunken eyes.

Guns roared all around me, splattering the nearest ghouls into black-blooded slurry. It wasn't enough. The creatures simply surged forward, being torn apart, until Murphy's gun clicked empty.

'Reloading!' she screamed, ejecting the weapon's magazine, hopping a step back as the ghoul she'd only wounded continued toward me.

Marcone's gun roared and that ghoul went away, but when he pumped the weapon it clicked on an empty chamber. He dropped it for the little submachine gun clipped to his harness, and for a second or two it cut through ghouls like a scythe, ripping in a great horizontal swath – and then it ran empty.

I stepped forward as another wave of ghouls bounded over those the gunfire had held off.

Murphy and Marcone had bought me time enough for the spell I'd been forming in my mind to meet with my will and congeal into fire. I whirled the staff overhead, and then brought it down gripped in both hands, striking its end to the stone floor as I cried, 'Flammamurus!'

There was a crackling howl, and fire ripped its way up out of the stones of the floor. It rippled out from the point of impact in a line running thirty or forty yards in either direction, a sudden fountain of molten stone that shot up in an ongoing curtain ten or twelve feet high, angled toward the ghouls charging us from the far side of the cavern. Blazing liquid stone fell down over them, among them, and the oncoming tide of screaming ghouls broke upon that wall of stone and fire with screams of agony and, for the first time, of fear.

The wall held off fully half the ghouls in the cavern and

screened us from Vittorio's sight. It also provided all the humans with plenty of light to see by.

'Hell's bells, I'm good,' I wheezed.

The effort of the spell was monumental, even with the Hellfire to help me, and I staggered, the light vanishing from the runes of my staff.

'Harry, left!' Murphy screamed.

I turned my head to my left in time to see a ghoul, half of its body a charred ruin, slam Hendricks aside as if the huge man had been a rag doll, and throw itself at me, while two more leaped over the group from behind, and tried to follow in its wake.

I was pretty sure I could have taken the ghoul, provided he wasn't much heavier than a loaf of bread and had no idea how to use those claws and fangs. But just in case he was heavier than he looked and competent at ripping things apart, I flung up my shield bracelet.

It sputtered into life for a second, and the ghoul bounced off it – and the effort it cost me nearly made me black out. I fell.

The ghoul recovered and thrashed toward me, even as I saw Thomas appear from the ranks of vampires and thralls and attack its two companions from behind. My brother's pale face was all but glowing, his eyes were wide with fear, and I hadn't ever seen him move that fast. He hamstrung both of the other ghouls with the blades in his hands – well, if hacking through three-quarters of the leg, including the thick, black thighbones, could be considered 'hamstringing.' He left them on the ground while other Raiths tore them to pieces. Thomas leaped at the lead ghoul.

He wasn't fast enough.

The ghoul came at me with a dreadful howl. I didn't have enough energy left to lift my body up off the floor and face my killer head-on.

Fortunately, I *did* have energy enough to draw the .44 from my duster pocket. I'd like to tell you that I waited till the last second for the perfect shot, coolly facing down the ghoul with nerves of steel. The truth is that my nerves were pretty much shot, and I was too *tired* to panic. I barely got the sights lined up before the ghoul's jaws opened wide enough to engulf my entire head.

I never consciously pulled the trigger, but the gun roared, and the ghoul's head snapped back before it crashed into me. There was pain and I suddenly couldn't breathe.

'Harry!' Thomas cried.

The weight vanished from my chest and I sucked in a breath. I got my left hand free and pounded at the ghoul with the .44.

'Easy!' Murphy shouted. 'Easy, Harry!' Her small, strong fingers caught my wrist and eased the gun out of it. I dimly realized that I was lucky it hadn't gone off again while I was thrashing around with it.

Thomas flung the ghoul off me, and it landed in a heap. The back upper quarter of its head was gone. Just gone.

'Nice shot,' Marcone noted. I looked back to see him lifting a pale and sweating Hendricks, getting one of the big man's arms over his shoulder and supporting his weight. 'Shall we?'

Thomas hauled me to my feet. 'Come on. No time to rest now.'

'Right,' I said. I raised my voice and called, 'Lara, get them moving!'

We started toward the gate, keeping the curtain of molten fire on our flank. It was hard just moving one foot in front of the other. It took me a while to notice that Justine was under one shoulder, supporting part of my weight, and that I was walking amidst the thralls, near the White King and his guard.

The vampires were still the outer guard, spread out over a half circle, in what amounted to a running battle. Only we weren't running. It was more of a steady walk, made all the more eerie by hellish light and shadow and desperation. Murphy's gun chattered several more times, and then fell silent. I heard the throaty bellow of my .44. I checked my hand and sure enough, my gun wasn't there.

'Leave them!' I heard Lara snap, her cold silver voice slithering around pleasantly in my ear. 'Keep the pace steady. Stay together. Give them no opening.'

We walked, the vampires growing more desperate and less human as the fight went on. Ghouls roared and screamed and died. So did Raiths. The cold subterranean air of the cavern had grown greenhouse hot, and it felt as if there weren't enough *air* left in the air. I panted hard, but it never seemed to get enough into my lungs.

I kept lifting one foot and putting it back down again, numbly noticing that Marcone was behind me with Hendricks, doing the same thing.

I glanced to my left and saw the fiery fountain of molten stone beginning to dwindle. It hadn't been an ongoing spell I had to keep pumping power into. That's the beauty of earth magic. Momentum. Once you get it moving, it doesn't slow down very quickly. I'd poured fire magic into all that stone and *forced* it to expand out of the earth around it. It had simply taken this long for the spell to play out.

But that's exactly what had happened. The spell was beginning to play out. Much as I had.

The curtain lowered slowly, thinning and growing less hot, and I could see ghouls behind it, ready to attack. I noted, idly, that they would be able to rush right into our group of dazed thralls, wounded gangsters, and weary wizards, with nothing much to oppose them.

'Oh, God,' Justine whimpered. She'd noticed, too. 'Oh, God.'

The ghouls had all seen the curtain lowering. Now they rushed forward, to the very edge of the fading curtain, seemingly uncaring of the molten stone on the floor, dozens of them, a solid line of the creatures just waiting for the first chance to bounce over and eat our faces.

A blast of green light flashed down the line. It went completely through two ghouls, leaving them howling on the floor, severed a third ghoul's arm at the shoulder, and continued on through the white throne, leaving a hole the size of a laundry basket in its back.

Ramirez had been waiting for them to line up like that.

He stood, his weight on one foot, at the far end of the lowering wall of flaming stone, on the ghoul side, arms akimbo. They whirled toward him, but Ramirez started lifting his arms alternately from his hip to extend before him, the motion like that of a gunfighter in the Old West, and every draw flung more silent green shafts of deadly light through the ghouls.

Those nearest him tried to rush forward for the kill, but Ramirez had their measure now, and he wasn't content to leave a single gaping hole, trusting that it would incapacitate them sufficiently. He hurled blast after hideously ruinous blast, and left nothing but a scattered pile of twitching *parts* of the first ghouls to rush him, and those beyond them suffered nearly as greatly. Fresh-spilled black ichor rushed back and forth across the cavern floor until it looked like the deck of a ship pitching on a lunatic sea.

'What are you waiting for, Dresden?' Ramirez shouted. 'One little bit of vulcanomancy and you get worn out!' A particularly well-aimed bolt tore the heads from a pair of ghouls at once. 'How do you like *that*?'

We all began hurrying ahead. 'Not bad,' I slurred back at him, 'for a virgin.'

His rate of fire had begun to slacken, but the gibe drew a fresh burst of ferocity out of Ramirez, and he redoubled his efforts. The ghouls howled their frustration and bounded away from the wall of fire, out of its treacherous light and away from the power of the Warden of the White Council ripping them to shreds.

'It hurts!' bellowed Ramirez drunkenly, flinging a last pair of bolts at a fleeing ghoul. 'Ow! Ow, it hurts! It hurts to be this *good*!'

There was a hiss of sound, a flicker of steel, and one of Vitto Malvora's knives hit Ramirez's stomach so hard that it threw the young man off his feet and to the ground.

'Man down!' Marcone shouted. We were close enough to the gate that I could see the pale blue light that spilled through it. Marcone waved his hand through a couple of signals and flicked a finger at Ramirez, then at Hendricks. The armed men – mercenaries, they had to be; no gang of criminal thugs was so disciplined – rushed forward, taking charge of the wounded, seizing Ramirez and dragging him back toward the gate, roughly pushing and shoving the thralls ahead and toward the gate.

I went to Ramirez, staggering away from Justine. The knife had hit him in the guts. Hard. Ramirez had worn a Kevlar vest, which wasn't much good for stopping sharp, pointy things, though it had at least kept the knife's hilt from tearing right into the muscle and soft tissue. I knew there were some big arteries there, and more or less where they were located, but I couldn't tell if the knife was at the right angle to have hit them. His face was terribly pale, and he blinked his eyes woozily as the soldiers started dragging him across the floor, and his legs thrashed weakly, bringing his own left leg up into his field of view.

'Bloody hell,' he gasped. 'Harry. There's a *knife* in my leg. When did *that* happen?'

'In the duel,' I told him. 'Don't you remember?'

'I thought you'd stepped on me and sprained my ankle,' Ramirez replied. Then he blinked again. 'Bloody hell. There's a *knife* in my guts.' He peered at them. 'And they match.'

'Be still,' I warned him. Vampires and thralls and mercenaries were falling back through the gate now. 'Don't move around, all right?'

He began to say something, but a panicked vampire kicked his leg as he went past. Ramirez's face twisted in pain and then suddenly slackened, his eyes fluttering closed. I saw his staff on the ground and grabbed it and pitched it through the gate after him, the men carrying him as the fight behind me got closer, while most of the retreating vampires still fought off the determined assault of the ghouls.

'How long?' I heard Marcone demand of one of the soldiers.

The man checked his watch — an expensive Swiss stopwatch, with springs and cogs, not some digital thing. 'Three minutes, eleven seconds,' the soldier said.

'How many charges?'

'Six doubles,' he replied.

'Hey,' I snapped at Marcone. 'Cutting it a little close, huh?'

'Any longer and they wouldn't accomplish anything,' Marcone replied. 'Can you walk?'

'Yes, I can walk,' I snapped.

'I could get someone to carry you,' Marcone said, his tone solicitous and sincere.

'Bite me,' I growled, and called, 'Murphy?'

'Here!' Murphy called. She was among the last of those retreating from the ghoul onslaught. Her boxy little Volvo of a gun was hanging by its strap on one shoulder, and she held my .44 in both hands, though it looked almost comically overlarge for her.

'Ramirez has got a knife in the stomach,' I said. 'I need you to look after him.'

'He's the other Warden, right?'

'Yeah,' I said. 'He's already through the gate.'

'What about you?'

I shook my head and made sure my duster was still covering most of me. 'Malvora is still out there. He might try to kill our gate, or try some other spell. I've got to be one of the last ones through.'

Murphy gave me a skeptical look. 'You look like you're about to fall over. You in any shape to do more magic?'

'True,' I said, and offered her my staff. 'Hey, maybe you should do it.'

She gave me a hard look. 'No one likes a wiseass, Harry.'

'Are you kidding? As long as the wiseass is talking to someone *else*, people love 'em.' I gave her half a smile and said, 'Get out of here.'

'How are we getting back out again?' she asked. 'Thomas led us there, but . . .'

'He'll lead you back,' I said. 'Or one of the others will. Or Ramirez, if some idiot doesn't kill him trying to help him.'

'If it's all the same to you, I'd rather you did it, Harry.' She touched my hand, and departed through the broad oval of the gate. I saw her hurry through ankle-deep snow beneath what looked like sheltering pine trees to Ramirez's side, where he lay limply on his cloak. The thralls looked confused, which of course they would be, and cold, which, given their wardrobe, of course they would be.

'That's all of ours!' shouted the soldier to Marcone. 'Two minutes, fifteen seconds!'

He had to shout. The nearest of the ghouls were about ten feet away, doing battle against, for lack of a more clichéd term, a thin white line of Raith, including my brother with his two blades spinning.

'Go!' Marcone said, and the soldier went through. Marcone, a fresh shotgun in hand, stepped up next to me. 'Dresden?'

'What are you hanging around for?'

'If you recall,' he said, 'I agreed to extract you alive. I'm not leaving until I have done so.' He paused and added, 'Provided, of course, that it happens in the next two minutes.'

From where I was standing, I could see three two-brick bundles of C4, detonators thrust into their soft surfaces, each fitted with old-fashioned precision timepieces. They were simple charges on the floor. The other three must have been shaped charges affixed to the cavern walls. I had no idea how much destruction was going to be wrought by them, but I didn't suppose it would be much fun to be there when they went boom. Alas, that the poor ghouls would most likely be staying for the fireworks.

'Thomas!' I called. 'Time to go!'

'Go!' Thomas shouted, and the other vampires with him broke from their line and fled for the gate, except for one, a tall female Raith who . . .

I blinked. Holy crap. It was Lara.

The other vampires fled past me, through the gate, and Thomas and his sister stood alone against the horde of eight-foot ghouls. Stood against it, and stopped it cold.

Their skin gleamed colder and whiter than glacial ice, their eyes blazed silvery bright, and they moved with blinding speed and utterly inhuman grace. His saber fluttered and slashed, drawing a constant stream of blood, punctuated by devastating blows of his kukri.

(Ah, right, that was the name of that inward-bent knife. I knew I'd remember it eventually.)

Lara moved with him, trailing her damp, midnight hair and shredded silk kimono. She covered Thomas's back like a cloak hung from his shoulders. She was no weaker than her younger brother, and perhaps even faster, and the wavy-bladed short sword in her hand had a penchant for leaving spills of ghoulish entrails in its wake. Together, the pair of them slipped aside from repeated rushes and dealt out deadly violence to one foe after another.

Ultimately, I think, their fight was futile – and all the more valiant and astonishing for being so doomed. No matter how lethal Thomas and Lara proved to be, or how many ghouls went screaming to the floor, their black blood continued to slither back into their fallen bodies, and the ghouls that had been taken down continued to gather themselves together to rise and fight again. Most of those who reentered the fight with renewed vigor and increased fury remained hideously maimed in some way. Some trailed their entrails like slimy grey ropes. Others were missing sections of their skulls. At least two entered the fray armless, simply biting with their wide jaws of vicious teeth. Beside the beauty of the brother and sister vampires, the ghouls' deformed bodies and hideous injuries were all the more monstrous, all the more vile.

'My God,' Marcone said, his voice hushed. 'It is the most beautiful nightmare I have ever seen.'

He was right. It was hypnotic. 'Time?' I asked him, my voice rough.

He consulted his own stopwatch. 'One minute, forty-eight seconds.'

'Thomas!' I bellowed. 'Lara! Now!'

With that, the pair of them bounded apart, apparently the last thing the ghouls had been expecting, and dashed for the gate.

I turned to go – and that was when I felt it.

There was a dull pulse, a throb of some power that seemed at once alien and familiar, a sickening, whirling sensation and then a sudden stab of energy.

It wasn't a magical attack. An attack implies an act of force that might be predicted, countered, or at least mitigated in some way. This was something far more existential.

It simply asserted itself, and by its very existence, it dictated a new reality.

A spike of thought slammed into my being like a physical blow – it wasn't any one single thought. It was, instead, a mélange of them, a cocktail of emotions so heavy, so dense, that it drove me instantly to my knees. Despair flooded through me. I was so tired. I had struggled and fought to achieve nothing but raw chaos, rendering the whole of my effort useless. My only true friends had been badly injured, or had run, leaving me in this hellish cavern. Those who currently stood beside me were monsters, of one stripe or another – even my brother, who had returned to his monstrous ways in feeding on other human beings.

Terror followed hard on its heels. I had been paralyzed, while surrounded by monsters of resilience beyond description. In mere seconds, they would fall on me. I had fallen with my face toward the gate, and though physical movement was beyond me, I could see that everyone, everyone had also pitched over onto the ground, vulnerable to the attack while the gate remained open. Vampires, thralls, and mortal warriors alike, they had all fallen.

Guilt came next. Murphy. Carlos. I had gotten them both killed.

Useless. It had all been useless.

Marcone's stopwatch lay on the ground near his limply outstretched hand. He'd fallen next to me. The second hand was sweeping rapidly downward, and the watches on the charges of C4, the nearest of them about ten feet away, did the same.

Then I understood it. This was Vittorio Malvora's attack. This hideous, paralyzing brew of everything darkest in the moral soul was what he had poured out, as the Raith administered desire, the Malvorans gave fear, and the Skavis despair. Vitto had gone beyond them all. He had taken all the worst of the human soul and forged it into a poisonous, deadly weapon.

And I hadn't been able to do a damned thing to stop him.

I lay staring at Marcone's stopwatch, and wondered which would kill us all first: the ghouls or the explosion.

41

Between 1:34 and 1:33, the backward-running hand of the stopwatch suddenly halted. Or it seemed that way. But several moments later, the hand twitched down to the next second, and the tick sounded more like a hollow thump. I just lay there staring at it, and wondering if this was how my mind was reacting to my own imminent death.

And then I thought that I'd had enough will to wonder about something, rather than just being crushed and suffocated by despair and terror. Maybe *that* was how I was reacting to my imminent death: with denial and escapist self-induced hallucinations.

'Not precisely, my host,' came Lasciel's voice.

I blinked, which was a lot more voluntary movement than I'd had a second before. I tried to look around.

'Don't try,' Lasciel said, her voice a little alarmed. 'You could harm yourself.'

What the hell. Had she somehow slowed down time?

'Time does not exist,' she said, her tone firm. 'Not the way you consider it, at any rate. I have temporarily accelerated the processes of your mind.'

The stopwatch *thud-thumped* again: 1:32.

Accelerating my brain. That made more sense. After all, we all use only about ten percent of our brain's capacity, anyway. There was no reason it couldn't handle a lot more activity. Well, except that . . .

'Yes,' she said. 'It is dangerous, and I cannot maintain this level of activity for very long before it begins inflicting permanent damage.'

I presumed that Lasciel was about to make me an offer I couldn't refuse.

Her voice became sharp, angry. 'Don't be a fool, my host. If you perish, I perish. I simply seek to give you an option that might enable us to survive.'

Right. And by some odd coincidence, might that option just happen to involve the coin in my basement?

'Why do you continue to be so *stubborn* about this, my host?' Lasciel demanded, her voice tight with frustration. 'Taking up the coin would not enslave you. It would not impede your ability to choose for yourself.'

Not at first, no. But it would finish up with me enslaved to the true Lasciel, and she knew it.

'Not necessarily,' she said. There was a tone of pleading to her voice. 'Accommodations can be reached. Compromises made.'

Sure, if I'm willing to go along with her every plan, I'm sure she'd be quite agreeable.

'But you would be *alive*,' Lasciel cried.

It didn't matter, given that the coin was buried in the stone under my lab anyway.

'Not an obstacle, my host. I can teach you how to call it to you within a few seconds.'

Thud-thump: 1:31.

A thud from behind me. Footsteps. The ghouls. They were coming. I could see part of Marcone's face, twisted in agony under Vittorio Malvora's psychic assault.

'Please,' Lasciel said. 'Please, let me help you. I don't want to die.'

I didn't want to die, either.

I closed my eyes for another second.

Thud-thump: 1:30.

It took an effort of will, and what seemed like several moments of effort, but I managed to whisper aloud, 'No.'

'But you will *die*,' Lasciel said, her voice anguished.

It was going to happen sooner or later. But it didn't have to be tonight.

'Then quickly! First, you must picture the coin in your mind. I can help you—'

Not like that. She could help me.

Silence.

Thud-thump: 1:29.

'I can't,' she whispered.

I thought she could.

'I *can't*,' she replied, her voice anguished. 'She would never forgive that. Never accept me back into her . . . just take the coin. Harry, just take the coin. P-please.'

I gritted my teeth.

Thud-thump: 1:28.

Again, I said, '*No*.'

'I can't do this for you!'

Untrue. She'd already partially shielded me from the effects of Malvora's attack. The situation was simple, for her: She could do more of what she'd already done. Or she could stand by and do nothing. It was her choice.

Lasciel appeared in front of me for the first time, on her hands and knees. She looked . . . odd. Too thin, her eyes too sunken. She had always looked strong, healthy, and confident. Now, her hair was a wreck, her face twisted with pain, and . . .

. . . and she was crying. She looked blotchy, and she needed a tissue. Her hands touched either side of my face.

'It could hurt you. It could inflict brain damage. Do you *understand* what that could mean, Harry?'

Never can tell. It might be nice to have brain damage. I already liked Jell-O. And maybe they'd have cable TV at whatever home they wound up sticking me in. Either way, it would be better than having my brains scooped out by ghouls.

Lasciel stared at me for a moment and then let out a choking little laugh. 'It's your brother. Your friends. That's why.'

If frying my brain got Murphy, Ramirez, Thomas, and Justine out of the mess I'd gotten them into, it would be worth it.

She stared at me for another long moment.

Thud-thump: 1:27.

Then a look of almost childish resentment came over her face, and she looked over one shoulder before turning back to me. 'I . . .' She shook her head and said, very softly, wonderingly, '*She* . . . doesn't deserve you.'

Deserved or not, the fallen angel wasn't getting me. Not ever.

Lasciel squared her shoulders and straightened. 'You're right,' she said. 'It *is* my choice. Listen to me.' She leaned closer, her eyes intent. 'Vittorio has been given power. That is how he can do this. He is possessed.'

I wished I could have raised my eyebrows. Possessed by what?

'An Outsider,' Lasciel said. 'I have felt such a presence before. This attack is drawn directly from the mind of the Outsider.'

Gosh, that was interesting. Not relevant, but interesting.

'It *is* relevant,' Lasciel said, 'because of the circumstances of your birth – because of *why* you were born, Harry. Your mother found the strength to escape Lord Raith for a *reason*.'

What the hell was she talking about?

Thud-thump: 1:26.

'There was a complex confluence of events, of energies, of circumstances that would have given a child born under them the potential to wield power over Outsiders.'

Which didn't make any sense. Outsiders were all but immune to magic. It took power garnered only from centuries of study and practice, wielded by the most powerful wizards on the planet, even to slow them down.

'Strange, then, don't you think, that you defeated one when you were sixteen years old?'

What? Since when? The only serious victory I'd had over a spiritual entity when I was that young had been when my old master had sent an assassin demon after me. It hadn't turned out the way DuMorne had been hoping.

Lasciel leaned closer. 'He Who Walks Behind *is* an Outsider, Harry. A terrible creature, the most potent of the Walkers, a powerful knight among their ruling entities. But when he came for you, you overthrew him.'

True. I had. It was all still a little blurry, but I remembered the end of the fight well enough. Lots and lots of kaboom, and then no more demon. And there was a burning building.

Thud-thump: 1:25.

'Listen,' Lasciel said, giving my head a little shake. 'You have the potential to hold great power over them. You may be able to escape the power now held over you. If you are sure it is what you want, I can give you an opportunity to defy Malvora's sending. But you'll have to hurry. I don't know how long it will take to throw it off, and they are almost upon you.'

After which, we were going to have a long talk about my mother and these Outsiders and their relation to the Black Court and exactly what the hell was going on.

Lasciel – Lash, rather – nodded once and said, 'I will tell you all that I can, Harry.'

Then she rose and stepped past me and toward the oncoming ghouls and Vitto Malvora. Her clothes made a slow, soft rustle as she stepped away from me, and Marcone's stopwatch went *thud—*

Tick, tick, tick . . .

For just a second, no more than a heartbeat or two. I remained impaled on that horrible pike of psychic anguish. Then an odd sensation fell over me, and I don't know precisely how to describe it, except to say that it felt like stepping from brutal, burning sunlight into a sudden, deep shadow. Then that horrible pain eased – not much, but enough to let me suddenly move my arms and my head, enough to know that I could act.

So I froze in place.

'Mine!' howled a voice, so distorted with lust and violence that it sounded like nothing human. 'She is mine!'

Footsteps came closer, *thump-drag, thump-drag.* I saw Vittorio's horribly burned leg go by in my peripheral vision. The sensation of shade began to fade at the edges, with the power of Vittorio's spell returning by slow degrees, like sunlight beginning to burn its way through a sheet of frosted glass.

'Little Raith bitch,' Vittorio snarled. 'What I do to you will make your father's blood run cold.'

There was the sound of a heavy blow. I twitched my head a tiny bit to one side to get a look at what was around me.

A lot of really huge ghouls, that was what, apparently no less fierce for being battered and torn by the battle. Vittorio stood over Lara, his face pale, his leg horribly burned. He had his right hand held out, the hand that projects energy, fingers spread, and I could still feel the terrible power radiating from them. He was maintaining the pressure of the spell that held everyone down, then – and I could see, from the reaction of the ghouls around him, that they were feeling the bite of the spell, too. It seemed only to make them flinch and cower a little, rather than incapacitating them entirely. Maybe they were more used to feeling such things.

He kicked Lara in the ribs, twice more, heavy and ugly kicks that cracked bones. Lara let out little sounds of pain, and I think it was that, more than anything, that let me push the paralyzing awl of hostile magic completely away from my mind. I moved one hand, and that slowly. From the lack of outcry, I took it that no one noticed.

'We'll put a pin in this, for now, little Raith bitch.' He whirled toward my brother. 'I had intended to find you, you know, Thomas,' Vittorio continued. 'An outcast like you, I assumed, might be inclined to throw in his lot with someone with a more equitable vision for the future. But you're like some sad dog, too ugly to be allowed into the house, but faithfully defending the master that holds him in contempt. Your end isn't going to be pretty, either.' He started to turn toward me, smiling. 'But first, we start with the busybody wizard.' He finished the turn, saying, 'Burns hurt, Dresden. Have I mentioned how much I hate being exposed to fire?'

No sense in wasting perfectly good irony. I waited until he said *fire* to spin and pull the trigger on Marcone's shotgun.

The weapon bucked hard – I hadn't had time to brace it properly – and slammed into my shoulder with bruising force only partly attenuated by my duster. The blast pretty well removed Vittorio's right hand at the middle of his forearm.

The way I hear it, amputation is bad for your concentration. It certainly wasn't good for Vittorio's, and you can't hold up the pressure on a spell like he'd been using without concentration. There was a sudden surge of particularly intense discomfort through the spell as Vittorio's physical trauma sent a flare of energy through it, like feedback on an enormous speaker. The ghouls howled in agonized reaction to the surge of discord, and it gave me a second or so to act.

I lashed out with both legs and got Vittorio in one of his knees – the one that wasn't all burned. A kick to the knees doesn't bother a vampire from the Red Court – their actual knees are all backward anyway. A Black Court vampire wouldn't have been anything but annoyed at having a hand blown off with a shotgun.

Vitto wasn't either.

When he wasn't drawing upon the power gained from his Hunger, he was pretty much human. And while I'm a wizard and all, I'm also a fairly big guy. Tall and skinny, sure, but when you get tall enough, even skinny guys are pretty darned heavy, and I've got strong legs. His knee bent in backward and he fell with a scream.

Before he could recover, I was up on one knee with the shotgun's stock against my shoulder and its long barrel against Vittorio's nose. 'Back off!' I shouted. I was going for cool and strong, but my voice came out sounding angry and not overly burdened with sanity. 'Tell them to back off! Now!'

Vittorio's face was twisted with surprise and pain. He blinked at the shotgun, then at me, and then at the stump of his right hand.

I couldn't hear or see the stopwatch anymore, but my head provided the sound effect. *Tickticktickticktick*. How much time was left? Less than sixty seconds?

Around me, the ghouls, recovered from their moment of pain, began to let out a steady, low growl, like the rumbling engines of several dozen motorcycles. I kept my eyes focused on their boss. If I took a moment to get a good look at all the bits of feral anatomy around me that might start ripping into my flesh at any second, I would probably cry. That would be unmanly.

'B-back!' Vittorio stammered. Then he said something in a language that sounded vaguely familiar, but that I didn't understand. He repeated it in a half scream, and the ghouls edged a couple of inches away from us.

Ticktickticktick.

'This is what happens,' I told Vittorio. 'I take my people. I go through the gate. I close it. You get to live.' I leaned into the shotgun a little, making him flinch. 'Or we can all go down together. I'm feeling ambivalent toward which way we go, so I'll leave it up to you.'

He licked his lips. 'Y-you're bluffing. Pull that trigger, and the ghouls will kill everyone. You won't l-let them die for the pleasure of killing me.'

'It's been a long day. I'm tired. Not thinking real clearly. And the way I see it, you got me pretty much dead to rights here, Vitto.' I narrowed my eyes and spoke very quietly. 'Do you really think I'll let myself go down without taking you with me?'

He stared at me for a long moment, and licked his lips. 'G-go,' he said, then. 'Go.'

'Thomas!' I shouted. 'Wakey, wakey! Now is not the time to lie down and die.'

I heard my brother groan. 'Harry?'

'Lara, can you hear me?'

'Quite,' she said. Thomas's older sister was already on her feet, from the sound, and her voice was coming from close behind me.

'Thomas, get Marcone and get him through the gate.' I gave Vittorio a fierce glare. 'Don't move. Don't even twitch.'

Vittorio, his face in agony, held up his left hand, fingers spread. He was bleeding, a lot, and started shivering. There wasn't any fight left in his face. He'd hit me with his best shot, and I'd apparently shrugged it off. I think it had scared the hell out of him. Losing his hand hadn't helped his morale any, either. 'Don't shoot,' he said. 'Just . . . d-don't shoot.' He shot a glance around at the ghouls and said, 'L-let them go.'

I heard Marcone let out a groan, and Thomas grunted with effort. 'Okay,' Thomas said from behind me. 'I'm through.'

I kept the gun on Vittorio and stood up, trying not to let the barrel waver. How many seconds did I have left? Thirty? Twenty? I've heard about people who can keep track of wild situations like this while keeping a steady count, but apparently I wasn't one of them. I took a step back, and felt Lara's back pressing against mine. From the corner of my eye, I could see that the ghouls had spread out all around us. If she hadn't been there, one of them could have blind-sided me without any trouble the second I was a couple of feet away from Vittorio. Gulp.

I took a step back, forcing myself to move smoothly, steadily, when my instincts were screaming at me to run.

'Three more steps,' Lara told me in a whisper. 'A little more to your left.'

I corrected the direction of my next step, trusting her word. One step more, and I could hear winter wind sighing behind me. Silver moonlight shone on the barrel of the shotgun.

And then I found out whether or not Cowl was actually there.

There was a surge of power, an abrasive scream against my arcane senses, and the offspring of a comet and a ptero-dactyl came hurtling out of the darkness at the far end of the cavern. My eyes had adjusted enough to see a dim oval of reddish light that outlined a heavily cloaked figure — Cowl, standing in his own gate.

'Master!' Vittorio cried, his voice slurred.

'Look out!' I screamed, and thrashed behind me with my arm as I ducked and lurched to one side, trying to sweep Lara out of the flying thing's path as I did. It missed us by inches, but we got out of the way.

Cowl's leathery, rasping voice hissed something in a slith-ering tongue, and a second surge of power lashed invisibly across the cavern — not at us, but at my *gate*.

And as quickly as that, my gate began to close, the opening sewing itself shut like a Ziploc bag – starting with the end closest to me.

Tickticktickticktick.

The gate was closing far more quickly than I could have gotten up and moved. I wasn't getting out. But Lara might.

'Lara!' I shouted. 'Go!'

Something with the strength of a freight train and the speed of an Indy car seized my duster and hauled on it so hard that it wrenched my neck and nearly dislocated my arms.

'Dresden!' called Marcone's voice from the closing gate. 'Nineteen!'

I hurtled through the air. Looking wildly around showed me that Lara had seized me and leaped for the far end of the collapsing gate.

'Eighteen!' came Marcone's shout.

Lara and I flew through empty and unremarkable air.

The gate had closed.

We missed it.

42

The only light was the dim scarlet glow from Cowl's gate, and everything had become blood and shadows. The eyes of dozens of ghouls burned like nearly dead coals as they turned toward us, reflecting that lurid luminescence.

'Lara,' I hissed. 'This cavern goes up in seventeen seconds, and there are ghouls in the tunnel out.'

'Empty night,' Lara swore. Her voice was thready with pain and fear. 'What can I do?'

Good question. There had to be . . . Wait. There might be a way to survive this. I was too tired to work any magic, but . . .

'You can trust me,' I said. 'That's what you can do.'

She turned her pale, beautiful, gore-smattered face to me. 'Done.'

'Get us to the tunnel's mouth.'

'But if there are ghouls there already—'

'Hey!' I said. 'Tick, tick!'

Before I'd gotten to the end of the first *tick*, Lara had seized me again and hauled us across the floor to the mouth of the tunnel. Behind me, Cowl was shouting something, and so was Vittorio, and the ghouls set up a howl and were running after us. Only one of the ghouls was close enough to get in the way, but Lara's wicked little wavy-bladed sword ripped straight across its eyes and left the monster momentarily stunned with pain.

Lara dumped me at the mouth of the tunnel, and I took a couple of steps back in, checking the smooth tunnel walls as I shook out my shield bracelet. That demonic flying thing of Cowl's banked around for another pass.

'What now?' Lara demanded. The ghouls were coming. They were nowhere near as fast as Lara had been, but they weren't far away.

I took a deep breath. 'Now,' I said. 'Kiss me. I know it seems weir—'

Lara let out a single, ravenous snarl and was abruptly pressed up against me, arms sliding around my waist with sinuous, serpentine power. Her mouth met mine and . . .

. . . ohmygod.

Lara had once boasted that she could do more to me in an hour than a mortal woman could in a week. But it ain't boasting if it's true. The first, searing second of that kiss was indescribably intense. It wasn't simply the texture of her lips. It was how she moved them, and the simple, naked *hunger* beneath every quiver of her mouth. I knew she was a monster, and I knew she would enslave and kill me if she could, but she *wanted* me with a passion so pure and focused that it was intoxicating. That succubus kiss was a lie, but it made me feel, within that single moment, strong and masculine and powerful. It made me feel that I was attractive enough, strong enough, *worthy* enough to deserve that kind of desire.

And it made me feel lust, a primal need for sex so raw, so scorching, that I felt sure that if I didn't find expression for that need – here and *now* – that I would surely go insane. The fires that surged up in me weren't limited to my loins. It was simply too hot, too intense for that, and my whole body felt suddenly aflame with need. Every inch of me suddenly supernaturally aware of Lara, in all her blood-soaked sensuality, in all her wanton desirability, pressed against me, the mostly transparent white silk of her gown doing less to conceal her nudity than the black blood of her foes.

Now, my body screamed at me. *Take her. Now. Fuck the stopwatch and the bombs and the monsters. Forget everything and feel her and nothing else.*

It was a close thing, but I held back enough to keep from forgetting the danger. The lust nearly killed me — but lust is an emotion, too.

I embraced that lust, allowed it to enfold me, and returned the kiss with nearly total abandon. I slid my right hand around the succubus's waist, and down, pulling her hips hard against me, feeling the amazing strength and elasticity and rondure of her body on mine.

With my left hand, I extended the shield bracelet toward the cavern, the bombs, the onrushing ghouls — and I fed that tidal force of lust through it, building up the energy I would need, some part of me shaping and directing it even as the rest of me concentrated on the mind-consuming pleasure of that single kiss.

The clocks stopped ticking.

The explosives went off.

Cleverness, determination, treachery, ruthlessness, courage, and skill took a leave of absence, while physics took over the show.

Tremendous heat and force expanded from the explosives. It swept through the cavern in an almighty sword of fire, laying low anything unfortunate enough to have remained within. I saw, for one flash-second, the outline of the ghouls, still charging us, unaware of what was about to happen, against the white-hot fireball that expanded through the chamber.

And then that blast hit my shield.

I didn't try to withstand that incredible sledgehammer of expanding force and energy. It would have shattered my shield, melted my bracelet to my wrist, and crushed me like an egg. The shield wasn't meant to do that.

Instead, I filled the space at the mouth of the cave with flexible, resilient energy, and packed layer upon layer of it behind the shield, and more of it all around us. I wasn't trying to stop the energy of the explosion.

I was trying to catch it.

There was an instant of crushing compression, and I felt the pressure on my shield like a vast and liquid weight. It flung me from my feet, and I held hard to Lara, whose arms gripped me in return. I began to tumble, blinded by the flame, and fought to hold the shield, now hardening it all around us, into a sphere, constricting it around us until we were pressed body-to-body. We hurtled up the tunnel, flung out ahead of the explosion like a ship ahead of a hurricane – or, more accurately, like a ball being fired down the barrel of a long, stony musket. The shield banged against the smooth walls, dragging more effort out of me. A single outcropping might have stopped our progress for a disastrous instant, shattering stone, shield, succubus, and shamus into one big mess. Thank God the vanity of Lara's family had made sure the walls of the tunnel were polished smooth and gleaming.

I didn't see the ghouls guarding the upper reaches of the tunnel, so much as I felt them hit the shield and be smashed aside and splattered like bugs, only to be consumed by the flood of fire washing up the tunnel after us. I don't know how fast we were going, beyond 'very.' The explosion flung us up the long tunnel, and out into the night air and up through the branches of a couple of trees – which shattered under the force. Then we were arcing through the night, spinning, with stars above us whipping by and a long tongue of angry flame emerging from the entrance to the Deeps below.

And all the while, I was locked in the heated ecstasy of Lara's kiss.

I lost track of what was happening somewhere near the top of the arc, right about when Lara's legs twined with mine and she ripped aside my shirt and hers to press her naked chest against me. I had just begun wondering what it was I'd forgotten about how kissing Lara was not the best idea when there was a horrible crashing sound that went on for several seconds.

We weren't moving. The shield wasn't under pressure, and I was so dizzy and tired that I couldn't string two thoughts together. I lowered the shield with a groan of relief that was lost in an answering moan of need from the succubus in my arms.

'St-stopped,' I said. 'Lara . . . st-stop.'

She pressed closer, parted my lips with her tongue, and I thought that I was going to explode, when she suddenly let out a hiss and recoiled from me, a hand flying to her mouth — but not before I saw the blisters rising from the burned flesh around her lips.

I fell slowly to my back and lay there gasping in the near-dark. There were several small fires nearby. We were in a building of some kind. There were a lot of broken things.

I was sure to get blamed for this one.

Lara turned away from me, huddling in upon herself. 'Bloody hell,' she said after a moment. 'I can't *believe* you're *still* protected. But it's old . . . My intelligence said Ms Rodriguez hadn't left South America.'

'She hasn't,' I croaked.

'You mean . . .' She turned and blinked at me, astonishment on her face. 'Dresden . . . do you mean to say that the last time you had relations with a woman was nearly four *years* ago?'

'Depressing,' I said. 'Isn't it?'

Lara shook her head slowly. 'I had just always assumed that you and Ms Murphy . . .'

I grunted. 'No. She . . . she doesn't want to get serious with me.'

'And you don't want to be casual with her,' Lara said.

'There's an outside chance that I have abandonment issues,' I said.

'Still . . . a man like you and it's been four *years* . . .' She shook her head. 'I have enormous personal respect for you, wizard. But that's just . . . sad.'

I grunted again, too tired to lip off. 'Saved my life just now, I suppose.'

Lara looked back at me for a moment and then she . . . turned pink. 'Yes. It probably did. And I owe you an apology.'

'For trying to eat me?' I said.

She shivered, and the tips of her breasts suddenly stood out against the white silk. She'd rearranged her clothes to cover them. I was too tired to feel more than a little disappointed about it. 'Yes,' she said. 'For losing control of myself. I confess, I thought that we were facing our last moment. I'm afraid I didn't restrain myself very well. For that, you have my apologies.'

I looked around and realized, dimly, that we were in some part of the Raith château itself. 'Hngh. I'm, uh. Sorry about the damage to your home here.'

'Under the circumstances, I'm inclined to be gracious. You saved my life.'

'You could have saved yourself,' I said quietly. 'When the gate was closing. You could have left me to die. You didn't. Thank you.'

She blinked at me as if I had just started speaking in alien tongues. 'Wizard,' she said after a moment. 'I gave you my word of safe passage. A member of *my* Court betrayed you. Betrayed us all. I could not leave you to die without forsaking my word – and I take my promises seriously, Mister Dresden.'

I stared quietly at her for a moment and then nodded. Then I said, 'I notice that you didn't go terribly far out of your way to save Cesarina Malvora.'

Her lips twitched up at the corners. 'It was a difficult time. I did all that I could to protect my House and then the other members of Court in attendance. More's the pity that I could not save that usurping, traitorous bitch.'

'You couldn't save that usurping, traitorous Lord Skavis, either,' I noted.

'Life is change,' Lara replied quietly.

'You know what I think, Lara?' I asked.

Her eyes narrowed and fastened on me.

'I think someone got together with Skavis to plan his little hunt for the low-powered-magic folks. I think someone encouraged him to do it. I think someone pointed it out as a great plan to usurp mean old Lord Raith's power base. And then I think that same someone probably nudged Lady Malvora to move, to give her a chance to steal Lord Skavis's thunder.'

Lara's eyelids lowered, and her lips spread in a slow smile. 'Why would someone do such a thing?'

'Because she knew that Skavis and Malvora were going to make a move soon in any case. I think she did it to divide her enemies and focus their efforts into a plan she could predict, rather than waiting upon their ingenuity. I think someone wanted to turn Skavis and Malvora against one another, keeping them too busy to undermine Raith.' I sat up, faced her, and said, 'It was you. Pulling their strings. It was you who came up with the plan to kill those women.'

'Perhaps not,' Lara replied smoothly. 'Lord Skavis is — was a well-known misogynist. And he proposed a plan much like this one only a century ago.' She tapped a finger to her lips thoughtfully and then said, 'And you have no way of proving otherwise.'

I stared at her for a long moment. Then I said, 'I don't need proof to act on my own.'

'Is that a threat, dear wizard?'

I looked slowly around the ruined room. There was a hole in the house, almost perfectly round, right through the floors above us and the roof four stories above. Bits and pieces were still falling. 'What threat could I possibly be to you, Lara?' I drawled.

She took in a slow breath and said, 'What makes you think I won't kill you right here, right now, while you are weary and weakened? It would likely be intelligent and profitable.' She lifted her sword and ran a fingertip languidly down the flat of the blade. 'Why not finish you right here?'

I showed her my teeth. 'You gave me your word of safe passage.'

Lara threw back her head in a rich laugh. 'So I did.' She faced me more directly, set the sword aside, and rose. 'What do you want?'

'I want those people returned to life,' I spat at her. 'I want to undo all the pain that's been inflicted during this mess. I want children to get their mothers back, parents their daughters, husbands their wives. I want you and your kind never to hurt anyone ever again.'

Right in front of my eyes, she turned from a woman into a statue, cold and perfectly still. 'What do you want,' she whispered, 'that I might give you?'

'First, reparations. A weregild to the victims' families,' I said. 'I'll provide you with the details for each.'

'Done.'

'Second, this never happens again. One of yours starts up with genocide again, and I'm going to reply in kind. Starting with you. I'll have your word on it.'

Her eyes narrowed further. 'Done,' she murmured.

'The little folk,' I said. 'They shouldn't be in cages. Free them, unharmed, in my name.'

She considered that for a moment, and then nodded. 'Anything else?'

'Some Listerine,' I said. 'I've got a funny taste in my mouth.'

That last remark drew more anger out of her than anything else that had happened the entire night. Her silver eyes blazed with rage, and I could feel the fury roiling around her. 'Our business,' she said in a whisper, 'is concluded. Get out of my house.'

I forced myself to my feet. One of the walls had fallen down, and I walked creakily over to it. My neck hurt. I guess being moved around at inhuman speed gives you whiplash.

I stopped at the hole in the wall and said, 'I'm glad to preserve the peace effort,' forcing the words out. 'I think it's going to save lives, Lara. Your people's lives, and mine. I've got to have you where you are to get that.' I looked at her. 'Otherwise, I'd settle up with you right now. Don't get to thinking we're friends.'

She faced me, her face all shadowed, the light of slowly growing fires lighting her from behind. 'I am glad to see you survived, wizard. You who destroyed my father and secured my own power. You who have now destroyed my enemies. You are the most marvelous weapon I have ever wielded.' She tilted her head at me. 'And I love peace, wizard. I love talking. Laughing. Relaxing.' Her voice dropped to a husky pitch. 'I will kill your folk with peace, wizard. I will strangle them with it. And they will thank me while I do.'

A cold little spear slid neatly into my guts, but I didn't let it show on my face or in my voice. 'Not while I'm around,' I said quietly.

Then I turned and walked away from the house. I looked blearily around me, got my directions, and started limping for the front gate. On the way there, I fumbled Mouse's whistle out of my pocket and started blowing it.

I remember my dog reaching my side, and holding on to his collar the last fifty yards or so down the road out, until Molly came sputtering up in the Blue Beetle and helped me inside.

Then I collapsed into sleep.

I'd earned it.

43

I didn't wake up until I was back home, and then only long enough to shamble inside and fall down on my bed. I was out for maybe six hours, and then I woke up with my whole back fused into one long, enormous muscle cramp. I made some involuntarily pathetic noises, and Mouse rose up from the floor beside my bed and jogged out of my room.

Molly appeared from the living room a moment later and said, 'Harry? What's wrong?'

'Back,' I said. 'My back. Freaking vampire tart. Wrenched my neck.'

Molly nodded once and vanished. When she came back, she had a small black bag. 'You were holding yourself sort of strangely last night, so after I dropped you off, I borrowed Mother's medicine bag.' She held up a bottle. 'Muscle relaxants.' A jar. 'Tiger Balm.' She held up a plastic container of dust. 'Herbal tea mix Shiro found in Tibet. Great for joint pain. My father swears by it.'

'Padawan,' I said, 'I'm doubling your pay.'

'You don't pay me, Harry.'

'Tripling it, then.'

She gave me a broad smile. 'And I'll be happy to get you all set up just as soon as you promise to tell me everything that happened. That you can, I mean. Oh, and Sergeant Murphy called. She wanted to know as soon as you were awake.'

'Give her a ring,' I said. 'And of course I'll tell you about it. Is there any water?'

She went and got me some, but I needed her help to sit

up enough to drink it. That was embarrassing as hell. I got more embarrassed when she took my shirt off with a clinical detachment, and then winced at all the bruises. She fed me the muscle relaxants and set to with the Tiger Balm, and it hurt like hell. For about ten minutes. Then the stuff started working, and the not-pain was a drug of its own.

After a nice cup of tea – which tasted horrible, but which made it possible to move my neck within ten or twenty minutes of drinking it – I was able to get myself into the shower and get cleaned up and into fresh clothes. It was heavenly. Nothing like a nightmarish near-death experience to make you appreciate the little things in life, like cleanliness. And not being dead.

I spent a minute giving Mister some attention, though apparently he'd slept with Molly, because he accepted maybe a whole thirty seconds of stroking and then dismissed me as unnecessary once he was sure I was in one piece. Normally, he needs some time spread across someone's lap to be himself. I ruffled Mouse for a while instead, which he enjoyed dutifully, and then got myself some food and sat down in the chair across from Molly on the couch.

'Sergeant Murphy's on the way,' Molly reported.

'Okay.'

'So tell me about it.'

'You first.'

She gave me a semiexasperated look, and started talking. 'I sat in the car being invisible for . . . maybe an hour? Mouse kept me company. Nothing much happened. Then bells started ringing and men started shouting and shooting and the lights went out. A few minutes later, there was a great big explosion – it moved the rearview mirror out of position. Then Mouse started making noise like you said he would, and we drove to the gate and he jumped out of the car and came back with you.'

I blinked at her for a minute. 'That sounds really boring.'

'But scary,' Molly said. 'Very tense.' She took a deep breath and said, 'I had to throw up twice, just sitting there, I was so nervous. I don't know if . . . if I'm going to be cut out for this kind of thing, Harry.'

'Thank God,' I said. 'You're sane.' I took a few more bites of food and then said, 'But I need to know how much you want to know.'

Molly blinked and leaned toward me a little. 'What?'

'There's a lot I can tell you,' I said. 'Some of it is just business. Some of it is going to be dangerous for you to know about. It might even obligate you in ways you wouldn't like very much.'

'So you won't tell me that part?' she asked.

'Didn't say that,' I said. 'I'm willing. But some of this stuff you'd be safer and happier not knowing. I don't want to endanger you or trap you into feeling you have to act without giving you a choice about it.'

Molly stared at me for a minute while I gobbled cereal. Then she frowned, looked down at her hands for a minute, and said, 'Maybe just tell me what you think is best. For now.'

'Good answer,' I said quietly.

And I told her about the White Court, about the challenge and the duel, about Vittorio's betrayal and how he gated in the ghouls and how I'd had my own backup standing by in the Nevernever.

'What?' Molly said. 'How did you do that?'

'Thomas,' I said. 'He's a vampire, and they have the ability to cross into the Nevernever at certain places.'

'What kind of places?' Molly asked.

'Places that are, ah,' I said, 'important to them. Relevant to them in a particular way.'

'Places of lust, you mean,' Molly said.

I coughed and ate more cereal. 'Yeah. And places where

significant things have happened to them. In Thomas's case, he was nearly sacrificed by a cult of porn-star sorceresses in those caves a few years a—'

'I'm sorry,' Molly said, interrupting. 'But it sounded like you said "cult of porn-star sorceresses."'

'Yeah,' I said.

'Oh,' she said, giving me a skeptical look. 'Sorry, then. Keep going.'

'Anyway. He nearly died there, so I knew he could find it again. He led Marcone and Murphy there, and they were camped out, waiting for me to open a gate.'

'I see,' Molly said. 'And you all ganged up on this Vittorio guy and killed him?'

'Not quite,' I said, and told her what happened, leaving out any mention of Lasciel or Cowl.

Molly blinked as I finished. 'Well. That explains it, then.'

'Explains what?'

'There were all kinds of little lights going by the windows all night. They didn't upset Mouse. I thought maybe it was some kind of sending, and figured the wards would keep it out.' She shook her head. 'It must have been all the little faeries.'

'They hang around all the time anyway,' I said. 'It just takes a lot of them before it's obvious enough to notice.' I chewed Cheerios thoughtfully. 'More mouths to feed. Guess I'd better call Pizza 'Spress and step up my standing order, or we'll have some kind of teeny faerie clan war over pizza rights on our hands.'

I finished breakfast, found my back stiffening again, after sitting still, and was stretching out a little when Murphy arrived. She was still in her party clothes from the night before, complete with a loaded backpack.

After kneeling down to give Mouse his hug, she surprised me. I got one, too. I surprised myself with how hard I hugged back.

Molly occasionally displayed wisdom beyond her years. She did now, taking my car keys, showing them to me, and departing without a word, firmly shutting the door behind her.

'Glad you're okay,' I told Murphy.

'Yeah,' she said. Her voice shook a little, even on that one word, and she took a deep breath and spoke more clearly. 'That was fairly awful. Even by your usual standards. You made it out all right?'

'Nothing I won't get over,' I told her. 'You had any breakfast?'

'Don't think my stomach is up for much, after all that,' she said.

'I have Cheerios,' I said, as if I'd been saying 'dark chocolate caramel almond fudge custard.'

'Oh, God.' Murphy sighed. 'How can I resist?'

We sat down on the couch, with Murphy's heavy bag on the coffee table. Murphy snacked on dry Cheerios from a bowl with her fingers. 'Okay,' I told her. 'First things first. Where is my gun?'

Murphy rolled her eyes and nodded at her bag. I got in and opened it. My .44 was inside. So was Murphy's boxy little submachine gun. I picked it up and eyed it, then lifted it experimentally to my shoulder. 'What the hell kind of gun is this?'

'It's a P90,' Murphy said.

'See-through plastic?' I asked.

'That's the magazine,' she said. 'You can always see how many rounds you have left.'

I grunted. 'It's tiny.'

'On a hyperthyroid stork like you, sure,' Murphy said.

I frowned and said, 'Full automatic. Ah. Is this weapon precisely legal? Even for you?'

She snorted. 'No.'

'Where'd you get it?' I asked.

'Kincaid,' she said. 'Last year. Gave it to me in a box of Belgian chocolate.'

I took the weapon down from my shoulder, flipped it over, and eyed a little engraved plate on the butt. '"We'll always have Hawaii,"' I read aloud. 'What the hell is that supposed to mean?'

Murphy's cheeks turned pink. She took the gun from me, put it in the bag, and zipped it firmly closed. 'Did we ever decide who blew up my car?'

'Probably Madrigal,' I said. 'You stood him up for that cup of coffee, remember?'

'Because he was busy kidnapping you and attempting to sell you on eBay,' Murphy said.

I shrugged. 'Vindictive doesn't equal rational.'

Murphy frowned, the suspicious-cop look on her face something I was long used to seeing. 'Maybe. But it doesn't feel right. He liked his vengeance personal.'

'Who then?' I asked. 'Vittorio wasn't interested in drawing out the cops. Neither was Lord Skavis's agent. Lara Raith and Marcone don't do bombs.'

'Exactly,' Murphy said. 'If not Madrigal, then who?'

'Life is a mystery?' I suggested. 'It was probably Madrigal. Maybe one of the others had a reason for it that we don't know. Maybe we'll never know.'

'Yeah,' she said. 'I hate that.' She shook her head. 'Harry, wouldn't a decent human being be inquiring after his wounded friends and allies about now?'

'I assumed if there was bad news, you'd have told me already,' I said.

She gave me a steady look. 'That,' she said, 'is so archetypically male.'

I grinned. 'How is everyone?'

'Ramirez is in the hospital. Same floor as Elaine, actually, and we're watching them both. Unofficially, of course.'

We meaning the cops. Murphy. Good people. 'How is he?'

'Still had some surgery to go, when I left, but the doctor said his prognosis was excellent, as long as they can avoid infection. He got his guts opened up by that knife. That can always be tricky.'

I grunted, and had my suspicions about where Molly had gone when she borrowed my car. 'He'll make it. What about that poor no-neck you abused?'

'Mister Hendricks is there with two of those mercenaries. Marcone has some of his people guarding them, too.'

'Cops and robbers,' I said. 'One big, happy family.'

'One wonders,' Murphy said, 'why Marcone agreed to help.'

I settled back on the couch and rubbed at the back of my neck with one hand, closing my eyes. 'I bribed him.'

'With what?' Murphy asked.

'A seat at the table,' I said quietly.

'Huh?'

'I offered Marcone a chance to sign on to the Unseelie Accords as a freeholding lord.'

Murphy was quiet for a moment, and then she said, 'He wants to keep expanding his power.' She thought about it a minute more and said, 'Or he thinks his power might be threatened from someone on that end.'

'Someone like the vampires,' I said. 'The Red Court had de facto control of prostitution in Chicago until Bianca's place burned down. And an agent of the White Court has just shown up and killed one of his prostitutes.'

'Are we sure it was Madrigal?'

'I am,' I said. 'No way to prove it, but he was the Raith involved in this mess.'

'That was more or less an accident,' Murphy said. 'Taking out one of Marcone's people, I mean.'

'She's just as dead,' I replied. 'And Marcone won't stand by when someone – anyone – kills one of his own.'

'How does becoming a . . . what was it? And how does it help?'

'Freeholding lord,' I said. 'It means he's entitled to rights under the Accords – like rights of challenge when someone kills his employees. It means that if a supernatural power tries to move in on him, he'll have an opportunity to fight it and actually win.'

'Are there many of these lords?'

'Nope,' I said. 'I had Bob look into it. Maybe twenty on the whole planet. Two dragons, Drakul – the original, not baby Vlad – the Archive, the CEO of Monoc Securities, some kind of semi-immortal shapeshifter guru in the Ukraine, people like that. The Accords let them sign on as individuals. They have the same rights and obligations. Most people who consider the idea aren't willing to agree to be a good, traditional host for, let's say, a group of Black Court vampires, and don't want to get caught up as a mediator in a dispute between the major powers. They don't want to make themselves the targets of possible challenges, either, so not many of them even try it.' I rubbed at my jaw. 'And *no one* who is just a vanilla human being has tried it. Marcone is breaking new ground.'

Murphy shook her head. 'And you were able to set him up for it?'

'You have to have three current members of the Accords vouch for you to sign on,' I said. 'I told him I'd be one of them.'

'You can speak for the Council in this?'

'When it comes to defending and protecting my area of responsibility as a Warden, I damned well can. If the Council doesn't like it, they shouldn't have dragooned me into the job.'

Murphy chewed on some Cheerios, scrunched up her nose in thought, and then gave me a shrewd look. 'You're using Marcone.'

I nodded. 'It's only a matter of time before someone like Lara Raith tries to push for more power in Chicago. Sooner or later they'll swamp me in numbers, and we both know SI will always have their hands tied by red tape and politics. If Marcone signs the Accords, he'll have a strong motivation to oppose any incursion – and the means to do so.'

'But he's going to use his new means to secure his position here even more firmly,' Murphy said quietly. 'Make new allies, probably. Gain new resources.'

'Yeah. He's using me, too.' I shook my head. 'It isn't a perfect solution.'

'No,' Murphy said. 'It isn't.'

'But he's the devil we know.'

Neither of us said anything for several minutes.

'Yes,' Murphy admitted. 'He is.'

Murphy dropped me off at the hospital and I headed straight for Elaine's room.

I found her inside, dressing. She was just pulling a pair of jeans up over strong, slender legs that looked just as good as I remembered. When I opened the door, she spun, thorn-wand in hand.

I put my hands up and said, 'Easy there, gunslinger. I'm not looking for any trouble.'

Elaine gave me a gentle glare and slipped the wand into a small leather case that clipped to the jeans. She did not look well, but she looked a lot weller than she had the last time I'd seen her. Her face was still quite pale and her eyes were sunken and bruised, but she moved with brisk purpose for all of that. 'You shouldn't sneak up on people like that,' she said.

'If I'd knocked, I might have woken you up.'

'If you'd knocked, you'd have missed out on an outside chance of seeing me getting dressed,' she shot back.

'Touché.' I glanced around and spotted her bag, all packed. My stomach twisted a little in disappointment. 'Shouldn't you be in bed?'

She shook her head. 'Have you ever tried to watch daytime television? I was *glad* when the set finally blew. I'd lose my mind just lying here.'

'How you feeling?'

'A lot better,' Elaine said. 'Stronger. Which is another reason to leave. I don't want to have a nightmare and have my powers kill some poor grampa's respirator.'

I nodded. 'So it's back to California?'

'Yes. I've done enough damage for one trip.'

I folded my arms and leaned against the door, watching her brush back her hair enough to get it into a tail. She didn't look at me when she asked, 'Did you get them?'

'Yeah,' I said.

She closed her eyes, shivered, and exhaled. 'Okay. That shouldn't make me feel better. It won't help Anna.'

'It will help a lot of other people in the long run,' I said.

She abruptly slammed the brush against the rail of the bed, snapping it. 'I wasn't *here* trying to help a lot of other people, dammit.' She glanced down at the brush's handle and seemed to deflate for a moment. She tossed it listlessly into a corner.

I went over to her and put a hand on her shoulder. 'This just in. Elaine isn't perfect. News at eleven.'

She leaned her cheek on my hand.

'You should know,' I said. 'I got reparations out of the White Court. A weregild for their dependents.'

She blinked at me. 'How?'

'My boyish charm. Can you get me contact information for the victims' families? I'll get somebody to get the money to them.'

'Yes,' she said. 'Some of them didn't have any dependents. Like Anna.'

I grunted and nodded. 'I thought we might use that money to build something.'

Elaine frowned at me. 'Oh?'

I nodded. 'We use the money. We expand the Ordo, build a network of contacts. A hotline for middle-class practitioners. We contact groups like the Ordo in cities all around the country. We put the word out that if people are in some kind of supernatural fix, they can get word of it onto the network. Maybe if something like this starts happening again, we can hear about it early and stomp on the fire before it grows. We teach self-defense classes. We help people co-ordinate, cooperate, support one another. We *act*.'

Elaine chewed on her lip and looked up at me uncertainly. 'We?'

'You said you wanted to help people,' I said. 'This might. What do you think?'

She stood up, leaned up onto her toes, and kissed me gently on the lips before staring into my eyes, her own very wide and bright. 'I think,' she said quietly, 'that Anna would have liked that.'

Ramirez woke up late that evening, swathed in bandages, his injured leg in traction, and I was sitting next to his bed when he did. It was a nice switch for me. Usually I was the one waking up into disorientation, confusion, and pain.

I gave him a few minutes to get his bearings before I leaned forward and said, 'Hey, there, man.'

'Harry,' he rasped. 'Thirsty.'

Before he was finished saying it, I picked up the little sports bottle of ice water they'd left next to his bed. I put the straw between his lips and said, 'Can you hold it, or should I do it for you?'

He managed a small glare, fumbled a hand up, and held on to the bottle weakly. He sipped some of the water, then laid his head back on the pillow. 'Okay,' he said. 'How bad is it?'

'Alas,' I said. 'You'll live.'

'Where?'

'Hospital,' I said. 'You're stable. I've called Listens-to-Wind, and he's going to come pick you up in the morning.'

'We win?'

'Bad guys go boom,' I said. 'The White King is still on his throne. Peace process is going to move ahead.'

'Tell me.'

So I gave him the battle's last few minutes, except for Lash's role in things.

'Harry Dresden,' Ramirez murmured, 'the human cannonball.'

'Bam, zoom, right to the moon.'

He smiled a little. 'You get Cowl?'

'Doubt it,' I said. 'He was right by his gate. When he saw me running for the exit, ten to one he just stepped back through it and zipped it shut. In fact, I'm pretty sure he did. If there'd been an open gate there, the blast would have been able to spread into it. I don't think we would have been thrown so far.'

'How about Vitto?'

'Vitto was pretty far gone even before the bombs went off. I'm pretty sure we nailed him, and those ghouls, too.'

'Good thing you had that army on standby, huh,' Ramirez said, a faint edge to his voice.

'Hey,' I said, 'it's late. I should let you get some rest.'

'No,' Ramirez said, his voice stronger. 'We need to talk.'

I sat there for a minute, bracing myself. Then I said, 'About what.'

'About how tight you are with the vamps,' he said. 'About you making deals with scumbag mobsters. I recognized Marcone. I've seen his picture in the papers.' Ramirez shook his head. 'Jesus Christ, Harry. We're supposed to be on the same team. It's called trust, man.'

I wanted to spit something hostile and venomous and well deserved. I toned myself down to saying, 'Gee. A Warden doesn't trust me. That's a switch.'

Ramirez blinked at me. 'What?'

'Don't worry about it. I'm used to it,' I said. 'I had Morgan sticking his nose into every corner of my existence for my entire adult life.'

Ramirez stared at me for a second. Then he let out a weak snort and said, 'All hail the drama queen. Harry . . .' He looked unhappy. 'I'm talking about you not trusting *me*, man.'

My increasingly angry retort died unspoken. 'Uh. What?'

Ramirez shook his head wearily. 'Let me make some guesses. One. You don't trust the Council. You never have, but lately, it's been worse. Especially since New Mexico. You think that whoever is leaking information to the vampires is pretty high up, and the less anyone in the Council knows about what you're doing, the better.'

I stared at him and said nothing.

'Two. There's a new player in the game. Cowl's on the new team. We don't know who they are, but they seem to have a hard-on for screwing over everyone equally – vampires, mortals, wizards, whoever.' He sighed. 'You aren't the only one who's been noticing these things, Harry.'

I grunted. 'What do you call them?'

'The Black Hats, after our Ringwraith-wannabe buddy, Cowl. You?'

'The Black Council,' I said.

'Oooh,' Ramirez muttered. 'Yours is better.'

'Thanks,' I said.

'So you can't trust our own people,' he said. 'But you're cutting deals with the vampires . . .' He narrowed his eyes. 'You think you might be able to find the traitor coming in from the other side.'

I put my finger on my nose.

'And the gangster?' Ramirez asked.

'He's a snake,' I said. 'But his word is good. And Madrigal and Vitto had killed one of his people. And I *know* he isn't working for Cowl's organization.'

'How do you know that?'

'Because Marcone works for Marcone.'

Ramirez spread his hands weakly. 'Was that so damned hard, Dresden? To talk to me?'

I settled back in my chair. My shoulders suddenly felt loose and wobbly. I breathed in and out a few times, and then said, 'No.'

Ramirez snorted gently. 'Idiot.'

'So,' I said. 'Think I should come clean to the Merlin?'

Ramirez opened one eye. 'Are you kidding? He hates your guts. He'd have you declared a traitor, locked up, and executed before you got through the first paragraph.' He closed his eye again. 'But I'm with you, man. All the way.'

You don't have much endurance after going through something like Ramirez had. He was asleep before he realized it was about to happen.

I sat with him for the rest of the night, until Senior Council Member Listens-to-Wind arrived with his team of medical types before dawn the next morning.

You don't leave an injured friend all alone.

The next day, I knocked on the door to the office at Executive Priority and went in without waiting for an answer.

'Tonight you will be visited by three spirits,' I announced. 'The ghosts of indictment past, present, and future. They will teach you the true meaning of "you are still a scumbag criminal."'

Marcone was there, sitting behind the desk with Helen Beckitt, or maybe Helen Demeter, I supposed. She wore her professionally suggestive business suit – and was sitting across Marcone's lap. Her hair and suit looked slightly mussed. Marcone had his third shirt button undone.

I cursed my timing. If I'd come ten minutes later, I'd have opened the door *in medias res*. It would have been infinitely more awkward.

'Dresden,' Marcone said, his tone pleasant. Helen made no move to stir from where she was. 'It's nice to see you alive. Your sense of humor, of course, remains unchanged, which is unsurprising, as it seems to have died in your adolescence. Presumably it entered a suicide pact with your manners.'

'Your good opinion,' I said, 'means the world to me. I see you got out of the Nevernever.'

'Simple enough,' Marcone said. 'I had to shoot a few of the vampires, once we were clear of the fight. I did not appreciate the way they were attempting to coerce my employees.'

'Hell's bells.' I sighed. 'Did you kill any of them?'

'Unnecessary. I shot them enough to make my point. After that, we had an adequate understanding of one another – much as you and I do.'

'I understand that you settled matters with Anna's killers, Mister Dresden,' Helen said. 'With help, of course.'

Marcone smiled his unreadable little smile at me.

'The people who did the deed won't be bothering anyone anymore,' I said. 'And most of the people who motivated them have gone into early retirement.' I glanced at Marcone. 'With help.'

'But not all of them?' Helen asked, frowning.

'Everyone we could make answer,' Marcone said, 'has answered. It is unlikely we could accomplish more.'

Something made me say, 'And I'm taking steps to prevent or mitigate this kind of circumstance in the future. Here and elsewhere.'

Helen tilted her head at me, taking that in. Then she nodded and said, very quietly, 'Thank you.'

'Helen,' Marcone said. 'Would you be so good as to excuse us for a few moments.'

'Won't take long,' I added. 'I don't like being here.'

Helen smiled slightly at me and rose smoothly from Marcone's lap. 'If it makes you feel any better, Mister Dresden, you should know that he dislikes having you here as well.'

'You should see how much my insurance premiums go up after your visits, Dresden.' He shook his head. 'And they call me an extortionist. Helen, could you send Bonnie in with that file?'

'Certainly.'

Helen left. Healthy brunette Bonnie, in her oh-so-fetching exercise outfit, bounced in with a manila folder, gave me a Colgate smile, and departed again. Marcone opened the folder, withdrew a stack of papers, and started flicking through them. He got to the last page, turned it around, slid it across the desk, and produced a pen from his pocket. 'Here is the contract you faxed me. Sign here, please.'

I walked over to the desk, took the entire stack, and started reading it from page one. You never sign a contract you haven't read, even if you aren't a wizard. If you are one, it's even more important than that. People joke about signing away their soul or their first-born. In my world, it's possible.

Marcone seemed to accept that. He made a steeple of his fingers and waited with the relaxed patience of a well-fed cat.

The contract was the standard one for approving a new signatory of the Accords, and though he'd had it retyped, Marcone hadn't changed a word. Probably. I kept reading. 'So you suggested the name Demeter for Helen?' I asked as I read.

Marcone's expression never changed. 'Yes.'

'How's Persephone?'

He stared at me.

'Persephone,' I said. 'Demeter's daughter. She was carried away by the Lord of the Underworld.'

Marcone's stare became cold.

'He kept her there in Hades, but Demeter froze the whole world until the other gods convinced him to return Persephone to her mother.' I turned a page. 'The girl. The one in the coma, who you're keeping in a hospital somewhere, and visiting every week. That's Helen's daughter, isn't it? The one who got caught in the crossfire of one of your shoot-outs.'

Marcone didn't move.

'Newspaper file on it said she was killed,' I said.

I read several more pages before Marcone answered. 'Tony Vargassi, my predecessor, I suppose, had a son. Marco. Marco decided that I had become a threat to his standing in the organization. He was the shooter.'

'But the girl,' I said, 'didn't die.'

Marcone went on, 'It put Vargassi in an awkward position. If the girl recovered, she might identify his son as the shooter, and no jury in the world would fail to send a thug to jail who'd shot a pretty little girl. But if the girl died, and it came back on Marco, he'd be looking at a murder charge.'

'And someone who murders little girls gets the needle in Illinois,' I said.

'Exactly. There was a great deal of corruption at the time—'

I snorted.

Marcone's little smile returned for a moment. 'Pardon me. Say instead that the Vargassis exerted their influence on official matters with a heavy hand. Vargassi had the little girl declared dead. He convinced the medical examiner to sign false paperwork, and he hid the girl away in another hospital.'

I grunted. 'If Marco got identified as the shooter and put up for trial, Vargassi could produce the little girl. Look, she's not dead. Mistrial.'

'One possibility,' Marcone replied. 'And if things went quietly for a while, he could simply delete her records.'

'And her,' I said.

'Yes.'

'Whatever happened to old Tony Vargassi?' I asked.

I saw a flash of Marcone's teeth. 'His whereabouts are unknown. As are Marco's.'

'When did you find out about the girl?'

'Two years later,' he said. 'Everything was set up through a dummy corporation's trust fund. She could have just . . .' He looked away from me. 'Just lain there. Indefinitely. No one would have known who she was. Known her name.'

'Does Helen know?' I asked him.

He was quiet for a moment more. 'I can't return Persephone from Hades. The child's death almost destroyed Helen – and her world is still frozen. If she knew her daughter was . . . trapped . . . just lying there in a half-life . . .' He shook his head. 'It would shatter her world, Dresden. And I shouldn't wish that.'

'I've noticed,' I said quietly, 'that most of the young ladies working here would be about the same age as her daughter.'

'Yes,' Marcone said.

'That isn't exactly a healthy recovery.'

'No,' Marcone said. 'But it's what she has.'

I thought about it while I kept reading. Maybe Helen deserved to know about her daughter. Hell, she probably did. But whatever else Marcone was, he was no fool. If he thought news of her daughter's fate might shatter Helen, he was probably right. Sure, she should know. But did I have the right to make that decision?

Probably not – even if Marcone wouldn't do his best to

have me killed if I tried. Hell, I probably had less right to decide than Marcone. He had way more invested in the girl and her fate than I did.

Because that was the secret I'd seen in a soulgaze with Gentleman Johnnie Marcone, years ago. The secret that gave him the strength and the will to rule the mean streets.

He felt responsible for the little girl who'd taken a bullet meant for him.

He'd taken over Chicago crime with ruthless efficiency, always cutting down on the violence. A couple of people had been hurt in gang-related crimes. The gangsters responsible hadn't been heard from again. I'd always assumed it was because Marcone had decided to manipulate matters, to make himself appear to be a preferable alternative to more careless criminals who might take his place if the cops took him down.

I'd never even considered the idea that he might actually give a crap about innocents being harmed.

Granted, that didn't change anything. He still ran a business that killed far more people than any amount of collateral damage. He was still a criminal. Still a bad guy.

But . . .

He was the devil I knew. And he probably could have been worse.

I got to the last page of the contract and found spaces for three signatures. Two of them were already filled.

'Donar Vadderung?' I asked Marcone.

'Current CEO of Monoc Securities,' Marcone replied. 'Oslo.'

'And Lara Raith,' I murmured.

'Signing on behalf of her father, the White King, who is obviously in charge of the White Court.' There was a trace of irony in Marcone's voice. He hadn't been fooled by the puppet show.

I looked at the third open line.

Then I signed it, and left without another word.

It isn't a perfect world. I'm doing the best I can.

'Hmmmm,' said Bob the Skull, peering at my left hand. 'It looks like . . .'

I was sitting in my lab, my hand spread open on the table, while the skull examined my palm.

I'd worn a mark there for years – an unblemished patch of skin amidst all the burn scars, in the perfect shape of the angelic sigil that was Lasciel's name.

The mark was gone.

In its place was just an irregular patch of unburned skin.

'It looks like there's no mark there anymore,' Bob said.

I sighed. 'Thank you, Bob,' I said. 'It's good to have a professional opinion.'

'Well, what did you expect?' Bob said. The skull swiveled around on the table and tilted up to look at my face. 'Hmmmmm. And you say the entity isn't responding to you anymore?'

'No. And she's always jumped every time I said frog.'

'Interesting,' Bob said.

'What's that supposed to mean?'

'Well, from what you told me, this psychic attack the entity blocked for you was quite severe.'

I shivered, remembering. 'Yeah.'

'And the process she used to accelerate your brain and shield you was traumatic as well.'

'Right. She said it could cause me brain damage.'

'Uh-huh,' Bob said. 'I think it did.'

'Huh?'

'See what I mean?' Bob asked cheerfully. 'You're thicker already.'

'Harry get hammer,' I said. 'Smash stupid talky skull.'

For a guy with no legs, Bob backpedals swiftly and gracefully. 'Easy there, chief; don't get excited. But the brain damage thing is for real.'

I frowned. 'Explain, please.'

'Well, I told you that the entity in your head was like a recording of the real Lasciel, right?'

'Yeah.'

'That recording was written in your brain, in portions you weren't using.'

'Right.'

'I think that's where the damage is. I mean, I'm looking at you right now, and your head has been riddled with tiny holes, boss.'

I blinked and rubbed my fingers over my scalp. 'It doesn't feel like that.'

'That's because your brain doesn't sense injuries. It manages sensing injuries for the rest of you. But trust me, there's damage. I think it wiped out the entity.'

'Wiped out . . . you mean, like . . .'

'Killed it,' Bob said. 'Technically, it was never alive, but it *was* constructed. It's been deconstructed, and . . .'

I frowned. 'And what?'

'And there's, um, a portion of you missing.'

'I'm sure I would have felt that,' I said.

'Not your body,' Bob said scornfully. 'Your life force. Your chi. Your soul.'

'Whoa, wait a minute. Part of my *soul* is gone?'

Bob sighed. 'People get all excited when you use that word. The part of you that is more than merely physical, yes. You can call it whatever you want. There's some missing, and it's nothing to panic over.'

'Part of my *soul* is gone and I'm not supposed to be worried about that?' I demanded.

'Happens all the time,' Bob said. 'You shared a bunch of

yours with Susan, and she with you. It's what protected you from Lara Raith. You and Murphy swapped some pretty recently, looks like — you must have gotten a hug or something. Honestly, Harry, you really ought to bang her and get it over wi—'

I reached under the worktable, drew out a claw hammer, and gave Bob a pointed look.

'Um, right,' he said. 'Back to business. Uh, your soul. You give away pieces of yourself all the time. Everyone does. Some of it goes out with your magic, too. It grows back. Relax, boss.'

'If it's no big deal,' I said, 'then why is it so interesting?'

'Oh, well,' Bob said. 'It *is* energy, you know. And I wonder if maybe . . . maybe . . . well, look, Harry. There was a tiny bit of Lasciel's energy in you, supporting the entity, giving you access to Hellfire. That's gone now, but the entity had to have had some kind of power source to turn against the essence of its own originator.'

'So it was running off my *soul*? Like I'm some kind of *battery*?'

'Hey,' Bob said, 'don't get all righteous. You *gave* it to her. Encouraging her to make her own choices, to rebel, to exercise free will.' Bob shook his head. 'Free will is horrible, Harry, believe me. I'm glad I don't have it. Ugh, no, thank you. But you *gave* her some. You gave her a *name*. The will came with it.'

I was quiet for a moment, then said, 'And she used it to kill herself.'

'Sort of,' Bob said. 'She chose which areas of your brain were going to take the worst beating. She took a psychic bullet for you. I guess it's almost the same thing as choosing to die.'

'No, it isn't,' I said quietly. 'She didn't choose to die. She chose to be free.'

'Maybe that's why they call it free will,' Bob said. 'Hey, tell me that at least you got a pony ride before the carnival left town. I mean, she could have made you see and feel *anything* at all, and . . .' Bob paused, and his eyelights blinked. 'Hey, Harry. Are you *crying?*'

'No,' I snapped, and left the lab.

The apartment felt . . . very empty.

I sat down with my guitar and tried to sort out my thoughts. It was hard. I was feeling all kinds of anger and confusion and sadness. I kept telling myself that it was the emotional fallout of Malvora's psychic assault, but it's one thing to repeat that to yourself over and over, and quite another to sit there feeling awful.

I started playing.

Beautifully.

It wasn't perfect performance — a computer can do that. It wasn't a terribly complex bit of music. My fingers didn't suddenly regain their complete dexterity — but the music became *alive*. My hands moved with a surety and confidence I usually felt only in bursts a few seconds long. I played a second piece, and then a third, and every time my rhythm was on, and I found myself seeing and using new nuances, variations on chords that lent depth and color to the simple pieces I could play — sweet sadness to the minor chords, power to the majors, stresses and resolutions I'd always heard in my head, but could never express in life.

It was almost like someone had opened a door in my head, like they were helping me along.

I heard a very, very faint whisper, like an echo of Lash's voice.

Everything I can, dear host.

I played for a while longer, before gently setting aside my guitar.

Then I went to call Father Forthill and tell him to come

over, so that he could pick up the blackened denarius as soon as I dug it out of my basement.

I picked up Thomas outside his apartment and tailed him as he crossed town. He took the El over toward the Loop, and hit the sidewalks again. He looked tense, and paler than usual. He'd blown an awful lot of energy killing those ghouls, and I knew he'd have to feed — maybe dangerously — to recover what he'd lost.

I'd called him the day after the battle and tried to talk to him, but he'd remained reticent, remote. I'd told him I was worried about him, after blowing that much energy. He'd hung up on me. He'd cut short two more calls since.

So, being as how I am a smart and sensitive guy who respects his brother's feelings, I was tailing him to find out what the hell he was trying so hard not to talk to me about. This way, I was sparing him all the effort and trouble of telling me about it by finding out all on my own. Like I said, I'm sensitive. And thoughtful. And maybe a little stubborn.

Thomas wasn't being very careful. I would have expected him to move around the city like a long-tailed cat at a rocking chair convention, but he sort of trudged along, fashionable in his dark slacks and loose, deep crimson shirt, his hands in his pockets, his hair hiding his face most of the time.

Even so, he attracted more than a little feminine attention. He was like a walking, talking cologne commercial, except that even silent and standing he was making women look over their shoulders at him, while coyly rearranging their hair.

He finally stalked into the Park Tower, and went into a trendy little salon-slash-coffee shop calling itself the Coiffure Cup. I checked a clock, and thought about following him in. I could see a few people inside, where a coffee bar backed up to the front window. A couple of fairly pretty girls were getting things set up behind the counter, but I couldn't see any more than that.

I found a spot where I could watch the door and loomed unobtrusively — which is easier than you'd think, even when you're as tall as I am. A couple of women whose hair and nails screamed 'beautician' came in later. The salon opened for business a few minutes after Thomas got there, and immediately began doing a brisk trade. A lot of evidently wealthy, terribly attractive, generally young women started coming and going.

It put me in a quandary. On the one hand, I didn't want anyone to get hurt because my brother had exerted himself so furiously on my behalf. On the other, I didn't particularly care to go in and find my brother lording it over a roomful of worshipful women like some dark god of lust and shadow.

I chewed on my lip for a while, and decided to go on in. If Thomas had . . . if he had become the kind of monster his family generally did, I owed it to him to try to talk some sense into him. Or pound it in. Whichever.

I pushed open the door to the Coiffure Cup and was immediately, pleasantly assaulted by the aroma of coffee. There was techno music playing, thumping bouncily and mindlessly positive. The front room contained the coffee bar, a few little tables, and a little podium next to a heavy curtain. Even as I came in, one of the young women behind the bar came out to me, gave me a bubbly, caffeinated smile, and said, 'Hi! Do you have an appointment?'

'No,' I said, glancing back at the curtains. 'Um, I just need to talk to someone. One second.'

'Sir,' she said in protest, and tried to hurry into my path. My legs were longer. I gave her a smile and outdistanced her, pushing the curtain aside.

The techno music grew a little louder as I went through. The back room of the salon smelled the way salons always do, of various tonsorial chemicals. A dozen styling stations, all in use, stood six on a side, marching up to a rather large and elaborate station on a little raised platform. At the base of the little platform was a pedicure station, and a young woman with a mud mask, and cucumber slices, and a body posture of blissful relaxation was lounging through a pedicure. On the other side, another young woman was under a dryer, reading a magazine, her expression heavy and relaxed with that postcoiffure glow. On the main chair on the platform, a deluxe number that leaned back to a custom shampoo sink, another young woman lay back with a blissful expression while having her hair washed.

By Thomas.

He was chatting with her amiably as he worked, and she was in the middle of a little laugh when I came in. He leaned down and said something in her ear, and though I couldn't hear the substance of it, it came across in an unmistakable just-us-girls kind of tone, and she laughed again, replying in a similar manner.

Thomas laughed and turned away, practically prancing over to a tray of . . . styling implements, I supposed. He came back with a towel and, I swear to God, a dozen bobby pins held in his lips. He rinsed her hair and started pinning.

'Sir!' protested the coffee girl, who had followed me into the room.

Everyone stopped and looked at me. Even the woman with the cucumbers over her eyes took one of them off and peered at me.

Thomas froze. His eyes widened to the size of hand mirrors. He swallowed, and the bobby pins fell out of his mouth.

All the women looked back and forth between us, and there was an immediate buzz of whispers and quiet talks.

'You have got to be kidding me,' I said.

'O-oh,' Thomas said. 'Ah-ree.'

One of the stylists glanced back and forth between us and said, 'Thomas.' (She pronounced it Toe-moss.) 'Who is your *friend*?'

Friend. Oy vey. I rubbed at the bridge of my nose with one hand. I was never going to get away from this one. Not if I lived to be five hundred.

Thomas and I sat down at a table over cups of coffee.

'*This?*' I asked him without preamble. '*This* is your mysterious job? *This* is the moneymaking scam?'

'It was cosmetology school first,' Thomas said. He spoke in a French accent so thick that it barely qualified as English. 'And night work as a security guard in a warehouse where no one else ever showed up, to pay for it.'

I rubbed at my nose again. 'And then . . . *this*? Here I'm thinking you've created your own batch of personal thralls while running around as a hired killer or something, and . . . you're washing *hair*?'

It was difficult to keep my voice quiet, but I made the effort. There were too many ears in that little place.

Thomas sighed. 'Well. Yes. Washing, cutting, styling, dying. I do it all, baby.'

'I'll bet.' Then it hit me. 'That's how you're feeding,' I said. 'I thought that took . . .'

'Sex?' Thomas asked. He shook his head. 'Intimacy. Trust. And believe me, next to sex, washing and styling a woman's hair is about as intimate as you can get with her.'

'You're still feeding on them,' I said.

'It isn't the same, Harry. It isn't as dangerous – more like . . . sipping, I suppose, than taking bites. I can't take very much, or very quickly. But I'm here all day and it . . .' He shivered. 'It adds up.' He opened his eyes and met mine. 'And there's no chance I'm going to lose control of myself. They're safe.' He shrugged a shoulder. 'They just enjoy it.'

I watched the woman who'd been under the hair dryer come out, smile at Thomas, and pick up a cup of coffee on the way out. She looked . . . well, radiant, really. Confident. She looked like she felt sexy and beautiful, and it was quite pleasant to watch her move while she did.

Thomas watched her go with what I recognized as his look of quiet possession and pride. 'They enjoy it a lot.' He gave me one of his brief, swift grins. 'I imagine there's a lot of husbands and boyfriends enjoying it, too.'

'But they're addicted to it, I'd imagine.'

'Some, maybe. I try to spread myself around as much as I can. It isn't a perfect solution—'

'But it's the one you've got,' I said. I frowned. 'What happens when you try to wash somebody's hair and it turns out that they're in love? Protected?'

'True love isn't as common as you'd think,' Thomas said. 'Especially among people rich enough to afford me and superficial enough to think that it is money well spent.'

'But when they do show?' I asked.

'That's why I've got all the hired help, man. I know what I'm doing.'

I shook my head. 'All this time and . . .' I snorted and sipped at some coffee. It was amazing. Smooth and rich and just sweet enough, and it probably cost more than a whole fast-food meal. 'They all think I'm your lover, don't they?'

'This is a trendy, upper-class salon, Harry. No one expects a man with a place like this to be straight.'

'Uh-huh. And the accent, Toe-moss?'

He smiled. 'No one would pay that much money to an American stylist. Please.' He shrugged. 'It's superficial and silly, but true.' He glanced around, suddenly self-conscious.

His voice lowered, and his accent dropped. 'Look. I know it's a lot to ask . . .'

It was an effort not to laugh at him, but I managed to give him a hard look, sigh, and say, 'Your secret is safe with me.'

He looked relieved. '*Merci*.'

'Hey,' I said. 'Can you stop by my place tonight after work? I'm putting something together that might help people if someone else starts something like those White Court bozos just tried. I thought maybe you'd want to be in on it.'

'Um, yeah. Yeah, we can talk about it.'

I sipped more coffee. 'Maybe Justine could help, too. Might be a way to get her out, if you want to do it.'

'Are you kidding?' Thomas asked. 'She's been working for a year to get closer to Lara.'

I blinked up at him. 'Hell's bells, I thought she was acting weird,' I said. 'She came on all zonked out, like the mindless party girl, but she dropped it a couple of times, where I could see. I just put it down to, well. Weirdness.'

He shook his head. 'She's been getting information to me. Nothing huge, so far.'

'Does Lara know about her?'

Thomas looked worried. 'She hasn't tipped to it yet. Justine is, as far as Lara is concerned, still one more helpless little doe.' He glanced up. 'I talked it over with her. She wants to stay. She's Lara's assistant, most of the time.'

I exhaled slowly. Holy crap. If Justine stayed in place, and was willing to report on what she knew . . . intelligence gathered at that level could turn the entire course of the war – because even if the White Court's peace proposal went through, it just meant a shift in focus and strategy. The vamps weren't about to let up.

'Dangerous,' I said quietly.

'She wants to do it,' he said.

I sighed. 'I take it you've been in touch with Lara?'

'Of course,' Thomas said. 'Given my recent heroism' — his voice turned wry — 'in defense of the White King, I am now in favor in the Court. The prodigal son has been welcomed home with open arms.'

'Really?'

'Well,' Thomas amended, 'with reluctant, irritated arms, anyway. Lara's miffed about the Deeps.'

'Guess the bombs weren't good for them.'

Thomas's teeth showed. 'The whole place just collapsed in on itself. There's a huge hole in the ground, the plumbing at the manor got torn up, and the foundation cracked. It's going to cost a fortune to fix it.'

'Poor Lara,' I said. 'No more convenient corpse-disposal facilities.'

He laughed. 'It's nice to see her exasperated. She's usually so self-assured.'

'I have a gift.'

He nodded. 'You do.' We sat quietly for a few minutes.

'Thomas,' I said, finally, gesturing at the room. 'Why didn't you tell me about this?'

He shrugged and looked down. 'At first? Because it was humiliating. I mean . . . working nights to put myself through cosmetology school? Starting my own place and posing as . . .' He waved a hand down at himself. 'I thought . . . I don't know. At first I thought you'd disapprove or . . . laugh at me or something.'

I kept a straight face. 'No. Never.'

'And after that . . . well. I'd been keeping secrets. I didn't want you to think I didn't trust you.'

I snorted. 'In other words you *didn't* trust me. To understand.'

His cheeks turned very slightly pink and he looked down. 'Um. I guess so, yeah. Sorry.'

'Don't worry about it.'

He closed his eyes and nodded and said, 'Thanks, Harry.'

I put a hand on his shoulder for a second, then dropped it again. Nothing else needed to be said.

Thomas gave me a suspicious look. 'Now you're going to laugh at me.'

'I can wait until you've turned your back, if you like.'

He grinned at me again. 'It's all right. I sort of stopped caring about it after I got fed steady for a few weeks straight. Feels too nice not to be starving again. Laugh all you want.'

I looked around the place for a minute more. The coffee girls were having a private conversation, evidently discussing us, if all the covert glances and quiet little smiles were any indication.

I couldn't help it. I burst out laughing, and it felt good.

About the author

A martial arts enthusiast whose resume includes a long list of skills rendered obsolete at least two hundred years ago, Jim Butcher turned to writing as a career because anything else probably would have driven him insane. He lives in Independence, Missouri, with his wife, his son, and a ferocious guard dog. You can visit Jim's website at www.jim-butcher.com

Find out more about Jim Butcher and other Orbit authors by registering for the free monthly newsletter at www.orbitbooks.net